Henry J. Morgan

Bibliotheca Canadensis

A manual of Canadian literature

Henry J. Morgan

Bibliotheca Canadensis
A manual of Canadian literature

ISBN/EAN: 9783337188818

Printed in Europe, USA, Canada, Australia, Japan

Cover: Foto ©Andreas Hilbeck / pixelio.de

More available books at **www.hansebooks.com**

BIBLIOTHECA CANADENSIS:

OR

A MANUAL OF CANADIAN LITERATURE.

BY

HENRY J. MORGAN,

FELLOW OF THE ROYAL SOCIETY OF NORTHERN ANTIQUARIES, COPENHAGEN;
CORRESPONDING MEMBER OF THE NEW YORK HISTORICAL SOCIETY.

"All we have to do, is * * * each for himself—you and you, gentlemen, and all of us—to welcome every talent, to hail every invention, to cherish every gem of art, to foster every gleam of authorship, to honour every acquirement and every natural gift, to lift ourselves to the level of our destinies, to rise above all low limitations and narrow circumscriptions, to cultivate that true catholicity of spirit which embraces all creeds, all classes, and all races, in order to make of our boundless Province, so rich in known and unknown resources, a great new Northern nation." HON. T. D. MCGEE: Address of Quebec, Vo., 1862.

OTTAWA:

PRINTED BY G. E. DESBARATS.

1867.

TO

THE HONORABLE

SIR JOHN ALEXANDER MACDONALD,

K.C.B., D.C.L, M.P.,

Prime Minister of Canada,

THIS VOLUME IS BY PERMISSION MOST RESPECTFULLY INSCRIBED

AS

A SLIGHT TRIBUTE TO HIS UNIVERSALLY ACKNOWLEDGED ABILITIES AS A
STATESMAN AND A SCHOLAR;

AND AS

SOME EXPRESSION OF GRATITUDE FOR VERY MANY KINDNESSES
RECEIVED AT HIS HAND.

BY HIS OBEDIENT AND FAITHFUL SERVANT,

HENRY J. MORGAN.

INTRODUCTORY REMARKS.

"'There are,'" says John Hill Burton, in his interesting work *The Book-Hunter*, "sometimes agreeable and sometimes disappointing surprises in encountering the interiors of books. The title-page is not always a distinct intimation of what is to follow." Now, however sensible I may be of the many demerits of this volume, resulting from various uncontrollable causes, I am yet convinced of its utility and benefit; and may therefore venture to indulge in the hope that it will prove the reverse of disappointing to the reader. And lest the title-page should not convey a sufficient knowledge of what are the contents of the book, I shall here proceed briefly to enumerate them:

First. An Alphabetical List of the authors of works, pamphlets and contributions to the periodical press, written in, or by natives of, or relating to the several Provinces, now constituting the Dominion of Canada, their history, affairs and resources; to which is prefixed brief biographical notices of the several authors, followed by a catalogue of their productions, the place and year of publication, the number of pages and the size of each work or pamphlet, the title and year of publication of the magazine, periodical, or journal in which the papers or contributions mentioned have appeared, with succinct notices of the press, or criticisms thereon from competent authorities.

Second. Brief biographical sketches of the principal Canadian journalists, or newspaper writers, past and present, detailing their services in the cause of the press, and their connection with public affairs generally.

The whole forming a compendious record or history of Canadian Bibliography or Literature, from the time of the Conquest of Quebec down to the present year.

There were various reasons which at the present time impelled the writer to take up the subject of Canadian Bibliography:—First, the not unworthy ambition to render some slight aid to the nascent Literature of our native country, by exhibiting to the rising youth of the New Dominion the extent of our intellectual development as evinced in the literary efforts which have from time to time been made in the country, and which would serve as examples and an incentive to those in the same field. It has been said by Dr. Johnson that "the chief glory of a nation lies in its authors," and it might well be added that no nation can be considered truly great which does not possess some literary power and excellence. "If we consider" says a writer in the *Canadian Magazine*, (Mont. 1824,)—a periodical which evinced more decided literary ability than any one which has succeeded it in this country—"the effect of science and literature on the minds of men, in drawing them nearer together in bonds of unanimity and social order, and in the formation of laws to govern, and at the same time, giving a proper idea of freedom to uphold their relative situation the one with the other; we shall find that the most enlightened ages have been the most productive of happiness, independence and glory."

There is just now, and has been for some years past, a perceptible movement on the part of the two great branches, French and English, which compose our New Nationality, and principally amongst the younger men, to aid the cause of Canadian Literature by their own personal contributions to that Literature. The present time is without doubt most opportune for such a movement. We are just entering upon the commencement of a new, and it is sincerely to be hoped,—a bright and glorious epoch in our history—an epoch which now sees us firmly implanted on the American Continent as a vigorous and highly promising State, Federally constituted, full of brilliant hopes and fond yearnings for national greatness and renown—of important achievements to be performed—of high purposes and resolves to create for Canada an independent position, and a name which shall be symbolical of wisdom and enlightenment worthy of our British lineage and antecedents.

Now more than at any other time ought the literary life of the New Dominion develope itself unitedly. It becomes every patriotic subject who claims allegiance to this our new northern nation to extend a fostering care to the native plant, to guard it tenderly, to support and assist it by the warmest countenance and encouragement.

Were I to write an essay on Canadian Literature and its claims to recognition and assistance, it would be an easy task to prove how thoroughly deserving it is of aid. Into such a paper I might introduce the names of natives of these once scattered and isolated appendages of the British Empire, who have by their works given new lustre to French, English and American Literature This alone would suffice to show that we have had, and still have, the proper elements of literary skill and excellence; and would serve to give the true idea which I wish to impress upon the attention of the reader. In this connection it should always be borne in mind that our Republican neighbours, when not much older than ourselves, and with a population which did not exceed to a very great extent the present population of the Dominion, had produced names in the many varied walks of Literature, which have long been justly famous throughout the civilized world, and have in no common degree assisted to win for Americans an acknowledged place amongst the most civilized and enlightened peoples.

A second and no slight reason for undertaking this volume has been the benefit which such a work would confer upon the professional man, the student and the general reader, as a book of reference. Thus, any one can easily become aware of what subjects have engaged the attention of our own authors and writers, and what has been written by strangers and others respecting the history, affairs, and resources of the several Provinces of Canada.

Another desire was that the relations of the literary men and journalists of the Dominion might by such a book become intimate by an acquaintance with, and knowledge of each other's works and services. By this means also they and others may be made aware of the approximate strength of the literary forces of the United Provinces.

A large number of the productions enumerated are pamphlets, and therefore to some extent ephemeral. But when we consider the degree of value which has been placed on pamphlets by the majority of bibliographers, as important links in the chain of history and affording knowledge on divers other important points, I think that it would have been most unwise on my part to have excluded them from notice. The elder D'Israeli gives the opinion of Myles Davis, a famous collector, upon Pamphlet Literature :

"There is scarce any class of people but may think themselves interested enough to be concerned with what is published in pamphlets, either as to their private instruction, curiosity and reputation, or to the public advantage and credit." *

An American writer, prefixing to his article a quotation from John Quincy Adams : "Posterity delights in details," relates : "I have known a journey to be made from New York to Cambridge, in a storm in January, mainly for the purpose of consulting an old funeral sermon, of which another copy could not be found in the country. It had probably never been asked for during the generations since it came to the library ; but it was now wanted in a law case involving near half a million of dollars. How many would think a funeral sermon worth sending to the library of Harvard College." "Men of eminent literary and scientific attainments," he states, "are daily searching for books, pamphlets, and papers which are considered worthless by many of our superficial ones. Many books, which are seldom read, are wanted to verify quotations and dates. The biographer and the historian want all the ephemeral pamphlets, newspapers, manuscript diaries and letters relating to the times and persons of which they write." †

In a work of a bibliographical character it is somewhat anomalous to include notices of newspaper editors and writers. In our young country, however, our principal newspapers may be considered as holding no unimportant position in Literature. We have not many periodicals of a purely literary kind ; and the morning journal may be said to be as much a literary as it is a political organ, and newspaper, in the general acceptation of the term. Besides, the majority of our journalists have been men of superior education and literary culture, who have themselves written works and pamphlets. A very distinguished author has recently remarked "that a hundred years hence the newspaper will be the only possible book." It is well then to preserve the germs of our future literature.

Some of the biographical sketches have extended to unusual length, and are much longer than others. In such cases, generally where the individual has figured largely in public life, it has been found difficult to reduce the record of his life and services, to shorter dimensions.

This volume is the result of many long hours of painstaking toil ; it may not be free from blemishes and imperfections, nor from serious omissions, which it is now too late to rectify. It is an effort in the cause of National Literature, and as such I send it forth, with all its failings, either to take its place on the library shelf, or to be cast to the trunk-makers.

In closing these remarks, I cannot sufficiently express my thanks to the various gentlemen in and out of the Dominion who have aided me by furnishing information relative to authors and books, and otherwise by personally assisting me in my undertaking. My special thanks are due for assistance in this way, and

* *D'Israeli's Curiosities of Literature.*
† Lemuel G. Olmstead : *Am. Historical Magazine,* (Feby., 1861.)

are hereby tendered to the Rev. George Patterson, Greenhill, Pictou, N. S.; Frederick Griffin, Esquire, Q. C., Montreal; T. D. Hodgins, Esquire, F. R. G. S., Deputy Superintendent of Education for U. C.; Rev. Æ. McD. Dawson, Ottawa; Hon. T. D. McGee, M. R. I. A., M. P., Montreal; Rev. W. Elder, A. M., Editor of the *Morning Journal*, St. John, N. B.; Beamish Murdoch, Esquire, Q. C., Halifax; T. B. Akins, Esquire, D. C. L., do.; Judge Marshall, do.; Rev. Henry J. McLardy, Ottawa; Alpheus Todd, Esquire and A. Gérin Lajoie, Esquire, Library of Parliament, Canada; Very Rev. Edmond Langevin, Vicar General, Rimouski; Rev. A. Cuoq, Seminary of St. Sulpice, Montreal; Rev. Robert Murray, St. John, N. B.; John A. Gemmill, Esquire, Ottawa; Joseph E. McDougall, Esquire, do.; Miss Whiteford, St. John's Newfoundland; Miss Jennings, Halifax; Thomas White, Esquire, Editor of the *Daily Spectator*, Hamilton.

H. J. M.

Ottawa, October, 1867.

" If with your pleasing occupation of looking for books, you possess the love of reading them, you may somewhere have met with the quaint old comparison, that, as geography and chronology are the eye and the ear, so Bibliography is both the hands of History; and, as these two poor hands are the slaves of the eye and ear, so Bibliography without distinction or reward ministers to the wants of History."—HENRY STEVENS: *Historical Nuggets.*

" At the period when nations, yet in their infancy, are animated by a creative genius, which endows them with a poetry and literature of their own, while it renders them, at the same time, capable of splendid enterprises, susceptible of lofty passions, and disposed to great sacrifices, the literature of other nations is unknown to them. Each draws from its own bosom that which best harmonizes with its nature. Eloquence, in such a nation, is the expression of natural sentiment; poetry, the play of an imagination yet unexhausted. Amongst such a people, no one writes for the sake of writing; no one speaks merely for the sake of speaking. To produce a deep impression, there is no need either of rules or examples. The orator touches the inmost soul of his hearer, because his words proceed from the depths of his own heart. The priest obtains a mastery over the conscience, and in turns awakens love or terror, because he is himself convinced of the truth of the dogmas which he inculcates; because he feels the duties he proclaims, and is only the organ of the inspirations within him. The historian places before the eyes of his readers the events of past times, because he is still agitated by the passions which produced them; because the glory of his country is the first passion of his heart; and because he wishes to preserve by his writings, that which his valour has contributed to acquire. The epic poet adds durability to these historical recollections, by clothing them in a language more conformable to the inspirations of his imagination, and more analogous to those emotions which it is his object to awaken. The lyric poet abandons himself to the transports of which he has so deep a sense; while the tragedian places before our eyes the picture of which his fancy has first formed a perfect conception. Manner and language, to such a creative genius as this, are merely the means of rendering its emotions more popular. Each seeks, and each discovers in himself that harmonious touch, to which all hearts must respond; each affects others, in pursuing only that which affects himself; and art becomes unnecessary, because every thing is supplied by nature and by feeling."—SISMONDI: *Literature of the South of Europe.*

Watt's Bibliotheca Brittanica, 5 vols.; Darling's Cyclopædia Bibliographica, 2 vols.; Quérard: France Littéraire; Manuel de Bibliographie Universelle; Lowndes' Bibliographers Manual, 9 vols.; Roorbach's Bibliotheca Americana, 4 vols.; Trubner's Guide to American Literature; Biographie Universelle; Allibone's Dictionary of Authors; Duyckincks Cyclopædia of American Literature; Faribault's Catalogue; Rich's Catalogue of Books relating to America; Stevens' Historical Nuggets; Appleton's American Cyclopædia; J. R. Smith's Catalogue of Books; London Catalogue, 4 vols; British Catalogue; Martin's Catalogue of Privately Printed Books; Ternaud: Bibliothèque Américaine; Tromel: Bibliothèque Américaine; Poole's Index to Periodical Literature; Kelly's American Catalogue; Bibliotheca America Nova; Gowan's Catalogue; Sampson Low's Catalogue; Notman's Portraits of British Americans; Lemoine's Maple Leaves; Lindsey's Life of McKenzie; Catalogues of the Library of Parliament, Can.; Men of the Time; Young's Colonial Literature; Bibaud's Panthéon Canadien; Murdoch's History of Nova Scotia; Dawson's Acadian Geology; Howe's Speeches and Letters; Logan's Geology of Canada; Dewart's Selections from Canadian Poets; Proceedings of the N. Y. Historical Society; Transactions of the Botanical Society, Can.; Transactions and Catalogue of the Literary and Historical Society, Quebec; London Monthly Review; London Athenæum; London Saturday Review; Edinburgh Review; North British Review; Westminster Review; Blackwood's Magazine; Fraser's Magazine; North American Review; American Historical Magazine; Canadian Journal; Upper Canada Law Journal; British American Journal; Bibaud's Bibliothèque Canadienne; Bibaud's Magasin du Bas-Canada; Presbyterian Magazine; Literary Garland; Répertoire National; Revue Canadienne; Canadian Naturalist; New York Albion; Canadian News; Colonial Magazine; Canadian Review; Provincial Magazine; Naval and Military Gazette; Les Soirées Canadiennes; Le Foyer Canadien; La Ruche Littéraire; Canada Medical Journal; Anglo-American Magazine; Journals of Education L. C. and U. C.; Acadian Recorder; Halifax Reporter; St. John Journal; Quebec Canadien; Quebec Gazette; Quebec Mercury; Quebec Chronicle; Montreal Minerve; Montreal Gazette; Montreal Herald; Montreal Daily News; Montreal Transcript; L'Echo du Cabinet de Lecture Paroissial; Hamilton Spectator; Kingston Daily News; Toronto Globe; Toronto Leader; Saturday Reader.

Explanation of Abbreviations.

A. Am. Mag., - *Anglo American Magazine.*
Abst. Proc. Geol. Soc., { *Abstract Proceedings Geological Society.*
Am., - - *America, American.*
Am. His. Mag., *American Historical Magazine.*
Am. Lit. Gaz., - *American Literary Gazette.*
Annals Ly. of Nat. His., { *Annals Lyceum of Natural History.*
Appd., - - - *Appointed.*
Appt., - - - *Appointment.*
Ass., - - - *Association.*
Athen., - - - *Athenæum.*
Atty., - - - *Attorney.*
B., - - - - *Born.*
B. A. Journ., - *British American Journal.*
B. N. A., - - *British North America.*
Bib. de Voyages, - *Bibliothèque des Voyages.*
Bish., - - - *Bishop.*
Bos., - - - *Boston.*
Brit., - - - *British.*
Brit. Am. Mag., - *British American Magazine.*
Brit. Can. Rev., - *British Canadian Review.*
Brit. and For. Med. { *British and Foreign Me-*
Chir. Rev., { *dical Chirurgical Review.*
Brit. Med. Journ., - *British Medical Journal.*
Can., - - - *Canada, Canadian.*
Can. Journ., - - *Canadian Journal.*
Can. Lit., - - *Canadian Literature.*
Can. Mag., - - *Canadian Magazine.*
Can. Med. Journ., - *Canada Medical Journal.*
Can. Merch. Mag., - { *Canadian Merchant's Magazine.*
Can. Nat., - - *Canadian Naturalist.*
Can. News, - - *Canadian News.*
Can. Rev. & Mag., - { *Canadian Review and Magazine.*
Cath., - - - *Cathedral.*
Ch., - - - *Church.*
Charlottet., - - *Charlottetown.*
Clergym., - - *Clergyman.*
Clk., - - - *Clerk.*
Co., - - - *Company, County.*
Cob., - - - *Cobourg.*
Col., - - - *Colonial.*

Col. Mag., - - *Colonial Magazine.*
Coll., - - - *College.*
Com., - - - *Commissioner.*
D., - - - *Died.*
Do., - - - *Ditto.*
Dub., - - - *Dublin.*
Ed., - - { *Educated, Editor, Edited, Editorship, Edition.*
Edin., - - - *Edinburgh.*
Edin. New Phil. Journ. { *Edinburgh New Philosophical Journal.*
Edin. Rev., - - *Edinburgh Review.*
Eng., - - - *England, English.*
Fam. Herald, - *Family Herald.*
Geo. of Can., - *Geology of Canada.*
Geol. Journ., - *Geological Journal.*
Glasg., - - *Glasgow.*
Gov. Genl., - - *Governor General.*
Govt., - - *Government.*
Gt. Brit., - - *Great Britain.*
Hal., - - *Halifax.*
Ham., - - *Hamilton.*
H. B. T., - *Hudson Bay Territory.*
H. & F. Rec. of Can. { *Home and Foreign Record of Canada Presbyterian*
Presb. Ch., { *Church.*
Irel., - - *Ireland.*
Journ., - - *Journalist.*
Journ. de l'Inst. Pub., { *Journal de l' Instruction Publique.*
Journ. Nat. His., - *Journal of Natural History.*
Journ. of Ed., - *Journal of Education.*
Kings., - - *Kingston.*
L. C., - - *Lower Canada.*
Leg. Assem., - *Legislative Assembly.*
Leg. Coun., - *Legislative Council.*
Lieut. Gov., - *Lieutenant Governor.*
Lit. Garland, - *Literary Garland.*
Lit. Gaz., - *Literary Gazette.*
Lit. & His. Soc., *Literary and Historical Society.*
Lon., - - *London.*

Mag., . . . *Magazine.*
Med. Chir. Jour., *Medical Chirurgical Journal.*
Mem., . . . - *Member.*
Mgr., . . . *Monseigneur.*
Min., ... *Minister.*
Mon. Rev., . . *Monthly Review.*
Mont., . . . *Montreal.*

Nat. His. Soc., - *Natural History Society.*
N. A. Rev., - *North American Review.*
N. B., . . *New Brunswick.*
N. D., . . *No Date.*
N. F. L., . . *Newfoundland.*
N. S., . . *Nova Scotia.*
N. Y., . . *New York.*

Obit., - . . *Obituary.*
Obst. Trans., - *Obstetrical Transactions.*

Path. Trans., - *Pathological Transactions.*
P. E. I., - *Prince Edward Island.*
Phil. Trans., - *Philosophical Transactions.*
Presb., - . . *Presbyterian.*
Proc. Aca. N. S., - { *Proceedings Academy of Natural Sciences.* }
Proc. Geol. Soc., *Proceedings Geological Society.*
Proc. Royal Geog. Soc., { *Proceedings Royal Geological Society.* }
Proc. Zool. Sec., *Proceedings Zoological Society.*
Prof., . . . *Professor.*
Provl. Mag., - *Provincial Magazine.*

Quar. Journ. Anthrop. Soc., { *Quarterly Journal Anthropological Society.* }
Quar. Jour. Chem. Soc., - { *Quarterly Journal Chemical Society.* }
Quar. Med. Journ., *Quarterly Medical Journal.*
Quar. Rev., - . *Quarterly Review.*

Que., . . . *Quebec.*
R. C., - . . *Roman Catholic.*
Rép. Nat., . . *Répertoire National.*
Rev., . . *Reverend.*
Rt. Rev., . . *Right Reverend.*
Sat. Reader, . *Saturday Reader.*
Sat. Rev., . . *Saturday Review.*
Secy., . . . *Secretary.*
Sch., . . . *School.*
Scot., . . . *Scotland.*
Scot. Lit. Gaz., - *Scottish Literary Gazette.*
Sill. Journ., . *Silliman's Journal.*
Sim. Col. Mag., *Simmond's Colonial Magazine.*
Soc., . . . *Society, Société.*
S. P. G. F. P., { *Society for the Propagation of the Gospel in Foreign Parts.* }
Supdt., . . *Superintendent.*
Tor., . . . *Toronto.*
Tp., . . . *Township.*
Trans., . . *Transcript.*
Trans. Am. Ant. Soc. { *Transactions American Antiquarian Society.* }
Trans. Bot. Soc. Can., - { *Transactions Botanical Society.* }
Trans. Irish Aca., *Transactions Irish Academy.*
Trans. N. S. Inst., - { *Transactions Nova Scotia Institute.* }
U. C., . . *Upper Canada.*
U. C. Law Journ., *Upper Canada Law Journal.*
Univ., . . *University.*
U. S., . . *United States.*
Wesl. Meth., . *Wesleyan Methodist.*
West Rev., . . *Westminster Review.*

or invade his personal privacy; that we have asserted what we believe to be the true fundamental principles of the British Constitution, so far as applicable to this colony; that, on this side of the great waters, as on the eastern, we have stood, with the spirit and pertinacity of an Englishman, by those great Whig principles, the practical enunciation of which has saved England alike from monarchical and from mob despotism. The creed of our youth, imbibed from descent, and from early associates, has been that of our maturer age; and if we have failed it is neither from want of love of liberty, nor from want of due honour to the royalty and the institutions which are its best and most glorious guarantees."

Either before or after this time he studied law and was admitted to practice as an advocate of L. C. For a brief period he did not write, and had no connection with the press. In 1849, however, he was induced to undertake the charge of the *Transcript*, of the same city, and continued its senior ed. up to the time of his death. He was also ed. of the *L. C. Agricultural Journal* for some time previous and up to that event. Mr. A. was a man, truly able and well educated; and had so prodigious a memory that no one, in his time, could be better entitled to be called, as he sometimes was, *a walking Encyclopedia!* From the notice of him in the *Gazette* to which we are indebted for much of the above, we learn that during the last year of his life his health and physical energies had been gradually, but perceptibly declining—though he retained his mental faculties up to the last. The same journal pays the following affectionate tribute to his character:

"As an English politician Mr. Abraham took his place in the Whig-radical school; but he—like the late lamented Lord Metcalfe—found the democratic element so strong in this country that he held an English radical might, with perfect consistency, be a Canadian conservative. So, during the time of his connexion with this journal, it was the staunch advocate of liberal-conservative views,—liberal in according and securing to all men their reasonable, constitutional liberties.—Conservative in so curbing innovation as to preserve intact the provincial connection with the mother country. Further we need not speak of his political career in this province—it is before the people in his writings. On the merits of those writings, their elegant

1*

epigrammatic style, the vast stores of useful and curious information which abounded in every thing he wrote, shining forth spontaneously from the overflowing treasury of his cultivated mind, we might say much, but time and space forbid us now. As a geologist and naturalist (particularly in his favourite branch of Natural History, Entomology) he had few equals in Canada—perhaps no superior on this continent. While by his writings he won the admiration of strangers as well as friends, in private life he was one of the most truly generous and kind-hearted—one of the most pure, honest, and sincere men whom it was ever our lot to know. Well may we look upon his loss to journalism as almost irreparable, and the large circle of friends who mourn his loss cannot hope to see his place in their affections again filled by such a man."

I. Some remarks upon the French tenure of "Franc-alleu roturier" and its relation to the Feudal and other tenures. *Montreal*, 1849 ; pp. 81. 8vo.

II. Tracks of a Chelonian Reptile in the Lower Silurian formation at Beauharnois. *B. A. Journ.* 1851.

"With the *Climactichnites* at Perth, there occurs also the *Protichnites* of Owen, the first discovery of which at Beauharnois was made by the late Mr. Robert Abraham, then editor of the Montreal *Gazette*, in which he gave an interesting description of these curious footprints."—SIR W. E. LOGAN : *Geo. of Can.*

ADAMS, J,
   I. Sketches of the Tête de Boule Indians. *Trans. Lit. & His. Soc.* (Quo.) vol. II.

ADAMS, LEVI, a Can. writer, supposed to have been a native of the Eastern Townships, L. C. D. at Montreal, of cholera, 21 July, 1832. Was admitted as an advocate in 1827. While still a student at law contributed to the *Canadian Review*, (1826), "*Jean Baptiste : a Poetic olio ; most respecifully inscribed to Stephen Sewell, Esq.*" Two tales—*The young Lieutenant*, and *The Wedding*, from the same pen, appear in vol. IV of the *Canadian Mag.* (Mon.) Mr. A. was a resident of Henryville, L. C.

ADAMSON, *Rev.* WILLIAM AGAR, *D. C. L.* A clergym. of the Ch. of Eng. in Can. B. in Dublin, Irel., 21 Nov. 1800. His father was Jas. Adamson, Esq., eldest son of the Rev. Christopher Adamson of Ballinalack, Co. Wesmeath and St. Marks, Dublin ; his mother the eldest daughter of Isaac Hutchinson, Esq., of

Violet Hill, Co. Wicklow. In July 1817, he entered Trinity Col., (Dub.), as a gentleman commoner and, in July 1821, graduated as A. B. In 1824, he was ordained and held the curacies of Lockeen and Parsonstown till 1826, when he was presented to the vicarage of Clonlea, Co. Clare. In 1833, he was promoted by the bish. to the vicarage of Ennis, the chief town of that county. In 1838, he was presented by the late Marquis of Normanby to the rectory of Kilcooly, Co. Tipperary. In 1840, having been appointed to the incumbency of Amherst Island, and chaplain to Lord Sydenham, the first Gov. Genl. of B. N. A., he came to Can., and at the union of the Provinces received the appointment of chaplain and librarian to the Legis. Council. Whilst the seat of government was at Montreal, Dr. A., who had received the degree of D. C. L. from McGill Univ. and also from the Univ. of Bishop's Coll. Lennoxville, held the office of assist. min. of Christ Ch. Cathedral, on resigning which to proceed to Toronto, he was presented by the inhabitants of Montreal of all religious denominations with two costly silver salvers, on which were one thousand dollars in gold. Since then, Dr. A. has been assist. min. of St. George's, (Tor.) and St. Paul's, Yorkville ; secretary to the Ch. Soc. of Quebec, afternoon lecturer in the Cathedral of the same city, and now holds a like appointment in Christ's Church, Ottawa. In 1824, Dr. A. married Sarah, second daughter of John Walsh, Esq., of Walsh Park, Co. Tipperary, by whom he has had nine children. As a preacher, he is one of the most eloquent and moving pulpit orators in Am. He occupies a foremost position in the nascent literature of Can. From an early age he has been a constant contributor to the periodicals of Gt. Brit. and Irel., chiefly to the *Dublin University Magazine* and *Blackwood*, and has sent communications to almost every literary serial attempted in Can. It would be an arduous task to enumerate the titles or subjects of one-tenth of these contributions.

I. The Fall of Man : a sermon. *New Irish Pulpit*, 1836, pp. 7.

II. A Sermon preached in St. George's Church, Kingston, 26th Sept. 1841, on the death of Lord Sydenham. *Montreal*, 1841, pp. 14, 8vo.

III. Things to be remembered : a sermon. *Do.* 1846, pp. 32, 4to.

IV. The Order for Divine Service daily throughout the year : a sermon. *Do.* 1847, pp. 15, 8vo.

V. The Churching of Women. *Do.* 1848, pp. 43, 8vo.

VI. Human suffering and Heavenly sympathy : a sermon. *Do.* 1852, pp. 30.

VII. A sermon preached in the Cathedral, Quebec, on the day set apart for humiliation and fasting on account of war between Great Britain and Russia. *Quebec*, 1854, pp. 14, 8vo.

"It is marked by all the fervid eloquence that distinguishes the Reverend preacher, and does equal credit to his head and heart."— *Gazette* (Mont.)

VIII. The decrease, restoration and preservation of Salmon in Canada. *Can. Journ.* 1857.

IX. Salmon Fishing in Canada. By a Resident. Edited by Colonel Sir J. E. Alexander, Kt., K. C. L. S. *London*, 1860, pp. 350, 8vo.

"The book is pleasantly and cleverly written. The author is evidently, as all anglers should be, a true lover of nature, and some of his descriptions of Canadian scenery are given with considerable effect. "— *Literary Gazette* (Lon.)

"One of the most agreeable sporting works of the season. "— *Bell's Life in London*.

ADDERLEY, *Rt. Hon.* C. B. A mem. of the House of Commons, lately Under Secretary of State for the Colonies.

I. Letter to the Rt. Hon. Benj. D'Israeli on the present relation of England with the Colonies, with preface on Canadian affairs. *London*, 1862, 8vo.

"While I acknowledge that this *brochure* has been written with great skill and ingenuity, and in a spirit of commendable moderation, I regret to be compelled, by a sense of duty to the North American Provinces, and the Empire at large, to question the soundness of the conclusions at which you have arrived."—JOSEPH HOWE.

AKINS, THOMAS BEAMISH, *D. C. L.* A barrister of N. S. and Com. of Records for that province.

I. Prize Essay on the history of the settlement of Halifax, at the Mechanics

Institute, 18th April, 1839. *Halifax*, 1847, pp. 62.

"There is an interesting little pamphlet, published by Mr. Akins, respecting the early settlement of Halifax, that is well worthy the perusal of those who feel interested in the early history of the town."—R. G. HALI-BURTON.

II. A sketch of the rise and progress of the Church of England in the British North American Provinces. *Do.* 1849, pp. 151, 8vo.

III. A brief account of the origin, endowment and progress of the University of King's College, Windsor, N. S. *Do.* 1865, pp. 84, 8vo.

ALCOCK, *Rev.* THOMAS, *A. M.*
I. An account of the bombardment and seige of Quebec. *Plymouth*, 1763. French version, *London*, 1770.

ALDER, *Rev.* ROBERT. A Wesl. Meth Min.
I. The substance of a sermon delivered at Charlottetown, on the death of Her Majesty Queen Charlotte. *Charlottetown*, 1819, pp. 40, 8vo.

II. A defence of the proceedings of the extra district meeting of the Wesleyan Missionaries. *St. John*, 1824, pp. 64, 8vo.

III. The substance of a sermon delivered at Montreal, March 25, 1827, on the death of His Royal Highness the Duke of York. *Montreal*, 1827, pp. 28.

ALDRIDGE, *Rev.* MR.
I. A narrative of the Lord's Wonderful Dealings with John Marrant, a black, (now going to preach the Gospel in Nova Scotia). Born in New York, in North America. Taken down from his own relation, arranged, corrected, &c. *London*, 1785, pp. 38, 8vo.

ALEXANDER, JAMES.
I. The Canadian Mercantile Test, a private and confidential document, issued by the compiler and proprietor to bankers and members of the Canada Trade Protection Society, on the express condition of its not being lent or contents exposed to non-subscribers, or any one unconnected with a subscriber's own business establishment. *Toronto*, 1859.

ALEXANDER, *Col. Sir* J. E., *K. C. L. S., F. R. G. S.* A well known Brit. officer

and writer. B. in Stirling, Scot., 16 Oct. 1803. He explored for and surveyed a portion of the military road, leading from Quebec to Halifax.

I. Transatlantic Sketches, comprising visits to the most interesting scenes in North and South America, and the West Indies. With Notes on Negro Slavery and Canadian Emigration : *London*, 1833, 2 vols. 8vo. ; *Philadelphia*, 1833, 8vo.

II. L'Acadie ; or, seven years' explorations in British America. *London*, 1849, 2 vols., pp. 345,—pp. 326, 8vo.

" Sir James Alexander left England in the spring of 1841, having received an appointment in the Staff of the Commander of the Forces in Canada. His military duties and his love of field sports induced him to make excursions in every direction, besides which, he occasionally crossed the frontier to visit the United States. Thus he had the opportunity of seeing great variety of scene and society. We find him at one time in the wildest part of the lakes, paying a visit to the notorious pirate and smuggler, Bill Johnstone ; at another time, housed in a comfortable hotel at New York, exchanging visits with the literary celebrities of that city. He is equally at home in the jovialities of a Canadian winter, and the rough sports of the backwoods. With equal alacrity he examines and relates the arrangements of educational establishments, and surveys the military positions made famous in the last American war. He is just what a soldier should be, incessantly attentive to his profession, but with active sympathy for others, and a judicious observer of what is passing before him."—*Colonial Mag.*

III. Salmon Fishing in Canada. By a Resident. Edited by Sir J. E. Alexander. *London*, 1860, 8vo.

ALEXANDER, *Sir* WILLIAM, *Kt.*, (*Earl of Stirling.*)
I. Copies and translations of the Royal Charters, etc., by which Nova Scotia and Canada were granted, in 1621, 1625 and 1628. *London*, 1831, fol.

Analytical statement of the case of Alexander, Earl of Stirling and Doran, his Official Dignities, peculiar Territorial Rights and Privileges in the British Colonies of Nova Scotia and Canada, with notes and observations. By Sir Thos. Banks. *Do.* 1832, pp. 132, 8vo.

Case of the Rt. Hon. Alexander, Earl of Stirling and Doran, respecting his title to Nova Scotia and other territorial possessions in North America (with Map.) By J. J. Burn. *Do.* 1833, 8vo.

" Sir William Alexander was born in 1580 in Clackmannanshire. He was made gentleman usher to prince Charles in 1613, viscount Stirling in 1630, and earl of Stirling in 1633. He died in 1640, and his grandson succeeded him, who in his turn was succeeded by an uncle named Henry. On the 10—20 September, 1641, King James the first of England (James the 6th of Scotland) granted all Nova Scotia (including what is now New Brunswick) to Sir William Alexander. This grant gives the name of Nova Scotia to the territory, and a copy of it in the original Latin is in the memorials of the English and French commissaries. It was probably issued under the great seal of *Scotland*. This grant was confirmed by another patent from Charles the first of England, dated 12th July, 1625. In 1635 a grant was made to lord Stirling of a district between Pemaquid and St. Croix, and also of Long Island, opposite to Connecticut, (1621). This last grant was made by the Plymouth council. Sir Ferdinando Gorges and captain John Mason, who were both active and interested in the English colonization, and were anxious to secure Acadie from the French, obtained a conveyance from the council of the New England company to Sir William Alexander of the territory included afterwards in his crown patent."—*Murdoch's His. of U. S.*

The trial of Lord Stirling, being Part II. of the Vindication of the Rights and Titles, political and territorial. of Alexander, Earl of Stirling and Doran, Hereditary Lieutenant General and late proprietor of Canada and Nova Scotia. By John L. Hayes, *Washington*, 1853, 8vo.

" We have already given our opinion on the pretensions of Lord Stirling, and can only add that the work before us gives evidence of much labour and outlay in its compilation; attached to the work is a large lithographed sheet containing the fac-similes of a number of French documents of more than a century old, bearing the seals of the British and French governments—a curiosity in itself."—*Mercury (Que.)*

ALGEN, F. (Boston).

I. Chemical examination of Algerite, a new mineral species, by T. S. Hunt, of the Geological Commission of Canada, including a description of the mineral. *Journ. Nat. His.* (BosL) 1848.

ALLAN, *Lieut.* ADAM.

I. The New Gentle Shepherd, reduced to English. *London and Fredericton*, 1798.

In this English version of Allan Ramsay's Pastoral, the author has added a third scene (of his own composition) to the 4th act of the drama. This version of the Scottish Pastoral is uncommonly scarce, and seems to have escaped the notice of Bibliographers.

ALLAN, *Hon.* G. W., *M. L. C.* of Can.

I. On the land-birds wintering in the neighbourhood of Toronto. *Can. Journ.* 1853.

II. Address as President of Canadian Institute. *Do.* 1856.

III.   Do.   *Do.* 1859.

ALLAN, *Rev.* J. A., a Can. poet and writer, residing at Ardath, Wolfe Island, U. C.

I. A Greek Lexicon.

II. Day Dreams by a Butterfly.— *Kingston*, 1854 ; pp. 156.

" 'Day Dreams' is a speculative and philosophical poem, and as such is not to be comprehended in a hasty and careless glance. It shows a high and rich intellect, without which imagination is never worth much; the true poetic spirit and power of expression are to be found there. It is not a poem of mere fancy or sentiment; it appeals to the highest faculties of our nature, and by them it must be judged."—CHAS. SANGSTER.

III. The Lambda-Nu Tercentenary Poem of Shakspeare *Stratford-upon-Avon*, 1864, pp. 46.

" One of the many poems written for the late Tercentenary of William Shakspeare. Mr. Allen could not fail, in a poem of this length, to write many fine passages, and many more still finer thoughts, so largely is he imbued with poetic sentiment, but which his philosophy so greatly interferes with. The poem is very unequal—perhaps intentionally so—some portions of it glowing with a warm redundant fancy, with deep suggestive thought ; and others, again, so lightly and even carelessly flung off, that the critical taste cannot fail to notice the wide discrepancy.   *   *   *   *

We can safely assert that Mr. Allan has done the fullest justice to his subject ; and have every hope that his poem will occupy a high place in the Tercentenary literature of the day. The poem is graced with a copy of the portrait of Shakespeare prefixed to the folio edition of his plays of 1623 by his personal friends Heminge and Condell."—*News* (Kings.)

ALLEN, ETHAN, an Am. Brig. Genl., who distinguished himself during the first Am. Revolutionary War. D. 1789.

I. A Narrative of Col. Ethan Allen's Captivity, from the time of his being taken by the British near Montreal. on the 25th day of September, in the year 1775, to the time of his exchange, on the 6th day of May, 1778. Containing his Voyages and Travels, with the most remarkable occurrences respecting himself, and many other Continental Prisoners of different ranks and characters, which fell under his observation in the course of the same ; particularly the destruction of the prisoners at New York, by General Sir William Howe, in the years 1776 and 1777 ; interspersed with some political observations written by himself, and now published for the information of the curious of all nations. *Newbury*, 1780, pp. 80, 8vo ; An. ed. *Walpole*, 1807, pp. 158, 12mo.; An. ed. *Albany*, 1814, pp. 144, 8vo.

ALLINE, *Rev.* HENRY. An individual who at one time occupied a prominent place in the religious affairs of N. S. B. in Rhode Island, 1748. D. at North Hampton N. H., 1784. In 1760, he went with his parents to N. S, and settled at Newport. Six years afterwards moved as he believed by the spirit, he commenced preaching without ordination, or recognizing any Ecclesiastical authority, but received the imposition of hands as an itinerant preacher, at Cornwallis, in 1779. From the time of his commencing to preach at Falmouth, he had refused any settled charge, and travelled through all or nearly all the then settled portions of N. S., and also some portions of the adjoining Provinces of N. B. and P. E. I. Refusing connexion with any religious denomination, he assailed the ministers of all sects as " poor dark ministers," and wherever he went caused divisions among their people, and formed societies after his own ideas. These were generally known as the " New Lights " and sometimes as " Allinites. " He held a number of strange tenets, such as the denial of creation out of nothing, and the denial of what he called corporeal hardness (i. e. of men having material bodies) before the fall, or even the existence of the material world He maintained that all the souls of men were not only actually created at the beginning of the world, but in Eden actually sinned and fell. He denied the Resurrection, of what he called " the elemental body." On some of the great doctrines of Christianity, he wrote a great deal ; but it is impossible to give a definite idea of his singular sentiments.

With such views, and pursuing such a course, he was regarded on the one hand by his followers with intense admiration, by those of other denominations as a heretic and an enemy both to the truth of God and the peace of the Church. He continued to labour incessantly, travelling and preaching, even after his health gave way. In the summer of 1783, he went to New Eng., where he died in the following year. Of his followers some joined the regular Baptists, but the majority became what are called " Free Christian Baptists," and " Free Will Baptists," two bodies which separated from each other some years ago, but which are almost identical in their tenets. A. is described as having an agreeable manner, and was an impressive and naturally eloquent preacher.

I. Two mites on some of the most important and much disputed points of Divinity, cast into the Treasury for the welfare of the poor and needy, and committed to the perusal of the unprejudiced and impartial reader. *Halifax*, 1781, pp. 342, 18mo.

II. A Sermon preached to and at the request of a Religious Society of young men, united and engaged for the maintaining and enjoying religious worship, in Liverpool on the 19th Nov., 1782. *Do.*

III. Sermon preached at Fort Medway. *Do.*, 1783, pp. 44, 8vo.

IV. The Anti-Traditionists. *Do.*, 1783 (?).

V. Another volume, title unknown.

VI. Life and Journals. *Boston*, 1806, pp. 180, 12mo.

The whole of this latter vol. was written by A., with the exception of the concluding part, describing his last sickness and death.

A Rev. gentleman of N S., in a letter to the author, remarks : " The first of these works exhibits his peculiar views. It is a singular book. In its statements of doctrines it is the most confused medley that one could imagine, almost resembling a sick man's dreams, and yet it is varied with the most impassioned, and I might say, eloquent appeals, when he touches on some of the grander or more tender topics of religion. In fact his religion was a religion of feeling, and his followers were characterized in their proceedings by fanatical extravagance, which disgusted sober-minded Christians. From his " *Life* " one has no doubt that he was a good man, but as little that he was a thorough fanatic. I have no doubt that by the earnestness and rousing nature of his preaching, he did much good 'in his day, particularly as much of the Province was at that time very destitute of preachers; but for the causes mentioned, his career was also attended with many evils. The few copies of his books that are in existence, are so prized by his admirers, that they could not be bought for their weight in gold."

AMBROSE, *Rev. John, M. A.* A clergym. of the Ch. of Eng. (St. Margaret's Bay, N. S.) Has written anonymously in prose and verse for local papers and contributed to the *Church Journal*, (N. Y.) During his under-graduate course at King's Coll., N. S., took the prize for English verse.

I. Some account of the Petrel—the Sea Serpent—and the Albicore—as observed at St. Margaret's Bay,—together with a few observations on Beach mound, or Kitchen-midden, near French village. *Trans. N. S. Inst.* 1864.

II. Observations on the Sea Birds frequenting the coast of St. Margaret's Bay. *Do.* 1864–5.

AMOS, A.
I. Reports of trials in the Courts of Canada, relative to the destruction of the Earl of Selkirk's settlement on the Red River; with observations. *London*, 1820, pp. iv and 388, 8vo.

AMSDEN, SAMUEL. A Can. journ. B. in London, Eng., Oct. 1820. D. at Dunnville. U. C., 1867. Was employed in the Customs in different capacities by the Can. Govt. Held the rank of Major in the Volunteer Militia. Was ed. and prop. of the *Independent*, (Dunnville), a conservative newspaper, from 1857 to 1866. As a public writer maintained a respectable position on the Can. newspaper press.

ANDERSON, DAVID.
I. Canada ; or, a view of the importance of the British American Colonies ; shewing their extensive and improveable resources, and pointing out the great and unprecedented advantages which have been allowed to the Americans over our own colonists ; together with the great sacrifices which have been made by our late commer-

cial regulations of the commerce and carrying trade of Great Britain to the United States, &c. *London*, 1814, pp. 355, 8vo.

ANDERSON, *Rt. Rev.* D., *D. D.* For a long time Bish. of Rupert's Land, recently resigned. Was President of the Institute of Rupert's Land, before which he read one or two interesting papers.

I. Seal of Apostleship, an Ordination sermon, preached at St. Andrews' Church, Red River. *London*, 1851, 8vo.

II. Notes of the flood at the Red River, 1852. *Do.* 1853, 12mo.

III. Journal of a visit to Moose and Albany. *Do.* 1854, 12mo.

IV. The net in the bay ; a journal by the Bishop of Rupert's Land. *Do.* 1854, fscap.

ANDERSON, JAMES, *F. R. S. E.* Was ed. of *The Farmer's Journal,* and of the *Trans. of the Board of Agriculture, L. C.* (Mont.)

I. The improvement of agriculture and the elevation in the social scale of both husbandman and operative. *Montreal*, 1858, pp. 22.

II. The Union of the British North American Provinces considered, in a letter addressed to the citizens of British America, by Obiter Dictum. *Do.* 1859.

ANDERSON, W. J., *M. D., M. R. C. S.,* (EDIN.) One of the Vice-Presidents of the Lit. & His. Soc. (Que.) Was connected with the newspaper press in N. S.

I. The Gold Fields of the world, our knowledge of them, and its application to the Gold Fields of Canada. *Quebec*, 1864, pp. 46, 12mo.

II. The Gold Fields of Nova Scotia. *Trans. Lit. & His. Soc.* (Que.) 1863–4.

III. On the coal-like Substance, or " Altered Bitumen," found in the excavations at Fort No. 3, Point Levis, and the presently accepted theories on the origin of Coals, Bitumens, and Petroleum Springs, with an account of the " Carboniferous System" of British North America. *Do.* 1865–6.

ANDREW, WILLIAM, *M. A.* A Can. journ. B. at Glasgow, 1804. D. at Aberdeen, 1862. Educated at Marischal Coll.,

Aberdeen. Was for some time Prof. of Mathematics in McGill Coll., and Rector of the High School (Que.) He filled the office of President of the Lit. & His. Society of that city several terms. Ed. the *Daily Chronicle* (Que.) for some years.

"Without remarkable brilliancy of style Mr. Andrew's productions were usually characterised by logical conclusion, and purity and elegance of diction."—*Daily News*, (Que.)

ANDREWS, F. H.

I. A collection of original Sacred Music; arranged in full score, with organ or piano-forte accompaniment. *Quebec*, 1848.

"This work is highly creditable, both to the Province and the author." *Gazette*, (Mont.)

ANDREWS, F. H., Jr.

I. Shipping Culler's. Lumberman's and Shipmaster's pocket ready reckoner for square timber. *Quebec*, 1853.

ANDREWS, ISRAEL D. Late Consul for the U. S. at St. John, N. B.

I. Report on the Trade and Commerce of the British North American Colonies, and upon the Trade of the Great Lakes and Rivers since 1829. Presented to the United States Senate. (With Atlas.) *Washington*, 1851, pp 775, 8vo. (Executive Document.)

Prepared for the U. S. Govt., at the time when the Reciprocity Treaty with B. N. A. was in contemplation.

"Our sole object in this brief notice is, to call attention to one of the most laboriously and faithfully prepared public documents that have ever seen the light. The author has been unwearied in his endeavours to prepare the way for a system of reciprocal free trade between the United States and the British Provinces. He shows that our existing tariff operates as a prohibitory duty with regard to many of the Exports from the Colonies, and, in that same proportion, cuts off the profits of the return sales; and that, were all restrictions removed, our ports would be the chief emporia of colonial commerce."—*N. A. Rev.*

ANGERS, F. REAL, a French Can. lawyer. B. 1813. D. at Quebec, Apl. 1860. Admitted to the bar at an early age. He was a reporter of the Parliamentary debates to the L. C. Assem. previous to the Union. In conjunction with Mr. Loranger, defended the *Censitaires* before the Seigniorial Court. From

1851.up to his death was one of the editors of the *Décisions des Tribunaux du Bas Canada,* (Que.)

I. Système de Sténographie, *Québec*, 1836, 8vo.

II. Les révélations du crime, ou Cambray et ses complices, Chroniques Canadiennes de 1834. *Do.* 1837, pp. 77.

ANNAND, *Hon.* WILLIAM. A N. S. journ. and politician. B., we believe, in the Co. of Halifax, N. S., which he has represented in the N. S. Parliament. Was associated with Mr. Howe in the ed. of the *Nova Scotian*, of which journal he is now proprietor. He is also ed. and prop. of the *Daily Chronicle*, (Hal.) Was for some time Provl. Secy. of N. S.

I. The Speeches and Public Letters of the Hon. Joseph Howe, [Edited] *Boston*, 1858, 2 vols., pp. 642—558, 12mo.

II. Confederation. A letter to the Right Honorable the Earl of Carnarvon, Principal Secretary of State for the Colonies. *London*, 1866, pp. 42, 8vo.

ANSPACH, *Rev.* LEWIS AMADEUS. "Late a Magistrate of Newfoundl. and Missionary for the district of Conception Bay."

I. Summary of the Laws of Commerce and Navigation, adapted to the present State, Government and Trade of the Island of Newfoundland. *London*, 1809, 8vo.

II. A history of the island of Newfoundland; containing a description of the island, the banks, the fisheries, and the trade of Newfoundland, and the coast of Labrador. (With two maps.) *Do.* 1819, pp. 512, 8vo.

APPLETON, LYDIA ANN.

I. Miscellaneous Poems, Moral and Religious, written on various occasions. *Toronto*, 1850, pp. 92.

ARCHBOLD, JOHN.

I. On the failure of the Apple Tree in the neighbourhood of Montreal. *Can. Nat.* 1862.

ARCHIBALD, A. K. (Colchester, N. S.)

I. Poems. *Boston*, 1848, pp. 200, 8vo.

ARCHIBALD, C. D. A Barrister, N. S. Resides in Eng.

I. British North American Railways. Letter to His Excellency the Rt. Hon. the Earl of Elgin and Kincardine. *Halifax*, pp. 11, 8vo.

II. Letter to the Duke of Newcastle, K. G., relating to the Intercolonial or Halifax and Quebec Railway. 1860, pp. 16, 8vo.

ARDAGH, W. D. A practising Barrister at Barrie, U. C. Ed. the *Upper Canada Law Journal*, (Tor.), from 1856 till 1857, when he became joint ed. with Mr. Harrison. Since 1866 has been joint ed. of the *U. C. Law Journal* and of the *Local Courts' and Municipal Gazette*, (Tor.)

ARFWEDSON, C. D.,
I. The United States and Canada in 1832, 1833 and 1834. *London*, 1834, 2 Vols. 8vo.

ARMOUR, ROBERT, jr. A Can. writer. B. 1809. D. at Montreal, 4th Oct., 1845. Was the eldest son of the late Mr. Robert Armour, a well known Can. publisher and bookseller, and had adopted the law as a profession. At the time of his death held the appointment of Law Clerk to the Leg. Council, Can. For some years he had ed. the *Gazette* (Mon.) In 1829, his father commenced the publication of the *Montreal Almanack and Lower Canada Register*, a very useful and well arranged annual, which was published for several years under the ed. of the above.

ARMSTRONG, JAMES, Advocate.
I. A treatise on the Law relating to Marriages in Lower Canada. *Montreal*, 1857, pp. 46, 8vo.

ARMSTRONG, *Major-Gen.* JOHN.
I. Notices of the war between Great Britain and America in 1812. *New York*, vol. I. pp., 263, 1836 ; 12mo. Vol. II. *Do.* 1840.

ARMSTRONG, WILLIAM. A Can. journ. B. and educated at Edinburgh, Scot. Studied law in his native city for some years, and in 1833, emigrated to Can. In the succeeding year he took up his residence in N. Y., and entered into business as a druggist, sometimes contributing to a newspaper published by a friend, called the *Scottish Journal.* In 1844 he returned to Can., establishing himself at Kingston, where in 1847 he first commenced his connection with the Can. press by joining the staff of the *British Whig*, as sub-ed. a position which he held until 1851, when he became ed. of *The Argus.* Two years afterwards, on the death of the

proprietor, Mr. A. purchased this newspaper, changing its name to the *Commercial Advertiser*, and under that name it took a prominent part in discussing the many important political movements of the day. In 1859 Mr. A.'s office being destroyed by fire, he purchased the *Herald* of the same city and united it with his other paper under the name of the *Herald & Advertiser*, which he continued to own and conduct up to a recent period. In politics Mr. A supported the policy of the Liberal Conservatives of U. C.

ASCHER, ISIDORE G., *B. C. L.* A Can. poet. B. in Glasgow, Scot., 1835. His early days were spent at Plymouth, Eng. When 8 years of age he came with his parents to Can., and was educated at the High Sch. of Montreal, in which city his family had taken up their residence. On leaving sch. he entered his father's counting house, but after a few years experience finding his occupation distasteful and irksome he abandoned the ledger for the law, and in due time was called to the Bar of L. C., receiving the degree of B. C. L. from McGill Coll. For some years he had been known as the author of many poetical pieces, among which were some beautiful and tender lyrics, which had appeared in the provincial press under his Christian name " *Isidore*." They had attracted a degree of attention, and called forth the well merited praise of several of the Can. newspapers. One western journal remarked :—

" 'Isidore' is the *nom de plume* over which some one occasionally writes for the Montreal papers, and we must confess that the pieces evince more genuine poetic feeling, melody of diction, and happiness of expression, than those of any Canadian poet we yet have had the fortune to peruse."

In 1863, at the solicitation of his friends and others, he collected those of his printed pieces which he no doubt considered as his best and, together with other new pieces, published them in a volume called *Voices from the Hearth.* The book was well received by the public and warmly commended by the press. The edition was speedily exhausted. Since 1864, Mr. A. has resided in Eng., where he contributes regularly to one or two of the leading London magazines. His later poems, some of which have been reproduced in the Can. newspapers, decidedly attest to a more matured and experienced hand, and are well worthy of their authorship. We believe that Mr. A. intends bringing out a new volume of Poems from the London press shortly.

I. Voices from the Hearth : a Collection of Verses. *Montreal*, 1863, pp. 168, 8vo.

"We must conclude, • • • , at the same time stating that we have not for a long while read a more pleasing collection of short poems, written with elegance, truth of sentiment, and genuine poetic feeling. • • It has made us for a few moments forget the mechanical life around us, and lose ourselves in that indescribable absence from sensual objects, which is a vision of our higher humanity."—*Colburn's Mon. Mag.*, (Lon.)

"The writer's muse is essentially of the household; and he cannot do better than to continue to worship its gods, for there he is emphatically at home."—*Athen.*, (do.)

"Mr. Ascher's poems are distinguished by a pleasant and lively fancy, by gay and cheerful feeling, often, however, overshadowed by a pathetic tenderness;—and at times they give evidence that the writer feels the deeper mysteries and passions of human nature and human life. The moral spirit throughout is of the highest; it is one of mildness, of goodness, and yet of uncompromising right; it is gracious, generous, and of the most ample liberality and charity; it is of the most comprehensive humanity, truly tolerant but never temporising."—HENRY GILES: *Boston Transcript.*

ASHBURTON, *Lord.* Ambassador to Am. in 1841. D. 1848.

I. Speech on the Second Reading of the Canada Government Bill. *London*, 1838, 8vo.

ASHE, *Commander* E. D., *R. N., F. R. S.* Has been Director of the Observatory at Quebec for many years. Is President of the Lit. & His. Soc. (Que.)

I. Water Power of Quebec. *Trans. Lit. & His. Soc.* (Que.) 1855.

II. Plan of raft to rescue passengers from sinking ships. *Do.* do.

III. Journal of a voyage from New York to Labrador to observe the Solar Eclipse. *Do.* do.

IV. Notes of a journey across the Andes. *Do.*, 1862.

V. Motions of the Top, Tectotum and Gyroscope. *Do.*, 1863-4.

VI. Result of observations for the determination of the latitude of the Quebec Observatory. *Do.* do.

VII. On the employment of the Electric Telegraph in determining the Longitude of some of the principal places in Canada. *Can. Journ.* 1859.

ASHWORTH, HENRY.
I. A tour in the United States, Cuba, and Canada. *London*, 1861, cr. 8vo.

ASSIKINACK, FRANCIS, "a warrior of the Odahwahs." Educated at U. C. Coll. Filled the office of Interpreter to the Indian Dept., Can.

I. Legends and traditions of the Odahwah Indians. *Can. Journ.*, 1858.

II. Social and warlike customs of the Odahwah Indians. *Do.*, do.

III. The Odahwah Indian language. *Do.*, do.

IV. Remarks on preceding paper. *Do.*, 1860.

ATCHESON, NATHANIEL, *F. A. S.* A London Solicitor. Was agent for N. S., in London, for some years.

I. American encroachments on British Rights ; or, Observations on the importance of the British North American Colonies, and on the late treaties with the United States ; with remarks on Mr. Baring's examination ; and a defence of the shipping interest from the charge of having attempted to impose on Parliament, and of factious conduct in their opposition to the American Intercourse Bill (with 2 maps). *London*, 1808 ; pp. about 370, 8vo.

II. Compressed view of the points to be discussed in treating with the United States of America [relating to the Boundary Question] (with maps). *Do.*, 1814, 8vo.

ATCHESON, R. S. Was Commissioner of Trust and Loan Company of U. C. for many years.

I. Letter on the means by which it is proposed to carry on the undertaking of the Trust and Loan Company of Upper Canada. *London*, 1845, pp. 12.

ATKINSON, *Rev.* T.

I. Christian Unity : a Sermon. *Quebec*, 1842, pp. 23.

ATKINSON, *Rev.* W. CHRISTOPHER, *A. M.*
Was Pastor of Presb. Ch., Mascreen, St. George's.

I. A historical and statistical account of New Brunswick, B. N. A. With advice to Emigrants. *Edinburgh*, 3rd Ed., 1844, pp. 14–284, 12mo.

ATTY, P. T. S.

I. Law and Lawyers in Canada West. *Ang. Am. Mag.*

AUBERT, R. P., *O. M. I.*

I. Le Rationalisme. *Rev. Can.* 1864.

AUBIN, N. A French Can. journ. B. at Paris, France, 1812. Came to Can. 1834. At the time of the Insurrection in 1837, commenced the publication at Quebec of a humourous and satirical paper called *Le Fantasque*, of which he was ed. The articles in this sheet displayed considerable pungency and wit, not unmixed with some amount of acritude, and directed, as they generally were, against the dominant party of the day, caused the latter some annoyance and trouble. In 1838, Mr. A. was arrested, and with his printer, incarcerated in the Quebec Gaol, and his press and types seized by the authorities, for the expression of his political views in *Le Fantasque.* After his enlargement he continued his paper up to 1845. In that year he founded *Le Castor*, a journal which enjoyed but a short existence, owing to the great fires which occurred shortly afterwards in Quebec. Subsequently he wrote for *Le Canadien*, and in 1862 founded and ed. *La Tribune* (Que.), as the organ of the L. C. section of the Macdonald-Dorion administration. This paper was but short-lived. Mr. A. is generally recognized as one of the ablest newspaper writers the French Cans. possess. He resided for some time in the U. S., and invented the plan of making gas from water, which has been adopted in some cities of the Union. He is the author of many miscellaneous poems, several of which, in addition to prose articles from his pen, are preserved in *Le Répertoire National* (Mont.) We give the titles of the latter.

I. La Chimie agricole mise à la portée de tout le monde. *Quebec*, 1847, pp. 116.

Répertoire National.

I. Une entrée dans le monde. 1848.

II. La Lucarne d'un vieux garçon. *Do.*

III. Monsieur Desnotes. *Do.*

IV. Petite Revue Parlementaire. *Do.*
[Containing sketches of Col. Gugy, L. J. Papineau, Andrew Stuart and A. N. Morin.]
V. Cours de Chimie. 1850.

AUBRY, AUGUSTE EUGÈNE. A French Can. journ. B. in France 14 July, 1819. Ed. *Le Courrier du Canada* (Que.) from 1859 until 1865, when he returned to his native country. Was prof. of the faculty of Law in Laval Univ.

Un contemporain—A. E. Aubry. Par L'Abbé H. R. Casgrain (with portrait). *Quebec*, 1865, pp. 103, sm. 4to.

AUBRY, M., *Avocat.*

I. Mémoire pour Michel-Jean-Hugues Péan, Captaine-Aide-Major des Ville et Gouvernement de Québec : *Paris*, Desprès, 1762, *in-4.*

" On trouve dans ce mémoire plusieurs
" détails intéressants sur les dernières opéra-
" tions militaires des Français dans le Canada.
" Pendant le même procès, on a imprimé
" plusieurs autres mémoires, savoir : ceux de
" M. le Marquis de Montcalm, du Sieur de
" Saint-Blin, et du Sieur de Boishébert, Com-
" mandants des Forts : du Sieur Varin, Com-
" missaire Ordonnateur, &c. Tous ces mé-
" moires sont très intéressants, en ce qu'ils
" font connaître le dernier état du Canada
" sous les Français."—*M. de Fontette.*

AUCHINLECK, GILBERT. Was one of the Editors of the *Ang. Am. Mag.* (Tor.), in which his history of the war first appeared.

I. A History of the war between Great Britain and the United States, in 1812–'13 and '14. *Toronto*, 1855, 8vo.

AUSTIN, F. W. G. An Advocate at the Quebec Bar. Has written largely in the local newspaper press on the Fish and Game of Can.

I. Remarks on the Fisheries Bill ; addressed to the Hon. A. Campbell, Commissioner of Crown Lands. *Quebec*, 1865.

" The whole question at issue is the one we have fought and are still fighting—Shall fixed nets be allowed to destroy our fisheries ?

Mr. Austin is, we believe, an officer of the Fish and Game Club, a sort of national society for preventing the fish and game from extermination, and a great deal of good has unquestionably resulted from the labors of these gentlemen."—*Field* (Lon.)

II. On some of the Fishes of the St. Lawrence. *Trans. Lit. & His. Soc.* (Que.) 1865-6.

AUTEROCHE, *L'Abbé* CHAPPE D'. An eminent French astronomer.

I. A voyage to California, to observe the transit of Venus ; by Mons. Chappe d'Auteroche. With an historical description of the author's journey through Mexico, and the Natural History of that Province ; also, a voyage to Newfoundland and Sallee, to make

experiments on Le Roy's Time-keepers. By M. de Cassini. *Paris*, 1772, 4to. English trans. *London*, 1778, pp. 215, 8vo.

AYLMER, *General* (5th) *Lord*, Gov. Genl. of B. N. A., from 1830 to 1835. B. 1775 ; D. 1850.

Public documents relating to his administration of the Government of Lower Canada. *London*, 1835, pp. 126, 8vo.

"Not printed for sale." *Rich.*

Address to Lord Aylmer from Public Bodies in Lower Canada, on his removal from the Administration of the Government of that Province, in the year 1835, with his answer. *Do.* 1847, 8vo.

Privately printed. *Do.*

B.

BACHELOT DE LA PYLAIE, M.
   I. Voyage à l'Isle de Terre-Neuve, contenant la Description des Isles voisines et des Vues générales sur leur Vegetation. *Paris*, 1825, pp. 131, 8vo.

BACKHOUSE, THOMAS, " Master of H. M. S. Thisbe."
   I. Surveys of the principal harbours on the coast of Nova Scotia. 1798.

BACON, AVERY D.
   I. A treatise on Bees ; their management, diseases and method of cure. *Aylmer, L. C.*, 1864.

BADDELEY, *Lieut.* F. H., Royal Engineers, (now Lieut. Genl., half pay.)
   I. On the Geology of a portion of the Labrador coast. *Trans. Lit. & His. Soc.* (Que.) vol. 1.
   II. On the Geonosy of a part of the Saguenay country. *Do. do.*
   III. Additional notes on the Geonosy of St. Paul's Bay. *Do.* vol. II.
   IV. On the Magdalen Islands. *Do.* vol. III.
   V. Geological sketch of the most S. E. portion of Lower Canada. *Do. do.*
   VI. Tabular view of Minerals which decrepitate with heat. *Do.* vol. IV.

"Lieutenant, now Major General Baddeley, of the Royal Engineers, when in Canada, now nearly forty years since, was an ardent promoter of Geological inquiry, and his services were made available to the Provincial Government in explorations in the region of the Saguenay, and in the peninsula of Gaspé. To him we are indebted for the first published notice of the Lower Silurian limestones on Lake St. John, Bay St. Paul, and Murray Bay, as well as of the existence of Gold in the drift of the Eastern Townships."—SIR W. E. LOGAN, *Geo. of Can.*, 1863.

BAGG, STANLEY CLARK, *N. P., F. N. S.* A Can. Numismatologist and Archeologist. B. at Montreal, 1820. In 1862 founded the Numismatic Soc., (Mont.), of which he is a Fellow. Mr. B. is President of the Numismatic and Antiquarian Soc., (Mont.), and a mem. of other local Literary, Scientific, National, Religious and Charitable bodies. He is also a mem. of the Numismatic Societies of London and Philadelphia, and a corresponding mem. of the State Historical Soc. of Wisconsin, U. S. He has written largely for the local press on subjects connected with his favorite studies, and is also the author of some *Hymns for Christmas, Good Friday, Easter and Ascension day.*

I. Notes on Coins : Being the first

paper read before the Numismatic Society of Montreal. *Montreal.*

" This very interesting paper well opened the proceedings of the Society as an introduction to the Study of Numismatics, showing its value and importance, as well as the interest which it excites by its connection with sacred and profane history. He dwells on the ' Widow's Mite ' in the Philadelphia Mint. ''—*Am. Hist. Mag., N. Y.*

" The author of this essay is known as an ardent and accomplished Numismatician, who is not only the founder of the Numismatic Society, but also the first to read a paper before it. The essay briefly reviews the objects of the Science, and contains many interesting notes on coins and medals."— *Medical Circular,* (Lond.)

II. Coins and Medals as aids to the study and verification of Holy Writ. *Do.,* 1863.

" In the present instance, by the pleasant occupation of a few minutes, well spared for the purpose, we have learnt more on the subject of medals and coins, and the use of Numismatics, than we had gathered in our whole life before, simply from having had our attention properly directed to it. We thank Mr. Bagg for showing the value of the science in reference to Holy Writ, and for giving his paper to us in so attractive a form."—*Echo,* (Mont.)

III. A Chronological Numismatic Compendium of Twelve Cæsars, and a summary of remarkable events from the birth of Julius Cæsar, B. C. 100, to the death of Saint John the Evangelist, A. D. 100   *Do.,* the Ides of March, A. D. 1864.

" A very useful numismatic table, intended principally to assist collectors of coins and medals in their historical researches, and also as a work of easy reference for the general reader. The names and titles of the twelve Cæsars, taken from their actual coins, are given in the abbreviated form in which they occur, and also in full, with English translations. Short biographical sketches of the emperors are added, together with summaries of the most remarkable events that, with a few exceptions, have been commemorated by the striking off of coins or medals during the 200 years over which the table extends."—*Journ. of Ed., L. C.*

IV. Canadian Archæology. *Do.,* 1864, pp. 9, 8vo.

V. Archæologia Americana. *Do.,* 1864, pp. 11, 8vo.

VI. The Antiquities and Legends of Durham, a lecture before the Numismatic and Antiquarian Society. *Do.,* 1866, pp. 21, 8vo.

BAILEY, J.
I. The Gold-Digger's Manual. *Quebec,* 1864.

BAILEY, Rev. JACOB, A. M.
I. The Frontier Missionary ; a Memoir of the Life of the Rev. Jacob Bailey, A. M., Missionary at Pownalborough, Maine, Cornwallis and Annapolis, N. S. (With illustrations, notes and appendix.) By Rev. W. S. Bartlett, *Boston,* 1853, 8vo.

" This work is of rare historical and antiquarian value, being largely composed of the diaries of Mr. Bailey, who was born in Massachusetts, in 1731 ; became a clergyman of the Church of England, was employed by the Society for Propagating the Gospel in Foreign Parts as a missionary in Maine, whence he was driven by the war of the Revolution, and took refuge as a royalist in Nova Scotia, where he discharged the duties of his profession till his death, in 1808, at the age of seventy-six."—DUYCKINCK.

BAILEY, LORING W., *A. M.* A N. B. Geologist. Prof. of Chemistry and Natural Science, Univ. of N. B.

I. Notes on New Species of Microscopical Organisms from the Para River, South America. *Cambridge, Mass.,* 1861, 8vo.

II. Notes on Diatomaceae from the St. John River. (From *Can. Nat.,)* 1863, pp. 4.

III. Report on the mines and minerals of New Brunswick, with an account of the present condition of mining operations in the Province. *Fredericton,* 1864, pp. 73, 2 Ed's.

IV. Notes on the Geology and Botany of New Brunswick. With a Geological Map. (From *Can. Nat.,)* *Do.,* 1864, pp. 17.

V. Observations on the Geology of Southern New Brunswick, made principally by Prof. L. W. Bailey, Messrs. G. F. Matthew and C. F. Hartt ; prepared and arranged, with a Geological Map, by L. W. Bailey. *Do.,* 1865, pp. 158.

" Without any invidious comparison, we may say that Prof. Bailey's report is distinguished for clearness, systematic arrangement, and careful attention to details ; and that its execution must have involved a large amount of laborious field-work."—*Can. Nat.*

BAILLAIRGÉ, C. P. F. A Can. Civil Engineer, Architect and Surveyor practising at Quebec.

I. Nouveau Traité de Géométrie et de Trigonométrie rectiligne et sphérique, suivi du toisé des surfaces et des volumes, et accompagné de tables de logarithmes des nombres et sinus, etc., naturels et logarithmiques et d'autres tables utiles. Ouvrage théorique et pratique illustré de plus de 600 vignettes, avec un grand nombre d'exemples et de problèmes à l'usage des Arpenteurs, Architectes, Ingénieurs, Professeurs et Elèves, etc. *Québec*, 1866, pp. xlviii—728—108, 4to.

"Cet ouvrage, le plus considérable de ce genre qui ait encore vu le jour en Canada, est appelé, croyons-nous, à jouir d'un grand succès. A la fois théorique et pratique, l'ouvrage de M. Baillairgé s'adresse à une classe nombreuse qui saura en apprécier toute la clarté et toute la simplicité de la disposition. Le but de l'auteur a été de rendre plus facile l'étude d'une partie des sciences mathématiques et d'éliminer des ouvrages suivis dans les écoles une foule de propositions qui en rendent les abords si ingrats et si arides. C'est ainsi qu'il a réduit de plus de moitié les deux cents et quelques propositions des six premiers livres d'Euclide; en outre, il a entièrement séparé le cinquième livre dont il a mis les théorèmes les plus importants au nombre des principes ou axiomes. C'est une voie nouvelle que M. Baillargé cherche à frayer à l'étude de cette science."—JOSEPH ROYAL: *Rev. Can.*

BAILLARGEON, *Rt. Rev.* C. F. Bish. of Tloa, Coadjutor and Administrator of the R. C. Diocese of Quebec. B. in Can. 26 April, 1798.

I. Le Nouveau Testament de Notre Seigneur Jésus Christ, traduit en français avec le commentaire littéral du P. de Carrière dans le texte et des notes explicatives, morales et dogmatiques pour en faciliter l'intelligence au public avec l'approbation de Mgr. l'Archevêque de Québec. *Québec*, 1846. 2d Ed. do., 1865, pp. xiv., and 817, 8vo.

"The translation of the Vulgate, of which we have here a remodelled edition, was undertaken at the instance of Mgr. Signay, when the author was still *curé* of Quebec, and published for the first time about the year 1846. In the former ed., besides numerous foot notes added by the translator, the commentaries of Père de Carrières had been interwoven with the text—an arrangement that proved embarrassing and defective. In expunging the commentaries from

the text for the present ed., it was found that many portions of the narrative, as translated, would require to be altered in consequence of the intended change, or because His Lordship believed they were susceptible of a more literal rendering, and the greatest part of the text has been retranslated accordingly. The work is enriched besides by the addition of notes to the 1600 contained in the first edition."—*Journ. of Ed. L. C.*

II. Recueil d'Ordonnances Synodales et Episcopales du Diocèse de Québec. *Do.* 1859; 2nd ed. (revised and corrected.) *Do.* 1865, pp. 316, 8vo.

BAILLIE, HUGH, LL.D., late Judge of the Court of Admiralty, (Eng.)

I. A letter to Dr. Shebear: containing a refutation of his arguments concerning the Boston and Quebec Acts of Parliament: and his aspersions upon the memory of King William and the Protestant Dissenters. *London*, 1775, pp .54, 8vo.

BAILLIE, THOMAS.

I. An account of the Province of New Brunswick; including a description of the settlements, institutions, soil and climate of that important Province; with advice to Emigrants. (With Map.) *London*, 1832, pp. 134, 12mo.

BAIRD, *Rev.* JAMES, *A. M.* Pastor of Carleton Presb. Ch., St. John, N. B. Ed. at Belfast, Glasgow and Edinburgh. Has published a Sermon in memory of the late Rev. Nicholas Murray, D. D., author of "*Kirwin's Letters,*" 1861; Notes of a tour in Canada and the United States 1863; and a lecture entitled "*Education in its higher relations*" 1866.

BAKER, HENRY. Owen Sound, U. C.

I. Translations and choice pieces from some of the best French and German authors. *Montreal*, 1867, pp. 286.

"The selections are as varied as they are admirable."—*Daily News*, (Mont.)

BALDWYN, AUGUSTA. A Can. poet. Is the daughter of the late Rector of St. John's, L. C. Miss B. has contributed poetical pieces to the periodical and newspaper press for many years. In 1839–40 she wrote for the *Literary Garland*, (Mont.), and about the same time for the *Christian Mirror* (Bos.) Subsequently poems from her pen appeared in the *Ladies' Repository*, and the *Cultivator* (Bos.), the *News* (St. John's,) and the *Family Herald* (Mont.)

I. Poems, *Montreal*, 1859, pp. 163, 12mo.

BALLANTYNE, R. M. A popular author of works of Fiction and Adventure.

I. Hudson's Bay ; or every-day life in the wilds of North America during six years residence in the territories of the Hon. Hudson's Bay Company. [With illustrations.) *Edinburgh*, 1848, 8vo.; 3rd Ed.. 1858, cr. 8vo. ; *New York.*

II. Snow flakes and Sunbeams ; or, the young Fur Traders, a tale of the Far North. *Do.* 1856, cr. 8vo. ; *New York.*

III. Ungava ; a tale of Esquimaux-Land. *Do.* 1857, 8vo. ; *New York.*

IV. Columbia Gold Fields. *Do.* 1858.

BANCROFT, *Rev.* CHARLES, *D. D.* Honorary Canon of Christ Ch. Cathedral, and Min. of Trinity Ch. (Mont.)

I. Sermon preached on the death of the Rev. Mark Willoughby. *Montreal*, 1847.

II. Farewell Sermon ; delivered at St. Thomas's Church, Montreal. *Do.* 1847, pp. 29.

III. Family Prayers; selected from various approved manuals. *Do.* 3rd Ed. 1857, pp. 96, 8vo.

BANCROFT, *Hon.* GEORGE. An Am. historian.

Inauguration of the Perry Statue, Sept. 10, 1860, including a history of the battle of Lake Erie, by G. Bancroft. *Cleveland O.*, 1861, 8vo.

BANKS, T. C.

I. Baronia Anglia Concentrata ; or, a Concentration of all the Baronies in Fee, deriving their Origin from Writ of Summons, and not from any Specific Limited Creation, showing the descent and Line of Heirship, as well of those Families mentioned by Sir William Dugdale, as of those whom that celebrated author has omitted to notice, &c. *London*, 1844 ; 2 vols., 4to.

" Pages 210–300 contain an Historical account of the first settlement of Nova Scotia, and of the foundation of the order of Nova Scotia Baronets, with the Charters in favour of Sir William Alexander."—J. R. SMITH.

BANNISTER, JOHN WILLIAM, " Rice Lake, U. C."

I. Sketches of Plans for Settling in Upper Canada, a portion of the unemployed Labourers of Great Britain and Ireland. 3rd Ed. *London*, 1826, pp. 39, 8vo.

II. On Emigration to Canada. *Do.*, 1831, 8vo.

BARCLAY, *Captain.*

I. Agricultural tour in the United States and Upper Canada. *London*, 1842, 8vo.

BARCLAY, CHARLES.

I. Letters from the Dorking emigrants who went to Upper Canada, in the Spring of 1832. (Edited.) *London*, 1833.

BARCLAY, *Rev.* JOHN, *D. D.* Min. of St. Andrews' Presb. Ch. (Tor.)

I. The Throne established by Righteousness : a sermon preached on the Queen's Birthday. *Toronto*, 1863, pp. 24, 8vo.

II. A Sermon preached on the occasion of the lamented death of the Hon. Archibald McLean, President of Her Majesty's Court of Error and Appeal for Upper Canada. *Do.* 1865, pp. 39, 8vo.

BARNSTON, GEORGE. An officer in the H. B. Co.'s Service. Resides at Montreal.

I. Remarks upon the Geographical Distribution of the Order Ranunculaceæ, throughout the British possessions of North America. *Can. Nat.* 1857,

II. Remarks on the Geographical Distribution of Plants in the British possessions of North America. *Do.* 1858.

III. Remarks on the Geographical Distribution of the Cruciferæ, throughout the British possessions in North America. *Do.* 1859.

IV. Geographical Distribution of the Genus Allium in British North America. *Do.* do.

V. Catalogue of Coleoptera collected in the Hudson's Bay Territories. *Do.* 1860.

VI. Abridged sketch of the life of Mr. David Douglas, Botanist, with a few details of his travels and discoveries. *Do. do.*

"A very interesting memoir."—BISHOP FULFORD.

VII. Recollections of the Swans and Geese of Hudson's Bay. *Do.* 1861.

VIII. Remarks on the Genus Lutra, and on the species inhabiting North America. *Do.* 1863.

"The name of Mr. Barnston is not unknown in Britain as that of a Scientific Collector, and his valuable contribution from this country may be seen in the Entomological Department of the British Museum."—BISHOP ANDERSON, of Rupert's Land.

BARNSTON, JAMES, *M. D.* Son of the above. B. at Norway House, H. B. Territory, 3 July, 1831. D. at Montreal, 20 May, 1858. In 1847 went to Edinburgh, where he studied medicine in the Univ. and in 1851, (being under age), passed the final examination for his degree with the highest honors; he also carried off several prizes, two of which were for Botany, his favourite study. During the 3rd year of his course he filled the post of House Surgeon to the Royal Maternity Hospital, which he resigned on passing his examination. After practising at Selkirk he, in 1852, proceeded to the continent of Europe where he resided for over a year, principally in Paris and Vienna. In 1853, he returned to his native country and commenced practice at Montreal. In 1857, he was appointed to the newly created chair of Botany in McGill Coll., which he held up to the time of his death. During his studies in Scot. he made a large collection of Botanical Specimens which he afterwards added to in Can.

I. General Remarks on the Study of Nature, with special reference to Botany. *Can. Nat.* 1857.

II. Hints to the young Botanist, regarding the collection, naming and preserving of Plants. *Do. do.*

III. Introductory Lecture to the course on Botany before Students of Arts and Medicine, McGill College. *Do. do.*

IV. Catalogue of Canadian Plants in the Holmes' Herbarium in the Cabinet of the University of McGill College. *Do.* 1859.

"Dr. Barnston held * * the office of Curator and Librarian to the Natural History Society. He was one of its most valued members, and foremost and most active friends. He read many interesting papers, and delivered many delightful and instructive lectures, before its members; and among those of his own age, whom he has left behind, we fear the Society will find few upon whom his mantle will fall."—*Can. Nat.*

BARNWALL.

I. The Game-Fish of the Northern States of America, and British Provinces. *New York*, 1862, 12mo.

BARR.

I. Journal of the weather at Montreal. *Phil. Trans.*, 1778.

BARRASS, *Rev.* EDWARD. A Wes. Meth. Min., Gananoque, U. C. Prior to coming to Can. from Eng., published "*A Gallery of Eminent and Popular men, or Sketches of some leading Temperance Advocates,*" and also "*A Gallery of deceased Ministers.*"

I Class Meetings : their origin and advantages. *Sherbrooke*, 1865, pp. 21.

BARRETT, M., *M. A., M. D.*

I. On the composition, structure and development of bone. *Can. Journ.*, 1865.

BARROW, JOHN.

I. Geography of Hudson's Bay : being the remarks of Capt. W. Coats, in many voyages thereto, between 1727 and 1751 ; with extracts from the Log of Capt. Middleton, on his voyage for the discovery of the North-West Passage, in 1741-2. (Ed.) *London*, 1852, 8vo.

BARROW, S.

I. Five hundred questions on the New Testament. *Kingston*, 1820, pp. 70.

BARTHE, GEORGES ISIDORE. A French Can. journ. B. at Ristigouche, (*Baie des Chaleurs*), 16th Nov., 1834. His father, originally a merchant at Carleton, N. B., became a navigator between the Antilles and the St. Lawrence. Ed. at Three Rivers where he also studied for and was (in 1855) admitted to the Bar. In 1852-3, ed. *L'Ere Nouvelle*, (Three Rivers.) In 1855, in conjunction with his brother (J. G. Barthe, whom see) established *Le Bas-Canada*, a semi-weekly journal, having for its principal object French emigration to this country. Its articles were ably written and often reproduced in the London and Paris newspapers ; it had a circulation in

2

France alone of over 500 copies. Unfortunately for the proprietors, who were only partly insured, the establishment and material of *Le Bas-Canada* were destroyed in an extensive fire which occurred at Three Rivers in 1856, and the paper never appeared afterwards. Early in 1857, Mr. B. established the *Gazette de Sorel*. at the town of that name, which he still continues to ed. and publish. Mr. B. possesses considerable talent as a writer, and is strongly attached to *nos institutions, notre langue et nos lois*. He naturally takes the warmest interest in the welfare of his race, and has laboured strenously to the end that his countrymen may occupy their proper place on this continent as a great and enlightened people.

BARTHE, J. G. A French Can. journ. B. at sea, about 1818, on board a vessel commanded by his father. Ed. at Nicolet Coll., and afterwards studied medicine at Three Rivers, which profession, however, he soon abandoned in favor of law. During his Coll. days Mr. B. contracted a habit of writing poetic effusions, to the neglect of severer studies. In 1837, he contributed lengthy pieces in verse, on political subjects and events, to the newspaper press, in which he dealt rather freely with the public occurrences of the day, taking the side of the so called " patriots," and thereby excited the hostility of the Govt. ; he was arrested and confined in Montreal gaol, on a charge of writing an obnoxious ode in honor of Papineau and the Bermuda exiles. Being released, Mr. B. was afterwards called to the Bar, and proceeding to Montreal, ed. *L'Aurore des Canadas*, from 1839 to 1845. He sat for Yamaska in the Leg. Assem. from 1841 to 1845 ; and was afterwards appointed Clk. of the Court of Appeals, L. C., a position which he held for 4 years. While in that office he conceived an idea in favour of an emigration from France to Can., and in furtherance of that object went to France to urge the matter upon the consideration of the proper authorities. He resided at Paris for 3 years, and there contributed to the *Gazette de France* and wrote and published his work on Can. After his return in 1855, he assisted his brother

on *Le Bas Canada*. During the *régime* of Mr. S. Macdonald, he ed. *Le Canadien*, then the organ of the French section of the cabinet. Mr. B. has contributed to *L'Avenir, Le Moniteur, Le Populaire*, and other French Can. newspapers.

I. Le Canada Reconquis par la France. *Paris*, 1855, pp. 483, 8vo.

" Un livre travesti et calomnié par un homme d'esprit, qui n'avait que de l'esprit, qu'il faudrait remettre à sa place dans notre littérature, c'est le *Canada reconquis par la France* de M. Barthe. Cette œuvre éloquente a coûté à son auteur une grande dépense de talent. Un goût sévère aurait dû sans doute restreindre, dans une certaine mesure, les prodigalités d'imagination, mais il fallait un talent abondant pour répandre ainsi tant de richesses sans les compter. Un écrivain économe de ses idées, bien rangé dans ses phrases aurait tiré plusieurs livres de ce seul ouvrage. Il y a dans le *Canada reconquis* de belles et amples idées, une verve, une imagination exubérante, des passages éloquents. Mais les côtés excessifs ont effacé les bons côtés et mis l'ouvrage à la merci d'un railleur."— HECTOR FABRE: *Trans. Lit. & His. Soc. Que.,* 1865-6.

BARTLETT, W. H.

I. Canadian Scenery, illustrated from drawings, by W. H. Bartlett. The literary department by N. P. Willis. *London*, 1842, 2 vols, 4to. Translated into French. *London* and *Paris*, 1857, 2 vols, 4to.

BARTON, J. KING. A native of Can. Was for some years a Clk. to Leg. Assem.

I. Io : a tale of the Ancient Fane. *New York*, 1851, 12mo.

BASS, CHARLES. A well known Shakspearean actor on the Brit. and Am. boards. Was manager of the Caledonian Theatre, (Edin.,) about 1829 ; his rendering of the character of *Falstaff* was considered one of the finest performances of the present century. D. at Hamilton, U. C., where he had taken up his residence some years previously, 1863.

" Bass is a spirited manager."—*Noctes Ambrosiance*, vol. IV.

I. Lectures on Canada, illustrating its present position, and shewing forth its onward progress, and predictive of its future destiny. *Hamilton*, 1863, pp. 45, 8vo.

" As essays upon an interesting subject, they emphatically possess the elements of popular success. The arguments are pleasingly logical and cogent—clothed, as they are, with gorgeous imagery, historical allusions and beautifully stirring quotations, rendering them delightfully readable and impressive."—*The Editor.*

BASTEROT, VICOMTE DE. A French traveller.

I. De Québec à Lima, journal d'un voyage dans les deux Amériques en 1858 et en 1859 *Paris*, 1860, pp. 336, 12mo.

BAYARD, R., *M. D.*

I. Exposition of facts relative to a case of croup, in a letter to Henry Cook, Surgeon. *St. John, N. B.*, 1826, pp. 33, 8vo.

II. A statement of facts as they occurred at the late annual meeting of the Diocesan Church Society ; with a reply to some mis-statements and expositions in the Rev. D. F. Coster's defence of the "Companion to the prayer book." *Do.* 1849, pp. 28, 8vo.

BAYFIELD, *Vice Admiral* HENRY WOLSEY, *R. N.* A celebrated naval Topographer. B. in Eng. Entered the navy in 1806 as a supernumerary volunteer, and after seeing considerable active service was appointed to the command of a gunboat on the Can. Lakes, towards the close of the war, in 1814. In the following year he assisted in the survey of Lake Ontario, and in 1817 became an admiralty surveyor, and was appointed to the survey of Lakes Erie and Huron, in which work he continued until 1823, when he commenced the survey of Lake Superior. In 1825 he returned to Eng. and was employed by the Admiralty to complete the charts of the Lakes. In 1827 he was appointed to the Survey of the St. Lawrence, on which he is still engaged. This great work has been extended so as to include the whole of the river and gulf of St. Lawrence, from Montreal through the Straits of Belle-isle to Cape St. Lewis on the Labrador coast, all tributary streams as far as they are navigable, the islands of Anticosti, Mingan, the Magdalens, P. E. I., Cape Breton, &c., the coast of N. S., westward to Halifax, including Sable Island. His charts of the St. Lawrence, &c., published by the Admiralty have been found singularly accurate in all

particulars. Admiral B. was a resident of Quebec from 1827 to 1841. He was one of the original members (and is now an honorary mem.) of Lit. and His. Soc. of that city, and took an active part in its transactions. He is also a mem. of the Astronomical Soc. of London and of the *Soc. Géologique de France.* Since 1841 he has resided at Charlottetown, P. E. I.

I. Sailing directions for the Gulf and River St. Lawrence. *London*, 2nd Ed., vol. I, 1843 ; vol. II, 1847, 8vo.

II. On the Geology of Lake Superior. *Trans. Lit. and His. Soc.* (Que.), 1829.

III. On coral animals in the Gulf of St. Lawrence. *Do.*, 1831.

"Admiral Bayfield's excellent maps of the lakes, river, and gulf of St. Lawrence have always been of the utmost aid to the Survey in such explorations as came upon the great water-lines of the Province. Their value however is not confined to the indication of geographical features. There is registered upon his charts, a considerable amount of accurate geological information, in the form of notes, which he has in many places given of the character of the rocks forming the coast. These notes have on some occasions immediately directed attention to points of interest, and at other times have saved much labor in tracing out the distribution of formations. It is understood that Admiral Bayfield, in his surveys of the St. Lawrence made, with the aid of Dr. Kelly, a considerable collection of organic remains, which were presented to various Societies and Institutions of Natural History. It is much to be regretted that these had not been figured and described before they were thus distributed, as we should thus probably have long ago obtained a knowledge of many fossils, the descriptions of which have been only recently published from specimens in the collections of the Survey. Admiral Bayfield has communicated to the Literary and Historical Society of Quebec, and to the Geological Society of London, various interesting papers on subjects connected with Canadian Geology, with the facts in which it will be found that we have on several occasions availed ourselves."—*Sir* W. E. LOGAN, *Geo. of Can.*, 1863.

BAYLEY, *Mrs.* H. Resided at Isle aux Noix, L. C. Wrote for the Eng. and Am. literary press. Contributed many tales, sketches and poems to the *Museum* (Mont.) 1832–34, of which we may mention the following :—*The Young Soldier, a sketch from life ; the*

Recruit ; Enthusiasm, or female friend-ship ; The Discovery, or the marriage prevented ; Maria, the Orphan ; Indo-lence, a moral tale ; Honesty the best policy, or the Baronet and the Miller ; *A West India sketch ; Female education.*

I. Tales of the Heath. *London.*

II. Scenes at home and abroad. *Do.*

III. Employment the true source of happiness. *Do.*

IV. Improvement, or a visit to Grandmaina. *Do.*, 1833.

"A sweet little book for children, and one really adapted for their holiday reading. * * It abounds in pious feelings and moral lessons, combined with general and useful information, put in the most pleasing and delightful form."—*National Standard* (Lon.)

BAYNE, *Rev.* JOHN, *D. D.* For many years Presb. min. at Galt, U. C. D. there Nov. 1859. Was eminent as a theologian and preacher. Several of his sermons have been published, and we understand a collection of the best of his pulpit discourses is soon about to appear.

I. Man responsible for his belief ; a lecture. *Galt*, 1851, pp. 32, 8vo.

BEACH, DAVID, *A. M.* A Can. journ. B. Tp. of South Gower, Co. Grenville, U.C., 1819. Completed his ed. at Victoria Coll. and had degree of A. M. conferred upon him. Conducted Hamilton High Sch. on leaving coll., and, in 1847, became Principal of the Newburgh Academy, a position which he held for 10 years. In 1857 assumed the duties of Head Master of the Prescott Grammar Sch., which he resigned in 1858. In 1854, while Principal of Newburgh Academy, became with Mr. Caton joint prop. and sole ed. of the *Index*, (Newb.) a weekly journal of Liberal politics, and continued as such until 1857, when he left New-burgh. In March, 1859, ed. the *Evening Courier*, (Kings.) a tri-weekly journal, which only existed for 4 months. In Aug., same year, Mr. B. took charge of the *Watchman*, (Whitby) which he conducted for 12 months, and, in 1861, he started the *Press* in the same town, which was doomed to but a brief spell of existence. In Dec. 1862, the *British American*, a daily paper, designed as an exponent of Liberal views, was

established at Kingston, and Mr. B. was invited to become its Ed., a position which he accepted and the duties of which he discharged until June, 1864, when, through continued ill-health, he was compelled to resign the post and to close his connection with the press.

BEADLE, D. W.
I. On the Natural History of the Salmon (*Salmo salar*), with remarks upon its economical importance and preservation. *Can. Nat.* 1856.

II. On the Classification of Fishes ; with particular reference to the Fishes of Canada. *Do. do.*

III. List of Coleopterous Insects collected in the County of Lincoln, C. W. *Do.* 1861.

BEATSON, *Lt. Col.*, R. S., Royal Engineers.
I. The Plains of Abraham : notes, original and selected. [With portraits of Wolfe and Montcalm.] *Gibraltar*, 1859, pp. 48, 8vo.

"An interesting little work."—*Chronicle* (Que.)

BEAUBIEN, HENRI DESRIVIÈRES.
I. Traité sur les lois civiles du Bas Canada. *Montreal*, 1832, 3 vols. 8vo.

BEAUDRY, *Rev.* HERCULES. A French Can. Priest. Is *Curé* of St. Constant, L. C.

I. Le Conseiller du Peuple, ou Ré-flexions adressées aux Canadiens-Fran-çais, par un Compatriote. *Montreal*, 1861, pp. 281, in-12.

"L'auteur qui a eu la modestie de taire son nom, mais dont le style et les idées accusent un talent distingué, un observateur attentif, et surtout, un homme de bien, s'adresse plus particulièrement au cultivateur et à l'ou-vrier. Il leur prêche les vertus civiques, leur indique les moyens de reconnaître leurs vrais amis, leur enseigne leurs devoirs comme chrétiens et comme citoyens, et les met en garde contre les piéges que l'on tend souvent à leur bonhomie et à leur bonne foi."—*Minerve*, (Mont.)

II. Nouveau Mois de Marie, dédié aux fidèles du Canada, par un Prêtre du diocèse de Montréal. *Do.* 1865, pp. 269, in-16.

"Tel qu'il est, ce livre ne convient pas seulement pour les exercices du Mois de Marie, mais c'est un excellent manuel qui pourra fournir en tout temps de pieuses prières et des réflexions utiles pour la vie chrétienne. Le Nouveau Mois de Marie a obtenu l'approbation unanime de NN. SS. les Evêques du Bas-Canada : rien ne pouvait mieux attester le mérite du livre, ni le recommander plus fortement à tous les fidèles."—*Rev.* A. NANTEL: *Rev. Can.*

III. Les Jeunes Converties, ou Mémoires des Trois Sœurs Debbie, Helen et Anna Barlow. Traduit de l'Anglais. *Do.* 1866, pp. xv–195, in-8.

" Ces pages forment un sujet de lecture très-pieux et très-attrayant, qui ne manquera pas d'avoir un intérêt tout particulier pour les jeunes personnes; car il leur rappellera le souvenir de jeunes compagnes qui, il est vrai, n'ont fait que passer au Couvent de la Congrégation."—*Rev. Can.*

BEAUDRY, J. U. A Commissioner for Codifying the Laws of L. C. A contributor to the *Revue de Législation et de Jurisprudence,* 1845, and to *L. C. Reports* since 1851.

BEAUFOY, *Mr.*

I. Mémoire au soutien de l'appel de de la fabrique de N. D. de Montréal. *Montréal,* 1867, pp. 29, 8vo·

I. Tour through parts of the United States and Canada. By a British Subject. *London,* 1828, pp. 141, 8vo.

Printed for private circulation.

BEAVEN, *Rev.* JAMES, *D. D.* Prof. of Metaphysics and Ethics in Univ. Coll. and Canon of St. James's Cathedral, (Tor.) Was formerly Prof. of Divinity in same Coll. Is a graduate of Oxford.

I. Account of the life and writings of St. Irenæus. *London,* 1841, 8vo.

II. Doctrine of Scripture on Religious Celibacy. *Do.* 1841.

III. Devotions for School boys. *Toronto,* 1845, pp. 32.

IV. Recreations of a long vacation; or, a visit to Indian Missions in Upper Canada. *Toronto,* 1846 ; *London,* 1847, 12mo.

V. Catechism of the Thirty-nine Articles of the Church of England. *London,* 1850 ; *New York,* 1853, 18mo.

VI. Elements of Natural Theology. *London,* 1850, 12mo.

VII. Questions on Scripture History. *Do.* 1850, 18mo. 4th Ed. *Do.* 1864.

VIII. Manual for visiting the sick. *Do.* 1852, 18mo.

IX. Help to Catechising. *Do.* 1859 18mo. ; Am. Ed. *New York.*

BEAVEN, Mrs. Wife of the above.

I. Devotions for school girls. *Toronto,* pp. 32.

BECKETT, S. B.

I. Guide-book of the Atlantic and St. Lawrence, and St. Lawrence and Atlantic Railroads. *Portland,* 1853, 12mo.

BEDARD, ISIDORE. The author of the Can. national song, *Sol Canadien terre chérie.* Was b. at Quebec about 1806. D. at Paris. France, 14 April, 1833. He early contributed poetical effusions to the press principally to *Le Canadien* newspaper, of which his father, the late Hon. Pierre Bedard, was prop. In 1830, he was returned to the L. C. Assem., but only sat in that body during one brief session, at the end of which he left for a tour in Europe, whence he never returned, dying abroad as above stated. He is buried in the cemetery of Montmartre.

" A son départ du pays, il n'avait guère pu que faire concevoir les plus belles espérances. On allait se disant que les principales qualités du père ralaient revivre dans le fils, et cela seul faisait le plus bel éloge qu'un jeune homme pût mériter. Cependant, la mémoire d'Isidore vivra aussi longtemps, dans la Nouvelle France, que celle de Rouget de l'Isle dans la vieille France. Le jeune Bedard a laissé quelques couplets qui ont eu le mérite de l'emporter, dans la faveur publique, sur tous nos autres chants patriotiques, très-nombreux pourtant et l'œuvre des talents les plus distingués parmi notre jeunesse lettrée. Ce n'est pas que la partie littéraire de ces couplets ne prête un peu à la critique, et que sous ce rapport ils ne soient inférieurs à quelques-unes de nos chansons patriotiques; mais Bedard sut, mieux, qu'aucun de ses concurrents, malgré les négligences du style, trouver le chemin des cœurs et faire vibrer la fibre nationale. C'est, il est vrai, ce qui fait le poète, le reste est du versificateur. Avec le temps, sans doute, notre jeune poète aurait apporté plus de soins et de goût à ses compositions." ETIENNE PARENT.

BEDARD, *Hon.* PIERRE. A French Can. politician and journ. B. at Charlesbourg, near Quebec, 14 Sept. 1763. D. 1827. He was one of the first of his race admitted to the Can. bar. In 1792, he was returned as a mem. to the first Parliament held in the Province. and long held a seat in that body. He eventually became the leader of the French opposition party, and both as a private mem. and leader displayed great ability. In 1806, he with others of his party founded the newspaper called *Le Canadien* (Que.), of which he became the chief ed. Both in Parliament and through the columns of his paper he waged a bitter and uncompromising war against the Eng. and the govt. In 1810, *Le Canadien* was seized by the authorities, and Mr. B., as its ed., was imprisoned. He was refused a trial. Being released after a long confinement, he tarnished his patriotism by accepting a judgeship from the same govt. which he had before so loudly condemned.

BEDARD, P. H.

I. Lettre à M. Chaboillez, Curé de Longueuil, relativement à ses " Questions sur le Gouvernement Ecclésiastique du district de Montréal." *Montréal*, 1823, pp. 40.

BEERS, W. GEORGE. A Can. writer on Sports and Pastimes. Has contributed largely to the periodical and newspaper press. In 1862-3 wrote a series of articles (20 in number) on " *Canadian Sports,*" for *Wilkes' Spirit of the Times,* (N. Y.), and for the *Brit. Am. Mag.* (for..) on " *The Voyageurs of Canada,*" and " *Canada in Winter.*" In 1863-4, to *Once a Week* (Lon.) ; in 1865, to *Harper's Mag.* on " *Pictures of Life and Character in Canada.*" In 1866, to the *Saturday Reader* (Mont.), and to various other periodicals. Mr. B. is also the author of an unpublished Comedy in 3 acts, called "*Bob Treacle, or Love and War.*"

I. The Game of Lacrosse ; containing the construction of the Crosse and the various methods of throwing and catching the ball, &c., reduced to rule. *Montreal*, 1860, pp. 40. (*A new and enlarged ed. in preparation.*)

The author had to reduce this wild and magnificent Indian field game to systematic rule, as it was void of laws ; the different players had no particular names ; and there was hardly any source from which to get practical information to assist in the writing. A writer in *Cumbers' Journal,* in 1862, under an article called "*A Rival to Cricket,*" makes free use of the book, often word for word, without any acknowledgement, and extols the Game, ranking it far above Cricket or Golf, and proposing its introduction into Eng. An Eng. sporting paper undertook voluntarily to introduce it into Eng. schools, with what success we cannot state.

BELANGER, L. Advocate, (Mont.)

I. Table Alphabétique et Analytique du Code Civil du Bas Canada. *Montréal,* 1867, pp. 88.

BELCHER, *Vice-Admiral Sir* EDWARD, *K. C. B., F. R. S., F. G. S.* A distinguished Brit. Admiral and Hydrographer. Is a grandson of the late Chief Justice Belcher of N. S. B. in N. S. 1799. Entered the navy in 1812 as a first class volunteer, and was soon afterwards appointed a midshipman. After having served in the defence of Gaeta and the battle of Algiers was, in 1819, appointed to the *Myrmidon* sloop, destined for the African station. In 1825, he became asst. surveyor to the Behring's Straits discovery expedition under Capt. Beechey in the *Blossom.* Promoted to the rank of commander in 1829, he served on the coast of Africa, and of Portugal, rendering on the latter service valuable assistance to the Brit. residents by protecting their property during the political troubles in Portugal. From Nov. 1836 to Aug. 1842, he was employed in the *Sulphur,* surveying vessel, of whose voyage round the world he has given an interesting account in his *Narrative.* In 1841, Com. B. rendered a series of important and brilliant services in China, having sounded and explored the various inlets of the Canton river, and made a reconnoissance which contributed in a great measure to the successes of Sir Hugh (now Lord) Gough and Sir H. F. Senhouse. On the same day, he caused the enemy to destroy 8 of his vessels. For these services he was appointed a Post Captain, and received the honour of knighthood. Afterwards he was engaged in the surveying service in the East Indies, and was severely wounded while assisting the Rajah of Sarawak, Sir James Brooke, in his efforts to subdue the pirates of Borneo. From 1852 to 1854, he commanded the expedition in search of Sir John Franklin, and on his return to Eng. was tried before a Court Martial for voluntarily abandoning his ships. The case against him was not legally supported, and he was acquitted.

I. On Nautical Surveying, an outline of the Duties of a Naval Surveyor ;

with cases applied to Naval Evolutions, Rules and Tables. *London*, 1835, 8vo.

II. Narrative of a Voyage round the World in H. M. S. *Sulphur*, from 1836 to 1843, including details of the Naval operations against China in 1840–1. (With Maps and Plates.) *Do.* 1843, 2 vols. pp. 892, 8vo.

"Among the countries visited by the "*Sulphur*," and which in the present state of science are invested with more particular interest, may be mentioned the California, Columbia River, the North West Coast of America, &c."

III. Narrative of the Voyage of H. M. S. *Samarang*, employed in surveying the Islands of the Eastern Archipelago, with Vocabularies of Languages, &c. (With Map and tinted plates.) *Do.* 1848, 2 vols. 8vo.

IV. The last of the Arctic Voyages ; being a narrative of the Expedition in search of Sir John Franklin, during the years 1852–53–54. (With Map and plates.) *Do.* 1855, 2 vols. R. 8vo.

V. Horatio Howard Brenton, a novel. *Do.* 1856, 3 vols. 8vo.

BELCHER, *Hon.* JONATHAN. First Chief Justice of N. S., to which office he was appointed in 1754. D. March 1776. Was a son of Governor Belcher, of Massachusetts. Graduated at Harvard Coll. 1728. Studied Law in the Temple. (Lon.), and rose to some eminence at the Eng. Bar. He acted as ed. of the Provincial Statutes N. S., many of which he had drafted.

I. The Laws of Nova Scotia. 1767.

BELCHER, *Rev.* JOSEPH, *D. D.* Ed. the *Christian Gem*, (Hal. 1845), a monthly periodical.

BELCOURT, *Rev.* GEORGE A. A French Can. writer on Indian languages. Is a priest of the R. C. Ch. stationed at Rustico, P. E. I. For the last 28 years has been preparing a Dictionary of the French and Ojibaway languages, with the etymology and roots of words, a work which may shortly be published. Has contributed largely to the Reports of the *Association pour la Propagation de la Foi pour le diocèse de Québec*, in a series of letters written from the R. C. mission of Red-River,—has also contributed to the *Trans. of the Historical Soc. of Minnesota* on the Traders and early Missionaries of the North West.

I. Principes de la langue des Sauvages appelés Sauteux. *Quebec*, 1839, pp. 146, 12mo.

II. Traduction du catéchisme et de cantiques dans la langue des Sauteux. *Do.* 1839, 18mo.

BELL, ANDREW, well known in Gt. Brit. and Am. as the author of " *Men and Things in America*" ; " *Historical Sketches of Feudalism, British and Continental* " ; " *Lives of the Illustrious* " ; " *New Annals of Old Scotland*," &c.

I. British-Canadian Centennium, 1759–1859. General James Wolfe, his life and death ; a lecture delivered at Montreal, Sept. 13, 1859, being the anniversary day of the Battle of Quebec, fought a century before, in which Britain lost a hero and won a province. *Montreal*, 1859, pp. 52, 8vo.

II. History of Canada, from the time of its discovery till the Union year 1840–1 ; translated from " l'Histoire du Canada " of F. X. Garneau, Esq., and accompanied with illustrative notes, &c. &c. *Do.* 1862, 2 vols. pp. 556–499, demy 8vo.

BELL, S. S.

I. Colonial Administration of Great Britain, 1859. *London*, 1859, 8vo.

BELL, ROBERT, *C. E., F. G. S.* Prof. of Chemistry and Natural Sciences, Univ. of Queen's Coll. (Kings.) Son of the following. B. in the Tp. of Toronto, June 1841. Ed. at the Grammar Sch., L'Orignal, and at McGill Coll. (Mont.) At the latter Institution attended various classes from 1858 to 1861, and in the spring of the last named year graduated as a C. E., having passed the preliminary examination in U. C. for P. L. S. in 1859 with the intention of following Engineering and Surveying. In 1857 he joined the Staff of the Geo. Survey of Can. under Sir William Logan, and has continued to be engaged on it since, exploring and surveying both topographically and geologically in all parts of the province from Gaspé to Lake Superior. In 1863, Mr. B. received his present appointment in Queen's Univ., he being at the time Lecturer on Geology in Morrin Coll. (Que.) He spent the summer of 1864 in Gt. Brit. practising chemical analyses under Prof. Lyon Playfair in the Univ. of Edinburgh, and attending the lectures of Profs. Balfour, Allman and others. He also attended the meeting of the Brit. Association at Bath, and met many of the leading scientific men of Eng. and the continent of Europe. In 1865, he made a complete Geological examination of the Great Manitoulin Island, besides topographical surveys of portions of it. We append a list of his writings :

I. Report on the Natural History of the lower St. Lawrence, the Saguenay and Lake St. John. *Report of Prog. Geol. Surv.* 1857.

" A Report of considerable merit."—*Can. Journ.*

II. Explanatory catalogue of the Animals and Plants of the Gaspé Peninsula. *Do.* 1858.

III. Natural History of the Gulf of St. Lawrence and the distribution of the Mollusca of Eastern Canada. *Can. Nat.* 1859.

"Mr. Bell's essay contains a very elaborate exposition of the vertebrated, molluscous and other animals of the St. Lawrence valley and Eastern Canada generally. It is an exceedingly useful and carefully drawn up paper ; and as the effort of so young a man, it cannot be too highly commended. Mr. Bell bids fair to occupy a distinguished position amongst Canadian Naturalists."—PROF. CHAPMAN : *Can. Journ.*

IV. On the occurrence of fresh water Shells in some of our Post Tertiary deposits. *Do.* 1861.

V. List (with notes) of recent land and fresh water Shells collected around Lakes Superior and Huron in 1859-60. *Do. do.*

VI. Catalogue (with notes) of Birds collected and observed around Lakes Superior and Huron. *Do. do.*

VII. Catalogue of Plants collected on the south and east shores of Lake Superior and on the north shore of Lake Huron. *Annals of Bot. Soc. Can.* 1861.

VIII. The Trees and Shrubs growing around Lakes Superior and Huron. *Do. do.*

IX. Lake Superior. *Chambers' Encyclopedia,* (Edin.)

X. On the Superficial Geology of the Gaspé Peninsula. *Can. Nat.* 1863.

XI. Roofing slate as a source of wealth to Canada. *Do. do.*

XII. On the Superficial Geology of Canada. *General Report Geol. Surv.,* 1863.

"In its compilation, (The General Report), the officers of the Survey have been materially assisted by Mr. Robert Bell, a young Canadian naturalist, first brought prominently forward by Sir William Logan.—*Can. Journ.*

XIII. Report to the Gaspé Bay Company on the Oil region of Gaspé. *New York,* 1865.

XIV. On the occurrence of Petroleum in Gaspé. *Do. do.*

XV. Report on the Manitoulin Islands. *Report of Pro. Geol. Surv.* 1866.

" Some, while admitting your ability, may hesitate to pronounce in your favour in consequence of your youth; but I have not considered you too young to entrust you with the independent control of the funds and men, necessary for distant explorations ; and I have every reason to be satisfied with your prudent and economical management, and with the scientific results of your investigations, which have in every instance, greatly advanced our knowledge of Canadian Geology."—SIR W. E. LOGAN : *Letter to Mr. Bell.*

" I anticipate much from his future career as a Naturalist."—PRINCIPAL DAWSON.

BELL, *Rev.* WILLIAM. Min. of the Pres. Congregation at Perth, U. C. Now dead.

I. Hints to Emigrants ; in a series of letters from Upper Canada. With a Map and Plans. *Edinburgh,* 1824, pp. 236 12mo.

BELLE, J. A. A., a Montreal advocate. Was one of the founders, in 1857, of the institution known as the *Cercle Littéraire.* In 1864 appointed Ed. of *L'Echo du Cabinet de Lecture Paroissial,* and has contributed largely to its pages. Several of his papers and lectures delivered and read at various times have been published in that periodical, amongst them one on *Intemperance* another on *Maury,* and a speech on Political Economy—*Le luxe est-il avantageux au progrès des nations.*

BELLEMARE, RAPHAEL. A French Can. Journ. and writer. Ed. at the Semimary of Nicolet, where he studied Theology for some years. In 1847 went to Montreal where he ed. *La Minerve* from that year until 1855, and is spoken of as being a very clear, concise and energetic writer. Leaving the newspaper press, he devoted his leisure to historical studies, more particulary those relating to our own country, a taste which he had acquired from a close friendship and intimacy with the late Commander Viger, the Can. Antiquarian. In 1857 he wrote in *La Minerve*, *Mémoire sur le Gouvernement du Canada il y a un siècle (Administration Bigot)*. His other papers are: *Mémoire sur les Vice-Rois du Canada* in the *Mémoires Soc. Hist.* (Mont.); *Mémoire sur Champlain* in the *Echo.* In 1860, 3 articles in reply to the London *Times*, on the Capitulation and the Treaty of Peace of 1763; and several articles criticising M. Bibaud's *Panthéon Canadien*. He was one of the founders and editors of the *Echo du Cabinet de Lecture paroissial* and was one of the founders of the *Soc. Historique de Montréal*, and is a mem. of the *Soc. des Antiquaires de Normandie*, and of the State Historical Soc. of Wisconsin.

BELLENGER, *Rev.* J. M.
I. Catéchisme dans la langue des Abénakis. *Quebec*, 1842; 12 mo.

BELT, THOMAS, (N. S.)
I. On some recent movements in the earth's surface. *Trans. N. S. Inst.* 1863.

II. List of Butterflies observed in the neighbourhood of Halifax, N.S. *Do. do.*

III. The Production and Preservation of Lakes by Ice Action. *Do.* 1864–5.

BENJAMIN, GEORGE. A Can. Journ. B. in Sussex, Eng., 15 April, 1799. D. at Belleville, U. C., 7 Sept. 1864. Founded the *Intelligencer*, (Bellev.), in 1834, of which he was ed. from that year until 1848. Under his management, as it has since, the paper consistently and fearlessly supported, and defended the Conservative party, the principles of which Mr. B. ever maintained and upheld. He held various office under the Municipal Govt. and the Crown, and from 1856 to 1863 was a mem. of the Leg. Assem. Can.

I. Short lessons for Members of Parliament, compiled from English and other publications. By a Canadian M. P. of experience in Legislative routine. *Quebec*, 1862, pp. 70, 8vo.

This pamphlet, published in French and English, contains the Rules and Practice of the Canadian Parliament on all public and private matters of Legislation.

BENJAMIN, L. N., *B. C. L.* An Advocate of L. C.
I. The St. Albans Raid, &c. *Montreal*, 1865, pp, 480.

"The official record of the examination of the St. Alban's Raiders before Judge of Sessions Coursol and Judge Smith, containing the text of all the proceedings, the arguments of Counsel, and the judgments of the judges corrected by themselves."—*Gazette* (Mont.)

BENNETT, *Rev.* JAMES. A Presb. Clergym. (St. John N. B.) B. in Co. Down, Irel. 1817. Ed. at Royal Belfast Institution and Belfast Coll. Studied for Divinity at Belfast, Glasgow and Edinburgh. Min. at Tassagh, Co. Armagh, 1844. Min. of St. John Presb. Ch. since 1854. His literary efforts consist of poetry, essays on various subjects, sermons and newspaper and mag. articles. Mr. B. ed. the *Colonial Presbyterian* (St. John) for 2 years, and many of his sermons and essays have appeared in its columns.

I. Sermon on Labour, its rights and duties. *St. John*, 1861, pp. 24.

II. "The Kirk" on Union of Presbyterians in New Brunswick, criticised in a series of letters. (Reprinted from the *Col. Presb.*) *Do.*, 1861, pp. 56, 4to.

BENT, JOHN.
I. Prohibition and anti-prohibition, being a series of letters written by the Revd. C. Tupper, and replies to the same. *St. John N. B.*

BERTHELOT, AMABLE. A Quebec Advocate. D. 1848. He was a mem. of the Assem. of L. C. previous to the Union, and is said to have been a good speaker. As a mem. of the Lit. and His. Soc. (Que.), he evinced much interest and activity in the objects and proceedings of that body.

I. Dissertation sur le Canon de Bronze, trouvé en 1826, sur un banc de sable, dans le Fleuve Saint-Laurent, au-devant de la paroisse de Champlain, dans le District des Trois Rivières. *Quebec*, 1827, 12mo.

" Dans la première partie de cet écrit, l'auteur entreprend de prouver, que Jacques Cartier ne fit pas naufrage sur un rocher, auquel une tradition erronée a conservé en Canada, le nom de ' *La Roche de Jacques Cartier*.' Dans la seconde partie, l'auteur conjecture que le Canon de Bronze ainsi trouvé, a dû appartenir à Verrazzani, et que c'est ce dernier qui fit naufrage dans ce même endroit.

" L'auteur a bien établi sa première proposition ; mais il n'en est pas de même à l'égard des conjectures qu'il hasarde sur ce canon, et du naufrage présumé de Verrazzani. Qu'on lise attentivement Marc Lescarbot ; on y verra tout au contraire, que la pantomime que l'auteur fait jouer aux sauvages dans leur entrevue avec Cartier, n'avait aucun rapport avec le naufrage de Verrazzani, mais que c'était, comme dit Lescarbot, ' *une finesse et ruse des sauvages pour empêcher Cartier de faire le voyage de Hochelaga*." G. B. FARIBAULT.

II. Essai de Grammaire Française suivant les principes de l'abbé Girard. *Do.*, 1842 pp. 60.

III. Dissertation sur la découverte des restes de la petite *Hermine*, avec une carte de Québec. *Do.*, 1844.

BERTON, G. F. S.
I. Reports of cases adjudged in the Supreme Court of the Province of New Brunswick, commencing in Hilary Term 1835. *Fredericton*, 1835.

BETHUNE, *Rt. Rev.* A. N., *D. D.*, *D. C. L.* Coadjutor Bish. of Toronto. Was for many years Archdeacon of Toronto and Rector of Cobourg, U. C. B. in Can. about 1800. Has written largely for the religious press; also on " *Church Property in Canada*" in the London *Times*, and on the subject of the " Clergy Reserves " to the *English Churchman* " (Lon.) He ed. the *Church* newspaper from 1837 to 1841, and again from 1843 to 1847.

I. Six Sermons on the Liturgy of the Church of England. *York*, *U. C.* 1829, pp. 76.

II. Sermon on the duty of loyalty. *Cobourg*, 1849, pp. 16.

III. Thoughts upon the Clergy Reserve question as now agitated : in a letter to the Hon. R. Baldwin, H. M's. Attorney General, U. C. *Toronto*, 1850, pp. 16.

IV. Four Sermons on the Holy Sacrament of the Lord's Supper. *Do.*, 1852, pp. 52.

V. Thirteen Lectures on Historical portions of the Old Testament. *New York*, pp. 213.

VI. Thirteen Lectures, Expository and Practical on the Liturgy of the Church of England. *Toronto*, 1862, pp. 170, D. 12mo.

VII. Charges to the Clergy of Archdeaconry of York ; 1849, 1852, 1855, 1856.

VIII. The Church of the Living God ; a sermon. *Toronto*.

BETHUNE, *Rev.* CHARLES J. S., *M. A.* Son of the preceding. A Graduate of Trinity Coll. (Tor.), and for some years Assist. Rector at Cobourg, U. C. Is well known as a Can. Entomologist. Was Ed. *pro tem.*, in 1861, of the *Journal of the Board of Arts and Manufactures, U. C.*, and is now a mem. of the Editing Committee of the *Can. Journal*. Has contributed many minor articles to the *Can. Nat.*, the *Can. Farmer* and the above periodicals. Is Secy. of the Can. Entomological Soc., and a corresponding mem. of the Entomological Soc. of Philadelphia and of the Soc. of Natural Sciences, Buffalo, N. Y.

I. Descriptions of some species of Nocturnal Lepidoptera found in Canada. *Can. Journal*, 1863.

II. Insect Life in Canada. *B. A. Mag.*, 1863.

III. Descriptions of three new species of Canadian Nocturnal Lepidoptera. *Proc. Entomological Soc. (Phil.)*, 1865.

IV. Nocturnal Lepidoptera found in Canada. Part II Homopteridæ. *Can. Journ.* 1865.

BETHUNE, *Very Rev.* JOHN, *D. D.* Dean of Montreal.

I. Letter to the parishioners of Christ's Church, respecting a tract intituled : " Lent Usages." *Montreal*, 1847, pp. 8.

II. Sermon on the occasion of the death of the late Chief Justice Reid. *Do.* 1847, pp. 17.

III. A sermon preached on the occasion of the primary visitation of the Rt. Rev. Francis Fulford, Lord Bishop of Montreal. *Do.* 1852, pp. 21.

BETTRIDGE, *Rev.* WILLIAM, *B. D.* of St. John's Coll. Cambridge, Rector of Woodstock, U. C.

I. A brief history of the Church in Upper Canada. *London*, 1838, pp. 143, 8vo.

BIBAUD, F. M. U. M., *LL. D.* A French Can. historical biographical and legal author. A son of the following. B. at Montreal, Nov.· 1824. Contributed some biographical sketches of celebrated Indian warriors to his father's *Mag. du Bas Canada.* He afterwards wrote for the *Mélanges Religieux* (Mont.) For several years he has been prof. of legislation in St. Mary's Coll. (Mont.) He is a corresponding mem. of the Historical Soc. of Michigan.

I. Les Sagamos Illustres de l'Amérique Septentrionale, précédé d'un Index de l'histoire fabuleuse de ce continent. *Montreal*, 1848, 8vo.

II. Catéchisme de l'histoire du Canada à l'usage des écoles. *Do.* 1853, 32mo.

III. Essai de Logique Judiciaire, ouvrage qui doit servir d'appréciation, et sur quelques points, d'antirrhétique de la logique judiciaire publiée à Paris en 1841, par M. Hortentius de St. Albin, juge au tribunal de la Seine, membre de la chambre des députés, &c. *Do.* 1853, 12mo.

IV. Les Institutions de l'histoire du Canada ou Annales Canadiennes jusqu'à l'an MDCCCXIX. *Do.* 1855, pp. 440, 8vo.

" It contains a concise history of America, its primitive inhabitants, its discovery and advancement: it exhibits much learning and labour in its compilation, and a great research into writers both European and American, on history, ancient and modern, and also on the natural history of Man, both on this Continent, and in the Old World." *Transcript* (Mont.)

V. Le Charlatanisme dans l'histoire, ou revue critique de l'histoire du Canada de F. X. Garneau. *Do.* 1855, 8vo.

VI. Dictionnaire Historique des Hommes Illustres du Canada et de l'Amérique. *Do.* 1857, pp. 389, 8vo.

" Ce travail doit coûter à son auteur des recherches considérables et formera une série de mémoires d'une très grande utilité pour ceux qui plus tard s'occuperont de l'histoire

du continent Américain et du Canada."— J. C. TACHÉ.

VII. Opuscules. *Do.* 1857, pp. 70, 12mo.

" Cette brochure nous est venue avec la continuation du *Dictionnaire Biographique*, et du *Supplément aux Travaux sur l'Histoire du Canada*, par le même auteur, ouvrages dont nous parlerons très au long lorsqu'ils seront terminés. Les opuscules se composent d'essais lus à l'*Œuvre des bons livres* ou à la *Société Philotechnique.* Ils ont pour titre, 1° Système politique des Jésuites au Paraguay, 2° Droits des gens, 3° Géologie, 4° Le Code Napoléon."—*Journ. de l'Inst. Pub. L. C.*

VIII. Tableau Historique des Progrès Matériels et Intellectuels du Canada. *Do.* 1858, pp. 50, 8vo.

IX. Bibliothèque Canadienne, ou Annales Bibliographiques. *Do.* 1858, pp. 52, 8vo.

X. Le Panthéon Canadien, (Choix de Biographies.) Dans lequel on a introduit les hommes les plus célèbres des autres Colonies Britanniques. *Do.* 1858, pp. 364, 8vo.

XI. Commentaires sur les Lois du Bas-Canada, ou Conferences de l'Ecole de Droit liée au Collége des RR. PP. Jésuites, suivis d'une notice Historique. *Do.* 1859, pp. 595, 8vo.

" It is the first compressed treatise on the law of Lower Canada that has been published ; and is remarkably clear, concise and comprehensive—an evidence of the industry, learning and ability of the author."— *Herald*, (Mont.)

XII. Tablettes Historiques Canadiennes. *Do.* 1859, pp. 39, 8vo.; 2nd Ed. *Do.* 1861, pp. 46, 8vo.

XIII. Les Machabées Canadiens. *Do.* 1859, pp. 28, 8vo.

XIV. Napoléon I et Napoléon III, parallèle historique. *Do.* 1860, pp. 22, 8vo.

XV. La Confédération du Sud. *Do.* 1864, pp. 119, 8vo.

BIBAUD, MICHEL. A French Can. historian and journ. B. at Côte des Neiges, near Montreal, 20 Jan'y., 1782. D. at Montreal, 3 Augt. 1857. Descended from an old and honorable French family which settled in New France. Ed. at the Coll. of St. Raphael, (Mont.), and subsequently at the new Coll. under M. Roque. After finishing his studies, he, for a time, devoted himself to teaching. He was an early contributor to the *Spectateur Canadien* whose politics, as a liberal, he thoroughly believed in. In 1815, he founded a journal called *L'Aurore des Canadas* (Mont.), which he conducted until discontinued in 1819; the *Courrier du Bas Canada* was established in its stead, which he also ed. In both these papers he strongly opposed the scheme for the Union of U. & L. Can. which was then propounded. His book of poetry was the first of the kind published in the French language in Can. In 1825, he established the *Bibliothèque Canadienne*, a periodical which enjoyed some popularity during its existence, but died early, in 1830. His next literary venture was the *Magazin du Bas Canada*, which was commenced in 1832, and lasted for 2 years. Another paper the *Observateur Canadien* followed. Again, we find him, in 1842, founding the *Encyclopédie Canadienne*, which expired in the same year. Much of his time was now taken up in writing his *History of Canada*, and preparing other works for the press; but he found leisure, nevertheless, to contribute to several of the leading journals of the day. Mr. B. during his long life undoubtedly did much to advance the literature of his native country, not only by the important works which he himself contributed to it, but also by his encouragement of all worthy literary exertion. His latter years were spent in the service of the Can. Geol. Survey as a French translator.

I. L'Arithmétique en quatre parties, comprenant l'Arithmétique Vulgaire, l'Arithmétique Marchande, l'Arithmétique Curieuse et l'Arithmétique Scientifique. *Montreal*, 1816.

II. Relation d'un voyage à la côte du nord-ouest de l'Amérique Septentrionale, dans les années 1810-14. Par G. Franchère, (Edited by M. Bibaud.) *Do.* 1820, 8vo. Translated into English. *New York*, 1854, 8vo.

III. Epitres, Satires, Chansons, Epigrammes, et autres pièces de vers. *Do.* 1830, 12mo.

IV. Histoire du Canada sous la domination Française. *Do.* 1837, 8vo; 2nd ed. *Do.* 1843, 12mo.

V. Histoire du Canada et des Canadiens sous la domination Anglaise. *Do.* 1844, 12mo.

"Mr. Bibaud has brought to his task a most commendable zeal, and untiring industry. He has carefully studied the various memoirs and documents which have been submitted to the world, connected with Canadian History, and sifted with a judicious hand the doubtful and untrue from the authentic. The result of his labours is a book that may be almost implicitly relied upon by the Student of our Colonial Annals. Beginning with the voyages of Cartier, and closing with the termination of the power of France in the Province, he has passed over no event which it is of importance to be acquainted with, and he has so condensed the whole that it is contained in one neat and convenient volume of about four hundred pages. It is a book which every Canadian should be perfectly acquainted with, as furnishing a most valuable record of the early struggles through which his country passed, and its gradual progress from a mere wilderness to a populous and important country. * * "The second volume begins with the period of its cession to England, and is continued to the commencement of the rebellion in 1837. Mr. Bibaud has been most industrious in his search after authentic records. He has also been most successful. When we add that he is possessed of a happy talent for compilation as well as for composition, we presume we have said enough to convince our readers that the work now noticed is well deserving of perusal and of preservation."—*Lit. Gar.*, (Mont.)

BIGNEY, MARK F. An Am. journ. B. at Pugwash, N. S. In 1848, went to New Orleans, U. S., where he has since resided, having been connected with the newspaper press of that city from that time up to the present. He first joined the staff of the *Son of Temperance*, and was subsequently connected with the *Live Oak*, *Delta*, *True Delta* and *Picayune*. In 1864, he became associate ed. of the *Daily Times*, the largest and most influential newspaper in the South. Mr. B. was official reporter to the Senate of Louisiana during one session.

I. The Forest Pilgrims and other poems. *New Orleans*, 1867, pp. 258. 16mo.

"Some of the purely imaginative pieces are of a high order of merit, and, when collected into a volume, they make a very agreeable addition to a library shelf of Southern literature."—*Picayune.*

BIGOT, *Sieur* F.

I. Mémoire ou Factum pour le Sieur F. Bigot, Intendant en Canada. *Paris*, 1763, 2 vols. 4to.

BIGSBY, JOHN J., *M. D., F. L. S., F. G. S.*

I. Notes on the Geography and Geology of Lake Huron. *London*, 1824, pp. 52, 4to.

" The publication before us, though, with that modesty peculiar to the author, it is only called *notes*, contains a full and complete Geographical and Geological description of Lake Huron, with its interesting group of islands. It was republished from the transactions of the Geological Society of London."—*Can. Rev. and Mag.* (Mont.)

II. A sketch of the Geology of the Island of Montreal. *Annals Ly. of Nat. His. N. Y.* 1826.

III. The Shoe and the Canoe, or Pictures of Travel in the Canadas illustrative of their Scenery and Colonial life, with facts and opinions on Emigration, State policy, &c. (With engravings.) *London*, 1850, 2 vols. 8vo.

" The position occupied by the author, as Secretary to the Commission appointed under the treaty of Ghent to survey and settle the boundary line between Canada and the United States, gave him advantages of becoming acquainted with the real condition of the border lands closed to mere travellers. Of these advantages Dr. Bigsby has made good use, and the results are evidenced in two volumes, replete with information faithfully illustrative of Colonial life and Colonial scenery. His duty carried him along a route seldom followed by his fellow countrymen. Lakes Simcoe, Huron and Superior, were visited by him; into a portion of South Hudson's Bay, and up the river Ottawa into Lake Nipissing, he penetrated, and visited the almost *incognita terra* of the highland of the St. Lawrence, below Quebec."—*Colonial Mag.*

" Among the pioneers in Canadian Geology, no observer was more accurate than Dr. J. J. Bigsby, Secretary to the Boundary Commissioners under the Treaty of Ghent. His range of investigation extended from Quebec to Lake Superior, and beyond the limits of the province in that direction; and he has accumulated and published a great store of facts, upon the exactness of which the greatest reliance can be placed. He is in consequence frequently quoted in this volume as an authority."—SIR W. E. LOGAN: *Geo. of Can.*, 1863.

BILLINGS, B., Jr., (Ottawa, U. C)

I. List of Indigenous Plants found growing in the neighbourhood of Prescott, C. W., under the nomenclature of Gray. *Can. Nat.* 1858.

II. Supplementary list to above. *Do.* 1860.

III. List of Plants observed growing principally within four miles of Prescott, C. W., and for the most part in 1860. *Trans. Bot. Soc. Can.* 1861.

BILLINGS, ELKANAH, *F. G. S.* A Can. Palæontologist and writer on Geological Science. B. on his father's farm in Tp. of Gloucester, near Ottawa, U. C., 5 May, 1820. His family on the paternal side came originally from Wales, and settled in the N. E. States. His father was born in Massachusetts during the Am. revolutionary war, shortly after which the family removed to Can. He received his education at Ottawa (then Bytown) and at Potsdam, N. Y. In 1840, he entered on the study of the Law in U. C., and in 1845 was admitted to practice, which he did from that time up to 1856 when he received the appointment, which he still holds, of Palæontologist to the Geological Survey of Can. While living at Ottawa, Mr. B. made a large collection of the Fossils which abound in the rocks of the neighbourhood. By studying these, he made himself well acquainted with the palæontology of the Silurian Rocks of Can. His first papers appeared in the *Citizen* of that city and in the *Can. Journal* (Tor.) In 1856, he established the *Can. Naturalist and Geologist*, a monthly scientific publication, of which he was sole ed., prop. and principal contributor for the first year. Since 1857, the *Naturalist* has been owned and published by the publishing house of the Messrs. Dawson (Mont.), and ed. by a committee of the Natural History Soc. of that city, of which committee Mr. B. has been a prominent and active mem. up to the present time. His most important memoirs are the 3rd and 4th *Decades* and the *Palæozoic Fossils* of the Can. Geol. Survey, in which nearly all the genera and species of Fossils described were discovered by himself. In 1858, he was elected a Fellow of the Geological Soc. (Lon.)

In 1862, he was awarded a medal in Class 1, by the Jurors of the Universal

Exhibition at London, for important services to science. In 1867, he was awarded the silver medal of the Natural History Soc. of Montreal for his "long continued and successful labours in Canadian science."

Canadian Naturalist.

I. Introductory—Elevation and subsistence of Land—Various Theories of the Earth—Origin of Stratified Rocks—European and American Formations—Geographical Distribution of the latter in Canada. 1856.

II. On the Nomenclature and Classification of the animal kingdom. *Do.*

III. Fossils of the Potsdam Sandstone, Sea-weeds, Shells, and footprints on the rock at Beauharnois. *Do.*

IV. On some of the characteristic fossils of the Lower Silurian Rocks of Canada. *Do.*

V. On the Crinoidea or Stone Lilies of the Trenton Limestone, with a description of a new species. *Do.*

VI. Fossils of the Upper Silurian Rocks, Niagara and Clinton groups. *Do.*

VII. Natural History of the Moose Deer (*Alces Americana.*) *Do.*

VIII. The Northern Reindeer, or Barren Ground Caribou (*Tarandus articus.*) *Do.*

IX. The Woodland Caribou (*Tarandus hastalis.*) *Do.*

X. On the Wapite, or Canadian Stag (*Elaphus Canadensis.*) *Do.*

XI. On the common Deer (*Cervis Virginianus.*) *Do.*

XII. On the Mule Deer (*Cervus Macrotis.*) *Do.*

XIII. On the American or Black Bear (*Ursus Americanus.*) *Do.*

XIV. On the Grizzly Bear (*Ursus Ferox.*) *Do.*

XV· On the White or Polar Bear (*Ursus Maritimus.*) *Do.*

XVI. On the Cinnamon Bear (*Ursus Cinnamomum.*) *Do.*

XVII. On the Fossil Corals of the Lower Silurian Rocks of Canada. *Do.*

XVIII. On some of the technical terms used in the description of Fossil Shells. *Do.*

XIX. On some of the Fossil Shells of the Niagara and Clinton Formations. *Do.*

XX. Ornithology ; technical terms. *Do.*

XXI. On the Robin, or Migratory Thrush (*Turdus Migratorious.*) *Do.*

XXII. On Black Duck (*Anas Obscura.*) *Do.*

XXIII. On the Wood Duck (*Anas Sponsa.*) *Do.*

XXIV. On the Green-winged Teal (*Anas Carolinensis.*) *Do.*

XXV. On the Blue-winged Teal (*Anas Discors.*) *Do.*

XXVI. On the Mallard (*Anas Boschas.*) *Do.*

XXVII. On a Sea Gull shot at Ottawa. *Do.*

XXVIII. On the Pigeon (*Ectopistes Migratoria.*) *Do.*

XXIX. On the species of Woodpeckers observed in the vicinity of the City of Ottawa. *Do.*

XXX. A chapter on Earthquakes. *Do.*

XXXI. On some of the Common Rocks of the British Provinces. *Do.*

XXXII. On some of the Lower Silurian Fossils of Canada. *Do.*

XXXIII. Natural History of the Wolf (*Canis Lupus*) and its varieties. *Do.*

XXXIV. On the Foxes of British North America. *Do.*

XXXV. On the Canadian Otter (*Lutra Canadensis*). *Do.*

XXXVI. On the Bob-link or Rice-Bird (*Dolichonyx orzivora*). *Do.*

XXXVII. Natural History of the Wolverine or Carcajou (*Gulo Luscus.*) *Do.*

XXXVIII. On the Loup Cervier, or Canadian Lynx (*Lynx Canadensis,*) and the Bay Lynx or Wild Cat of the United States (*Lynx Rufus*). *Do.*

XXXIX. Natural History of the Racoon. (*Procyon Lotor*). *Do.*

XL. On some of the Game Birds of Canada. *Do.*

XLI. On the insects injurious to the wheat crop. *Do.*

XLII. Description of Fossils occurring in the Silurian Rocks of Canada. *Do.*

XLIII. On the Tertiary Rocks of Canada, with some account of their Fossils. *Do.*

XLIV. On the American Buffalo (*Bison Americanus*). *Do.*

XLV. On the Musk Ox (*Ovibos Moschatus*). *Do.*

XLVI. The Rocky Mountain Sheep (*Ovis Montana*). *Do.*

XLVII. On the Skunk (*Mephitis Chinga.*) *Do.*

XLVIII. On the Canada Porcupine (*Hystrix dorsata.*) *Do.*

XLIX. On the Northern Hare (*Lepus Americanus.*) *Do.*

L. On the Mammoth and the Mastodon. *Do.*

LI. On the several species of Squirrels inhabiting the British Provinces. *Do.*

LII. On the great Horned Owl (*Bubo Virginianus.*) *Do.*

LIII. The Snowy Day Owl (*Surnia Nyctea.*) *Do.*

LIV. The enemies of the Wheat Fly. *Do.*

LV. Fossils of the Hamilton Group. *Do.*

LVI. On the Iron ores of Canada and the cost at which they may be worked. 1857.

LVII. On the Natural History of the Rossignol or Song Sparrow (*Fringilla Melodia. Do.*)

LVIII. Notes on the Natural History of the M untain of Montreal. *Do.*

LIX. On the Muskrat (*Fiber Zibethicus.*) *Do.*

LX. On the Wood Chuck (*Arctomys Monax.*) *Do.*

LXI. On the "Fisher" or Pekan. "Pennants Marten" (*Mustela Canadensis.*) *Do.*

LXII. On the Beaver (*Castor fiber.*) *Do.*

LXIII. On the Genera of Fossil Cephalopoda occurring in Canada. *Do.*

LXIV. New Genera and Species of Fossils from the Silurian and Devonian formations of Canada. 1858.

LXV. On some new Genera and Species of Brachiopoda, from the Silurian and Devonian Rocks of Canada, 1859.

LXVI. Description of a new Genus of Brachiopoda, and on the Genus Cyrtodonta. *Do.*

LXVII. Fossils of the Calciferous Sandrock, including those of a deposit of white limestone at Mingan, supposed to belong to the formation. *Do.*

LXVIII. Descriptions of some new species of Trilobites from the Lower and Middle Silurian rocks of Canada. *Do.*

LXIX. Fossils of the Chazy Limestone, with descriptions of new species. *Do.*

LXX. Description of a new Palæozoic Starfish of the genus Palaster, from Nova Scotia, 1860.

LXXI. Description of some new species of Fossils from the Lower and Middle Silurian Rocks of Canada. *Do.*

LXXII. New species of Fossils from the Lower Silurian Rocks of Canada. *Do.*

LXXIII. On some new species of Fossils from the Limestone near Point Levi, opposite Quebec. *Do.*

"This paper contained the discoveries on which the changes in the view entertained of the Quebec group of rocks were mainly based. It marks an era in the Lower Silurian Geology of Canada and illustrates the pre-eminent value of fossils as guides to the ages of rocks."—BISHOP FULFORD: *Address before Nat. His. Soc. Mon.* 1861.

LXXIV. On certain theories of the formation of mountains. *Do.*

"A very good exposition of the prevailing views, with some valuable theoretical deductions."—*Idem.*

LXXV. On some of the Rocks and Fossils occurring near Phillipsburg, Canada East. 1861.

LXXVI. On the occurrence of Graptolites in the base of the Lower Silurian. *Do.*

LXXVII. Remarks upon Prof. Hall's recent publication, entitled "Contributions to Paleontology." 1862.

LXXVIII. Notes on some of the

habits of the pine boring beetles of the genus Monohamacus. *Do.*

LXXIX. On the Parallelism of the Quebec Group with the Llandeilo of England and Australia, and with the Chazy and Calciferous formations. 1863.

"An interesting view."—Principal Dawson.

LXXX. On the remains of the Fossil Elephant found in Canada. *Do.*

" * * * * of especial value, as for the first time giving accurate descriptions and figures of these remains, and identifying our species with that known to American Naturalists as *Elephas Jacksoni*. In this paper, Mr. Billings has worthily followed up, with reference to the extinct elephantine animals of Canada, the able investigations of Dr. Falconer on the general distribution of these animals."—Principal Dawson: *Annual Address before Mont. Nat. His. Soc.*

LXXXI. Description of a new species of Phillipsia from the lower Carboniferous rocks of Nova Scotia. *Do.*

LXXXII. On the Genus Stricklandia ;—proposed alteration of the name. *Do.*

Canadian Journal.

I. On some new genera and species of Cystidea from the Trenton Limestone. 1854.

"This, we believe, was the first Palæontological paper ever written by a Canadian. Would do credit to the transactions of the most distinguished societies in Europe and America."—*Can. Journ.*

II. On the Fossil Corals of the Devonian Rocks of Canada West. 1859.

III. On the Devonian Fossils of Canada West. 1860.

Silliman's Journal.

I. Note on a new Trilobite from the Potsdam Sandstone. Vol. 30.

II. Additional note on Potsdam Fossils. *Do.*

III. On the age of the Red Sandstone formation of Vermont. Vol. 32.

In this article the age of a great and important formation of rock was first determined.

IV· Further observations on the age of the Red Sandrock of Vermont. *Do.*

V. On Prof. J. Hall's claim of priority in the determination of the age of Red Sandrock series of Vermont. Vol. 35.

VI. On the Genus Centronella, with remarks on some other genera of Brachiopoda. Vol. 36.

VII. On the Classification of the subdivisions of McCoy's Genus Athyris, as determined by the laws of the Zoological Nomenclature. Vol. 44.

Official Reports and Works.

I. Report on the arrangement and classification of the Geological Museum, with numerous descriptions of new Fossils. pp. 98. *Rept. of Survey for* 1853–4–5–6. 1857.

"In the first part of report we have a very able Analytical review of the palæontological relations of the Anticosti rocks. This is succeeded by detailed descriptions of a great number of newly determined forms, embracing not only new species, but many new genera. Scattered through these descriptions, we find the germ of much new thought."— *Can. Journ.*

II. Report on Organic Remains. pp. 44. *Do.* 1858.

"All Silurian palæontologists will estimate the value of the lists, descriptions, and figures of Canadian fossils by that able naturalist, Mr. Billings, in his report of 1858, helping as they do, to a comparison of the Old World forms of the other side of the Atlantic with those of Europe—a subject the interest of which will be best understood by those who know that, while many American forms are identical with ours, others differ just so much that palæontologists disagree as to whether they are different species or mere varieties. Those who are able to appreciate Mr. Darwin's remarkable book on the *Origin of Species* will see the importance of this subject."—*Sat. Rev.* (Lon.)

III. 1. Monographs of Lower Silurian Cystideæ and Asteridæ. 2. A description of the genus *Cyclocystoides*, by Messrs. J. W. Salter and E. Billings. *Decade III of Canadian Organic Remains*, 1858.

IV. A Monograph of the Lower Silurian Crinoidea ; with wood cuts and lithographed plates. pp. 72. *Decade IV.* 1859.

"The species described, of which the greater part are new, amount to about fifty. The detailed description of these is very properly preceded by a brief essay on the history and structure of Crinoideæ generally, a plan not only convenient in itself, as explanatory of special terms, and in adding completeness of the work, but also of the greatest assistance to the student ; more especially in a country like this, where books of reference are not always procurable, and in which so few public libraries exist."—*Can. Journ.*

V. Palæozoic Fossils; with 401 woodcuts. *Montreal*, 1865, pp. 426, royal 8vo.

"It contains descriptions of 443 new species, with re-descriptions or farther details of about 50 others previously published in the Reports of the Survey or in the Scientific periodicals of the Province."—*Introd. to Atlas of Survey*, 1865.

VI. Catalogue of the Palæozoic Fossils of Anticosti, with descriptions of some of the species. *Montreal*, 1866.

BINNEY, *Rt. Rev.* HIBBERT. Lord Bishop of N. S. B. in N. S. 1819. Ed. at King's Coll. (Lon.) Was afterwards successively scholar and fellow of Worcester Coll. Oxford, where he graduated 1st class mathematics, and 2nd class classics 1842; M. A. 1844; appointed tutor of that coll. 1846, and bursar in 1848; ordained a deacon 1842; a priest 1843; and consecrated 4th Bish. of N. S. 1851.

I. Charge to the Clergy of Nova Scotia. *Halifax*, 1854, pp. 32, 8vo.

II. Do.   *Do.*   1858, pp. 48, 8vo.

III. Do.   *Do.*   1862, pp. 39, 8vo.

IV. Do.   *Do.*   1866, pp. 44, 8vo.

V. A Pastoral Letter, including correspondence between the Rev. G. W. Hill and himself. *Do.* 1866, pp. 48, 8vo.

BINNEY, W. G.
I. Catalogue of land and fresh-water univalve Mollusks collected in British America, by Messrs Ross, Kennicott and Drexler, and deposited in the Smithsonian Collection. *Proc. Aca. N. S. Phil.* 1861.

BIRKMYRE, *Rev.* J., *A. M.*
I. A Sermon on the Sanctification of the Lord's Day. *Fredericton*, 1840, pp. 16, 8vo.

BLACHFORD, *Lt. Col.*
I. The Ultimatum. A short tale with a long moral. *London, U. C.*, 1867, pp. 32, 12mo.

BLACHFORD, M., Hydrographer.
I. Sailing directions for the Gulf and River of St. Lawrence, giving a particular description of all the harbours, islands, anchorages, rocks,

shoals and other dangers. *London*, 1842, pp. 95, 4to.

BLACK, *Rev.* JAMES, Min. of the Pres. Ch. at Seneca, U. C.
I. Unity of Mankind; a lecture. *Caledonia, V. C.*, 1865, pp. 26.

BLACKIE, *Rev.* ALEXANDER, *D. D* A Presb. Min. in the U. S. B. at Pictou, N. S., and was ed. at the Academy there under the late Dr. McCulloch. Was for some years Pastor of the Associate Reformed Pres'b. Ch., Boston, where he still resides.

I. The Philosophy of Sectarianism; or, a classified view of the Christian sects in the United States; with notices of their progress and tendencies. Illustrated by historical facts and anecdotes. *Boston*, 1854, pp. 362, 8vo.

"Some of your views I fully accept, although myself bred and continuing in Congregationalism; and all of them indicate thought, earnestness and sincerity."—*Hon.* RUFUS CHOATE: *Letter to Author.*

II. A Catechism on Praise. *Do.* 1854. 4th ed. pp. 32, 8vo.

"In very short bounds, he has presented a very clear and satisfactory vindication of the use of the Scripture Psalms, and these alone, as the matter of praise in the worship of God."—*Covenanter.*

III. A Catechism on Church Government. *Do.*

IV. The Schools, or, a comparative statement of the relative position and distinctive principles of the new, old, older and oldest schools of Presbyterians, in the United States. *Do.* 1860, pp. 59, 12mo.

V. The Organ and other musical instruments, as noted in the Holy Scriptures. *Do.* 1865, pp. 22, 8vo.

BLACKWOOD, THOMAS.
I. Remarks on the constitution of the Canadas, Civil and Ecclesiastical, with a view to its amendment. By a Layman of the Church of Scotland.

BLAIN DE ST. AUBIN, EMM. A native of France and a graduate of the Univ. of Paris. Has composed some musical compositions, and contributed some interesting fragments to the periodical literature of Can. since his residence in the Province. Two lectures: *La Guerre—Les Milices Canadiennes*, and

Passé, Présent et Avenir probable de la "Langue Française au Canada," recently delivered by him, have been published in the French press and are much admired, not only for their historical interest, but also for the pure and graceful language in which they are written.

BLAIN, *Rev.* D. B.
   I. Short memoir of Rev. J. McGregor, D. D., prefixed to his Gaelic poems. *Pictou,, N. S.,* 1861.

BLAKE, *Hon.* W. H., late Chancellor of U. C. Was a mem. of the Leg. Assem. during one Parliament, and Solicitor Genl. U. C. from April 1848 to Sept. 1849.
   I. Separate Report of Mr. Blake's Speech on the Rebellion Losses. *Montreal,* 1849.

BLANCHARD, JOTHAM. A N. S. journ. B. at Peterboro, New Hampshire, U. S., 15th March, 1800. D. in N. S. 1840.
   His grandfather, Jotham, had left the United States during the Revolutionary War, and settled at Truro with two sons, Jonathan and Edward, and several daughters, then young. After the war, Jonathan returned to New Hampshire, and there married. Jotham was their eldest child, and when he was 15 months old, his parents with him removed to Truro, where the old people with their family were still residing. Here he spent his early days, and was thus by education at least a Nova Scotian. He received his collegiate education under Dr. McCulloch at the Pictou Academy, and was one of the first class of students at that institution. He studied law with Thomas Dickson, of Pictou, and was admitted to the Bar on the 18th October, 1821.
   In the year 1827, Mr. B. was mainly instrumental in establishing at Pictou the first newspaper published in N. S. out of Halifax. It was called " *The Colonial Patriot,*" and was anonymously edited by him. It had for its motto, "*Pro rege, pro patria.*" In exposition of its motto and principles, it stated,

"We reverence the British Constitution and honour the King as its head, but we feel assured, that the best way of showing true regard to the King is by advancing the interests of his subjects. All governments are designed for the general good of the people, and that government deserves most praise which most effectually succeeds in this object; and we boldly assert that he who pretends to support the dignity of the government and the honour of the Crown at the expense of the general happiness, alike commits treason against the King and his subjects,—he betrays the people and dishonours their Sovereign.

"In politics we shall side with the most liberal system, * * * Having witnessed the beneficial effects resulting from an unshackled press in Britain, we shall always advocate the same system here.

"We will discuss the interests of Pictou. * * We shall raise our voice on behalf of the whole Province, * * And our humble efforts shall always be at the command of our sister colonies, when we think their just rights attacked or disregarded or in danger of being compromised by the negligence or inertness of the great body of the people, or the adroitness or the power of the few."

The paper thus established soon excited attention by the bold stand which it took as an advocate of Liberal politics. *It was the first paper of the kind published in the Lower Colonies.* The newspapers in Halifax were devoted to the news of the day, containing only some common-place remarks on public events, and to have made any remarks in condemnation of the conduct of those in authority was then deemed high treason. But Mr. B. by the study of English politics, on which excitement then ran high in the mother country, embraced very warmly the principles for which Brougham and his compatriots were there contending, and deeply imbibed their spirit; impressed with the much greater subservience of the people in general to the few in power which existed here, he threw his whole soul into the work of securing for the popular will that control over public affairs for which the Reformers in Britain were contending. Those measures of Reform which the Reformers in Can. and N. S. afterwards succeeded in carrying, *the Colonial Patriot was the first paper in the Lower Provinces to advocate.* Mr. B. wielded the pen of a ready writer. He wrote rapidly, but his writings were marked by great vigour and independence. The principal part of the political writing in that paper emanated from his pen. These are marked by what Mr.

Howe happily styled " racy vitupera-
tion." He was, however, aided by
others. The political questions of the
day were then mixed up with the
Pictou Academy discussion. In fact
that was the battle ground of party.
This drew in several Presbyterian
clergymen to his aid, especially Dr.
McCulloch and Rev. Thos. Trotter,
both of whom wrote articles on the
public events of the day.

The principles which the *Colonial
Patriot* advocated, and the free spirit
in which it assailed those in power,
soon brought it into notice. The
extreme radical, or as they were
then deemed, revolutionary views
which it advocated, were received in
some places with horror, at a time when
the excesses of the first French Revolution were still fresh in the minds of
men. We recollect of hearing of an
old Scotch minister being in company
with Mr. B. one evening, and hearing
him in his earnest way advocating his
political views, lifting up his hands
in holy amazement, and exclaiming,
" Daring Innovator !"

But a circumstance which gave Mr.
B. and the paper special notoriety,
was the publication of what was called
" the Canadian letter." There being
at that time much political agitation
in Can., its condition and affairs occupied a prominent place in the *Patriot's*
discussions. It commented freely on
the unconstitutional ground taken by
Lord Dalhousie in rejecting a second
time the Speaker chosen by the
people's representatives; and maintained that if the people were true to
themselves they must triumph in the
end. He was for a time a warm admirer of Mr. Papineau, though doubtless had he lived till the outbreak in
Canada in 1837, he would, like all the
Reformers in N. S., have condemned
the course taken by the French Canadian leader at that time.

Not long after the report of the proceedings of the Can. Parliament, at
which Mr. Papineau was a second time
rejected, reached N. S., an extract from
a private letter from a gentleman in
that province, was published in the
Canadian Spectator, in which the spirit
of the popular party was applauded,

3•

and assurance was given that whatever the enslaved press of N. S.
might say upon the subject, the great
majority, who knew the merits of
the conflict, thought well of the objects they had in view and in general
of the means they took to accomplish
them. It was stated that whilst in the
Legislature of N. S. there was a growing spirit of independence, there was
still far too much servility to men in
power ; and though the existing state
of things in Can. was much to be de-
precated, it was desirable that some of
their spirit should come this way.

" A moderate quantity of it now might
supersede the necessity of more hereafter.
As prevention is preferable to remedy, I am
in hopes a little of it will creep our way
before a greater share of it be required."

This extract was copied into the Halifax papers. The writer was denounced as a political libeller, not fit
to crawl on free soil, and his opinions
were characterised as disloyal and dangerous. Over a *nom de plume*, Mr. B.
defended the extract of which he was
the author, but disavowed the legitimacy of the comments which were
made upon it and the inferences drawn
from it. Such was the feeling excited
in high circles, that Mr. B. did not
trust the office with the knowledge of
the authorship of what he wrote, and
therefore employed a friend as scribe,
in whose hand writing the manuscript
went to the press.

Mr. Joseph Howe, at that time editor
and publisher of the *Nova Scotian*, was
prominent amongst the assailants of
the principles which the writer of the
Canadian letter advocated, and a controversy was maintained which did more
for the elucidation of the principles
of the liberal or reform party and their
establishment in N. S. than any thing
that had previously transpired. Mr.
Howe was then a young man, just beginning his career as a journalist.
Even his early writings gave indications of the talents he possessed, although he had not reflected deeply
upon political questions. He was naturally connected with the official party,
his father being both Queen's Printer
and Postmaster General, and Mr. Howe,
was brought out as the chosen cham-

pion of that party. But the result of his controversy with Mr. B. was, that he became a convert to the views, which he at that time denounced, and in the advocacy of which he afterwards became so prominent and so celebrated as a Reformer. He has acknowledged that he received his first impressions of liberal politics from Jotham Blanchard; not approving of them at first, the more he thought upon them the better he liked them, and, at last, fully embraced and acted upon them.

Mr. B. in the course which he pursued encountered very violent hostility. Besides opposition in the press, and burning in effigy he was, though not robust, the subject of violent personal assault, which however drew from his pen a castigation of the assailant, compared with which any person of ordinary feeling would have preferred Mr. B.'s bodily assault; even when he set up as a candidate for the house of Assembly, a worthy magistrate, who had independence enough to propose him at the hustings, was immediately dismissed from the Commission of the Peace.

In the year 1830, he entered the house of Assem. as a member for the county of Halifax, which then embraced what now forms the three large counties of Halifax, Colchester and Pictou, comprehending nearly one-third of the province. The contest was most violent, it being a time of great excitement, and the whole government influence being brought to bear especially against Mr. B., one of the four opposition candidates, so that when the poll was adjourned from Halifax, he was at the foot, but through his popularity in the county districts, now forming the counties of Colchester and Pictou, was triumphantly returned.

For 5 years he proved an energetic member of the house. His voice was ever raised on behalf of measures of public improvement, and he was instrumental in carrying various important measures. The subject which engaged him most heartily was the support of the Pictou Academy. Both in the Legislature and in the columns of the *Colonial Patriot*, he was its leading advocate and champion. The govern-

ment still continuing hostile to the institution, he was in the year 1831 sent by its friends to Britain to lay its claims before the British Government.

His labours were too great for his bodily strength; and though he was in Halifax during the Session of 1836, the last of that house, and able to attend at his rooms to local county business, he was unable to sit in the house. Not long after, in 1838, his mind also gave way, and he sank into a state of mental imbecility from which he never recovered.

BLANCHET, FRANCOIS, *M. D.* A French Can. medical practitioner and politician. B. at St. Pierre, Rivière du Sud, L. C., 1776. D. at Quebec, 26th June, 1830. Shortly after completing his ed. at the Seminary (Que.), he proceeded to N. Y. where he studied his profession and obtained his degree. After his return to Can. was elected to Parliament where he warmly espoused the popular side. He took part in the editing of *Le Canadien* (Que.), and was with others arrested and imprisoned by the Governor. He introduced the first education bill passed in L. C.

I. Recherches sur la médecine ou l'application de la chimie à la médecine. *New York*, 1800, 8vo.

II. Appel au Gouvernement Impérial et aux Habitants des Colonies Anglaises dans l'Amérique du Nord, sur les prétentions exorbitantes du Gouvernement Exécutif et du Conseil Législatif de la Province du Bas Canada; par un Membre de la Chambre d'Assemblée. *Québec*, 1824, pp. 70, 8vo.

BLANEY, *Captain.*

I. An excursion through the United States and Canada, during the years 1822 and 1823. By an English Gentleman. *London*, 1824, pp. 511, 8vo.

BLEASDELL, *Rev.* WILLIAM, *M. A.* A Clergyman of the Ch. of Eng. Now Incumbent of Trenton, U. C. Several of his sermons have been published in the local press.

I. The Indian Tribes of Canada. *Can. Journ.*, vol. 3.

II. The Great Trent Boulder, its botanical and geological associations. *Trans. Bot. Society of Can.*

III. Papal Supremacy, a Sermon. *Belleville*, 1853.

IV. History of Trenton. *Hastings Directory*, 1864-5.

BLISS, HENRY, *Q. C.* A native of N. B. Is a Barrister of Lincoln's Inn. Resides in London, Eng. Acted for many years as agent in Eng. for N. S.

I. On Colonial Intercourse, with Appendix. *London*, 1830, pp. 111, 8vo.

II. Letter to Sir Henry Parnell, Bart., M. P., on the New Colonial Trade Bill. *Do.*, 1831, pp. 37, 8vo.

III. Statistics of the Trade, industry and resources of Canada, and the other Plantations in British America, *Do.* 1833, pp. 169, 8vo.

BLYTH, STEPHEN CLEVELAND. (Boucherville L. C.)

I. A narrative of remarkable occurrences connected with the death of Louis XVI, late King of France. Translated from the French of the Abbe Edgeworth de Firmont. *Montreal*, 1812, pp. 36. .

BOARDMAN, GEORGE A. (St. Stephen N. B.)

I. Catalogue of the birds found in the vicinity of Calais, Me., and about the islands at the mouth of the Bay of Fundy. *Proc. Nat. His. Soc.* (*Bos.*), 1862.

II. A list of birds and animals found in the Southern part of the Province of New Brunswick. Monro's *His.*, &c., *of B. N. A.*, 1864.

BOLDUC, *Rev.* J. B. Z. A French Can. Priest. In charge of the parish of St. Roch's. (Que.)

. I. Mission de la Colombie. Lettre et Journal. *Quebec*, pp. 95.

BOLLAN, WILLIAM. Agent for Massachusetts in England, from 1745 to 1762.

I. Coloniæ Anglicanæ illustratæ ; or the acquest of dominion and the plantation of colonies made by the English in America, with the rights of the colonies examined, stated and illustrated. *London*, 1762, pp. X and 141, 4to.

II. The ancient right of the English nation to the American fishery ; and its various diminutions ; examined and stated. *Do.*, 1764, pp. 105, 4to.

III. The importance of the Colonies of North America, and the interest of Great Britain with regard to them, considered. Together with remarks on the stamp duty. *Do.*, 1766, pp. 46, 4to.

BOLTON, E. C., and WEBBER, H. H.

I. The Confederation of British North America. (With Maps.) *London*, 1866, pp. 149.

BOND, J. WESLEY.

I. Minnesota and its Resources ; to which are appended Camp Fire Sketches, or Notes of a trip from St. Paul to Pembina and Selkirk Settlement on the Red River of the North. (With Map, &c.) *New York*, 1853, 12mo.

"We have seen no work respecting the north-west of equal value to this."—*Christian Intelligencer.*

BOND, *Rev.* WILLIAM, and BANCROFT, *Rev* CHARLES.

I. Sermons on the death of the Rev. Mark Willoughby. *Montreal*, 1847, pp. 43.

BONNER, JOHN. An Am. author and journ. B. at Quebec, 1828. Has resided at N. Y. for some years past, where he has ed. *Harper's Weekly*, and also been on the ed. staff of the *Daily Herald*.

I. The Registry Laws of Canada. *Quebec*, 1851.

II. Child's history of the United States. *New York*, 1855, 2 vols, 18mo.

"This American history is freely written, and contains a fair account of the settlement in America of the early Puritans, of their trials and misfortunes, and of their after prosperity and liberty."—*Athen.* (Lon.)

III. Child's history of Rome. *Do.*, 1856, 2 vols. 16mo.

IV. Child's history of Greece. *Do.*, 1857, 2 vols. 16mo.

"Into ·..... in these books, the idea of which was suggested by Charles Dickens's Child's History of England, Mr. Bonner has infused a critical spirit into an engaging, lively narrative."—DUYCKINCK.

V. The Old Régime and the Revolution, translated from the French of DeTocqueville.

BONNYCASTLE, *Sir* RICHARD HENRY, *Kt.* An Eng. Military Officer. B. 1791. D. 1848. Commanded the Royal Engineers in Can. from 1837 to 1839, and was knighted for his defence of Kingston, U. C., in the former year. He possessed considerable literary and scientific acquirements.

I. Excursion in Canada, or Canada, in 1831. *London*, 1841, 2 Vols. 8vo.

II. Newfoundland in 1842. *Do.* 1842, 2 vols. pp. 367 and 351, p. 8vo.

" Published under the sanction of the British Government, and comprises a full account of this most important colony."— *Athen.* (Lon.)

III. Canada and the Canadians in 1846. *Do.* 1846, 2 vols. p. 8vo.

" There is excellent advice, as well as information of a practical kind, which ought to be treasured up by the intending emigrant."—*M. Chronicle,* (Lon.)

IV. Canada as it was, is, and may be. *Do.* 1852, 2 vols. p. 8vo.

BORLAND, *Rev.* JOHN. A Wes. Meth. min., (Brantford, U. C.) Has written on Roman Catholicism and other controversial religious topics for the Provincial press.

I. Universalism. *Sherbrooke*, 1848, pp. 153, 8vo.

II. Sermons and tracts published at various times.

BORRETT, GEORGE TUTHILL., *A. M.* Fellow of King's Coll., Cambridge.

I. Out West ; a series of letters from Canada and the United States. *London*, 1866. pp. 294.

BORTHWICK, *Rev.* J. DOUGLAS, a clergym. of the Ch. of Eng. (Hochelaga L. C.); formerly a master in the High Sch. (Mont.), and a prof. in the Huntingdon (L. C.) Academy.

I. Examples of Historical and Geographical Autonomasias; for the use of Schools. *Montreal*, 1858, pp. 16.

II. A Cyclopædia of History and Geography. *Do.* 1859, pp. 251, 8vo.

" It is just the sort of book the scholar is always requiring at his elbow, and the general reader will find it a great convenience."— *Gazette,* (Mont.)

III. The British American Reader. *Do.* 1860, pp. 288, 8vo.

" The best we have seen for use in the British American Colonies."—*Idem.*

" It does the greatest credit to the industry and taste of Mr. Borthwick."—*Journ. of Ed., L. C.*

IV. The Harp of Canaan ; or, Selections from the Poets on Bible historical incidents. *Do.* 1866, pp. 269, 8vo.

V. The Battles of the World. *Do.* 1866, pp. 500, 8vo.

" To Teachers and Academical Students it will prove most useful, embracing as it does, the whole of the principal battles, by land and sea, that have ever taken place, from the earliest recorded action of which we have in history any distinct and reliable information, to the very last event of any military importance which has transpired previous to its going to press."—*Trans.* (Mont.)

BOSWORTH, *Rev.* NEWTON, *F. R. A. S.* A Baptist Min. D. at Paris, U. C. 14 July, 1848.

I. Hochelaga Depicta ; the early history and present state of the City and Island of Montreal. *Montreal*, 1839, 12mo.

" A most useful book."—*Lit. Garland.*

BOTSFORD, GEORGE. A Barrister. N. B.

1. Rules and Statutes regulating the practice of the Court of Chancery in New Brunswick—now the Supreme Court in Equity. Also Rules made in the Supreme Court since the publication of Allen's Rules in 1847. *St. John, N. B.*, 1866, pp. 178.

BOUCHER, ADÉLARD J. A French Can. writer (Mont.) His lectures before the " *Cabinet de Lecture Paroissial*" of that city, in 1858, on " *The Eloquence of the Fine Arts* " and " *The Battle of Chateauguay,* " and, in 1861. on " *The Influence of Catholic Charity,*" have been published in the organ of that association, and the first also in pamphlet form, *(Mont.* 1858.) In 1862, he acted as Musical critic to the same periodical. Mr. B. established in April 1863, cojointly with Messrs. J. A. Manseau and Gustave Smith, a monthly musical review called " *Les Beaux Arts,*" to which he contributed until it suspended publication in 1864. In Jany. of the latter year, he became one of the directors of *La Revue Can.,* in which articles from his pen have appeared—

I. Tableau Synoptique et Synchronique de l'Histoire du Canada, indiquant les principaux événements qui se sont passés dans cette Colonie depuis son premier établissement jusqu'à l'administration de Son Excellence Sir Edmund Walker Head (depuis, 1534 jusqu'à 1854.) *Montreal*, 1858; second edition same year.

BOUCHER-BELLEVILLE, J. P. A French Can. journ. and author (St. Remi, L. C.) Published and ed. *L'Echo du Pays*, (St. Charles, L. C.) from 1835 to 1836 ; *Le Glaneur* in 1837, and ed. in 1839-40, *L'Aurore des Canadas* (Mont.) Since then has written many articles on subjects connected with religion, politics and agriculture in the French press of Montreal.

I. Les Principes de la langue Française, en deux parties, suivis des Règles de la versification Française. *Montreal*, 1831 ; 2nd Ed. *St. Charles, L. C.*, 1835 ; 3rd Ed. *Montreal*, 1848 ; 4th Ed. *Do.* 1855, pp. 119, 12mo.

II. Les Principes de la Langue Latine, en deux parties, suivis des Règles de la versification Latine. *Do.* 1832, pp. 86, 12mo.

III. Dictionnaire des Barbarismes et des Solécismes les plus ordinaires en ce pays, avec le mot propre ou leur signification. *Do.* 1855, pp. 23, 8vo.

"Is a remarkable work and very useful. It was entirely a want in Canada. In filling up the gap the anonymous lexicographer has accomplished a meritorious task."—*L'Avenir.*

BOUCHER-BELLEVILLE, *L'Abbé* J. BAPTISTE. A R. C. priest. B. at Quebec, 1761. D. at Laprairie, of which he had been for 47 years *Curé*, 6 Sept. 1839.

I. Le Cantique à l'usage des Missions. Has passed through many editions.

II. Manuel abrégé de Controverse, traduit de l'Anglais de J. Mannock. *Quebec*, 1806.

BOUCHER, CYRILLE. A French Can. journ. D. 9 Oct. 1865. Was connected in an ed. capacity with the Montreal French newspaper press for some years. Left a novel in MS. "Emilie de Brunoville," which we understand is soon to be published.

BOUCHER DE LA BRUÈRE, fils. Was ed. of the *Courrier de St. Hyacinthe* from 1861 to 1862.

I. St. Hyacinthe ; a Lecture. *St. Hyacinthe*, 1859, pp. 16, 12mo.

II. Le Canada sous la domination Anglaise. *Do.* 1863, pp. 80, 8vo.

III. Esquisse Historique de l'Instruction en Canada. *Rev. Can.* 1866.

BOUCHETTE, *Lieut. Col.* JOSEPH. An eminent Can. Surveyor and Topographer. B. in Can. 1774. D. at Montreal, 9 April 1841. Was a son of Commodore Bouchette, also a native of Can., an officer in the Provincial Navy. In 1790, he entered the office of his uncle Major Holland, then Surveyor Genl. of B. N. A., as a draftsman. In the following year he joined the Provincial Navy, in which service he remained until 1796. In that year he was placed in command of an armed row-galley on the St. Lawrence for the purpose of detecting certain treasonable practices, in which object he was successful. In 1803, he was appointed Deputy Surveyor Genl., and in the following year Surveyor Genl of L. C. During the Am. war of 1812, Mr. (now Col.) B. raised a corps called "The Quebec Volunteers," and during the continuance of the campaign, was employed in carrying despatches from head-quarters to the Major Genl. commanding in U. C. ; he was also charged " with secret instructions to report on the general defensive state of the frontier, whether possessing any interesting posts, and at the same time to reconnoitre and ascertain the position and strength of the enemy as he proceeded." He also rendered various other important services to the Crown at this critical period. In 1815, he proceeded to Eng. for the purpose of personally superintending the publication of his Topographical Maps and *Topographical description of Lower Canada*. A copy was presented by the author in person to the Prince Regent, to whom the work, by permission, was dedicated. On this occasion Mr. Fennings Taylor informs us, Col. B. was recommended by the Duke of Kent for the honour of Knighthood. While in Eng. he received the appointment of Surveyor Genl. under the articles of the Treaty of Ghent, for establishing the boundary between His Majesty's possessions in Am. and the U. S. ; and at the instance of the Commissioners and the agent under that treaty prepared a project of operations for the year 1817, which he submitted to the board at Boston. The results of his labours, during that year was conveyed to the board of Commissioners in extensive and explanatory plans, sections, and reports, for which he received their approval and commendation, and upon which the strongest arguments of His Majesty's Agent were chiefly grounded, in claiming the whole extent of country north of Mars hill ridge of highlands. which is that pointed out by Col. B. as the legitimate boundary between that part of the Brit. possessions and the territory of the U. S. And although the Ashburton Treaty has since yielded to the pretensions of the U. S., to a boundary much further north, and coming within a few miles of the St. Lawrence. it is now generally admitted that the line of boundary pointed out by Col. B. was that upon which the Brit. negotiator should have insisted. In 1827, with a view of ascertaining the statistics of L. C., he visited all parts of the province, and devoting himself to long and laborious researches, deducted explanatory reports and tabular statistical statements that met with the marked approbation of His Majesty's representative in that colony.

Availing himself of these several tours as a means of perfecting his topographical work on L. C., he solicited from the seigneurs copies of the plans of their respective *fiefs* and seigneuries, and was enabled to compile maps of the province still more voluminous and correct than the former ; and desirous of rendering the information thus acquired as generally useful as possible, not only to the government, but to the public in the mother country and the colony, he repaired to Eng. in 1830, under the formal sanction and support of the Provincial Legislature, and with the approbation of the Executive Govt., to superintend the publication of his new work on the topography, geography, and statistics of L. C., which grew out of the materials studiously collected during the previous 15 years with a view to the accomplishment of that object. His works were printed and published in Eng., on a scale of magnificence which rendered them costly to the author, and too expensive for general circulation. For his first work the Soc. of Arts and Sciences

(Lon.) elected him a corresponding mem. and awarded him their " Gold Isis Medal." His second work " *The British Dominions in North America*," and the maps which accompanied it, were by special permission dedicated to the late king William IV, and was received by that monarch from the author in person. Col. B. was received with favour and distinction at Court, owing doubtless to the friendship of his early patron the late Duke of Kent, whose royal influence and protection followed him in every phase of his career in Eng.

I. A Topographical description of the Province of Lower Canada, with remarks upon Upper Canada, and on the relative connection of both provinces with the United States of America. *London*, 1815, pp. xv–640–lxxxvi, r. 8vo. Plates 17.—Also in French.

The following Maps accompany this work:—

I. Topographical Maps of Lower Canada in two sections. *First*—District of Quebec, Three Rivers and Gaspé. *Second*—The district of Montreal.

II. Geographical Map of British America, and of the United States.

" The interior of Lower Canada being so little known beyond the limits of the province, a belief that a detailed account of it would not only be useful by shewing its present state, but by bringing it under more general notice, might possibly assist in the developement of its vast resources, has led to the construction of a Topographical Map upon a large scale, and to the publication of the following book to illustrate the same more fully. The result of several years of continued labour is now presented to the world, but not without its author's feeling the greatest diffidence in bringing his work before the tribunal of public opinion, of whose decisions even the most scientific and accomplished often feel a dread. The manner and method of the performance must speak for themselves, but of the subject matter it may be worth while to say a few words ; and on this point he may perhaps be pardoned for a little self-gratulation. when he notes with confidence the authenticity and correctness of the materials he has had to work upon, which principally consist of the valuable documents and official records, that in his capacity of Surveyor General of the Lower Province, are lodged with his department, and which he has been permitted the free use of. These, as accurately descriptive of the date and extent of the feudal tenures, and of all the grants made by the English Government, may consequently be relied upon; besides this source, a long period of professional field service has enabled him to acquire a very critical local knowledge of almost every part of the province, and to verify the same by numerous Surveys, and careful observations on the nature, quality, and properties of the best and most valuable tracts; and from which he ventures to believe he has been able to present a body of information, relative to this part of the British Trans-Atlantic Dominions, that has, up to this period, been sought for in vain from any other work. Nothing has been admitted into the description without mature reflection, nor anything but what he entertains a well grounded confidence is borne out by the actual state of the country. What is said of the Province of Upper Canada is the substance of notes and memoranda made in that country very recently, as well as a knowledge obtained of it during an anterior service of six years as an officer of the Provincial Navy upon the lakes; these have been corroborated and enlarged from other sources of undeniable intelligence and veracity."—*Author's Preface.*

" A work of so much authority and importance."—*N. A. Rev.*

II. The British Dominions in North America, or a topographical and statistical description of the Provinces of Upper and Lower Canada, New Brunswick, Nova Scotia, the Islands of Newfoundland, Prince Edward, and Cape Breton, including considerations on land granting and Emigration, and a Topographical Dictionary of Lower Canada; to which is annexed the statistical tables and tables of distances, published with the author's Maps of Lower Canada, in consequence of a vote of the Provincial Legislature. Embellished with vignettes, views, landscapes, plans of towns, harbours, &c., containing also a copious Appendix. *London,* 1831, 3 vols. 4to.

The following Maps accompany this work:—

I. Topographical Map of the District of Quebec and Three Rivers.

II. Topographical Map of the District of Montreal.

III. Geographical Map of British America and of the Northern, Western and Central States of America.

" Of the maps which accompany this work, we can speak in terms of unmeasured approbation. They depict all that is known of the northern part of the great continent of America, with accuracy and clearness, while the information they accord is various 'and minute."—*West. Rev.*

" Colonel Bouchette's work ought to be in every public library in the empire, for it is by it that the truest conception can be formed of the value of our *North American Dominions,* which very shortly will become the subject of deep and anxious consideration in Parliament.'—*Fraser's Mag.*

BOUCHETTE, JOSEPH, *Jr.* Son of the preceding. Is Deputy Surveyor Genl. of Can.

I. Table of Trigonometrical solutions of Right Angle, plane Triangle, computed on the Logarithmic number 2,000,000. *Montreal,* 1827, pp. 12.

II. Tables showing the difference of Longitude in time at the most important places between the Atlantic and Pacific Oceans in the British North American Dominions and the Northern section of the United States. *Toronto,* 1857.

BOUCHETTE, R. S. M. Com. of Customs, Can. Was in his early days one of the editors of *Le Libéral,* a newspaper published in Quebec in 1837.

I. Weights and Measures. *Trans. Lit. and His. Soc.* (*Que.*) 1863.

BOUGAINVILLE, LOUIS-ANTOINE DE.

I. Notice Historique sur les Sauvages de l'Amérique-Septentrionale. [*Dans les Mémoires de l'Institut National des Sciences et des Arts.* Tome III.]

" C'est le même M. *De Bougainville* qui servit en Canada, comme Aide-de-Camp, sous le Marquis de Montcalm. Il est décédé à Paris, le 31 août, 1811, à l'âge de 82 ans."—FARIBAULT.

BOULTON, *Hon.* D'ARCY. A Can. Judge. B. 20 May, 1759. D. at Toronto, 23 May, 1834. Was Solicitor Genl. of U. C. in 1805, acting Attorney Genl. in 1815, and appointed a Puisne Judge, Court of King's Bench of same Province in 1818.

I. Sketch of His Majesty's Province of Upper Canada, (with map.) *London,* 1805, pp. 99, 4to.

BOULTON, HENRY JOHN.

I. A short sketch of the Province of Upper Canada, for the Information of the Labouring Poor throughout England. To which is prefixed thoughts on Colonization. *London,* 1826, s. 8vo.

BOULTON, H. J., Jr.

I. The drainage of land, and its necessity in the present state of the agricultural interests of Canada. *Toronto*, 1859, pp. 12.

II. On thorough land drainage, and the results of actual operations in Canada. *Do.*, 1860, pp. 8.

BOURASSA, NAPOLÉON, A French Can. author and painter. B. at L'Acadie, L. C. Was one of the founders of *La Revue Canadienne* (Mont.,) of which he is still, we believe, one of the conductors. Is favorably known in Can. by his works as a painter.

Revue Canadienne.

I. Le Carnaval à Rome (Souvenirs de Voyage,) 1864, pp. 8.

II. Quelques Réflexions critiques à propos de l'*Art Association of Montreal. Do.*, pp. 12.

III. Causerie Artistique sur l'Exposition de l'*Art Association of Montreal*, 1865, pp. 10.

IV. Causerie Artistique. *Do.*, pp. 5.

V. Jacques et Marie, souvenir d'un peuple dispersé. 1865-66, pp. 294. (Since published in book form.)

" Le style de M. Bourassa est charmant. C'est un heureux mélange de sincérité dans le sentiment, d'originalité ou d'entrain dans l'idée, de grâce et de vivacité dans l'expression. On n'écrit pas plus naturellement. Aucun effort, point de prétention. L'écrivain laisse la plume aussitôt qu'il cesse de sentir, ou s'il continue, c'est à son corps défendant. Il faut qu'il soit de belle humeur pour écrire des choses gaies, ou ému pour écrire des choses émouvantes ; nulle feinte n'altère son idée, ne masque son sentiment. Bien différents de ces auteurs qui ne s'orientent qu'une fois la plume à la main et pour qui une phrase en amène une autre. Ne leur demandez pas ce qu'il vont écrire : ils ne vous le diront que lorsqu'ils l'auront écrit.

" Ce style pur, charmant, est chez M. Bourassa un don de nature, une grâce d'écrivain ; il ne s'est point laborieusement formé. il s'est modelé tout naturellement sur la pensée de l'écrivain. Son imagination est douce, ample et riche ; elle embrasse aisément les larges horizons, mais, même en son vol le plus puissant, elle ne perd pas de vue la réalité, le coin de terre d'où elle s'est élevée dans les airs, le détail familier. Le drame national se déroule dans toute sa grandeur et sa variété sous les yeux du spectateur ; en avant et jusqu'au sein des masses populaires groupées dans le fond de la scène éclatent librement les incidents caractéristiques de la vie réelle. L'artiste excelle à la fois dans la fresque et dans le tableau de guerre."—HECTOR FABRE : *Rev. Can.*

BOURGEOIS, Sœur MARGUERITE.

I. Vie de la Vénérable Sœur Marguerite Bourgeois, institutrice, fondatrice et première Supérieure de la Congrégation de Notre Dame de Montréal. *Montreal*, 1818, 12mo.

BOURGET, Rt. Rev. IGNACE. R. C. Bish. of Montreal. B. at Pointe Levi, L. C., 30 Oct. 1799. On one of his missions to Rome, Pius IX appointed him Assistant to the Pontifical Throne.

I. Mandement contre les Sociétés secrètes. *Montreal*, 1846.

II. Le Cérémonial des Evèques, commenté et expliqué, par les usages et les traditions de l'église romaine. *Do.*, 1855.

A critical notice of this book appeared in the *Revue Théologique* (Paris). to which his lordship replied at some length in the same periodical.

III. Instruction Pastorale sur l'indépendance et l'inviolabilité des Etats Pontificaux. *Do*, 1860, pp. 52.

" Cette brochure contient un exposé complet, écrit avec talent et conviction, de tout ce qui concerne la question romaine."—*Journ. de L'Inst. Pub.*, L. C.

BOURINOT, JOHN GEORGE. A N. S. Journ. B. at Sydney, N. S., Oct. 24, 1834. Is the eld. son of John Bourinot. Esq., for many years mem. for Cape Breton in the Assem. N. S., and now a Senator for the Dominion of Can. Ed. at Trinity Coll. (Tor.,) where he took the Wellington and other scholarships. He first became connected with the newspaper press at the age of 21 ; was Parliamentary reporter for the *Leader* (Tor.,) and wrote for several Am. journals and periodicals. Until quite recently was chief ed. and prop. of the *Evening Reporter*, (Hal.) This journal was established in 1860 as a general newspaper. It has been eminently successful and has now a circulation only exceeded by one paper in the Lower Provinces. In politics it has always been independent. It has been a firm advocate and staunch supporter of the Union of the B. N. A. Colonies, the Intercolonial Railway and other great projects which its conductors believe would promote the welfare and prosperity of this portion of the British Colonial Empire. Mr. B's. style as a writer is inclined to be bold and vigorous ; his diction is pure, and unalloyed by the slang phraseology which marks many of our Provincial newspapers. He bids fair to take a high position on the press of the New Dominion of Can. For some years he has been Chief Official Reporter to the Leg. Assem. of N. S., which is one of the few provinces that has adopted the plan of giving the debates in an official form.

I. Debates and proceedings of the House of Assembly, during the third session of the twenty-third Parliament of the Province of Nova Scotia. *Halifax*, 1866, pp. 315. Large 4to.

II. Confederation of the Provinces of British North America. *Do.*, 1866, pp. 18, 8vo.

BOURNE, *Rev.* GEORGE. In 1829, Mr. B. was awarded a prize medal by the Soc. for the Encouragement of Arts and Sciences of Quebec, for an Essay on Literary and Scientific Institutions ; and an honorary medal by the same body, for an Essay on Political Economy.

I. The Picture of Quebec. *Quebec*, 1829, 18mo. Another ed., revised. *Do.*, 1831.

II. Lorette, the daughter of a Canadian nun. *London*, 1836, 12mo.

BOUTHILLIER, JEAN ANTOINE.
I. Traité d'arithmétique à l'usage des écoles. *Quebec*, 1809, New Ed., 1862, pp. 180.

BOVELL, JAMES, *M. D., M. R. C. P. (Lon.)* A medical practitioner at Toronto. Is Prof. of Physiology and Chemistry in the Univ. of Trin. Coll. in that city. Was for a time Junior Physician to the Barbadoes General Hospital. Has contributed to the Medical press of the Province.

I. Communion for the sick. *Toronto.*

II. Constitution and Canons of the Synod of the Diocese of Toronto. with explanatory notes and comments. *Do.*, 1858, pp. 52.

III. Preparation for the Holy Communion. *Do.*, 1859, pp. 294, 18mo. 2 eds.

IV. Outlines of Natural Theology, for the use of the Canadian Student. *Do.* 1859, pp. 660. Demy 8vo.

" The work • • • unlike the general character of Dr. Bovell's writings, is strictly a compilation from various sources, put together in accordance with the author's special views ; • • • a book not intended for the critical investigation of the scientific inquirer, to whom the facts brought forward in it must necessarily be familiar, but one offered to the student of Natural Theology, as a convenient and accessible text-book, in the prosecution of his studies. • • • As a treatise of undoubted merit, and as a home product both of pen and press, it well deserves the attention of all interested in the progress of Canadian Literature."—*Prof.* CHAPMAN : *Can. Journ.*

V. Outlines of the History of the British Church. *Do.* 1860, pp. 150. Demy 18mo.

VI. Passing thoughts on Man's relation to God and God's relation to Man. *Do.* 1862, pp. 427, 18mo.

VII. A Plea for Inebriate Asylums ; commended to the consideration of the Legislators of the Province of Canada. *Do.*, 1862, pp. 50, 4to.

British American Journal.

I. Report of Medical cases occurring in the Toronto General Dispensary, 1848.

II. Observations on the climate of Barbadoes, and its influence on Disease: together with Remarks on Angioleucitis or Barbadoes leg. *Do.*

III. Chemical Remarks on two cases of Tumour on the Uterus complicating Parturition, 1849.

Canadian Journal.

I. On the transfusion of milk, as practised in Cholera, at the Cholera Sheds, Toronto, July, 1854—1855.

II. Passing visits to the Rice Lake, Humber River, Grenadier's Pond, and the Island. By Dr. Goodby and J. Bovell, M. D. *Do.*

III. Notes on some points in the anatomy of the Leech, 1856.

IV. Note on the preservation of some Infusoria with a view to the display of their Cilia, 1863.

BOWEN, NOEL H., *N. P.*, (Que.)

I. An Essay on the social condition of the Coast of Labrador. *Trans. Lit. & His. Soc.* (Que.) Vol. 4.

II. An historical sketch of the Isle of Orleans, being a paper read before the Lit. & His. Soc. *Quebec*, 1860, pp. 40, 8vo.

"Conceived in an excellent spirit, and is well recommended by its literary merit."— *Journ. of Ed. L. C.*

BOWLES, G. J.

I. On the occurrence of Pieris Rapæ in Canada. *Can. Nat.* 1864.

BOWLES, *Captain* W., *R. N.*

I. Suggestions for the speedy and secure conveyance of our Reinforcements to Canada. *London*, 1837, pp. 12.

BOWLES, SAMUEL. Ed. of the Springfield (Mass.) *Republican.*

I. Across the Continent; a summer's journey to the Rocky Mountains, the Mormons, and the Pacific States, with Speaker Colfax. *Springfield*, 1866, pp. 452, 8vo.

BOXER. F. N., *C. E.* (Mont.)

I. Reminiscences of the Boundary Survey between Canada and the United States, from the spring of 1843 to 1845. *Trans. Lit. & His. Soc.* (Que.) 1855.

II. Handbook of the Victoria Bridge. *Montreal*, 1860, pp. 114, 12mo.

BOYD, JOHN. An extensive merchant (St. John, N. B.) most popularly known in his capacity as a lecturer and as an amateur writer for the provincial press. Mr. B. commenced life in 1838, when 11 years of age, by entering a large importing house in his native city, and has risen through the various grades of the mercantile profession until he is now become one of the leading partners in the firm. After the tedious and toilsome labours of the "busy season" he has sought recreation in writing and in preparing lectures, addresses and speeches on various popular subjects connected with History, Biography and Literature. These have been read and delivered, and in every instance repeated, in some cases from 15 to 18 times, in different parts of the Lower Provinces and the U. S. to crowded and intelligent audiences. They have yielded large sums in aid of various useful works and charities; in no instance has Mr. B. himself consented to receive payment for his services as a lecturer. The titles of his lectures are as follows :—" *British Seamen and their claims on us ;*" " *What the World worships ;*" " *On a right knowledge of Character ;*" " *The Russian War ; its cause and probable consequences :*" " *The Men who make a Country ;*" " *The Social and Moral evils of Strikes ;*" " *The Old World and the New : a Contrast ;*" " *Great Britain ; the Hope of the world ;*" " *What the wild waves are saying ;*" " *Go it while you're Young ;*" " *Robert Burns ; the man and the poet ;*" " *The British Pulpit in 1859 ;*" " *A Night in the House of Commons ; From London to Paris in 1863 ;*" " *George Stephenson, his life and its lessons ;*" " *A new Lesson for the day,*" " *The Confederation of British North America.*" etc. His lectures have appeared in the provincial journals. Mr. B. has also written a series of sketches for the *Journal* (Bost.) entitled " *Letters from Abroad,*" and various other fugitive pieces for the press.

I. Railways in New Brunswick, published by the Chamber of Commerce, (St. John, N. B.)

BOYD, JOHN A., *M. A.* A Toronto Barrister. Is a graduate of the Univ. there, where he took the prize for Eng. verse.

I. A Summary of Canadian History; from the time of Cartier's Discovery to the present time. *Toronto*, pp. 123, 1860; 18th Thousand, 1865.

" The author has accomplished, with complete success, the difficult task of compressing into the compass of little more than a hundred pages an accurate and connected relation of the chief incidents connected with Canadian history from the time of Cartier's discovery to the present day. It is written in a pleasing and attractive style, and not only comprehends an interesting notice of such leading events in the history of the Province as are to be found in the various bulky volumes already written on the subject : but our examination satisfies us that the author has gone for his materials to the original sources ; and his facts and dates are not only well arranged and placed in an attractive form for reference, but he has also corrected errors which have been repeated by one writer after another, in volumes of much greater pretension. * * * * We should be glad to learn that the same pen which has been so well employed on this little summary, was engaged on a full critical survey of the interesting story of Canadian discovery, settlement, and progress, through all the interesting events of its three historic centuries."—Prof. D. Wilson: *Can. Journal.*

BOYD, JOHN P. Brig. Genl. in the Am. Army during the War of 1812.

I. Documents and facts relative to military events during the late war. 1816, 8vo.

BOYS, WILLIAM FULLER ALVES, *LL. B.* A practising barrister at Barrie, U. C.

I. A Practical Treatise on the Office and Duties of Coroners in Upper Canada, with an Appendix of Forms. *Toronto*, 1864.

"It embraces the whole subject of the Coroner's judicial duties, and supplies all that is necessary for a Canadian Coroner to know. Were it in our power to aid the circulation by any testimony of our approbation we would almost be at a loss for words sufficiently strong and emphatic. In our judgment it is one of the most comprehensive works on Coroners extant, for no English work contains all the subjects Mr. Boys has dealt with."—*U. C. Law Journ.*

BROMLEY, WALTER. "Late Paymaster 23rd Regt., or Royal Welsh Fusiliers. Superintendent of the Lancasterian or Royal Acadian Institution, Halifax," which he had founded.

I. Two addresses on the deplorable state of the Indians; one delivered at the Free-Masons' Hall, Aug. 3, 1813, the other at the Royal Acadian School, March 8, 1814, at Halifax, in Nova Scotia. (Published for the benefit of the Indians.) *London*, 1815, pp. 71, 12mo.

II. An Appeal to the virtue and good sense of the Inhabitants of Great Britain, &c., in behalf of the Indians of North America. *Halifax*, 1820, pp. 57, 8vo.

N. B.—This work contains very interesting letters addressed to the author, by several pious and benevolent persons in England and America, on the important subject of the civilization of the Indians.

III. A Catechism of Geography; in two parts. *Do.* 1822, pp. 132, 8vo.

IV. The English Grammar made Easy. *Do.* 1822, pp. 104, 8vo.

V. General Description of Nova Scotia. *Do.* 1825.

BRACKENRIDGE, H. M.

I. History of the late war between the United States and Great Britain, *Philadelphia*, 8vo. French translation, *Paris.* 1820, 2 vols. 8vo.

BRADFORD, JOHN.

I. Address to the inhabitants of New Brunswick, Nova Scotia, occasioned by the mission of two Ministers, John James and Charles William Milton, sent out by the Countess of Huntington from her College in South Wales. *London*, 1788, 8vo.

BRANNAN, JOHN.

I. Official letters of the Military and Naval Officers of the United States during the war with Great Britain, in the years 1812–1815; with some additional letters and documents elucidating the History of that period. *Washington*, 1823, 8vo.

BRANT, JOSEPH. A celebrated Mohawk Chief. B. in Ohio about 1742. D. in U. C. 24 Nov. 1807. He received a good education in Conn., through the aid of Sir William Johnson. In the campaign of Lake George in 1755 he took part on the British side, and also in several subsequent skirmishes. On the death of Sir W. Johnson he became Secy. to Col. Guy Johnson, Superintendent Gen. of Indians; and on the breaking out of the Am. revolution was instrumental in carrying over the Indian tribes to the Royal cause. He received a commission in the British army and served under Sir Guy Carleton, the then Governor of Can. In 1786 he visited England and was received with great distinction; while there published the "Book of Common Prayer," with the translation of the "Gospel of St. Mark," into the Mohawk language. He also collected funds for a church, which, it is said was the first built in U. C. The latter part of his life was spent at Burlington Bay, at the head of Lake Ontario, where he lived on a tract of land granted to him by the Brit. Govt.

I. The Book of Common Prayer, and administration of the Sacraments, and other Rites and Ceremonies of the Church, according to the use of the Church of England. Together with a collection of occasional Prayers, and divers sentences of Holy Scripture, necessary for knowledge and practice. Formerly collected, and translated into the Mohawk language under the direction of the Missionaries of the Society for the Propagation of the Gospel in Foreign Parts, to the Mohawk Indians. A new edition. To which is added the Gospel according to St. Mark. Translated into the Mohawk language by Capt. Joseph Brant, an Indian of the Mohawk nation (with plates), *London*, 1787, pp. iii and 500, 8vo.

Life of Joseph Brant, Theyendanega, including the border wars of the American Revolution. By William L. Stone, *New York*, 1838, 2 vols. New Ed. *Do.* 8vo. 1865.

BRASS, JOHN.

I. The art of ready reckoning, or mental and practical arithmetic reduced to a system. *Toronto*, 1351.

BRASSEUR DE BOURBOURG, *L'Abbé*. A French priest who lived some time in Quebec about the year 1851—has published important works on Archæological subjects, principally on the antiquities of Mexico, and is a constant contributor to the *Revue Orientale et Américaine*.

I. Histoire du Canada, de son Eglise et de ses missions, depuis la découverte de l'Amérique jusqu'à nos jours, écrite sur des documents inédits, compulsés dans les archives de l'archevêché de Québec. *Paris*, 1852, 2 vols. 8vo.

II. Esquisse biographique sur Mgr. de Laval. *Quebec*, 1855.

BREAKENRIDGE, JOHN. Was a Barrister of U. C. Has been dead for some years.

I. The Crusades and other Poems. *Kingston*, 1846, pp. 327.

"This volume possesses considerable poetic merit, though portions of it are somewhat prosaic and diffuse in style. It is distinguished, both in choice of subjects and treatment, by a martial and chivalrous spirit."—DEWART : *Can. Poetry*.

BRECKENRIDGE, JAMES. A teacher at Georgetown, U. C.

I. Poems. *Toronto*, 1860, pp. 256.

BRENAN, *Hon.* DANIEL.

I. Remarks on Education. *Charlottetown*, 1856, pp. 61, 8vo.

BRETT, THOMAS.

I. Treatise on Light, Vision and Colours, comprising a theory on entirely new principles. *Toronto*, 1358, pp. 106.

BREWER, T. M., *M. D.*

I. A few ornithological facts gathered in a hasty trip through portions of New Brunswick and Nova Scotia, in June, 1850. *Journ. Nat. His.* (Bos.) 1852.

BRIDGES, JOHN GEORGE, *M. D.* A Can. journ. B. in Eng. D. at Aylmer, L. C., 1841. Ed. with marked ability *The Caledonia Springs Mercury*, 1839–40. In 1841 established *The Ottawa Advocate and Sydenham and Dalhousie Advertiser*, (Aylmer), upon which occasion he was entertained at a public dinner by the inhabitants of Aylmer. He did not live long to benefit by his undertaking, dying only a few months afterwards.

I. Digest of the British Constitution.

BRIGGS, THOMAS. (Kingston, U. C.)

I. Description of the Curculio, its mode of destroying fruit, and the various means employed to check its progress. *Trans. Bot. Soc. Can.* 1861.

BRISTOW, WILLIAM. A Can. journ. B. in Birmingham, Eng., 25 Dec., 1808. Mr. B. commenced his connection with Can. journalism as a contributor to the *Union*, (Que.) a small paper, established in 1836, to secure the return to Parliament of the late Mr. Andrew Stuart. In 1841 he contributed to the *Gazette* (Que.) a series of letters, advocating the principles of Responsible Govt. affirmed in the Resolutions of the Hon. R. Baldwin in the Can. Legislature. When the Free Trade Associatio (Mont.) established the *Economist* in 1846, Mr. B. became a leading and a frequent contributor to its ed. columns. In 1849 the storm of party strife was at its highest, and the Rebellion Losses Bill with the burning of the Parliament buildings and other incidents stirred the public mind from its lowest depths; the Ministerial or Reform party was almost without a representative in the press of Montreal. Mr. Hincks having, during his position of Minister perforce retired from the ed. chair of the *Pilot*, a Montreal journal which he had vigorously occupied during several years. The Conservative press, ably represented by

Messrs. Kinnear, Abraham, Fleet, Turner and others, launched their daily thunders for some time with deadly effect on almost silent opponents. In this condition of affairs, Mr. B., whose experience with the press had been of the limited nature related, was invited by the leaders of the party to take the ed. chair of the *Pilot* newspaper, then the property of Mr. Rollo Campbell, who had recently purchased it from Mr. Hincks. Mr. B. accepted the charge, and it was generally conceded that he fulfilled his arduous duty with ability and discretion under all the trying events that ensued. When the movement, now generally admitted as most injudicious, in favor of annexation with the U. S. with the consent of Gt. Brit. was instituted, Mr. B. was strenuous in his opposition to it, and largely contributed by his arguments, continued in every successive issue of the *Pilot* in bringing the entire project into public disfavour. His connection with the *Pilot* continued at different intervals until 1854, when it ceased. Shortly after the General Election of 1854, at which he was an unsuccessful candidate for Montreal, he established a journal—published, at first tri-weekly and subseqently daily—called the *Argus*. It was continued for about 4 years. Its politics were in decided opposition to the Ministry under the various *replatrages* which prevailed during that space of time, and its columns were devoted to an exposure of alleged abuses and the advocacy of Departmental and Financial reforms. After the relinquishment of the *Argus*, he became ed. of the *Transcript*, for about 2 years. This terminated his ed. connection with the press, although he has the reputation of having furnished occasional articles to several public journals.

Although Mr. B. is known as thoroughly conversant with literature generally, his writings have been principally, so far as we are aware, conveyed through the press. On two occasions he delivered a public lecture. The first was on a Free Trade subject, during the time he contributed so largely to the *Economist*. The second was before the Mechanics' Institute (Mont.) during the *furore* of the annex-ation movement in 1849. The subject was the future condition and prosperity of Can., and in handling it, the lecturer whilst studiously refraining from directly adverting to annexation, so collocated his arguments and illustrations as to refute those adduced in favour of the radical change attempted to be introduced. This lecture which was published at the request of the auditors, found its way to the public journals, and was largely quoted from and eulogized strongly in the *Times* (Lon.) the *Colonial Mag.* and other British periodicals. The then Secy. for the Colonies, Earl Grey, also addressed to Lord Elgin, Gov. Genl., a flattering eulogy on the production, requesting him to convey his hearty sentiments of approbation to the author.

Mr. B. has occupied various positions of trust and importance in the Province. In 1837 he was Secy. of the Constitutional Association (Que.), and in that capacity was largely instrumental in causing Mr. Andrew Stuart to be despatched to Eng. to urge on the Imperial Govt. legislation for the Union of the Canadas. In 1848 he was a mem. of a Commission appointed to enquire into the conduct and management of the Provincial Penitentiary. In 1862 he was a mem. of the Financial and Departmental Commission, whose report has been published.

BROCK, *Maj. Genl. Sir* ISAAC, *K. B.* A celebrated Brit. soldier. B. in Guernsey 6 Oct. 1769. Killed in action whilst in command of the Brit. force at the battle of Queenston heights, 13 Oct. 1812. Was President and Administrator of the Govt. of U. C.

Papers relative to the reconstruction of his monument. *London and Montreal*, 1839, 8vo.

Family Records, containing memoirs of the late Sir Isaac Brock. *Guernsey and London*, 1845, 8vo.

Life and correspondence of Major General Sir Isaac Brock, K. B. By F. B. Tupper, *London*, 1845, 8vo.

BROCKLIN, P. C. VAN.
  I. Proposed Commercial Law. 1859, pp. 12.

BROMME, TR.
  I. Reisen durch die Vereinigten

Staaten und Ober Canada. *Baltimore*, 1834, 3 vols. 8vo.

BROOKE. *Mrs.* FRANCES. An Eng. Novelist and Dramatist. B. 1745. D. 1789. She was the daughter of the Rev. Mr. Moore, and wife of the Rev. John Brooke, Rector of Colney, in Norfolk. She resided for some years in Can. and among other works wrote

I. The History of Emily Montague, [a novel]. *London*, 1769, 4 vols. 12mo.

" The gifted author, Frances Brooke, dedicated her effusions to the then Governor General of Canada, Lord Dorchester, and also wrote another work entitled Lady Julia Mandeville. * * * The history of Emily Montague presents to the reader, together with a racy description of Canadian scenery, a most romantic account of colonial courtships, flirtations, &c. The reader is initiated into Quebec society as it existed in the good olden times, &c. The whole work consists of a series of letters, a large portion of which have been written and dated from Sillery, near Quebec."—*Brit. Can. Rev.* (Que.)

BRONDGEEST, J. T.
I. On Mines and Mining, especially referring to the mining districts on the great lakes of North America. *Sim. Col. Mag.* 1848.

II. On the Preservation of Food. *Can. Journ.* 1853.

BROUGHAM, *Rt. Hon. Lord.* A famous Brit. statesman and author. B. in Edinburgh, 1778.

I. Speech in the House of Lords, Thursday, Jany. 18, 1838, upon Canada. *London*, 1838, p. 61, 8vo.

II. Speech upon the Ashburton Treaty, delivered in the House of Lords 7 April, 1843. *Do.* 1843, 8vo.

BROUN, *Sir R., Bart.*
I. The Baronetage of Scotland and Nova Scotia. *Sim. Col. Mag.* 1845.

BROWN, *Rev.* ANDREW, *D. D.*
I. The Perils of the Time, and the purposes for which they are appointed; a sermon preached on the last sabbath of the year 1794. *Halifax*, 1795.

BROWN, *Hon.* GEORGE. A Can. Statesman and Journ. B. in Edinburgh, Scot., 29 Nov. 1818, where he was ed. He early entered mercantile life in London, but his occupation proving uncongenial he soon retired from it and accompanied his father the late

Mr. Peter Brown (whom see) to N. Y. Here he joined the ed. staff of the *British Chronicle*, established by his father in 1842. His writings in that journal attracted attention in Can., and when in the following year his father was invited by the Free Ch. party in U. C. to proceed there and found a newspaper in the interest of that important religious body, the subject of our notice accompanied him to Toronto. To the ed. columns of the *Banner*, as the new journal was called, he was one of the chief contributors, while it existed. But it was soon found that, as a political organ, the *Banner* owing to its religious character could never obtain a general circulation ; and in 1844 the Reform party wanting an organ which would be more directly under the control of its leaders than any paper which then existed, the *Globe* was projected and established by Mr. G. B. to meet the want.

" The ability with which the new journal was conducted " says Mr. Fennings Taylor, in his sketch of Mr. B. " became at once apparent. It received the support of the great reform party of Upper Canada. From a weekly, it speedily became a tri-weekly and then a daily paper, and from that time until now it has, we believe, no superior in circulation, and no equal in influence among the newspapers of the Province.

" The signal triumph of the liberal party at the elections, in 1847, was not a little due to the advocacy which their cause received from the new journal ; nor was it a matter of surprise that it should have become the organ of the Lafontaine-Baldwin government, when that administration was formed in March, 1848.

" The indignation which was naturally occasioned in England in 1850, when the Pope issued his bull, erecting a Roman Catholic hierarchy in the United Kingdom, was not without its effect on Mr. Brown. The spirit of Lord John Russell's famous letter to the Bishop of Durham fired his mind with a zeal which. however, was rather characterized by ardor than by policy. Indeed he felt too strongly to be discreet. He would meet Papal aggression with Protestant resistance ; and, regardless alike of party considerations or political consequences, he thence forward became the uncompromising exponent of what he termed ' broad Protestant principles.' It has been observed elsewhere that the public opinion of Canada appears to be in the highest degree sensitive to the public opinion of the two great European nations from which its population has mainly sprung. Thus the violence which preceded and accompanied the passing of the Reform Bill of England, gave shape to the greater violence which characterized the Provincial troubles of 1837-38. The revolution in France, in 1848, created the philosophical revolutionary party of Canada, which, for want of another name, is conveniently designated the 'rouge' party; and the Papal aggression Act of 1850 had the effect of gathering under one political banner the various bodies of nonconformists, whose aggressive Protestantism appears to be as fully allied with political feeling as with religious sentiment. Thus when the anger of Lord John Russell had been rebuked by wisdom or silenced by fear; when, as Leech portrayed him in *Punch*, he ran away from the consequences of his own cry, the animosity of his Canadian imitators continued unabated; and such phrases as 'Papal aggression' and 'Protestant ascendancy.' continued to be reverberated through our community with perilous persistency, until the evils which they exaggerated seemed to threaten its peace."

In 1851 Mr. B. was returned to Parliament as a mem. of the Leg. Assem., in which he has since, with but slight interruption, continued to sit. Both in the columns of his paper, and in his place in Parliament he was a constant and unswerving advocate of " Representation by Population," for the people of U. C., and it was mainly owing to his zealous endeavours that that great principle was at length conceded by the opposite political party in the Union Negotiations of 1865. The *Globe* has also been successful, since its first establishment, in being the means of having various necessary reforms effected in the administrative, departmental and municipal government of the Province—it has contended strongly against monopolies of every kind, both great and small. The abolishing of all unnecessary oppressive enactments and of all measures having a tendency in any way to retard the commercial, industrial and general prosperity of Can., has also been the assiduous and, we believe, the sincere object of that great organ of public opinion. From the time of the formation of the Can. Coalition in 1865 until the final passage of the " British North America Act of 1867 " by the Imperial Parliament, the *Globe* gave a strong and steady support to Confederation. In 1864 Mr. B. established

4

the *Canada Farmer*, a weekly agricultural journal, which had been previously published by the Board of Agriculture of U. C. Mr. B. was for several years the leader of the Reform party in U. C. For a few days in June, 1858 he was Prime Minister of the Province; in 1865 he again took office in the Taché-Macdonald ministry in order to carry out the Union of B. N. A., from which administration he retired early in 1866.

I. The American War and Slavery; a speech delivered at Toronto. *Manchester*, 1863, 12mo.

" One of the best speeches I have read on the subject (the contest in Am.,) is one by Mr. Geo. Brown, a member of your Parliament, which has recently been reprinted here by the Union and Emancipation Society of Manchester."—JOHN STUART MILL: *Letter to Author*.

BROWN, *Hon.* JAMES. Late Surveyor Genl. N. B.

I. New Brunswick, as a home for Emigrants, &c., a prize essay. *St John*, 1860, pp. 21.

BROWN, JAMES B.
I. Views of Canada and the Colonists, embracing the experience of an eight years' residence; views of the present state, progress and prospects of the colony; with detailed and practical information for intending emigrants. *Edinburgh*, 1851, 12mo.

BROWN, JOHN. D. 1766.
·I. Sermon on religious liberty. To which is prefixed an address to the principal inhabitants of the North American Colonies, on occasion of the Peace. *London*, 1763, 4to.

BROWN, *Rev.* LUNDIN, *D. D.*
I. Prize Essay on the Physical features and capabilities of British Columbia. *New Westminster*, 1863.

" Shows not only great ability, but contains a vast amount of useful and original information."—*Can. News.* (Lon.)

BROWN, PETER. A Canadian journ. B. in Scotland, about 1784. D. at Toronto, 1863. In his earlier years was a merchant in Edinburgh, and an active politician on the Liberal side. Meeting with difficulties in business, he in 1838, emigrated with his family to N. Y., where he contributed to the ed.

columns of the *Albion*, and afterwards became ed. and prop. of the *British Chronicle*. In 1843, at the solicitation of the prominent ministers and members of the Free Ch. in Can., Mr. B. removed to Toronto, and established the *Banner*, as an independent organ of liberal Presb. views in Ch. and State. The first number appeared on the 18 Aug. 1843, and the journal was successfully maintained for many years under his editorship with great vigour and ability. From 1844 up to 1849, Mr. B. also contributed largely to the ed. columns of the *Globe*, owned by his son.

"It may not be for us to speak publicly in praise of one so near and so beloved. And yet, ought his literary associates of many years, who knew him well, to be debarred from laying a tribute on the bier of one once so prominent among Canadian journalists, to the uprightness of his character, his love of justice, his hatred of wrong, his clear judgment, his manly firmness, and his genuine kindness of heart? Mr. Brown was possessed of a large and generous mind—ever on the side of freedom. He was a good classical scholar, and an earnest student to the last week of his life. He was an accurate historian, and especially in the constitutional and biographical history of the past century he was thoroughly versed. As a writer, he was vigorous and logical in thought, bold in expression, but ever, even in the heat of controversy, kind and courteous in his language." —*Globe*, (Tor.)

I. The Fame and Glory of England Vindicated. By Libertas. *New York* and *London*, 1842, pp. 306·

"This was intended as a reply, and it proved a most successful reply, to the well-known production of Mr. C. Edwards Lester: 'The shame and glory of England.'"—*Idem*.

BROWN, R. Resided for many years at North Sydney, Cape Breton, as Supdt. of the mine of that place. He resigned his situation 2 years since, owing to failing health, and returned to Eng. He wrote the notice of the Geology of N. S. in Haliburton's *History* of that Province which for the time was very accurate and valuable.

I. On the Geology of Cape Breton. (2 papers.) *Proc. Geol. Soc.* (Lon.) 1843-44.

II. On a group of erect Fossil-Trees in the Sydney Coal-formation, Cape Breton. *Geol. Journ.* (*Do.*) 1846.

III. On the Gypsiferous Strata of Cape Dauphin, Cape Breton. (*Do.*) 1847.

IV. Description of an upright Lepidodendron, with Stigmaria-roots, Sydney. (*Do.*)

V. Description of erect Sigillariæ, Sydney. (*Do.*) 1848.

VI. On the Lower Coal-measures of the Sydney Coal-field. (*Do.*) 1849.

BROWN, SAMUEL R. An Am. author and journ. Was a volunteer in the War of 1812.

I. A View of the Campaigns of the North Western Army, &c. *Burlington*, 1814, 12mo.

II. History of the War of 1812. 2 vols.

BROWN, THOMAS STORROW. B. at St. Andrews, N. B., 1803. Descended from an U. E. Loyalist. Has occupied many important positions in Can., more particularly in the city of Montreal, with the commercial interests of which he has always been prominently identified. In 1832, in conjunction with others, re-established the *Vindicator* (Mont.) newspaper, to which he largely contributed, often taking the place of its regular ed., up to 1837. Mr. B. also contributed in 1833 to the *Advertiser*, the first daily journal established in Mont. Having taken an active part in the Rebellion of 1837, holding the rank of "General" of the "Sons of Liberty," a body of the insurgents, and participated in the actions of St. Charles and St. Denis, he succeeded in eluding the British forces and gaining the U. S. In 1838 he proceeded to Florida, and from 1839 to 1842 ed. and managed the *Florida Herald* (St. Augustine.) He returned to Canada, in 1844; resides at Montreal and occasionally writes for the daily press. It is said he contemplates writing a history of the events of 1837.

I. Report on Cholera and Emigration. *Montreal*, 1832.

II. History of the Grand Trunk Railway. *Quebec*, 1864, pp. 100, 8vo.

BROWN, W. DAWSON.
I. Virgil's Æneid translated into Verse. Books 5th and 6th. *Montreal*, 1864-66, pp. 57 and 59.

" Considering the matter in all its bearings, I cannot but think that Mr. Brown has achieved a self-imposed task of great difficulty, and that he has effected his object, remarkably well."—A. H. : *Gazette* (Mont.)

BROWNE, CALVIN, and CHADWICK, EDWARD MANION, Barristers at Law, U. C.

I. Osgoode Hall Examination Questions, given at the examinations for call with or without Honors, and for certificates of Fitness, with concise Answers ; and the Students Guide, a collection of Directions and Forms for the use of Students at Law and Articled Clerks. *Toronto*, 1862, pp 400, 8vo.

"So far as we have been able to judge, the questions are answered with much care. The authors not only have given us the particular answer to each question, but very wisely referred to the authority upon which the answer is given. In this way a person in doubt as to the correctness of a particular answer, is enabled to satisfy his mind and so remove the doubt."—*U. C. Law Journ.*

BROWNE, HENRY.

I. Geometrical diagrams, being the whole of the first six books of Euclid at one view. *Toronto*, 1866.

BROWNING, SAMUEL.

I. Poems, (including a voyage to Quebec, in two cantos). *London*, 1846, 8vo.

BRUCE, JOHN. An Inspector of Sch's. in L. C. D. Jan. 1866. His lectures on "*Education*," "*Physical Culture*," "*Language*," "*Advantages of Union of Teachers*," "*Teaching Power*," "*Astronomy*," and various articles on educational topics have appeared in the *Journ. of Ed. for L. C.*

BRUNET, *L'Abbé* OVIDE. A French Can. Botanist. Is Prof. of Botany at the Laval Univ. (Que). Has travelled extensively in Europe and Am. in the pursuit of this branch of Science.

I. Voyage d'André Michaux en Canada. *Quebec*, 1861, pp. 27, 8vo. [Translated into English by Dr. Sterry Hunt, *Can. Naturalist*, and in pamphlet form.]

II. Notice sur les Plantes de Michaux et sur son voyage au Canada et à la Baie d'Hudson d'après son journal manuscrit et autres documents. *Quebec*, 1863, pp. 44, 8vo.
4*

" This valuable tract will prove a treat to our botanists, as the range of plants is not entirely confined to Canada, and the life belongs as well to American as Canadian biography.—*Am. His. Mag.*

III. Enumération des genres de plantes de la Flore du Canada, précédée des Tableaux analytiques des familles, et destinée aux élèves qui suivent le cours de botanique descriptive donné à l'Université Laval. *Do.* 1863, pp. 45, 12mo.

" We received with much interest the little work just issued by the learned professor at Laval University * * * * * * Prof. Brunet has the reputation of being an enthusiastic botanist, particularly well acquainted with the historical botany of Lower Canada, and zealous in promoting the science, so that with the aid of other earnest labourers that we know to be found in Quebec, the flora of that district ought to become well known."—*Can. Journ.*

IV. Catalogue de Plantes Canadiennes. *Do.* 1865, pp. 200, 8vo.

V. Histoire des Picea qui se rencontrent dans les limites du Canada. *Do.* 1867, pp. 16, 8vo.

VI. Catalogue des Végétaux ligneux du Canada. *Do.* 1867, pp. 64, 8vo.

BRUNTON, *Rev.* WILLIAM.

I. The Judgments of God, a call to Repentance ; a sermon on the occasion of Fasting and Prayer on account of the Cholera Morbus. *Montreal*, 1832.

BRUYAS, *Rev.* JAMES, S. J. Missionary on the Mohawk.

I. Radices Verborum Iroquæorum. *New York*, 1863, pp. 123, 8vo.

" The manuscript of Father Bruyas, from which this is printed, was found at a mission near Montreal, and it gives for the study of the Mohawk language an immense aid."—*Am. His. Mag.*

BRYANT, HENRY, *M. D.*

I. Account of a recent visit to the Coast of Labrador. *Proc. Nat. His. Soc.* (*Bos.*) vol. 7.

II. Notice of a visit to Green Island, off the mouth of Chester Bay, Nova Scotia, by the Rev. I. Ambrose, M. A. Halifax, *Do.* do.

III. Remarks on some of the Birds that breed in the Gulf of St. Lawrence. *Do.* vol. 8.

BRYDONE, JAMES MARR, *Surgeon, R. N.*

I. Narrative of a voyage with a

party of emigrants, sent out from Sussex in 1834 by the Petworth Emigration Committee, to Montreal, thence up the River Ottawa and through the Rideau Canal to Toronto, Upper Canada. (With Map.) *Petworth, Eng.* 1833, pp. 66, 8vo.

BUCHANAN, A. C. Brit. Emigration Agent, Can.

I. Emigration practically considered with detailed Directions to Emigrants proceeding to British North America. *London*, 1828, 8vo.

BUCHANAN, *Hon.* ISAAC. A Can. statesman and writer on protection and cognate subjects. B. at Glasgow, Scot., 21 July, 1810, and is the fourth son of the late Peter Buchanan, Esq., an eminent merchant of Glasgow. Ed. at the Glasgow Grammar Sch. When only 15 years of age entered into business in the employment of a large firm engaged in the West India and Honduras trade. Before he arrived at the age of 20 he was taken into the firm as a partner, and in 1833 was wholly entrusted with the Can. branch. He was the pioneer of the wholesale trade in Western Can., having as early as 1831 established a branch of his house at Toronto. He subsequently established another branch at Hamilton, and a third at London. In 1811 he was returned to Parliament for Toronto. He sat for Hamilton from 1857 to 1865, and was President of the Executive Council for a short period in the latter year. He has been President of the Boards of Trade of Toronto and Hamilton, respectively.

During the time he sat in Parliament, Mr. B. either introduced or was prominently identified with many measures and schemes for the improvement of the trade and currency of the Province. He is the recognized standard-bearer of Protection, and has for many years been the President of the Association for the Promotion of Canadian Industry. He has written largely both in Britain and Can. on subjects connected with Political Economy, Labour and Money. The subjoined is a very imperfect list of his various valuable and interesting writings.

I. New Political course suggested to the Metropolitan Trades. 1850.

II. Moral consequences of Sir R. Peel's unprincipled and fatal course, disquiet, overturn and revolution. Chiefly from the newspaper writings of Isaac Buchanan. *Greenock, Scot.*, 1850.

III. A Thoroughly British Legislature wanted, or, in other words, Legislation combining patriotism and popularity; seeing that British public opinion in the Government is our only security against a Revolution, as being the only security for Protestantism, or British (as opposed to Foreign) authority, in the Monarchy, and for protection to the British as opposed to the foreign laborer; foreign principles and interests being the only things cared for by our present aristocratic and eminently anti-British, if not wholly unprincipled, legislators, who (quaking for their own monopolist and tyranical church) could not be expected to adopt the honest and straightforward, or British, course of confining Cardinal Wiseman's authority to aliens—by making every man render himself an alien by submitting to any such unlawful or anti-British authority, even if the Roman were the true faith—any more than they could be expected to undo the other work of their own hands, and repudiate political economy as a science of which circumstances are the only facts—thus no longer leaving our Home Trade at the mercy of the Foreign Exchanges. Being newspaper writings by Isaac Buchanan. *Greenock*, 1850, pp. 32.

IV. The Crisis of Sir Robert Peel's mission; his assertion of the omnipotence of Parliament, in the room of the omnipotence of principle, moral and constitutional, must—if we would prevent unfortunate legislation becoming a cause of Revolution, after losing the Colonies and our supremacy on the sea—precipitate universal suffrage. Democratic legislation, however, as being synonymous with shielding the labour and fixed property of the country from the alien money-power, is the best, or only permanent security for monarchy in the Executive, in these days of revolution ; and, without thanking Sir R. Peel, we might take courage—if we only had a man such as we lost in Lord George Bentinck, or like William Pitt, at the helm—from the facts that the Constitution has invariably been strengthened by the widening of the Franchise, whether in the time of King John, Charles I., or the more recent Reform Bill, and that the Navigation Law was the work of Oliver Cromwell and the Long Parliament, while our Colonial system, although it may date its nominal origin from Queen Elizabeth, owed all its vitality and development to the extreme democracy of the great Rebellion,—Our universal suffrage should also be used to elect the Upper House, which is at present without moral weight in the country, Peers and Baronets, with their sons, being eligible as members of it hereafter. From the newspaper writings of Isaac Buchanan. *Do.* 1850, pp. 16.

V. The True Policy in Canada of a Patriotic Ministry. *Quebec*, 1860, pp. 4, fol.

VI. Britain the Country. *versus* Britain the Empire. Our Monetary distresses—their legislative cause and cure. *Hamilton, C. W.*, 1860, pp. clxiv-288, 8vo. (*New ed. preparing.*)

" If, however, the title displays eccentricity, the work itself is full of such thought as will enter largely into the reflections of the future historian of the ' Rise and Progress ' or of the ' Decline and Fall ' of the British Empire : for it is a review of the economical legislation of the last twenty-five years."—FENNINGS TAYLOR : *Portraits of Brit. Am's.*

VII. Militia Brochure ; our Battalion organization should not be as Volunteers but as a Militia force. *Do.* 1863, pp. 15.

VIII. The Relations of the Industry of Canada, with the mother country and the United States,—being a speech by Isaac Buchanan, Esq., M. P., as delivered at the late demonstration to the Parliamentary Opposition at Toronto,—together with a series of articles in defence of the national sentiments contained therein, which originally appeared in the columns of the " Hamilton Spectator," from the pen of Mr. Buchanan ; to which is added a speech delivered by him at the dinner given to the Pioneers of Upper Canada, at London, C. W., 10 Dec., 1863. Now first published in a complete and collected form, with copious notes and annotations, besides an extended introductory explanation, and an appendix containing various valuable documents. Edited by Henry J. Morgan. *Montreal*, 1864, pp. 546, 8vo.

" A collection of the *Speeches and Writings of the Hon. Isaac Buchanan*, edited by Mr. Henry J. Morgan, has been published at Montreal, by Mr. John Lovell. They relate to the politics of Canada—with which Mr. Buchanan has been connected for many years—and afford much useful information as to the industrial interests of the provinces. Their favorite topic is political economy. which Mr. Buchanan discusses with practical knowledge and with warm enthusiasm. Their style, though unpolished, is forcible ; and though occasionally tinged with partisan bitterness, their spirit is candid and manly. Their writer is the foremost merchant of Canada, and is noted no less for his patriotism than for his experience in business, and his general information. His faithful services, in the Canadian Parliament, and in other official stations, have won. the honorable esteem of his fellow-citizens. He speaks, therefore, with authority as to the Canadas : and students of politics therein will find his writings instructive in no common degree."—*Albion*, (N. Y.)

" We have been agreeably disappointed in this work, for instead of finding it ' flat, stale and unprofitable,' like too many of the books and pamphlets which find their way to our *sanctum*, it is replete with information of vast importance, and of vital and absorbing interest. Previous to meeting with this work, we had fallen into the very prevalent error of supposing that the doctrines of the English Economists or Free Traders had long since been established on a solid and immutable basis, and that it would be little short of insanity to impugn the soundness of their principles or to question the social advantages which—the advocates of " free trade " assert—are inseparably connected therewith. ' Free Trade,' as advocated by the Manchester School, we now find, means simply the free import of raw materials, and *the substitution of foreign for domestic labor.* The work before us has completely dispelled the " fog " which has hitherto prevented our looking this subject full in the face, and has caused our adoption of principles, without sufficient inquiry or investigation, which we should, with clearer light and under better guidance, have long since repudiated."—*Monitor*, (Charlottetown.)

" Our industrial relations with Canada are so intimate as to make the book interesting to us, and a mere glance at a few of its pages assures us that the reader will find matter for grave reflection, interspersed with much of the free, bold, tart, defiant language of antagonism, born and bred of liberty and Constitutional Government."—*Knickerbocker Mag.*, (N. Y.)

IX. The British American Federation a necessity ; its Industrial policy also a necessity. *Hamilton*, 1865, pp. 48, 8vo.

X. Memorial to the Commercial Convention at Detroit. *Do.*, 1865, 8vo.

This *brochure* was printed, but has not been distributed or published. It contains a memorial on the subjects to be considered by the Convention, with an appendix of extracts from his former writings, &c.

XI. A Government Specie-paying Bank of Issue and other subversive Legislation, proposed by the Finance Minister of Canada. *Do.*, 1866, pp. 24.

BUCHANAN, JAMES. Late H. B. M. Consul at N. Y.

I. Sketches of the History, Manners and Customs of the North American Indians, with a plan for their amelioration. *New York*, 1824, 2 vols in one, pp. 182-156, 8vo.

II. Continuation of the above. *Do.*, 1824.

" It is intended to submit a plan to the British public for the amelioration and civilization of the American tribes. The plan is to locate the different tribes, upon a grant from His Majesty of the extensive ground lying between the 44th parallel of North lat. and Lakes Huron and Simcoe, the Indians to be governed by a council of their own, &c." —*Can. Mag.* (Montreal.)

III. Reasons submitted in favour of allowing a transit of merchandize through Canada to Michigan, without payment of duties ; with observations as to the importance of the River St. Lawrence for extending the trade of the Canadas and British Commerce generally. *Toronto*, 1836.

IV. Letter addressed to Sir F. B. Head, Lt. Governor of Upper Canada, on the construction of Railroads in that Province. *Do.*

V. Letter to the Rt. Hon. Sir Chas. Bagot, Governor Genl. of B. N. A., with a view to preserve from contami-

nation and crime destitute and neglected female children, containing plan and estimate. *New York*, 1842, pp. 14.

VI. Letter on Free Trade and Navigation of the St. Lawrence, addressed to the Earl of Elgin and Kincardine, *Toronto*, 1846, pp. 31.

BUCKE, R. MAURICE, M. D., C. M. (Sarnia, U. C.)

I. The Correlation of the Vital and Physical Forces. A Prize Thesis. *Montreal*, 1862, pp. 22. Lar. 4to.

BUCKINGHAM, JAMES SILK. A well known author and traveller. B. at Flushing. near Falmouth, Eng., 1786. D. in London, 1855.

I. Canada, Nova Scotia, New Brunswick and the other British Provinces in North America, with a plan of National Colonization (with map and plates). *London*, 1843, pp. 540, 8vo.

" He possesses a happy facility of clothing his thoughts in language, and a quick and discerning eye to perceive whatever is worthy of note or comment in the Countries through which he passes."—*Lit. Garland.*

BUCKINGHAM, WILLIAM. A Can. Journ. B. in Eng., where he served on the staff of the Halifax *Guardian* for 4 years. Mr. B. came to Can. many years since, and was connected with the *Globe* (Tor.) for a considerable period. In the autumn of 1859, in conjunction with Mr. William Caldwell, he conceived the project of establishing a newspaper in the very heart of the chartered territory of the Hudson's Bay Company. The enterprise was beset with difficulties of which " gentlemen of the press," " who sit at home at ease," can have very little conception. A newspaper publisher from Detroit had already attempted the experiment, but taking the Lake Superior route, broke down with his heavy material at Sault Ste. Marie, at the very commencement of his journey, and gave up the project in despair. Mr. B. and his colleague adopted the wiser plan of setting out for the Red River Settlement *via* St. Paul and Pembina. Their printing press, types, paper, ink, and every other newspaper requisite were conveyed in ox-carts—the only mode of transportation at that time known to the country. The journey was tedious and laborious, lasting about 6 weeks, and extending through a territory wholly unopened beyond the frontier settlements of Minnesota, and occupied by treacherous Indians. The destination was, however, reached at last in safety, and early in the following year, the first number of *The Nor'-Wester*, published immediately under the walls of Fort Garry, attested the success of the undertaking. Occupying by many hundred miles the most advanced position amongst journalists, it has no "contemporary" to fight or compete with; but acts the better part of making known the advantages and resources of the country, and of demanding for the people the right, which cannot be much longer delayed, of self-government. Speaking of the enterprise when it was first set afoot, the late W. L. Mackenzie, the veteran journalist of U. C., said in his *Message*,—"I was once the most western "editor, bookseller, and printer in "British America; but *The Nor' Wester* "is a thousand miles beyond me." Leaving *The Nor' Wester* an established institution at Red River, Mr. B. returned to Can. in 1861 and renewed his connection with the Provincial press, editing the Norfolk *Reformer* for about 18 months, when in 1862 he became private secretary to the Hon. M. H. Foley, then Postmaster Genl., a position from which he retired in the following year to assume the ed. and proprietorship of the *Beacon*, (Stratford, U. C.), in which he still continues. During the recent conference in London between the delegates from the B. N. A. Provinces and the Imperial Authorities, preparatory to the passing of the Confederation Act, Mr. B. was present and acted as official reporter of the proceedings on behalf of Can.

BUCKLE, JOHN.

I. Letter to Viscount Melbourne on the Ordinance of the Earl of Durham, Governor of Canada. *London*, 1839, pp. 32.

BUEL, *Hon.* A. W.

I. Free Navigation of the St. Lawrence; a Report made to the House of Representatives. *Washington*, 1850.

BUELL, WILLIAM. A Can. journ. B. in Elizabethtown, U. C., 18 Feby. 1792. D. at Brockville, U. C., Sept. 1862. Was ed. and prop. of the *Recorder*, (Brockville), from 1822 to 1849. Is said to have possessed much power and vigour as a writer. Was a steady supporter of the liberal party. Sat in the U. C. Parliament with but a short interruption from 1828 to 1836.

BULKLEY, *Captain*, Secy. of the Province of N. S. Was the first ed. of *The Nova Scotia Chronicle and Weekly Gazette*, the first paper published in N. S., it having been established in Jany. 1769.

BULLER, CHARLES, *M. P., Q. C.* A leading Eng. lawyer and statesman. B. 1806. D. 1848. Was Secy. to Lord Durham during his Administration in Can., a large portion of whose *Report*, Mr. B. was generally supposed to have written.

I. Responsible Government for Colonies. *London*, 1840.

BULLOCK, *Very Rev.* WILLIAM, *A. M.* A Ch. of Eng. Min., N. S. Is Dean of Halifax, and Min. of St. Luke's, there.

I. The Baptist answered. The doctrine of Infant Baptism as taught in the Scriptures and practised in the Church. *Boston, U. S.*, 1843, pp. 18, 8vo.

II. The Ruler's Daughter raised. A funeral discourse (on the occasion of the death of Miss Bliss.) *Halifax*, 1851, pp. 11, 8vo.

III. Songs of the Church. *Halifax*, 1854, pp. 235; *London*, 1855, 8vo.

BUNBURY, —.
I. On a Fossil Fern from Cape Breton. *Geol. Journ.* (Lon.) 1849.

BURGESS, JAMES.
1. The present and past position and future destiny of the world, as set forth in Prophecy. *Toronto*, 1863.

BURGESS, *Hon.* TRISTRAM.
1. Battle of Lake Erie, with notices of Com. Elliot's conduct in that engagement. *Providence*, 1839, pp. 132, 12mo.

BURGOYNE, JOHN. An Eng. Genl. B. about 1730. D. in London, 4 June 1792. In 1777, was appointed to command the army which was to penetrate from

Can. into the U. S., which army he was compelled to surrender to the Am. force at Saratoga.

I. A State of the Expedition from Canada, as laid before the House of Commons, by the Author, and verified by evidence ; with a collection of authentic documents, and an addition of many circumstances which were prevented from appearing before the House, by the prorogation of Parliament; written and collected by himself, and dedicated to the Officers of the Army he commanded. *London*, 1780, 4to. *with maps.*

II. A Supplement to the same : containing General Burgoyne's orders respecting the principal movements and operations of the Army, to the raising of the Seige of Ticonderoga. *Do. do.* 4to. *New York.*—Privately reprinted, 1865.

BURKE, LUKE.
I. Phrenological Enquiries ; Parts 1 and 2. *Quebec*, 1840, pp. 40.

BURN, DAVID, late Deputy Registrar for the Co. Wentworth, U. C.
I. Colonial Legislation on the subject of Education ; two Letters originally published in the Hamilton *Gazette.* *Toronto.* 1841, pp. 16.

BURNABY, *Rev.* ANDREW, *D. D.* Archdeacon of Leicester and Vicar of Greenwich, Eng. D. 1812.
I. Travels through the middle settlements of North America, in the years 1759 and 1760 ; with observations on the state of the Colonies. *London*, 1775, 8vo.; 3rd ed. considerably enlarged *Do.* 1792-9. French translation : *Lausanne*, 1778, 8vo.

BURNS, *Rev.* GEORGE, *D. D.* A. Presb. Min. B. in West Lothian, Scot., Oct. 1790. Ed. at Edinburgh Univ. In 1817, became Min. of St. Andrew's Ch. St. John N. B. where he remained for 17 years. Is now stationed at Corstorphine in his native county in Scot. Received the degree of D. D. from the Univ. of St. Andrews in 1817. Contributed for some years to the *Christian Instructor* and the *Church Witness.* (Edin.)
I. A View of the Principles and Forms of the Church of Scotland as by law established. Addressed to the Presbyterian Congregation of St. John. *St. John*, 1817, pp. 32, 8vo.

II. Letter addressed to the Rev. James Milne, A. M., in consequence of his Remarks on Dr. Burns's view of the Principles and Forms of the Church of Scotland, &c. *Do.* 1818.

III. Lectures and Sermons delivered in the Scots Church of St. John. on several ordinary occasions. *Do.* 1820, pp. 388, 8vo.
A 2nd Ed. has recently appeared at Edinburgh.

IV. Prayers for the Closet and Family; with remarks on Prayer. *Do.* 1832, 12mo. 2nd Ed. *Edinburgh*, 1862, 16mo.

V. Treatise on Baptism. *Do.*

VI. Pastor's Gift to his Parish families; prayers. *Edinburgh*, 1839, 12mo.

BURNS, *Rev.* J., *D. D.*
I. Notes of a tour in the United States and Canada, 1817. *London*, 1848, 18mo.

BURNS, *Rev.* ROBERT, *D. D., F. R. S.* (Edin.) A Min. in the Can. Presb. Ch. (Tor.), and Emeritus Prof. of Church History in Knox Coll., same city. B. at Barrowstowness, West Lothian, 13 Feb. 1789. Is an elder brother of the preceding. He studied at Edinburgh Univ. and was ordained Min. of the Laigh Kirk, Paisley, in July 1811. Here he laboured for nearly 34 years, when, in 1845, in response to a call made to him from Toronto, he removed with his family to Can. Besides taking an active part in all the leading affairs of his Ch. he manifested a warm interest in the advancement of the B. A. Provinces, and as Secretary of the Glasgow Colonial Soc. did much to open up an emigration to Can. In 1844 he, with the late Principal Cunningham, were deputed by the Free Ch. of Scot. to visit the Churches in the U. S. and Can., and it was mainly owing to this official visit and the cordial reception given them that Dr. B. accepted the call which he received in the following year. He was Pastor of Knox's Ch. (Tor.), from 1845 to 1856, when he was appointed to the chair which he still holds in Knox Coll. He has been twice Moderator of the Church in Can.

In 1828 he received the degree of D. D. from the Univ. of Glasgow; he is also a Fellow of the Royal Society, Edin., and a member of the Antiquarian and other learned Societies. Dr. B. has written largely on Church history and churchmatters. He edited *Wodrow's Church History* in 4 vols. and collected the *MSS* of Wodrow and other old divines, some of which were published by the Wodrow Society. He was also ed. of the *Christian Instructor* (Edin.) for three years and contributed many literary and theological papers to its pages.

I. Essay on the Propagation of Christianity in the East. 1813. 2nd Ed.

II. Illustrations of Providence in late events; a Sermon. 1814. 2nd Ed.

III. A Letter to Dr. Chalmers, on the distinctive Characters of Protestantism and Popery. 1817.

IV. An Essay on the Eldership. 1818.

V. Historical Dissertations on the Poor. *Edinburgh*, 2nd Ed. 1819, 8vo.

VI. Trail's Guide to the Lord's Table, with Life, &c., 1820.

VII. Bonar's Genuine Religion, the best friend of the people, with Life, &c. 4th Ed. 1821.

VIII. Active Goodness beautifully exemplified in the Life and labours of the Rev. T. Gouge. 1821.

IX. Cecil's Visit to the House of Mourning, with Introductory Essay. 1823.

X. Cecil's Address to Servants, with Introductory Essay. 1823.

XI. Henry's Address to Parents on Baptism, with Life and Preface.

XII. Brown of Wamphray on Prayer, with Life of the Author.

XIII. Brown on the Life of Faith, with Preface. 1825.

XIV. Treatise on Pluralities. 1824.

XV. Speech on the Roman Catholic Claims. 1825.

XVI. Three Letters to a Friend on the Moral Bearings of the Bible Society Controvery. 1827.

XVII. Sober Mindedness; a Sermon to the Young. 1828.

XVIII. A Voice from the Scaffold; an Address on the Execution of Brown and Craig. 3rd Ed. 1829.

XIX. The Gareloch Heresy Tried. 3rd Ed. 1830.

XX. A Letter in Vindication of the above. 1830.

XXI. Wodrow's History of the Sufferings of the Church of Scotland; with Life, Notes, and Preliminary Dissertation. 4 vols. 1830.

XXII. Jehovah the Guardian of his own word; a Sermon before the Society in Scotland for propagating Christian Knowledge. 1830.

XXIII. Memoir of the Rev. Pliny Fisk, Missionary to Palestine, with Preface and Notes.

XXIV. Bellamy's Letters and Dialogues, on the Nature of Love to God, Faith in Christ, and Assurance of Salvation; with Introductory Essay.

XXV. Vindication of Church of Scotland. *Paisley*, pp. 57.

XXVI. Defence of Religious endowments. *London*, pp. 24.

XXVII. Plea for the Poor of Scotland. *Paisley*, 1841, pp. 36.

XXVIII. Memoir of Professor McGill of Glasgow University. *Edinburgh*, pp. 358, 12mo.

XXIX. Report of Visit to Canada and Nova Scotia. *Do*. 1844, pp. 50.

XXX. Farewell Sermon on leaving Paisley. *Toronto*, 1845, pp. 20.

XXXI. Reply to Dr. Cahill on the Eucharist. *Do*. 1863, pp. 24.

BURNS, *Hon.* R. E., a Puisne Judge of the Court of Queen's Bench, U. C. D. 1863.

I. Letter to the Hon. Robert Baldwin on the subject of Division Courts. *Toronto*, 1847.

BURNS, *Rev.* R. F., *D. D.* A Min. of the Can. Presb. Ch., and son of Rev. Dr. Burns, (Tor.) B. in Paisley. Ed. at Glasgow Univ. Studied Theology partly in Edinburgh, under Dr. Chalmers, and partly at Knox Coll. (Tor.) Has contributed largely to the religious and secular press of this country and elsewhere, principally to the *Can. Presbyterian Record of the Presbyterian*

Church in Canada, Scottish Guardian (Glas.) *News of the Churches*, (Lon.) In April, 1867, Dr. B. was inducted as pastor of the First Presb. Ch. of Chicago, U. S.

I. Lecture on the Maine Law. *Kingston*, 1853, pp. 11.

II. Progress and Principles of the Temperance Reformation. *Do.* 1857, pp. 12.

III. On Christian Liberality. *Hamilton*, 1857, pp. 8.

IV. Six Tracts on Various Subjects. *St. Catharines*, 1863-4, pp. 24.

V. Maple Leaves from Canada to the grave of Abraham Lincoln—an address. *Do.* 1865, pp. 40, 8vo.

VI. Contributions to *Canada Presbyterian* on " Whitefield," " Howell," " Harris," " Carlyle and Emerson," "Newman and Parker," "Conscience," and " Man's Responsibility for his belief."

VII. " On Russia." *An. Am. Mag.* 1854.

BURNS, W. SCOTT.
I. Principles of Book-keeping by single and double entry. *Toronto*, 1844-5, pp. 140, D. 12mo.

II. Connection between Literature and Commerce. Two Essays read before the Lit. and His. Soc. of Toronto. *Do.* 1845, pp. 16, 8vo.

BURTIS, W. R. M. A N. B. writer, residing at St. John. N. B. Contributed several tales to *The Amaranth*, a N. B. periodical. Ed. the *Temperance Telegraph* from 1841 to 1843; and has written considerably for various local newspapers on subjects of national importance.

I. Prize Essay on the history of New Brunswick. Read before the St. John Young Men's Debating Society, 1837.

II. Grace Thornton ; a tale of British America. *The Guardian Magazine*, (St. John) 1860.

III. New Brunswick, as a home for Emigrants ; with the best means of promoting Immigration, and developing the resources of the Province. An Essay published by the St. John Mechanics' Institute. *St. John*, 1860, pp. 50, 12mo.

IV. The New Dominion ; a poem. *Do.* 1867.

BURTON, *Rev.* J. E., *A. B.*, (*T. C. D.*) Missionary at Rawdon, L. C.

I. Essay on Comparative Agriculture ; or a brief examination into the state of Agriculture as it now exists in Great Britain and Canada. *Montreal*, 1828, pp. 107, 12mo.

For this essay the author received an honorary medal from the Soc. for the Encouragement of Arts and Sciences, (Que.)

BUTEL-DUMONT, GEORGE MARIE, Avocat.
I. Conduite des Francais par rapport à la Nouvelle-Ecosse ; traduit de l'Anglais de Jeffreys, avec des notes. *London*, 1765, in-12.

BUTLER, SAMUEL.
I. The Canada Guide. *London*, 1858.

BUTLER, T. P., *B. C. L.* Advocate, L. C.
I. Alphabetical Index to the Statutes passed by the Parliament of Canada since the date of the Consolidated Statutes (1859) ; with an Appendix shewing the Amendments to all the Consolidated Statutes. *Ottawa*, 1867.

C.

CADIEUX, *Very Rev.* LOUIS MARIE. A R. C. priest. B. at Montreal, 1785. D. at Rivière Ouelle, L. C., 13th June, 1838. Was Vic. General. (Three Rivers.) Contributed to *L'Ami de la Religion*, of the latter place.

I. Observations sur un écrit intitulé :

Questions sur le gouvernement ecclésiastique du district de Montréal, par un prêtre du diocèse de Québec. *Three Rivers*, 1823.

CAIRD, JAMES. A mem. of the House of Commons, Gt. Brit.
I. Prairie Farming in America, with

notes by the way on Canada and the United States. *New York*, 1858, 12mo.

CALDWELL, MAJOR HENRY. Father of the late Sir John Caldwell, Bart.

I. The Invasion of Canada in 1775. *Quebec*, 1865, pp. 19.

A short account of the seige of Quebec by Arnold and Montgomery written in the year following that event.

CALDWELL, MORGAN. A Can. Journ. Ed. the *Prototype* (Lon. U. C.), a daily conservative journal, from 1861 until recently. Is now practising as a barrister in Toronto.

CALKIN, J. B. Teacher of Eng. and the Classics in the Provincial Normal Sch. Truro, N. S. Has contributed to the *Journal of Education* N. S. Is now preparing a General Geography for the press.

I. The Geography and History of Nova Scotia. *Halifax*, 1st Ed. 1859 ; 2nd Ed. 1864, pp. 110. 12mo.

This book has been adopted as a text book in the Sch's. of N. S.

CALVERT, G. H. An Am. author.

I. Oration on the 40th anniversary of the battle of Lake Erie. *Providence*, 2nd Ed. 1854, 8vo.

CAMERON, *Rev.* J. A Presb. Min. N. S.

I. Is Election a doctrine of the Bible ; a discourse. *Halifax*, 1862, pp. 29, 8vo.

CAMERON. *Hon.* JOHN HILLYARD, *D. C. L.*, *Q. C.* A Can. lawyer and statesman. B. at Beaucaire, France, 14 Apl., 1817. Came to Can. when a child with his father, an officer in the Brit. Army. Ed. at U. C. Coll. Called to the Bar in 1838. Was reporter to the Court of Queen's Bench, U. C., from 1843 to 1846. Is distinguished as a *Nisi Prius* Counsel. Sat in Can. Assem. with little or no interruption, from 1846 until the Union of 1867. Was Sol. Genl., with seat in the Cabinet, from 1846 to 1848. Is Grand-master of the Orangemen of B. N. A., Chancellor of the Univ. of Trinity Coll. (Tor.), and Treasurer of the Law Soc., U. C.

I. Digest of Cases determined in the Upper Canada Court of Queen's Bench from the Michaelmas Term, 10 Geo. IV. to the Hilary Term, 3 Vic. *Toronto*, 1840, 8vo.

II. The Rules of Court and Statutes

relating to Practice and Pleading in the Court of Queen's Bench, Upper Canada, together with the Criminal and other Acts of general reference and a few practical points. *Do.* 1844, pp. 448, 12mo.

III. Reports of Cases determined in the Queen's Bench and Practice Courts in U. C. from 7 to 8 Vic. *Do.* 1845, r. 8vo.

IV. Address on installation as Chancellor of the University of Trinity College. *Do.* 1864, pp. 8.

CAMERON, *Hon.* MALCOLM. A Can. politician. B. Apl. 1808. Entered the Leg. Assem. U. C. in 1836 ; after the Union sat for various constituencies in same chamber up to 1860, when he was elected to Leg. Coun. Was successively Asst. Com. of Public Works, President of Ex. Coun. and Postmaster Genl. Is now Queen's Printer of Can. Founded the *Bathurst Courier*, (Perth) in 1834, which he conducted for 3 years ; he also assisted in establishing the *North American* and the *Huron Signal* newspapers.

I. Speech on the Intercolonial Railway. *Quebec*, 1862.

II. Reminiscenses of a Voyage to British Columbia ; a lecture delivered before the Young Men's Mutual Improvement Association. *Do.* 1865, pp. 23, 8vo.

CAMERON, *Rev.* ROBERT. B. in Co. Oxford, U. C., 1839. Has served as correspondent for various political newspapers. Since March, 1865, has ed. the *Baptist Freeman*, (Woodstock, U. C.), a religious journal.

CAMPBELL, *Rev.* A. DIGBY.

I. Lecture on the ancient Catholic Faith contrasted with the modern creed of the Church of Rome. *Montreal*, 1850, pp. 32.

CAMPBELL, F. W., *M. D.*, *L. R. C. P. L.* Associate ed. of the *Canada Medical Journal and Monthly Record of Medical and Surgical Science*, (Mont.)

CAMPBELL, *Mrs.* ISABELLA, a resident of Quebec.

I. The Inner Life.

II. Rough and Smooth, or Ho ! for the Australian Gold diggings. *Quebec*, 1865.

"Mrs. Campbell is a shrewd observer, and her account of the condition of such portions of the land of gold she visited—of the city of Melbourne, the oven diggings, and the diggers—are very graphic and interesting."—*Sat. Reader.*

CAMPBELL, P.

I. Travels in the Interior Inhabited parts of North America. In the years 1791 and 1792. In which is given an account of the manners and customs of the Indians, and the present war between them and the Federal States, the mode of life and system of farming among the new settlers of both Canadas, New York, New England, New Brunswick, and Nova Scotia, interspersed with anecdotes of people, observations on the soil, natural productions, and political situation of these countries. Illustrated with Copper Plates. *Edinburgh*, 1793, pp. 10—387.

CAMPBELL, ROLLO. For some time prop. of the now defunct *Pilot* (Mont.) newspaper.

I. Two Lectures on Canada ; delivered in the Sheriff Court Hall, Greenock, Scotland, on Jan. 20th and Jan. 23rd. 1857. Reprinted from the Greenock Ed. *Toronto*, 1857, pp. 47, 12mo.

CAMPBELL, W. D. C. (Que.)

I. A method of determining the Index errors of Thermometer Scales. *Can. Journ.* 1856.

CANNIFF, WILLIAM, M. D., M.R.C.S. (Eng.) B. near Belleville, U. C. Ed. at Victoria Coll. (Cobg.) Studied medicine at the Sch. of Medicine (Tor.) and at the Univ. of N. Y., in which last Institution he took his degree. He received the appointment of House Surgeon to N. Y. Hospital, which he afterwards resigned and went to Eng. Walked the London Hospitals and took the diploma of the R. C. S. (Lon.) In 1856, he passed the Army Medical Board and was appointed to do duty in the R. Artillery. At the close of the Crimean War withdrew from the service, travelled through Britain, France and Germany, attending the Hospitals of Edinburgh, Dublin and Paris. On his return from Europe, commenced the practice of his profession at Belleville. He received a call to the chair of General Pathology in the Medical department of Victoria Coll. ;

and at the request of the Dean undertook the professorship of Surgery in the same institution, which however he resigned in 1863. During the Am. war visited the hospitals at Washington. Returned to Belleville where he now practises. We believe that he is preparing for early publication a " History of the Bay of Quinté."

I. Case of Resection of the ankle joint performed at Toronto. *B. A. Journ.* 1862. Reported on in *Lancet*, (Lon.)

II. An extraordinary case of Chorea. *Do. do.*

III. The Surgery of the American war, as witnessed at Washington, and in the Army. *Lancet* (Lon.)

IV. False Anchylosis of the lower jaw of some twenty years standing. *Can. Med. Journ.*

V. A Manual of the Principles of Surgery, based on Pathology for Students. *Philadelphia*, 1866, pp. 402, 8vo.

"Altogether this book bears evidence of careful study and preseverance, devoted to this particular branch of the science of the healing art, and will be found of use by the student, as enunciating the doctines of masters of the science of surgery, with much that is the result of patient and pains-taking observation."—*Can. Med. Journ.*

CARAYON, P. AUGUSTE, (Company of Jesus.)

I. Première Mission des Jésuites au Canada. Lettres et documents inédits. *Paris*, 1864, pp. 304, 8vo.

CARDEN, Rev. R. A. A min. of the Ch. of Eng.

I. Words of comfort to the bereaved ; a sermon. *Quebec*, 1854.

CAREY, DANIEL. A Can. poet and journ. Founded in 1857, the *Vindicator* (Que.), a journal of moderate conservative politics, which he ed. until it was discontinued in 1864. He was also ed. of the *Monitor*, a literary weekly. As a literary man he is best known by his poetical contributions of which a historical ballad, *The Battle of St. Foye*, a didactic poem which appeared in the *New Era* (of which Mr. McGee was Ed.) one on *Confederation* and another on the *Pioneers of Canada*, are the most celebrated. We understand Mr. C. is preparing for publication, a work on Can. history, for popular use.

CARMAN, JOHN WALMSLEY. A Can. Journ. B. in Co. Prince Edward U. C., 1834. In 1854, established the *Reformer* (Napanee, U. C.,) a weekly newspaper, which he conducted until 1858, when he removed to Belleville, taking the office and plant with him, and there founded the *Independent*, a semi-weekly and weekly journal. In Nov. 1862, disposed of that paper by sale and started the *Daily British American* (Kingston), of which for a time he was Ed. and Prop. Mr. C. has always been identified with the Liberal party in politics.

CARNEY, RICHARD. Sheriff of Algoma Dist., Can. In 1853, established and ed. the *Times* (Owen Sound.)

CARPENTER, PHILIP P., *B. A.*, *Ph. D.* Hon. Secy. of the Montreal Sanitary Association.

I. On the Relative Value of Human Life in Different Parts of Canada. *Can. Nat.* 1859.

II. On the Vital Statistics of Montreal. *Do.* 1867.

Also in pamphlet form.

CARROLL OF CARROLTON, CHARLES. An Am. patriot. B. at Annapolis Ind. 1737. D. 1832. In Feby., 1776, he was appointed a commissioner with Dr. Franklin and Judge Chase, to proceed to Can. on a political mission, to induce the inhabitants of that country to unite with the revolted colonies. As is well known, the object of the mission failed.

I. Journal of Charles Carroll, of Carrolton, during his mission to Canada, in 1776, as one of the Commissioners with Chase and Franklin from Congress; with a memoir and notes, by Brantz Mayer. *Baltimore*, 1845, pp. 84, 8vo.

Published by the Maryland His. Soc.

CARROLL, *Rev.* JOHN. A Wesl. Meth. min. (Guelph, U. C.) Has been a constant contributor to the *Christian Guardian* (Tor.) and to the *Wesleyan Mag.*

I. The Stripling Preacher, or a sketch of the life and character, with the theological remains of the Rev. Alexander S. Byrne. Written and compiled at the request of the Conference. *Toronto*, 1852, pp. 255, 12mo.

"The author has succeeded admirably in furnishing the Wesleyan community with an interesting addition to biographical literature."—*Ch. Guardian.*

II. The Besieger's Prayer; or a Christian Nation's appeal to the God of Battles, for success in a righteous war: a sermon preached on the occasion of the "General Fast." *Do.* 1855, pp. 25.

"An able and lucid sermon."—*Can. Evangelist.*

III. Past and Present, or a description of persons and events connected with Canadian Methodism for the last forty years. By a Spectator of the scenes. *Do.* 1860, pp. 331, 12mo.

"It is not without value as a contribution to the history of Methodism in the North, and affords very entertaining and profitable family reading."—*Ch. Advocate.*

IV. Reasons for Wesleyan Belief and Practice, relative to Water Baptism. *Peterborough*, 1862, pp. 52.

"There is a great deal of thought, fact, and argument crowded into a small space."—*Ch. Guardian.*

CARRUTHERS, J.

I. Retrospect of Thirty-six years' residence in Canada West: Being a Christian journal and narrative. *Hamilton*, 1861, pp. 253.

CARRY, *Rev.* JOHN, *B. D.* A clergym. of the Ch. of Eng., (Holland Landing, U. C.)

I. Sermons, Doctrinal, Devotional and Practical. *Quebec*, 1859, pp. 202, 8vo.

CARSON, JAMES, *M. D.* (Liverpool, Eng.)

I. Reasons for Colonizing the Island of Newfoundland. *Greenock*, 1813, 8vo.

II. A Letter to the members of Parliament, on the Address of the inhabitants of Newfoundland to the Prince Regent. 1813, 8vo.

CARTER, EDWARD, *Q. C.* A Montreal advocate. Was for a short time joint Clk. of the Peace for that District.

I. A Treatise on the Law and Practice of Summary Convictions and Orders of Justices of the Peace in Upper and Lower Canada. *Montreal*, 1856, 8vo.

CARTER, GEORGE. Organist at Christ Ch. Cath., (Mont.)

I. A Selection of Anthems as sang

in the Cathedrals of Montreal, Toronto and Quebec. *Montreal*, 1865, pp. 59.

"The Anthems selected in this little volume are mostly from the Psalms, the Collects and the Holy Scriptures. The music to which they are set is from composers of various creeds, classes and countries. * * * It is one of the prettiest little *brochures* ever issued from our Provincial press."—*Transcript*, (Mont.)

CARTIER, *Hon.* GEORGE ETIENNE, *C. B.*, *Q. C.* A French Can. Statesman. B. at St. Antoine, L. C., 6 Sept. 1814. Has held various offices in successive Can. administrations, was once Premier, and has been Atty. Genl. L. C., for the third time since 1862. Is now Minister of Militia of the Dominion of Can. Author of the popular French Can. song *O Canada ! Mon Pays, Mes Amours !* (*Rep. Nat.* 1848), since published with music, and of other songs.

CARTWRIGHT, GEORGE.

I. Journal of Transactions and Events, during a residence of nearly sixteen years on the Coast of Labrador ; containing many interesting particulars, both of the country and its inhabitants, not hitherto known, with charts. *Newark*, (Eng.), 1792, 3 vols. 4to.

"This journal is written with care and fidelity ; the style of the author is plain and manly ; he delivers his sentiments with freedom, and with confidence asserts only those circumstances which, with his own observation, he knew to be facts. The author commenced his voyage from England in 1770. He was brother of the celebrated Major Cartwright."—*Rich.*

CARTWRIGHT, JOHN.

I. American Independence the interest and glory of Great Britain ; with reflection on the Boston and Quebec Acts. In a series of letters to the Legislature. *London*, 1774, pp. 92, 8vo.

"This writer asserts that the distance of the colonies renders it impossible to govern them by authority of Parliament, and that therefore a law should be passed declaring them free and independent states."—*Mon. Rev.* (Lon.)

CARTWRIGHT, R. J. A mem. of the Leg. Assem., Can.

I. Remarks on the Militia of Canada. *Kingston*, 1864, pp. 46, 8vo.

CARVER, J. Commanded a company of Provincial troops during the war with France in Am., prior and up to the conquest of Can.

I. Travels through the interior parts of North America, in the years 1766, 1767, and 1768. (Illustrated.) *London*, 1778, pp. 544, 8vo. ; 3rd ed. *Do.* 1799 ; *Boston*, 1797. Translated into French, *Paris*, 1784, 8vo.

CARY, THOMAS. A Can. journ. B. near Bristol, Eng., 1751. D. at Quebec, 1823. He started in life in the service of the East India Co. Subsequently emigrated to B. A., became a tutor to several persons who afterwards attained honorable distinction, and was admitted a mem. of the bar of N. S. He was a man of varied and scholarly attainments ; and possessed considerable ability and skill as a public writer. In 1805, founded the *Mercury*, (Que.) This paper originated from a desire to express the sentiments, sympathies and predilections of the British inhabitants of Quebec, who, at that time, formed a small but wealthy and influential portion of the community. The object was that that section of the people should have a non-official organ of their opinions, and be enabled to protest against such acts of power as they objected to, and to oppose the writings of their adversaries in respect of politics and nationality with equal freedom. Under Mr. C., the *Mercury* at once became what it has ever since continued to be, the consistent and unswerving advocate of high tory and episcopalian principles.

He conducted his journal with the most dauntless intrepidity. His style was at once classical, terse and vigourous ; his mode of attack—and he was even readier with the sword than with the shield, though master of both—was, in the taste of his day, modelled after Junius. But, if in the manner he followed the teachings of the great satirist, in the matter he was essentially original ; and his boldness brought him several times into collision with the House of Assembly. Stuart, Van Felson, Papineau and D. B. Viger, while leaders of opposition, were all subject to the lash of his sarcasm. One of his compositions,—abounding in ironical compliments directed against the late Sir James (then Mr.) Stuart, who at that time led the Leg. Assem., while Mr. C. was the literary defender of the then Chief-Justice Sewell and the Leg. Coun.—was pronounced a libel and breach of privilege, by a nearly unanimous vote of the Assem. On another occasion, the speaker's warrant having been issued for his apprehension, he remained concealed till the close of the session in a secret apartment ingeniously constructed in his residence, and from his hiding place poured forth his philippics upon his political opponents, like a high tory and amiable Marat—we say amiable, for he was a man of decided benevolence of heart. Unterrified by the sergeant-at-arms, then a much more formidable personage than now-a-days, the *Mercury* continued its course ; and, with its principles, descended from father to son, and from son to grandson, of its first proprietor.

CASAULT, *Rev.* L. J. 1st Rector of Laval Univ. (Que.) D. at Quebec, 1862.

Souvenir consacré à la mémoire vénérée de M. L. J. Casault, premier recteur de l'Université-Laval. *Quebec*, 1863, pp. 58.

CASE, *Rev.* ALBERT.

I. The principles of Odd Fellowship; a sermon. *Montreal*, 1845, pp. 15.

CASE, *Rev.* GEORGE. Wes. Min. Moulinette, U. C.

I. Our " Constitutional Rights " vindicated : or an argument for the legal proscription of the traffic in Alcoholic beverages. In six letters to the Hon. F. Hincks. *Toronto*, 1854, pp. 22.

CASE, *Rev.* WILLIAM. A Meth. Min. D. at Alnwick Mission, U. C., 19 Oct, 1855.

I. Jubilee Sermon delivered at the request and before the conference in London, C. W, 6th June, 1855. *Toronto*, 1855.

This embodies the reminiscenses of 50 years as a Meth. Min. in the rugged fields of Can., during its early history.

CASGRAIN, *L'Abbé* H. R. A French Can. author. Is a son of the late Hon. Charles Casgrain. B. at River Ouelle, L. C. 1831. Ed. first at the College of Ste. Anne de la Pocatière and then at the Quebec Seminary where he studied Divinity for the R. C. Ch., and in due course was admitted to the priesthood. As an author he first became known to the public through his volume of Can. Legends. There is apparent in this work great richness of imagination which however is disfigured by want of the natural in his scenes and characters. This defect, he has succeeded in overcoming in his later productions. His most successful literary performance, is the history of *La Mère Marie de l'Incarnation*, which has been justly pronounced one of the most remarkable books published in Can. The life of this most excellent woman has much of the romantic in it. Allied to one of the first families in France, becoming in turn first a wife, then a mother and finally a widow, she abandoned all the comforts and luxuries of her elevated position, to cross the seas to the uncivilized regions of New France in order to devote the remainder of her existence to a religious life. The recital of her labours and struggles with the privations and disappointments which met her, up to the final establishment of the Monastery of the Ursulines (Que.), of which she became first superior, is full of the liveliest interest. The style of the author is elaborate, more so, in fact, than we could wish in a work of this description. For this work l'Abbé C. has received a medal from His Holiness the Pope in recognition of its literary merits. Mr. C. has done much towards creating a correct taste in Literature and the Arts amongst his countrymen, and is regarded as one of the most graceful and finished writers which the French Canadians possess. His miscellaneous writings have appeared nearly altogether in the pages of *Les Soir. Can.* and *Le Foy. Can.* (Que.) M. Casgrain has lately made a voyage to France in search of documents concerning Champlain, the founder of Quebec.

I. Légendes Canadiennes. *Quebec*, 1861, pp. 425, 12mo.

" Ce joli volume, imprimé avec une élégance toute européenne, contient trois légendes, dont deux ont été publiées dans le *Courrier du Canada* et reproduites en Europe, comme nous l'avons déjà fait savoir à nos lecteurs, et dont la troisième remplit les dernières livraisons des *Soirées Canadiennes.* Le *Tableau de la Rivière Ouelle,* les *Pionniers* et *La Jongleuse,* sont d'intéressants récits d'aventures arrivées dans les premières années de la colonie ; écrites dans un style coloré et élégant, elles forment un petit groupe plein de charme et de poésie, dont la valeur sera surtout bien appréciée par ceux qui connaissent nos belles paroisses de la rive sud du St. Laurent, au-dessous de Québec. Elevé dans un de ces sites grandioses, au sein d'une famille chrétienne et d'une société distinguée, M. l'Abbé Casgrain a gardé un touchant souvenir et des belles scènes champêtres et des récits émouvants qui ont amusé son enfance. Un voyage en Europe, qu'il fit plus tard, comme il le raconte dans une sorte de prologue à sa dernière légende, lui a révélé à lui-même toute la valeur littéraire de ses souvenirs, et l'a engagé à les écrire. Ce sont là d'heureuses circonstances, tout au profit de notre . littérature, qui s'est enrichie par là d'un bien aimable volume."—*Journ. de L'Inst. Pub.*

II. Notice biographique sur le Chevalier Falardeau. [With a Portrait of the Chevalier] Par Eugène de Rives. *Do.* 1862, pp. 96, 4to.

III. Histoire de la Mère Marie de l'Incarnation, Première Supérieure des Ursulines de la Nouvelle France. Précédée d'une esquisse sur l'histoire religieuse des premiers temps de cette colonie. *Do.* 1864, pp. 467, 8vo.

"M. l'Abbé Casgrain a écrit cette histoire avec cette richesse, cette originalité et quelquefois même avec cette hardiesse de style qui distinguent ses autres productions. Il a en même temps apprécié, en homme versé dans la connaissance de la vie intérieure, cette existence si visiblement soutenue par le souffle d'en haut et dont les vertus séraphiques et l'active énergie ont laissé non seulement des souvenirs qui ne s'effaceront jamais, mais encore des œuvres qui se continuent sous les auspices et comme sous l'égide protectrice de son ombre."—D. H. SENECAL: *Rev. Can.*

"This is certainly the handsomest work we have yet seen from the Canadian press, and well deserves its dress. The Teresa of New France, whose biography her son portrayed in the 17th, and Charlevoix in the 18th, had her claims on the 19th, and Canada, in one of her most gifted sons, a litterateur of exquisite taste, of rich and classic language, pays the tribute of his country to the heroine whose exalted piety and devotion can rouse even the sons of the Puritans to admiration. Mr. Casgrain

weaves into his narrative all the grace and beauty of style called for in our day, without neglecting the accuracy of historical details or the pious element, the omission of which, as a pervading atmosphere in such a life, would be a misconception of the subject."— *Am. His. Mag.* (N. Y.)

"Il me reste à porter sur l'ouvrage et sur le talent de l'auteur un jugement d'ensemble. J'ai déjà indiqué, chemin faisant, une partie de ce qui me reste à dire, j'ai reconnu et loué l'éclat de certaines qualités et donné le signalement de quelques uns des défauts. La première qualité de M. Casgrain est l'imagination ; ses principaux défauts sont le goût de la déclamation dans le style, l'amour de certains mots sonores dans la phrase, le respect du convenu dans le récit, le culte de la pose dans ses héros. Son imagination est tour à tour brillante, évoquant les plus belles images, gracieux, donnant aux choses un tour délicat et charmant, touchant et faisant naître sans efforts les plus vives impressions, les émotions les plus profondes. Cette imagination ne peut que se développer, devenir sûre d'elle-même, en restant hardie, s'élever à mesure qu'elle s'astreindra aux lois d'un goût sévère. Il y a une plus grande dépense d'imagination dans les *Légendes* que dans *l'Histoire de la Mère de l'Incarnation,* cependant même comme imagination, je préfère l'*Histoire* aux *Légendes.* La profusion est moins grande, mais l'abondance est plus réelle ; l'éclat est plus tempéré, mais il est plus solide ; il éblouit moins à première vue, mais la lumière qu'il projette est plus pure et elle ne lasse pas. L'éclairage artificiel est magnifique dans les *Légendes,* et ce qui y manque c'est plutôt un coin obscur, une page simple où l'esprit se puisse reposer un instant de toutes ces splendeurs ; mais dans l'*Histoire de la Mère de l'Incarnation,* ce sont de purs rayons qui éclairent et qui font bien vite pâlir les quelques lumières douteuses qui cherchent encore à se glisser çà et là. Le sujet a porté bonheur à l'auteur et lui a fait sentir la nécessité d'être plus simple, plus sévère ; il n'a pas voulu étaler, à côté de la belle prose du 17e siècle de son héroïne, les ornements fanés du romantisme. Son imagination avait aussi moins à s'exercer, en ce sens que dans les *Légendes,* où il fallait créer une fable, composer une trame, tandis qu'ici il n'y avait qu'à suivre les phases successives de la vocation et de l'existence de la Mère de l'Incarnation. Le talent s'est ployé aisément aux règles du sujet, et en le voyant dans le cadre un peu sévère, mais élégamment sculpté, suspendu aux murs blancs d'un couvent, on croirait qu'il y a été placé en naissant et l'on ne devinerait pas de suite qu'il a glissé autrefois, sur la pente de la légende, vers le roman."— HECTOR FABRE : *Rev. Can.*

IV. Un Contemporain—A. E. Aubry. *Do.* 1865, pp. 103, 4to.

V. Un Contemporain—F. X. Garneau. Avec un portrait photographique et un autographe. *Do.* 1866, pp. 135, sm. 8vo.

VI. Découverte du Tombeau de Champlain, par MM. les abbés Laverdière et Casgrain. *Do.* 1866, pp. 13, 8vo. (with Plans, &c.)

VII. Un Contemporain—G. B. Faribault. *Do.* 1867, pp. 123, sm. 8vo.

VIII. Vies des Saints. *Ottawa*, 1867, pp. 750, 4to.

CASSEGRAIN, ARTHUR. A French Can. who wrote a report of l'Abbé Ferland's course of lectures on Can. History as delivered at Laval Univ. which originally appeared in *Le Courrier du Canada*, (Que.) and was extensively copied; also a series of articles on University education, in the same journal. He is the author, conjointly with Mr. P. A. Dionne, of a humorous poem, *La Tauride*, (*Rev. Can.* 1864.) Another of his poetical pieces on the 100th anniversary of the Battle of St. Foy, was highly eulogized by the French poet Sempé.

I. La Grand-Tronciade. *Ottawa*, 1866, pp. 96, 12mo.

"Le travail de M. Cassegrain n'est pas toutefois sans aucun mérite. Les personnages qu'il nous présente sont assez vraisemblables : ses tableaux ne sont pas dépourvus de couleurs. Cet ouvrage lui servira de marche-pied pour atteindre plus haut, M. Cassegrain a une diction assez facile et il serait injuste de ne pas admettre qu'il se rencontre, par endroits, d'assez jolis vers : mais pour qu'un poème soit tolérable, il faut que les bons vers ne soient pas l'exception. Emporté par la vapeur, M. Cassegrain ne semble pas voir les barrières que la prosodie met invariablement sur la voie où s'élancent les poètes, et il arrive au bout du vers avec tant d'ardeur, que ne pouvant s'arrêter, il *enjambe* sur le voisin, fort surpris de son audace. Son respect pour la rime ne va pas jusqu'à l'idolâtrie. J'ai rencontré maintes syllabes finales très-mécontentes de se voir courbées sous le même joug et forcées de chanter de concert. Pour terminer, je dirai que je ne crois pas que M. Cassegrain soit sorti victorieux de sa lutte contre le vieux proverbe : *Qui trop embrasse mal étreint.*"— L. P. LEMAY : *Rev. Can.*

5

CATTERMOLE, WILLIAM.
I. The advantages of emigration to Canada, being the substance of two Lectures, delivered at the Town-hall. Colchester. *London*, 1831.

CAUCHON, *Hon.* JOSEPH. A French Can. statesman and journ. B. in Quebec. Dec. 1816. Received his education at the Seminary of his native city. At the termination of his sch. studies, entered on that of the law and was finally admitted as an advocate ; he has however never practised his profession. Mr. C. has sat uninterruptedly in the Leg. Assem. since 1844 ; held the offices of Com. of Crown Lands and Com. of Public Works at separate times. Since Jany. 1866 he has been Mayor of Quebec. Whilst still a sch. boy, began writing for the newspaper press, contributing to *Le Liberal* (Que.) Gaining strength with his pen he afterwards edited *Le Canadien*, the leading organ of the French Canadians, during the temporary absence of its regular ed., Mr. Parent, and was engaged in writing for it when the paper was suppressed by the Govt. In 1842 founded *Le Journal de Québec*, which has since become in point of circulation and influence one of the foremost and most enterprising newspapers published in either language in Can. Of this paper Mr. C. has been the chief ed., and he has divided the principal portion of his time and attention between his journalistic and legislative duties. It is generally conceded that he occupies a first place in the ranks of French Can. journalists.

" He is one of the most clear and nervous of our public writers ; and to his other high merits unites a well stored and cultivated mind on almost every branch of knowledge. Besides an indomitable will, Mr. Cauchon possesses great individuality of character : determination which no opposition can intimidate ; industry which no labor can exhaust, and perseverance which no discouragement can appal. He moves vehemently as well as persistently, towards the point he wishes to arrive at. Such movement, moreover, appears to be impelled by the unrestrained despotism of his thoughts ; thoughts which know neither friend nor counsellor outside of the fervid brain in which they are generated. The matter of his speech harmonizes with its temperature. He rarely persuades ; he seeks rather to destroy than to convince ; to expose the weakness of his adversary's argument rather than exhibit the strength of his own. He does not resort to sophistry, being careful only to assert truth, or what he believes to be truth. He conciliates by accident, while he controls by habit. Force is his normal condition, and intellectual activity is the life of that condition. He delights in mental gymnastics, and enters with zest, and from sheer love of the exercise into the arena of controversy. Though he lacks the flexible qualities which go to make a leader popular, he possesses the forcible ones which make an ally valuable. He is a powerful associate and a dangerous opponent."—FENNINGS TAYLOR : *Portraits of Mr. Am's.*

I. Notions Elémentaires de Physique, avec planches. *Quebec*, 1841, 8vo.

II. Etude sur l'Union Projetée des Provinces Britanniques de l'Amérique du Nord. Reproduite du *Journal de Québec. Do.* 1858, pp. 36, 8vo.

III. L'Union des Provinces de l'Amérique Britannique du Nord. *Do.* 1865, pp. 152, 8vo. (See *Macaulay, G. H.*)

" The Unionists of all these Provinces have good reason to welcome among the champions of their cause, so able, resolute and judicious an advocate as Mr. Cauchon."
—*Gazette*, (Mont.)

" There is no man in Lower Canada to whom the duty of laying before his countrymen a bold, vigorous defence of the resolutions of the Conference could be better entrusted than to Mr. Cauchon. His long career as a public man, and the important positions which he has held in the government of the Province, and in the discussions of every question of importance which has agitated it during the last twenty years, had endeared him to his fellow subjects—the French Canadians of Lower Canada—and entitled him to speak to them, as one who had never hesitated when their interests were involved, never remained silent when their character was assailed. Never having betrayed them in the past, he was entitled to ask at their hands a fair and full hearing now ; and it is a matter of sincere congratulation, that in the district of Quebec where his power most circulates, and where his influence is most felt, the vote in favour of the resolutions of the Conference will be all but unanimous. If the scheme shall be successful, a large portion of the merit of bringing it to a successful termination will be due to the earnest and patriotic effort of Mr. Cauchon to induce its acceptance at the hands of the Lower Canadians."—*Spectator*, (Hamil.)

CAWDELL, JAMES M. Formerly an officer in the Brit. Army. D. at Toronto, 13 July, 1842. Published for a short time. *The Rose-Harp*, (York U. C.) a Mag., to which he contributed.

CAYLEY, *Hon.* WILLIAM. Inspector Genl. of Can. from 1845 to 1848, and again from 1854 to 1858.

I. Finances and Trade of Canada at the beginning of 1855. *London*, 1855, pp. 40, 8vo.

CELLEM, ROBERT.
I. Visit of His Royal Highness the Prince of Wales to the British North American Provinces and United States in the year 1860. Compiled from the Public Journals. *Toronto*, 1861, pp. 438, 8vo.

CHABOILLEZ, *Rev.* M.
I. Réponse à la lettre de P. H. Bédard ; suivie de quelques remarques sur les " Observations " imprimées aux Trois Rivières. *Montréal*, 1824, pp. 70.

CHAGNON, GODFREY, *N. P.* (L'Assomption, L. C.)
I. Précis de diverses Ordonnances du Conseil Spécial, et d'Actes de la Législature de la ci-devant Province du Bas Canada. *Montréal*, 1842, pp. 108.

CHALMERS, GEORGE. The author of a number of political, historical, and other works. B. at Fochabers, Scot., 1742. D. 1825.

I. Political Annals of the present United Colonies, from their settlement to the Peace of 1763 : compiled chiefly from Records, and authorized often by the insertion of State Papers : *London*, 1780, 4to.

Republished with additions and an introduction. *Boston, U. S.* 1845, 2 Vols. 8vo.

" You will sometimes see the work of Chalmers referred to. It is an immense, heavy, tedious book, to explain the legal history of the different colonies of America. It should be consulted on all such points. But it is impossible to read it. The leaves, however, should be turned over, for curious particulars often occur, and the nature of the first settlement and original laws of each colony should be known. The last chapter, indeed, ought to be read. The right to tax the Colonies became a great point of dispute. Chalmers means to show that the sovereignty of the British Parliament existed over

America, because the settlers, though emigrants, were still English subjects and members of the Empire."—*Prof. Smyth's Lect. on Mod. Hist.*

CHAMBERLAND, J. B. E.

I. Dissertation familière calme et intègre sur la question d'un hâvre de refuge dans le bas du fleuve St. Laurent. *Québec*, 1857.

CHAMBERLIN, BROWN, *M. A., D. C. L.* A Can. Journ. B. at Frelighsburg L. C., 26 March, 1827. Ed. there and at St. Paul's Sch., (Mont.) Admitted to the bar of L. C. in 1850, but abandoned law 2 years afterwards for the profession of journalism. Is a Fellow and Mem. of the Senate of the Univ. of McGill Coll. and President of the Board of Arts and Manufactures L. C. Has Contributed to the *University Mag.* (Dub.) Has been joint ed. and prop. of the *Gazette*, (Mont.) to which he had previously been law reporter, and an occasional contributor, since 1852. Was a Com. from Can. to the London Exhibition of 1862. The following letter has recently been addressed to the conductors of *Gazette*, by the Rev. Chas. Kingsley, the distinguished author and scholar:

"EVERSLY RECTORY, ENGLAND.

"DEAR SIR,—Some unknown friend has sent me from time to time, for some years past, the *Montreal Gazette and Canadian Mail*.

"Allow me, at this crisis, to tender him through your columns my hearty thanks; and to tender to you, at the same time, the expression of my respect for your paper.

"Loyalty and patriotism are qualities on which I shall not compliment you. They seem to be native to Canadians; and it would be an impertinence on my part to praise you for possessing that which you would be ashamed to want.

"But I must compliment you on the sound sense with which you are treating the question of the 'Reciprocity Treaty.' As an old freetrader, I cannot but believe that the United States are making a mistake injurious to themselves but ultimately most beneficial to you; that the present change will issue in your finding new and more profitable markets for your productions, and will connect you more closely with that old world whose history is not yet quite played out.

"Let me compliment you also on the noble attitude which Canada is assuming at this moment, an attitude which you have (as far as I have read) always recommended; and, it may be materially assisted by your gallant but moderate exhortations.

"England will be, now and henceforth, truly proud of her child; and all the more proud because in Canada seems to be solved at last that 'Irish problem' which has so sadly troubled us at home.

"As long as the system of politics and society carried out in Canada can convert such men as Mr. McGee, (whom I mention with much respect) and can rally in support of the Throne and Constitution thousands, not only of Protestant English and Scotch, but of Catholic French and Irish, Canada will be in a position which many a kingdom of the old world may well envy; and one which will surely, if she continues as she has begun, make her a mighty and happy State.

"I remain, Dear Sir,

"Your faithful servant,

"CHAS. KINGSLEY."

I. A Lecture delivered before the Mercantile Library Association of Montreal on the British North American Colonies. *Montreal*, 1853.

II. Report upon Institutions in London, Dublin, Edinburgh, and Paris, for the promotion of Industrial Education. *Do.* 1859.

CHAMBERS, WILLIAM. A well known Scot. author and publisher.

I. Narrative of a tour in British America and the United States. *Edinburgh*, 1854, cr. 8vo.

CHAMPION, RICHARD. "Late Deputy Paymaster Genl. of His Majesty's Forces"

I. Considerations on the present situation of Great Britain and the United States of America, with a view to their future Commercial Connexions. Containing remarks upon the Pamphlet published by Lord Sheffield, intituled : "Observations on the Commerce of the American States"; and also on the Act of Navigation, so far as it relates to those States. Interspersed with some observations upon the state of Canada, Nova Scotia and the Fisheries; and upon the Connexion of the West Indies with America, &c. *London*, 2nd Ed., 1784, 8vo.

CHAPMAN, EDWARD J., *Ph. D., F. C. S.* Prof. of Mineralogy and Geology in Univ. Coll. (Tor.) Filled the chair of Mineralogy in Univ. Coll. (Lon.), for some time, prior to receiving his present appointment.

I. Songs of Charity and other poems. *London*, 1839, 12mo.

5 *

II. Practical Mineralogy. *Do.*, 1843, 12mo.

III. Description of Characters of Minerals. *Do.*, 1844, 12mo.

IV. A Song of Charity. *Toronto*, 1857.

"Craving as we do a native poetry, if we are to have Canadian poetry at all, the Song of Charity takes us by guile. The dedication * * 'to kinds friends in Orillia, Canada West,' tell us that the poem was 'composed in chief part, during a summer's holiday, on the waters and amidst the islets of little Lake Couchiching.' Here accordingly is genuine native inspiration. We are gliding, with the author in his birch canoe, over the picturesque lake, and hailing the Indian as he silently paddles past us, under the lee of the wooded islands, from the prettily named Orillia—so called after a favorite native flower—to his own scattered Indian lodges at Rama. [Quoting from one of the poems *A Canadian Summer's Night* the writer proceeds :] Now this is a genuine Canadian scene, such as no fire-side traveller or fancy-visioned poet of old world wanderings or library book-dust, could possibly call into being. The dark recesses of the pine-woods and the shadows of the lake-fringing Sumach, the monotonous call of the Whip-poor-will, the soft and musical night-song of the frogs, the fitful gleaming of the firefly dancing in the cedar-swamp, the prowling night owl noiselessly listening to the mocking note—half a whistle and half a coo—of the tree-frog ; each one of these shows the touch of a Canadian pencil, such as the most labored study of the home poet would in vain attempt. In this direction alone lies the path in which poetic success is worth welcoming among us."—PROF. D. WILSON: *Can. Journ.*

V. Examples of the application of Trigonometry to Crystallographic Calculations, drawn up for the use of Students in the University of Toronto. *Do.*, 1860.

VI. A popular and practical Exposition of the Minerals and Geology of Canada. *Do.*, 1864.

Canadian Journal.

I. Note on the object of the Salt Condition of the Sea. 1855.

II. A review of the Trilobites; their characters and classification. 1856.

III. On the occurrence of the genus Cryptoceras in Silurian Rocks. 1857.

IV. On atomic constitution and Crys-

talline form as classification characters in Mineralogy. *Do.*

V. Deposition of native metals in vein fissures, &c., by Electro-chemical agency. (Read before Am. Ass. for Advanc. of Science.) 1858.

VI. On the assaying of coals by the blowpipe. *Do.*

VII. On some new Trilobites from Canadian Rocks. *Do.*

VIII. On the Hypostoma of Asaphus Canadensis, and on a third new species of Asaphus from Canadian rocks. 1859.

IX. Note on the occurrence of Asaphus Megistos in Canadian rocks, with additional remarks on Asaphus Hincksii. *Do.*

X. A popular exposition of the Minerals and Geology of Canada. 1860.

XI. On the Geology of Belleville and the surrounding district. *Do.*

XII. On a new species of Agelacrinites, and on the structural relations of that genus. *Do.*

XIII. Sketch of the Geology of Hastings County, Canada West. *Do.*

XIV. Note on Stelliform Crystals, with special reference to the crystallization of snow. 1861.

XV. Some notes on the drift deposits of Western Canada, and on the ancient extension of the Lake area of that region. *Do.*

XVI. On the Klaprothine or Lazulite of North Carolina. *Do.*

XVII. Additional note on the occurrence of fresh water shells in the upper drift deposits of Western Canada. *Do.*

XVIII. On the position of Lievrite in the Mineral series. 1862.

XIX. Note on the occurrence of Allanite in Canadian rocks. 1864.

XX. Note on the presence of Phosphorus in iron wire. *Do.*

XXI. Contributions to Blowpipe Analysis. 1865.

XXII. On some minerals from Lake Superior. *Do.*

"Professor E. J. Chapman, of Toronto University, so favorably known for his contributions to mineralogy, has advanced the science of geology in the province, not only by his lectures in connection with the University, but by such field Explorations as he has had an opportunity to make; and by his communications to the *Canadian Journal* on various points relating to his investigations of the Drift and the Silurian formations of Western Canada, of which we have availed ourselves."—Sir W. E. Logan: *Geo. of Can.* 1863.

CHAPMAN, *Hon.* H. S. A Can. Journ. and writer. B. at Kennington, Surrey, July, 1803. Came to Can. in 1823. Asst. Commissioner to enquire into the condition of the hand-loom weavers in Eng. 1838. Called to the Eng. bar 1840. Judge of the Supreme Court of New Zealand from Nov. 1843 to March 1852, when appointed Colonial Sec. of Tasmania. Throwing up this latter position, in 1854 he established himself at Melbourne where he practised his profession. Being elected to the Assem. he became Attorney Genl. in 1857, again in 1858, a third time in 1859, and finally received the appointment of Judge of the Supreme Court in 1862. He is now Judge in New Zealand. In 1833 established the *Daily Advertiser* (Mont.) the first daily newspaper published in B. A. Connected with it was the *Courier*, published twice a week, and the *Weekly Abstract*, the latter journal published for the Eng. mail; all of these were strong advocates of the Liberal cause of that day. As Ed. of these journals Mr. C. displayed great vigour and ability and materially assisted the cause of the political party to which he belonged. Their publication ceased on Mr. C. proceeding to Eng. in 1834, as the bearer of a petition from the inhabitants of L. C. to the Imperial Legislature. As a writer for the Eng. periodical press he was the means of rendering important services to Can. and B. A. He is the author of articles in the *Encyclopædia Brittanica*, and of several works on law and government which have appeared since he left this country.

I. A Statistical Sketch of the Corn Trade of Canada. (Reprinted from the *Brit. Farmer's Quarterly Mag.*) *London*, 1832, pp. 47.

II. Thoughts on the Money and Exchanges of Lower Canada. *Montreal*, 1832, pp. 64, 8vo.

III. Petition from Lower Canada, with explanatory remarks. *London*, 1834.

This pamphlet was printed for circulation amongst members of Parliament previous to a debate in the House of Commons on the affairs of L. C.

IV. Letter to the Editor of the *Monthly Repository* in answer to an article in that periodical on Canada. *Do.* 1835, pp. 8.

V. Recent occurrences in Canada. (Reprinted from the *Monthly Repository.*) *Do.* 1836, pp. 16.

VI. The Trade of the Canadas. *Scot. Monthly Mag.* (Glas.) 1836, pp. 52.

VII. The Trade of Nova Scotia, &c. *Do.*, 1836, pp. 16.

VIII. The Timber monopoly. *Lond. and West. Rev.*, 1836, pp. 32.

IX. Progress of events in Canada. (Reprinted from *Do.*) *London*, 1837, pp. 16.

X. The Canadian Question. *Dub. Rev.* pp. 36.

XI. Canadian Boat Songs ; with descriptions of Canadian scenery, manners, &c. *Scottish Mag.* (Glas.)

CHAPPELL, EDWARD, *Lieutenant R. N.*

I. Narrative of a voyage to Hudson's Bay, in His Majesty's ship Rosamond: containing some account of the North-Eastern Coast of America, and of the tribes inhabiting that remote region. *London*, 1817, 8vo.

II. Voyage of His Majesty's Ship Rosamond to Newfoundland and the Southern Coast of Labrador, of which countries no account has been published by any British Traveller since the reign of Queen Elizabeth. *Do.*, 1818, 8vo.

CHARNOCK, JOHN H. Took the prize of the Royal Agricultural Soc. (Eng.), for an essay on the *Farming of the West Riding of Yorkshire*, and other papers on *Drainage*, &c. Was instrumental in securing the passage of the public Drainage Act in Eng., and was appointed an Asst. Com. for carrying the same into effect. Since his residence in Can. has contributed occasionally to the newspaper press on subjects of public importance.

CHANDONNET, *Rev.* THOMAS AIMÉ. A R. C. Priest.

I. Discourses delivered at Notre-Dame de Québec, during the Triduum of the Society of St. Vincent-de-Paul, 1863. Translated from the French. *Quebec*, 1864, pp. 52, 8vo.

CHAUVEAU, *Hon.* PIERRE J. O., LL. D. Supdt. of Education for L. C. B. at Quebec, 30 May, 1820. Ed. at the Seminary of that city where he went through a complete course of studies. On leaving that institution he entered on the study of the law, and in due time was admitted to practice. In 1844, he was returned to Parliament where he continued to hold a seat up to 1855, in which year he was appointed to the office which he still holds—Superintendent of Education for L. C. He was twice in office—first as Solicitor Gen. for L. C., and secondly as Provincial Sec. As a literary man his talents first attracted attention by his poems in *Le Canadien* (Que.) from 1838 to 1841. Many of these were afterwards collected and republished in *Le Rep. Nat.* (Mont.) He also contributed from 1847 to 1850 in prose and verse to *Le Castor, Le Fantasque, Le Canadien* and *La Revue Canadienne*, the latter a literary miscellany published at (Mont.) From 1841 to 1852, he was the Can. correspondent of *Le Courrier des Etats-Unis*, (N. Y.) His letters to that journal on the political and other topics of the day which engaged public attention in the Province, deservedly drew forth favorable comment. In 1856, he founded in connection with his department *Le Journal de l'Instruction Publique* and *The Journal of Education for L. C.*, 2 periodicals admirably suited to the objects for which they are intended. Of the first named he is the principal ed., but he writes frequently for both, Many interesting articles from his pen have appeared in their columns. Dr. C. is also an occasional contributor to *Les Soirées Can.* (Que.) He is a corresponding mem. of the Academy of Sciences (New Orleans.)

I. Charles Guérin, roman de mœurs Canadiennes. *Montreal*, 1852, pp. 359, 8vo.

"Un précieux ouvrage."—*Bib. Universelle par Denis, Paris.*

"Disons-le de suite, Charles Guérin est un bon livre, que tout Canadien ou étranger lira avec plaisir et qui ne sera pas plus déplacé dans la bibliothèque de l'homme de lettres que dans celle de la mère de famille. C'est une histoire vraie, touchante et naïve de la vie humaine. Le héros principal exprime admirablement le deuxième acte de notre existence. Irrésolutions, romantisme, fluctuations, ennuis, agitations sans cause, tels sont les éléments avec lesquels M. Chauveau a pétri le caractère du jeune homme qu'il met en scène. Bien des gens se réfléchiront dans cette peinture et en loueront, comme nous, la délicatesse de touche."—*La Ruche Litt.* (Montreal.) The work was also favourably reviewed by Mr. de Puibusque in *L'Union* (Paris.)

II. Discours prononcé le mercredi, 18 juillet, 1855, à la cérémonie de la pose de la pierre angulaire du monument dédié, par souscription nationale, à la mémoire des braves tombés sur la plaine d'Abraham, le 28 avril, 1760. *Quebec*, 1855, pp. 12.

"L'éloquence a brillé de tout temps d'un vif éclat parmi nous, mais en dehors de la chaire. il ne nous en reste qu'un chef-d'œuvre de M. Chauveau à l'occasion de la pose de la première pierre du monument de Ste. Foye."—HECTOR FABRE.

III. Relation du Voyage de S. A. R. le Prince de Galles en Amérique. reproduite du Journal de l'Instruction Publique du Bas Canada, avec un appendice contenant diverses adresses, correspondances, etc. *Montreal*, 1861, pp. xxviii—148.

An Eng. translation of this book was published at the same time.

"This is the most valuable work on the subject that has as yet been published."—*Journ. of Ed.*, U. C.

"Of Mr. Chauveau we need not speak. Already well known as one of the foremost *littérateurs* in Canada, he has by his labors in the cause of education, entitled himself to a high rank in the annals of his country."—*Am. His. Mag.*

CHENEY, MRS. HARRIET V. A contributor to Can. periodical Literature. B. in Massachusetts, U. S. Prior to taking up her residence in Can. produced several works in her native country:—*The Sunday School, or the Village Sketches*, written in conjunction with her sister Mrs. Cushing ; *A Peep at the Pilgrims in 1636, a tale of the Olden Times*, afterwards republished in London where it was very favorably reviewed ; *The*

Rivals of Acadia ; Sketches from the Life of Christ; and *Confessions of an Early Martyr.* Contributed many well written tales and sketches to the *Literary Garland,* (Mont.) From 1847 to 1851 ed., with her sister, *The Snow Drop,* (Mont.), a monthly juvenile mag.

CHERRIEN, C. S., *Q. C.* A Montreal advocate of long standing. Many of his addresses on various topics have appeared in *L'Echo du Cabinet de Lecture,* (Mont.) In 1863 he was offered the Chief Justiceship of L. C., which he declined.

I. Mémoire contenant un Résumé du Plaidoyer sur les questions soumises par l'honorable L. T. Drummond, Procureur Général de Sa Majesté pour le Bas Canada à la décision des juges de la cour du Banc de la Reine et de la Cour Supérieure, en vertu des dispositions de l'Acte Seigneurial de 1854. *Montreal,* 1855, pp. 110, 8vo.

II. Discours prononcé dans l'Eglise Paroissiale de Montreal dans la grande démonstration des Catholiques en faveur de Pie IX. *Do.,* 1860, pp. 21.

III. Discours sur la Confédération. *Do.,* 1865, pp. 13.

CHERRIMAN, JOHN BRADFORD, *M. A.* Prof. of Mathematics and Natural Philosophy, Univ. Coll. (Tor.) Is a graduate of Cambridge ; took a high rank as a Wrangler at that Univ. in 1845, and was subsequently elected to a fellowship in St. John's Coll.

I. Plane Trigonometry as far as the Solution of Triangles. *Toronto,* 1865.

Canadian Journal.

I. On the Atmospheric Phenomena of Light. 1852.

II. On the Provincial Currency. 1853.

III. On the variations of Temperature at Toronto. *Do.*

IV. General Meteorological Register of the Provincial Magnetical Observatory, Toronto. 1854.

V. Mean Meteorological Results at Toronto, during the year 1854. 1855.

VI. Report on the Solar Eclipse of May, 26th, 1854. By Profs. Cherriman and Irving. 1855.

VII. On the Reduction of the General Equation of the Second Degree in Plane Co-ordinate Geometry. 1856.

VIII. Note on the Composition of Parallel Rotations. 1857.

IX. Note on the Propositions of Pythagoras and Pappus. 1858.

X. Note on Guldins Properties. 1863.

XI. Note on Poinsot's memoir on Rotation. Do.

XII. Note on Trilinears. 1864.

XIII. Notes on do. 1865.

CHESSHYRE, HENRY T. N.
I. Canada in 1864 : a handbook for settlers. *London,* 1864, 12mo.

CHEVALIER, H. EMILE. A French writer. Resided for some years in Can. Founded in 1853 *La Ruche Littéraire* (Mon.), a Mag., of which he was ed. from its commencement until it ceased publication in 1859. He also served successively as ed. of *La Patrie* and *Le Pays.* (Mont.) Returned to France in 1859.

I. L'Héroine de Chateauguay, épisode de la guerre de 1812. *Montreal,* 1858, pp. 95.

" A pleasing and interesting addition to our native literature."—*Leader,* (Tor.)

II. Le Pirate du Saint Laurent. *Do.*

III. Les Trappeurs de la Baie d'Hudson. *Do.* 1858, pp. 167.

IV. Le Foyer Canadien ou le mystère dévoilé. [Translated from the English of E. Clemo.] *Do.* 1858.

V. Legends of the Sea : Thirty-nine men for one woman. [Translated from the French of H. E. Chevalier.] *New York,* 1863, 12mo.

La Ruche Littéraire.

I. L'Ile de Sable : Episode de la Colonisation du Canada. 1854.

II. La Huronne de Lorette. *Do.*

III. La Langue Française et la Nationalité Canadienne. 1859.

IV. Histoire d'une famille Canadienne depuis l'an mil six cent six, jusqu'à l'an mil huit cent cinquante. *Do.*

V. La Presse Franco-Américaine. *Do.*

CHEWETT, W. C., *M. D.* For sometime connected with the *Ang. Am. Mag.*

(Tor.), to which he frequently contributed. The following are some of his contributions to that periodical : *The Student's Vision, a fancy for Christmas' Eve*, 1852 ; *Queenston Suspension Bridge* ; *Aristendeen, a story* ; *The Thousand Isles*, 1853 ; *The Tale of a Scrap* ; *What is Man? a dream*. 1854.

CHILDE, McALPINE and KIRKWOOD.
I. Report on the Harbour of Montreal. *Montreal*, 1858.

CHINIQUY, *Rev.* CHARLES. A writer on Temperance and religious topics. B. at Kamouraska, L. C., July 1809. Ordained a priest in the Church of Rome, Sept. 1833. In 1835 established the first Temperance Soc. which existed amongst the French Can. people. From 1847 to 1849 by command of the Bish. of Montreal he journeyed throughout Can. advocating the principle of Temperance from the pulpit. In 1850 M. C. was invited to proceed to the U. S. to labour in behalf of his countrymen residing in the Union ; and in the succeeding year the Bish. of Chicago entrusted him with the task of conducting his fellow compatriots to the Far West for the purpose of there founding a R. C. Colony, in which object he was entirely successful, having succeeded in establishing them at St. Anne, Kankakee, Illinois, where he became their pastor. In 1857 he seceded from the Ch. of Rome taking over his parishioners with him. M. C. contributed to the *Mélanges Religieux* from 1846 to 1856, and to *L'Avenir* from the latter year to 1858.

I. Manuel de la Société de Tempérance, dédié à la jeunesse Canadienne. *Montreal*, 2nd Ed. 1847, pp. 183, 8vo ; 4th Ed., *Do.*, 1849.

" The author has treated well his subject, and we only regret, that so much of a religious character has been imparted to the work, that its general use will, of necessity, become much restricted, and its utility proportionately diminished." *B. A. Journ.*

II. L'Ennemi de la Sainte-Vierge et de Jésus-Christ est l'église de Rome. *Chicago*, 1863, pp. 42.

CHISHOLME, DAVID. A Can. journ. B. in Rosshire, Scot., about 1796. D. at Montreal, 24 Sept., 1842. He studied for the legal profession. Emigrated to Can. in 1822. Lord Dalhousie the then Gov. Genl. whose particular and confidential friend he was, conferred upon him the office of Clk. of the Peace for the District of Three Rivers. For the remainder of this notice we are indebted to the *Gazette* (Mont.), of which he was ed. during the last 5 years of his life :

" Thoroughly versed in the constitutional law and practice of his native land, and indignant at the bold assumptions and encroachments of the House of Assembly, he volunteered fearlessly in defence of those institutions, which he felt to be the birthright and heirloom of every Briton, wherever British rule prevails. To the cause of constitutional government and British connection his indefatigable pen was ever devoted. He nailed these colours to the mast, and stood by them without fear, hesitation, or compromise, to his latest hour. The opposition of a constant and incorruptible adversary, was not forgotten by those, who felt no simpathy with his motives, and possessed not the magnanimity to forgive the publicity of their castigation. To the hostility of the House of Assembly, may be clearly traced and justly ascribed his destitution, in November, 1836, of the office he held in the District of Three Rivers. From that period, almost without interruption, Mr. Chisholme has continued to edit the *Montreal Gazette*. His contributions to these columns have been characterised by great and varied research, by sound and uncompromising constitutional principle, by the frank and fearless repudiation of all speculative theories and new fangled notions ; accompanied ever by the most gentlemanly courtesy towards his contemporaries."

I. The Lower Canada Watchman. *Kingston*, 1829, 32mo.

II. Observations on the rights of the British Colonies to Representation in the Imperial Parliament. *Three Rivers*, 1831, pp. 301-xxii, 18mo.

" Again, the Liberals, and even the moderate Conservatives, urge upon the mother country the importance and the necessity of a represention in Parliament. • •
A treatise written at Montreal about fifteen years ago is supposed to contain the earliest statement of this claim."—*N. A. Rev.*, 1848.

III. The Annals of Canada. *Do.* pp. 150.

This is a history of the events of 1837-8, and had it been completed it would have been the most accurate and impartial account of the Rebellion extant.

CHRISTIE, A. J., A. M.

I. The Emigrant's Assistant : or Remarks on the agricultural interest of the Canada's. Containing an account of the most effectual means of assisting settlers on their arrival in the country; observations on the different tenures by which lands are held in both provinces; directions for procuring grants of waste lands, and some account of the different methods of clearing them, collected from documents and various papers furnished for the information of the Montreal Emigrants Society in the year 1820. With an Appendix exhibiting the latest official orders of Government respecting the granting of waste lands, forms of petitions, location tickets, &c. *Montreal*, 1821, 2 vols. 12mo.

CHRISTIE, Rev. GEORGE. Presb. Min. (Yarmouth.) N. S.

I. The want of India, as manifest in the spiritual and social degradation of her people ; a lecture. *Halifax*, 1859, pp. 32, 8vo.

CHRISTIE, ROBERT. A Can. historian. B. at Windsor, N. S., 1788. D. at Quebec, 13 Oct., 1856. He was ed. at his native place. For sometime he followed Mercantile pursuits in Halifax, subsequently proceeded to Can., and took up his residence at Quebec. He studied for and was admitted as a mem. of the bar. In course of time he entered the Assem. of L. C. as mem. for Gaspe. During the violent party contests which for so long a period characterised the proceedings of that body and which reached a crisis in the rebel ion of 1837, Mr. C. was distinguished for the warmth and pertinacity with which he upheld the Conservative cause. Whether his political conduct upon all occasions was justifiable, or not, it drew down upon him the especial animosity of the more numerous party to which he was opposed. In 1829, he was expelled from the House for having by his advice to the Governor, caused the dismissal of a number of its members from the Magistracy and other offices held by them, in consequence of their votes and speeches in Parliament. His constituents triumphantly re-elected him, but on presenting himself to take his seat he was again expelled, and it was not until the Union of the Provinces that he again sat in Parliament. In 1854 he was defeated by his old constituency, and withdrew from public life. Mr. C. was a regular contributor to the *Gazette* (Que.) during Mr. Neilson's time ; latterly he lent the aid of his pen to the *Mercury*.

I. Memoirs of the Administration of the Colonial Government of Lower Canada, by Sir James Henry Craig and Sir George Prevost, from the year 1807 until the year 1815 ; comprehending the Military and Naval operations in the Canadas, during the late war with the United States of America : *Quebec*, 1818, pp. 150, and appendix 9, 8vo.

" These memoirs are very interesting, and, although intended to please the ruling power, impartially written."—LATERRIÈRE.

II. A Brief Review of the Political State of Lower Canada, since the Conquest of the Colony to the present day ; to which are added, Memoirs of the Administration of the Colonial Government of Lower Canada by Sir Gordon Drummond and Sir John Coape Sherbrooke : *New York*, 1818, 8vo.

III. Memoir of the Administration of the Government of Lower Canada by the Right Honorable the Earl of Dalhousie, G. C. B., comprehending a period of eight years, from June, 1820, till September, 1828 ; together with a Memoir of the Administration of the Honble. Sir Francis N. Burton, G. C. H. during a portion of the above period. *Quebec*, 1829, 8vo.

IV. A History of the late Province of Lower Canada, parliamentary and political, from the commencement to the close of its existence as a separate Province ; embracing a period of fifty years, that is to say : from the erection of the Province, in 1791, to the extinguishment thereof, in 1841, and its reunion with Upper Canada, by Act of the Imperial Parliament. *Do.*, vols. I and II, 1849; vol. III, 1850 ; vol. IV, 1853 ; vol. V, 1854 ; vol. VI, 1855.

Volume IV. bears the following title :— Interesting public documents and official correspondence, illustrative of, and supplementary to the History of Lower Canada. It is prefaced by a memoir of the public life of the Hon. H. W. Ryland, confidential Secy. to Lord Dorchester when Gov. in Chief of B. N. A., and includes copious extracts from Ryland's Correspondence and Papers, with other documents on the affairs of the Province from 1789 to 1833 ; the whole numbered from 1 to 158. No. 159, is a note by Jacques Viger, Esq. "Sur la prise du Village de St. Régis par les Américains durant la dernière guerre avec les Etats-Unis." Nos. 160 and 161, are correspondence concerning the Rebellion in L. C., and the conduct of MM. D. B. Viger, Wolfred Nelson, L. J. Papineau, &c.—New ed. of the complete work : *Montreal*, 1866, 6 vols., 8vo.

" The whole work shewing ability, industry, and favorable opportunities of obtaining information."—*Gazette*, (Que.)

" We regard with a particular sort of affection these volumes of an old freind of long ago, who although not one of the great men, was one of the features and distinctive characters, for many years, of the House of Assembly, before and after the Union. He had many troubles with it in the old times, and was more than once unjustly and harshly dealt with by the old House of Assembly of L. C., as he shews in these volumes. He was yet a simple and single minded man, with almost no guile, at times exhibiting that particular kind of courage which led him to butt his head against the stone wall of superior power. He dressed quaintly—in the style of a former generation ; and as in his dress, so in his manners, he never adapted himself to the times. He was a man of great industry as these volumes show. He was not the most polished of writers, nor was his style that which was 'most economical of his reader's time and attention.' But as a repertory of old and curious facts, which cannot elsewhere be so conveniently found, concerning the history of Lower Canada, up to the period of the Union, including the troubles which culminated in the rebellion, Mr. Christie's volumes are very valuable. He furnishes copies of old despatches, old speeches, old newspaper articles, &c., which had force in their day ; which are now very interesting to read ; and which are very valuable as *pieces* or *memoires pour sercir*."—*Gazette*, (Mont.)

CHRISTMAS, *Rev.* HENRY.
I. The Emigrant Churchman in Canada. By a Pioneer of the Wilderness. (Ed. by Mr. Christmas.) *London*, 1849, 2 vols. f. 8vo.

CHURCH, PHARCELLUS.
I. Mapleton, or more work for the Maine Law. *Montreal*, 1853.

CHURCH, THOMAS.
I. The History of the great Indian War of 1675 and 1676 ; also, the old French and Indian Wars, from 1689 to 1704 ; with notes by S. G. Drake. Revised Ed. *Hartford*, 1854, 8vo.

CHURCHILL, *Rev.* CHARLES, *A. M.* A Wesl. Missionary.
I. Memorials of [Wesleyan] Missionary life in Nova Scotia. *London*, 1845, pp. 206, 12mo.
II. India : its past history, present position and future prospects ; a lecture. *Halifax*, 1858, pp. 35, 8vo.

CLARK, THOMAS.
I. Sketches of the Naval History of the United States ; from the commencement of the Revolutionary War to the present time. To which is added a List of the British Vessels captured since the Declaration of War, June 18, 1812. *Philadelphia*, 1813, 12mo.

CLARKE, CHARLES. A Can. Journ. B. at Lincoln, Eng., Nov. 1826. Came to Can. in 1844. Ed. the *Journal and Express*, (Ham.), from 1848 to 1850. Subsequently contributed to the *North American*, writing the letters of " Reformator," and to the *Mirror*, *Examiner*, *Warder* (Dundas), and *Canadian* (Ham.) Was also Ed. of the *Backwoodsman* (Elora) for some time.

CLARKE, *Rev.* JAMES FREEMAN, *D. D.* A Unitarian clergym. at Boston, U. S.
I. History of the Campaign of 1812, and Surrender of the Post of Detroit. *New York*, 1848, 8vo.

CLARKE, JAMES PATON, *Mus. Bac.* A Graduate of King's Coll. (Tor.) Author of various musical compositions of acknowledged merit, some of which were published in the *Ang. Am. Mag.*, (Tor.)
I. Canadian Church Psalmody ; consisting of Psalm-tunes, chants, anthems, &c. *Toronto*, 1845, pp. 116.
II. Lays of the Maple Leaf. *Do.*
III. " Arise O Lord God," an anthem. *Do.* pp. 46.

CLARKE, *Rev.* W. B. A clergym. of the Can. Presb. Ch. Is min. of Chalmer's Ch. (Que.) Has contributed to *Waymarks in the Wilderness*, (Ham.), the *Canadian Presbyter*, *Good News* and the *Home and Foreign Record of the Can. Presb. Ch.* Is the author of various tracts and addresses, published in Scot. and Can.

I. Book of Family Worship, and Helps to Devotion.

This work was originally published in a small and cheap form, at Edinburgh, by T. Nelson & Sons, under the title of "The Cottage Prayer book." 2nd ed. *Edinburgh*, 1848. 3rd ed. *London*, 1863, pp. 270, 12mo.

II. Asleep in Jesus, or words of consolation to bereaved parents. 1st ed. *London*, 1852. 2nd ed. *Philadelphia*, 1853. 3rd ed. *London*, 1863, pp. 138.

III. The Promise of the Spirit; being eight discourses delivered at various times. *Prescott, U. C.*, 1863.

"Your tract on the Spirit is just what is needed, in these times of deadness on the one hand, and fanaticism on the other."— REV. W. TAYLOR, *D. D.*: *Letter to the Author.*

CLARKE, *Rev.* WILLIAM FLETCHER. A Can. journ. B. in Coventry, Eng., 31 March, 1824. Studied for the ministry in the Congregational Academy, (Tor.), and was ordained in Oct. 1844. Has been pastor of the Congregations at Burford, Norwich and London, U. C., and is now pastor at Guelph. In 1855-6, was chairman of the Congregational Union of Can. In 1859, went as Missionary to Brit. Columbia whence he returned in less than a year, and settled at Guelph. In 1854, Mr. C. founded the *Canadian Independent*, the organ of the Congregational body in Can., of which he was for 2 years ed. and prop. In 1863 was agricultural ed. of the *Witness*, (Mont.) For the past 2 years has ed. *The Sunday School Dial*, (Tor.), a small religious monthly for children. In 1865, on the establishment of *The Canada Farmer*, by Mr. Brown, Mr. C. was appointed its Ed. in Chief, a position which he continues to hold. For some years he has been Can. correspondent of the *Patriot*, (Lon.)

I. Two Sermons on Baptism.

II. "In Memoriam:" a sketch of the life of the late Rev. John Roaf.

III. The History of Non-conformity in England in 1662.

CLAUDET, M.

I. Handbook of British Columbia, and Emigrants' guide. *London*, 1862.

CLEMENTI, *Rev.* VINCENT, *A. B.*, (Cantab:) A min. of the Ch. of Eng. (Lakefield U. C.) Is eldest son of the late Muzio Clementi, the celebrated musical composer. Has been a contributor on subjects of local and general importance to the *Review* (Peterborough, U. C.), for many years. He has also contributed occasionally to the *Can. Journal* and the *Can. Naturalist.*

I. Lakefield Tracts. The Great Doxology; a sermon. *Peterborough, U. C.*, 1864.

II. Do. do. St. John the Divine; a sermon. *Do.* do.

CLEMO, EBENEZER. A Can. novelist. B. in London, Eng., about 1831. D. at Morristown, N. J., 1860. Came to Can. in 1858 and for a time was reduced to extreme poverty. His circumstances were somewhat improved by being engaged to write 2 works of fiction for a Can. publisher. He was the inventor of making paper pulp from straw, and at the time of his death was engaged in directing the erection of machinery on an extensive scale for carrying out his important invention. He is spoken of as being a man of considerable ability and much general information.

I. The Life and Adventures of Simon Seek; or Canada in all shapes. By Maple Knot. *Montreal*, 1858, pp. 179, 12mo.

"The author of Simon Seek evidently possesses in no mean degree, all the requisites of a successful and popular novelist; and we hail the advent of this work amongst us as an earnest of better things for our literature of Canada; for there can be no doubt, if the succeeding efforts of 'Maple Knot' sustain the promise of Simon Seek, we shall soon be able, at least, to boast a novelist, and a novelist of whom we may well be proud."— *Can. Merch. Mag.*

II. Canadian Homes; or the Mystery solved. A Canadian tale. *Do.* 1858, pp. 136, 12mo.

CLINCH, *Rev.* JOSEPH H., *A. M.* A clergym. of the Episcopal Ch., now Chaplain to the City Institution (Bos., U. S.) B. at Trinity, Newfoundland, Jan. 1806.— Was for some years engaged in commercial pursuits in his native colony, but in 1826 entered King's Coll. Windsor, N. S., to study divinity, and in 1829 was admitted to the Priesthood. Was Rector of St. Matthew's (Bos.) for 22 years.

I. The Captivity in Babylon and other poems. *Boston*, 1840, pp. 115, 8vo.

II. A Churchman's answer; a sermon preached at Digby. *Do.* 1812, pp. 24, 8vo.

III. Epistola Poetica ad Familiarem. *Olicana*, MDCCCLXIV, pp. 18, 8vo.

CLUNY, ALEXANDER.

I. The American Traveller; or Observations on the present state, culture, and commerce of the British Colonies in America, and the further improvements of which they are capable, with an account of the Exports, Imports and Returns of each Colony respectively, and of the numbers of British Ships and Seamen, Merchants, Traders and Manufacturers employed by all collectively: together with the amount of the Revenue arising to Great Britain therefrom. In a series of letters, written originally to the Right Hon. the Earl of * * * * * * * * by an old and experienced Trader (with map.) *London*, 1769; pp. 122, 4to. Translated into French : *Amsterdam*, 1783.

"The author was the first to give accurate intelligence of Hudson's Bay."—RICH.

COATS, *Captain* W.

I. The Geography of Hudson's Bay : being the remarks of Captain W. Coats, in many voyages to that locality, between 1727 and 1751. With extracts from the log of Capt. Middleton on his voyage for the discovery of the North-West passage in 1741-42. Edited by John Barrow. *London*, 1852. (Published by the Hakluyt Society.)

COBBETT, WILLIAM. An Eng. politician and writer. D. 1835.

I. Letters on the late war between the United States and Great Britain, with miscellaneous writings on the same subject. *New York*, 1815, 8vo.

COCHRAN, *Hon.* A. W., *D. C. L.*, *Q. C.* A Can. lawyer. B. at Windsor, N. S., 1792. D. at Quebec, 11 July, 1849. Held various prominent and honorable public positions in L. C. Contributed to the ed. columns of the *Mercury* (Que.)

I. Prize Essay on the Hyperboreans. *Trans. Lit. & His. Soc.* (Que.) 1837.

II. Inaugural address as President of Library Association. *Quebec*, 1844.

III. Notes on the measures adopted by Government, between 1775 and 1786, to check the St. Paul's Bay Disease. *Trans. Lit. & His. Soc.* (Que.) 1855.

COCHRAN, *Rev.* JAMES C., *A. M.* Bishop's Chaplain, N. S. Son of the following. Edited the *Church Times* (Hal.)

I. A Sermon in reference to the death of the Rt. Rev. John Inglis, D. D., Lord Bishop of Nova Scotia. Preached at Lunenburg. *Halifax*, 1850, pp. 13, 8vo.

II. A New Year's address to the congregation of the Bishop's Chapel. *Do.* 1863; pp. 15, 8vo.

COCHRAN, *Rev.* WILLIAM, *D. D.* For many years Vice-President and Prof. of Languages, Logic and Rhetoric in King's Coll., Windsor, N. S. B. in the North of Irel., about 1745. D. at Windsor, N. S., 4 Augt. 1833. Ed. at Trinity Coll. (Dub.) where he subsequently received the degree of D. D. In 1784 became Prof. of Languages in Columbia Coll. (N. Y.) where he remained until his removal to N. S., in 1787. At Columbia Coll. he had for pupils many youths who afterwards greatly distinguished themselves, such as Governor DeWitt Clinton, John Randolph. Drs. Hossack and Jones, Chancellor Jones, &c. After his death his son prepared and advertised an account of his life, but the book so far has not appeared.

I. Fast sermon, preached in the church at Falmouth, N. S. *Halifax*, 1795; 8vo.

II. Journal of the Thermometer, Hygrometer, Barometer, Winds and Rain, kept at Windsor, N. S. *Trans. Irish Acad.* IX, 133.

COCKBURN, *Lt.-Col.*, *R. A.*

I. Picturesque guide to Quebec and its environs. *Quebec*, 1831, pp. 42.

COCKINGS, GEORGE.

I. War ; an heroic poem. From the taking of Minorca, by the French, to the raising the seige of Quebec, by General Murray. *London*, 1760, 8vo.

II. The Conquest of Canada, or the Seige of Quebec ; a tragedy. *Do.*, 1766, 8vo.

"We know nothing of this writer in connection with America except that he wrote a portion of his poem on War in Newfoundland, in the winter of 1758; that the second edition of his performance was published at Portsmouth, 'in Piscataqua, or New Hampshire Colony, in America, in 1761,' the first having appeared in London in 1760, and the third 'in Massachusetts Colony, in 1762'"— DUYCKINCK.

CODERRE, J. EMERY, *M. D.*

I. Examen Médico-légal des procès d'Anaïs Toussaint, de Joseph Bérubé et de Césarée Thériault, et précis de procédures à suivre dans les cas d'empoisonnement par l'arsenic et le phosphore. *Montreal.*

COFFIN, *Lieut.-Col.* WILLIAM F. Formerly Sheriff of the District of Montreal, now and for some years past Ordnance Land Agent in Can.

I. 1812 ; the war and its moral : a Canadian Chronicle, vol. I. *Montreal*, 1864, pp. 296, 8vo. (*Vol. II in preparation.*)

"The descendant of U. E. loyalist and connected by various ties of intermarriage with other men who left their homes and property and home ties for the sake of the old flag—the son of one who served under that flag here and elsewhere—and a gallant and enthusiastic volunteer officer himself, one of the first, if not the very first to don the uniform when the force was organized in Canada, Col. Coffin had many reasons urging him to undertake this book. *

The fame of the men who fought our battles in 1812-15, has been too much neglected among us. The story of the war has always been told either too much from an English, or regular service point of view, or from that of our then American foes. Like an old Mortality in modern soldierly and cavalier guise, Col. Coffin has been digging out the moss which hid the inscriptions on the tomb-stones of the men of 1812, here and there adding a new tablet to honor the name of a hero altogether unheeded and forgotten, here and there freshening up the inscription on the monuments already set up in the grave yards of our memory. Interspersed with the narrative of the war are fragments of the family annals of the U. E. Loyalists, and of the French Canadian noblesse engaged in the conflict, lending an additional and personal interest to the story. Of the American troops and officers, Col. Coffin speaks at once with the chivalry of a soldier, and the honesty of a historian. The present volume brings his chronicle down from the beginning of the war to the latter part of 1813, including the disaster of Moravian town in the West, and the Chateauguay victory in the East. He had traced the war from the capture of Mi-

chilmackinac by Roberts, and the skirmish of Tarontee, where Mr. Cass earned his renown—has told the story of the surrender of Detroit, of the battles of Queenstown Heights, Frenchtown, Fort Erie, Ogdensburg, York, Fort George and Newark, Beaver Dam, Sackett's Harbor, Stoney Creek, Thorold, Fort Schlosser, Black Rock, Isle aux Noix, Champlain, Fort Meigs, Fort Stevenson, the Thames or Moravian town, and Chateauguay, together with the naval engagements on the sea and lakes. As he pauses, our fortunes in the far west seemed disastrous ; this victory in the East gave new zeal and heart to Canadian resistance. Mr. Coffin's personal sketches lend life and animation to the story, but the fault of the book is, nevertheless, these too florid. and too elaborately worked up biographical episodes, leading us away from the current of the narrative. And yet there are very few of them we should care to spare from the volume.—*Gazette*, (Mont.)

" Ce premier volume se termine à la bataille de Chateauguay, si courageusement gagnée par les Canadiens le 26 Octobre, 1813, et dont nous sommes si fiers. C'était alors au milieu de la guerre.

Ce premier volume nous fait vivement désirer la publication du second, qui sera le dernier, croyons nous. C'est une œuvre importante, et qui sera lue avec intérêt et avec plaisir.

L'auteur a puisé dans beaucoup de documents encore inédits et dans la conversation de quelques acteurs dans ce beau drame, une foule de détails précieux qui mettent encore plus en relief les caractères divers de tous ceux qui ont figuré dans cette guerre. Ces détails donnent à l'histoire l'attrait d'un roman. Les noms de Brock, de Salaberry, de Duchesnay, de Sheaffe, de McDonell, de Rolette, de Tecumseh, et d'une foule d'autres, ce présentent tour-à-tour aux lecteurs, noms célèbres, et qui seront répétés avec admiration et avec orgueil tant que vivra la race Canadienne. Cette admiration s'accroît encore lorsqu'on peut, comme dans le livre de M. Coffin, suivre jour par jour et pas à pas, chacune de leurs actions, dans cette lutte difficile qui a fait leur gloire et notre salut."—J. A. N. PROVENCHER : *Rer. Can.*

COGSWELL, CHARLES, *M. D., A. B., F. L. S.* B. in N. S. Is a Graduate of King's Coll. Windsor, and a *L. R. C. S.* (Edin.) Practises his profession in London, Eng.

I. Medical Statistics of Nova Scotia. *Boston Med. Almanac,* 1840.

II. On the Ætiology of sea-sickness. *Lancet* (Lon.) 1845.

III. On the history of Chloroform as

an anæsthetic agent. *Med. Gazette* (Do.) 1847.

IV. On the propagation of Cholera by contagion. *Do.* 1849.

V. On the eudosmotic action of Medicines. *Lancet*, 1852.

VI. On the influence of hydrocyanic acid on the larynx and tractea. *Do. do.*

VII. On the local action of Poisons. *Do. do.*

VIII. On the active properties of Hemlock. *Ass. Med. Journal* (Lon.) 1853.

IX. On the kind of Education best suited for Nova Scotia. *Trans. N. S. Lit. & Scien. Soc.* 1859.

X. On Nova Scotia in its sanitary aspect as a military and naval station. *Lancet*, 1862.

COGSWELL, *Hon.* HENRY H.

I. Views relative to the construction of a railway from Halifax to Quebec by the British Government; as the most efficient and economical means of promoting the prosperity of the British North American Colonies; and securing their continued connection with the Imperial Government and their establishment in a Federal Union. *Halifax*, 1852; pp. 6, 8vo.

COGSWELL, *Rev.* WILLIAM, *A. M.* A clergym. of the ch. of Eng. in N. S. Son of the preceding. B. in N. S. 1810. D. 5 June, 1847. Ed. at King's Coll., Windsor, and was for 14 years curate of St. Paul's, (Hal.) He possessed great eloquence as a pulpit orator.

I. We shew the Lords death till He come; a sermon. *Halifax*, reprinted 1836; pp. 15, 8vo.

II. Seven lectures on the Acts of the Apostles, delivered in St. Paul's church, Halifax. *Do.* 1839; pp. 174, 8vo.

III. Sermons at Halifax, Nova Scotia. *London*, Vol. I., 1839; pp. 497, 8vo.

IV. A Sermon preached before the Nova Scotia Philanthropic Society, on the occasion of their celebrating the nuptials of Her Most Gracious Majesty Queen Victoria with His Royal Highness Prince Albert. *Halifax*, 1840; pp. 15, 8vo.

"An immense concourse is said to have thronged the church during the delivery of the sermon, which was listened to with pride

and delight. Its fervent piety, its ardent patriotism, its sentiments of loyalty, its glowing eloquence, its rich mellifluent language, and beautiful figures, are stated by a Halifax contemporary to be such as to render this effusion of poetic prose one of the most delightful productions that have been issued from the Provincial press."—*Gazette* (Mont.)

V. Four Sermons preached in the Parish Church of St. Paul, during the season of Advent, A. D., 1840. *Do.* 1841.

VI. Sermons at Halifax, Nova Scotia. *London*, 1847; pp. 505, 8vo.

COKE, *Lieut.* E. T.

I. A Subaltern's Furlough; descriptive Scenes in various parts of the United States, Upper and Lower Canada, New Brunswick, and Nova Scotia, during the summer and autumn of 1832. *New-York*, 1834; 2 vols, 12mo.

COLBY, M. F., *A. M., M. D.* (Stanstead, L. C.)

I. An abstract of the new physiological and pathological views, as set forth in a work intituled : New views of the functions of the digestive tube &c., (now preparing for press.) *Stanstead*, 1860.

COLLINS, FRANCIS. A Can. journ. B. in Irel., 1801. D. at Toronto 4 Sept. 1834. Ed. the *Canadian Freeman* (York), an opposition paper. Was tried for libel by the govt. of U. C. in 1828, and sentenced to fine and imprisonment. He was possessed of considerable ability. Charles Lindsey gives the following account of him :

"Being disappointed in the attempt to dispose of his services to the government, he sometime afterwards commenced the publication of an opposition paper, a very slight acquaintance with which will convince any one that in spite of his natural ability he sometimes mistook coarseness for strength of language. He was an excellent reporter, and several years acted officially in that capacity, as the servant of the House. It was not his habit to write his articles. He put them in type as he composed them."

I. An abridged view of the Alien Question unmasked. By the Editor of the *Canadian Freeman. York, U. C.*, 1826; pp. 16.

COOK, *Capt.* JAMES. The celebrated circumnavigator. B. 1728. Killed in a skirmish with the natives of the Sandwich Islands, 1779.

I. Directions for Navigating on part

of the south coast of Newfoundland. *London*, 1766, 4to.

II. Observation of an Eclipse of the Sun at Newfoundland. *Phil. Trans.*, 1767.

Cook, *Rev.* John, *D. D.* Min. of St. Andrew's Presb. Ch. (Que.) Principal of Morrin Coll. in that city.

I. Early Moral and Religious Education; a lecture. *Quebec*, 1849, pp. 29.

Cook, John Wilson. Advocate, (Que.) Son of the preceding.

I. On the History of Canada. *Trans. Lit. & His. Soc. (Que.)* 1866.

Cooney, *Rev.* Robert, *D. D.* A Wes. Meth. Min. (St. Catharines, U. C.) B. in Ireland about 1800. Is a convert from the Ch. of Rome. Has written extensively for the religious and secular press of Can. and the Maritime Provinces, in all of which Provinces he has been stationed in the exercise of his ministry.

Lectures.

I. The Benefits to be derivable from a judicious course of reading.

II. Science in connection with the Bible.

III. Her Majesty, Queen Victoria.

IV. The Rise and Progress of Great Britain.

Sermons.

V. On lay Preaching.

VI. The Glory of the God of Israel displayed. *Halifax*, 1836, pp. 34, 8vo.

VII. The Judgment Seat of Christ. *Do.* 1838, pp. 23, 8vo.

VIII. The authenticity of the Sacred Scriptures.

IX. The Lord is on our side, delivered in the Wesleyan Chapel, Odelltown, Nov. 9, 1839 ; being the first Anniversary of the Battle fought at the above place, between the Insurgents and the Loyal Volunteers. *Montreal*, 1840.

" This pious, loyal and patriotic discourse is dedicated to, and published at the request of Lieut. Col. Taylor, C. B., and the Officers, non-commissioned Officers and privates of the LaCole, Odelltown and Hemmingford, Volunteer Corps, who so gloriously and triumphantly defended their hearths and

Constitution, on the 9th of November, 1838, against a combined attack of marauders from the United States, and native insurgents who are well described by Mr. Cooney, as one of the most ungrateful race of men that ever lived."—*Gazette*, (Mont·)

X. A Compendium History of New Brunswick and of the District of Gaspé. *Halifax*, 1832, pp. 287, 8vo. 2nd Ed.

XI. The Autobiography of a Wesleyan Methodist Missionary. *Montreal*, 1856, pp. 406, 8vo.

Cooper, Charles W. A Toronto Barrister. B. in Eng. In 1842 founded the Literary and Historical Soc., (Tor.) Has long been a frequent contributor to the newspaper and periodical press of Can. on miscellaneous subjects. Was Sec. in 1849 of the Central Committee of the " British American League," and wrote what are known as the "League Articles" in the *Patriot*, (Tor.,) and other newspapers. Contributed to the *Maple Leaf* Mag. during its existence. Is legal ed. and reporter to the *Globe*, (Tor.)

I. Remarks on the proposed abolition of the Court of Chancery. *Kingston*, 1851, pp. 19.

"The writer has treated the subject in an upright, honorable and candid manner."—*Sun*, (*Picton.*)

II. A Prize Essay on the Features and Resources of the United Counties of Frontenac, Lennox and Addington. *Do.*, 1856, pp. 105, 8 vo.

Several public spirited inhabitants of the counties above named having offered a prize of £100 for the best essay on the above subject, Mr. C. was declared the successful competitor, and in addition to the prize awarded, received a vote of thanks from the corporation of Kingston, together with a present of £25.

III. Canadian Tales from a Canadian Pen : Frank Woods, or Twice Married. *Toronto Colonist*, 1859.

IV. Equity Digest. *Toronto*, 1866.

Cooper, *Rev.* H. C., *B. A.* Rector of Etobicoke. Ed. the *Echo*, (Tor.,) for two years previous to 1861.

I. Sermon on the Husbandman's dependence upon Almighty God, preached in St. George's Church, Etobicoke, Oct. 23, 1853, pp. 11.

COOPER, ROBERT. A Can. journalist. Brother of the two preceding. B. in Eng. D. at Goderich, U. C., June 19, 1866. Ed. at the Charter House School, (Lon.), came to Can. early in life, and adopted the law as a profession. In 1846 ed. the *British Canadian*, (Tor..) a leading conservative paper, evincing decided marks of ability as a writer. Subsequently was ed. of the *Herald*, (Lon., U. C.) He also contributed to the *Maple Leaf* and the *Anglo American Mag.* of the former city. One of his earlier successes was the obtaining of the gold medal of the Prov. Ag. Ass. for the best essay on agriculture. In 1856, he was appointed County Judge of the United Counties of Huron and Bruce.

I. Rules and Practice of the Court of Chancery of Upper Canada. *Toronto,* 1851, 8vo.

II. The Farming Interest, and the influence of agricultural societies; an essay. *A. Am. Mag.,* 1852.

COPLESTON, *Mrs. EDWARD.*

I. Canada : Why we live in it, and why we like it. *London,* 1861, pp. 121.

CORDNER, *Rev.* JOHN. A well known Unitarian Clergyman ; pastor of the Ch. of the Messiah, (Mont.) B. in Ireland. Ed. the *Bible Christian* from 1844 to 1849, and the *Liberal Christian* from 1854 to 1858, both being monthly periodicals published at Mont. Has written extensively for the newspaper and periodical press of Can. and the U. S.

' I. Jesus : a Christmas sermon preached at Montreal. *Montreal,* 1851, pp. 14, 8vo.

II. Christ the Son of God. A discourse in review of the Rev. Dr. Wilkes' sermon, intituled, "Who is Christ?" *Do.* 1851, pp. 28, 8vo.

III. The Philosophic origin and Historic progress of the doctrine of the Trinity ; a lecture delivered at Montreal. *Do.,* 1851, pp. 22, 8vo.

IV. The Foundations of Nationality; a discourse preached at Montreal. *Do.* 1856, pp. 28, 8vo.

V. The Vision of the Pilgrim Fathers; an oration spoken before the new England Society of Montreal. *Do.* 1857, pp. 54, 8vo.

VI. The Christian idea of Sacrifice ; a discourse preached at the dedication of the Church of the Messiah, Mont. *Do.* 1838, pp. 29, 8vo.

VII. Righteousness exalteth a Nation ; a discourse concerning the relation of morality to national well-being, preached at Montreal. *Do.* 1860, pp. 19, 8vo.

VIII. The American Conflict : an address spoken before the New England Society of Montreal. *Do.,* 1865, pp. 48, 8vo.

"This is a discourse which might well have the two nations—with all their sections and parties for audience—not an oration or a poem, but the right word, spoken in the right spirit, in the right time and place."— *Daily News,* (Lon.)

CORMACK, W. E.,

I. A Journey across the Island of Newfoundland, the only one ever performed by a European. *St. Johns',* 1856.

CORNWALLIS, K. An Am. author and journ. B. in Eng.

I. New Eldorado ; or, British Columbia. *London,* 1858, post 8vo.

II. Panorama of the New World. *Do.* 1859, 2 vol. post, 8vo.

III. Royalty in the New World ; or the Prince of Wales in America. *New York,* 1861, c. 8vo.

CÔTÉ, *Rev.* C. H. O., *M. D.*

I. Un mot en passant à ceux qui ont abandonné l'église romaine et ses traditions. 1848.

Memoirs of the Rev. C. H. O. Côté, M. D., with a memoir of Mrs. M. P. Côté, and a History of the Grand Ligne Mission. C. E. By the Rev. N. Cyr, *Philadelphia,* 1853, *pp.* 144, 18mo.

CÔTÉ, J. O., *N. P.* A Clk. in the Privy Council Office, Can.

I. Political Appointments and Elections in the Province of Canada. 1841 to 1860. *Quebec,* 1860, pp. 81. r. 8vo.; New ed. *Ottawa,* 1866, pp. 130, r. 8vo.

COTTLE, T. J., *F. R. C. S., (Eng.)*

I. Coccothraustes Vespertina—Evening Grosbeak. *Can. Journ.,* 1855.

II. The Mastodon Giganteus. *Do.*

III. Grus Americana and Grus Canadensis : are they the same bird in different stages of growth ? *Do.,* 1859.

IV. Capture of two birds of unusual occurrence, in Upper Canada. *Do. do.*

V. List of birds found in Upper Canada. *Can. Nat. Do.*

VI. On the two species of Astacus found in Upper Canada. *Can. Journ.*, 1863.

COUES, ELLIOTT.

I. Notes on the Ornithology of Labrador. *Proc. Aca. N. S.* (Phil.) 1861.

COUGHLAN, Rev. L.

I. An account of the work of God in Newfoundland, North America. In a series of letters. To which are prefixed, a few choice experiences, some of which were taken from the lips of persons who died triumphantly in the faith. *London*, 1776, pp. 192, 12mo.

COULOMBE, Sister ADÈLE.

Vie d'Adèle Coulombe, religieuse hospitalière de l'Hôtel-Dieu de Montréal, en Canada. *Tours, France*, 1863, pp. 267, 12mo.

COUPÉ DE SAINT DONAT, ALEXANDRE.

I. Histoire de l'Etablissement des Français dans l'Amérique du Nord. *Paris*, 1823, in-8.

COUPER, WILLIAM. A Can. Entomologist. Has studied the insects of Canada since 1844. In 1856, he took a prize at Toronto, for the best methodically arranged collection of insects. Since that time his leisure has been devoted in the investigation of the Geographical distribution of Coleoptera of the temperate regions of North America. He compiled lists of this order of insects, collected by himself at Toronto, which were published in the *Canadian Journal*; contributed several miscellaneous articles on Entomology to the *Canadian Naturalist*. In a late number of the *Naturalist* he describes eleven new species of Coleoptera, and also a new moth of the genius ALYPIA (*Alypia Langtonii* COUPER). In the late *Transactions* of the Lit. & His. Soc. (Que.), Mr. C. published lists of Coleoptera and Diptera taken at Quebec and other parts of Lower Canada. He was one of the earliest promoters of this branch of Natural Science in Canada, one of the founders of the Quebec Branch of the Entomological Soc. of Canada, and for some years Assistant Secy. of the former body.

6

COVENTRY, GEORGE. B. near London, Eng. Is the author of "*Enquiry into the Letters of Junius, shewing that Lord George Sackville was the author*, London, 1825"; "*An Essay on Tythes, shewing they are contrary to the Christian Dispensation*, Do., 1830."; and various contributions to the periodical and newspaper press, written and published prior to his emigration to Can. Has written many essays on political, financial, agricultural and horticultural subjects, and poetical pieces for the Can. press. He is best known as the collator and compiler of historical manuscripts and documents, for the Library of Parliament, Can. Mr. C. resides at Cobourg, U. C.

COWDELL, THOMAS D.

I. A Poetical Journal of a Tour from British North America to England, Wales and Ireland, interspersed with Reflections Natural, Moral and Political. To which are subjoined Two Pieces of the Intended Jubilee. *Dublin*, 1809, pp. 76, 12mo.

II. A Poetical Account of the American Campaigns of 1812 and 1813. *Halifax*, 1815, pp. 139, 8vo.

COX, Rev. F. A., D. D., LL. D. and *Rev.* J. HOBEY, *B. D.*

I. The Baptists in America; a narrative of the deputation from the Baptist Union in England, to the United States and Canada. *London*, 1836, 12mo. Reprinted same year at *New York*, pp. 476.

COX, ROSS.

I. Adventures on the Columbia River, including the Narrative of a Residence of six years on the western side of the Rocky Mountains, among various Tribes of Indians hitherto unknown, together with a journey across the American Continent. *London*, 1831, 2 vols. 8vo; *New York*, 1832, pp. 335.

"Mr. Cox is well known in this Province to many of those gentlemen whose names are mentioned in his pages, and he appears by education to have been well fitted to describe the scenes he visited, and the dangers he passed through."—*Gazette*, (Mont).

COXE, RICHARD S.

I. Extent and Value of the Possessory Rights of the Hudson's Bay Company in Oregon, South of Forty-Ninth Degree. *Montreal*, 1849, pp. 51, 8vo.

'Cozzens, Frederic S.

I. Acadia ; or, a month with the Blue Noses. *New York*, 1859, pp. 329, 12mo

Craig, Daniel H. " Telegraph Agent, N. Y. Associated Press."

I. A Review of " An exposition of the differences existing between different presses and different lines of telegraph respecting the transmission of foreign news." *Halifax*, 1850, pp. 29, 8vo.

Craigie, William, M. D. A Can. Medical practitioner. B. in Aberdeendshire, 1790. D. at Hamilton, U. C., 1863. Studied for medical profession at Marischal Coll. Aberdeen, and at the Universities of Edinburgh and Dublin. Contributed Monthly Meteorological reports to *Spectator* (Ham.) for a number of years, and also reports on same subject to the *Smithsonean Miscellaneous Collections*.

I. Mean Results for each Month for eleven years, (1835 to 1845 inclusive), of a Register of the Thermometer and Barometer, kept at Ancaster, C. W. *B. A. Journ.*, 1846.

II. List of Indigenous plants found in the neighbourhood of Hamilton, with the dates of their being found in Flower and examined. *Can. Journ.* 1854.

III. Mean Results of the Meteorological observations at Hamilton. *Do.* 1857-8-9-60-61.

Cramp, *Rev.* John Mockett, *D. D.* A Baptist clergym. B. at St. Peter's, Isle of Thanet, Eng., 25 July, 1791. After usual sch. education entered Stepney Coll. (Lon.), where he studied for the Baptist Ministry. Pastor of the Baptist Ch., Dean street, Southwark, 1818 ; at St. Peter's, with his father, also a min. of the same denomination, from 1827 to 1842 ; Pastor of the Baptist Ch., Hastings, Sussex, 1842 ; President of the Baptist Coll. (Mont.) from 1844 to 1849 ; has been President of Acadia Coll., N. S., since June 1851. Ed. the *Register*, (Mont.), a weekly religious journal, from 1844 to 1849, when it ceased publication ; ed. the *Colonial Protestant*, a monthly mag., in conjunction with Rev. W. Taylor, D. D., from 1848 to 1849, when it was also discontinued. Was general ed. of the *Pilot*

(Mont.) newspaper from 1849 until he removed to N. S. Dr. C. has also contributed to a large extent to various other religious and secular journals. He has recently published a history of the Baptists of N. S. in the *Christian Messenger* (Hal.) He is undoubtedly the most learned man of that body in the Lower Provinces.

Sermons.

I. Bartholomew day commemorated.

II. Funeral Sermon for George III.

III.   Do.   do.   IV.

IV.   Do.   William IV.

V. On the Signs of the Times.

VI. The Inspiration of the Scriptures.

VII. The Scripture doctrine of the Person of Christ. (Two Sermons.)

VIII. On Weekly Communion in the Lord's Supper.

Works.

IX. A Text-Book of Popery, comprising a brief history of the Council of Trent, its Doctrinal Decrees and Catechism. *Dublin*, 1831, 12mo. ; enlarged, *London*, 1839, 8vo. ; 3rd. Ed., *Do.* 1851, 12mo., pp. 568. Am. Ed., *New York*, 1831, 8vo.

" A complete exposure of the imposture of the Papal religion by authorities the most unexceptionable, the most decisive, the most condemning."—Mendham : *Memorials of the Council of Trent. It is a library in itself.—* Bishop Copleston.

X. The Reformation in Europe. *Do.* 1844, pp. 388, 18mo.

XI. Lectures for the Times. *Do.* 1844, pp. 308, 12mo.

XII. The Inaugural Address and Introductory Lecture to the Theological course. *Halifax*, 1851, pp. 52, 8vo.

XIII. Scripture and Tradition. *Do.* pp. 94, 18mo.

XIV. A Portraiture from Life. By a Bereaved Husband. *Do.* 1862, pp. 18, 8vo.

XV. The Great Ejectment of 1862 ; a lecture. *Do.* 1862, pp. 40, 8vo.

XVI. A Catechism of Christian Baptism. *Do.* 1865, pp. 90, 18mo.

Crantz, David.

I. The History of Greenland, including an account of the Mission carried on by the United Brethren in that country, from the German of David Crantz, with a continuation to the present time, illustrative notes, and an appendix, containing a sketch of the Mission of the Brethren in Labrador. *London*, 1820, 2 vols. 8vo.

"First published in German in 1765 and in English in 1767."—Rich.

CRAWFORD, *Rev.* ALEX.

I. Believer in Immersion as opposed to Unbeliever Sprinkling, in two Essays. *Charlottetown*, 1827, pp. 135, 8vo.

CRAWFORD, W. N.

I. Views on the subject of systematic British Pauper Immigration to Canada. Represented to the Parliament and People of Great Britain, and her Canadian Colony. *Montreal*, 1840, pp. 28.

CRAWLEY, *Rev.* EDMUND A., *A. M.* A prof. in Acadia Coll., N. S., of which he was one of the founders. In 1839 contributed to the *Free Press* (Halifax) a series of letters on Education, shewing especially the value of a rural situation for higher education and the necessity of the principle of assessment for common schools. ·

"Although compelled to differ from the able Professor in some of his sectarian views, the earnest zeal these letters exhibit in favour of a general and practical system of education, founded on assessment, and the blending of religious and secular institutions—the two pillars on which an effective and useful system can alone be reared,—entitled him to respect, and I gladly avail myself here, as I intend to do in subsequent times, of some of his illustrations."—G. R. YOUNG : *Col. Literature, &c.*

I. A Treatise on Baptism containing a reply to Mr. Elder's Letters on Infant Baptism. *Halifax*, 1835, pp. 197, 8vo.

CREMAZIE, JACQUES, *LL. D.* Has been for some years Recorder of the City of Quebec, and Dean of the Faculty of Law, Laval Univ. same city.

I. Les lois criminelles Anglaises, traduites et compilées de Blackstone, Chitty, Russell, et autres criminalistes; arrangées suivant les dispositions introduites dans le code criminel de cette Province par les statuts provinciaux 4 et 5 Vic. c. 24, 25, 26 et 27, comprenant aussi un précis des statuts penaux de

6 *

la ci-devant Province du Canada. *Québec*, 1842, 8vo.

II. Manuel de Notions utiles sur les droits politiques, le droit civil, la loi criminelle et municipale, les lois rurales, etc. *Do.* 1852, 12mo. ,

III. Notions élémentaires de cosmographie et de météorologie accompagnées de leçons sur l'usage des globes. *Do.* 1857, pp. 71.

CREMAZIE, JOSEPH OCTAVE. A French Can. poet.

I. Promenade de Trois Morts, poésie. *Soir. Can.* 1862.

"Il est difficile d'assigner un rang à chacun de nos poëtes. Comment cependant refuser la première place à celui, dont il n'est plus permis de prononcer le nom, et qui, dans sa pièce des *Morts* et dans la première partie de la *Promenade des trois morts*, a donné d'éclatants témoignages d'un talent si supérieur?"—HECTOR FABRE : *Can. Lit.*

CREVIER, J. A., *M. D.* A medical practitioner (St. Césaire L. C.)

I. Etudes sur le Cholera Asiatique. *Montréal*, 1866, pp. 16.

CRISP, *Rev.* THOMAS, *A. B.* Ch. of Eng. Min. at St. George's (Hal.) Dead.

I. Is Peter or Christ the Rock ? a sermon. *Halifax*, 1859, pp. 16, 8vo.

II. The men of the age; a lecture. *Do.* 1859, pp. 25, 8vo.

CROFT, HENRY, *D. C. L., F. C. S.* Prof. of Chemistry and Experimental Philosophy Univ. Coll. (Tor.) Completed his scientific education at the Univ. of Berlin.

I. Course of Practical Chemistry, as adopted at University College, Toronto. *Toronto.* 1860.

"Although various treatises on Chemical Analysis exist, many of these are too extensive for general use, and others are not readily procurable in this country ; and thus, Professor Croft's very excellent manual will supply the Canadian student with a long felt want."—*Can. Journ.*

"In Forensic Chemistry he is without an equal in the Province."—HON. DR. CHAUVEAU.

Canadian Journal.

I. Gas Patents. 1852.

II. The Mineral Springs of Canada. 1853.

III. On some new Salts of cadmium

and the iodides of barium and strontium. 1856.

IV. On the Hydrate of Hydrosulphuric acid. *Do.*

V. Report on Copper Implements found near Brockville. *Do.*

VI. Note on the Oxalate of Manganese. 1857.

VII. On the Action of air on Alkalic arsenites. 1858.

VIII. Note on the Oxalate of Iron. 1861.

IX· Thallium. 18 ۱.

X. Chemical Notes. 1865.

CROFTON, WALTER CAVENDISH. A Clk. in the Court of Chancery, U. C. Was formerly in the Can. Civil Service.

I. Brief sketch of the life of Charles Baron Metcalfe to the period of his resigning the office of Governor General of the British North American Colonies in 1845. By Uncle Ben. *Kingston*, 1846, pp. 37.

II. Sketches of the Thirteenth Parliament of Upper Canada. By Erienensis. *Toronto*, 1840, pp. 32. 12mo.

" After favouring us with one or two slight notices of the first Parliaments of *Upper Canada*, and of the more recent ones, we are presented with a list of the Members of the present House of Assembly, of their personal appearance and peculiarities, political opinions, and general public character—the latter at times diverging, and very improperly, in our opinion—into sketches of private life. The production, therefore, ought to have been called "*Random Sketches of the House of Assembly of Upper Canada*," in humble imitation of those of the House of Commons, published not long since in *England*."—*Gazette*, (Mont.)

CROIL, JAMES. A Can. author, residing at Archerfield, Morrisburgh, U. C. B. at Glasgow, Scot.

I. Practical Agriculture ; a lecture, 1858.

II. An Essay on the County of Dundas ; 1859.

This received the first prize from the Board of Agriculture, U. C.

III. Our Country, Past and Present ; a lecture delivered at the time of the "Trent difficulty." 1862.

IV. Modern improvements in Agriculture ; an address delivered before

the South Grenville Agricultural Society, 1863. *Can. Agriculturist.*

V. Dundas, or a sketch of Canadian History. *Montreal*, 1861, pp. 351, 8vo.

"A capital book of its class • • • creditable at once to the author and to the press of Montreal."—*Herald* (Glas.)

"His very comprehensive sketch of Canadian history—for he commences with the discovery of the American Continent by Columbus and concludes with the Prince of Wales' visit of last year—is alike creditable to his powers of research and of discrimination, in selecting the more important and salient events of so extended a period for his narrative ; while his equally comprehensive remarks upon the physical peculiarities of our country—its climate, soil, geological structure and natural history—are replete with knowledge both useful and entertaining to the Canadian reader. Mr. Croil's work is a welcome and valuable contribution to our Anglo-Canadian literature."—*Herald* (Mont.)

CROSKILL, JOHN H. A N. S. journ. B. 1810. D. 1855. Was originally a carpenter by trade. In 1840 established the *Morning Post* (Hal.) which, in 1845. he issued as a daily journal, it being the first daily newspaper ever published in N. S. From the latter year until 1848 he was Queen's Printer. In 1851 he established another paper called the *British North American*, which had but a brief existence.

I. A Comprehensive Outline of the Geography and History of Nova Scotia. *Halifax*, 1838, pp. 76, 12mo.

CUGNET, FRANÇOIS JOSEPH. An eminent Can. Jurisconsult. Was Counsellor to the Superior Council under the French Govt. in Can., an office which he retained up to the capitulation of Montreal in 1760. In the same year Genl. Murray appointed him "*Procureur-Général et Commissaire de la Cour et Conseil de guerre dans toute l'entendue de la côte du Nord de son gouvernement comme homme de bonnes mœurs et capacité en fait de loi.*" He lost this office in 1763, on the establishment of Eng. Law in the Province. Shortly afterward he was compensated with another office in connection with the Leg. Council ; and Sir Guy Carleton appointed him principal ed. in preparing "*An abstract of the Royal Edicts and Declarations, &c., in force in the Province of Quebec during the time of the French Government*, which was favorably noticed by the chief law officers of the crown in Eng. D. Sept., 1789.

I. An abstract of the several Royal Edicts and Declarations, and Provincial Regulations and Ordinances in force in the Province of Quebec in the time of the French Government; and of the Commissions of the several Governors-General and Intendants of the said Province during the same period, faithfully collected from the Registers of the Superior Council of Quebec, by Francis Joseph Cugnet, Esquire, Secretary to the Governor and Council of the said Province for the French language. *London*, Folio, 1772.

II. Réponse aux observations faites par M. Frs. Jos. Cugnet, sur le plan d'acte de parlement dressé par M. Frs. Masères. *Londres*, 1773, fol.

III. Traité de la Loi des Fiefs ; qui a toujours été suivie en Canada depuis son établissement, tirée de celle contenue en la *Coutume de Prevôté et Vicomté de Paris*, à laquelle les Fiefs et Seigneuries de cette Province sont assujettis, en vertu de leurs titres primitifs de concession, et des Edits, Règlements, Ordonnances et Declarations de Sa Majesté très-Chrétienne, rendus en conséquence ; et des différents jugements d'Intendants rendus à cet égard, en vertu de la Loi des Fiefs, et des dits Edits, Règlements, Ordonnances et Declarations. *Quebec*, 1775, pp. xiv—183, sm. 4to.

IV. Extraits des Regitres du Conseil Supérieur, et des Regitres d'Intendance, concernant la Justice, et des Reglements de Police. *Do.* 1775, pp. 106, 4to.

V. Traité de la Police qui a toujours été suivi en Canada, aujourd'hui Province de Québec, depuis son établissement jusqu'à la Conquête, &c. *Do.*, 1775, pp. 188, sm. 4to.

CUMMINS, E. H.

I. History of the late war between the United States and Great Britain, with a critical appendix, &c. *Baltimore*, 1820, 8vo.

CUMMINS, JOHN S. A Can. journalist and novelist. Ed. the *Chronicle & News*, (King..) for some years. D. some years. Had been an officer in the British Mer-

chant service. Served in the Can. Militia during the Rebellion of 1837. Contributed to *Barker's Magazine*, (King.)

I. Altham, a tale of the Sea. *Lon.* 1848, 2 vols., post 8vo.

CUNNINGHAM, JOHN P.

I. Remarks on the Mineralogical character of the Seigneury of Rigaud, Vaudreuil, District of Quebec. Dedicated to the proprietors, Charles and Alexander DeLery, Esquires. *Montreal*, 1847.

CUOQ, *Rev.* A. A French Can. Philologist. Is a priest of the R. C. Ch. Formally labored as a missionary among the Indian tribes of N. A. Is now attached to the Seminary of St. Sulpice, (Mont.)

I. Jugement erroné de M. Ernest Renan sur les Langues Sauvages. Par N. O. *Montreal*, 1864, pp. 23, in-8.

"Tel qu'il est, ce travail scientifique n'en reste pas moins un nouveau quoique modeste monument philologique, attestant une fois de plus le merveilleux accord des sciences, avec le récit inspiré des Livres Saints.—Jos. ROYAL : *Rev. Can.*

"Renan, as a professor of Semitic languages, naturally exalts the object of his studies; the Indo-European stands next with him. In one of his works he says: 'To imagine a savage race speaking a semitic or Indo-European language is a contradictory fiction to which no one versed in the laws of comparative philology and the general theory of the human mind, will lend himself.' The discredit thus thrown on American languages has elicited this Canadian reply, defending the two great languages of Canada and the Northern States—the Algonquin and Iroquois—from the imputation of being discordant cries, variable or unphilosophic."— *Am. His. Mag.* (N. Y.)

II. Études Philologiques sur quelques langues sauvages de l'Amérique. Par N. O., ancien missionnaire. *Do.* 1866, pp. 160, 8vo.

"The book now before us is one that displays an amount of information on the subject of the Indian tongues rarely to be found at this day—information which is conveyed to the reader in a manner as clear as it is concise. Our author enters upon his work with the spirit and force of a philologist. We learn from his preface that, some three years ago, he published in Montreal a pamphlet in reply to some strictures of the famous M. Renan, who had chosen to treat the Indian languages in the erroneous and flippant style he used with respect to other and higher subjects. This brochure attracted considerable attention, and the author received an urgent invitation from Paris to lay before its men of learning fuller details on the grammatical system of the Indian languages of America. The present work constitutes an admirable compliance with the request. He says: 'Twenty years of a sojourn among the Iroquois and Algonquins have sufficed to give us some conception of the idioms of these people; and we think we can offer, with confidence and without presumption, this first work from the pen of a poor Missionary, to men of learning in general, and in particular to the Indianologists of each continent.'

"The author informs us that it requires eighteen characters to represent all the Algonquin sounds—namely, A, B, C, D, E. G, H, I, J, K. M, N, O, P, S, T, S, Z. Twelve characters suffice for the Iroquois language—namely, A, E, F, H, I, K, N, O, R, S, T, S. The character 'S' is equivalent to the ou of the French and our English w. In both languages all the letters are pronounced, for there are neither mutes nor quiescents. The 'C' and 'G,' which in the principle languages of Europe have a double articulation, have only one in the Algonquin. The vowel 'E,' has always the sound of the French É (é fermé.) The 'C' in Algonquin has the sound of 'ch' in French, or 'sh' in English. The 'G' is hard as in the Greek. The 'N,' Algonquin, at the end of a word, is not nasal, but pronounced as in Latin, but it has the French nasal sound when at the end of a syllable that does not terminate a word. The 'N,' Iroquois, at the end of a word or syllable, is always nasal. * * *

"We must here draw to a close, and reiterate our opinion that this work displays a thorough acquaintance with the Algonquin and Indian languages, and is such a work as will meet with favour from all who take an interest in the study of philology."—Transcript, (Mont.)

CURRIE, Rev. DUNCAN D. A Wes. Meth. min., N. B.

I. A Catechism of Baptism. New York, 1854, pp. 50; 2nd Ed. 1855.

CURRIE. Mrs MARGARET GILL.

I. Gabriel West. and other Poems. Fredericton N. B. 1866.

"They manifest both culture and poetic feeling. The story of Gabriel West, an early

Loyalist soldier, is well told, and the entire collection such as colonists should appreciate and encourage."—Journal (St. John N. B.)

CURTIS, Lieut. ROGER.

I. Particulars of the country of Labradore. Phil. Trans. 1774.

CUSHING, Mrs. E. L. A Can. authoress, residing at Montreal. B. in Massachusetts, U. S. Previous to coming to Can. wrote several works which were produced in the U. S. Was a contributor to the Literary Garland (Mont.) for many years, and near the demise of that popular periodical was entrusted with its ed. management. In conjunction with her sister, Mrs. Cheney, ed. the Snow Drop, a monthly juvenile Mag., from 1847 to 1851. Has written for various other Can. periodicals.

I. Esther, a Dramatic poem.

"A work of deep interest."—MRS. HALE.

CUTHBERT, Ross. A mem. of the Quebec bar. Long dead. Sat in the L. C. Legislature.

I. An Apology for Great Britain in allusion to a Pamphlet intituled: "Considérations sur les effets qu'ont produits en Canada, la conservation des établissements du pays, les mœurs, l'education, &c., de ses habitans; et les conséquences qu'entraînerait leur décadence par rapport aux intérêts de la Grande Bretagne." Quebec, 1809, 8vo.

II. New theory of the Tides. Do., 1810, 8vo.

CYNOSURIDIS, ALPHONSE.

I. Mémoires d'un vieux garçon. Montreal, 1865, pp. 48.

CYR, Rev. N. A native of Can. Is now pastor of the French Protestant Ch. Philadelphia. He was, for upwards of 14 years, ed. and prop. of Le Semeur Canadien (Mont.), a religious, political and literary journal.

(See Côté, Rev. C. H. O.)

D.

DADE, *Rev* C., *M. A.* A min. of the Ch. of Engl. Incumbent of Georgetown U. C.

    I. Remarks on the Law of Storms. *Can. Journ.*, 1860.

    II. Notes on the Cholera Seasons of 1832 and 1834. *Do.* 1862.

DAINVILLE, D.

    I. Beautés de L'Histoire du Canada, ou Epoques mémorables, traits intéressants, mœurs, usages, coutumes des Habitants du Canada, tant indigènes que Colons, depuis sa découverte jusqu'à ce jour. *Paris*, 1821. *in*-12.

DALLAS, ANGUS. (Tor.)

    I. Appeal on the Common School Law, its incongruity and maladministration setting forth the necessity of a minister of Public Instruction, responsible to Parliament. *Toronto*, 1858, pp. 32.

    II. Outlines of Chemico-Hygiene and Medicine; or the application of Chemical results to the preservation of Health and cure of disease. *Do.* 1860, pp. 119.

DALRYMPLE, ALEXANDER, *F. R. S.* An eminent Scot. Hydrographer. D. 1808.

    I. Plan for promoting the Fur trade and securing it to this country, by uniting the operations of the East India and Hudson's Bay Companies. *London*, 1789, 4to.

DALTON, THOMAS. A Can. journ. B. in Eng. D. at Toronto, 26 Oct. 1840. Was for many years prior and up to his death, ed. and prop. of *The Patriot* (Tor.), then the leading Conservative journal in U. C. Of a strong and fervid mind, he displayed indefatigable zeal as a public writer in strengthening the tie between Can. and the Mother Country; his efforts were unflinching to crush every measure calculated to disturb the harmony that should always exist between the Parent State and her dependencies. Mr. D. was considered the most vigorous public writer of his day in the Upper Province—he was one of the first to advocate a Confederation of all the B. A. Colonies and his political foresight has been strikingly evinced in the fulfilment of many of his predictions. We close this brief and imperfect notice of this distinguished writer with the following tribute to his worth, taken from a Toronto journal:—

    " In the cause of his country, he was sometimes ardent to a degree which all his friends could not approve. But those who knew him best, were the most convinced of the sincerity with which he declared his opinions upon the public questions of the day. He was an Englishman in heart and mind, as well as by birth—was proud of his Saxon lineage—was proud of British freedom, which he considered the light of the world, and the best adapted to carry forward the human family from improvement to improvement in all time to come. In private life he was friendly, amiable and cheerful."

DALTON, WILLIAM.

    I. Travels in the United States of America and part of Upper Canada. *Appleby, Eng.*, 1821, pp. 256, cr. 8vo.

DAMBOURGÈS, *Col.* FRANÇOIS. A French gentleman who emigrated to Can. in 1763. B. at Salies 1742. D. at Montreal, 13 Dec. 1798. He sat in the first parliament of L. C. As an officer in the Can. Volunteers he greatly distinguished himself.

    Le Colonel Dambourgès. Etude historique Canadienne. *Québec*, 1865, pp. 58, 8vo.

DANA, J. F., *M. D.*

    I. An account of some experiments on the root of the Sanguinaria Canadensis. *Ann. Ly. Nat. His. (N. Y.)* 1828.

DANSEREAU, ARTHUR, *B. C. L.* A French Can. journ. B. at Contrecœur, L. C., 1844. Admitted to the Bar, L. C., 1865. Has contributed many meritorious poetical pieces and prose articles to the newspaper press, and delivered various lectures on subjects of public interest before *L'Institut Canadien* (Mont.) Is one of the Editors of *La Minerve* (Mont.)

    " Mr. Dansereau nous a donné une lecture sur le souverain Pontife et sur les derniers événements de l'Italie; il a captivé l'attention dans une travail remarquable par l'abondance des aperçus, la fermeté des convictions, enfin l'eclat du style."—*L'Echo du Cab. de Lec.*

I. Annales Historiques du Collége de L'Assomption depuis sa fondation.— Première livraison. *Montreal*, 1864, pp. 44, 8vo.

DARBY, JOSEPH.

I. Letter on the subject of British Colonial Fisheries. 1853, pp. 16, 8vo.

II. Wreck of the Schooner Arno. *Halifax*, 1858, pp. 6.

DAREY, P. J., *M. A.* Prof. of French language and literature in Univ. of McGill Coll. (Mont.) Is a corresponding mem. of the *Soc. Impériale Géologique de Vienne.*

I. The Students' Companion to the study of French. *Montreal*, 1863, pp. 143.

II. Commission Géologique du Canada. Rapport de Progrès depuis son commencement jusqu'à 1863 ; Traduite de l'Anglais. *Do.*, 1864, pp. xxvi—1043, r. 8vo.

DARLING, *Rev.* W. STEWART. A clergym. of the Ch. of Eng. Assist. min. of the ch. of the Holy Trinity. (Tor.) Contributed much in prose and verse to the *Church* newspaper, *Streetsville Review*, *Churchman's Friend*, *Church Press*, *Brit. Am. Mag.* and other journals and periodicals.

I. Sketches of Canadian Life, Lay and Ecclesiastical, illustrative of Canada and the Canadian Church. By a Presbyter of the Diocese of Toronto. *London*, 1849, pp. 310. 8vo.

II. Papers on the unpopularity of Religious Truth. *Toronto*, 1857, pp. 85.

III. The Emigrant's ; a tale (in verse). [Reprinted from the *B. A. Mag.*] *Do.*, 1863, pp. 39, 8vo.

IV. Papers on Music as applied to the service of the Church. [Reprinted from the *Toronto Leader*]. *Do.*, 1863, pp. 32.

DARNELL, *Rev.* HENRY FAULKNER, *M. A.* A clergym. of the Ch. of Eng. (St. John's, L. C.) B. in London, Eng., 1831. Is a son of Rev. J. Darnell, of Tunbridge Well's. Was privately ed. Ordained both priest and deacon by Archbishop Musgrave of York. Appointed Rector of St. John's, L. C., 1861. Has contributed a great many pieces in prose

and verse to the *Echo* and the *Gazette* (Mont.) He also wrote for the *Brit. Am. Mag*, [See *Children ; Wet Blankets ; The Maple ; Sir Everard's Hound, a ballad ; The Wreather's ; The Elements at strife :* and *Chapter from the life of a Threepenny piece ;* the latter one of the most effective stories in that periodical.]

I. Songs by the way : a collection of original poems for the comfort and encouragement of Christian pilgrims. *Montreal*, 1862, pp. 186, 8vo.

"Canada writers do not suffice, it seems, to freeze up Helicon. The aim of this volume is the same as that of Miss Proctor's delightful book of *Legends and Lyrics*, to brighten common lives, and ease common burdens. Every such effort is commendable, and we doubt not more than ' one Christian Pilgrim ' will be grateful to the Rector of St. John's for his words of encouragement and sympathy."—*Church Monthly* (Bos.)

"I trust it will have a large circulation, which it deserves, and prove to very many a favoured instrument to elevate their taste and warm their devotion."—BISHOP HOPKINS. (Vermont) *Letter to Author.*

II. Verses in memory of the Right Rev. G. J. Mountain, Lord Bishop of Quebec. *St. John's, L. C.*, 1863, pp. 7.

"These verses express in a beautiful manner the deep sorrow the death of this venerable prelate has occasioned, and serve as another illustration of the respect and affection entertained for him."—*Herald* (Mont.)

DARROCH, *Rev.* JOHN, *A. M.* A Presb. clergym. (Lochiel, U. C.) Has written for the Scottish, Am. and Can. periodical press.

I. Caraid A' Ghaidheil ; a discourse on the life of the late Reverend Norman MacLeod, D. D., of St. Columba Parish, Glasgow, &c. *Glasgow*, 1863, pp. 42.

"It is an interesting contribution to Celtic Literature ; and if as a contemporary has observed, it is the first contribution to that literature from across the Atlantic, we have also to remark as a second characteristic feature, that we believe it to be the first funeral sermon that has appeared in Gaelic print."—*Herald* (Glas.)

DARTNELL, GEORGE H.

I. On the Duration and Expectation of Life in Canada compared with other countries. *Can. Journ.*, 1854.

DARVEAU, L. M., (Que.)

1. Histoire de la *Tribune*. *Quebec*, 1863, pp. 16.

DAUBENY, CHARLES, M. D., F. R S.
I. Journal of a tour through the United States, and in Canada, made during the years 1837-38. *Oxford*, 1843, pp. 231, 8vo.

"Printed for private circulation only."

D'AUBERTEUIL, HILLIARD.
I. Essais Historiques et Politiques sur les Anglo-Americans. *Bruxelles*, 1782, 3 vols. 8vo.

DAVID, A. H., M. D. A medical writer, (Mont.) Founded the *Canada Medical Journal* in 1852, of which he was co-ed. for 1 year. Has contributed to nearly all of the Can. medical serials.

DAVIES, Rev. B., LL. D.
I. On the origin of the name "Canada." *Can. Nat.*, 1861.

DAVIES, Maj. Gen. THOMAS, F. R. S., F. L. S.
I. An account of the Jumping Mouse of Canada. (*Dipus Canadensis.*) *Trans. Linn. Soc.*, 1798.

DAVIES, W. H. A., (Mont.) D. 1867.
I. Notes on the Esquimaux Bay and the surrounding country. *Trans. Lit. & His. Soc.* (Que.,) 1855.

"An interesting paper."—*Sim. Col. Mag.*

II. Notes on Ungava Bay and its vicinity. *Do.*

DAVIES, P. M.
I. History of the War of 1812-15. *New York*, 1836.

DAVIDSON, G. M.
I. The Fashionable Tour and Guide to Travellers through the Northern and Middle States and Canada. *Saratoga*, 1830., 12mo.

D'AVRAY, J. MARSHALL. Prof. of Modern Languages and Literature, Univ. of N. B.
I. Official Reports as Chief Superintendent of Schools. *Fredericton*, 1853-4-5-6 and 7.

II. Public Lectures on Education.

III. Three Encœnial Orations in University of N. B.

DAWSON, Rev. ÆNEAS MCDONELL. A Can. author. B. in Scot., 30 July, 1810. Connected on both father's and mother's side with old historic families. Maternal grandfather for a long time heir presumptive to the honours of the ancient house of Glengarry. The name originally Deasson. Studied for Ch. of Rome at the Diocesan Seminary, Paris, under the celebrated Abbé Frère, who numbered amongst his pupils Messrs. Gillis and Dupanloup, both of whom afterwards became Bishops in the Ch. Ordained Priest, 1835. Was in Mission of Dumfries from 1835 to 1840; laboured from latter year till some time afterwards in northern missions of Edinburgh, and subsequently took up residence in that city. For sometime before coming to Canada, in 1855, had separate charge of the Counties of Fife, Kinross and Clackmannan which he was forced to resign owing to the overwhelming nature of the duties connected therewith. During all this time he was the means of rendering much useful service to the cause of his Ch. Since his residence in Can. has had charge of the parish of St. Andrew's (City of Ottawa), but now preaches at the Cathedral. Mr. D. is well known as a lecturer on interesting and popular topics ; nearly all his lectures have appeared in the local journals after their delivery. He has also contributed various poetical pieces to the provincial press, evincing much power and beauty.

I. "Maître Pierre." Conversations on Morality. Translated from the French of M. Delcassott. *Paris* 1836 ; *Liverpool*, 1838, pp. 192, 8vo.

II. The Parish Priest and his Parishioners, or answers to popular prejudices against religion. Translated from the French of M. B. D'Exauvillez. *Glasgow*, 1842.

"This is a very beautiful little work in defence of religion, admirably agreeing with its title, and suited to the purpose for which it was written. It contains a picture of a village in the North of France which by the disastrous events of the Revolution has been deprived of the benefits of Religious instruction for one whole generation. so that the very name and knowledge of Religion have died out amongst its people, and it is treasured up in their memories only as an unknown thing, a fit subject of laughter and jeers. * * Into this parish is sent a pious, humble, zealous and intelligent clergyman, M. Vincent; and the author sets forth with a good deal of dramatic skill how he first overcomes by his suavity and christian meekness, the bitter hatred with which he is at first welcomed, and then by degrees vanquishes the irreligious prejudices of his parishioners, until at last he has the happiness of reforming his entire parish and restoring it to faith and virtue. The principal characters of the village are sketched with sufficient distinctness to give a real dramatic interest to the various turns of the argument and to relieve it from the dryness which is inseparable from a long train of syllogisms. It is not merely a series of logical arguments, but a succession of scenes in which the reader is made to feel that the considerations insisted on are not merely true in themselves, but are adapted to the spiritual condition of the persons to whom they are addressed. We are thus not only satisfied that the logic is sound, we understand also how and why the village has been compelled to yield to its cogency."—FREDERICK LUCAS, M. P.: *Tablet* (Lond.)

III. The Pope considered in his relations with the Church, temporal sovereignties, separated churches, and the cause of civilization. Translated from the French of Count Joseph De Maistre. *London*, 1850, pp. 369, 8vo

" The best translated book that I have ever read."—BISHOP GILLIS : (Edin.)

IV. Letters to a Russian Gentleman on the Spanish Inquisition. Translated from the French of Count Joseph De Maistre. *Do.*, 1851, pp. 114, sm. 8vo.

V. The Temporal Sovereignty of the Pope in relation to the State of Italy. *London* and *Ottawa*, 1860, pp. 227, 8vo.

" The character and history of the Sovereign Pontiff, the remarkable events of his reign, the testimony borne by Protestants themselves to the purity of his motives and the earnestness of his efforts to ameliorate the lot of his subjects ; these, and a multitude of other matters more or less connected with the subject, are set forth by Mr. Dawson with force, lucidity and eloquence. As a whole, the work is most creditable to the rising literature of Canada."—*Weekly Register* (Lond.)

" We commend it to the careful study of the Catholics of Canada. If the facts therein adduced are not startling by their novelty, they are, at least, convincing by the excellence of their arrangement, and the lucidity of the arguments which the author thereon bases."—*True Witness* (Mont.)

VI. Lament for the Right Rev. James Gillis. D. D., Bishop of Edinburgh, &c., &c., &c., and other poems. *Do.*, 1864, pp. 58, 8vo.

" In the narrow compass of a newspaper notice we can hardly do justice to the merits of these compositions. The style, as may be supposed, is chaste, finished, and delicately worded. Imagination, the true charm of verse, the author possesses in an eminent degree ; and the poetic fire, giving life, spirit and force, is by no means of the smouldering kind."—*Union* (Ottawa.)

" It contains several pieces of considerable poetic beauty. * * * The style is vivid and forcible, and the sentiments are worthy the reverend author.—*Weekly Register* (Lond.)

VII. St. Vincent de Paul ; a lecture delivered before the St. Vincent de Paul Society of Ottawa. *London*, 1865, pp. 69, 8vo.

" A very beautiful lecture. The author is most enthusiastically interested in his exhibition of the admirable virtues of the humble and holy St. Vincent, and carries his audience with him."—*Tablet*, (N. Y.)

VIII. Lines for October. [*Solitude ; Royalty at Ottawa ; The Volunteers who fell at the Battle of Ridgeway.*] *Ottawa*, 1866.

DAWSON, JOHN WILLIAM, *M.A.*, *LL.D.*, *F.R.S., F. G. S.* A Can. author and geologist. Is Principal and Vice Chancellor of the Univ. of McGill Coll. (Mont.) B. at Pictou, N. S., 13 Oct. 1820. Is the son of Scottish parents who had emigrated to N. S., some years previous to his birth. His father, Mr. James Dawson, from 1835 until 1840, owned and conducted a paper called *The Bee* (Pictou.) He received the primary portion of his education at the sch. and coll. of Pictou and completed it at the Univ. of Edinburgh, at which institution he directed his attention chiefly to the study of natural history and practical chemistry, and received the degree of M. A. During his residence at the Univ. he contributed some papers on geological subjects to the Edinburgh press. In 1842, having returned home on the completion of his studies, he accompanied Sir Charles Lyell on his geological exploration of N. S., and as one of the results of the experience he gained on that expedition transmitted several papers to the Geological Soc. (Lon.), describing points of interest in the geology of his native province. Shortly afterwards the Govt. of N. S. entrusted him with the direction of a geological survey of some of the coal fields of that Province. His report will be found in the *Journals of the Legislative*

Assembly, N. S. About this time he delivered a course of lectures on natural history at Dalhousie Coll. (Hal.) In 1850 he was appointed to the newly created office of Superintendent of Education for N. S., which he held for upwards of 3 years, during which time he put in operation the new Sch. Act, and otherwise laid the foundation of the admirable system of sch. education which obtains there. During the second visit of Sir Charles Lyell to the Province Dr. D. accompanied him to the "South Joggins" section, and dis covered therein the first reptilian remains found in the live freestone of Am. In 1853, he was appointed one of the directors of the new Normal Sch. (Hal.), and shortly afterwards was one of a commission appointed to enquire into the condition of King's Coll., Fredericton. In 1855, Dr. D. was ap pointed to his present position as Prin cipal of the Univ. of McGill Coll. In addition to his being a fellow of the Royal and the Geological Societies (Lon.), Dr. D. is also a corresponding mem. of the Academy of Natural Sciences, Philadelphia; of the Am. Academy of Arts and Sciences; of the Am. Philosophical Soc.; of the Natural History Soc. (Portland); of the Natural History Soc. (N. B.); of the Can. Insti tute; of the Natural History Soc. (Mont.) (of which he has been several times President); and a Fellow of the Mont real Literary Club.

" In these seasons of intercolonial courtesy, and with the prospect of more intercolonial intercourse, it is pleasing to note that the Principal of one of our prominent Universities represents a contribution, so to speak, by Nova Scotia to Canada, the property of the former Province by birth, and of the latter by adop tion. How thoroughly Principal Dawson has adapted himself to his new home and his new duties are matters of knowledge to many and of observation to all. Shunning notoriety for its own sake, he has found his pleasures in his duty,—to the fulfilment of which duty, all his energies, intellectual and physical, have, we believe, been unceasingly devoted. College work all day, and work enough too, such work as wayward youth may not intermit, such work as mature manhood must not leave undone; close, exacting, continuous work, such as a hurrying, progressive age requires to be done, and done speedily."—FENNINGS TAYLOR : *Por traits of British Americans.*

" Let me say how fortunate we are in hav ing among us Principal Dawson, of Montreal, whose merits are so well known to every reader of the volumes of Lyell and the Quar terly Journal of the Geological Society of London."—SIR R. I. MURCHISON: *Address Brit. Ass.* 1865.

I. Handbook of Geography and Na tural History of Nova Scotia: *Pictou,* 1848 ; 6th Ed. 1863 pp. 95.

II. Reports on Schools of Nova Sco tia. *Halifax,* 1850-1-2.

III. Acadian Geology; an account of the Geological Structure and Mine ral Resources of Nova Scotia, and por tions of the neighbouring Provinces of British America. [With a map and illustrated views.] *Edinburgh and Lon don,* 1855, pp. 458, 8vo. *2nd Ed. pre paring.*

" Apart from from its local value, the work is not without many points of general interest; and in its masterly treatment of the leading questions which come under re view, it may be referred to with profit by all interested in the progress of geological in quiry."—*Can. Journ.*

" The little work which stands next on our list, although of a very different character from the preceding, is not unworthy of rank near it, being one of those valuable contri butions to the Geology of important yet dis tant regions of the globe, which are now con tinually being furnished by the zeal and in telligence of local observers; and which not only serve to extend our knowledge of the constitution of a given portion of the earth's crust, and to point out the modes in which that knowledge may be turned to practical account, but also in many cases, as in the present, furnish us with new and valuable evidence, in regard to problems of the highest interest to the geological speculator."—*West minster Review.*

" There is in especial one work of perma nent interest,—'Acadian Geology, or an Account of the Geological Structure and Mineral Resources of Nova Scotia,' by John William Dawson,—which issued last year from the press, and which, both from its great intrinsic merits, and the circumstance that it was written in a distant colony, we ought to have noticed long ago,—that strik ingly shows how much may be effected in the scientific walk by an ardent mind and a fresh and active curiosity in even new and wild countries, far from the sympathy and coun sel of minds engaged in similar pursuits. Mr. (now Professor) Dawson's volume has not only high scientific merits, but also very considerable literary ones. It is the work of a man who has *made* himself a naturalist and geologist, but who was previously a scholar and tasteful writer; and so his 'Acadian Geology' is not only a curious, but also a very readable book."—HUGH MILLER: "*Edinburgh Witness.*"

IV. Inaugural discourse on the course of Collegiate Education in British North America. *Montreal*, 1855, pp. 29.

V. Contributions toward the improvement of Agriculture in Nova Scotia, *Pictou*, N. S., 1853, pp. 99 ; 2nd Ed., with practical hints on the management and improvement of Live Stock, compiled from Youatt, Johnston, Young, Peters, Stephens, &c. *Halifax*, 1856, pp. 280.

"It forms a compendium of useful information in the various branches of agriculture and husbandry, which if properly studied, cannot fail of being largely useful to the Nova Scotia farmer."—*Church Times.* (Hal.)

VI. Archaia ; or Studies of the Cosmogony and Natural History of the Hebrew Scriptures. *Montreal* and *London*, 1860, pp. 400, 8vo.

"Dr. Dawson is certainly entitled to a prominent place among the scanty band of combatants who are gifted with this rare faculty of double vision. He is at once a Geologist of no mean distinction, and a firm believer in the inspiration of the Hebrew Scriptures ; a combination of which it has been well observed, that were it more commonly to be met with, there would be more faith on the earth and also more Philosophy."—*Literary Gazette*, (Lon.)

"We have read this volume with great pleasure. There are some things in it with which we do not agree, but every page bears testimony to the substantial literary, scientific and theological attainments of its author. There are no attempts to look asquint at any of the important topics discussed. Candour, good sense and a fine Christian spirit, happily distinguish Principal Dawson's work from many which on both sides of the Atlantic have been written on the same subject. We were aware of Dr. Dawson's accomplishments as a Geologist, but we were not prepared to accord to him that varied learning, evidences of which are apparent in this volume."—*North British Rev.*

"Whatever opinions may be entertained of the speculations which this volume contains, there will, we are persuaded, be but one opinion as to the thoroughness with which its topics have been discussed, the patient labour which has been bestowed on every section, the eloquence with which many of its truths are stated, and the wide and accurate knowledge of contemporary science which it manifests. Our author has

not given crude and ill-digested speculations to the world, or claimed the attention of his fellows to that which he himself has not completely mastered, or regarding which he has not something new and important to say."—*Can. Nat.*

VII. Air-Breathers of the Coal Period : a descriptive account of the remains of land animals found in the Coal Formation of Nova Scotia, with remarks on their bearing on theories of the formation of coal and of the origin of species with illustrations. *Montreal* and *London*, 1863, pp. 81. 8vo.

"In the pamphlet before us, scientific descriptions are given of the creeping, crawling, and flying tenants of the dark luxuriant forests of the coal period of Nova Scotia, and allusion is also made to the origin and mode of accumulation of coal. The greater part of the subject matter has already appeared in the *Canadian Naturalist and Geologist*, in detached numbers. The publication of these interesting and valuable descriptions in their present form will prove particularly useful to the geologist, and especially to those who may be induced to search for new species of air-breathers in the vast unexplored coal fields of British America and the United States."—*B. A. Mag.*

VIII. First Lessons in Scientific Agriculture for schools and private instruction. *Montreal*, 1864, pp. 208, 8vo.

"Both in design and execution it surpasses any work of a similar kind extant."—*Colonial Farmer* (Fredericton.)

IX. On some points in the History and Prospects of Protestant Education in Lower Canada ; a lecture. *Do.*, 1864, pp. 20.

X. Duties of Educated young men in British America. Annual University Lecture. *Do.*, 1865.

Haszard's Gazette.

I. Geological Excursion in Prince Edward Island. 1842.

Proceedings of the Royal Society of Edinburgh.

I. On the Boulder formation and Superficial Drift of Nova Scotia. 1847.

II. On the mode of Occurrence of Gypsum in Nova Scotia. *Do.*

New Philosophical Journal (Edinburgh.)

On the Meriones and Arvicola of Nova Scotia. 1856.

Proceedings and Journal of the Geological Society of London.

I. On the Lower Carboniferous or Gypsiferous formation of Nova Scotia. 1843–4.

II. On the Newer Coal formation of the Eastern part of Nova Scotia. *Do.*

III. Notice of some Fossils found in the Coal formation of Nova Scotia. 1846.

In the same year a paper was communicated by Mr. Bunbury: *Notes on the Fossils communicated by Mr. Dawson.*

IV. On the new Red Sandstone of Nova Scotia ; map and section. 1847.

V. On the colouring matter of Red Sandstones, and the White Beds associated with them. 1848.

VI. Notice of the Gypsum of Plaster Cove. *Do.*

VII. On the Metamorphic and Metalliferous Rocks of the east of Nova Scotia. 1849.

VIII. Notice of the occurrence of upright Calamites, near Pictou, N. S. *Do.*

IX. Notes on the Red Sandstone of Nova Scotia. 1852.

X. On the remains of a Reptile and a Land shell in an erect Fossil tree in the Coal measures of Nova Scotia. By Messrs. Lyell, Dawson, Wyman and Owen. *Do.*

XI. On the Albert Mine, New Brunswick. *Do.*

XII. On the Coal Measures of the South Joggins. 1853.

XIII. On the Structure of the Coal field of Pictou. 1853.

XIV. Notice of the discovery of a Reptilian Skull in the Coal of Pictou. 1854.

XV. On a Modern Submerged Forest at Fort Lawrence in Nova Scotia. *Do.*

XVI. On the Lower Carboniferous Coal Measures of British America. 1858.

XVII. On the vegetable structures in Coal, (plates.) 1860.

" A communication of no ordinary interest. * * * Many new and exceedingly interesting details are brought out by these investigations, rendering Dr. Dawson's paper one of the most valuable contributions to our knowledge of the Carboniferous flora, that has appeared for some time."—*Can. Journ.*

XVIII. On the occurrence of Reptilian Remains, with a Land shell and Myriapod, in the Coal measures of Nova Scotia. 1860.

XIX. Notice of the discovery of additional Remains of Land Animals in the Coal measures of the South Joggins, N. S. 1861.

XX. On the Flora of the Devonian Period in North Eastern America. 1862.

XXI. Further observations on the Devonian Plants of Maine, Gaspé and New York. 1863.

XXII. Notice of a new species of *Dendrerpeton,* and of the Dermal coverings of certain Carboniferous Reptiles. 1863.

" This paper referred to new facts ascertained in the course of re-examination of the remains of Reptiles from the Coal formation of Nova Scotia, and first to the characters of a new and smaller species of *Denrerpeton,* for which Dr. Dawson proposed the name of *D. Oweni.*"—*Journ. Geol. Soc.* (Lon.)

XXIII. On the structure of certain Organic remains (*Eozoon Canadense*) in the Laurentian Limestones of Canada, —(two plates.) Feby., 1865.

" This Fossil (discovered by Sir W. E. Logan) was examined in 1864, by Dr. Dawson, of Montreal, who detected in it by the aid of the Microscope the distinct structure of a Rhizopod or Foraminifer. Dr. Carpenter and Prof. T. R. Jones have since confirmed this opinion. * * * * * On this oldest of known Organic remains Dr. Dawson has conferred the name of *Eozoon Canadense.*"— LYELL.

XXIV. On the conditions of accumulation of Coal, more especially as illustrated by the Coal formation of Nova Scotia and New Brunswick. May, 1866, pp. 70, and 8 plates.

Canadian Naturalist.

I. On the Geological Structure and Mineral Deposits of the Promontory of Maimanse, Lake Superior. Vol. II.

II On the Varieties and mode of preservation of the Fossil, known as Sternbergiæ. *Do.*

III. On the Newer Pliocene and Post Pliocene Deposits of the vicinity of

Montreal, with notices of Fossils recently discovered in them. *Do.*

IV. Things to be observed in Montreal and its vicinity. Vol. III.

V. Coal in Canada—The Bowmanville Discovery. *Do.*

VI. A week in Gaspé. *Do.*

"A very interesting paper."—*Can. Journ.*

VII. On Sea Anemones and Hydroid Polyps from the Gulf of St. Lawrence. *Do.*

VIII. Additional notes on the Post-Pliocene Deposits of the St. Lawrence Valley. Vol. IV.

"Taken in connexion with the author's former researches on this subject, the present paper will be found of no ordinary value to the student of Canadian Geology."—*Can. Journ.*

IX. On the Microscopic Structure of some Canadian Limestones. *Do.*

X. On a new species of Stickleback (*Gasterosteus gymnetes*) *Do.*

XI. On Fossil plants from the Devonian Rocks of Canada. Vol. V.

XII. On the Tubicolous Marine Worms of the Gulf of St. Lawrence. *Do.*

XIII. On the Silurian and Devonian Rocks of Nova Scotia. *Do.*

XIV. Notice of Tertiary Fossils from Labrador, Maine, &c. *Do.*

XV. Notes on Aboriginal Antiquities recently discovered in the Island of Montreal. *Do.*

XVI. Notes on the Geology of Murray Bay, Lower St. Lawrence. Vol. VI.

"The local geology of a very interesting region, showing the characters of several important formations in very good natural exposures."—BISHOP FULFORD.

XVII. On the Pre-carboniferous Flora of New Brunswick, Maine and Eastern Canada. *Do.*

XVIII. Additional notes on Aboriginal Antiquities found at Montreal. *Do.*

XIX. On the recent discoveries of gold in Nova Scotia. *Do.*

XX. Notes on the Flora of the White Mountains, in its Geographical and Geological relations. Vol. VII.

XXI. On an Erect Sigillaria and a Carpolite from the Joggins, Nova Scotia. *Do.*

XXII. On the footprints of Limulus. *Do.*

XXIII. Zoological Classification; or *Calenterata and Protozoa versus Radiata. Do.*

XXIV. On the Antiquity of Man; a Review of 'Lyell and Wilson.' Vol. VIII.

XXV. Synopsis of the Flora of the Carboniferous Period of Nova Scotia. *Do.*

XXVI. Annual address as President of the Natural History Society of Montreal, 1864.

XXVII. Elementary views of the classification of animals. *Do.*

XXVIII. On the Fossils of the Genus Rusophycus. *Do.*

XXIX. On the Post Pliocene Deposits of Rivière du Loup and Tadousac, 1865.

American Journal of Education.

I. Natural History in its Educational Aspects. Lecture before the Natural History Society of Montreal. 1857.

II. Biographical sketch of James McGill, 1859.

"Amidst his many arduous duties connected with the University of McGill College, Dr. J. W. Dawson has still found time to devote attention to many points in Canadian geology. His investigations into the character of our Post-tertiary deposits have greatly extended our knowledge of the subject; while his study of the land plants of the Devonian rocks of North America has given a new interest to this series of deposits. He was first incited to an examination of this flora by the numerous specimens which he found ready for examination in the collection of the survey from the Gaspé sandstones; and the species found in Gaspé although few in number, naturally suggested inquiry into the vegetable remains of equivalent rocks in other parts. Goeppert in his memoir on the flora of the Silurian, Devonian and Lower Carboniferous rocks of Europe and America, enumerates in 1860, fifty nine species as known, in the Devonian series up to that date. In 1859, D. Dawson described six species from specimens collected by himself, and by the Geological Survey, in the Devonian rocks of Gaspé. In 1861, he added fifteen other species from Perry, in Maine, and from St. John, in New Brunswick. In 1862, having had placed in his hands the collections of the New York Survey, and those made by Messrs. Matthew & Hartt, at St. John, in New Brunswick, he raised the number of American species to sixty nine; and in a paper read before the Geological Society of London, in May, 1863, he has added to these thirteen more, including two from Gaspé; making the whole number of species in the Devonian flora of Eastern North America eighty two, belonging to thirty-five genera. Of these species eight had previously been recognised in Europe, and about ten of them had been more or less perfectly noticed or figured in reports on American Geology. On the subject of the Post-tertiary deposits, we have availed ourselves not only of Dr. Dawson's published observations, but of various manuscript notes which he has kindly placed in our hands. In his investigations of these deposits, Dr. Dawson has more than doubled the number of species of invertebrate animals previously known in them; and Mr. J. F. Whiteaves, so well known as a naturalist, has kindly aided in preparing a catalogue of these fossils."— SIR W. E. LOGAN: *Geology of Canada,* 1863.

DAWSON, S. J., *C. E.*
I. Report on the exploration of the country between Lake Superior and the Red River Settlement, and between the latter place and the Assiniboine and Saskatchewan. (With maps.) *Toronto,* 1859, pp. 45, Large 4to.

DAY, *Hon.* C. D., *LL. D.* Is a retired Judge from the Superior Ct. L. C., and now a Com. for the Consolidation of the Civil Law of same Province.
I. Address at the Provincial Industrial Exhibition. *Montreal,* 1850.

DAY, *Mrs.* C. M.
I. Pioneers of the Eastern Townships; a work containing official and reliable information respecting the formation of settlements; with incidents in their early history, and details of adventures, perils and deliverances. *Montreal,* 1863, pp. 171, 4to.

DAY, SAMUEL PHILLIPS. An Eng. author and newspaper correspondent. Served as correspondent in Can. for the *Herald,* in 1863-4, and for the *Morning Post,* (Lon.), in 1865.
I. English America; or, Pictures of Canadian Places and People. *London,* 1864, 2 vols, p. 8vo.

DEACON, W. F. A N. B. writer. (St. John.)
I. Murder will out, or confessions of a Village Apothecary.

II. The Author; or, sketches from Life. *St. John,* 1866, pp. 64.

DEARBORN, *Genl.* HENRY. "An officer in the Am. Revolution, the author of a M S. journal of his expedition to Canada, imprisonment in Quebec, expedition to Wyoming, and other adventures during the war, printed in his life by his son." DUYCKINCK.

DE BELLEFEUILLE, E. LEF. A French Can. author and writer. A mem. of one of the oldest and most honorable families in the Province. Is an advocate practising at the Montreal Bar. His connection with the press dates from 1859 when he commenced contributing to *L'Ordre* (Mont.) of which he eventually became co-ed. In that journal in 1859-60 appeared his translation into French of Madame Leprohon's tale of *Ida Beresford,* and in 1861, his translation of the novel of the *Manor House of Villerai,* by the same lady. This latter translation also appeared in book form. In 1859 Mr. DeB. in a discussion which took place before the *Cabinet de Lecture* (Mont.) as to which of the four arts— Eloquence, Poetry, Music and Painting should be awarded pre-eminence, sustained the art of Poetry; his address on the occasion appeared in *L'Echo* and drew from *Le Courier du Canada* the following tribute:—

"As regards the advocate of Poetry we had not up to this time any grounds for believing him a poet; we had always seen him reposing in matters of fact, as the columns of several journals shew; but after the tide of poetic eloquence which his mouth as well as his pen has poured out on this subject; after the accents in turn, tender, playful, energetic, noble and exalted, which he has uttered from his soul, like a lyre which produces every note, we are compelled to acknowledge that if he busies himself with everything else as well as he has done with poetry, he does it with satisfaction as well as with taste."

In 1864 he assisted in establishing *La Revue Canadienne* (Mont.) of which he has since been one of the directors. For that periodical he has written a considerable number of essays, &c.,— one of which on the *Code Civil du Bas Canada* was extended to some length and displayed great legal acumen. Its production had the effect of modifying the proposed legislation of the Codification Commission respecting marriages by the Catholic priesthood.

"I have read this work with the serious attention merited by the subject of which the writer treats and which interests so deeply both religion and civil society. I am happy that the first cry of alarm that the press has uttered upon this important subject, is found in a publication only just commenced and which holds out such brilliant hopes for the future, and that this cry has been made by a young man of the world, by a young lawyer, by a young Canadian who belongs to one of the most honorable families of our land. When one has one foot in the grave, he always entertains high hopes for the future when he leaves behind him many young men determined to devote the talents which Divine Providence has so liberally bestowed upon them, in defending all the principles of religion and all the laws of the land which their fathers have bequeathed to them."— † Ig., Evêque de Montréal.

I. Thèse sur les Mariages Clandestins ; soutenue le 28 Nov. 1859, dans les Salles de l'Ecole de Droit du Collége Ste. Marie. *Montréal*, 1860, pp. 110, in-12.

"This learned dissertation does much honour to your talents. In my opinion it is destined to be of great service to your fellow countrymen in enlightening them on a question which affects in the highest degree both religion and the public morals. • • • I shall preserve this work with care as a precious manual which I shall be glad to consult on many occasions."— † C. F., Bishop of Tloa.

"It is an important work which has required great research, and which shows a remarkable aptitude for the exposition and discussion of the most abstract and subtle points and questions. This work is a very striking evidence of the powerful studies which its author knows how to draw, as well as so many other literary articles in *L'Ordre* which always shew an earnest writer, and one careful of correctness and literary elegance. Mr. DeB. loves philosophy and sound reasoning, but he is not exclusive and he thinks that the beautiful has something to do with the truth ; that they should go hand in hand ; that their alliance is of the most legitimate and honorable nature and that it never enters into the category of those clandestine unions which he has so forcibly attacked and branded."—*L'Echo du Cab. de Lec. Paroissiale.*

II. Le Manoir de Villerai ; (translated from the English of Madame Leprohon.) *Do.* 1861, pp. 405, in-12.

III. Code Civil du Bas Canada d'après

le rôle amendé déposé dans le bureau du greffier du Conseil Législatif, tel que prescrit par l'Acte 29 Vict. chap. 41, 1865. Augmenté des autorités citées par les Codificateurs dans le projet soumis à la Législature ; d'un précis des changements introduits par le Code Civil dans les lois du Bas Canada. *Do.* 1866, pp. lxxxiv—612, in-18.

"The work of editing this useful volume has been ably performed by Mr. DeBellefeuille."—*Herald,* (Mont.)

La Revue Canadienne.

L. Code Civil du Bas Canada, Législation sur le Mariage. (4 articles.) 1864-5.

II. La Question Mexicaine. 1865.

III. L'Incursion de St. Albans. *Do.*

IV. Le Démembrement de la Paroisse de Montréal. 1866.

V. La Nouvelle Législation du Bas Canada. *Do.*

VI. Discours sur l'Emprunt Romain. *Do.*

VII. Deux Questions de Dîmes. *Do.*

De Blackford, Dominique.

I. Précis de l'état actuel des colonies Anglaises dans l'Amérique Septentrionale. *Milan*, 1771, pp. 99, 12mo.

A compilation from Douglas and Kalm.

De Boilieu, Lambert.

I. Recollections of Labrador Life. *London*, 1861, pp. 251, 8vo.

De Boisthibault, Doublet.

I. Les Vœux des Hurons et des Abenaquis à Notre-Dame de Chartres, publiés pour la première fois d'après les manuscrits des Archives d'Eure-et-Loir avec les Lettres des Missionnaires Catholiques au Canada, une Introduction et des Notes. *Paris*, 1857.

De Boucherville, C. B. A French Can. author. Was, we believe, one of the founders of *La Revue Canadienne.* (Mont.)

I. Le Pont de Pierre. *Ref. Nat.* 1848.

II. Programme d'étude pour la formation d'une Banque Agricole Nationale pour le Bas Canada. *St. Hyacinthe*, 1862, pp. 23.

III. The system of Credit Foncier, annexed to the Report of the Special Committee appointed by the Legislative Assembly to enquire into the expediency of establishing it in Lower Canada, *Quebec*. Sess. Paper. (In French and English) 1863, pp. 177, 8vo.

IV. Une de perdue, deux de trouvées. Roman, *Rev. Can.* 1864-5, pp. 418, 8vo.

De Courtenay, J. M.
I. The Culture of the Vine and Emigration. 2nd. Ed., *Quebec*, 1863, pp. 53, 8vo.
II. The Canadian Vine Grower. *Toronto*, 1866.

De Fenouillet, Joseph Emile. A French Can. journ. B. at Hyères, France, 1806. D. at Montreal, 30 June, 1859. Was connected with the *Epoque*, (Paris.) Was a prof. at the Univ. of Bonn, and wrote a series of letters on Germany for *L'Univers* (*Do.*) Came to Can. 1854, and for 2 following years ed. *Le Journal de Quebec*. He contributed some papers on the Fine Arts to *Le Journal de L'Inst. Pub.* (Mont.) At the time of his death held a professorship in the Laval Normal Sch.

DeGaspé, Philippe Aubert. A French Can. author. B. at Quebec, Oct. 30, 1786. Is the descendant of a noble French family which settled in New France during our early history. He held the office of sheriff of Quebec for some years. Has resided for a considerable period at St. Jean Port Joli, L. C., of which he is Seignior.

I. Les Anciens Canadiens. *Quebec*, 1863, pp. 411, 8vo.

Translated into English. *Do.*

"This is an historical romance in which many old legends and family traditions are wrought into a connected story. The narative is enriched by many graphic and peculiarly interesting descriptions of the old manners of the country; and the *dénouement* is, we are assured, founded on fact. Many historical anecdotes and documents are added in the notes that accompany the work."— *Journ. of Ed. L. C.*

"A story illustrative, as its title imports, of old Canadian manners. M. de Gaspé is, as he tells us himself, a septuagenarian, born only eight-and-twenty years after the conquest of La Nouvelle France, at a time when the traditions and customs of the French settlers must have still been fresh. Tales of this character stereotype features which history cannot chronicle, and render a service which in the absence of contemporary me-

moirs and literature, is not to be undervalued. The narrative which is rather designed as a vehicle for this pictorial object, than directed to the excitement of any thrilling interest, is not wanting, however, in spirit or movement. Much credit is due to the translator. The work is rendered into good flowing and easy English, and bespeaks not only a perfect knowledge of both tongues, seldom possessed by those who undertake the task, but a power of thinking out the ideas of one tongue in another, still more rare, combined with much freedom of style and mastery of language."— *Dublin Rec.*

II. Memoires. *Ottawa*, 1866, pp. 563, 8vo.

"Né le 30 Octobre, 1786, les souvenirs personnels de M. de Gaspé embrassent une période de plus de soixante-dix ans, et sa jeunesse s'étant écoulée au mileu des témoins oculaires de la conquête, il a été à même de recueillir parmi eux les tristes mais glorieuses traditions de cette époque encore obscure de notre histoire. Cela fait en tout une période d'un siècle entier, dans laquelle l'aimable chroniqueur a butiné au courant de la plume, racontant sa vie en y mêlant celle de ses amis, et les récits de ses contemporains ; et cela avec une verve toute gauloise et une aisance parfaite.

Placé par sa naissance aux premiers rangs de la vieille aristocratie canadienne, qui, au temps de sa jeunesse, prolongeait encore, autour des gouverneurs anglais, l'existence de la cour vice-royale, il s'est nourri de ses traditions, qui sont pour lui des traditions de famille ; il a pris part à ses fêtes, il a vu passer et disparaitre tour à tour à ses côtés les illustrations du rang, de la beauté et du talent qui faisaient l'ornement de cette fière et puissante société du temps passé et il s'est plu à les faire revivre dans ses Mémoires.

Observateur fin et délicat, il a su faire un choix judicieux parmi les matériaux sans nombre qui ont dû se présenter à son souvenir. Ce qui fait bien souvent le succès des mémoires, ce sont les révélations scandaleuses, les médisances bien apprêtées ; mais je vous défie d'en trouver une seule dans le livre de M. De Gaspé ; pour éviter de dire du mal de ses contemporains, il n'a fait que les portraits de ses amis, et il les a peints avec la touchante mémoire du cœur."— S. Lesage : *Rev. Can.*

DeGaspé, Philippe Aubert, Jr. A son of the preceding. Was Reporter to the House of Assem., N. S. D. at Halifax, 7 March, 1841.

I. L'Influence d'un Livre, roman de Mœurs Canadiennes. *Quebec*, 1837, 12mo.

De Guise, Charles, *M. D.*
    I. Légende Canadienne. Le Cap au Diable. *St. Anne de la Pocatière*, 1863, pp. 45.

Dejean, *Rev. M.* An Indian missionary.
    I. Anichinabek Amisinaki-Kaniwa. The Indian book. (Contains a vocabulary of 40 words in French and Ottawa) *Detroit*, 1830, pp. 106, 12mo.

De La Ponterie, Ferdinand. A native of France. Was for some years connected in an ed. capacity with *La Patrie* and *La Minerve* (Mont.) In 1864 was appointed Inspector of Finance in Mexico, and we believe, established an official journal there.

Delaroche, Peter. Missionary.
    I. The Gospel of Christ preached to the Poor. *Lunenburg, N. S.*, 1773, pp. 99, 8vo. Reprinted : *Halifax*, 1787, pp. 96, 8vo.

Delessert, —.
    I. Les Indiens de la Baie d'Hudson, promenades d'un artiste parmi les Indiens de l'Amérique du Nord, depuis le Canada, jusqu'à l'Ile de Vancouver ; imité de l'Anglais. *Paris*, 1861. pp. vii-273, 18mo.

DeLorimier, Chas. C.
    I. Trois jours de Fêtes Littéraires. Thèses oratoires développées par les élèves du Collège Ste. Marie, à l'inauguration de leur nouvelle salle académique, les 10 et 12 Juillet, 1865. *Montreal*, 1865, pp. 45, 8vo.

    "M. Ch. C. de Lorimier a vraiment un joli talent d'écrivain, et, ce qui vaut mieux encore, la mémoire du cœur ; c'est avec ces deux choses qu'il s'est fait l'historiographe des *Trois jours de fêtes littéraires* au Collège Ste. Marie, en juillet dernier, et il a dignement et brillamment rempli sa tâche."— Joseph Royal : *Rev. Can.*

DeMarconnay, Leblanc. A French Can. journ. B. in France. Came to Can. in 1833 or 1834. In 1837, in conjunction with M. Gosselin, founded *Le Populaire*, of which he became ed. This journal was discontinued in the following year. He was also for a time ed. of *La Minerve* and of *L'Ami du Peuple* ; all three papers being published at Montreal. His comedy was performed at the Theatre Royal, (Mont.) He returned to France.
    I. Valentine, ou la Nina Canadienne. *Montreal*, 1836, pp. 52.

Demers, *Very Rev.* Jerome. For 18 years Superior of the Seminary (Que.) B. at St. Nicholas, L. C., about 1774. D. at Quebec 17 May. 1853. Created Vicar General 1825. Wrote several treatises on the natural sciences for the use of the scholars of the seminary, which have never been printed.

    I. Institutiones Philosophicæ ad usum studiosæ juventutis. *Quebec*, 1835, pp. 395, 8vo.

Dempsey, Richard. A Barrister of U. C. Was Co. Atty. and Clk. of the Peace for York & Peel, U. C. D. some years.

    I. Observations upon the duties of Magistrates. *Toronto*, 1860, pp. 82, 8vo.

Denison, *Lt. Col.* George T., Jr., *LL. B.* A Can. Volunteer officer. B. at Bellevue, (Tor.) Aug. 31, 1839. Ed. at U. C. Col. ; matriculated at Trinity Coll., same city ; and went through the law course in the Univ. of Toronto where, in 1861, he obtained his degree, and in same year was called to the Bar. Has served as an officer in the Volunteer Cavalry of U. C. since 1854. In 1866 attained the rank of Lt. Colonel in the service. During March of that year was on active service with his troop during the Fenian excitement which then prevailed, and in June of the same year when the Province was invaded by O'Neil and his followers, was ordered to the scene of operations. On this latter occasion, although he left Toronto eighteen hours after the last of the other corps ordered to the same destination, he was the first to enter and take possession of Fort Erie. In Aug. and Sept. following was again detailed with his troop for frontier duty, and rendered very efficient service as commanding officer of a chain of out-posts on the Niagara river, and as chief intelligence officer to the Govt.

    I. The National Defences ; or Observations on the best defensive force for Canada. *Toronto*, 1861, pp. 32, 8vo.

    "Captain Denison has collected very valuable facts and arguments in favor of cavalry as a defensive force ; the reasons for supporting such a force in Canada ; and hints on its organization."—*Leader*, (Tor.)

II. Canada : Is she prepared for War? or a few remarks on the state of her defences. By a Native Canadian. - *Do.* 1861, pp. 24, 8vo.

III. A Review of the Militia Policy of the present administration. By Junius, jr. *Hamilton,* 1863, pp. 45, 8vo.

IV. Manual of Outpost Duties, with instructions for the defence of detached houses, villages, bridges, &c., for the use of the volunteers. *Toronto,* 1866, pp. 61, 12mo.

"Though addressed to the volunteers of Canada it would be well if our citizen soldiers became acquainted with the contents of this admirable compilation. Major Denison has sought for his information from the best authorities, and has spared no pains to make his manual complete, and of a practical character. The gallant gentleman's industry, combined with his lucid style, has produced a work of higher merit than its modest appearance would lead one to suppose. The subject is discussed in two parts: Part one dealing with the question of Outpost Duty, and the remaining part treating of the Defence of Outposts. Major Denison is not content with giving instruction to one branch of the service, his manual being applicable to both cavalry and infantry ; indeed, the duties of sentries are treated at some length, but not more than their importance justifies. Chapters in the first section of the book are devoted to formation of chain of outposts, posting videttes and sentries and their duties, patrols and relieving outposts, picquets, &c., while part second contains general principles of defensive works, plan of temporary works, details of execution, obstruction and defence of buildings, villages and bridges. By those members of our volunteer force who are not satisfied with merely becoming acquainted with routine drill, Major Denison's Manual of Outpost Duties will be read and studied with pleasure."—*Public Opinion,* (Lon.)

"Major Denison has produced a little volume which, brief though it be, contains a large amount of information lucidly conveyed, as to the duties of officers and men engaged on outpost service."—*London Rev.*

V. History of the Fenian Raid on Fort Erie, with an account of the Battle of Ridgeway. *Do.*, 1866, pp. 92, 8vo.

"A large amount of labour has been bestowed upon this work. The utmost care has been exercised in collecting and verifying facts. There is throughout proof of an independent and dispassionate mind ; and hence the narrative is valuable, alike for the information it contains, and the manner in which it is expressed."—*Globe,* (Tor.)

7 *

DENNYS, N. B. Royal Navy.

I. An account of the Cruise of the St. George on the North American and West Indian Stations, during the years 1861–1862. *London,* 1863.

DENBY, E. H.

I. A Preliminary Report on the Treaty of Reciprocity with Great Britain, to regulate the trade between the United States and the Provinces of B. N. A. *Washington,* 1866.

II. Letter to Hon. W. H. Seward on the Relations of the United States with the British Provinces, and the actual condition of the question of the fisheries. *Do.* 1867.

DERBYSHIRE, ALEXANDER. An U. C. farmer.

I. A Journey to the West and back again. *Picton,* 1865, pp. 189.

DEROME, FRANÇOIS MAGLOIRE. A French Can. journ B. at Montreal, 1821. Ed. at St. Ann's Coll. where he distinguished himself, carrying off the prize for composition in French Prose and Verse. Whilst studying law contributed some articles to the French Can. newspaper press which attracted attention, and established his reputation as a public writer. His regular connection with the press commenced , in 1851 as ed. of the *Mélanges Religieux* (Mont.) to which he had previously been a contributor. *Le Canadien* in noticing his appointment spoke of him as " a man of rare information and talents," and that he " wrote French with an elegance and a purity uncommon to this country." The office of the *Mélanges Religieux* having been destroyed by fire in 1852, the paper was discontinued. In 1854 he succeeded the late Mr. Ronald Macdonald as ed. of *Le Canadien,* (Que.,) then the organ of the Hincks–Morin Administration. In 1857 he terminated his journalistic career and accepted the office of Prothonotary and Clk. of the Crown and Peace for the District of Rimouski, a position which he still holds. Mr. D. held a high place as a political writer ; he was something more than the ordinary Can. Ed.; he was no time-server and sycophant, approving of every act of the party whose general policy he supported. He wrote purely from conviction and did not fail to record his disapproval when his moral scruples would not allow him to do otherwise. In style he is clear, forcible and eloquent, displaying at the same time a perfect knowledge and command of his native language. Very general regret was manifested by his *confrères* of the newspaper press at the termination of his connection with it. *La Patrie,* (Mont.,) said :

" We say adieu to a man whose character and talents have honored the Canadian press. Mr. Derome is a man of study and a man of taste devoted to the principles of order of which *Le Canadien* is one of the staunchest supporters."

Mr. D. is the author of a large number of poetical pieces some of which were reproduced in the *Rep. Nat.,* (Mont.) 1848. He occasionally contributes to *Le Foyer Can.* and *La Revue Can.*

I. Manuel élémentaire et pratique de l'art agricole, ou notions pratiques sur l'agriculture. *Montreal,* 1853.

DE ROOS, *Hon.* FREDERICK FITZGERALD, *Lieut. R. N.*

I. Personal Narative of Travels in the United States and Canada in 1826 with remarks on the present state of the American Navy. (With plates). *London,* 1827, 8vo.

DE ROTTENBURG, *Col. Baron* GEORGE, *C. B.* B. in U. C. Is a retired officer from the British army in which he served for many years. Was Adjutant General of Militia in Canada, and from 1858 to 1861 Colonel of the 100th Regiment.

I. The supposed self-luminosity of the Planet Neptune. *Can. Journ.* 1856.

II. On an occultation of Spica Virginis by the moon. *Do.* 1857.

III. Solar Spots observed at Toronto, in January, February and March, 1858. 1858.

DEROTTENMUND, *Count* EDOUARD SYLVESTRE. A European Geologist who resided in Can. for some years. B. 1813. D. at Montrieux, lake of Geneva, 1858.

I. Report to Mayor and Corporation of Quebec, on the nature of combustible materials to be found in that city. *Quebec,* 1855.

II. Report on the Exploration of Lakes Superior and Huron. *Can. Sess. Papers,* 1856.

" We look in vain for a single new fact of any practical or scientific value."—*Can. Journ.*

DESAUTELS, *Mgr.* JOSEPH. A priest in the Ch. of Rome. " Chap. S. d'Honneur de SS. P. IX. Chan. H. de Montréal. Curé de Varennes, B. C."

I. Manuel des Curés pour le bon gouvernement temporel des Paroisses et des Fabriques dans le Bas Canada, etc.. avec un chapitre sur la dîme. *Montréal,* 1864, pp. 688, 8vo.

" Accept my thanks for the conscientious work that your zeal has prompted you to undertake. It is full of clear, solid and incontestible principles. I have earnest hopes that this grain of mustard seed may soon become a great tree, on the branches of which the birds of Heaven may lodge."— † IG. BISHOP OF MONTREAL : *Letter to Author.*

II. Des biens et revenus des Fabriques dans le Bas Canada. *Rev. Can.* 1864.

DESBARATS, GEORGE E., Jr., *LL. B.*

I. L'Esclavage dans l'Antiquité, et son abolition par le Christianisme. Etude faite devant le Cabinet de Lecture de Montréal. *Quebec,* 1858, pp. 19. 8vo.

DES BARRES, *Col.* JOSEPH F. W. A celebrated Eng. military officer and hydrographer. B. 1722. D. at Halifax. N. S., 24 Oct., 1824. Entered the army in 1756, and saw considerable active service in Am. In 1758 was engaged in the expedition against Louisbourg. Was present at the seige of Quebec, and subsequently acted as directing engineer in restoring and improving the fortifications of the conquered city. His services in the same and other useful works were brought into requisition in N. S., Newfoundland, and N. Y. It was, however, as a surveyor of the coasts and harbours of the colonies that he chiefly distinguished himself. The want of correct charts of the coast of N. A., for the use of the fleet engaged in carrying on the Am. Revolutionary War, began at this time to be felt, and on Earl Howe representing the immediate necessity of their being prepared, D. was selected to adapt the surveys of Holland, De-Brahm, and others, to nautical purposes. These were published in the work whose title is given below. In 1784, he was appointed Gov. of Cape Breton, with the Military command of that and P. E. I.; soon after he commenced building the town of Sydney, and opened and worked the valuable coal fields at the entrance of the river. In 1804, he became Lieut. Gov. and Commander in Chief of the latter Island.

I. The Atlantic Neptune, published for the use of the Royal Navy of Great Britain. *London*, 1777, 2 vols. atlas fol.

Vol. I. contains : "The Sea Coast of Nova Scotia ; exhibiting the diversities of the coast and face of the country near it : the bank, rocks, shoals, soundings, &c. Together with remarks and directions for the conveniency of navigation and pilotage."

Vol. II. "Charts of the coast and harbours in the gulf and river of St. Lawrence from surveys taken by Major Holland, Surveyor Genl. of the northern district of North America, and his assistants."

"The most splendid collection of charts, plans, and views, ever published."—RICH.

II. Des Barres—Cape Breton. *Do.* 1804.

" Privately printed and suppressed."— COL. ASPINWALL.

DESBRISAY, CHARLES MASSE. A N. S. poet. B. at Halifax, July, 1805. D. at Boston, U. S., 1847. Ed. in Eng. ; studied law there and was admitted as an attorney and solicitor. It is stated that he disliked the practice of the profession he had chosen, and abandoned it on his return to his native country, which occurred after a few years residence in London. His general abilities were of a high order, and his literary attainments varied and extensive. From the same authority, (*Provl. Mag.*) we gather that :

" For many years of his life his mind was deeply shadowed by melancholy. His poetry is all of a serious nature, more or less imbued with his own religious feelings ; we consequently meet with but little variety of sentiment and expression. He wrote very rarely, and then but to express some exquisite thought of the moment, connected with the great subject to him of such vital importance."

DE SOLA, *Rev.* ABRAHAM, *LL. D.* Minister Hebrew Cong., Prof. of Hebrew and Oriental Literature, Univ. of McGill Coll. (Mont.) B. in London, Eng. His father, the late Rev. D. A. De Sola, one of the most learned of modern Hebrew divines, was author of several valuable works, well known to Biblical scholars, chief of which was, perhaps, his new translation of the Scriptures, with a copious and learned commentary. Dr. De S. had the advantage of the partial supervision of his eminent father in his oriental studies which he also pursued under the celebrated Dr. Loewe, orientalist to the Duke of Sussex and oriental examiner to the Royal College of Preceptors. Without neglecting his classical and other studies, he displayed at a very early age a decided preference for oriental literature, receiving a special diploma for his progress therein. His taste for science and abstruse study led him to master some of the modern languages also. This taste was, no doubt, promoted by the circumstance that his father possessed an extensive and valuable library, more especially in his favorite department, was himself a great linguist and close reader, and was constantly receiving at his house, the visits of eminent *literati*. It was probably from the latter circumstance, chiefly, that the reputation of Dr. De S. extended most favourably, so that eulogistic notices of him appear in various literary journals before he had attained his twentieth year, before which period, also, he had received some very flattering calls to fill honourable appointments, among them, was the charge of the Montreal Hebrew Congregation, which he accepted. Prior to his departure for Montreal, however, he had been rather actively employed in the literary world around him. He had been for some time co-editor of *The Voice of Jacob* with Dr. Benisch ; and while he assisted his father in his official duties, lectured at various establishments on the Semitic languages, Biblical Antiquities, &c. He had also been actively employed in aiding various literary institutions in the metropolis, especially, in assisting to found the Sussex Hall Literary Institution, of which he remained one of the Directors until he left, Eng. He arrived in Montreal Jany. 1847, and although his time was necessarily chiefly devoted to his official duties, he still found leisure to contribute to various magazines in the U. S., and during the same winter he gave one of the course of lectures at the Mercantile Library Association. Thereafter he was called upon by that Association and the Mechanics' Institute every succeeding winter, while they continued to give a course, and he always acceded to the request of these institutions, the Literary Club, and some institutions in sister cities, when his leisure permitted him. His desire to promote the study of Natural Science led him to devote himself very zealously to the Natural History Society, then in a languishing and all but dying state. By warmly interesting himself in it, and inducing others to do so, he assisted greatly to promote its interests and vitality. The reports of the society show that besides an occasional address at its conversaziones he has lectured on " *The Cosmogony;*" " *The Ancient Hebrews as promoters of the arts and sciences;*" " *The Zoology of the Scriptures;*" " *The Botany of the Scriptures,*" and kindred topics. In 1848 he was appointed Prof. of Hebrew and Oriental Literature in the Univ. of McGill College; the press of the Province universally applauding the fitness of the appointment. But multifarious official duties have not prevented Dr. De S. from wielding a most industrious pen. In 1850 he wrote, by request, for the *British American Journal of Medical and Physical Science,* a series of articles " *On the employment of Anæsthetics in Midwifery,*" the popular objections to their use being, at that time, very rife. He also wrote in consecutive numbers of the same Mag. a notice of Dr. Dawson's "*Archaia.*" In 1852 he contributed to the " *Canada Medical Journ.*" a series of articles which were published regularly as long as the Mag. appeared, on " *The Sanatory Institutions of the Hebrews.*" These learned papers attracted very general attention and were reproduced by the *Dublin Medical Journal* " and some other scientific journals, and the Jewish periodicals. They were criticised most favorably by the press, even where writers differed from him. Dr. DeSola has also published the following :—"*A*

Selection of Sermons, Addresses and Reviews;" " *Hebrew Authors and their Opponents;*" " *An Inquiry into the Early Settlement of the Jews in England;* " " *The Jews of Persia under Mahommed Shah;* " " *Biography of Rev. D. A. De Sola,*" (the above published in Philadelphia 1847–1865.) A translation of Zedners " *Auswahl aus Hebraischen Schriftstellern,*" and Elias Levitas' " *Habachur* " (a Hebrew grammatical work). Hanagids " *Introduction to the Talmud,*" and "*The Jewish Calendar* " published in N. Y. & Montreal. He has also published a couple of religious educational books and some occasional pieces written in Hebrew and other languages. Besides his literary activity, Dr. De S. has uniformly identified himself with every movement calculated to promote the intellectual advancement of the community in which he lives. He has been elected honorary member of various literary and scientific societies both in Europe and America; and the good will of his friends, both around him and abroad, has made him the recipient of several presentations and testimonials of a valuable and flattering character. For the above, we have been indebted to some biographical notices of Dr. De S. contained in the "*Hebræische Bibliographie* " of Dr. M. Steinschneider in Berlin, the *Tijdschrift* in Amsterdam, Holland; the *Hebrew Observer* and *Chronicle,* London, England; the *Occident* in Philadelphia, and other publications. We conclude with the following from a Canadian writer :

"The Rev. Doctor is a gentleman of high intellectual powers combined with that bearing and open urbanity of manner, which, whenever it appears, is sure to elicit profound respect and at the same time to attract the highest esteem. Of consistent and liberal views which, however, he never obtrudes, he commands the confidence and respect of other religious denominations, and has obtained the warm friendship of many of their leading clergy. Indeed, there are few of the professional men of Montreal who are more extensively or more favorably known, or who centre in themselves more true humility combined with sound scholarship."

DESSAULLES, *Hon.* LOUIS A. A French Can. author and journ. B. at St. Hyacinthe, L. C., Jan. 1819. Ed. there and at the col. of Montreal. Sat for Rougemont in the Leg. Coun., Can., from 1856, until appointed Joint Clerk of the Crown and Peace, (Mont.,) in 1863. Was editor in chief of *Le.Pays*, (Mont.,) the organ of the *Rouge* party of 1. C. Wrote in that paper several series of elaborate articles. 1st. in 1861, "*On the sovereign right of the people to control the government of the country;*" 2ndly. in 1862, "*On the temporal power of the Pope;*" 3rdly- in same year, "*On the mismanagement displayed in connection with the erection of the public buildings at Ottawa.*" All written in a moderate liberal spirit, but which nevertheless were strongly animadverted upon by his adversaries. Mr. D. was president of *L'Institut Canadien*, (Mont.,) for some years and has delivered various lectures and addresses before that institution.

I. Rouge et Noir. *Montreal*, 1848.

This pamphlet was written in vindication of Mr. L. J. Papineau who, in 1847-8 was violently attacked by the Lafontaine and Nelson party for his conduct at St. Denis during the Rebellion of 1837.

II. Six Lectures sur l'annexion du Canada aux Etats-Unis. *Do.*, 1851, pp. 199, 4to.

III. Galilée, ses travaux scientifiques et sa condamnation : Lecture publique faite devant. *Do.*, 1856, pp. 50, 4to.

IV. A Messieurs les electeurs de la Division de Rougemont. *Do.*, 1858, pp. 66, 8vo.

This is an address to his constituents on the political transactions of the day.

V. Discours sur L'Institut Canadien prononcé, par l'Hon. L. A. Dessaulles, Président de l'Institut, à la séance du vingt-trois de décembre, 1862, à l'occasion du dix-huitième anniversaire de sa fondation. *Do.*, 1863, pp. 21, 4to.

VI. La Guerre Américaine, son origine et ses vraies causes. *Do.*, 1865, pp. 341, 32s.

D'ESTIMAUVILLE, *Chevalier* ROBERT. D. at Quebec, about 1829. Was for some years a member of the L. C. Leg.

I. The Enquirer, *Quebec*, 1821.

II. Cursory view of the Local, Social, Moral and Political State of the Colony of Lower Canada. *Do.*, 1829, 8vo.

DEVINE, THOMAS, *F. R. G. S.* Head of Surveys, U. C. Dept. of Crown Lands, Canada.

I. Description of a new Trilobite from the Quebec group. *Can. Nat.* 1863.

"The fossil now described was of special interest, as giving the complete characters of a genus previously known only by parts of the body."—*Can. Nat.*, 1863.

DEWART, *Rev.* EDWARD HARTLEY. A min. in the Wes. Meth. Ch., (Tor.) Poetical contributions from his pen are to be found in the *Christian Guardian*, (Tor.,) though he has written for several other journals.

I. Thoughts on the relation of Baptized Children to the Church, and the duty and responsibility which it involves. *Toronto*, 1861.

II. Selections from Canadian Poets; with occasional critical and biographical notes, and an introductory essay on Canadian Poetry. *Montreal*, 1864, pp. 304, 8vo.

"This book ought at least to convince those who are not disposed to believe—and we hold that there are many even among the best informed—that we have in this Canada a few writers of verse whose productions, had they appeared in British or American periodicals would have won for their authors literary renown of no mean order. * * *

"What Mr. Dewart has done he has done well. His choice has been most judicious: his introductory essay affords ample food for thought to those who take an interest in our literature; his critical notes are always in excellent taste, and his preface at once fully explains his object. * * *

"He is certainly entitled to the lasting gratitude of all who take an interest in Canadian literature."—*Chronicle*, (Que.)

III. Songs of Life, a collection of original poems. (*In preparation : to be published at Edinburgh*, 1867.)

DE WETTE, L.

I. Reise in den Vereinigten Staaten und Canada im Jahr, 1837. *Leipzig*, 1838, 8vo.

DEWHURST, E. R. A Can. Journ. Was on the staff of the *Herald*, (Brantford), in 1855, and in same year joined the *Courier* of same town as Asst. Ed., a position which he held until 1862. In 1864 established the *Welland Telegraph* which he still continues to own and edit. Is a Liberal Conservative in politics.

Dick, Alexander. (Woodstock, U. C.)

I. Splores of Halloween—Twenty years ago. *Woodstock*, 1867, pp. 22, 18mo.

Dick, Rev. Robert, D. D. A Baptist clergym. and writer, now residing in U. S. In 1849 established a monthly journal, called the *Unfettered Canadian* (Brockville,) "asserting the right and duty of every man to investigate and choose for himself in relation to the philosophy and means of health." Its chief object was the defeat of an oppressive medical monopoly bill then before Parliament, which it was instrumental in accomplishing. Founded in 1854 the *Gospel Tribune*, (Tor.), also a monthly journal, "for alliance and intercommunication throughout Evangelical Christendom," which he ed. until its publication was brought to a close in 1858.

Dinning, John G.

1. Book-keeping by Single and Double Entry for the use of Schools, exemplified in three sets of books, and adapted to the use of the Farmer, Mechanic, Retail Tradesman and the Merchant, with a variety of useful Commercial Forms. *Montreal*, 1861.

Dixon, Major F. E. 2nd Batt., Queen's Own Rifles, Toronto.

I. The Volunteer's Active Service Manual ; or Internal economy and standing orders for Volunteers when on active service ; with bugle calls and forms of all reports, returns, &c., necessary for the government of a Volunteer Battalion, and shewing the every day duties of the various grades of rank and command. *Toronto*, 1867, pp. 131, 8vo.

' " It seems to contain everything which in addition to drill, is necessary for volunteers to know of internal economy, while, at the same time, we can discover in it nothing superfluous or unnecessary." — *Telegraph*, (Tor.)

Dixon, Captain George, R. N.

I. A voyage round the world ; but more particularly to the North-West coast of America, performed in 1785-6-7-8, in the King George and Queen Charlotte, by Captains Portlock and Dixon. *London*, 1789, 4to.

Dixon, James.

I. Tour through a part of the United States and Canada, with notices of Methodism in America. *New York*, 1849.

Dixon, John. "Missionary."

I. Baptismal Regeneration exhibited in the Prayer Book of the Church of England. *Halifax*, 1850, pp. 15, 8vo.

Donaldson, J. A. Govt. Emigrant Agent, (Tor.)

I. Practical hints on the cultivation and treatment of the Flax plant, expressly for the use of the Canadian farmer. *Toronto*, 1865.

Donnelly, William, M. D. Surgeon R. N.

I. Diary of Practical Observations on Malignant Cholera at New York. *Halifax*, 1832, pp. 44, 8vo.

Dorion, E. P. Chief French translator, Leg. Assem. Can.

I. Affaire-Pelletier. La Reine *vs.* Prudent Pelletier. Procès pour meurtre. *Quebec*, 1853, pp. 100.

II. Historique des fonds de retraite en Europe et en Canada. *Quebec*, 1862, pp. 94.

Dorion, Jacques Edmond, M. D. A French Can. journ. B. at St. Ours L. C. 1827. Proceeding to the U. S. at an early age to pursue his professional studies, he there founded and ed. *La Ruche Canadienne ; La Feuille d'érable ; Le Citoyen* and *L'Union.* The last named journal was published in the interest of the Democratic party at Ogdensburg, N. Y. previous to the Am. Rebellion of 1860. From 1861 to 1865 ed. *Le Courrier d'Ottawa.* Dr. D. is the author of various lectures delivered before several national associations in the U. S. and Can. He has also written several novels :—*Le Brave Edouard, légende de la Vallée du Richelieu* 1837 ; *Un Échappé de Prison*, etc. He is the founder of *La Soc. St. Jean Baptiste* at Burlington, Plattsburg, Ogdensburgh and other places in the U. S.

I. L'Éducation populaire, besoin des Ecoles du Soir pour la classe ouvrière ; a lecture delivered before *L'Institut Français* of N. Y., and printed by request of the Committee. *New York*, 1853.

Dorion, Jean Baptiste Eric. A French Can. journ. and legislator. B. at St. Anne de la Perade L. C. 16 Sept., 1826. D. at L'Avenir L. C., 1 Nov., 1866.

Ed. at his native place. He early gave his attention to politics, and in 1848 in conjunction with Mr. P. Blanchet and one or two other gentlemen of advanced political views established *L'Avenir*, (Mont.) newspaper, which, while it lasted, was held as the most uncompromising organ of the *Rouge* party in L. C. Some years before his death he established another journal *Le Défricheur*, at L'Avenir, L. C., a village which he had founded and settled, and named after his first paper. This journal was started mainly for the purpose of promoting colonization amongst the French Can. rural population, many of whom he induced to leave the parishes along the St. Lawrence, and settle on the more fertile lands in the Eastern Townships. Mr. D. was one of the most forcible writers on the *Rouge* press. He held the presidency of the *Institut Canadien* (Mont.) for 3 years. He sat in the Leg. Assem. Can. from 1854, until 1857, and again from 1861 until the close of the last Parliament. He excelled as a stump orator, and during his time rendered very useful service to his party.

Dorion, V. P. W. A French Can. journ. B. 1827. Admitted to the Bar L. C., 1850. Has been President of the *Institut Canadian* (Mont.) Was one of the Ed's. of *L'Avenir* (Mont.), a liberal newspaper. Is now joint prop. and ed. of *Le Pays*, (do.,) also a Liberal journal.

D'Onsonnens, Eraste. A French Can. writer, (Mont.) Has contributed several tales and sketches to the French Can. newspaper and periodical press. See *Esquisses Indiennes* in *La Patrie*, 1856 ; *Angélina* in *La Guêpe*, 1860. He has also delivered lectures on different occasions before the *Institut Canadien* (Mont.)

I. Felluna. *Montreal*, 1856, 18mo.

"Three literary essays which in our opinion possess considerable merit."—*L'Avenir*.

II. Une Apparition. *Do*., 1860, 18mo.

"This romance is written with a great deal of cleverness and in a very elegant style. The author has real merit as a literary man."—*Gazette* (Sorel.)

Dory, *Rev*. John. A Presbyter of the Ch. of Eng., and Missionary from the incorporated S. P. G. F. P.

I. A Sermon preached at the opening of Christ's Church at Sorel, in the Province of Canada, on Sunday the 25th day of December, 1785. *Montreal*, 1786, pp. 14, 8vo.

Doucet, N. B., *N. P.*

I. Fundamental principles of the laws of Canada, as they existed under the Natives ; as they were changed under the French Kings, and under the domination of England. The Custom of Paris, the text and a literal translation; the Statutes changing the Jurisprudence of Canada, &c. *Montreal*, 1843, 8vo.

Dougall, James.

I. The Canadian Fruit Culturist. 1867.

Douglas, *Captain* A. G.

I. Leçons de chimie de Sir Humphrey Davy, traduites en Français, dédiées aux Sociétés d'Agricultures du Bas Canada. *Montreal*, 1824, 8vo.

II. Dix-neuf années en Canada. 1831.

Douglas, *Maj. Genl. Sir* Howard. A distinguished Eng. Officer. Was Lieut. Gov. of N. B. for some years.

I. Considerations on the Value and Importance of the British North American Provinces. *London*, 1831, 8vo.

Douglas, *Rev.* James, *B. A.* A Min. of the Presb. Ch., (Que.) Is Vice President of the Lit. and His. Soc. there.

I. The Belief of the Ancient Egyptians regarding a future State. *Trans. Lit. and His. Soc.* (Que.) 1862.

II. The Gold Fields of Canada. *Do.*, 1863-4.

III. On two Mummies from Thebes, in Upper Egypt. *Do.*, 1864-5.

IV. Opening address. *Do.*, 1865-6.

Douglas, John. Assist. Surgeon of the 8th Foot ; placed on half pay, 1816.

I. Medical topography of Upper Canada. *London*, 1819, pp. 126, 8vo.

Doutre, Gonzalve, *B. C. L.* A French Can. lawyer at the Montreal Bar. B. at Montreal, 12 July 1842. Graduated at Univ. McGill Coll. in 1861. Admitted to the Bar in Aug., 1863. While still a Law Student was made President of the Law Institute and endeavoured to persuade the members of the Bar to adopt more stringent measures in connection with the mode of admission to the Bar, with the view of preventing the overcrowding of the profession with useless and sometimes unworthy members. A large number of students feeling that such measures would prevent their admission to the Bar, attacked Mr. D. with more than ordinary impetuosity. On the 4 May, 1866, still persevering in his project of reform, he submitted to a meeting of the members of the Bar (Mont.), a series of resolutions proposing amendments to the Law concerning the Bar. These resolutions were referred to a special committee, of which he was one as Secy. They were favorably reported on by that committee who submitted a Bill intended to be substituted for the law then in force. That Bill was transmitted to all the sections of the Bar and approved by them, and Mr. D was deputed to the seat of government with the view of promoting the passage of a law which embodied all his suggestions. Finally on the 15th Augt., 1866, the new law was sanctioned with certain amendments which, however, did not affect the principal changes proposed. Since then the general council of the Bar of L. C., composed of all the Bâtonniers of the several sections, has appointed him their Secy., an office which also gives him a seat in the General Council. Thus ended the agitation for reforms which appeared impracticable when he was merely a student. The stringent examinations for admission to the Bar have since had their effect, the admissions being less numerous, which may lead one to hope that the legal profession will not be so over-crowded as formerly.

Having been a mem. of the *Institut Canadien* since 1858, he successively performed the duties of Recording Secy., Treasurer, Corresponding Secy. and Secy. of the Dept. of the Museum, which, under his management, has been much enlarged. The *Institut* was favored with valuable donations from several Govts. of Europe and of this continent. As Corresponding Secy. he had an agent appointed at Paris to communicate with H. I. H. Prince Napoleon, one of the patrons of the *Institut*, and with the scientific institutions of France. Since the appointment

of this agent the communications between the *Institut Canadien* and France have become regular and have produced important results for the *Institut*. Mr. D. has delivered several lectures under the patronage of the *Institut* and the Law Soc. Several of his lectures have been published by the press, some in *Le Pays*. One *On the Principle of Nationalities* led to a lively discussion among the French papers in L. C., and was printed in pamphlet form. Mr. D. has, at different periods, written in *Le Pays* upon various subjects, more particularly upon the administration of justice, the mode of admission to the Bar, on the abolition of capital punishment, monomania, numismatics, the *Institut Canadien*, and the Law Institute.

DOUTRE, JOSEPH, *Q. C.* A French Can. lawyer and journ. B. at Beauharnois, L. C., 11 March, 1825. Mr. D. had scarcely left Coll. in 1843, before he commenced his connection with the press as a contributor to *Les Mélanges Religieux* (Mont.), the subject of his first essay being a pointed attack on Sir Chas. Metcalfe, the then Gov. Gen. In 1844 he wrote for *L'Aurore des Canadas*, and in 1848, having attached himself in politics to the side of Mr. L. J. Papineau, he laboured long and earnestly on behalf of the Liberal party through the columns of *L'Avenir* then the organ of Mr. P. Some biographical sketches of leading public men which appeared in that paper are from his pen. He took an active part in the establishment of *Le Pays* (Mont.), and for a long period lent to the new journal his powerful aid in its ed. columns. Mr. D. has been a contributor to nearly every Liberal journal published in the French language in L. C., and there can be no doubt that he has rendered very material assistance as a journ. to the Liberal cause. He has also written for *Le Courrier des Etats Unis* and the *Tribune* (N. Y.), and for the *Lower Canada Jurist* (Mont.) In 1852 he was elected President of *L'Institut Canadien* (Mont.), and did much while he held that office towards infusing new life and vigour into the operations of the Institution. It was through his efforts that it became an incorporated body, and that the splendid additions to its library, &c., from the Imperial collections in France were obtained. He has delivered many lectures and addresses before the *Institut*. We append a list of his more purely literary efforts. Of late he has devoted himself almost exclusively to his profession as an advocate, and in 1866 was counsel for the celebrated E. T. Lamirande, the defaulting cashier of the Bank of France, at Poictiers.

I. Les Finances de 1812. *Montreal*, 1844, pp. 500.

II. Le Frère et la Sœur, a legend. [Originally published in *La Revue Canadienne*.] *Rép. Nat.*, 1848.

III. Le Concours Boucherville. 1851.

IV. Les Sauvages du Canada. 1852.

Dowdall, *Commander* P. S.

I. Narrative of the Loss of the Brig Charles, on her Passage from Liverpool to Newfoundland, and Miraculous Delivery of the Master and two of the Crew in an open boat. *Liverpool*, 1812, 8vo.

Downs, A.

I. On the Land Birds of Nova Scotia. *Trans. N. S. Inst.*, 1864-5.

Doyle, MARTIN.

I. Hints on Emigration to Upper Canada, especially addressed to the middle and lower classes. *Dublin ; London*, and *Edinburgh*, 1832.

Doyle, WILLIAM, *LL. B.*

I. Some account of the British Dominions beyond the Atlantic ; containing chiefly what is most interesting and least known, with respect to those parts ; particularly, the important question about the North-West passage is satisfactorily discussed. *London*, 1770, 8vo.

Drake, B.

I. Life of Tekumseh, and of his brother the Prophet, with an historical sketch of the Shawnee Indians. *Cincinnati*, 1855, 12mo.

Drapeau, STANISLAS. A French Can. writer. Has identified himself specially with the Colonisation movement in L. C., and rendered material service in promoting that important work. He was for many years connected with the French Can. press, and founded several

journals which in their day exerted some influence upon public opinion. For several years he has held a position in the Bureau of Agriculture, Can.

I. Appel aux Municipalités du Bas Canada. La Colonisation du Canada envisagée au point de vue National. *Québec*, 1858.

" De l'utilité et du patriotisme."—*Canadien*, (Que.)

II. Religion et Patrie ! Association de Secours pour venir en aide aux défricheurs du Sol. Projet de constitution. *Do.*, 1859, pp. 8, 12mo.

" Cette magnifique Association n'est pas seulement, nous sommes heureux de le dire, à l'état de projet. Etablie déjà dans plusieurs paroisses du bas du fleuve, elle a déjà fournie ses preuves, et l'expérience a démontré qu'elle pourrait opérer un bien incalculable ; déjà les résultats les plus consolants sont venus couronner ses efforts. C'est ce dont on a pu juger par les différents écrits do son fondateur, Mr. Drapeau."—*Minerve*, (Mont.)

III. Considérations sur les Classes Ouvrières et la Colonisation. *Do.*, 1860, pp. 24, 12mo.

IV. Etudes sur les développements, de la Colonisation du Bas Canada depuis dix ans (1851—1861.) Constatant les progrès des défrichements, de l'ouverture des chemins de Colonisation et du développement de la population Canadienne-Française. (Avec Cartes.) *Do.*, 1863, pp. 600, 8vo.

" • • • • Le livre que Mr. Stanislas Drapeau vient de publier à Québec, sur les progrès de la colonisation franco canadienne, est une œuvre éminemment utile et nationale. Nous connaissons de longue date M. Drapeau, qui est un des agents les plus actifs et les plus habiles de la colonisation canadienne, nul ne pouvait traiter cette question avec plus d'autorité et d'expérience. Nous pensons que tous les Canadiens liront attentivement ce livre, car il s'agit de l'affaire essentielle et vitale du pays."—E. RAMEAU: *L'Economiste Français.*

V. Coup-d'œil sur les Ressources productives et la richesse du Canada, suivi d'un "Plan d'Organisation" complet et détaillé, relatif à la Colonisation. Destiné à faire suite aux "Etudes sur la Colonisation." *Do.*, 1864, pp. 36, 8vo.

" Il est grandement temps que nous nous réveillions de notre apathie et que nous nous occupions sérieusement de l'organisation du département de la colonisation. Mr. Drapeau dans une brochure remarquable étudie la question avec connaissance de cause."—*Rev. Agricole.* (Mont.)

VI Observations sur la brochure de MM. les Abbés Laverdière et Casgrain relativement à la découverte du tombeau de Champlain. *Do.*, 1866, pp. 28, 8vo.

VII. Le *Journal de Québec* et le Tombeau de Champlain. *Do.*, 1867, pp. 8vo.

DRAPER, *Hon.* W. H., *C. B.* Chief Justice of Ontario. Sat in Can. Parliament from 1841 to 1845. Held the office of Atty. Genl., U. C., for some years.

I. Speech in defence of the chartered rights of the University of King's College, delivered at the bar of the Legislative Assembly of Canada, Nov. 24, 1843. *Toronto.* pp. 17.

II. Correspondence between the Hon. W. H. Draper and the Hon. R. E. Caron ; and between the Hon. R. E. Caron and the Hons. L. H. Lafontaine and A. N. Morin. *Montreal*, 1846, pp. 36. 8vo.

III. Report on Mission to England respecting the Hudson's Bay Territory. *Sess. Pap.*, 1858.

IV. Upper Canada King's Bench Reports 1729-31. *Toronto.* 2nd ed. vol. I., 1861, pp. 526 ; vol. II. 1862, pp. 548, 8vo.

Canadian Journal.

I. Address delivered at the Annual Conversazione of the Canadian Institute. 1853.

II. Annual Address as President of the Can. Institute. 1857.

III. Do. Do. 1858.

DRAPER. WILLIAM GEORGE. *M.A.* Judge of the Co. of Frontenac, U C. Son of the preceding. Contributed to the *Ang. Am. Mag.* (Tor.) *The Origin of Sea-Sickness ; Cruise of the Challenge, or a New Year's day in France*, and *A Curious Narrative.*

I. Rules of the Courts of Queen's Bench and Common Pleas ; the Municipal Court Rules ; the County Courts Equity Extension, and the new Division Court Rules ; together with a complete compilation of the Criminal Law of this Province. *Toronto*, 1855, 12mo.

II. The New Rules of Practice, and the proposed New Rules of Pleading of the Queen's Bench and Common Pleas, Upper Canada, with Schedule of Forms, and Table of Costs under the Common Law Procedure Act, 1856 ; with Notes. *Do.*, 1856.

III. Short sketch of the History of Kingston. *Kingston*, 1862, pp. 28.

IV. A handy book of the Law of Dower, with Statutes, Forms, Pleadings, &c. *Toronto*, 1863, pp. 140.

"It is well written, well arranged and well got up."—*U. C. Law Journ.*

DREW, BENJAMIN.

I. A North-side view of Slavery : the Refugee ; or, the narratives of fugitive slaves in Canada, related by themselves ; with an account of the history and condition of the coloured population of Upper Canada. *Boston*, 1856, crown 8vo.

DRISCOLL, FREDERICK. An Am. newspaper writer. B. at Montreal, 1830. Established and ed., in 1862, *The Spirit of our Times* (Mont.), devoted to "Sports and Arms." Was Foreign Ed. of the *World* (N. Y.) for 1 year. Served as war correspondent in the late Am. Rebellion for the *Tribune* (N. Y.), at different places during the continuance of hostilities, and subsequently as special correspondent in Mexico and Can. for the same journal. Is still, we believe, connected with the N. Y. press.

I. Ideas on Military Tactics. *Montreal Gazette*, 1860.

II. Memoirs of a Canadian. *Do. do.*

III. The Twelve Days Campaign. An impartial account of the final campaign of the late war. *Montreal*, 1866.

"He writes very graphically and well, and, as he is thoroughly read in military matters, his description of one of the greatest events of modern times cannot but prove valuable to the student and general reader. A reference map of the country in the vicinity of Richmond accompanies the work ; so that the reader can follow the movements of the two armies step by step, and understand the position and nature of their manœuvres. A very suggestive chapter on the defences of Canada and the Lower Provinces is also given. Mr. Driscoll believes that in cases of a serious attack by a great power like the United States, at least 150,000 men would be required for the defence of Canada alone, which, if properly backed by Great Britain, could be held against all comers—the Townships, of course, excepted. His considerations are well put, and will likely meet with attention at the hands of military men, to whom and to the militia we heartily commend them."—*Gazette* (Mont.)

IV. Sketch of the Canadian Ministry *Do.*, 1866, pp. 130, 12mo.

"This sketch is meant to be only a brief review of the members of the ministry. To the notice of each member distinguished for speech is added a specimen of his oratorical talent, taken from some late speech of the gentleman."—*Preface.*

DRUMMOND, A. T., B. A., LL. B.
I. Contributions to the local Flora of Kingston. *Trans. Bot. Soc. Can.* 1861.

II. On the economical uses of Sticta Pulmonaria Hoffm. *Do.*

III. Observations on Canadian Geographical Botany. *Can. Nat.* 1864.

DUANE, WILLIAM.
I. Canada and the Continental Congress, an annual address before the His. Soc. of Pensylvania. *Philadelphia*, 1850, pp. 20.

DU CALVET, PIERRE.
I. Appel à la Justice de l'Etat, ou Recueil des Lettres au Roi, au Prince de Galles et aux Ministres: avec une lettre à Messieurs les Canadiens, où sont fidèlement exposés les actes horribles de la violence arbitraire qui a régné dans la Colonie, durant les derniers troubles, et les vrais sentiments du Canada sur le Bill de Québec, et sur la forme de Gouvernement la plus propre à y faire renaître la paix et le bonheur public. Une lettre au Général Haldimand lui-même; enfin une dernière lettre à Milord Sydney : *Londres*, 1784, 1 vol. 8vo.

"Cet ouvrage fut publié à Londres, en 1784, après que M. *Du Calvet* eut échoué dans les plaintes qu'il avait portées au Roi et à ses Ministres, contre le général Haldimand. M. *Du Calvet*, Protestant Français, était resté en Canada après sa cession à la Grande-Bretagne, en 1763. Il était dans le commerce, et avait été nommé Magistrat pour la Ville de Montréal, sous le Gouvernement Anglais; mais il ne fut pas longtemps sans se trouver engagé vis-à-vis les Magistrats, ses collègues, dans une série de querelles et de haines qui eurent leur origine dans l'absolutisme du gouvernement d'alors: pouvoir qui est fréquemment mis en jeu dans des circonstances analogues. M. *Du Calvet* fut finalement emprisonné à Québec, comme favorisant les

Bostonnais, pendant deux ans et huit mois, qui finirent le 2 Mai, 1784. Après son élargissement il se rendit en Angleterre, pour obtenir justice contre le Gouverneur. Son ouvrage contient quelques Documents intéressants relativement aux époques qui précédèrent l'établissement d'une Constitution Représentative, dans le Bas Canada, dont M. *Du Calvet* était un aussi ardent partisan, qu'il était vigoureusement opposé à l'Acte, communément appelé le Bill de Québec de 1774. Le tableau que M. *Du Calvet* lui même nous donne de ces époques et des acteurs qui y figuraient est probablement surchargé, et dans bien des cas ses portraits sont absolument des caricatures.

"Dans cet ouvrage M. *Du Calvet* parle d'un autre ouvrage qu'il qualifie de *Mémoire*, (de 284 pages) qu'il avait aussi fait imprimer à Londres peu de temps auparavant, et dont il avait envoyé plusieurs exemplaires en Canada, par les premiers vaisseaux au printemps de l'année 1784. Il paraîtrait que ce *Mémoire* donne plus en détail tout ce que l'auteur eut à souffrir durant son emprisonnement; mais je n'ai pu m'en procurer le titre."—G. B. FAIRBAULT.

II. The Case of Pierre Du Calvet, Esquire, of Montreal, in the Province of Quebeck, containing, (amongst other things worth notice) An account of the long and severe Imprisonment he suffered in the said Province, by the order of General Haldimand, the present Governour of the same, without the least offense, or other lawful cause whatever. To which is prefixed, a dedication of it in the French language, (Mr. Du Calvet not understanding English) to the King's Most Excellent Majesty, humbly imploring the protection and countenance of His Majesty's Royal Justice in his endeavours to procure some compensation for the injuries he has received. *London*, 1784, 8vo.

DUMESNIL, CLÉMENT.
I. De L'Abolition des droits Féodaux et Seigneuriaux au Canada. *Montréal*, 1849.

II. Réflexions préliminaires des vrais principes politiques. *Do.*, 1849.

DUNBAR, JAMES. A Can. journ. B. in 1833. Son of an officer in the Brit. Army, who died in India. In 1851, while studying for the Bar, became Law Reporter to the *Mercury* (Que.), a position, however, which he relinquished in a short period. From 1854 to 1857 ed. the *Daily Chronicle* of the same city, and through unremitting toil and the force of his talents as a writer raised the character of that journal to a high standard.

DUNCAN, F.
I. Our Garrisons in the West (North America.) *London*, 1864, post 8vo.

DUNCAN, *Rev.* JOHN M.
I. Travels through part of the United States and Canada (with plans.) *Glasgow*, 1823, 2 vols, 8vo ; Am. ed., *New York, do.*

DUNDONALD, THOMAS COCHRANE, (10th) *Earl of.* A distinguished Brit. Admiral. B. 1775. D. 1862.
I. Notes on the Mineralogy, Government and condition of the British West India Islands and North American Maritime Colonies ; with a statistical chart of Newfoundland, contrasting the circumstances of the French and British Fisheries. *London*, 1851, 8vo.

DUNKIN, *Hon.* CHRISTOPHER, *Q. C., D. C. L.* A Can. legislator and advocate. B. in Eng. Received his education at the London Coll. and the Univ. of Glasgow. Was Asst. Provincial Secy. for L. C. for some time. Is one of the governors of the Univ. of McGill College. Sat in the Can. Parliament from 1857 until the Union of 1867. In latter year was appointed Treasurer of Province of Quebec.
I. British American Politics. *N. A. Rev.*, 1839, pp. 59.
II. Address at the Bar of the Legislative Assembly of Canada on behalf of certain proprietors of Seigniories of Lower Canada against the second reading of the bill intituled : " An Act to define Seigniorial rights in Lower Canada, and to facilitate the redemption thereof." *Quebec*, 1853, pp. 109, 8vo.
III. Case (in part) of the Seigniors of Lower Canada, submitted to the Judges of the Court of Queen's Bench and of the Superior Court for Lower Canada. *Montreal*, 1855, 8vo.
IV. Memorandum relative to the Militia system. *Ottawa*, 1866.

DUNLOP, WILLIAM, *M. D.* A well known Scot., and Can. *littérateur.* B. at Greenock, Scot. about 1795. D. at Lachine, near Montreal, 28 June, 1848. Came to Can. in 1826, with Mr. John Galt. in the service of the Canada Company, which Mr. G. had succeeded in forming in London, and continued a resident of the Province during the remainder of his life. After taking up his residence in Can. he resumed his contributions to *Blackwood's Magazine*, and among other things wrote " *The Autobiography of a Rat,*" for that popular periodical. He was also a frequent contributor to the native literary and political press—among the former class to the *Canadian Literary Magazine* (York) and the *Literary Garland* (Mont.) He founded in 1836 the City of Toronto Literary Club, before which he lectured on various subjects of interest. In 1841 he was elected to the Can. Parliament as member for the County of Huron, which he continued to represent until he resigned in 1846. For the following sketch of the early career of this very able and gifted man we are indebted to *Fraser's Magazine* (Vol. V.) Vol. VII. of the same periodical contains an admirable likeness of the subject of this notice :

" But leaving questions of pedigree to heralds, we find Dunlop a surgeon in the Connaught Rangers in early life, and, as he mentions in this little book, actively engaged in the campaigns of 1813, 1814, and 1815, against the Yankees, in what was then generally known by the name of Mr. Madison's war. Forgotten, out of America, as the battles of that war are now-a-days, there was some hard partizan fighting, in which the doctor, laying down the lancet for the bayonet, and inflicting wounds instead of curing them, played no conspicuous part. Peace being proclaimed, and the treaty of Ghent (which, as he observed, 'came upon them suddenly,' and, we may add, much to their grief,) having put an end to American campaigning, he went with his regiment to Calcutta, exchanging the blanket coat for the muslin jacket, and using brandy and water to keep out the intense heat of India with as much activity as he had formerly employed it to keep off the intense cold of Canada. Manifold were his occupations in the land of the Moguls. In addition to his medical and military duties—his convivial and charioteering occupations, he edited a newspaper, and contracted to clear the island of Saugur, falling with equal fury upon Silk Buckingham and the tigers. After having killed some incredible quantity of the latter nuisances (whence, and not from any resemblance to that king of cats, he has the name of Tiger,) the jungle fever subdued him, and he was obliged to come home on half-pay, 'one of the cankers of a calm world,' as Pierre expresses it. He fixed first in Edinburgh, where he gave a course of lectures on medical jurisprudence, the mixture in which of fun and learning, of law and science, blended with rough jokes, and anecdotes not always of the most prudish nature, will make them long live in the memories of his hearers. He also wrote sketches of Indian life, and other papers for *Blackwood*, under the signature of Colin Ballantyne, R. N., a *nom de guerre* under which, we believe, he figured in India during his controversies with Buckingham, whom he ever and anon delighted in calling the cobbler. Tired, however, as we suppose everybody must be of Edinburgh, he came to London, having for his *compagnon de voyage* the future editor of the *Quarterly Review*. He here lived a most miscellaneous life, turning his hand to everything. He edited, for a short while, the *British Press*, a journal now gone to sleep ; but could not like the business of a morning paper, as it interfered too much with other occupations of a more agreeable kind. He never suffered the composition of 'leaders' to interfere with the composition of works of a more fluent kind, and, accordingly, the *British Press* sometimes appeared sadly shorn of its 'leads.' The accession of M. de Villèle to power occurred during the time of the Tiger's editorship, and we need hardly say it was one of the most important events that had happened since the restoration of the Bourbons. The news arrived in London at night, and all the other newspapers were next morning full of remarks on the event, written with the sharpest acumen, the deepest knowledge, the profoundest political sagacity—in short, with all the magnificence of talent that usually adorns the best public instructors, and at wondrous length. The Antigallican Doctor, being, in all probability, more interested in the affairs of Jamaica than in those of France, dismissed the whole concern in a whiff : 'We perceive' said he, 'that there is a change of ministry in France ;—we have heard of no earthquakes in consequence.' Not another word ! Beyond question, it was treating the matter most philosophically, and, indeed, as all political affairs ought to be treated by men of sense ; but it suited not the views of the proprietors of the paper. Some impertinence was attempted, which, of course, was out of the question with Dunlop, and he left the concern.

"He then published an edition of Beck's *Medical Jurisprudence*, an American work, to which he wrote a preface, and appended many curious notes ; and started a Sunday newspaper for the India interest, intitled the *Telescope*, the history of which would be a comedy of the drollest kind. It did not succeed badly, but at the end of a year he was tired of it ; and having become connected

with the joint stocks of those days—our history has now reached the famous year of 1825—he figured in Brick, Iron, Salt, and other companies, as secretary or director. He personally superintended the salt works of this last named company somewhere in Cheshire ; but as Tiger is an honest fellow—a strictly honest fellow, in every sense of the word—it is perfectly unnecessary for us to add that he made nothing of the bubbles, except what salary he may have received. The future biographer of Dunlop will have to recount that at this time he founded a club of a most peculiar description, which he called by the picturesque title of 'The Pig and Whistle ;' but the time is not yet ripe for the history of that celebrated association."

I. Statistical Sketches of Upper Canada ; by a Backwoodsman. *London*, 3rd ed., 1833, 12mo.

" For its bulk, this is the clearest and most satisfactory treatise we have met with on the subject. It is brief, lucid, practical, complete, and cheap."—*Atlas* (Lon.)

"A pleasanter little book never came out of the press—full of information of all kinds, full of reading, full of sagacity, full of humour. It is a voice speaking to us from the forests of Canada—from the centre of woods that have seen generation after generation of men pass away into the ocean of eternity, as Niagara dashes into the gulf below ; and pleasant does that voice burst upon our ears, even as the voice of a friend whom we thought we had lost for ever. We may say, with Solomon, 'As cold waters to a thirsty soul, so is good news from a far country.' "—*Fraser's Mag.*

DUNN, JOHN. "Late of the Hudsons Bay Company. Eight years a resident in the country."

I. History of the Oregon Territory and British North American Fur Trade, with an account of the habits and customs of the principal native tribes of the northern continent. (With map.) *London*, 1844, pp. 359, 8vo.; *Philadelphia*, 1845, 8vo.

DUNSCOMB, J. W. Collector of Customs, (Que.)

I. Provincial Laws of the Customs. *Montreal*, 1844, 8vo.

II. Canadian Custom-house guide. Do. do.

DUPLESSIS, FRANCOIS XAVIER. A Jesuit Missionary. Born at Quebec, 15. Jan, 1694. D. at Paris, France. Evinced so much talent and zeal in his work as a Jesuit that he was summoned to Europe by his confrères to assist them in that wider and more extended field. He taught philosophy at Arras, and subsequently became apostolic missionary in French Flanders where he greatly distinguished himself by his missions and writings.

I. Avis et pratiques pour profiter de la mission et en conserver le fruits à l'usage des missions. *Paris*, 1742, 2 parties, in-12.

II. Lettre au suject des calomnies publiées par l'auteur des " Nouv. ecclésiastiques." *Do.*, 1745, in-4.

III. Représentation de la Croix Miraculeuse plantée sur le rempart de la ville d'Arras, par les soins du R. P. François Xavier Duplessis, de la compagnie de Jésus et Missionnaire Apostolique. *Do.*

DUPONT. *Hon.* JOHN. Chief Justice of St. John's Island, 1770. Had been an assistant judge of the Supreme Court, N. S. In 1766 prepared an edition of the Laws of N. S. for the govt. of that Province.

DUQUET, J. N.
I. Le Véritable petit Albert, ou secret pour acquérir un trésor. *Québec*, 1861, pp. 143.

D'URBAN, WILLIAM STEWART M. Formerly of Montreal. Now residing in Eng.

I. Notice of the occurrence of the Pine Grosbeak and Bohemian Chatterer, near Montreal. *Can. Nat.*, 1856.

II. Notes on the Land Birds observed round Montreal during the winter of 1856-7. *Do.*, 1857.

III. Notes on insects now injuring the crops in the vicinity of Montreal. *Do. do.*

IV. On the Order of Lepidoptera, with the description of two species of Canadian Butterflies. *Do. do.*

V. Description of Four Species of Canadian Butterflies. *Do. do.*

VI. Description of a Canadian Butterfly, and some remarks on the Genus Papilio. *Do.* 1858.

VII. Observations on the Natural History of the valley of the River Rouge, and surrounding townships in the Counties of Argenteuil and Ottawa. *Do.* 1859.

"Giving catalogues of the animals of a district but little known."—BISHOP FULFORD.

VIII. A systematic list of Coleoptera found in the vicinity of Montreal. *Do. do.*

IX. A systematic list of Lepidoptera collected in the vicinity of Montreal. *Do.* 1860.

X. Addenda to Natural History of the valley of the River Rouge. *Do.* 1861.

XI. Catalogue of Plants collected in the counties of Argenteuil and Ottawa, in 1858. *Do. do.*

"A valuable catalogue of the plants of that part of Canada."—BISHOP FULFORD.

"A young naturalist of considerable attainments and ability."—*Report Nat. His. Soc.* Montreal, 1857.

DURHAM, *Rt. Hon., the Earl* of (1st Earl.) A British statesman. B. 12 April, 1792. D. 1840. Was Governor General and High Commissioner of B. N. A., in 1838.

I. Report and Despatches on the affairs of British North America. *London*, 1839, pp. 423 folio ; *Montreal*, 1839, 8vo.

A translation of this document into French appeared at *Quebec* in 1840, pp. 78, 8vo.

[SUBJECTS — *Lower Canada* : Animosities between French and English Races—Jealousy between British Settlers and the Assembly—French Nationality not preservable amidst Anglo Saxon States. *American Colonies generally* : Defect of the Colonial System of Government—Evils of committing Details of Government to Colonial Department—Inefficient Administration of Justice. *Upper Canada* : Failure of Sir F. Head's Policy—Clergy Reserves—State of Society adverse to the principle of a Dominant Church. *Eastern Provinces and Newfoundland* : Working of the System of Government—Disposal of Public Lands—Emigration—Operation of Passengers Act—Union of the Two Provinces proposed.]

DURNFORD. *Miss* MARY.
I. Family Recollections of Lieut. Genl. E. W. Durnford. Printed for ↑ ● ↓ circulation. *Montreal*, 1863.

Dussieux, L. Prof. in the Imperial Univ., Paris.

I. Le Canada sous la domination Française d'après les archives de la marine et de la guerre. *Paris*, 1855, 8vo. New Ed., 1862.

Duvan, J. H. A N. S. writer. Has contributed many papers on History, Literature and Art to the periodical and serial press at home and abroad. An earnest advocate for the Union of the B. N. A. Colonies, he suggested the name of *Norland* for the Confederation of 1867.

Dwight, Jr., Theodore.

I. The Northern Traveller; containing the routes to the Springs, Niagara, Quebec, and the Coal Mines, with the tour of New England, &c. *New York*, 6th ed., 1841, 12mo.

E.

Earnshaw, James.

I. Abstract of various Penal and other Statutes relative to the Customs, from 28th Edw. III, to 32 Geo. III ; together with the laws in and subsequent to 1780, relating to the Southern, Greenland, and Newfoundland Fisheries. *London*, 1793, Vol. I., 8vo.

Earnshaw, William.

I. Digest of the Laws relating to the British American and West Indian Colonies. *London*, 1819, 8vo.

Edgar, James. A Lawyer, Woodstock, N. B.

I. New Brunswick ; a prize essay. *St. John*, 1860, pp. 37.

Edgar, James D. A Toronto Barrister. Has been President of the Ontario Literary Soc. of that city. Is Legal Ed. of the *Globe* (Tor.), and of the *Trade Review* (Mont.) Has lectured on various literary subjects in different places in U. C.

I. The Insolvent Act of 1864, with Tariff, Notes, Forms, and a full Index. *Toronto*, 1864, pp. 142.

"The volume contains all that is necessary to make it a useful, complete, and reliable manual of our insolvency law."— *U. C. Law Journ.*

II. An Act to amend the Insolvent Act of 1864, with annotations, notes of decisions, and a full index. *Do.*, 1865.

" Will be found a useful postscript to the former book. *Idem.*

III. A Journal for Oil Men and Dealers in Land, (with Map of the Oil Districts.) *Do.*, 1866.

Edmundson, W. G. A Can. journ. In 1840 published and ed. the *British American Cultivator*, the first journal devoted exclusively to agriculture published in the Province. It existed but 3 or 4 years.

Edwards, George.

I. Poems. *Clarence, U. C.*, 1867, pp. 50, 8vo.

Edwards, Wm. H.

I. Descriptions of certain species of Diurnal Lepidoptera, found within the limits of the United States and of British America. *Proc. Aca. U. S.*, (Phil.) 1861.

II. Second paper. *Do.*, 1862.

III. Third paper. *Do.*, do.

Elder, *Rev.* Samuel. A N. S. poet. B. in N. S. D. at Philadelphia, about 1853. Was a son of the Rev. W. Elder, a clergyman of the ch. of Eng., (whom see.) Studied for the Baptist ch. at Acadia Coll., Wolfville, N. S., where he distinguished himself in every department of learning. Completed his studies about 1846, and was for some years min. of the Baptist Ch., (Fredericton.) From a well-written and eloquent notice of him in the *Provincial Magazine*, (Hal.,) we extract the following :

" As he had made choice of the ministry as a profession, theology in a great measure usurped the place of lighter matter, and afforded but little time for poetical indulgence, but his mind was so active, that during his college life he found leisure to weave together chaste and beautiful ideas in smooth and elegant version. He contributed a large number of poems to the journal in connection with his denomination, above the signature of *L. R.*, and though all were more or less imbued with the same spirit of religious fervour, they possessed strong originality and a command of language rarely equalled in one so young in literary pursuits. * * * The most elaborate and lengthy poems of Mr. Elder that have come under our notice, are those entitled, ' *External nature coloured by the Soul's own Emotions*,' and ' *The Expulsion of the Acadians from their Native Land*,' both written for and delivered at anniversary meetings of Acadia College."

ELDER, *Rev.* WILLIAM. A clergyman in N. S. B. in Hants Co., N. S., Nov., 1784. D. in Cape Breton, 1848. In 1834 left the Baptist denomination and joined the Ch. of Eng. In addition to the following he published two sermons whose titles we have been unable to obtain.

I. Infant Sprinkling weighed in the balance and found wanting. In five letters addressed to the Rev. George Jackson ; being a reply to his letters in defence of Infant Sprinkling. *Halifax*, 1823, pp. 56, 8vo.

II. A series of Letters on Infant Baptism. *Do.*, 1834.

ELDER, *Rev.* WILLIAM, A.M. A N. B. journ. Is a min. in the Presb. Ch. Greatly distinguished himself as a student at Belfast Coll., at the Universities of Glasgow and Edinburgh, and at the New Coll. of the latter city. Of late he has devoted himself principally to journalism, being the ed. of the *Colonial Presbyterian* and of the *Morning Journal* (St. John, N. B.) The latter has only recently been established; both journals have taken a high place amongst our Provincial newspaper press. Mr. E. is a bold, earnest and logical writer ; he possesses a cultivated and refined taste, and is regarded as occupying a first position amongst Brit. Am. journalists.

ELGIN & KINCARDINE, JAMES BRUCE, *Earl of*, (Eighth Earl of Elgin and Twelfth Earl of Kincardine.) An Eng. statesman and diplomatist. B. in London, July 20, 1811 ; D. at Dhurumsala, Cashmere, Nov. 25, 1863. Gov. Gen. of B. N. A. from 1847 to 1854.

I. Condition and Prospects of Canada in 1854, as pourtrayed in his despatches to Her Majesty's Principal Secretary of State for the Colonies. *Quebec*, 1855, pp. 83, 8vo.

ELLEGOOD, REV. J., M.A. A clergym. of the Ch. of Eng. Incumbent of St. James's (Mont.)

I. Sleeping in Jesus ; a sermon. *Montreal*, 1854, pp. 17.

ELLIOT, T. F. Asst. Secy. of State for the Colonies. Eng.

I. The Canadian Controversy ; its origin, nature and merits. *London*, 1838, pp. 84, 8vo.

ELLIS, J. V. Ed. of the *Evening Globe*, (St. John, N. B.)

I. New Brunswick as a home for Emigrants, &c., a prize essay. *St. John*, 1860, pp. 60.

ENGLEHEART, G. D. Private Secy. to the late Duke of Newcastle, Secy. of State for the Colonies.

I. Journal of the Visit of H. R. H. the Prince of Wales to America, in 1860. Privately printed. *London*, 1861.

ENSLIN, CHRISTIAN. A Can. Journ. In 1840, established and ed. *The German Canadian*, (Berlin, U. C.) published in the German language.

ERMATINGER, EDWARD. Ed. the *Standard*, (St. Thomas, U. C.) from 1844 to 1846, and another journal for 3 years. Was 10 years in the service of the Hudson's Bay Co., and traversed the territory from the Atlantic to the Pacific several times. He is the author of the well known letters of *British Canadian*, which appeared in the *Spectator*, (Ham.), some years since, and which were extended in that journal for a considerable time.

I. The Hudson's Bay Territories ; a series of letters on this important question. *Toronto*, 1858, pp. 32.

II. Life of Colonel Talbot, and the rise and progress of the Talbot Settlement ; with sketches of the public characters and career of some of the most conspicuous men in Upper Canada, who were either friends or acquaintances of the subject of these memoirs. *St. Thomas*, 1859, pp. 230, 8vo.

ESSON, *Rev.* H.

I. Strictures on the present method of teaching the English Language;

and suggestions for its improvement. *Toronto*, 1852, pp. 31.

Evans, J. D., *P. L. S.*
I. A Chart of Geology, designed specially to illustrate the Geology of Canada. *Toronto*, 1866.

Evans, William. A Can. writer on agriculture. B. at Carana, Irel., Nov. 22, 1786; D. at Montreal, 1857. Emigrated to Can. in 1819, and established himself at Montreal, where he was Sec. to the first Agricultural Soc. founded there. In 1837 contributed a series of letters to the *Courier* on his favorite study, which were afterwards published in pamphlet form. In the following year established the *Canadian Quarterly, Agricultural and Industrial Mag.*, which after a short time had to be abandoned from want of support. In 1842 he ed. the *British American Cultivator*, (Tor.,) and, in 1843, having returned to Montreal he there founded the *Canadian Agricultural Journal*, published in both languages, of which he became ed., a position which he continued to hold up to within a short time of his death. He frequently contributed to the *Gazette*, (Mont.,) upon the subject of Agriculture, &c. In 1853, he was appointed Sec. and Treas. of the Board of Agriculture, L. C.

I. A Treatise on the Theory and Practice of Agriculture, adapted to the cultivation and economy of the animal and vegetable productions of agriculture in Canada. *Montreal*, 1835, pp. 297, 8vo.

The Legislature of L. C. made an appropriation of £215 for the translation and publication into the French language of this work.

II. Supplement to a Treatise on the Theory and Practice of Agriculture. *Do.*, 1836, pp. 317, 8vo.

III. Agricultural Improvements by the education of those who are engaged in it as a profession. *Do.*, 1837.

IV. Suggestions sur la sub-division et l'économie d'une ferme, dans les seigneuries du Bas-Canada, avec divers plans et dessins. *Do.*, 1854.

"It has been our fortune to meet few worthier or more patriotic men than he, few more diligent in the promotion, to the uttermost of his ability, of the prosperity of this his adopted country. Enthusiastically devoted to agricultural pursuits, it has been his endeavor for many years past to raise the standard of agriculture in Lower Canada from the position to which it had sunk, to teach and to lead the way in a system by which the worn out farms of the long settled districts might recover their fertility, and farming in the eastern province be made to rival in profitableness that of the west. Nor have his efforts been altogether in vain, we hope." *Gazette*, (Mont.)

Everest, *Rev.* Robert.
I. A journey through the United States and part of Canada. *London*, 1855, 8vo.

F.

Fabre, Hector. A French Can. journ. B. at Montreal. The son of a well known bookseller there. Was sometime ed. of *L'Ordre*, (Mont.) From 1862 to 1866 had ed. management of *Le Canadien*, (Que.) In May, 1867, founded a new journal—*L'Evénement*, (do.), of which he is ed. and prop. He writes freely, gracefully and vigorously, and has obtained a very high position as a public writer and *littérateur*.

I. Esquisse biographique sur Chevalier de Lorimier. *Montréal*, 1856, pp. 15.

II. Ecrivains Canadiens.—L'Abbé Casgrain. *Rev. Can.* 1865.

III. Le cœur et l'esprit. *Do.*, do.

IV. Ecrivains Canadiens.—N. Bourassa. *Do.* 1866.

V. On Canadian Literature. *Trans. Lit and His. Soc.* (Que.) 1866.

A very able essay.

Fahey, James, Jr.
I. The Political History of Canada; a lecture. *Dundas*, 1867.

"An eloquent address."—*Times*, (Ham.)

FAILLON, *L'Abbé*. A French biographical writer and historian. Is a mem. of the order of St. Sulpice. Came to Can. in 1854, where he resided for several years pursuing his literary studies and researches. He now lives in France.

I. Vie de Mme. D'Youville, fondatrice des Sœurs de la Charité de Villemarie dans l'île de Montréal, en Canada. (With portrait and illustrations). *Villemarie*, 1852, pp. 491, 8vo.

II. Vie de la Sœur Bourgeoys, fondatrice de la Congrégation de Notre-Dame de Villemarie, en Canada, suivie de l'histoire de cet Institut jusqu'à ce jour, et précédée d'une introduction (Illustrated.) *Paris*, 1853, 8vo.

III. Vie de M. Olier, fondateur du Séminaire de St. Sulpice et de la Colonie de Montréal. *Do.*, 1853, 2 Vols. 8vo ; Abridged ed. *Montreal*, 1866, pp. 190, 12mo.

IV. Vie de Mlle. Mance, et histoire de l'Hotel-Dieu de Villemarie, dans L'île de Montréal, en Canada. *Villemarie*, 1854, 2 Vols. pp. 271—373, 8vo.

V. L'Héroïne Chrétienne du Canada, ou vie de Mlle. Le Ber. *Do.*, 1860, pp. 404, 8vo.

VI. Histoire de la Colonie Française en Canada, (with maps.) *Paris*, 1865, 1st vol. pp. 551, ; 2nd vol. pp. xxiv—568 ; 3rd vol., 1866, pp. xxiii—548, 4to.

Vol. III brings the narrative down to 1672 only.

"According to the custom of the Congregation of St. Sulpice of which he (L'Abbé Faillon) is a distinguished member, he has published anonymously the various works which have already made him known and esteemed by historical writers as a historian of great industry, extensive research, as well as vigorous and original views. Montreal is especially the subject of his labors; his previous works, * * * all illustrating the history of Montreal, by giving the chronicle of its most venerable institutions. In his history he develops the history of that city, on which previous historians have been less ample in detail, the Sulpitians having printed very little touching that city, and the Jesuit Relations, those annual volumes on Canada, scarcely alluding to Montreal, no Fathers of their society being stationed there, whose reports would have been a sort of chronicle. A Sulpitian, Mr. Dollier de Casson, wrote a history of Montreal down to 1672, but it has not been published and was not apparently used by Charlevoix or earlier writers. This affords Mr. Faillon a comparatively new field of labor, and his work will thus be a most valuable contribution to Canadian history. It is most creditable to the historical taste of that province that is has produced within so brief a period three so important histories as those of Messrs. Garneau, Ferland and Faillon.

"At the close of his first volume, under the unpretending titles of Notes, Mr. Faillon gives several very interesting discussions of debated questions on Cartier, the place of his wintering, the language of the people of Hochelaga and Stadacona, the family of Champlain, &c."—*Am. His. Mag.* (N. Y.)

FAIRBANKS, CASSIE. (Dartmouth, N. S.)
    I. The Lone House ; a poem, partly founded on fact. *Halifax*, 1859.

FAIRBANKS, CHARLES R.
    I. Reports and Papers relating to a Canal, intended to connect the Harbour of Halifax with the Basin of Mines; Remarks on its Nature and Importance, and a Plan and Section. Also the Report of a Survey for Canals between St. Peter's Bay and the Bras d'Or Lake, in Cape Breton ; and the Bay of Fundy and Bay of Verte. (With 2 maps.) *Halifax*, 1826, pp. 58, 8vo.

FARIBAULT, GEORGE BARTHÉLEMI. A French Can. Archæologist. B. in Quebec, 3 Dec. 1789. D. there, 21 Dec. 1866. His paternal ancestor in this country, a Parisian notary, had come to Can. in 1757, and held the office of Secy. to the army under the Marquis DuQuesne. He received the primary portion of his education from a Scotch schoolm. in his native city, but he was indebted to his own unaided exertions for the chief portion of his learning. Having studied law he was admitted to the practice of his profession in 1811. During the war with the U. S., in 1812, he served in the ranks of the Can. Militia against the enemy. In 1822, he entered the service of the Leg. Assem. of L. C. first as one of the staff of extra writers and was promoted through various grades until he finally became Asst. Clerk to the House in 1832, a position which he retained after the Union until 1855, when he resigned the office and was granted a pension. From an early age he had taken an interest in Can. Archæological pursuits. In 1837 he published his *Catalogue* which is still regarded as an authority by Am. bibliographists. It was while engaged in making the collection of works relating to the early history of Am. and Can. for the Can. Parliamentary Library, which unfortunately was destroyed by fire in 1849, that he obtained the materials for that useful work. In 1851 he was appointed by the Leg. Assem. to proceed to Europe to make a second collection for the Library, to replace that which had been destroyed, in which mission he was eminently successful. He was one of the original founders and for some time President of the Lit. and His. Soc. (Que.,) under the auspices of which body many important documents and manuscripts relating to the early history of Can. were reproduced, ed. by Mr. F. A list of these is given below. In acknowledgment of his services to the Soc. and the cause of Can. history and literature generally the Soc. have had his portrait painted and hung up in their library. Before his death Mr. F. presented his large and valuable collection of manuscripts, maps and plans, and his private library, which contained many rare and interesting works on our early history, to the Laval Univ. where they now are. A portrait of him was also painted for the hall of that institution, by order of the Univ. authorities. In 1859, being the 100th anniversary of the conquest of Quebec and the death of Wolfe and Montcalm, the generals of the Eng. and French armies engaged in the battle, Mr. F. succeeded in having placed over the last resting place of the French general, a suitable monument to his memory, which contains an appropriate inscription.

I. Catalogue d'ouvrages sur l'Histoire de l'Amérique et en particulier sur celle du Canada, de la Louisiane, le L'Acadie, et autres lieux, ci-devant connus sous le nom de Nouvelle-France ; avec des notes bibliographiques, critiques, et littéraires. En trois parties. *Québec*, 1837, pp. 207, 8vo.

" The compiler, an advocate of Quebec, is known as a corresponding member of the " *Société Littéraire de Québec,*" and is a most diligent contributor to the " *Mémoires Historiques*" published by that Society. Till Mr. Rich called attention to the work in 1846, it

was but little known beyond the confines of Canada ; and M. Ludewig, who first saw a copy of it in the library of Mr. J. Sparks, of Cambridge, Mass., could not meet with one for sale in the United States ; but had no difficulty in obtaining the work on application to the publisher. The merit of the catalogue, which evinces great diligence and aptitude, is greatly enhanced by its valuable notes to the more important articles ; and though, as regards those of earlier date, there is but little added to our former stock of information, still what is said is to the point ; whilst, as regards those of more recent date, the bibliographical notices are in every way most satisfactory. M. Ludewig thus sums up the contents of the volume :

" *Part I.* pp. 1-155. Ouvrages avec les noms des auteurs, par ordre alphabétique, (with supplement and alphabetical index.) 796 articles.

" *Part II.* pp. 157-184. Ouvrages sans noms d'auteur, classés d'après l'ordre chronologiques de leur publication, (from 1505-1836.) 178 articles.

" *Part III.* pp. 185-207. Cartes, plans et estampes."—TRÜBNER : *Guide to Am. Literature.*

" J'ai lu d'un bout à l'autre votre Catalogue raisonné et annoté d'ouvrages sur l'histoire de l'Amérique et particulièrement du Canada. Ce beau travail d'un bibliophile consciencieux m'en a plus appris en quelques pages que certaines histoires en trois ou quatre gros volumes ; et sa place est déjà marquée dans ma bibliothèque à côté de mon ami Ternaux-Compans, le premier bibliographe Américain de Paris."—ADOLPHE DE PUIBUSQUE : *Letter to Author.*

Publications of the Lit. and His. Soc.

I. Mémoires sur le Canada, depuis 1749 jusqu'à 1760. En trois parties, avec Cartes et Plans Lithographiés. *Québec*, 1838, 8vo.

II. Collection de Mémoires et de relations sur l'Histoire du Canada, d'après des manuscrits récemment obtenus des Archives et Bureaux Publics en France. *Do.*, 1840, 8vo.

III. Mémoires sur l'Etat présent du Canada. M. Salon. 1667.

IV. Mémoires sur le Canada d'après un manuscrit aux Archives du Bureau de la Marine, à Paris. *Québec*, 1736.

V. Considérations sur l'Etat présent du Canada. M. de Beauvart. 1758.

VI. Histoire du Canada, par M. l'Abbé de Belmont, à la Bibliothèque du Roi à Paris, entre les années 1713 à 1724.

VII. Relation du Siège de Québec en 1759, écrite en 1765.

VIII. Jugement Impartial sur les Opérations de la Campagne en Canada, en 1759.

IX. Reflections Sommaires sur le Commerce qui se fait en Canada.

X. Histoire de l'Eau-de-Vie en Canada, 1705.

XI. Voyages de Découverte au Canada, entre les années 1534 et 1542, par Jacques Cartier, le Sieur de Roberval, Jean Alphonse de Xantoigue ; suivis de la description de Québec et de ses environs en 1608. *Québec*, 1843, 8vo.

XII. Documents sur Jacques Cartier. *Do.*, 1860, 8vo.

XIII. Dessins Historiques destinés à illustrer les voyages de Jacques Cartier en Canada. *Paris*, 1860, 4to.

XIV. Mémoire du Sieur de Ramezay, Commandant, Québec, au sujet de la reddition de cette ville, le 18me Septembre 1759, d'après un MS. aux Archives du Bureau de la Marine à Paris. *Québec*, 1861, 8vo.

Un Contemporain—G. B. Faribault, par l'Abbé H. R. Casgrain, (with portrait.)— *Québec*, 1867. pp. 123, sm. 8vo.

FAIRFLAY, FRANCIS.
I. The Canadas as they now are. *London*, 1833.

FALKNER, *Mrs.* RHODA ANN. (Maiden name, *Paige*.) A Can. Poet. B. at Hackney, near Lond. Eng., 1826. D. near Cobourg, U. C., 1863. Her education was necessarily limited, owing to the emigration of her parents to Can. when she was only 6 years of age— and there being little sch. instruction to be obtained in their new home on this side of the Atlantic, but such were her natural abilities, and so carefully were they cultivated, that she early shewed the possession of a rare intellect, and soon manifested a strong taste for the beauties of poetry. At 13 she made her first attempts at composition in the *Star* (Cobourg) and afterwards published a collection of her pieces in book form. She contributed the story of *An Hour on the Ice* to the *Maple Leaf*, (Tor.) Marrying in 1856, her family and other cares usurped the place of poesy, and with the exception of one or two stray pieces her pen was comparatively idle, from that time up to her melancholy and untimely death.

I. Wild Notes from the Backwoods. By R. A. P., *Cobourg*, 1850, pp. 62.

" The selections from Mrs. Faulkner, in this collection, disclose the true spirit of poetry."—DEWART.

FALLOON, *Rev.* DANIEL, *D. D.*, *LL. D.* A min. of the Ch. of Eng., in Can. B. in Ireland. D. at Montreal, Sept. 1862. In addition to the works whose titles are given below he was the author of a series of letters reviewing and refuting portions of the *History of the Reformation*, by Dr. Merle D'Aubigné, which appeared in the *Morning Courier* (Mont.) in 1843, and which were subsequently printed in pamphlet form.

I. An Historical View of the Church of England, exhibiting her original principles, subsequent corruption, and reformation from the errors of Popery, *Dublin*, 1830, 2 Vols. pp. 1238, 8vo.

II. Dialogues on the Apostolic Church : or a discussion respecting the worship, legal establishment, hierarchy and institutions of the Church under the Christian dispensation. *London*, 1837, pp. 421, 12mo.

III. History of Ireland, Civil and Ecclesiastical, from the earliest times till the death of Henry II. Edited by Rev. John Irwin, A. M. *Montreal*. 1863, pp. 399, 12mo.

FAUCHER DE SAINT MAURICE, N. H. E. Has contributed various pieces in prose and verse to the newspaper press, and is now engaged on a novel to be called : *Pauvre fleur folle.*

I. Organisation militaire des Canadas. *Québec*, 1862, pp. 38.

II. Cours de Tactique. *Do.*, 1863. pp. 110.

III. De Québec à Mexico, *Rev.* n. 1866–67.

FAY, H. A.
I. Collection of the official accounts in detail of all the battles fought by sea and land, between the navy and army of the United States and the navy and army of Great Britain, during the years 1812–1815. *New-York*, 1817, 8vo.

FEATHERSTONHAUGH, G. W.

I. Observations on the Treaty of Washington, with the Treaty annexed. (With Map). *London*, 1843, 8vo.

FENETY, CHARLES. (Sackville, N. B.) Lived for some years in Australia, where he contributed some prose articles to the newspaper press. It is understood that he has a volume of poems nearly ready for the press.

I. Betula Nigra : a poem. *Halifax*, 1855, 8vo.

FENETY, GEORGE E. A N. B. journ. In 1839 established the *Commercial News*, (St. John), the first tri-weekly or penny newspaper started in the Maritime Provinces, which he conducted up to 1863, a period of 24 years, when he was appointed Queen's Printer for N. B. and disposed of his paper to the present proprietors. In politics the *News* was liberal.

I. The Lady and the Dress Maker ; or a peep at Fashionable Folly. A story founded on circumstances that occurred some time since in this city. By a " Bluenose." *St. John*, 1842, pp. 24, 8vo.

II. Political Notes and Observations, or a glance at the leading measures that have been discussed in the Assembly of New Brunswick, under the administrations of Sir W. M. G. Colebrooke, Sir E. W. Head, Hon. J. H. T. Manners-Sutton, and Hon. A. H. Gordon. *Do.* 1867.

" These notes will pass current all over the Province at least. They embrace just such matters in the political history as the people wish to recall, and the particulars of some of which are in danger of being lost, owing to the want of historical archives in the province, or even complete sets of all the newspapers which have been published during our brief history." — *Morn. Journ.* (St. John.)

FENWICK, G. E., *M. D.* Associate ed. of the *Can. Medical Journal and Monthly Record of Medical and Surgical Science.* (Mont.)

FENWICK, *Rev.* THOMAS. A clergym. of the Can. Presb. Ch., (Metis, L. C.) Has contributed in prose and verse to the newspaper press on subjects connected with Temperance and Religious matters, above the *nom de plume* of " *Hydrophilus*" and " *Blue Bonnett.*"

FERGUSSON, *Hon.* ADAM, of Woodhill, Perthshire, Scot., and of Woodhill, U. C. B. in Scot. 1782. D. at Woodhill, U. C., 1862. Appd. a Life mem. of the Leg. Coun. Can. June 1842, having previously been a mem. of the Leg. Coun. of U. C. Had been a prominent mem. of the Whig party in Scot. Was a Magistrate and Deputy Lieut. of Perth shire, a Director of the Highland Soc. and distinguished for his efforts to improve Scottish Agriculture. In Can. supported the Reform party, did much for the cause of Agriculture, and for some time was President of the Provincial Agricultural Ass. U. C.

I. Practical Notes made during a tour in Canada and a portion of the United States, in 1831, to which are added Notes made during a second visit to Canada in 1833. *Edinburgh*, 2nd Ed. 1834, pp. 426, 8vo.

" To the Agricultural emigrant, we can recommend no better guide then Mr. Fergusson's book :—unambitious in style, it is level in every capacity ; strong in its collection of useful information, and correct in its general reflections, it is admirably calculated to direct the steps of the enterprising capatalist, in common with the humble artizan or labourer, who bring nothing to our stores but unconquerable energy and perseverance. Some authors think it necessary for the purpose of ingratiating themselves and their subject with their readers, to represent every thing *en couleur de rose* ; but Mr. Fergusson has neither erred in this way, nor has he dwelt, like some croakers we wot of, upon the *désagréments* attendant upon a removal from thickly peopled and well cultivated England to the isolation and wildness of a Canadian forest. Having travelled with the intention of settling in the Upper Province, the author was necessitated, for his own sake, to examine with minuteness and circumspection, everything of importance or value, and of the results of this, the reader reaps the full benefit."—*Gazette*, (Mont.)

FERLAND, *L'Abbé* J. B. A., *A. M.* A Can. historian. B. at Montreal, 25 Dec., 1805. D. at Quebec, 8 Jan., 1864. He was descended from the family of Freland, of Poitou, France, a mem. of which was one of the early settlers on the isle of Orleans, near Quebec. His father, Anthony Ferland, dying young, his mother, Elizabeth Lebrun de Duplessis, daughter of one of the four French advocates who remained in Can. after the conquest, removed, in

1813, to Kingston, where young F. was ed. under the care of M. Gaulin, afterwards Bishop of that diocese, who, perceiving his growing talents secured his entrance into the Coll. of Nicolet. Here he attracted the notice of Bish. Plessis, and shortly after the completion of his studies he was apptd. Secy. to the Bish. Relinquishing that important office subsequently, he became Prof. of Arts, Rhetoric and Philosophy at Nicolet. In 1828 he was admitted to the priesthood, and upon the day of his admission was appointed Vicar of Quebec. He exercised the ministry subsequently at Rivière du Loup, St. Roch de Quebec, St. Isidore, St. Foye, St. Anne de Beaupré and St. Féréol. In 1834, during the cholera which then prevailed, he was Chaplain to the Marine and Emigrant Hospital. (Que.) In 1841 he returned to Nicolet as Supdt. of Studies, and in 1848 succeeded as Superior of that institution. From 1850 he was attached to the Cathedral of Quebec, was mem. of the Bishop's Council, Military Chaplain, and Dean of the Faculty of Arts and Prof. of Can. and Am. History in Laval Univ. The remainder of this notice we extract from an interesting sketch of the Abbé which appears in the *Am. Historical Mag.* (1865), in which periodical there is also an excellent portrait of him :

" His studies were not pursued at the sacrifice of the slightest duty, or what a sensitive conscience could consider as such. Being very methodical, his day was distributed with precision, and he followed his plan of life with unswerving regularity.

" Yet his modesty kept him long comparatively unknown. Rich in study, style, facts and ideas—conscientious, accurate, it was not till after the age of forty that he appeared as a writer,

" The trashy history of Canada by Brasseur de Bourbourg had so misrepresented his early protector, Bishop Plessis, that Mr. Ferland entered the arena in a review full of ability and erudition. The familiarity he displayed with the sources of Canadian history, his pleasing style, his masterly grasp of the whole subject, drew on him felicitations from all sides, and a general wish was expressed for a history of Canada from his pen.

" He followed this by his " *Notes sur les Registres*," opening the neglected field of family history in Canada, and giving a most interesting little sketch even to the general reader. His ' *Journal d'un Voyage sur les*

Côtes de la Gaspésie,' appeared in 1861, and an article on ' *Labrador*,' published in the Annals of the Association for the Propagation, of Quebec, which he edited for some years, was reprinted in a volume styled ' *La Littérature Canadienne*.' These placed him among the first Canadian writers, and are remarkable for their charming style and irresistible interest.

" His ' *Cours d'Histoire du Canada*," of which the first volume appeared in 1861, resulted from his series of lectures at the University Laval. Appointed Professor in the Faculty of Arts, June 10, 1855, and elected Dean of the Faculty, March, 18, 1864, he had the honor of inaugurating the public courses of the University. From 1858 to 1862, he drew an attentive audience to the lectures, in which he unrolled the dramatic history of his native province. The interval between his appointment and the opening of the course was spent in part in a visit to Europe, devoted to exact, minute, and scrupulous examination of the public archives and private collections.

"His work was hailed by all Canadians as a most noble contribution to their literature ; ' the noblest monument yet erected to their national glories ; ' and he displayed in it all the qualities of a great historian. Exact and persistent in research, every accessible source had been explored : his judgment, matured by study and discipline, enabled him to grasp the subject and treat it in a masterly manner; while his natural gaiety of disposition gave his writings a charm that render his work not only the most thorough history of Canada that has yet appeared, but also the most attractive in style.

"Mr. Garneau's work, so creditable to that author, had initiated the new era of history in Canada. Mr. Ferland brought to the field of historic literature, patience, research, skill, and narrative power ; and no one showed greater respect to Mr. Ferland than his brother historian.

" Unfortunately Mr. Ferland was not spared to complete his work. During its progress he published the life of Monseigneur Plessis in 1863, and just after its appearance in July, 1863, he was struck with paralysis. His naturally strong constitution enabled him to recover from this first attack, and his friends hoped for his ultimate recovery ; but his sedentary life and close application had determined the character of the malady, which had but given a manifestation of its power. On Sunday, the 8th of January, 1864, after saying mass and preaching at St. Patrick's Church, he suddenly sank down. He was at once taken to his room, and in spite of all medical aid, expired between ten and eleven o'clock at night.

" His second volume was going through the press at the moment of his death, and will, it is hoped, be completed by a competent hand, to give us all the labours of one whose lectures threw so much light on Canadian history, rectified so many errors, dissipated so many obscurities."

I. Observations sur un ouvrage intitulé : "Histoire du Canada, &c., par l'Abbé Brasseur de Bourbourg. *Québec*, 1853, pp. 79 ; 2nd ed. *Paris.*

II. Notes sur les Régistres de Notre-Dame de Québec. *Do.*, 1854, pp. 75 ; 2nd Ed. *Do.*, 1863, pp. 100, 8vo.

III. Cours d'Histoire du Canada. Première partie, 1534–1663. *Do.*, 1861, pp. xi-522 ; vol. II. *Do.*, 1867, 1663–1759, pp. 620, 8vo.

" Le cours de M. Ferland, dont nous reproduisons les premières leçons, formera une histoire du Canada d'un genre tout-à-fait différent de celle que nous avons déjà. Les détails, les citations et les recherches, qui surchargeraient une histoire proprement dite, sont surtout à leur place dans une série de leçons qui, si nous en jugeons par la période comprise dans ce gros volume, formeront un ouvrage très-étendu. Plus qu'aucune autre peut-être l'histoire du Canada peut y gagner à être traité de cette manière ; il n'est personne, du reste, qui, après avoir lu le bel ouvrage de M. Garneau, n'aimera à en lire un autre rempli de détails intéressants qu'il eut été impossible de consigner dans un travail historique plus concis."—*Journ. de l'Inst. Pub., L. C.*

" M. Garneau prie M. Ferland de vouloir bien accepter ses hommages et en même temps ses remerciments pour le premier vol. de son Cours d'Histoire qu'il a eu la complaisance de lui envoyer. Mr. Garneau est passé chez M. Ferland pour lui exprimer personnellement toute sa reconnaissance et parler avec lui de leur chère patrie, mais il n'a pas été assez heureux pour le rencontrer. M. Garneau aurait voulu causer avec une des lumières du Canada sur la foi qu'on doit avoir en notre nationalité et sur les moyens à suivre pour en assurer la consommation. Celui qui a su développer avec tant d'exactitude nos origines historiques doit être pénétré plus qu'un autre des sentiments de cette foi. Son livre, quel que soit l'avenir de ses compatriotes sera toujours le témoignage d'un principe révéré par tous les peuples et rendra la mémoire de son auteur plus chère à la postérité."—Samedi, 24 août, 1861. F. X. GARNEAU : *Letter to author.*

" Aussi grand citoyen que saint prêtre, esprit large, cœur dévoué, consacrant sa vie à élever, à côté de l'œuvre de M. Garneau, un temple où sont déposées les cendres de nos martyrs, où vivra à jamais leur mémoire bénie."—HECTOR FABRE : *Can. Lit.*

IV. Journal d'un Voyage sur les Côtes de la Gaspésie. *Soir. Can.*, 1861.

V. Lettre sur la mission du Labrador. [No. 13 of *Rapp. sur les missions du diocèse de Québec.*] Reprinted in *Litt. Can.*

VI. Notice biographique sur Monseigneur Joseph Octave Plessis, Evêque de Québec. *Foy. Can.*, 1863, pp. 248, 8vo.

Translated into English by T. B. French. *Quebec*, 1864, 8vo.

VII. Louis Olivier Gamache. *Litt. Can.*, 1863.

FERRES, JAMES MOIR. A Can. journ. B. at Aberdeen, Scot. Ed. at the Grammar Sch. there, and at Marischal Coll. Emigrated to Can. in 1833. In the beginning of 1835 a number of loyal gentlemen in Missisquoi, (where Mr. F. then resided,) established a newspaper called the *Missiskoui Standard*, to counteract the effects of the party who supported the 92 Resolutions of the House of Assem. of 1834, Mr. F. accepting the post of ed., a position which he occupied until the close of 1836. During the exciting times of that and the following year he assisted Mr. Thom on the *Herald*, (Mont.,) and was one of the ed's. of that paper with Mr. Weir, while the latter lived, and continued in the same capacity after his death, from 1839 to 1842. In 1848 he purchased the *Gazette*, (Mont.,) from Mr. Abraham, and was its ed. until 1852, when he disposed of his interest in that paper to the present proprietors and retired from journalistic life. All these papers were conducted upon Conservative principles. Mr. F. sat in Parliament from 1854 to 1861 when he declined re-election, and accepted his present appointment as one of the Inspectors of Prisons, &c., for Can.

FERRIE, *Hon.* ADAM, M. L. C., Can. D. 1864.

I. Appendix to Captain Synge's pamphlet entitled "Canada in 1848, &c." being a letter to Earl Grey. *Montreal*, 1847, pp. 7.

FERRIE, *Rev.* WILLIAM, *A. M.* Was min. of St. David's Ch., St. John, N. B. Author of *Life of Rev. John Carstairs, &c.* Now residing in Prescott, O.

I. The Cream of Scottish History ; with an appendix shewing the state of the extinct Peerage of Scotland in 1746. *St. John, N. B.*, 1857, pp. 48, 8vo.

II. The Papacy : its present Chronological position and consequent policy and prospects ; a lecture. *Halifax*, 1858, pp. 23, 12 mo.

FIDLER, *Rev.* ISAAC, *D. D.* "For a short time Missionary of Thornhill, on Yonge street, near York, U. C."

I. Observations on Professions, Literature, Manners, and Emigration in the United States and Canada, made during a residence in 1832. *London*, 1833, pp. 434, 12mo.; re-printed, *New York*, 1833, 18mo.

FIELD, *Rt. Rev.* EDWARD, *D. D.* Appointed Lord Bishop of Newfoundland, 1844.

I. A Charge delivered to the Clergy of Bermuda in the Easter week, 1849. *St. John's*, 1850, pp. 50, 8vo.

FINCH, J.

I. Travels in the United States of America and Canada. *London*, 1833, 8vo.

FINN, HENRY J. An Am. author and actor. B. at New York, 1782 ; D. 1840. Made his first appearance as an actor in Am., at Montreal, in 1811.

I. Montgomery ; or, the Falls of Montmorenci, a new national drama. *Boston*, 1821.

FISET, LOUIS JOSEPH CYPRIEN. A French Can. poet. B. at Quebec, 1827. He is descended from one of the oldest and most honorable French families in Can., his father, (the late Hon. Louis Fiset), held various offices of importance, including that of district judge of Quebec. Mr. F. was educated at the Seminary of his native city and at Dr. Wilkie's sch. At the former he was eminently successful in the departments of French composition, literature and eloquence. He studied law and was duly admitted as an advocate, but, so far, has never practised his profession. In 1861 he was appointed Joint Prothonotary, (Que.) During his school days he had imbibed a taste for literature—he had a strong poetic vein which he cultivated with success. With years his powers became more fully developed, and some of the most finished and graceful epic poems and lyrics in the realms of French Can.

poesy have emanated from his pen. The majority of his pieces have appeared in *La Ruche Litteraire*, (Mont.,) *Les Soirées Can.* and *La Litt. Can.*, (Que) His prose essays have been confined to the pages of *Le Journal de l'Ed. Pub.*, (Mon.,) and the leading Quebec journals published in the French language. Upon the occasion of the visit of the Prince of Wales to Can., in 1860, Mr. F. was selected to write the Ode of Welcome from his native city to the Royal Visitor for which he received the thanks of H. R. H. Mr. F. assisted in founding *L'Institut Can.* (Que.,) of which he afterwards became President, and in 1856, whilst holding that office offered £30 for the best essay on the subject : "*Quels seraient les moyens à adopter pour créer en Canada une littérature nationale, et quels avantages en résulterait-il pour le pays.*"

"M. L. J. C. Fiset, imagination charmante au vol gracieux, poete délicat au vers élégant."—HECTOR FABRE, *Can Lit.*

FISHER, JOHN CHARLTON, *LL. D.* A Can. journ. B. at Carlisle, Eng., 23 Oct., 1794. D. at sea, when returning to Can., 10 Augt., 1849. He ed. the *Albion* (N. Y.) for some years, a journal of which he was the founder. In 1823 he accepted the ed. management of the *Official Gazette* (Que.) and with it the office of Queen's Printer, under the administration of Lord Dalhousie. This paper he conducted up to 1831, when a demand was made upon him to change his political articles, which were found not altogether in unison with the policy and views of the ruling party of the day ; the peremptory character of the request led to his retirement from the *Gazette*, which thereafter was made, what it had previously been in name only, a vehicle for official announcements and appointments. Dr. F. next ed. the *Mercury* of the same city, and, in 1841, established a journal of his own, called the *Conservative*. During the existence of the *Canadian Magazine* (Mont.), from 1823 to 1825, he contributed to its pages. He was President and an active and zealous mem. and promoter of the Lit. & His. Soc. He is spoken of as having been an elegant and forcible writer, and a classical scholar of the highest order.

I. Note on the Ancient English or Anglo-Saxon language. *Trans. Lit. & His. Soc.* (Que.) Vol. III.

FISHER, PETER. B. at Staten Island, N. Y., about 1783. D. in N. B., 15 Augt., 1848. Was the son of an U. E. loyalist.

I. History of New Brunswick, 1829.

FITZGERALD, *Rev.* D., *A. B.*, (T. C. D.) Rector of Charlottetown, P. E. I.

I. A Lecture on the Reformation. *Charlottetown*, 1859, pp. 94, 8vo.

FITZGERALD, JAMES EDWARD.

I. Vancouver's Island, the Hudson's Bay Company and the Government. *London*, 1848, pp. 30.

II. Charter and Proceedings of the Hudson's Bay Company. *Do.*, 1849, 12mo.

FITZGIBBON, *Col.* JAMES. A retired half pay officer from the Brit. army. Rendered important services during the Am. war of 1812. Was for many years Clk. of Leg. Council, U. C. Created a "Military Knight" of Windsor 1850, where he died some years since.

I. An Appeal to the people of the late province of Upper Canada, on his claims for public services. *Montreal*, 1847, pp. 65, 8vo.

II. Documents, selected from several others, showing the services rendered by Col. Fitzgibbon, while serving in Upper Canada, between the years 1812 and 1837. *Windsor*, 1859, pp. 15.

FITZWILLIAM, WILLIAM, of Fairfield, N. B.

I. The Quoddy Hermit; or, Conversations at Fairfield on Religion and Superstition. *New Brunswick*, 1842.

FLEMING, *Mrs.* ANN CUTHBERT. A Can. authoress. D. 1860. A native of Scot. Came to Can. in 1815 or 1816, having separated from her first husband a Mr. Knight. For several years kept a Ladies' Sch. at Montreal, to the press of which city, including we believe the *Literary Garland*, she was a contributor. She married there Mr. James Fleming, a younger brother of John F. (whom see.)

I. Home, a Poem. *Edinburgh*, 1815, pp. 98, 12mo.

II. A Year in Canada, and other poems. *Do.*, 1816, pp. 126, 12mo.

III. Views of Canadian Scenery.

IV. First book for Canadian children. *Montreal*, 1844.

"Admirably adapted for the object with which it has been compiled."—*Lit. Garland.*

V. The Prompter. *Do.*, 1844.

"It is meant, chiefly, for the use of teachers, to whom it affords many useful hints, the fruits of the experience and observation of the author.—*Idem.*

VI. Progressive Exercises on the English language, to correspond with the Prompter. *Do*, 1845.

FLEMING, JOHN. A Can. merchant. B. in Aberdeenshire, Scot., about 1786. D. of cholera, at Montreal, 30 July. 1832. He was a resident of Montreal for 29 years, and at his death was head of the old-standing commercial firm of Hart, Logan & Co., and President of the Bank of Montreal. He had formed a valuable and unique library of about 11,000 volumes which it is believed he intended eventually to bequeath to McGill Coll., but his sudden death prevented an intention so patriotic from being carried out, and the collection was disposed of by public auction in 1843. In 1809 Mr. F. gained the medal of the *Soc. Littéraire de Québec* for an Ode on the Birthday of His Majesty, King George the Third. He was a contributor to the *Canadian Review*, (Mont.) in which first appeared the following work, from his pen :

I. The Political Annals of Lower Canada, being a Review of the Political and Legislative History of that Province. By a British Settler. *Montreal*, 1828, pp. lxxviii–180, 8vo.

"A work as full of information as it is of prejudice against the French Canadians."—LATERRIÈRE.

FLEMING, *Mrs.* M. A. (formerly Miss Early.) An Am. authoress. B. at Portland, St. John, N. B., 15 Nov., 1840. While still attending sch. being only 17, she contributed a story, *The Last of the Mountjoys, a tale of the days of Queen Elizabeth*, to the *Mercury* (N. Y.), which was so well received that it elicited from the prop. of the paper an invitation to the authoress to become a regular contributor to the *Mercury*. Since then she has been a mem. of the staff of that well known popular journal, and under the *nom de plume* of "*Cousin May Carle ton*" has written some hundreds of sketches, in addition to her serial novels and stories. Many of the latter have been reproduced on the other side of the Atlantic, some have been dramatized and performed on the stage with success, and nearly all have been republished in book-form by Brady (N. Y.) In 1865, Miss E. married Mr. John W. Fleming, an Engineer, and has since taken up her permanent residence in N. Y. We subjoin a list of her principal writings:

Mercury (N. Y.)

The Rover Chief, 1859 ; *Edith Percival*, 1860 ; *Gipsy Gower*, do. ; *Sybil Campbell, or The Queen of the Isle*, 1861 ; *Erminie, or The Gipsy's Vow*, 1862 ; *Silver Star*, 1863 ; *Victoria, or The Heiress of Castle Cliffe*, do. ; *La Masque, or The Midnight Queen*, 1864 ; *Hazelwood*, do. ; *Miriam*, 1865 ; *Nathalie Marsh*, do. ; *Eulalie*, 1866.

Metropolitan Record.

Three Cousins, 1860 ; *Georgia's Doom*, 1861 ; *Hagar Clyde*, 1862 ; *The Sisters of Torwood*, 1863 ; *New Year's Eve*, 1864.

Pilot (Bos.)

Ellie Moore, 1862 ; *Fairy May*, 1863.

FLEMING, PETER, *C. E.* For sometime in the employment of the Dept. of Public Works, Can. He surveyed some of the St. Lawrence Canals.

I. A System of Land Surveying.

II. A Method of Measuring a base line by angular observation.

III. On the St. Lawrence Canals, and gradual diminution of the Discharge of the St. Lawrence. *Montreal*, 1849.

IV. Geometrical Solutions of the Quadrature of the Circle. *Do.*, 1850.

V. Geometrical Solutions of the lengths and division of Circular Arcs, the quadrature of the circle, trisection of the angle, duplication of the cube, and the quadrature of the hyperbola. *Do.*, 1851, pp. 39.

FLEMING, SANDFORD. A Can. Civil Engineer and Surveyor. B. at Kirkaldy, Scot. Leaving sch. at an early age he devoted himself to the study of surveying and engineering, which professions he has constantly followed. In 1845, he emigrated to this country and took up his residence in U. C. He took

an active part in establishing the Canadian Institute (Tor.); he was on the engineering staff of the Northern Railway, U. C. from 1852 to 1863, during the greater portion of which time he was chief engineer of the road. In the latter year he was appointed by the inhabitants of Red River settlement to act as agent on their behalf in Can. and Gt. Brit. as the bearer of a memorial from them " on the subject of opening up such a line of road as would afford to that settlement free access without being dependent on a foreign country." He accordingly proceeded to Eng. to urge the matter upon the attention of the Imperial authorities, and received a cordial reception from the Duke of Newcastle, then Colonial Sec. In 1863, he was nominated by the Govts. of Can., N. S., N. B. and subsequently by that of the mother country to act as Chief Engineer of the Intercolonial Railway Survey, between Can. and the Lower Provinces. Owing, however, to some disagreement between the Provincial Govts., this appointment was not carried out. The survey was made, in the following year, under instructions from the Govt. of Can. Since the autumn of 1864, Mr. F. has held the position of Chief Railway Engineer for the Province of N. S., residing at Halifax, and simultaneously with the Exploratory Survey for the Intercolonial Railway between Rivière du Loup and Truro, has carried on the execution of Railway extensions in that Province. Besides his reports on various works, projected and effected, Mr. F. has written many communications to the newspaper press on subjects connected with his profession. He has also contributed many interesting and instructive papers to the *Can. Journ.* (Tor.) [See *The Prospectus* of that periodical ; *the Toronto Harbour, its formation and preservation ; General Railway Termini in Toronto, and projected Esplanade works ; Davenport Gravel drift ; On permanent way of Railways ; Valley of the Nottawasaga, with reference to ancient Lake Beaches, &c.*]

I. Preliminary Report on the projected North West Railway of Canada, with a description of the extent, physical features, soil and settlement of the country through which it is proposed to be constructed, showing the importance of the valley of the Saugeen, as a field for commerce and railway enterprise. *Toronto*, 1857, pp. 86.

II. Practical Observations on the construction of a continuous Line of Railway from Canada to the Pacific Ocean, on British Territory; a letter. *Do.*, 1862, pp. 35.

This is contained in Prof. Hind's work: *A Sketch of an Overland Route to British Columbia, Toronto*, 1862.

" We have no hesitation in ascribing to Mr. Fleming's letter a high degree of practical importance, and considering it as greatly increasing the value of Prof. Hind's very useful work."—*Can. Journ.*

III. Memorial of the People of Red River to the British and Canadian Governments, with remarks on the Colonization of Central British North America, and the establishment of a great Territorial road from Canada to British Columbia. *Quebec: Sess. Papers*, 1863, pp. 57, 8vo.

IV. Report on the Intercolonial Railway Exploratory Survey, made under instructions from the Canadian Government in the year 1864. (With maps.) *Quebec*, 1865, pp. 160, 8vo.

"Mr. Fleming divides his survey into two sections—one called the Nova Scotia division and the other the Canada and New Brunswick. The first division embraced an examination of a route from Truro, to which point a railway is now constructed. Mr. Fleming proceeds to describe six routes, the great object being to avoid the Cobequid Hills. He finally concludes that an available route to intersect the New Brunswick Railway east of Moncton can be found, the length of which would be 109 miles. Mr. Fleming settled on a central route for the other frontier, or the Canada and New Brunswick division of the railway to connect Rivière du Loup with the New Brunswick Railway. This route follows the old Grand Trunk survey from Rivière du Loup to Trois Pistoles, thence southward it keeps to the east of the St. John River, in a course towards the city of St. John, generally direct until it reaches the river opposite to Fredericton. The proposed line then strikes to the east round by the head of the Grand Lake, and then south, intersecting the New Brunswick Railway at Apohaqui station, a joint on that railway to the east of St. John, thus joining the immediate portion of the railway constructed between that joint and Moncton, where connection would be made with the proposed Nova Scotia line. Mr. Fleming

estimates the cost of proposed line per mile, after giving the approximate quantities of excavation, masonry, iron, &c., required to complete the grading and bridges, as follows: —Clearing, grubbing, draining, &c., £1,000; superstructure, embracing ballast, 5,000 cubic yards rails and joints, 70*l.* per yard; spikes, cross-ties, track laying, and an allowance of 10 per cent. additional for siding, $10,500; station accommodation, £1,000; engineering, $1,500; rolling stock, £3,000; contingencies, including miscellaneous services and reserve fund for extra rolling stock, £6,000; total, $23,000—producing a total mileage charge of $23,000, which will be considered uniform throughout and common to all lines. The total expenditure which he thinks a liberal estimate is as follows:— Truro to Moncton—the Nova Scotia division of the survey—uniform mileage charges above referred to, estimated 109 miles at $23,000 per mile, $2,507,000; bridging and grading, estimated from quantities, deducing from exploration survey, $2,693,000; total estimate, Truro and Moncton division, $5,200,000. Rivière du Loup to Apohaqui, New Brunswick and Canada division of the survey, uniform mileage charges, 340 miles at $23,000 per mile, $7,820,000; bridging and grading, estimated from quantities deduced from exploratory survey, $7,615,500; total estimate Rivière du Loup to Apohaqui, $15,435,500; grand total, $20,635,500—is an average of $46,000 per mile. Mr. Fleming enters into an examination of the different routes—15 routes,—closing with that of Major Robertson, 70 miles of which route along the Bay of Chaleurs he resurveyed last summer. He thinks this route not to be so difficult as was supposed and judges that it would not cost more than $40,000 per mile, or for the whole route from Rivière du Loup to Truro $20,000,000. In his proposed route, Mr. Fleming has kept at the narrowest point as distant from Maine as Maine is from the Grand Trunk in Canada along the St. Lawrence. He enters pretty fully into the commercial advantages of different routes, holding the view that as a frontier route would accommodate the largest amount of local traffic, and in the highest degree would serve the purpose of Canada in winter as an outlet for heavy through freight. He gives tables to show that communication could be established between New York and London by extending the railway from Rivière du Loup to Shippigan, in the Bay of Chaleurs, so that passengers could be set down in 171 hours, or nearly four days less than the lowest mean average of passages. The maximum grade in the central route from Rivière du Loup to the New Brunswick Railway is 40 feet per mile.—*Can. News*, (Lon. Eng.)

"Mr. Fleming has evidently entered on his work with enthusiasm, and though he had to grapple with a perfect maze of conflicting projects, he has canvassed the merits of each in an able manner, and embodied much valuable information as to the country through which the lines are intended to pass."—THOMAS AIRD: *Dumfries-shire Herald.*

FLEET, WILLIAM HENRY. A Can. journ. Ed. the *Transcript*, (Mont.) for some years. Now d.

I. How I came to be Governor of the Island of Cacona : with a particular account of my administration of the affairs of that island. Respectfully dedicated to my fellow-labourers in the Colonial Vineyard. By the Hon. Francis Thistleton, late Governor of the Island of Cacona. *Montreal*, 1853; *New York*, 1854, pp. 218, 8vo.

"It is evidently intended as a satire upon Colonial Governors and their administrations; and upon the present Canadian Government, in particular. * * * There is undoubtedly some wit and humour in the work, but the satire too often provokes a yawn in place of a smile."—*Brit. Col.* (Tor.)

FLETCHER, EDWARD TAYLOR. As early as 1834 contributed poetical pieces to the *Mercury* (Que.,) and from 1837 to 1839 to the *Literary Transcript* of the same city, under the signatures of "*Korah*," "*Tabitha*," and his own initials. From 1839 to 1845 was a steady contributor to the *Literary Garland*, in prose and verse; his contributions included some clever papers on the Literature of Northern Europe and on the songs of the Polish Peasantry, with literal translations of the originals. In 1853 the Lit. & His. Soc. (Que.) awarded him their prize medal offered for public competition for the best poem on a subject connected with Am. history. This poem *The Lay of Leif Eirckson*, has, however, never to our knowledge been printed. Mr. F. possesses considerable powers as an ethnologist, linguist and translator. He has for some years held an appointment in the Surveyor's Branch of the Crown Land Dept., Can.

I. The Twenty Years Seige of Candia. *Trans. Lit. & His. Soc.* (Que.) Vol. IV.

"A pleasing narrative."—*Can. Journ.*

II. On Languages as evincing special modes of thought. *Do.*

III. Essay on Language. Read before Toronto Literary Association. *Toronto*, 1857.

IV. The Lost Island of Atlantis. Read before the Lit. & His. Soc. *Quebec*, 1865, pp. 26. Also in *Trans. of Soc.*

FLETCHER, *Hon. Mr. Justice.* D. at Sherbrooke, L. C., 11 Nov. 1844.

I. On the modes of reducing the apparent distance between the Moon and the Sun or a Star, in Lunar observations, to the true distance, for the purpose of ascertaining the longitude. *Trans. Lit. and His. Soc.* (Que.) 1855.

Investigation of the Rules contained in Judge Fletcher's paper. By Valentine Daintry. *Do. do.*

FLETCHER, *Rev.* JOHN, *M. A.* A min. of the Ch. of Eng. Incumbent of Oakville, U. C. Has written in the newspaper press *On the correctness of the authorized translations of the Sacred Scriptures ; On Bible Reading versus Bible Burning ; &c.*

I. Letter to the Wesleyan Methodists of the Mission of Mono. *Toronto*, 2nd Ed., 1854, pp. 52, 12mo.

II. Address on Christian unity delivered in the Methodist Preaching House North Adjala. *Do.*, 1854, pp. 17, 12mo.

"According to my own views and convictions it appears to me that you have clearly and fully established every point which you have undertaken to prove and that on every point your authorities are decisive and your arguments unanswerable."—*Rev.* JAMES JONES, *D. D: Letter to the Author.*

III. Comparisons of the creeds of the Catholic and Roman Catholic Churches ; a Sermon. *Do.*, 1862, pp. 18, 12mo.

"The discourse will be found an excellent compendium of the Catholic and Scriptural character of our own church with reference to the claims of the church of Rome."—*Echo* (Mont.)

FOLEY, *Hon.* MICHAEL HAMILTON. A Can. politician and journ. B. in Sligo, Irel., about 1819. Came to Can. with his parents in 1832, and for some time taught sch. in Louth, U. C. In 1845 commenced the study of the law; in due time was admitted to practice as an Atty. and within a few years has been admitted as a Barrister. He sat in the Leg. Assem. from 1854 to 1863 and held office on 3 separate occasions as Postmaster General. From 1845 to 1853 he successively ed. the *Advocate* and the *Messenger* (Simcoe), and the *Herald* (Brantford), all published in the Reform interest.

FOND, S. P., *M. D.* A Can. poet. From 1862 to 1865 was on the staff of regular contributors to the *Waverly Mag.* (Bos.) in which many of his pieces appeared. Has contributed to the *Gazette* (Thorold); *Post* (St. Catherines); *Examiner* (Peterborough); and other country papers. Several of his poems are reproduced in Dewart's *Selections*. It is understood that Dr. F. is preparing a volume of his poems for publication.

"Mr. Ford was born and brought up in the neighbourhood of Peterboro. His poetry is distinguished by purity and elevation of moral sentiment, strong human sympathies and sweetness and gracefulness of style."— DEWART.

FORRESTER, *Rev.* ALEXANDER, *D. D.* Late Superintendent of Education, N. S.; now Principal Normal Sch., Truro. Has written a large number of pamphlets on Education, and is about to publish a large work on the same subject.

I. Duty of the Legislature of Nova Scotia with respect to Collegiate Education. *Halifax*, 1852, pp. 18, 8vo.

FORSTER, JOHN REINHOLD, *LL.D.*, *F.R.S.*, *F.A.S.* An eminent Eng. Naturalist. D. 1792.

I. Account of several quadrupeds from Hudson's Bay. *Phil. Trans.*, 1772.

II. Account of the birds sent from Hudson's Bay. *Do*.

III. Of some curious fishes from Hudson's Bay. *Do.*, 1773.

FORSYTH, J. BELL. A Quebec merchant. I. A Few Months in the East; or a glimpse of the Red, the Dead and the Black seas. By a Canadian. [With plates.] *Quebec*, 1861, pp. 181, 8vo.

"Mr. Forsyth, the author of this interesting little work, is eminently a practical man; it has been his aim to show, that with the great facilities modern improvements have placed within reach of every traveller, a voyage to the east may be accomplished with comparative ease and safety."—*Jour. of Ed., L. C.*

FOSDICK, H. M., *C. E.*

I. Report of the Chief Engineer, on the survey of the line for the Quebec and Saguenay Railway. Containing also a statement of the resources of the country through which it passes, and the general advantages to be derived therefrom ; with the proposed organization and By-Laws for the management of the Company. *Quebec*, 1854, pp. 68.

FOSTER, WILLIAM A., *LL. B.* Barrister at Law, Toronto. Has contributed in an editorial capacity to several Eng. and Can. newspapers and periodicals. In 1867 served as correspondent at the Paris *Exposition Universelle*, and on the Continent of Europe, for the *Telegraph*, (Tor.,) and other Can. newspapers.

I. The Canadian Confederation. *West. Rev.*, 1865.

"A valuable essay."—*Reader*, (Lon.)

II. The Canadian Confederation and the Reciprocity Treaty. *Do.*, 1866.

FOTHERGILL, CHARLES. A Can. journ. A native of Yorkshire, Eng. D. at Toronto, 22 May, 1840. Was for some time previous to 1824, King's Printer of U. C., and ed. and published the *Upper Canada Gazette* (York.) He was dismissed from his office for giving utterance from his place in the Assembly of U. C., of which he was a member, to some independent opinions respecting the administration of the govt. of the Province, at that time. He is spoken of as being a man of good education and considerable ability. At his death was ed. of the *Palladium* newspaper.

FOURNIER, JULES. A Montreal Merchant. B. in France. Since 1864 has occasionally contributed to *La Minerve* (Mont.); wrote a series of articles in that journal above the signature of *Auguste Vérité*. Mr. F. has also acted as Can. correspondent for some French newspapers.

I. Le Canada, son présent et son avenir ; Politique et Finance. *Montréal*, 1865, pp. 14.

II. Les Assurances au Canada. *Do.*, 1865, pp. 47, 8vo.

FRAME, *Miss* ELIZA. A N. S. authoress. Has contributed in prose and poetry to the local press.

I. Descriptive Sketches of Nova Scotia. By a Nova Scotian. *Halifax*, 1864, pp. 250.

"The verses are smooth, musical and pure in sentiment. The sketches are at the same time rich, racy and graphic."—*News* (St. John, N. B.)

FRANK, JACOB H.

I. Great Recipes for the cure of all diseases of Horses ; together with a treatise on taming and general treatment. *London, C. W.*, 1858, pp. 36.

FRASER, *Rev.* DONALD, *A. M.*

I. Leaves from a Minister's Portfolio. *Montreal*, 1853.

FRASER, *Col.* MALCOLM. An officer in Wolfe's army. D. 1815, aged 82 years.

I. Extract from a manuscript journal relating to the seige of Quebec in 1759, kept by Col. Malcolm Fraser. *Quebec*, 1865, pp. 37.

FRANCHÈRE, GABRIEL, *fils*. A Can. traveller. B. at Montreal, 1786. D. at St. Paul's, Minnesota, U. S., 12 Apl., 1863. Was one of the founders of the settlement of Astoria, which had to be abandoned owing to the Am. War of 1812. On his return to Can. in 1814 crossed the Rocky Mountains long before any Am. or many Europeans had attempted the feat. Was a mem. of the Am. Fur Co., and at his death was the last survivor of the Astoria Expedition.

I. Relation d'un voyage à la côte du Nord-Ouest de l'Amérique Septentrionale, dans les années 1810-1814. *Montreal*, 1820, pp. 284. Translated into English and ed. by J. V. Huntingdon. (With Illustrations.) *New York*, 1853, pp. 376, 8vo.

"Comme document historique, comme travail littéraire, l'œuvre de M. Franchère est pleine d'attraits, et d'utilité. La modestie avec laquelle le voyageur parle de son ouvrage ajoute un nouveau prix aux qualités qui le distinguent.

"Sans doute un littérateur consommé aurait dépensé grande quantité d'esprit et de pages pour rendre compte d'une exploration comme celle que fit M. Franchère ; mais nous sommes certain que jamais il n'aurait, malgré toutes ses connaissances, donné à son elucubration autant de fraîcheur et d'originalité qu'on en remarque dans le livre soumis à notre examen.

"Quoique abondantes, les peintures sont toutes marquées au coin de la diversité ; quoique fréquentes, les scènes de terre et de mer brillent toujours et par le pittoresque du fait lui même, et par la gracieuse simpli-

cité de l'expression. Bref, le voyage de M. Franchère est un livre qui se recommande autant par l'utilité qui en constitue le fond que par les agréments qui en parent la forme.—*La Ruche Litt.* : (Mont.)

"The great value of this work, as an authentic and decisive narrative of critical events, was strongly attested by Colonel Benton, in the great debate of 1846, on the Oregon boundary question. It is a pleasant narrative, simply told. Irving made much of it in his Astoria."—*Atlas*, (Boston.)

"The De Foe-like simplicity of the style, its picturesque descriptions of personal adventure, and of the features of the countries traversed by the author, confer an interest on this narrative, apart from that which springs from its historical value."—*Evening Post*, (N. Y.)

FRECHETTE, LOUIS HONORÉ. A French Can. poet. B. at Levis, L. C. 16 Nov., 1839. Ed. at the Seminary (Que.), at St. Ann's Coll. and at Nicolet Seminary. In 1864 was admitted as an Advocate of L. C. Mr. F. first began contributing short lyrical pieces to the press in 1858, and subsequently wrote for *Les Soirées Can.* and *Le Foyer Can.* (Que.) He dramatized the story of *Félix Poutré, ou L'échappé de la Potence, épisode de la Révolution Canadienne de* 1838, which has been repeatedly performed in public at Quebec and Montreal. In 1861 was appointed one of the Ed's. of *Le Journal de Québec*, and, in 1865, established *Le Journal de Levis*, of which he was Ed. for some time. Since the fall of 1866 has been a resident of Chicago, where he is connected with the newspaper press.

I. Mes Loisirs. *Québec*, 1863, pp. 204, 8vo.

"I have read your poems with great pleasure. * * * It is a great honour for you to be the first French Canadian in this field—the pathfinder through an unexplored land of songs ! You have all my best wishes."—H. W. LONGFELLOW : *Letter to Author.*

"What constitutes the greatness of French literature is its extension, hence its diversity. Paris alone was not the point of the great names which honor its literature. Our idiom with its inherent vitality gives lustre on its outskirts to works which its centre would not disavow. Whenever a French heart throbs, whenever a French mind thinks, then, rest assured, you will find an impassioned or an energetic pen. Has not Chambery produced the two De Maistres ? Geneva, Jean Jacques Rousseau ? Constantinople, Andre Chenier ?

The Mauritius, Parny? It is therefore without surprise that we see Canada, that new France so French, in despite of foreign dominion, giving birth to writers worthy in every respect of its glorious metropolis. I shall select one amongst a hundred, on account of his youth and on account of his genius, which sheds on his fatherland a gleam of his own glory."—THEODORE VIBERT: *Tribune Lyrique* (Paris).

FREEPORT, ANDREW.
  I. Case of the Hudson's Bay Company. *London*, 1857, 8vo.

FRESHMAN, *Rev.* CHARLES, *D. D.* A German Wes. Meth. Min. (Hamilton, U. C.) Late Rabbi of the Jewish Synagogue, (Que.)
  I. The Pentateuch; its genuineness and authenticity proved and defended by facts and arguments against the hypothetical criticisms, historical and literary of Bishop Colenso. *Toronto*, 1864, pp. 140.
  "I have read your pamphlet with interest and profit. Your statement of the arguments in favor of the high authority and accuracy of the books of Moses is clear and satisfactory, and your evidence of the high antiquity of the art of writing appears to be quite conclusive; while your suggestions as to the probable composition of the book of Genesis are worthy of careful and critical examination."—REV. W. ORMISTON, D. D.: *Letter to Author*.

FRIEL, HENRY J. A Can. journ. Contributed to the *Literary Garland* (Mont.) (See *Ottawa Sketches; The Misanthrope* and various other tales and miscellaneous pieces from his pen in that Mag.) Was Ed. and Prop. of the *Union* (Ottawa) from 1856 to 1866, when the paper ceased to be published. Is a terse and vigorous writer of undoubted ability.

'RY, A. A.
  I. Report of the case of the Canadian prisoners; with an introduction, on the Writ of Habeas Corpus. *London*, 1839, 8vo.

'ULFORD, *Rt. Rev.* FRANCIS, *D. D.* Lord Bish. of Montreal, and Metropolitan. B. at Sidmouth, Eng., 1803. Ed. at Tiverton grammar sch.; subsequently entered Exeter Coll. Oxford, where he graduated B. A. in 1824 and was elected a fellow in 1825. Rector of Trowbridge from 1832 until 1842; Rector of Croydon from last mentioned year

until 1845, when he became min. of Curzon Chapel, Mayfair, where he remained until his appointment in 1850 to the newly created separate See of Montreal. He was also Chapln in to the Duchess of Gloucester; and ed., for a time, the *Colonial Church Chronicle*. In 1860 his lordship was appointed Metropolitan bishop of Can. In 1850 he received the degree of D. D. from his *alma-mater*. He has been President of the Natural History Soc., and of the Art Association, (Mont.)
  I. Plain sermons on the Church and her services. *London*, 1837-8, 2 Vols., 8vo.
  II. Progress of the Reformation in England. *Do.*, 1841, 12mo.
  III. Pastoral letter addressed to the clergy of his Diocese, *Montreal*, 1851, pp. 16.
  IV. A Charge delivered to the clergy of the Diocese of Montreal, at the Primary Visitation. *Do.*, 1852, pp. 25.
  V. Sermon at the consecration of Horatio Potter, D. D., to the Episcopate. Preached by appointment in Trinity Church, New York. *New York*, 1854, pp. 31.
  VI. A Charge delivered to the clergy of the Diocese of Montreal, at the Triennial Visitation. *Montreal*, 1855, pp. 38.
  VII. Five Occasional Lectures delivered in Montreal. *Do.*, 1859, pp. 118, 8vo.
  [Contents: I. *Inaugural address to Church of England Association for Young Men of Montreal*. II. *Some remarks on Colonial Institutions*. III. *On Taste and Style in Literature* (with note). IV. *Some recollections of a visit to Abbotsford, and of Sir Walter Scott and his contemporaries*. V. *The state and prospects of Science and Literature in Montreal*.]
  VIII. A Letter to the Bishops and Clergy of the United Church of England and Ireland in Canada. *Do.*, 1862, pp. 30.
  IX. Sermons, Addresses and Statistics of the Diocese of Montreal. *Montreal, London*, and *Cambridge*, 1865, pp. xiv-308, 8vo.
  [Contents: *Sermons*, The Holy Catholic Church a Visible Body; The Interpretation of Law, and the Rule of Faith; The House of God; The Church one body in Christ;

The Witnesses for God's Truth; A Good Man's Death; The Victor's Crown; Worldly Wisdom; Worldly Conformity; The Lord our Righteousness; The Christian's Harvest; Fasting and Almsgiving; The Mystery of the Christian Life; Active Religion; A Word in Season.]

X. Sermon preached at the General Ordination held by the Right Rev. the Lord Bishop of Oxford, in the Cathedral Church of Christ. Oxford, 23rd Dec., 1866. *Oxford*, 1867.

FULFORD, FRANCIS DRUMMOND. Son of the preceding.

I. The Mis-application of Labour; a lecture. *Montreal*, 1859, pp. 15.

FULLER, *Rev.* T. BROCK, *D. D., D. C. L.* A min. of the Ch. of Eng. (Tor.) Formerly Rector of Thorold, U. C.

I. The Roman Catholic Church not the Mother Church of England; or the Church of England the Church originally planted in England. *Cobourg*, 1844, pp. 19.

II. Religious excitements tried by Scripture, and their fruits tested by experience; a sermon preached in 1842. 2nd Ed., *Toronto*, 1856, pp, 20.

III. Forms of Prayer. *Do.*, 1865, pp. 15.

FURLONG, *Rev.* WILLIAM. Presb. min. (Cornwallis, N. S.)

I. On the Transfiguration; a sermon. *Halifax*, 1864, pp. 16, 8vo.

FUTVOYE, GEORGE, *Ph. D., Q. C.* Permanent Clk. of the Crown Law Dept., C., since May, 1851. Was Clk. to the Corporation of the City of Quebec for some years, and has held various other offices of trust and importance in the Province.

I. A. Corn. Celsi Medicinæ, Libri viii., ad omnium veterum et recentium exemplarum fidem diligentissime emendati, quibus accedunt Index Librorum et Capitum, Tabula characterum ponderumque, cura et studio Georgii Futvoye, Ling. Profess. *London*, 18mo.

II. A Literal Interlineal Translation of the First Four Books of Celsus (from the above Text); with order of Latin words and original text; being the parts fixed on for the examination of

Medical Students at the British Navy Board, the Apothecaries' Hall, &c., &c. *Do.*, 12mo.

III. The Eight Books of Celsus on Medicine, originally translated by James Greive, M. D. A new edition carefully revised, with copious explanatory Notes. *Do.*, 12mo.

IV. A Literal Translation of the Pharmacopœia Londinensis (MDCCCXXXVI.) *Do.*, 1837, Royal 32mo.

"Eminently adapted to the purpose for which it is intended, as it is strictly close to the original, and at the same time free from the stiffness which renders literal translations in general so disagreeable."—PROFESSOR DRUITT, M. D.

V. A Collection of one thousand Latin prescriptions, containing every variety of form, according to the Nomenclature of the Pharmacopœia Londinensis 1836. *Do.*, 1837.

"A careful perusal of this book, will not only familiarise students with the forms of prescriptions used by the most eminent medical men, but will also exercise a spirit of inquiry as regards the nice judgment, of which the prescriptions, without a specification of the complaints to which they apply, afford intrinsic evidence."—*Parthenon.*

VI. Genera-nominum; or, a new and brief mode of learning the genders of Latin nouns. *Montreal*, 7th Ed., 1849; *Ottawa*, 8th Ed., 1866.

"Mr. Futvoye's Tract, though a trifle, is a desideratum in its way. Its conciseness is its great merit. We have here the substance of the '*Propria quoe Maribus*,' in the smallest compass possible. So BRIEF that a person of *common* capacity may commit it to memory in a few hours, and so INTELLIGIBLE, that the *dullest* may apply it."—*Academic Chronicle.*

"Not only novel, but exceedingly useful." *Scientific Gazette.*

VII. Lower Canada Law Almanac. *Quebec*, 1859. (Continued for several years.)

"C'est un tableau parfaitement compilé de tout ce qui peut être utile aux avocats et aux hommes d'affaires."—*Journ. de l'Inst. Pub. L. C.*

FYFE, *Rev.* R. A., *D. D.* Baptist Clergym. Is Principal and Prof. of Theology in the Can. Literary Institute, Woodstock, U. C. Has contributed to the periodical press of the U. S. (See *Canadian Affairs* in *Christian Rev.*, 1850; *Yeast—a Problem*, in the *New Eng. Rev.*, 1852.)

He has also written considerably for the newspaper press during the last 20 years, and for 3 years had the ed. control of the *Can. Baptist.* (Tor.)

I. An Address on Temperance. *Providence, R. I.,* 1351, pp. 24.

II. Spiritualism; a lecture. *Milwaukee, Wis.,* 1854, pp. 34.

III. The Secret Things of God and man's rule of duty; a sermon. *Toronto,* 1856, pp. 19.

IV. Baptist Sentiments confirmed by the testimony of the most learned Pedo-Baptists. *Do.,* 4th Ed., 1859, pp. 24.

V. The Teaching of the New Testament in regard to the Soul and the Nature of Christ's Kingdom. *New York* and *Toronto,* 2nd Ed., 1859, pp. 120.

G.

GAGNON, ERNEST. A French Can. musical author. B. at Rivière du Loup (en haut), L. C., 7 Nov., 1834. He early studied music, first at home, afterwards at the Coll. of Joliette, and subsequently in Mont. and Que. In 1853, was appointed Organist of the Parish Ch., St. John's Suburbs, in the last mentioned city, where he continued until he became organist to the R. C. Cathedral in the Upper Town, in 1864, which position he still holds. In 1857 was appointed Prof. of Music at the Laval Normal Sch. (Que.), and in the fall of that year proceeded to France where he studied his art for nearly a year, travelling subsequently through Italy, Sweden and Eng. Mr. G. has contributed occasionally to the *Journal des Maîtrises* (Paris), and has written articles at different times on subjects connected with music, for *Le Courrier* (Que.); of these articles we may particularize 3 which deservedly drew forth the praise of competent critics :— " *La Musique chez les Sauvages du Canada*," " *Étude sur Verdi*," and *Causerie Artistique*." In addition to these he is the author of several pieces of light music, which have been published.

MUSIC.

I. Ave Maria (*Sola and Chorus for 4 voices.*)

II. Stadaconé (*Indian dance for piano.*)

III. L'incarnation de la Jongleuse, (*Piano and violin.*)

IV. Souvenir de Venise (*Piano.*)

V. Chant des Voltigeurs (*Solo and chorus.*)

VI. Chansons Populaires du Canada. Recueillies et publiées avec annotations, etc. *Québec,* 1865, pp. 376, 8vo.

"This compilation of popular Canadian songs with music, and the excellent annotations by Mr. Gagnon, supplies a valuable addition to Canadian literature."—*Leader,* (Tor.)

"Par cette compilation M. Gagnon a rendu à notre pays un immense service, car nos chansons forment peut-être encore à l'heure qu'il est le plus clair de notre gloire, aux yeux de l'étranger."—HECTOR FABRE : *Can. Lit.*

GALBRAITH, THOMAS.

I. New Monetary theory. The absolute depreciation of Gold demonstrated to the extent of 50 per cent ; the prevalent monetary theory overturned ; the true nature of Money defined. *Montreal,* 1863, pp. 28.

GALE, SAMUEL. An Eng. officer. Was Asst. Paymaster to the Forces in Am. in 1770. After the revolution removed to Can. Subsequently became secy. to the Gov. Gen. of Can. D. at Farnham, L. C., 27 June, 1826.

I. An Essay on the nature and principles of public credit. *London,* 1784, 8vo.; 2nd Essay, *Do.,* 1785; 3rd Essay, *Do.* ; 1786 ; 4th Essay, *Do.,* do.

GALE, *Hon.* SAMUEL. Son of the above. For many years a Judge of the Court of Queen's Bench, L. C. B. at St. Augustine, Florida, U. S., 1783. D. June, 1865.

9*

I. Nerva, or a Collection of Papers published in the *Montreal Herald*. *Montreal*, 1814, pp. 45, 8vo.

"He wrote a series of letters to the Montreal *Herald* (in those days the organ of the stoutest conservatism) over the signature of "*Nerva*, which produced a strong impression on the public mind at the time."—*Gazette* (Mont.)

GALLATIN, *Hon.* ALBERT, *LL. D.* An Am. statesman. B. 1761. D. 1849.

I. Synopsis of the Indian Tribes within the United States, East of the Rocky Mountains, and in the British and Russian Possessions in North America. *Trans. Am. Ant. Soc.* Vol. II.

II. The Right of the United States of America to the North-Eastern Boundary, claimed by them. Principally extracted from the Statements laid before the King of the Netherlands, and revised by Albert Gallatin ; with an Appendix and 8 maps. *New York*, 1840, pp. 178, 8vo.

III. A Memoir on the North Eastern Boundary, in connexion with Mr. Jay's Map. Together with a Speech on the same subject by the Hon. Daniel Webster. (With Map.) *Do.*, 1843, pp. 74, 8vo.

GALT, *Hon.* ALEXANDER TILLOCH, *D. C. L.* A Can. statesman. Son of the late John Galt, the well known author of *Lawrie Todd ; The Annals of our Parish*, and many other popular works of fiction. B. at Chelsea, Eng., 6 Sept., 1817. Sat in the Leg. Assem. Can., with but one short interruption, from Apl., 1849 to the Union of 1867. Was Min. of Finance from 1858 to 1862 and again from 1864 to 1866, when he resigned office. Appointed to the same position in the Confederate Govt. of the Dominion of Can., 1867. Contributed to *Fraser's Mag.* in his younger days. Was long an earnest and eloquent advocate for a Federal Union of the B. N. A. Provinces.

I. Letter to the Chairman &c. of the North American Colonial Association on the St. Lawrence and Atlantic Railroad, with appendix and a map of the British possessions in North America. *London*, 1847, pp. 40.

II. Report upon the Memorial of the Chamber of Commerce of Sheffield. *Quebec*, 1859.

III. Canada, 1849 to 1859. *London*, 1860 ; 2nd Ed. *Quebec*, 1860, pp. 44, 8vo.

IV. Speech at the Chamber of Commerce, Manchester. *London*, 1862, pp. 18.

V. Speech on introducing the Budget, together with statistical and financial statements. *Quebec*, 1862, pp. 48, 8vo.

VI. Speech on the proposed Union of the British North American Provinces. delivered at Sherbrooke. *Montreal*, 1864, pp. 24, 8vo.

VII. Speech on bringing down the Financial Statement. *Quebec*, 1865, pp. 12, 12mo.

VIII. Speech on introducing the Budget. *Ottawa*, 1866, pp. 43, 12mo.

GALT, JOHN. A distinguished Eng. novelist. B. 1779. D. 1839. Was Commissioner of the Canada Land Co., and resided in Can. from 1826 to 1829. Founded the town of Guelph, U. C.

I. The Canadas—Topographical Information for emigrants. *London*, 1836, 12mo.

GANNETT. *Rev.* EZRA S., Min. (Bos.)

I. The faith of the Unitarian Christian explained, justified and distinguished ; a discourse at the dedication of the Unitarian Church, Montreal. *Boston*, 1845, pp. 40.

GARDINER, RICHARD. "Captain of Marines on board H. M. S. *Ripon*."

I. Memoirs of the Siege of Quebec, and of the Retreat of Monsieur De Boulamarque from Carillon to the Isle aux Noix, in Lake Champlain ; from the Journal of a French Officer, on board the Chezine frigate, taken by His Majesty's ship the Ripon,—Compared with the accounts transmitted home by Major General Wolfe and Admiral Saunders ; with occasional remarks. *London*, 1762, 4to.

The above is taken from Faribault. Watts gives a different title and date : "Memoirs of the Seige of Quebec, Capital of all Canada. From the Journal of a French Officer &c. *London*, 1761, 4to."

GARLAND, RICHARD. (N. S.)

I. Some thoughts on the nature, objects and management of Joint Stock Libraries. *N. D.*, pp. 7, 8vo.

ARNEAU, ALFRED. Son of the historian. Assisted his father in preparing the 3rd ed. of his *Histoire du Canada.* Has written some admirable pieces in verse which have appeared in the Que. and Mont. papers. His principal contributions have been to the *Foyer Can.* (Que.)

I. Les Seigneurs de Frontenac. *Rev. Can.*, 1866.

"M. Alfred Garneau, versificateur brillant, ciseleur habile."—HECTOR FABRE.

ARNEAU, FRANÇOIS XAVIER. A Can. historian. B. at Quebec, 15 June, 1809. D. there, 3 Feb. 1866. He was ed. at the Quebec Seminary, and on leaving sch. studied for the notarial profession. In 1828, made a tour through a portion of the New Eng. States, and in 1831, visited Eng. and France. On this latter journey he expected that he should have to return to Can. in the same year, and having visited Paris, was in London preparing to embark for home, when he accidentally met with Mr. D. V. Viger, the delegate from the Assem. of L. C. to the Imperial Govt. who retained him in Eng., as his Secy. During his stay in London, Mr. G. made the acquaintance of several prominent literary men, amongst others, Dr. Schirma, prof. of moral philosophy at the Univ. of Varsovia, Thomas Campbell, the poet, and McGregor the historian and statist; also of Mrs. Gore the authoress, and of the Polish exiles Prince Czartoriski, Gen. Pac, and Ursin Niemcewicz, the poet. He was admitted as a mem. of the Literary Association of the Friends of Poland, of which Campbell was president. In the following year he accompanied Mr. Viger from London to Paris, visited the Academy of Sciences and met many of the *Savants* of that institution. In 1833, he returned to Can. Some very interesting fragments respecting his voyage to Europe were written for *Le Journal de Québec* by Mr. G. so late as in 1855. We have been particular in noticing the main incidents of this visit to the old world, because from various causes, principally the literary society into which he was thrown, it exercised a strong influence toward the formation of his literary character. Several stray poems which he had written and never published were now produced in the Quebec journals. Some of them have been preserved by Mr. Huston in his *Recueil de Littérature Canadienne,* (Mont. 1848.); we quote the opinion of L'Abbé Casgrain, in his sketch of Mr. G., respecting their literary merits:

"Ces poésies respirent, en plusieurs endroits, les sentiments qui l'animaient au sujet de la nation dont il devait bientôt entreprendre d'écrire l'histoire.

"Ou peut citer parmi les plus remarquables: *Les Oiseaux Blancs, L'Hiver,* et *Le dernier Huron.*

"Mais ces essais qui auraient pu suffire à la réputation d'un autre, et qui lui assuraient une place distinguée parmi nos littérateurs, n'étaient qu'un acheminement à l'œuvre capitale de sa vie."

It was in 1840 that he commenced writing the history of his native country, a work which will perpetuate his name in the literature of Can. for all time. The 1st volume appeared at Quebec in 1845; the 2nd in 1846; and the 3rd, bringing our history down to the establishment of constitutional government in 1792, in 1848. It was at once favorably received by a large portion of the Can. population and by the French press of both Can. and France. The *Nouvelle Revue Encyclopédique,* of Firmin Didot, of Paris, (1847) reviewed it very approvingly. The State of N. Y. having obtained in the interim from the Eng. and French governments a copy of their official correspondence with the Colonies in N. A, Mr. G. proceeded to Albany to consult the documents, rightly judging that they would throw considerable additional light upon the history of Can. With the aid of Dr. O'Callaghan, who has since published the correspondence, &c., under the title of *The Documentary History of New York,* Mr. G. was entirely successful in his mission and the result of it was a second ed. of the *History of Canada,* revised and corrected from the correspondence in question, bringing the history down to the Union of the Canadas in 1840, published by Mr. Lovell in 1852. The new ed. was received with great favour and approbation by the public and the press. M. Th. Pavie devoted an article to it of 26 pages, in the *Revue des deux Mondes;* Dr. Brownson, one of 20 pages in his *Quarterly Review,* and M. Moreau, one of nearly 30 pages in the *Correspondant* of Paris. A third ed. of the work appeared at Quebec in 1859. and a translation from this into Eng., by Mr. Bell, which Mr. G. considered very faulty, was published at Montreal in 1860. The *History of Canada* of Mr. G. will ever be considered, a standard work. It has been quoted and given as an authority by such writers in the old and new worlds as Henri Martin, E. Rameau, G. Bancroft, Francis Parkman, Winthrop Sargent, L. Dussieux,

&c., and by most of our own *literati.* The first named in his *Histoire de France* thus speaks of Mr. G's work:

"Nous ne pouvons quitter sans émotion cette *Histoire du Canada,* qui nous est arrivée d'un autre hémisphère comme un témoignage vivant des sentiments et des traditions conservés parmi les Français du Nouveau-Monde après un siècle de domination étrangère. Puisse le génie de notre race persister parmi nos frères du Canada dans leurs destinées futures, quels que doivent être leurs rapports avec la grande fédération anglo-américaine, et conserver une place en Amérique à l'élément français."

In 1864, Mr. G. contributed the conclusion of his history to the *Revue Canadienne* which drew from Count Montalembert, the distinguished French orator and author the following: J'ai été surtout frappé d'un travail intitulé: *Une conclusion d'histoire,* par M. Garneau. Je dirais volontiers, avec ce patriotique écrivain 'Que les Canadiens soient fidèles à eux-mêmes,' et j'ajouterai qu'ils se consolent d'avoir été séparés par la fortune de la guerre de leur mère patrie, en songeant que cette séparation leur a donné les libertés et des droits que la France n'à su ni pratiquer, ni conserver, ni regretter!"

In conclusion we give the opinion of L'Abbe Casgrain on Mr. G. as a writer:

"Le style est à la hauteur de la pensée, et révèle un écrivain d'élite. Il a de l'ampleur, de la précision et de l'éclat: mais il est surtout remarquable par la verve et l'énergie. C'est une riche draperie qui fait bien ressortir les contours, dessine les formes avec grâce, et retombe ensuite avec noblesse et dignité. Il s'y mêle par fois, disent certains critiques français, une sorte d'archaïsme, qui loin d'être sans charme, donne, au contraire, au récit je ne sais quel caractère d'originalité à la fois et d'autorité.

"Mais le style de l'histoire du Canada se distingue surtout par une qualité qui fait son véritable mérite et qu'explique l'inspiration sous laquelle l'auteur a écrit. C'est dans un élan d'enthousiasme patriotique, de fierté nationale blessée, qu'il a conçu la pensée de son livre, que sa vocation d'historien lui est apparue. Ce sentiment, qui s'exaltait à mesure qu'il écrivait, a empreint son style d'une beauté mâle, d'une ardeur de conviction, d'une chaleur et d'une vivacité d'expression, qui entraînent et passionnent,—surtout le lecteur Canadien. On sent partout que le frisson du patriotisme a passé sur ces pages."

Mr. G. for many years up to within a short time of his death held the office of City Clk. to the Corporation of Quebec. Previous to this he had been an official in the employment of the Can. Legislature. He was an honorary mem. of several foreign as well as Can.

literary bodies. It is proposed to raise a national monument over his remains.

Un contemporain : F. X. Garneau. Par l'Abbé H. R. Casgrain. (With portrait and autograph.) *Quebec,* 1866, pp. 135, sm., 8vo.

GARVIE, WILLIAM. A N. S. journ. Ed. at Edinburgh, Scot., and at Halifax. His earliest contributions to the press consisted of several lyric poems in connection with the leading episodes of the Crimean War. Has been connected as ed. with several N. S. newspapers, and is now one of the ed's. and prop's. of the *Citizen* (Hal.) Was for some years Secy. to the N. S. Literary and Scientific Soc.

I. The Light and the Shadows : or Christianity the ideal of our race ; a lecture. *Halifax,* 1860, pp. 38, 12mo.

II. Barney Rooney's letters on Confederation, Botheration and Political Transmogrification. *Do.,* 1865, pp. 56, 12mo.

GASS, PATRICK.

I. A Journal of the Voyages and Travels of a corps of discovery under the command of Capt. Lewis and Capt. Clarke, of the army of the U. S., from the mouth of the Missouri through the interior parts of North America to the Pacific Ocean during the years 1804, 1805, and 1806. Containing an authentic relation of the most interesting transactions during the Expedition, a description of the country, and an account of its inhabitants, soil, climate, curiosities, and vegetable and animal productions, with geographical and explanatory notes by the publisher. *Pittsburgh,* 12mo, 1807.

Reprinted : *London,* 1808 ; 4th Edition. *Philadelphia,* 1812, 12mo.

GAVIN, *Rev.* D.
I. Le pouvoir temporel et spirituel du Pape. *Montréal,* 1852.

GEDDES, *Rev.* J. GAMBLE, *M. A.* Rector of Hamilton, U. C.

I. The Ministerial Character ; a sermon. *Toronto,* 1857, pp. 13.

GEDDIE, *Rev.* JOHN. A Presb. missionary. B. at Banff, Scot., but was taken when an infant to N. S. by his parents. He was ed. under Dr. McCulloch, licensed to preach in 1837, and ordained at Cavendish, P. E. I., in the following year. He was the founder of the Foreign Mission scheme of the Presb. Ch., N. S., the first missionary on the New Hebrides group, and the first to reduce to writing the language of any of the Islands composing the group. As early as 1843 he wrote letters to the *Presb. Banner*, urging upon the Presb. body the duty of establishing a mission to the Heathen, and in 1846 left N. S. as the first missionary to the South Seas. In July, 1848, he settled on the island of Aneiteum, one of the New Hebrides group, and having taken with him a printing press and the other necessary materials, he soon (being an amateur printer), commenced printing school books, hymns and portions of scripture in the language of the natives. His labours, from the commencement, have been most successful in bringing a people of the most savage character under the benign influence of Christianity. But his greatest work there has been the translation of the whole New Testament into their language, which he performed with the assistance of the Rev. John Inglis, a missionary who followed him 3 years after his departure. He has also translated portions of the old Testament; amongst others the Book of Psalms which was printed last year at Halifax. His letters to the *Missionary Register*, from 1850 to 1861, and to the *Presb. Record*. (both of N. S.). since then, giving an account of the islands, their inhabitants, etc., and his labours as a missionary, are models in their way, clear, concise, giving facts in a simple way, and manifesting a fine christian spirit.

I. Memorial to the Very Reverend the Synod of the Presbyterian Church of Nova Scotia. *Pictou*, 1844, pp. 4, 4to.

II. Summary of Information relative to the proposed mission to New Caledonia. *Do.*, 1846, pp. 12, 8vo.

III. The Universal diffusion of the Everlasting Gospel ; a sermon. *Do.*, 1846.

GEIKIE, *Rev.* A. CONSTABLE. A Presb. Clergym. Formerly of Galt, U. C. Now residing in Australia. Contributed largely to the Can. newspaper press.

I Notes on the population of New England. *Can. Journ.*, 1856.

II. Canadian English. *Do.*, 1857.

GEIKIE, JOHN C.
I. Reply to a Special Report of the Superintendent of Education on the theory and working of his educational repository of school and other text books, maps, apparatus and libraries. *Toronto*, 1858, pp. 30, 8vo.

II. George Stanley ; or Life in the Woods. A Boy's Narrative of the adventures of a Settler's family in Canada. (Edited.) *London*, and *Boston*, 1864, 16mo.

GENAND, JOSEPH AUGUSTE. A French Can. journ. B. at Montreal, Dec. 1839. The son of a Swiss officer who served under Napoleon I. Ed. at St. Mary's Coll. (Mont.) Was one of the joint Ed's of *L'Ordre*, (Mont.), a liberal newspaper, from 1861 to Augt. 1866, when he became Ed.-in-Chief of that journal. Mr. G. is the author of *Essai sur Montcalm ; L'Irlande ; Essai sur le R. P. de Ravignan* and several other papers which have appeared in *Le Journal de l'Inst. Pub.* and *L'Echo du Cab. de Lect.*

I. Antoinette de Mirecourt, [traduit de l'Anglais.] *Montréal*, 1865, pp. 342, 12mo.

"Mr. Genand has translated this novel with the fidelity and spirit of a scholar and translator."—ALLID: *Sat. Reader.*

GEORGE, *Rev.* J., *D. D.* Presb. Min. (Stratford, U. C.)
I. The Poetic Element in the Scottish Mind ; a lecture. *Kingston*, 1857.

GERIN-LAJOIE, A. A French Can. author. B. at Yamachiche, L. C., Augt., 1824. He received his education at the Seminary of Nicolet, where, in his 18th year, he wrote the tragedy of *Le Jeune Latour* which was performed at the institution during the collegiate exercises. In 1845, having previously commenced the study of the law, he became connected with *La Minerve*, the oldest journal published in the French language in Montreal ; he served as translator and reporter and finally was promoted to the chief editorship of that paper, a position which he held until Augt., 1847. In the following year he was admitted to practice at the bar.

During his residence in Montreal Mr. L. took an active part in establishing *L'Institut Canadien* of which he became President, and was for 2 or 3 years re-elected to that office. As an ordinary mem. of that body he delivered several interesting lectures before it, some of which have been published. In 1852 he was appointed one of the French translators in the Leg. Assem. and sub-sequently was transferred to the Library of Parliament as Assist. Librarian, a position for which, from his literary tastes and pursuits, he is eminently fitted. Mr. L. has contributed, both in prose and verse, to many of the French Can. periodicals and journals; his principal efforts of late have appeared in *Les Soirées Can.* of which he was one of the ed.-directors, and *Le Foyer Can.*, of which he was one of the founders and one of the ed's. His chief work is the novel of *Jean Rivard*, which appeared in the above perio-dicals. In this work he has success-fully endeavoured to give a true picture of French Can. life and cha-racter. The hero, from whom the story takes its name, is a young man who has just completed his education at coll., and who looks around him on entering the great theatre of life for a profession or calling to which he shall devote himself. Finding that all are greatly overcrowded, and that nothing is to be gained but much to be lost, by tying himself down to any particular one of them, passing a life of uselessness and inactivity, with no field or scope for ambition or the obtaining of distinction, he conceives the idea of entering the back-woods as a pioneer of civilization and by hard work, energy and pluck carve out a name and a fortune for himself in the primeval forest. He carries his project into execution, and with £50 as his capital commences and is ready to undergo all hardships and privations in his cherished purpose. He meets with hard struggles and many obsta-cles, but his indomitable will conquers all things which oppose him in his determination. Fortune smiles upon his efforts and his unconquerable spirit, others follow him in his course, and settle in the section of the country which knows him as its founder and

father, the wilderness which he en-tered but a few years before becomes a populous and growing community—Jean Rivard is a wealthy man, he mar-ries the girl of his heart and is returned to Parliament. The story is a simple one simply told and therein is its chief charm and attraction, but the romance is not wanting. There are many pha-ses of character introduced, and a fine moral sentiment runs through the en-tire book.

I. Le Jeune Latour, tragédie en trois actes. *Montréal*. 1344.

II. Catéchisme politique, ou élé-ments du droit public et constitutionnel du Canada, mis à la portée du peuple. *Do.* 1851, 8vo.

III. Jean Rivard, le défricheur Cana-dien. *Soirées Con.*, 1862, et *Foy. Can.*, 1864.

" We heartily wish that every young man in our Province who feels tempted to try his fortune in a foreign land, or in the more common of the learned Professions, rather than win his way to independence by the cultivation of the soil, had an opportunity of perusing the pages of this admirable story. It details the hardships and success of the new settlers, points out sources of enjoy-ment and profit, and inspires the doubting or desponding by the prospects of approach-ing comfort and independence."—REV. W. ELDER : *Journal*, (St. John, N. B.)

" Le style est simple, natural et gracieux : M. Lajoie montre une grande connaissance du caractère Canadien, et quelques-uns de ses tableaux de genre sont parfaits."—*Journ. de l'Inst. Pub.*

" En outre des *Anciens Canadiens*, deux romans ont fondé le genre et fixé le cadre du roman canadien, *Charles Guérin et Jean Rivard.* Si les deux héros de MM. Chauveau et Gérin-Lajoie sé fussent rencontrés dans le monde, ils eussent été amis ou parents, car, dans la fiction, ils ont un air d'intimité. Les deux histoires sont vraies, intéressantes, bien conduites, les personnages sont naturels, la couleur locale bonne ; cependant le grand succès obtenu par Jean Rivard a fait, jus-qu'à un certain point, défaut à Charles Guérin, qui, avec des portées plus brillantes, est inférieur à son heureux rival, comme étude exacte des mœurs canadiennes."—HECTOR FABRE : *Litt. Can.*

GÉNIN, ELZEAR. A French Can. journ-Brother of the preceding. Was for a short time on the staff of *Le Journal de Québec*. In 1865, became ed. of *Le Canada*, (Ottawa), where he remained until Augt. 1866, when he joined *La Minerve*. (Mont.) in the same capacity. In 1866, visited Europe, and was present in London during the sittings of the B. N. A. Confederation Conference. His letters to *La Minerve* during his stay abroad are full of interest.

I. La Gazette de Québec. *Québec*, pp. 65. 1864,

II. Relations Commerciales entre les Etats-Unis et le Canada (étude historique.) *Rev. Can.* 1865-6.

GESNER, ABRAHAM, *M. D., F. G. S.* A N. S. Geologist. B. in Cornwallis, N. S., towards the close of the last century. D. at Halifax, 29April, 1864. His father the late Colonel Gesner, was a native of Rockland County, N. Y., and an immediate descendant of the philosopher Conrad Gesner, of Zurich, Switzerl. At the commencement of the revolutionary war, which separated the Am. States from Gt. Brit., the Gesner family joined the Royalists, and 4 brothers entered the British Army. At the close of the war the father of Dr. G. and his twin brother settled in N. S., having lost all their patrimonial property by their attachment to the British Crown. Their losses and claims were not paid by the British Govt., although fully advocated by the late Duke of Wellington and other military men of high standing. *

In early life Dr. G. displayed a taste for learning. His opportunities to obtain an education were limited and he was altogether a self-made man. Natural history was his favorite pursuit. An opportunity was offered him of visiting the coasts of South Am. and the West India Islands, between 1818 1821, and he was twice shipwrecked in making voyages to that part of the world, where he had opportunities of examining a variety of tropical productions and numerous volcanic and coral formations. He afterwards commenced the study of medicine, went to Europe and obtained the honors of the medical profession. He was a pupil of the late Sir Astley Cooper, John Abernethy, and the most eminent men of the day. His leisure hours in Eng. were devoted to chemistry and geology. In 1835 he commenced an authorized geological survey of the Province of N. B., which was discontinued in 1842, in consequence of a disagreement between the Legislature and the Executive Govt. The survey was inadequately provided for, no assistant was employed and the work was never completed. In the mean time he collected a valuable museum of natural history which is now the property of the St. John's Mechanics' Institute. He was a public lecturer on different branches of science for many years. He also accompanied Sir Charles Lyell on his first tour to the principal places of geological interest in N.S., and especially to the Cumberland Coal field and the remarkable fossiliferous deposits of the "Joggins," which Sir Charles and other writers have since described with much minuteness: but of which Dr. G. had published an account as early as 1836. He devoted much labor to the developement of the resources of his native Province, and wrote a series of articles, on this subject in the *Mining Journal* (Lon.), and in other periodicals. In 1846 Dr. G made a geological survey of P. E. I., for the Govt., and in that year, he first extracted lamp oils from coals. From 1848 to 1851 he was occupied in analyzing the bitumen of Trinidad and other natural productions of the West India Islands, under the direction of the late Earl of Dundonald, then Admiral on the N. A. and W. I. Stations. He also accompanied his Lordship in his explorations of the coasts of N. S., Newfoundl. and Labrador, in reference to the fisheries and geology of the shores. Dr. G. was the discoverer of Kerosene Oil, * and the modes of extracting oils from coals and other bituminous substances. He established two extensive manufactories of the oils in N. Y., where he took up his residence in 1852, and the invention has been extended almost over the world. In 1862, Dr. G. returned to N. S., re-explored a considerable part of the Province, and published an account of her gold mines. He made many communications to the

---

* A biography of Colonel Henry Gesner, appeared in *Chambers Edin. Journal* about 11 years ago.

* See last census of the U. States, published in the *Scientific Am.* about Sept., 1862.

Scientific Societies of Europe and Am., of several of which he was an hon. mem.

I. Remarks on the Geology and Mineralogy of Nova Scotia ; with a new map of Nova Scotia, Cape Breton, Prince Edward Island, and part of New Brunswick. *Halifax* and *London*, 1836, pp. 272, 8vo.

" The author has been desirous to supply some of the testimony afforded among the rocks of Nova Scotia, which support the opinions, and correspond with the discoveries of distinguished naturalists in Europe. But more especially has his object been, to arouse the attention of the inhabitants of the Province, to a due estimation of the advantages they possess, and the resources Providence has placed within their reach."—*Extract from the Preface.*

" The Mineralogy and Geology of Nova Scotia, was the guide-book of Sir Charles Lyell in his geological survey of Nova Scotia, and after the most thorough examination was pronounced by him to be exceedingly correct."—*Men of the Time*, N. Y., 1852.

" The work before us is of peculiar value, as entering both into those valuable details [on the Natural Resources of N. S.], and paying great attention as to the topography of the Province, in which any particular circumstance is mentioned. These are drawn up succinctly and perspicuously, and are evidently the work of one who well understands the subject. The book is likely to be of essential benefit to Nova Scotia itself, and, we will add, to persons who carefully peruse it with a view to profit from the information it communicates. Besides the matter more properly included in the plan of the work, there is a brief but luminous ' Introduction to the Study of Geology,' with summaries of the various theories on the subject, and a similar introduction on that of Mineralogy. There are also a good map and two plates by way of illustration.—We would willingly extract largely from this clever work, but both the subject and our space forbid it."—*Albion*, (N. Y.)

II. First, Second, Third and Fourth Reports on the Geological Survey of the Province of New Brunswick. *St. John*, 1836-42, pp. 102, 8vo.

III. Report on the Londonderry Iron and Coal Deposits. *Halifax*, 1846, pp. 4, 8vo.

IV. New Brunswick ; with notes for Emigrants, comprehending the early History, an account of the Indians' Settlement, Topography, Statistics, Commerce, Natural History, Geology, social and political state, and contemplated Railways of the Province. *London*, 1847, pp. 388, 8vo.

" A very valuable and interesting acquisition to all who contemplate emigration, and to those who have friends in the Province, as well as forming a permanent addition to the library of reference."—*Critic*, (Lon.)

" We believe we may say confidently that few works have been more carefully prepared, or more thoroughly and laboriously digested and arranged than this history of the fine and fertile Province of New Brunswick—one of the nearest and most important of our British North American Provinces. We have, until now, had no complete history of this Province, and Dr. Gesner's scientific and literary talents, and his personal knowledge of the Province, acquired during a protracted geological survey of five years, on which he was engaged for the local government—all admirably fitted him for the important task which he has undertaken, and acquitted himself of so creditably."—*Sim. Col. Mag.*

V. The Industrial Resources of Nova Scotia, comprehending the Physical Geography, Topography, Geology, Agriculture, Commerce, contemplated Railways, &c., of the Province. *Halifax*, 1849, pp. 341, Large 8vo.

VI. A Practical Treatise on Coal, Petroleum and other distilled Oils. *New York and London*, 1861, pp. 134, 8vo. ; 2nd Ed. Revised and enlarged by G. W. Gesner. *Do.* 1865.

VII. The Gold Fields of Nova Scotia. *Halifax*, 1862, pp. 12, 8vo.

Miscellaneous.

On the Gypsum of Nova Scotia. *Geol Journ.* (Lon.) 1848.

Wild Scenes in New Brunswick. *Sim. Col. Mag.*, 1844.

Prince Edward's Island and its resources. *Do.* 1847.

Report on the Geology of Prince Edward Island. *Do.* do.

On the Commerce and Industry of New Brunswick. *Do.* do.

On Elevations and Depressions of the earth in North America. *Journ. Geol. Soc.* (Lon.) 1861.

GIBB, *Sir* GEORGE DUNCAN, *Bart.*, M. A., M. D., LL. D., F. G. S. An Eng. Medical author and writer. B. at Montreal Dec. 25, 1821. He was the eldest son of Thomas Gibb, Esq., who in early life had been an officer in H. M. Ordnance, and afterwards was engaged in commercial pursuits. Dr. G. lost his father when a mere boy, and with his brother and sister was carefully and religiously brought up by his mother, a daughter of James Ellice Campbell, Esq., an extensive timber merchant and ship builder at Hochelaga, a couple of miles below Montreal. He received his education at the well known Grammar Sch. of the Rev. Dr. Black, and afterwards under his successors Messrs. Howden and Taggart. On leaving sch. he entered on the study of law, but as his early tastes and predilections were for the profession of medicine he abandoned it, and after a probationary course of figures in the counting house of a well known wholesale Scotch firm, now extinct, he entered McGill Coll. as a student in Medicine and Arts. After some years study he took his degree of Doctor of Medicine in May, 1846. In the following year he paid a visit to Europe, remaining abroad until 1849, when he returned to Montreal and commenced to practise. With others, he was the originator of the St. Lawrence Sch. of Medicine, and held the Chair of Institutes of Medicine, giving a special course of lectures besides, on Comparative Anatomy. So energetic were the lectures at this sch., that a goodly number of students was obtained at the first session ; and the successful efforts of the teachers, together with the disinclination of students resident in the city to go long distances to attend lectures, were the chief means of bringing the medical faculty of McGill Coll. into the town. Besides his labours as a medical lecturer, Dr. G. was attached to the Montreal Dispensary, which he helped to found, and on his leaving Can. to settle in London in the spring of 1853, after practising for 4 years in Montreal, he was unanimously elected Consulting Physician to it. Whilst in his native city he delivered lectures each winter before the Natural History Soc., Mercantile Library Association, Addisonian Literary Soc. and other bodies, upon some of the divisions of Natural History, Comparative Anatomy and allied subjects. He was Curator and Librarian of the Natural History Soc. for 4 years, and devoted much time and attention to the arrangement of the Society's collection, presenting to that body, before he left, the greater portion of his private museum, numbering nearly 1500 various specimens in Natural History, and miscellaneous objects of interest and curiosity. At the anniversary meeting of the Soc. held 18 May, 1853, the following resolution was unanimously passed and afterwards extracted from the minutes and forwarded to Dr. G., through the hands of Major Lachlan, the president :

"That this Society, having learned with regret, that Doctor George D. Gibb is about to leave Canada, avails itself of this occasion to acknowledge his numerous valuable contributions to its Museum, and his labours on its behalf as Curator ; and to express its best wishes for his future success and welfare : while at the same time it would express its thanks for the numerous valuable lectures on Natural History delivered by him before the Society. (Signed) R. LACHLAN, Prest. N. H. S., Jos. T. DUTTON, Secretary."

During the years of his pupillage Dr. G. amassed a very fine Physiological and Pathological Museum, chiefly, however, whilst holding office as Assist. House Surgeon and Apothecary in the General Hospital : this fine collection was disposed of to the French Sch. of Medicine in Montreal, and is a good example of what untiring industry and perseverance will accomplish. Besides being a Governor, for some years, Dr. G. succeeded Mr. LaRocque as Secy. to the Montreal General Hospital, which he resigned with all his other appointments before leaving for Eng. On this occasion an affectionate farewell address was presented to him by his colleagues in the St. Lawrence Sch. of Medicine. At the period of his departure he was President of the Pathological Soc. of Montreal, of which he was the original founder, and had filled the office of Secy. to the Medico-Chirurgical Soc. He was Surgeon to the 3rd Battalion of Montreal Militia, his commission bearing date 14 July, 1847. This was in some measure a reward for his services as a Volunteer during the rebellion of 1837. On settling in London, amongst others to whom Dr. G. had letters, was the late Mr. G. J.

Guthrie, the celebrated Army Surgeon, who introduced him to Mr. Harevell at the Westminster Ophthalmic Hospital. This latter gentleman induced him to join the Medical Soc. of London as a Fellow—the oldest Soc. in London, which in times past had numbered Jenner and other distinguished men amongst its Fellows. The Soc. at the period we speak of (1853) offered great facilities to young and aspiring physicians to become known and to distinguish themselves, and Dr. G. was not slow to avail himself of these advantages. He immediately became an active contributor and debater, and the estimation in which he was held, was shown by his being elected on the Council of the Soc. 16 months after his election as a Fellow, a circumstance unprecedented in the annals of the Soc. Dr. G. has the happy knack of making a friend out of the most casual acquaintance, and his great personal popularity may, in a great measure, be due to this faculty. As a writer for the medical press, his services were sought as a sub-ed. firstly of the *Medical Circular* and afterwards of *The Lancet*. The reports of disease and clinical records from all the hospitals in the Metropolis, were exclusively under his management in the latter journal, and for 10 years (to the end of 1865) did he laboriously and assiduously edit this special department of the *Lancet*, and as his duties involved almost daily visits to some one or other of the hospitals, wherein everything curious or interesting was brought under his notice, he became acquainted (with but few exceptions) with all the hospital physicians and surgeons in London, and also in various parts of the kingdom. He was attached to 2 dispensaries, the St. Pancras Royal and West London, the post of physician to the former of which he held for 6 years, but resigned it on moving to the west or fashionable end of London. He subsequently was appointed Physician to the West London Hospital at Hammersmith; and on the occurrence of a vacancy in the Assistant Physicianship of the Westminster Hospital, opposite Westminster Abbey, he successfully contested the appointment with an Oxford graduate, who had the support of all the Clergy

and Barristers who were on the Board of Governors; so strenuously did he exert himself upon this occasion and so popular was his name, that he secured a majority of two-thirds of the votes over his opponent who did not in consequence go to the poll. The appointment to this ancient hospital Dr. G. considers one of the most important events in the history of his medical career. He now became associated with its medical sch. as one of the lecturers on Forensic Medicine. and resigned his other office of Physician to the West London Hospital, not wishing to retain two appointments. About this time the Council of the Laval Univ. (Que.), recognising his position in the mother country as an illustrious Can., and in consideration of the attention he has always paid to students and graduates of Medicine from Can., conferred the honorary degree of Doctor of Laws upon him. Dr. G. has been a great observer and recorder of facts, this habit was imbibed when a youth, for he was early accustomed to roaming about and studying appearances presented by nature both as regards the animal and mineral world. In his excursions he regularly noted down the various phenomena presented to his notice, and the features of the country over which he travelled, and doubtless if he had had the opportunity of attending lectures on Geology at that time, he would have made a good practical worker in that branch of science, for he was early at work studying the organic remains of the Lower Silurian Rocks, upon which we may say he was born; as it is, he has published several geological memoirs of interest. The records which he had preserved have been of the greatest service to him through life, and he has continued the plan to the present time of writing up his excursions and journeys whether for scientific or other purposes. He accumulated the materials. before leaving Can., of a small work never yet published, with the proposed title of " Geological Rambles around Montreal and its vicinity," which we hope he may some day have the leisure to complete and publish. In 1864 he published a monograph upon Hooping Cough, which he dedicated by permission to the late Earl of Elgin, whose friendship and acquaintance he enjoyed. This was one of many other publications of his, and the list of his writings which follows, shows that when others have slept Dr. G. has been at work. A systematic mode of life, regular hours and abstemious habits, have enabled him to carry all this out, without any great effort or strain upon his bodily or mental faculties; a source of change and relief was always at his command in visiting some spot where nature might be studied, and the system freshly invigorated. On his first visit to Europe he became a pupil at St. Bartholomew's Hospital (Lon.) and the Coll. of Surgeons (Dub.) : he was admitted a Licenciate of the latter body, after public examination, and took the diploma in midwifery. He witnessed the effects of the Revolution of June, 1848, in Paris, when all the hospitals were crowded with the wounded, and published a series of 123 cases, with remarks. He became an active Fellow of the Parisian Medical Soc. and read papers before it. Besides his degrees in Medicine and Arts from McGill Coll., Dr. G. holds that of the Royal College of Physicians (Lon.) ; he is also a Fellow of the Geological, Royal Medical and Chirurgical, Pathological, Anthropological, New Sydenham and other Societies (Lon.) He is at this time Senior Vice President of the Medical Soc. (Lon), and on the Council of several others. He is an honorary mem. of the Literary and Philosophical Soc. (St. Andrews), of the Kent Archæological Soc., a life mem. of the British Association for the Advancement of Science, and the British Medical Association. A mem. of the Academy of Sciences of Rome, and of Stockholm ; of the Natural History Societies (Bos. and Mont.), Literary and Historical Soc. (Que.), of the Medical Soc. of Virginia, Canadian Institute, Numismatic Soc. (Mont.) and various other bodies. Likewise a Fellow of the College of Physicians and Surgeons L. C. He has achieved a reputation of a European character for affections of the throat and windpipe, and has contributed largely to the literature of those subjects. He introduced several of the Bromides into Medicine as therapeutic agents, more especially the Bromide of Ammonium, an agent which promises to be of lasting benefit, in the relief of a large number of diseases. In relation to these we may remark that Dr. G.'s knowledge is essentially practical, for he was the best chemical student of his day in McGill Coll., and before taking his degree was offered the appointment of Chemist to the Geological Survey of Can., which he declined, not wishing to devote himself exclusively to that branch of science. He was the first to discover the characteristic crystal of Diabetic sugar, the presence of sugar in the fluid of certain dropsies, and the almost invariable presence of sugar in the urine of hooping cough. He has demonstrated that the epiglottis or valve at the top of the windpipe in 11 per cent of mankind, instead of being always erect or vertical is pendent, which to some extent accounts for the frequency of throat diseases. Dr. G. was the first in London to remove little tumours from within the larynx by the mouth, a feat he has now done some 18 or 20 times, which no other man living has accomplished, and which perhaps has helped more than any thing else to make his name celebrated in the annals of Medicine throughout the globe. In May, 1867, Dr. G. succeeded to the baronetcy of Gibb of Falkland, Fife, Scot.

List of Works and Contributions to the Press.

Case of Charbon or Malignant Pustule. *B. A. Med. Jour.*, 1845, vol. 1.

Treatise on morbid state of the Urine, with the chemical and other means of diagnosis ; together with some general remarks on Urinary Diseases. *London*, 1846, fcap., 8vo.

Evidence at a Coroner's Inquest in a case of fatal poisoning by Laudanum. *B. A. Med. Jour.*, 1846.

Monthly Meteorological Reports for upwards of 2 years (from March 1845 to end of May 1847,) taken in the City of Montreal. *Do.*, vols. 1, 2 and 3.

Cases of Gun Shot Wounds, occurring in Paris in June 1848 :

No. 1. *Head and Neck*, 19 cases. *Do.*, vol. 4.

No. 2. *Chest and Abdomen*, 19 cases. *Do.*, do.

No. 3 *Extremities*, 85 cases. *Do.*, do.

Report of the Sick on board of the ship "*St. George.*" bound from Liverpool to New York, with 338 steerage passengers. Numerous cases, and remarks on Ventilation. *Do.*, 1849.

Case of Comminuted Fracture of the Pelvis, with symptoms of fracture of the neck of the Thigh bone. Union of the bones complete by the 16th week. Fatal attack of Typhus fever. *Do.*, 1849.

The specimen is preserved in the Museum of the Royal Coll. of Surgeons, (Lon.)

Case of serious Apoplexy, with specimens of diseased heart, arteries and brain. *Do.*, do.

Lusus Naturæ—Fœtus of a Turkey with four legs and four wings. *Do.*, 1850.

Cyanopuon, or Cyanuret of Iron in the purulent discharge, in a case of chronic disease of the Breast, with a summary of cases published. *Do.*, do.

Fracture of the Thyroid Cartilage through the Pomum Adami. *Do.*, do.

Cancerous Tumour of the Neck, simulating Scrofula; hypertrophy of the Spleen. *Do.*, 1851.

Examination of the Sap of the Sugar Maple Tree, the *Acer Saccharinum* of Linnæus, with an account of the preparation of the Sugar. *Do.*

Reprinted as a pamphlet. Copied in full in several of the local and township newspapers.

"Dr. Gibb has brought to bear on this subject a mind fully embued with its interest and importance, and displays in the mode of his investigation an amount of chemical knowledge and scientific research highly gratifying to perceive in one who, we presume, like most practitioners in this country must, for the greater portion of his time, be employed in the more active and practical discharge of his professional duties."— *U. C. Med. Journ.*

On the Presence of Sugar in Pus. *Can. Med. Jour.*, 1852.

Experiments on the Livers of Birds, in relation to the presence of Sugar. *Do.*

Hereditary Insanity characterized by periodical attacks. Sudden Death and Coroner's Inquest. *Do.* 1853.

Shad Flies at Montreal. *Lancet*, (Lon.) 1853.

Epilepsy and Delirium Tremens. Read before Med. Soc. (Lon.) *Do.* do.

Protoxide of Copper, a new test for Sugar. Exhibited before Physiological Soc., 1853.

On the successful treatment of Cholera in Canada. *Lancet*, 1854.

On the relation that fat bears to the presence of Sugar in the Livers of Mammalia and Birds. Read before the Physiological Soc. *Do.* do.

Treatise on Hooping Cough; its complications, pathology, and terminations; with its successful treatment by a new remedy. London, 1854, pp. 395, fcap., 8vo.

"In his preface to the work, the author makes a kind of apology for presenting it to the profession. This, we believe, was scarcely necessary, for it possesses a quality which, at the present time above all others, should ensure it a welcome. It is thoroughly a practical work. Dr. Gibb's work is a valuable addition to medical literature."— *Lancet.*

"We now take our leave of Dr. Gibb, assuring him of our deep respect for the erudition and research displayed in his Treatise, and thanking him for the positive addition he has made to our knowledge."— *Quar. Jour. Med. Science,* (Dub.)

"We have read Dr. Gibb's work with attention, and are impressed with the industry, impartiality, and modesty of its author."— *Ranking's Abstract.*

London Correspondence of the *Medical Chronicle* or *Montreal Monthly Journal*, five letters in Volume 2. May 5, 1854, to 9th Feb., 1855.

Sugar present in the fluid of Ascites, from a case of Bright's Disease of the Kidneys. *Med. Times.*, 1854.

Nitric Acid in Hooping Cough; a letter in the *Association Med. Jour.*, 1854.

Small Calculi (*Phlebolites*) taken from between the coats of the Vagina in a coloured woman. *Path. Trans.*, 1854, vol. 5.

A paper supplemental to the above appeared in the *Montreal Med. Jour.* for Nov., 1854.

Epilepsy and Delirium Tremens in the same person, a case, brought before Med. Soc. of London. *Lancet*, 1854.

Cranium of a Female extensively diseased from Syphilitic periostitis with loss of bones of the nasal cavity. *Path. Tran.*, do.

Exastosis of the Zygoma. *Do.* do.

Cancer of the Uterus and Bladder; an ovarian tumour adherent to the posterior wall of the Uterus, &c. *Do.* do.

Replies to Questions on Diseases of the Eye, in connection with Industrial Pathology; made to the Soc. of Arts. *Jour. of Soc. of Arts,* do.

On the Pathology of Saccharine Assimilation. Read before the Medical Soc. (Lon.) 1855. *Lancet.*

This memoir was copied in the *Jour. Hebdomadaire de Paris* and reprinted in Paris as a separate work, with the Title "*De l'Assimilation du Sucre sous le point de vue de la Pathologie*, par George D. Gibb, etc." *Paris, 1855, 8vo.*

"A subject which has for a number of years engaged the attention of the author. The labour and research which he has bestowed in the accumulation of material is worthy the highest commendation."— *Med. Jour.* (Mont.)

Ancient Indian Arrows; are they poisoned? Physiological Society. *Med. Circular*, 1855.

Skull of the Babyrussa and the use of the upper tusks. *Do.* do.

Imperforate Rectum ; retention of Meconium, producing perforation of cæcum and fatal peritonitis. *Do.* do.

Case of Labour, foot presentation, with unusual twisting of the cord. Med. Soc. of London, 10th Nov., 1855. · *Lancet*, do.

Case of Suppurative Phlebitis in an infant a few days old, with post mortem softening of the stomach. *Do.* do.

Epidemic of Small Pox in Quebec, supposed to depend upon the opening of an Intramural Cemetery, 214 years old. *Quar. Jour. Public Health*, do.

Sanguineous Clot in the Right Corpus Striatum, Atheromatous disease of the Cerebral Blood-vessels, Fatty degeneration of the Heart and Liver. *Path. Trans.*, do.

Lungs containing small vomicœ, tubercles and dilated bronchical tubes, in a case of Pertussis complicated with Varicella. *Do.* do.

Unique Congenital Malformation, associated with umbilical Hernia, and a Pendulous artificial Anus. *Do.* do.

Ovarian Tumour weighing 106 lbs ; great elongation of the cervix uteri and vagina. *Do.* do.

This remarkable case has been quoted in various works in different Countries.

Edited Hospital Reports and Clinical Lectures in the *Med. Circular* for 15 months ending 31st March, 1856.

Specimens of acute pleuro-pneumonia with effusion from a female cat. Med. Soc. of London. *Lancet*, 1856.

Fœtus of between 4½ and 5 months which lived half an hour. Med. Soc. of London, 3rd May, 1856. *Do.* do.

On a case of Poisoning by Sulphate of Zinc, recovery. *Do.* do.

Calculus from the Bladder of a Field Mouse. *Path. Tran.* do.

Lobar Pneumonia of whole of left lung, and carnification of the right lung of an infant. *Do.* do.

Proliferous Ovarian Cyst, associated with Medullary Cancer and Melanasis in the liver, one suprarenal capsule and lymphatic glands. *Do.* do.

Congenital extroversion of the Bladder in an infant ; incurable nature of the affection. *Lancet*, 1857.

The living Infant was exhibited before the Pathological Society on 7th April. *Path. Tran.*, do.

Double sub-pericranial Cephalhaematoma. *Do.* do.

Remarkable fossil (Marine) Vegetable remains found in a bed of clay, at Tingewick, in Buckinghamshire. Forwarded with a description to the Canadian Institute at Toronto. Read before the Institute 4th April. *Can. Jour.*, 1857.

Adipose Tumour above the left Hip, the size of a fœtal head, growing 17 years, successfully removed. *Med. Chron.*, do.

Cannot enlargement of the middle lobe of the Prostate gland be removed by the Lateral operation of Lithotomy ? *Lancet*, do.

On a case of Poisoning by 12 drachms of Laudanum ; rejection from the stomach 9 hours after without symptoms of narcotism, recovery. *Do.* do.

Fibrous Tumour of the Uterus. A Clinical Record in *Do.* do.

The new diseases Drapetomania, and Dysæsthesia Ethiopis. A letter in *Do.* do.

Geological Features of the South Coast of England, from Brighton to Hastings. *Can. Nat.*, do.

Fall on the edge of a broken dish, wounding the neck, and severing the common carotid artery ; ligature of both ends, recovery. *Lancet*, do.

Pertussal Glucosuria, a Clinical Record in *Do.*, 1858.

Also a Letter on the same subject. *Do.* do.

Dichotomous Thumb, a Clinical Record in *Do.* do.

On the existence of a Cave in the Trenton limestone at the Côte St. Michel, on the Island of Montreal. *Can. Nat.*, do.

Fall across a chair by an 8 months pregnant woman, with laceration of the genitals, and escape of the liquor amnii ; regeneration of the fluid, and delivery beyond the full time. *Lancet*, do.

The Oyster conglomerate bed, at Bromley in Kent. *Geologist*, do.

Geological Map of Shetland, compiled from Hibbert and other sources. Exhibited before the Geological Soc. (Lon.) 1858.

Not published.

On the Generation of Sounds by Canadian Insects. *Can. Nat.*, 1859.

Crystals of Diabetic Sugar from Urine, with plates. *Archives of Med.*, 1858.

The author was the first to discover the characteristic crystal of Diabetic Sugar, and receives his full credit for it in the various works treating upon the subject.

Menstruation during Lactation and Pregnancy ; a Clinical Record in the *Lancet*, do.

Congenial Hemiplegia in a still born child, in a case of Placental and funis presentation. *Do.* do.

Cirrhasis of the Liver ; the Gall bladder filled with 4 biliary calculi, one of them encysted. *Path. Tran.*, do.

Calculus of Inspissated Bile, associated with Fibrous Tumours of the Uterus. *Do.* do.

Mulberry Calculi studded with Crystals, from the kidney of a horse. *Do.* do.

Neuralgia and Paraplegia, supposed to depend upon the long continued use of Arsenic, of which a trace was found in the liver and bones. *Do.* do.

Sugar in the Tears from a case of Diabetes. *Do.* do.

Death of the discoverer of the footprints of Birds in the New Red Sandstone of Connecticut. Letter in *Lancet*, 1859.

A case illustrating the fatal influence of Grief in Labour. *Obstet. Trans.*, do.

A chapter on Fossil Lightning. *Geologist*, do.

Reprinted as a pamphlet.

Nitric Acid in Hooping Cough. Letter in *Med. Times*, 1859.

Complete ossification of the Thyroid and Cricoid Cartilages. *Path. Tran.*, do.

Hydrarthrosis of the left thyro-hyoid articulation, and dislocation of the os hyoides. *Do.* do.

Farres Cancerous tubercle of the Liver and lesser curvature of the stomach ; gall bladder filled with pus and a calculus. Weight of liver 16 pounds. *Do.* do.

Epidemic Sudamina in a family of 8 persons. *Lancet*, do.

Copious secretion of Milk in the Breasts of an Infant. A Clinical Record in *Do.* do.

The number of Children a woman can bear. Clinical Record in *Do.* do.

On Canadian Caverns. Read before Brit. Assoc. for Advancement of Science, at Aberdeen, on 16 Sept., 1859. Abstract in *Trans.* of the Assoc. *Geologist* for April, May and June, 1860. Reprinted as a separate work with 8 plates. *London*, 1861, pp. 28, 8vo.

" I hope that your very clear description of those striking Caverns, will lead other explorers to detect fossil remains in them." SIR RODERICK MURCHISON : *Letter to Author.*

" I am much obliged to you for your paper on Canadian Caverns which I had already read, and regretted there were not more fossil bones."—SIR CHARLES LYELL : *do.*

Cancer of the Liver, Lungs and Pleura ; the Uterus and Bladder ; conjoined with Albuminuria of one kidney and saccharine urine of the other. *Path. Tran.*, 1859.

London Correspondence of the *Med. Chronicle* or *Montreal Monthly Journal*, letters in 1855-6-7-8 and 9.

The Natural History, Properties and Medical uses of the Sanguinaria Canadensis. Lengthy paper read before the Medical Soc. (Lon.) An abstract of it appeared with the discussion in the *Lancet*. The condensed paper as read appeared in *Brit. Med. Jour.* That part of the paper comprising the description, composition and preparations of the Sanguinaria was published in the *Pharmaceutical Journal* for March, with a wood cut. The account of its Physiological effects, properties and medical uses, appeared in the *Med. Jour.* (Glas.) for July, whilst that part of it relating to its Natural History has appeared in the *Can. Nat.* for 1866.

On Diseases of the Throat, Epiglottis and Windpipe ; including Diphtheria, displacement of the Cartilages, etc. ; their symptoms, progress and treatment. *London*, 1860, fcap., 8vo.

" The diseases which form the subjects of this volume are essentially of that kind which mere theoretic knowledge cannot assist the least in describing ; they are about as necessarily demonstrative as are diseases affecting the skin. We heartily recommend this proof of Dr. Gibb's observation and diligence to the favourable notice of our readers."— *Lancet.*

" We recommend this book as containing a sensible and well-written account of most diseases of the throat. The treatment recommended is essentially practical ; it is moderate, yet efficient. To many of the profession this small volume would prove in the hour of anxiety a valuable resource."— *Brit, and For. Med. Chir. Rev.*

" We are tempted to quote more largely from this valuable and elegantly-written volume ; but, on consideration, prefer to recommend its purchase by every practitioner, to be read entire, and then carefully placed in his library for reference."—*Quar. Med. Jour.* (Dub.)

On the Atheromatous Expression. *Lancet*, 1860.

Extensive calcification of the Arteries, with abnormal distribution of their trunks ; and other examples illustrating the atheromatous and calcareous expressions. *Path. Tran.*, do.

On Saccharine Fermentation of the milk within the Female Breast. Read before the Brit. Assoc. for Advan. of Science at Oxford, in June, 1860. *Arch. Med.* and *Brit. Med. Jour.*

The Laryngoscope : its value in healthy and diseased conditions of the Throat and Windpipe. *Lancet*, do.

Translated for the New Sydenham Society, of " Du Laryngoscope et de son empire en Physiologie et en Médecine, par le Docteur J. N. Czermak, Prof. de Physiologie à l'Université de Pest." Edition Française. *Paris*, do.

Pelvic Cellulitis after a first pregnancy followed by suppuration at the back and front parts of the Vagina, recovery. *Obstet. Tran.*, do.

Necrosed Cartilage expectorated in a case of Syphilitic laryngitis ; use of the Laryngoscope in the diagnosis of the condition of the glottis. *Path. Tran.*, do.

London Correspondence of the *Indian Lancet* or *Medical Officers' Journal*, (Lahore, Northern India.) 16 letters (bi-monthly) from 3rd Nov., 1860, to 18th June, 1861.

Calcification of the Cartilages of the Larynx including the Arytenoid. *Path. Tran.*, 1861.

Laryngitis in a white lipped Peccary. *Do.* do.

Cartilages of Wrisberg in the larynx of a Mona Monkey. *Do.* do.

Large amount of Chlorides with deposits of Cystine, lithates and oxalate of lime, in the urine in a case of long continued sweating. *Archives of Med.*, do.

Internal Cranial Exastosis in a case of Epilepsy, fatal from Delirium Tremens. *Path. Tran.*, do.

Fistulous communication between the Bladder and small Intestine through a peritoneal abscess ; cure. *Lancet*, do.

Removal of a Needle from beneath the skin of the belly of a Child. *Do.* do.

Hemorrhage from the Ears in Hooping Cough, its real cause. *Brit. Med. Jour.*, do.

On the arrest of Puparial Metamorphosis of the Vanessa Antiopa. *Brit. Assoc. for Advan. of Science*, at Manchester, Sept. 1861. See its *Tran.*

Fracture of the Os Hyoides which had united faultily. *Do.* do.

Horse Shoe Kidney affected with Bright's disease. *Path. Tran.*, do.

Inflammatory Disease of the Skin of the head and upper part of the body of an 8 months fœtus, with exudation of plastic lymph. *Obstet. Tran.*, do.

Diphtheria associated with Parotitis, recovery. *Path. Tran.*, 1862.

On the Diseases and Injuries of the Hyoid or Tongue Bone. Numerous wood cuts. *London*, 1862, 8vo.

" If any man has a right to the title of ' Specialist' in its best sense, Dr. Gibb may claim the hyoid bone and parts adjacent as his own special province. We can truly say, that no library is complete without Dr. Gibb's unpretending little book, since the most voluminous systematic works would be searched in vain for the unique information it contains "—*Med. Times.*

" The entire style of his essay bears witness to the manner in which he pursued his studies, as well as to his habits of observation and descriptive powers. We sincerely recommend it to the attention of the profession, who will find it a striking contrast to much of the book-making going on at the present time."—*Med. Press*, (Dub.)

Hypertrophy of the Spleen, with thick fibrous deposits on its entire convex surface. *Path. Tran.*, 1862.

Atrophy of the Spleen. *Do.* do.

Constituents of Bone in a case of Mollities Ossium. *Do.* do.

Enormous distension of the belly from the effects of a severe and extensive burn. *Do.* do.

A visit to Reculver in Kent. *Geologist*, do.

Empyema simulated by extra-thoracic abscess in a phthisical patient. *Lancet*, do.

Idiopathic Tetanus from sitting on the Grass ; recovery in three weeks. *Do.* do.

London Correspondence of the *B. A. Med. Jour.* (Mont.), 1860-1-2.

Acute Inflamation of the vocal cords as seen by the Laryngoscope, producing complete Aphonia, rapidly cured by local treatment. *Lancet*, 1862.

On the Physiological effects of the Bromide of Ammonium. *Brit. Assoc. for Advan. of Science*, at Cambridge, Oct. 1862. See its *Trans.*

The normal position of the Epiglottis as determined by the Laryngoscope. *Do.* do.

Destruction of the Epiglottis and right Arytenoid Cartilage, with necrosis of some of the other Cartilages. *Path. Tran.*, do.

Clinical Remarks on 2 cases of arrest of development and deformity of the vocal organs in adult deaf mutes, examined with the Laryngoscope. *Med. Times*, do.

Polypoid growths removed from the larynx, by means of the laryngost ecraseur. *Path. Tran.*, do.

Ulceration of the Membrane covering the turbinated bones, the cause of epistanis for 13 years, as seen with the rhinoscope. *Do.* do.

Paralysis of the throat and larynx following diphtheria, permitting of a view with the Laryngoscope of the bifurcation of the trachea ; good recovery. *Lancet*, do.

On a case of sudden Aphonia from cold ; autolaryngoscopy ; a circle of redness round the vocal cords ; cure after self application of topical treatment. *Do.* do.

Illustrations of the application of the Laryngoscope. Read before the Med. Soc. of Lon., Dec. 1862. *Do.* do.

A Splenic tumour, weighing 15lbs., removed from a live dog. *Path. Tran.*, do.

Fibro-cellular polypus of the larynx, the size of a pea, successfully removed. *Do.* do.

Congenital deformity and arrest of development of the larynx in an adult deaf mute. *Path. Tran.*, 1863.

Congenital deformity in a deaf and dumb boy. *Do.* do.

Deformity of the larynx with a double voice, the result of a wound of the left vocal cord. *Do.* do.

Deformity of the larynx and alteration of speech from small pox. *Path. Tran.*, do.

The Value of the Bromide of Ammonium as a remedial agent in certain diseases. *Lancet*, do.

Cutaneous eruption in an Infant, supposed to be from Hereditary Syphilis; cure chiefly through medication of the breast milk of the mother. *Do. do.*

Anæmia from great enlargement of the liver and spleen, disease of the heart, and phthisis; good effects for a time of the Bromide of Ammonium; fatal result. *Do. do.*

Tuberculous ulceration of the Larynx, especially involving the right vocal cord, in a phthisical patient, seen by the aid of the laryngoscope. *Do. do.*

Loss of Voice of some months duration; speedy recovery through the local use of Nux Vomica. *Do. do.*

Laryngeal Ecraseur, for the removal of small tumours from the interior of the larynx. Exhibited before Med. Soc. (Lon.) January, 1863. *Do. do.*

Peculiar form of Tumour of right false vocal cord, containing a piece of neerased cricoid cartilage which was expelled in coughing. *Path. Tran.*, do.

Tuberculous Ulceration of the larynx, especially involving the right vocal cord in a phthisical patient. *Do. do.*

Aphonia and Dysphonia from tuberculous ulceration of the fallicles of the epiglottis, larynx and trachea, in the first stage of phthisis pulmonalis. *Do. do.*

Aphonia following phthisis and pneumonia; tuberculous ulceration of the larynx and disease of the vocal cords. *Do. do.*

On the Influence of Musical and other sounds upon the larynx as seen by the aid of the Laryngoscope. A Lecture delivered before the *Musical Soc.* (Lon.), profusely illustrated by diagrams. An abstract appeared in *Lancet* and *Social Science Review*, do.

Elephantiasis Graecorum and Leontiasis, affecting the throat as well, and seen by the aid of the Laryngoscope. Showed the patient. *Path. Tran.*, do.

Spontaneous Expulsion of an elongated polypus from the left vocal cord. *Do. do.*

Ulceration and destruction of the Turbinated bones and floor of the right nostril, with exudation of fibrine. *Do. do.*

Organic Aphonia and Dysphonia for 22 months from several fallated growths in the true and false vocal cords. *Do. do.*

Organic Aphonia for 5 years from a tumour of the right vocal cord. *Do. do.*

Organic Aphonia for 3 years from tumours about vocal cords. *Do. do.*

Varying Aphonia from 2 small growths on the surface of the left cord. *Do. do.*

Impaction of a piece of Walnut shell below the glottis, seen by the aid of the Laryngoscope. *Do. do.*

Cases of Disease of the Thyro-hyoid articulation and ligament; with Clinical remarks. *B. A. Jour.*, do.,

Destruction of the free portion of the epiglottis, aryteno-epiglottidean folds, arytenoid cartilages and vocal cords. Incurable Aphonia. *Do. do.*

Total loss of Epiglottis, Aphonia from ulceration of larynx and pharynx. *Do. do.*

Larynx of a child affected with Diphtheria, chiefly involving the epiglottis. *Do. do.*

Branchoede bulging the trachea inwards, near the bifurcation as seen with the laryngoscope; neuralgic pains of the neck and elsewhere. *Lancet*, do.

The influence of Tobacco on the Mucous Membrane. A letter in *Do.* do.

Crackling of the Joints in a pregnant woman. *Do. do.*

Illustration of the causes of Hoarseness and Loss of Voice. Paper read at Bristol before the *Brit. Med. Assoc. B. M. Jour.* Nov. 1863.

Report on the Physiological effects of the Bromide of Ammonium, made to the Brit. Assoc. for Advanc. of Science at Newcastle, Aug., 1863. Published in full in the *Trans.*

Further observations on the Normal position of the Epiglottis. *Do. do.*

On voluntary closure of the Glottis independently of the act of breathing. *Do. do.*

Cases of Whooping Cough treated with the Bromide of Ammonium. Clinical record in *Lancet*, do.

The Laryngoscope: Illustrations of its Practical Application and description of its Mechanism. With 35 wood engravings. London, 1863, 8vo. 2nd Ed.

"Dr. Gibb was an authority on affections of the throat long before the introduction of the Laryngoscope, and translated for the *New Sydenham Society* the monograph of Czermak on the employment of this instrument. His skill in the examination of the Laryngeal apparatus, and in the treatment of its disorders and diseases, was, therefore, obtained under unexceptionably favourable circumstances. In this work he gives to the profession some of the results of his large experience. In some of the cases these have been so successful that we may place them in the first rank of surgical triumphs, whether we consider the relief afforded the patient, or the judgment and skill displayed by the operator."—*Lancet*.

"Dr. Gibb's name is already favourably known to the profession in connection with the subject of laryngoscopes, and the *brochure* which he has now published may be, perhaps, looked upon as one of the most important, in a practical point of view, which has hitherto been written on the subject in England."—*Med. Jour.* (Glas.)

" This *brochure* contains much that is new and worthy of being known ; the cases of disease in which polypi of the larynx were removed by the écraseur are of particular interest and value."— *Deutsche Klinik.*

Subglottic oedema of the Larynx associated with phthisis laryngea et pulmonalis. *Path. Tran.,* 1863.

Destruction of the free portion of the epiglottis from ulceration and disease of the throat for four years; good recovery. *Do.* do.

Constrained hoarseness for 18 months, depending upon a warty growth of the larynx, removed with the laryngeal écraseur; cure. *Do.* do.

Loss of voice, with an occasional whisper, for 15 months, from a warty growth at the back of the larynx, which was successfully removed. *Do.* do.

Exhibited a living male infant, with large swellings over the hip and shoulder joints of a doubtful nature. *Do.* do.

Functional Aphonia of 10 years duration, hereditary in its nature. *Do.* do.

A pin removed from the larynx ; a tooth brush bristle extracted from the Tonsil ; and a case of United Fracture of the Pomum Adami. Med. Soc. of London. *Lancet,* 1864.

Mr. Durham's case of Mucous Cyst of the Epiglottis. Letter in *Do.,* 1863.

Suppurating snuffles in an infant taking on the character of Ozæna. *Do.* do.

Lecture on the Laryngoscope delivered before the Medical Profession, by request, at Nottingham, August, 1863.

The substance of this extemporaneous lecture is scattered throughout the author's writings.

Lecture on Affections of the Throat, with the practical use of the Laryngoscope, delivered extempore, before the Western Med. and Surg. Soc. of London, Dec., 1863, also by request. Abstract in *Brit. Med. Jour.,* 1864.

Silver Shomers. Letter in *Medical Times,* do.

On Albuminuric Aphonia. *Lancet,* do.

On Subglottic Oedema of the Larynx. Paper read before the Med. Soc. of London, 1864.

This is incorporated in the second edition of the author's work on the Throat.

Case of Acute Epiglottiditis. *Path. Tran.,* do.

Report of Dr. Murchison's case of Necrosis of the Hyoid Bone. *Do.* do.

Constriction and thickening of the trachea and larger bronchi, associated with growths in the larynx. Tracheotomy, inability to keep in a tube ; fatal result. Hospital Report in *Lancet; Ranking's Abstract,* with woodcuts, do.

Worms from the nose and frontal sinuses. *Path. Tran.,* do.

On Diseases of the Throat and Windpipe, as reflected by the Laryngoscope : a complete manual upon their Diagnosis and treatment. Embellished with 116 engravings. *London,* 2nd Ed., Fools., 8vo., cloth pp. 481.

" From the introduction of the laryngoscope into note in this country, the author of this book possesses exceptionable opportunities of becoming very thoroughly acquainted with its use under the tuition of Czermak himself, the English translation of whose valuable monograph was very ably edited by Dr. Gibb for the New Sydenham Society. He had made the affections of the throat his study long before the ingenious professors at Prague introduced the laryngoscope, and, therefore, had a vantage-ground in commencing his investigations by aid of the new instrument. * * * * The special character of Dr. Gibb's work is that it is eminently practical—such a book as the practitioner desirous of learning and using the laryngoscope might study with advantage, since it just gives what he wants. There is no parade of antiquarian lore, no abstruse disquisition on the laws of reflection and the principles of illumination ; but just a straightforward setting down in print of the observations and experience of one of the most accurate and skilful of the numerous practitioners who are devoting themselves to the study of the laryngoscope in England, France and Germany."—*Lancet.*

" Dr. Gibb has most laboriously and ably investigated the whole subject of which his work treats, both by research in books and museums, and by personal observation ; and he has put together a great amount of information in a form which is pleasing and instructive. He may safely entrust his labours and reputation into the hands of his professional brethren, in the confidence that he will receive from them his full share of credit for having enlarged our knowledge of throat diseases."—*Brit. Med. Jout.*

Large growth of the Larynx partly removed by the mouth and partly through the Pomum Adami. *Path. Tran.,* 1864.

Detached Necrosis of Cricoid Cartilage. *Do.* do.

Gibb's Pocket Laryngoscope. Exhibited before the Med. Soc. of London, April 4th, 1864.

Some remarkably hypertrophied and diseased skulls from the Museum of Westminster Hospital. Exhibited and described before the Anthropological Society. *Quar. Jour. Anthrop. Soc.,* do.

The Effervescing Bromide of Ammonium. Letter in *Lancet,* do.

On the various forms assumed by the Glottis. Read before Brit. Assoc. for Advancement of Science at Bath, September. Abstract in its *Trans.,* but published in full in *Lancet,* do.

Essential points of difference between the larynx of the negro and that of the white man. Read at the same meeting of the Brit. Assoc. See Abstract in its *Trans.*

The paper was afterwards brought before the Anthropological Soc. of London in January 1865, and is published in fu'l wi h engravings in the 2nd Vol.

of its *Memoirs.* The larynx of a Negro was exhibited before the Med. Soc. of London, on 11 January, 1864, by the author, and its particularities carefully pointed out and noted at the time.—See the *Lancet.*

Note on the action of the Bromides of Lithium, Zinc. and Lead. Brit. Assoc. at Bath. Same time as the 2 previous communications, 1864.

Remarkable instance of a growth springing from the Epiglottis, which was successfully removed with the aid of the Laryngoscope. *Med. Chir. Tran.,* do.

Necrosis of Turbinated Bones and part of the Nomer, treated by aid of the Rhinoscope. *Path. Tran.,* do.

On Throat Cough: its causes and treatment. *London,* 8vo., 1865.

The subject was first brought before the Med. Soc. of London in a paper by the author, 1864.

Facility in the use of the Laryngoscope: the Instrument in its social aspect. *Brit. Med. Jour,* 1865.

Portions of ossified tracheal rings, expelled some months after tracheotomy. *Path. Tran.,* do.

Primary Cancer of the larynx, destroying the epiglottis, as seen with the laryngoscope. *Do. do.*

Muscles and Tendons forcibly pulled from the wrist by machinery. *Do. do.*

Refutation of the dogma recently propounded that food comes into contact with the vocal cords in deglutition. Brit. Assoc. for advancement of Science at Birmingham, Septem., 1865. See *Trans.*

The first attempt in England to remove a growth from the larynx through division of the pomum Adami. Brit. Med. Association at Leamington, Aug., 1865. *Brit. Med. Jour.*

Two Tumours removed from the Larynx in a case of long standing Aphonia. Instantaneous cure. *Path. Tran.,* 1865.

Laryngeal fluid pulverizers. 2 Letters in *Lancet,* do.

Fibrinous cast of the Trachea and Bronchi, expelled in a case of croup. *Path. Tran.,* do.

A tape worm expelled with its head. *Do. do.*

Ed. the Hospital Mirror and Clinical Records of the *Lancet* for the last 10 years, and relinquished his labours in this department of that journal, the end of the year 1865. During these 10 years, Dr. G. regularly supplied, on an average, at least 6 columns of hospital matter each week. This is equivalent to 3120 columns, for the 520 weeks, or to *two volumes of the Journal of* 760 *pages each !!!*

From the year 1851, to the end of 1865, Dr. G. has written 97 Critiques and Reviews on Medical and Scientific works, in the *Lancet* and *other journals,* not exclusively medical.

Numismata Medica et Physica: Medals of Medical Men, Philosophers, Hospitals, Medical Schools and Colleges of Great Britain and her Colonies. Small 4to. *In preparation.*

GIBSON, *Rev.* JAMES. Ch. of Eng. Missionary, (Uxbridge, U. C.)

I. Bochim, or the Weepers; a sermon preached on the day of humiliation on account of the Indian mutiny. *Toronto,* 1858, pp. 24.

GIBSON, JOHN. A Can. Journ. Ed. the *Literary Garland,* (Mont.), a monthly Mag. devoted to the advancement of general literature, of which he was also Joint Publisher, from 1843 to 1850. Besides his ed. labours Mr. G. occasionally contributed to the Mag. The first tale in the first volume is from his pen. In 1840, established in same city *The Commercial Messenger, and British Canadian Literary Gazette.*

GIBSON, *Rev.* J. C.

I. Sermon preached in St. Paul's Church. *Woodstock,* N. B., 1857. pp. 11, 8vo.

GIBSON, T. A., *M. A.* First Master, High Sch., (Mont.)

I. Geography of Canada. *Montreal,* 1854.

Described as a very poor production.

GIDNEY, ANGUS M. A N. S. journ. and poet. B. at Jemseg, N. B., 4 May, 1803. When still a child went with his family to N. S. where he has since resided. Until he attained the age of manhood was engaged in agricultural pursuits; and is almost wholly self-taught. Was for several years a sch. master. At 18 began to contribute in prose and verse to the newspapers. In 1843, became Ed. of the *Nova Scotian,* (Hal.) which had previously been under the able management of Mr. Joseph Howe. In the autumn, the paper changed hands and Mr. Annand became its prop. and principal ed., Mr. G. being his assist. In the following year Mr. A. established the *Morning Chronicle* which he published conjointly with the *Nova Scotian,* and Mr. G. was associated with him as parliamentary reporter and general assist. on both papers. and remained in those capacities when Mr. Howe subsequently assumed the chief ed. of them. In 1845, purchased the *Herald* (Yarmouth), liberal in politics, which he conducted until 1851, when he retired for a time from the field of journalism. He still, however, contributed largely to the magazines and newspapers of the Lower Provinces, taking part in most of the political discussions of the day, and in addition, furnishing many articles of a purely literary character. He also wrote a work of fiction, *The Refugee's Daughter* in 43 chapters, which appeared in the *Transcript* (Liverpool N. S.) in 1857-8. In 1859, his son and another gentleman having started the *Acadian*, (Digby.) Mr. G. became its Ed. for a year, and in 1861, took up the same position on the *Register* (Bridgetown.) In Oct. 1863 he, together with his son, established the *Free Press* at the last named place, which he still conducts. He is the author of many beautiful verses which have appeared from time to time in the columns of the newspaper press, and have been generally admired and extensively copied.

GILBERT, *Rev.* E. Rector of St. Andrews, N. B.

    I. Sermon on 2 Cor. 13, 13, 1813, pp. 123, 8vo.

GILL, *Prof.* THEODORE, *M. A.* (Washington, D. C.)

    I. Synopsis of the Fishes of the Gulf of St. Lawrence and Bay of Fundy. *Can. Nat.* 1865.

GILL, W., Engineer.

    I. Pocket guide for the management of steam boilers. *Toronto*, 1866.

    " A treatise which covers all the practical details connected with the careful working of boilers."—(Tor.)

GILLELAND, J. C.

    I. History of the late War between the United States and Great Britain. *Baltimore*, 1817, 12mo.

GILLESPY, WILLIAM. A Can. Journ. B. at Little Corby, near Carlisle, Eng. 1824. Came to Can. in 1842. In 1846, became a contributor to the *Liberal*, a weekly paper, and afterwards to the *Herald*, both of Hamilton. In the year following commenced his career as a political writer on the *Courier*, (Brantford,) to which he also contributed a short tale. In 1848 joined the staff of the *Spectator*,

(Ham.) but returned to the *Courier* in a few months, and shortly afterwards undertook the ed. control of the *Times*, (Lon. U. C.) In 1850 again went on the *Spectator* with which he was connected for the next 16 years, during nearly the whole of which time he occupied the ed. chair. In 1855, the *Spectator* became a daily journal and Mr. G. was part prop., 6 years later he assumed the sole proprietorship, a position which he held when he disposed of the paper in Sept. 1864 to the present prop's. Mr. G. has always been associated with the Conservative party, and the journals with which he has been connected have all strenuously supported the principles of that political body. He has acted as a correspondent for various newspapers including the *Can. News*, (Lon.)

    I. Fugitive Poetry: *Hamilton*, 1846, pp. 100, 8vo.

GILLIES, *Rev.* A. C. A min. of the Can. Presb. Ch. B. in Lotbinière, L. C., 1834. Ed. at Knox Coll. (Tor.) Has contributed in prose and verse to a large number of newspapers in the Western Province. His principal writings, however, on subjects of ethical philosophy and religion have appeared in the *Good News* and the *Evangelist.*

    I. Daily Meditations; a collection of poems. *Kingston*, 1860, pp. 96, 4to.

GILLIS, *Rt. Rev.* JAMES, *D. D.* Cath. Bishop of Edinburgh, Scot. B. at Montreal. 7 Apl., 1802. D. at Edinburgh, 24 Feby., 1864. Ed. at the Sulpician Seminary of his native city, at the Coll. of Aquorties, Scot., and in Paris. Being ordained priest in 1827, he commenced his spiritual labours in Edinburgh where his talents for pulpit eloquence soon attracted considerable notice. So highly were his merits thought of that Bish. Patterson, who died in 1831, solicited his appointment as his coadjutor, with the right of succession. The prayer was not then granted by the Sovereign Pontiff, but in 1837 he was named Bish. of Limyra and Coadjutor of the Eastern District of Scotland. In 1851, he succeeded Bish. Carruthers as Catholic Bishop of Edinburgh and the adjoining territory, comprising five of the ancient bishoprics of Scotland. To recount the many pious and great works of this distinguished and highly gifted prelate would occupy too large a space in a work of this description, and we will merely give the following epitome of his character from the funeral oration delivered over his remains.

"Only now," said the preacher on the occasion, "have we begun to understand what we have lost. The testimony of the last few days has proclaimed to us all that Scotland and the Church have at once lost a son eminent for talents, for eloquence, for taste, for art, for polish—for all that adorns the life of a man and the cause which he served."

I. The Gild of St. Joseph, Edinburgh, and an Appendix containing various papers on the present condition of the working classes of the community, and its possible improvement. *Edinburgh*, 1843, pp. 859, 8vo.

II. A Letter to the Editor of the *Caledonian Mercury*, (Edin.), 1845.

III. A Letter on the same subject to the Rev. Fred. Monod. *Do.*, 1845.

IV. A Protestant answer to the Rev. Mr. Thomson's query : " Why is Tahiti, that Eden of Protestantism, at this moment, a desolation ?"—With notes. *Do.*, 1845, pp. 54, 8vo.

V. A Discourse on the Mission and influence of the Popes, delivered in St. Mary's Catholic Church, Edinburgh, on the day of solemn thanksgiving for the return to Rome of His Holiness Pope Pius IX. *Edin. and London*, pp. 31, 8vo.

VI. A Letter to the Moderator of the Free Church of Scotland, containing a refutation of certain statements made in the last General Assembly of the same Church, by the Rev. Frederick Monod, and a few strictures on the Rev. Dr. Cunningham's second edition of Stillingfleet's " Doctrines and Practises of the Church of Rome," with an appendix. *Do.*, 1846, pp. 218, 8vo.

VII. A Discourse delivered at the opening of St. Giles' Catholic Church of Cheadle, on 1st Sept., 1846.

VIII. A Discourse delivered in St. Mary's Catholic Church, Glasgow. Dec. 10th 1846, at the funeral of the Right Reverend Father in God, Andrew Scott, D. D., Bishop of Eretria and Vicar Apostolic of the Western District of Scotland. *Glasgow*, 1847.

IX. Facts and Correspondence rerelating to the admission into the Catholic Church of Viscount and Viscountess Fielding with " Review," &c. *Edinburgh and London*, 1850, pp. 162, 8vo.

X. A Discourse delivered (1851) by request, before a very numerous meeting of the Catholics of Dublin.

" He was listened to with marked approbation, and received the unanimous applause of the vast assembly."

XI. Reclamations, setting forth the claims and rights of the Scottish Catholic Church to the whole property of the Scotch Benedictine Monastery at Ratisbon, &c.

"This able work was submitted to the late Lord Palmerston, who became completely convinced of.the justice of the claim in question, and used his powerful influence in support of it, with the Bavarian Government."

XII. A Letter to the Right Honble. the Lord Provost, of Edinburgh, animadverting on a speech made by his Lordship, on the Education Bill, then before Parliament. *Edinburgh*, 1853.

XIII. Three Sermons delivered (May 1851) in the St. George's Cathedral, London.

These sermons have been spoken of as "very beautiful." They were much admired by the Congregation of St. George's.

XIV. A Sermon delivered in the Cathedral of Amiens, on occasion of the translation of the Relics of St. Theodosia, in presence of the Emperor and Empress of the French, &c. 1853.

XV. A Pastoral Letter explanatory of the Dogma of the Immaculate Conception. *Edinburgh*, 1855.

XVI. A Pastoral Letter in behalf of the British sick and wounded in the Crimean War. *Do.*, 1855.

In this letter, Bishop Gillis enjoined prayers for the soldiers of the allied armies who had fallen in battle, or by sickness, and exhorted the people to make liberal contributions, both in money and clothing, for those who were laid up in the Hospitals.

XVII. Lecture on Education delivered at St. Mungo's, Glasgow. *Do.*, 1856.

XVIII. A Paper on the subject of Burns' pistols, which Dr. Gillis presented to the Antiquarian Society of Scotland. *Do.*, 1859.

XIX. A Discourse delivered in the Cathedral of Orleans, on occasion of the anniversary celebration of the deliverance of that City in 1429, by Joan of Arc. *Do.*, 1857.

This splendid oration by its power and eloquence produced a thrilling effect on the audience.

XX. A Letter to the Right Honble. Sir John McNeil, with regard to the education of Pauper children.

XXI. A Pastoral Letter on the distressed state of the Cotton districts. *Edin.*, 1862.

XXII. A Sermon preached at the opening of St. Peter's Italian Church, Hatton Garden, London, 1863.

The last sermon which Bishop Gillis ever delivered.

GILMORE, *Rev.* GEORGE, *A. M.* A Presb. min. B. in Co. Antrim, Irel., about 1720. D. at Horton, N. S., Sept., 1811. He laboured for some years in the New Eng. States. At the Revolution he espoused the loyal side, fled to Can., and subsequently removed to N. S.

I. A Sermon preached before a Lodge of Free and Accepted Masons, at Sorrel, in Canada, on the day of St. John the Evangelist, 1783. *London*, 1788.

"The following discourse was composed and delivered at Sorrel in compliance with a request made by a number of Freemasons, whose beneficence and charity were not wanting to the preacher after his arrival in Canada, and is published by the desire of sundry gentlemen, who have heard and read it with approbation."—*Advertisement.*

GILPIN, ALFRED. (N. S.)
I. Epistola Poetica ad amicum. *Olicanæ*, MDCCCLXIV.

GILPIN, *Rev.* EDWIN, *D. D.* Min. Ch. of Eng. (Hal.)
I. On the Principles of Unity in the Church of God ; a sermon. *Halifax*, 1837, pp. 18, 8vo.

GILPIN, J. BERNARD, *A. B., M. D., M. R. C. S.* Resides at Halifax.

I. Lecture on Sable Island ; its past history, present appearance, natural history, &c., delivered before the Halifax Athenæum Society. *Halifax*, 1858, pp. 24.

II. On Introduced Species of Nova Scotia. *Tran. Ins. Nat. Scic., N. S.*

III. On the Gaspereaux. *Do.*, 1865.

GINGRAS, *Rev.* LEON, *D. D.* A French Can. priest. B. in Can., 1804. D. at Paris, France, May, 1860. Admitted to holy orders in 1831. In the following year became prof. of belles-lettres in the Seminary (Que.), of which he was shortly afterwards appointed director. In 1844 he visited Europe and the Holy Land. While in Rome the degree of doctor of divinity was conferred upon him. Returning to Can. he resumed his duties in the Seminary, but owing to ill-health was compelled to proceed to Europe a second time, when he died shortly afterwards.

I. L'Orient, ou Voyage en Egypte, en Arabie, en Terre-Sainte, en Turquie et en Grèce. *Québec*, 1847, 2 vols, pp. 472–556, 8vo.

GINQUET, *Rev.* A. J. A French Priest. B. near Nancy, France, 1796. D. 21 Feby., 1846. Came to Can. in 1835. Ed. *Les Mélanges Religieux* (Mont.), for upwards of 2 years.

GIROD, AMURY. A Swiss emigrant. Took part in the Rebellion, in 1837, and died by his own hand.

I. Traité d'Agriculture (d'Evans) adapté au climat du Bas-Canada, traduit. *Québec*, 1831.

II. Conversations sur l'Agriculture, par un habitant de Varennes. *Do.*, 1834.

III. Notes diverses sur le Bas Canada. *Village Debartzch*, 1835, pp. 129.

GIROUARD, DÉSIRÉ, *B. C. L.* A Montreal advocate.

I. Essai sur les Letters de Change et Billets Promissoires. *Montréal*, 1860, pp 256, 8vo.

"I have read attentively your Essay on Bills of Exchange, &c., and I take pleasure in acknowledging that you have, with very rare talent, collected all that could possibly be written on this subject which could interest Lower Canada. The opinions you express on the laws relating to the subject, and on the decisions of the tribunals, show that your essay is the result of profound study on your part. Your book should be in the hands of every trader and business man. It would certainly be of great benefit to them. It will also be very useful to lawyers and judges.

Permit me to hope that your book may prove to you a sure and certain guarantee of an honorable and brilliant career at the bar.—CHIEF JUSTICE LAFONTAINE.

II. Etude sur l'Acte concernant la Faillite, 1864. *Do.*, 1864, pp. 103.

" La brochure de M. Girouard, presqu'aussi considérable que celle dont nous venons de parler, (M. Abbott,) se recommande par des commentaires et des discussions utiles sur la même loi de 1864 *concernant la faillite.* Ce travail dans lequel l'auteur fait preuve d'un talent remarquable et de connaissances étendues est précédé de remarques préliminaires dont quelques-unes expriment le regret de voir de si notables altérations s'opérer dans notre droit et compliquer dans une certaine mesure le fonctionnement des règles courtes et simples du droit commun et nos lois *statutaires.*"—D. H. SÉNÉCAL : *Rev. Can.*

III. Contrainte par Corps. *Rev. Can.*, 1865.

GLACKMEYER, EDWARD.

I. An alphabetical list of the Laws of Canada. *Toronto*, 1859, pp. 16.

GLADMAN, GEORGE. In 1857-8 had direction of the expedition appointed by the Can. Govt. to explore the country between the head of Lake Superior and the Red River Settlement.

I. Report on the Exploration of the country between Lake Superior and the Red River Settlement. With maps and plans. *Toronto*, 1858, pp. 425, 8vo.

[This volume in addition to the report of the director contains the separate reports of Mr. S. J. Dawson, as Surveyor, of Prof. H. Y. Hind, as Geologist and Naturalist, and of Mr. W. H. E. Napier, C. E., as Engineer of the Expedition.]

GOBINEAU, *Count* A. DE.

I. Voyage à Terre-Neuve. *Paris*, 1861, pp. 309, 8vo.

GODFREY, ARTHUR W.

I. Letters and Correspondence on the Halifax and Quebec Railroad, between some of the members of the Imperial and Colonial Governments, &c. *Halifax*, 1847.

GOGSWELL, J.

I. History of the Revolutions in Europe from the subversion of the Roman Empire in the West to the Congress of Vienna, from the French

of William Koch, with a continuation to the year 1815 by H. Schoël. Revised and corrected by J. GOGSWELL ; with a sketch of the late Revolutions in France, Belgium, Poland and Greece. *Kingston*, 1842, 8vo.

GOLDIE, T. W. "Assist. Commissary Gen."

I. The Mosaic Account of the Creation of the World and the Noachian Deluge, geologically explained. 2nd Ed., *Quebec*, 1856, pp. 52.

GOLDSMITH, OLIVER. A N. S. poet, and " collateral descendant of the author of the Deserted Village." B. in the Co. of Annapolis, N. S. Entered the Commissariat Department as a Clk. and eventually attained the rank of Commissary Genl. D. abroad many years since. He had much inclination to Literature, and it is said, had collected materials for a biographical work on the distinguished men of his native Province.

I. The Rising Village. A Poem. With a Preface by the Bishop of Nova Scotia. *London*, 1825, pp. 48 ; another ed. *St. John, N. B.*, 1834, pp. 144, 18mo.

"In looking over the title page of this little poem, a strong and lively feeling of interest is excited, when professedly the production of not only the namesake, but a descendant of the Great Oliver, whose name can never be mentioned without emotions of respect and admiration, and whose literary efforts always pourtrayed nature without deviating from truth : *nihil tegitit quod non ornavit.* * The striking similarity of the subject to one so ably handled by that masterly and pleasing writer, almost leads the fancy of the reader to identify the amiable elegance of its style with that which so highly characterizes

' Sweet Auburn, loveliest village of the plain,'

and impress us with the conviction, that the author is indeed worthy of the relationship he bears to that great genius. With respect more particularly to the present production, we find much to commend in the manner and strict adherence to truth with which various scenes are pourtrayed ; and whose fidelity of description plainly evinces, both an intimate acquaintance with, as well as a correct conception on the part of the writer of the subject on which he has founded this pleasing poem. The sweetness of versification and happy smoothness of expression that pervade it throughout, stamp it as the production of a polished and well cultivated

---

* Epitaph, Westminster Abbey.

taste. And we are truly glad to hail among ourselves the possessor of talent which, even in this first sample, has marked itself so far above mediocrity."—*Can. Rev. and Mag.* (Mont.)

GOODMAN, W. F.

I. Contrast of British America with the United States and Texas. *London*, 1846, 8vo.

GOODRICH, S. G. The well-known " Peter Parley."

I. Peter Parley's Tales about Canada. *London*, 1839, 16mo.

GORDON, *Hon.* A. H., *C. M. G.* Lieut. Gov. of N. B. for some years up to 1866.

I. Wilderness journeys in New Brunswick in 1862-63. *St. John, N. B.*, 1864, pp. 64.

GORDON, *Rev.* GEORGE N. A Presb. Missionary from N. S. B. at Cascumpeque, P. E. I., 1822. In 1855 he went out to the South Seas as the second missionary of the Presb. Ch. of N. S., and in 1857, settled on the island of Erromanga, the scene of the martyrdom of John Williams. Here he continued to labour till he and his wife were murdered by the savages in 1861. From the time of his being accepted as a missionary, and even before, until his death he wrote much, which was published principally in the *Presb. Witness* and the *Missionary Register*. His last published letter was on the subject of Evangelical Christendom, published in London, in 1861. He was the first to reduce the language of Erromanga to writing. He prepared and printed several small school books and scripture extracts. He also translated the Gospel of Luke, which has since been printed. He had also translated the book of Jonah and part of the Acts of the Apostles.

The last Martyrs of Erromanga ; being a memoir of the Rev. George A. Gordon and Ellen Catherine Powell, his wife. By Rev. James D. Gordon. *Halifax*, 1863, pp. 294, 12mo.

" This timely and valuable contribution to our Missionary literature will we trust be eagerly welcomed by the church, and be perused by all who feel an interest in the great cause to which we are committed, and the good, true men who having taken their lives in their hands, fought well the good fight of faith, and fell doing brave battle in the service of the Prince of Peace. If any men

deserve to be held in grateful remembrance by the Presbyterian Church of the Lower Provinces, they are those noble hearted young men, one Gordon and Matheson and Johnston, who sacrificed all they held dear on earth to be our missionaries to far foreign lands, who stood fearlessly in posts of imminent peril, never deserting their trust, falling at last with their armour on, and wielding the 'sword of the spirit."—*Mission. Record.* (Hal.)

GORDON, *Rev.* HENRY. Presb. Min. at Gananoque, U. C.

I. Christ as Redeemer, the delegated King and Head of Creation. *London*, 1857, pp. 20.

GORDON, *Rev.* JAMES D. A Presb. missionary from N. S. Younger brother of George N. G. B. at Cascumpeque, P. E. I. Went as a missionary to the South Seas from N. S. in 1863 and in the following year was settled at the same place where his brother was killed.

I. Halifax : its Sins and Sorrows. *Halifax*, 1862, pp. 41, 12mo.

II. The Sandal Trade and Traders of Polynesia. *Do.*, 1862, pp. 16, 12mo.

(See *Gordon*, Rev. G. N.)

GORDON, *Mrs.*

I. Outlines of Chronology, for the use of schools. *Montreal*, 1859, pp. 80.

GONE, MONTAGUE.

I. Observations on the Disturbances in Canada. *London*, 1838, pp. 38, 8vo.

GORRIE, ALEXANDER, *N. P.*

I. A Synopsis of the Laws of Letting and Hiring ; or, the Contract of Lease, in Lower Canada. *Montreal*, 1848, pp. 33, 8vo.

GOSSE, P. H. An Eng. Naturalist. Now dead.

I. The Canadian Naturalist : a series of conversations on the Natural History of Lower Canada. *London*, 1840, pp. 360, sm. 8vo.

" It was a pretty idea, to make the English public acquainted with Canada by a series of conversational dialogues for each month in the year, noting the more prominent objects in the kingdom of natural history, and interweaving pleasing descriptive anecdotes of climate, customs, manners, scenery, &c. The wood-cuts are real adornments to a text which could well afford to stand without embellishments."—SIM : *Col. May.*

GOSSELIN, CHARLES.

I. Petit Traité de Grammaire Anglaise, à l'usage des écoles primaires. *Québec*, 1861, pp. 80.

GOSSELIN, LÉON. A French Can. journ. D. at Montreal, 1 June, 1842. Some time ed. of the *Minerve* and the *Spectator*. (Mont.) In 1837 was one of the founders of *Le Populaire*, in the same city, a liberal sheet which had but a short existence. Mr. G. was an advocate of L. C. and a man of education and ability.

GOSSELIN, Mrs. MARY, (Graddon.) Wife of the above. Ed. the *Museum* (Mont.), a monthly literary publication, from its commencement in 1832 until 1834, when it ceased publication.

GOSSIP, WILLIAM. (Hal., N. S.)

I. On the Rocks in the vicinity. *Trans. N. S. Inst.*, 1864.

II. On the occurrence of the Kjockkenmœdding, on the shores of Nova Scotia. *Do.* do.

III. Enquiry into the Antiquity of Man. *Do.* 1864–5.

IV. Field Excursion. *Do.* do.

GOUIN, L. F. (Three Rivers, L. C.)

I. A new system of French and English Pronunciation, with or without a Master. *Montreal*, 1859, pp. 213, 12mo.

GOUINLOCK, G. & J.

I A complete system of Practical Arithmetic. *Hamilton*, 1843.

GOULD, NATHANIEL.

I. Sketch of the Trade of British America. *London*, 1833, pp. 20.

GOURLAY, ROBERT FLEMING. A name well known in the early political history of U. C. B. in Scotland, 1784. D. in Edinburgh, 1 Augt. 1863. He came to Can. in 1817, where he had acquired property by marriage; and commenced statistical enquiries into the capabilities of the Province, in the course of which he became aware of the existence of various abuses:

"He then proposed that a Commission should be appointed to proceed to Great Britain, to have these abuses rectified; and held public meetings for that purpose,— accounts of the proceedings at which were published in a pamphlet, which was generally approved of by the people of the Province; but, by those in power, was considered as having a seditious tendency, and he was therefore arrested, and put on his trial for sedition, at Kingston; but, being acquitted, he was again tried at Brockville, with however, a similar result. He, then, had to proceed to New York on business; and, on his return was imprisoned in the gaol at Niagara, where ill treatment, in being confined in a cell for five weeks (in all eight months,) in the dog days, debarred from the sight of, or communication with his friends, his Counsel, and the Magistrates of the District, threw both his body and mind into such a state, as to render him totally unfit to defend himself, upon his trial, or even to comprehend his arraignment. The result of the trial was, that he was banished from the Province for life, under pain of death, should he return,— his alleged crime being that he neglected to quit the country upon the order of a single Magistrate acting under an unjust construction of an unconstitutional Statute, most illegally exercised." *

Mr. G. retired to the U. S. whence he shortly after proceeded to Eng. The Can. Govt. granted him a pension for his losses and sufferings, which he refused. After his decease the arrears of pension up to the day of his death were paid to his family. In 1859, Mr. G. issued the prospectus of a work to bear the following title: "The Recorded Life of Robert Gourlay, Esq., now Robert Fleming Gourlay, with Reminiscences and Reflections, by himself, in his 75th year."

I. The Banished Briton, and the Neptunian. *Boston*, 1805, 8vo.

II. Principles and Proceedings of the Inhabitants of the district of Niagara, for addressing his Royal Highness the Prince Regent, respecting claims of Sufferers in the war, lands to Militiamen, and the general benefit of Upper Canada. *Niagara*, 1818.

III. General Introduction to Statistical Account of Upper Canada, compiled with a view to a grand system of Emigration, in connexion with a reform of the poor laws. *London*, 1822, pp. DIV.—47, 8vo.

IV. Statistical Account of Upper Canada. (With maps.) *Do.* do. Vol. I. pp. 625—xx. Vol. II. 704—cxxix.

"From this censure [inaccuracy and want of information] however, we must exempt

* Report of Select Committee Leg. Assembly, to whom was referred the petition of Mr. G.

Mr. Gourlay, who wrote a really valuable and useful statistical account of the Province." Dr. Dunlop.—(*Backwoodsman*.)

V. Appeal to the Common Sense, Mind and Manhood, of the British Nation. *Do*. 1826, 8vo.

VI. Letters on Emigration Societies in Scotland, written in 1828 and 1829.

VII. Chronicles of Canada, 1818. *St. Catharines, U. C.* 1842, pp. 40.

VIII. Canada, and Corn Laws, or no Corn Laws, no Canada. *Edinburgh*, 1852, pp. 12.

IX. Case before the Legislature, with his Speech delivered on 1st July, 1858. *Toronto*, 1858, pp. 29.

X. Manual of Individual, or Family Worship. *Edinburgh*, 1856, 8vo.

GOURLAY, WILLIAM. Resided many years in Can. Was at one time a merchant at Ayr., Scotl.

I. A Guide to the Canadas, containing useful and practical information for those who propose emigrating to the British Possessions in North America. *Ayr*, 1833, pp. 82, 12mo.

GOWAN, JAMES R. Judge of the Co. Court, of Simcoe, U. C.

I. An Analytical Index to the Upper Canada Division Courts' Acts, and to the Rules and Forms in use in the several Division Courts in Upper Canada, as approved by the Judges of the Superior Court of Common Law. *Toronto*, 1855.

" Judge Gowan has here rendered signal service to all connected with the Local Courts, or interested in their efficient working by placing within their reach the means of easy reference to the Statutes, Rules and Forms, now in force."—*U. C. Law Journ.*

II. Canadian Constable's Assistant. *Do*.

GOWAN, OGLE R. A Can. public man. B. at Wexford, Irel. Came to Can. about 1829. Has always been associated with the Orange Institution, and was for 20 years Grand Master of the Order in B. A. Sat in the Can. Parliament, for a lengthened period previous to, and after the Union, and has filled several important public positions. Previous to coming to this country wrote several pamphlets on religious questions which were published in

Dublin :—*The Kings Vision*, 1821 ; *Catholic Relics*, 1822 ; *The Pope's Bull*, 1822 ; *The Primate's answer*, 1822 ; *The Real Truth-teller*, 1825 ; *Defence of Orangism*, 1825. He was also from 1822 to 1825, ed. of the *Antidote*, and of the *Sentinel*, from 1825 to 1829, both weekly newspapers. In Can. he has ed. the *Brockville Statesman*, a weekly, from 1829 to 1851 ; and the *Patriot* and the *British Empire* (Tor.), from 1851 to 1855.

I. Responsible or Parliamentary Government ; a political pamphlet ; *Toronto*, 1st ed., 1830 ; 2nd ed., 1839, 8vo.

II. Orangeism,—its Origin and History. *Do*., 1859, 3 Vols.

GRAHAM, *Rev.* HUGH, *A. M.* A Presb. min. B. at Statehench, West Calder, Scot., 1758. D. at Stewiache, N. S, 1829. Entered Univ. of Edinburgh, and afterwards studied Theology under John Brown of Haddington. Came to N. S. in 1785, where he afterwards resided.

I. Sermon and Addresses delivered at the induction of the Rev. John Waddell to the collegiate charge of Truro, and the sermon preached on, the Sabbath following. *Halifax*, 8vo, 1799.

II. The Relation and Relative Duties of Pastor and People, illustrated in two sermons. *Do*., 1799, 12mo., pp. 54.

III. A Warning to Youth, or an address to the rising generation, being the substance of a sermon. *Pictou*, 1824.

Mr. G. also wrote an unpublished work called " Notitia, or Notices concerning the state of the Church and Religion in Nova Scotia in former and later times."

GRAHAM, J. D.
I. Tides in Lake Huron. *Mem. Am. Aca. A. and S.*, Vol. VI.

GRAHAM, JOHN H., *M. A.* Principal of St. Francis Coll., Richmond, L. C., and Fellow of the University of McGill Coll., (Mont.)

I. Letters in reply to the Superintendent of Education for Lower Canada. Reprinted from the *Montreal Herald*. *Montreal*, 1865, pp. 16, 8vo.

II. Letters on Public Education in Canada. *Do*., 1866, pp. 28, 8vo.

III. Arithmetic. *Do*., 1866.

GRANET, B., *LL. D.*

    I. Exercises upon all the French Verbs. *Montreal*, 1858.

GRANT, ALEXANDER. Clk. and Reporter to the Court of Error and Appeal, and Registrar and Reporter to the Court of Chancery, U. C.

    I. Reports of Cases adjudged in the Court of Chancery of Upper Canada. *Toronto*, 1850–65. II. Vols., 8vo.

    · II. Reports of Court of Error and Appeal of Upper Canada. *Do.*, 1866. 2 Vols., 8vo.

GRANT, CHARLES, *Vicomte de Vaux.*

    I. Proposals for a subscription to form Colonies in Canada of French Emigrant Loyalists, and Ecclesiastics now in England; pp. 8, 8vo.

    II. Adresse à toutes les puissances de l'Europe, sur l'état présent et futur de la noblesse, et du clergé Français. Particulièrement au Gouvernement Britannique, sur les moyens d'assurer à ces deux corps l'existence la plus convenable aux circonstances, moyennant un plan d'établissemens dans le Canada, les plus avantageux possibles, soit au Commerce Britanique soit aux Loyalistes. *Londres*, 1794, pp. 109.

GRANT, *Rev.* GEORGE MONRO, *A. M.* Min. of St. Mathews Presb. Ch. (Hal.) A native of Pictou, N.S., at the Academy of which town he received his primary education. While a student at Glasgow Univ., contributed to the *Glasgow University Album*, (1853-9), a literary periodical, conducted by students. He is noted for his literary tastes.

    I. Sermon preached at St. Mathews. *Halifax*, 1865, pp. 16, 8vo.

    II. Sermon preached at the National Scotch Church Saint Mathews, Halifax, on the morning of the first Sunday of 1866. *Gal. V. I. Do.* pp. 16, 8vo.

    III. Reformers of the Nineteenth Century; a lecture. *Do.* 1867, pp. 32, 8vo.

GRANT, HENRY CLARK. A Can. journ. B. at Kingston, U. C., 1810. Established in 1838, the *Western Herald and Farmer's Magazine*, (Sandwich, U. C.), a conservative journal, of which he was ed., from the above year until 1842, when he removed to London, U. C., taking his printing materials with him. He there founded the *Herald*, which, however, he soon abandoned. In 1848, he started the *Artizan*, (Tor.,) a non political paper which was subsequently merged in the *Provincial Telegraph*, a tri-weekly, which afterwards became a daily, and was eventually discontinued. This journal formed the first earnest attempt at establishing a daily newspaper in Toronto. Mr. G. was ed. of the *Daily News*, (King.) for some time up to 1860, when his connection with the press ceased.

GRANT, JAMES ALEXANDER, *M. D., F. G. S., F. R. C. S.* B. in Invernesshire, Scot, 1829. Came to Can. with his parents 1830. Ed. at the Univ. of Queen's Coll. (King.) in arts, and at McGill Coll. (Mont.) in medicine; at the latter institution he received the degree of M. D., in 1854. Practices at Ottawa. Dr. G. is, we believe, one of the few members of the profession in Can. who have obtained the high degree, F. R. C. S. of Edinburgh. He is also a Fellow of the Geological Soc.; a mem. of the Royal Coll. of Phys., and of the Royal Coll. of Surg. (Lond.,); a corresponding mem. of the Academy of Natural Sciences, Philadelphia; and of the Botanical Soc. of Can.

Medical Chronicle, (Mont.)

    I. Punctured wound of the anterior lobe of the brain, through the orbital plate of the frontal bone. 1856.

    II. Compound comminuted fracture of the Femur Ligature of the Femoral artery. 1857

    III. Punctured wound of the Pleura Costatis, pleuritic effusion; iodine injection. 1858.

    IV. Carcinoma Medullare. 1859.

    V. Notes of cases of poisoning. *Do.*

    VI. Twins with single Placenta. *Do.*

Brit. Am. Journ., (Mont.)

    VII. Notes of Surgical cases. 1860.

    VIII. Unique Anchylosis of the knee joint forward at a right angle. 1861.

    IX. Tetanus and poisoning by Strychnine contrasted. *Do.*

X. Obstruction of the bowels; concretion found in the appendix veroniformes. *Do.*

XI. Notes of Surgical cases. 1862.

XII. New treatment of Rheumatism by the Boletres Laricis Canadensis. *Do.*

XIII. Notes of Obstetrical cases. *Do.*

Can. Med. Journ. (Mont.)

XIV. Puerfural mania, the result of metritic irritation, from imperfectly developed Scarlatina Exanthema. 1865.

XV. Protracted uterine gestation. *Do.*

Med. Times and Gazette, (Lond.)

XVI. The treatment of skin diseases. 1863.

XVII. Disease termed "Black leg" as observed amongst the Ottawa Lumbermen. 1864.

XVIII. Excision of the knee joint. 1865.

Can. Nat. & Geol.

XIX. The Geology of Ottawa. 1864.

GRANT, *Mrs.* J. P. A Can. poet. Contributed to the *Literary Garland* during the time of its existence.

I. Stray Leaves; a collection of Poems. *Montreal*, 1865, pp. 166.

GRANT, T. H. (Que.) Has written anonymously for the newspaper press on subjects of Provincial importance, and is the author of an *Essay on the Reciprocity Treaty. Trade Rev.*, (Mont.) 1865.

GRASETT, G. R., *M. D.* Secy. and Librarian to the Medico-Chirurgical Soc. (Tor.), and a mem. of various other scientific and literary bodies in the Province. B. in Portugal 1811. D. at Toronto, 1847.

I. On the Diarrhœa of Infants. *B. A. Journ.* 1845.

II. On Poisoning by Opium. *Do.* 1847.

GRASSET DE SAINT SAUVEUR, JACQUES. A French author. B. at Montreal, 16 April, 1757. D. at Paris, France, 3 May, 1810. Was a son of André Grasset Saint Sauveur, Secy. to the Marquis DeVaudreuil, and of Marie Josephte Quesnel Fonblanche. When a youth was taken to Paris where he was ed.

at the Coll. of St. Barbe. He entered the diplomatic service and was for many years Vice Consul of France in Hungary and the Levant.

I. Costumes Civils actuels de tous les peuples connus. *Paris*, 1784, et suiv.; 4 vol. in-4o., ornés de 305 pl.; il y a une ed. in-8.

II. Tableaux de la Fable représentés par figures, accompagnés d'explications. *Do.* 1785, in-4.

III. Tableau cosmographique de l'Europe, de l'Asie, de l'Afrique, et de l'Amérique, avec histoire générale et détaillée des peuples sauvages. *Do.* 1787, in-4.

IV. L'Antique Rome, ou description historique et pittoresque de tout ce qui concerne le peuple romain dans les costumes civils, militaires et religieux, dans les mœurs publiques et privées, depuis Romulus jusqu'à Augustule. *Do.* 1796, 2 vol., in-4, avec 50 pl.

V. Encyclopédie des voyages, contenant l'abrégé historique des mœurs, usages, habitudes domestiques, religions, &c. *Do.* 1795–96, 5 vols., in-4, avec 432 planches coloriées.

VI. Les amours du fameux Comte de Bonneval, pacha à deux queues, connu sous le nom d'Osman, rédigé d'après quelques mémoires particuliers. *Do.* 1796, in-18.

VII. Le Sérail, ou histoire des intrigues secrètes et amoureuses du Grand Seigneur. *Do.* 1796, 3 vol., in-18.

VIII. Fastes du peuple français, ou tableaux raisonnés de toutes les actions héroïques et civiques du soldat et du citoyen français. *Do.* 1796, in-4.

IX. Waréjulio et Zelmire, histoire véritable, traduit de l'Anglais. *Do.* 1796, in-12.

X. Costumes des représentants, des membres des deux conseils, du directoire exécutif, des ministres, des tribunaux. *Do.* 1796, in-8.

XI. Les trois manuels, ouvrage moral, écrit dans le goût d'Épictète : Manuel des infortunés ; Manuel des indigens ; Manuel de l'homme honnête. *Do.* 1796, in-18.

XII· Les Amours d'Alexandre et de Sultane Amazille. *Do.* 1797, 2 vol., in-18.

XIII. Description des peuples de l'Europe, etc. *Do.* 1798, in-4.

XIV. Description des principaux peuples d'Asie, contenant le détail de leurs mœurs, coutumes, usages, etc. *Do.* in-4.

XV. Esprit des Ana, ou de tout un peu. *Do.* 1801, 2 vols., in-12.

XVI. Voyages pittoresques dans les quatre parties du monde. *Do.* 1806, in-4.

On y retrouve plusieurs des planches de l'Encyclopédie des voyages.

XVII. Les archives de l'honneur, ou notices historiques sur les généraux, officiers et soldats qui ont fait la guerre de la révolution. *Do.* 1306, 4 vol., in-8.

XVIII. Plantes usuelles indigènes et exotiques. *Do.* 1307, 2 vol., in-4.

XIX. Muséum de la Jeunesse, ou Tableau historique des sciences et des arts. *Do.* 1809-11, un fort vol. in-4, avec des figures color.

"Cet ouvrage a été publié en 24 livraisons : les 6 premières l'ont été par Grasset, et les 18 autres, après sa mort, par Babié."— QUÉRARD.

GRAY, *Rev.* ANDREW. A Wes. Meth. Min. in N. S. Has frequently contributed to the *Provincial Wesleyan* (Hal.), since 1862.

I. Baptism : its nature and subjects; being the substance of the arguments generally used by Pedo-baptists. *Halifax*, 1864, pp. 16, large 4to. 2nd Ed. in press.

GRAY, *Rev.* ARCHIBALD, *A. M.* A N. S. poet. Is Min. of the Ch. of Eng., and Rector of Digby, N. S.

I. Shades of the Hamlet, and other poems. *Woburn, Mass:* 1852.

"We have arisen from the perusal of Mr. Gray's poetry with a vivid conviction that we had been holding converse with a Master Spirit, and in the very threshold of our observations we will venture to affirm that in the judgment of all capable of appreciating poetic beauty it will add no small degree of honour to the lustre of our native genius. * * * A charm seems to be thrown over every subject and theme which have been touched by the plastic hand."—*Prov. Mag.* (Hal.)

GRAY, B. G. A native of N. S.

I. Extra-territorial Incidents of Colonial Legislation. *Boston*, 1863, pp. 22, 12mo.

GRAY, HUGH. A resident in Can. for several years.

I. Letters written from Canada during a residence there in the years 1806, 7, and 8; shewing the present state of Canada, its productions, trade, commercial importance and political relations. Illustrative of the laws and manners of the people, and the peculiarities of the country and climate; exhibiting also the commercial importance of Nova Scotia, New Brunswick and Cape Breton ; and their increasing ability, in conjunction with Canada, to furnish the necessary supplies of Lumber and provisions to our West India Islands. *London*, 1809, 8vo.; 2nd ed. *Do.*, 1314.

GRAY, *Rev.* I. W. D., *D. D.* A clergym. of the Ch. of Eng. Is Rector of Trinity Ch., St. John, and Canon of the Cathedral of Christ's Ch. Fredericton, N. B. In 1350 founded the *Church Witness* (St. John) of which he was ed. for 6 years. Is author of various sermons and other pamphlets not contained in the following list.

I. A Brief View of the Scriptural authority and Historical evidence of Infant Baptism, and a reply to objections urged in the Treatise of E. A. Crawley, A. M. *Halifax*, 1837, pp. 308, 12mo.

II. A Reply to the Rev. F. Coster's defence of the "Companion to the Prayer Book." *St. John*, 1849, pp. 48, 8vo.

III. A Reply to the statement of the Rev. Mr. Wiggins, A. M., showing the causes which have led to his retirement from the curacy of St. John. *Do.*, 1851, pp. 48, 8vo.

IV. A Letter to Members of the Church of England, in reply to a letter from Edward Maturin, M. A., late curate of St. Paul's, Halifax. *Do.*, 1859, pp. 124, 8vo.

V. Sermons on the 2nd Advent, preached at Trinity Church, St. John, in December, 1864. *Do.*, 1865.

GRAY, *Rev.* PATRICK. A Min. of the Can. Presb. Ch. (King.) Has contributed articles on religious subjects to the *Good News* (Prescott), and is the author of various poetical fragments.

I. The New Heavens and the New Earth. *Prescott*, 1861, pp. 40, 8vo.

"It is an inquiry into what the Bible teaches respecting the future dwelling and state of the righteous. The author is inclined to believe that this earth on which we dwell, purified from the curse, will be the abode of saints hereafter. He shews that in whatever locality the saints may dwell, their condition will be one of physical, intellectual and moral perfection. The pamphlet evinces in the author a cultivated mind and heart, judiciousness, and an acquaintance with the teachings of science which are related to the subject of which he treats."—*Can. Day Star* (Mont.)

GRECE, CHARLES FREDERICK. A Can. writer on Agriculture. B. in Eng. D. near Montreal. Came to Can. in 1806, under the auspices of the British Govt., for the purpose of introducing the cultivation of hemp into L. C., and with that view bought, and until he died, lived on, a farm at Long Point, near Montreal, which is still known as *Grece's Point*. He was a mem. of the Montreal and Quebec Agricultural Societies. Some of his papers on the subject of hemp were published in the *Trans. of the Soc. of Arts*, and the silver medal of the Soc. was awarded to him for them.

I. Essays on Husbandry, addressed to the Canadian Farmers. *Montreal*, 1817.

II. Facts and Observations respecting Canada, and the United States of America, affording a comparative view of the inducements to Emigration presented in those countries. To which is added an appendix of Practical Instructions to Emigrant Settlers in the British Colonies. *London*, 1819, pp. xv and 172, 8vo.

GREEN, *Rev.* ANSON, *D. D.* A Wes. Meth. min. In 1854 wrote a series of letters in the *Christian Guardian* (Tor.), descriptive of a visit to Europe, which have been promised for publication in pamphlet form.

I. The Minutes of the Wesleyan Conference. *Toronto*, 2 Vols., 12mo.

These volumes contain the statistics, official documents and correspondence of the conference from its first organization to the year 1858.

GREEN, WILLIAM. Secy. of the Soc. for the Encouragement of Arts and Sciences, founded at Quebec by Lord Dalhousie,

and a corresponding mem. of the Soc. of Arts of London. Now d.

I. On Colouring materials produced in Canada. *Trans. Lit. & His. Soc.* (Que.) Vol. I.

This paper obtained for the author the Isis medal of the Society of Arts, (Lon.)

II. Notes on the country about the Falls of Montmorenci. *Do.* do.

III. Processes used in Dying, among the Huron Indians. *Do.* Vol. II.

IV. Textile substances in use among the North American Indians. *Do.* do.

V. Pigments of Canada. *Do.* Vol. III.

GREEN, WILLIAM PRINGLE, *R. N.* A native of N. S.

I. Fragments from Remarks of Twenty-five years in every Quarter of the Globe, on Electricity, Magnetism, Aeroliths, and various other Phenomena of Nature, &c., &c.—*London*, 1833, pp. 24, 8vo.

GRESLEY, *Rev.* W.

I. The Danger of Dissent. *Toronto*, pp. 16.

GREY, *Sir* CHARLES EDWARD, *Kt., G. C. H.* A Brit. diplomatist. Was one of the Commissioners appointed in 1835 for the adjustment of Can. affairs. B. 1785.

I. Remarks on the proceedings as to Canada in the present session of Parliament: by one of the Commissioners. *London*, 1837, pp. 67, 8vo.

Appendix contains the address of the Leg. Assembly to the Governor 3 Oct., 1836, &c. and the 92 Resolutions of 21 Feby., 1834.

GREY, HENRY GEORGE (Third) *Earl.* A Brit. statesman; Colonial Secy. from 1845 to 1852, in Lord John Russell's Administration. B. 1802.

I. Colonial Policy of Lord John Russell's administration, from 1846 to 1852. Second edition, with additions. *London*, 1853, 2 vols., 8vo.

"A hand-book of modern colonial policy, which no person desirous of understanding the present state and future prospects of our Colonies can omit to read."—*Edin. Rev.*

GRIFFIN, FREDERICK, *Q. C.* A Can. author. B. at Montreal. Admitted to the Bar of L. C. 1824, and was in partnership with the late Stephen Sewell, K. C., from that time until the death of the latter in 1832. Created Q. C. in 1854.

I. Junius Discovered. *Boston*, 1854, pp. 310, 8vo.

"It is much to accomplish, in being able to produce a claimant [Thomas Pownall, Governor of Massachusetts Bay] for the laurels of Junius, concerning whom many arguments tend to suggest that he *may be* the true one. And this much we conceive Mr. Griffin to have established."—*Can. Journ.*

GROULX, LOUIS THOMAS. Prothonotary and Clk. of the Crown and Peace for the District of Joliette, L. C. B. at St. Laurent, L. C., Dec. 1819. Admitted as an Advocate 1843. Has written a number of stray poetical pieces in *La Minerve, L'Avenir, La Gazette de Sorel,* and other papers.

I. Mes Loisirs, 1848, pp. 48.

II. Epitre à Son Altesse Royale le Prince de Galles. 1860, pp. 40.

III. Epitre à Son Altesse Royale le Prince Alfred Ernest Albert, en visite au Canada. 1861, pp. 19.

IV. Poisson d'Avril, 1865. Rèveries d'un joueur de Pigeon-hole. 1865, pp. 51.

GROVE, *Miss.*

I. Little Grace, or Scenes in Nova Scotia. *Halifax*, 1846, pp. 178, 8vo.

GUNN, DONALD. A resident of Red River Settlement, (H. B. T.) Has contributed to the *Miscellaneous Collections of the Smithsonian Institution* on subjects connected with the Natural History of the North West. Is a corresponding mem. of the Smithsonian Institution, and a mem. of the Institute of Rupert's Land.

GURNETT, GEORGE. A Can. Journ. B. at Horsham, Sussex, Eng., about 1791. Previous to 1828 established and ed. the *Gore Gazette* (Ancaster, U. C.), which was the only Conservative journal in the Western Province for some time. Removing to York, now Toronto, he in 1829 founded the *Courrier of Upper Canada,* of which he was ed. and prop. until 1837, when being elected Mayor of the city he disposed of the paper. He was Clk. of the Peace and Police Magistrate (Tor.), at the time of his death.

H.

HAGARTY, *Hon.* JOHN HAWKINS, *D. C. L.* A Puisné Judge of the Court of Queen's Bench, U. C. Has been President of the Canadian Institute (Tor.)

I. Thoughts on Law Reform. *Toronto.*

II. Annual Address as President of Can. Institute. *Can. Journ.* 1862.

HAIGHT, *Miss* JENNIE E. A Can. poet. Miss H. began when very young to contribute to newspapers and magazines. In 1853-4 was the Can. correspondent of *The Olive Branch,* (Bos.,) and at the same time a regular contributor to the *Maple Leaf,* (Mont.) Her pieces have appeared in nearly every newspaper in Can.; several of them are to be found in Dewart's *Selections.*

"We give below one of these earnest appeals [*A Voice from the Life Forge*] that, meet them where we will, reflect honor alike on the head and heart of the writer; so earnest, in fact, that we are led to exclaim, 'Thank God that one Canadian woman is capable of

writing so well, and with aim so high!' For there is genuine womanly sincerity, womanly feeling, and deep sympathy with all that enobles our nature, in this thoughtful strain; there is a largeness of heart, and a burning desire to assist the fellow-traveller over the rough and intricate paths of the wearisome journey of life."—CHARLES SANGSTER: *The Can. Muse.*

HALE, *Hon.* J.

I. Observations on Crickets in Canada. *Trans. Lit. & His. Soc.* (Que.) Vol. I.

HALIBURTON, ROBERT G., *M. A., F. S. A., F. R. S. N. A.* A N. S. author. B. in N. S in 1833. Son of the late T. C. Haliburton, Esq., M. P., the distinguished novelist. (see *post.*) Studied at King's Coll., Windsor, in his native Province, where he graduated M. A. Is a Barrister of N. S., but abandoned law after one year's practice. While at the Bar was retained as leading counsel by the proprietors during the sitting of the P. E. I. Land Commission. Mr. H. was Secy. to the N. S. Commissioners for the London International Exhibition of 1862. He has also occupied several other important positions, and was Vice President of the N. S. Institute of Natural Sciences. He is a Fellow of the Royal Soc. of Antiquaries (Eng.,) and of the Royal Soc. of Northern Antiquaries (Denmark.) The idea of endeavouring to trace the popular customs and superstitions of nations to their origin was suggested to Mr. H. in 1853, by the discovery that many of those found in the old world, also exist among the Indian Tribes of Am. The attempt was regarded by the late Mr. Prescott and Sir Henry Ellis, F. R. S., librarian of the Brit. Museum, as an important but almost hopeless task ; the origin of such observances having been hitherto regarded as lost in the mists of the most remote antiquity. Mr. H. nevertheless devoted the leisure of several years to collecting materials, a most tedious and laborious task, and in 1863, published a short paper " *On the Unity of Origin of the Human Race proved by the Universality of Certain Superstitions.*" This was intended more for an amusing paper than a learned disquisition on one of the most important scientific questions of the day, but it met with a very favourable reception from some eminent scientific men. Among others Prof. Max-Muller, of Oxford, regarded the comparison of customs as being as likely to throw light on the history of man as the study of the science of language. His next was a paper published in the *Trans. of the N. S. Institute of Natural Sciences for* 1863 " *On the Festival of the Dead,*" or All Halloween, All Saints & All Souls, (Oct. 31st, Nov. 1st & 2nd), which was found to be celebrated for three days or rather for an Eve or vigil and two days among almost all nations, from Polynesia to Europe, being partly a thanksgiving and partly a commemoration of the dead. Very many coincidences in its observance in different quarters of the globe proved most remarkable and far too striking to be assigned to accident or chance. But the most interesting point that was brought to light, was that this Festival is generally observed in Nov. north and south of the Equator in the

11

old world and in the new. This could not be explained by anything yet known to us, as respects the history of man. and it seemed probable that the festival must have been regulated in some very simple manner, such as by the rising or setting of some stars or by some such phenomenon everywhere observable. The singularly universal reverence for the 7 stars, or for " the sweet influences of the Pleïades'" which existed even in the time of Job, naturally suggested those stars to the mind of Mr. H.; and his search was after a time rewarded by finding a primitive calendar in the South Sea Islands regulated by those stars, from Nov. to May, when they are visible in the evening above the horizon being called the season of " Pleïades above," and the rest of the year when those stars are invisible in the evening being termed the " Pleïades below." In Australia, also, a festival commencing in the evening and lasting 2 days is held in Nov. when those stars " are most distinct" i. e. when they are on the *meridian* at *midnight*, and is called the Corroborree of the Pleïades, the stars which they revere as being " very good to the blacks," being almost their only object of worship. Traces of this primitive reverence for the Pleïades or of this simple mode of regulation of the year by those stars were subsequently found in Borneo, Mexico, Egypt and India. In the most ancient calendar in the world that of the Brahmins of Tirralore the month of Nov. was called the month of the Pleïades. It became evident that this year of the Pleïades was the primitive calendar used by the common ancestors of the human race and that all other calendars had been based upon it, and that each nation as it branched off from the parent stock carried with it in its wanderings over the globe this primitive festival and the memory of the calendar by which it was regulated preserving and transmitting to their descendants a reverence for " the sweet influences " of those stars, which from the very birth of time itself must have been " for signs and for seasons and for days and years." It was discovered that the Mexicans, Egyptians and the Hebrews must have associated the memory of the Deluge with the same night, viz., on which the Pleïades are most conspicuous or are on the meridian at night. These conclusions were worked out by Mr. H. step by step, and the results were gradually printed in 1863, as his investigations progressed, in a paper or rather a journal of investigations of 104 pages, which was sent to a few scientific societies and to persons interested in such matters. While preparing this paper, however, it was not only apparent to Mr. H. that the year and its festivals were regulated by the Pleïades, but also that the chronology and the cycles of the ancients had some reference to those stars, he therefore turned his attention to this point.

A festival or calendar regulated by the fixed stars would of course be affected by the procession of the Equinoxes i. e. in every period of between 71 and 72 years, the fixed stars would gain one degree in their revolutions and would be on the meridian at midnight one degree later after every such period. A festival, regulated by this phenomenon, would also be progressive as regards the seasons and would take place one day later in the same period. The ancients it is perfectly clear knew this and attached a peculiar importance to a truth which they believed, and apparently not without good reason, was a gift from the Deity; and under the form of prehistoric chronology they preserved the rule as to the revolution of the fixed stars which they supposed would gain one degree in 72 years and 360 degrees (i. e. making a total revolution around the seasons) in 25920 years (72 X 360), and this vast lapse of time they regarded as a great year or cycle. The fact that the number 72, which is so conspicuous in the History of the Noah of the Chinese, Hindoos, and Egyptians appears also in connection with the Noah of inspired narrative, whose immediate descendants commentators agree were 72 in number, led Mr. H. to infer that the same peculiarity would pervade the prehistoric chronology of the Hebrews, and the results bore out his conjecture. The period from the creation to the deluge 1656 years makes 23 periods of 72 years each; assuming the 7 days of

creation to be similar periods of 72 years each, we have a total of 30 periods (2160 of our years), or a great month. 12 of them makes exactly 25,920 the great year of antiquity and the period in which the ancients from Scandinavia to China believed that the revolution of the fixed stars takes place. The results of these further investigations were privately printed in March 1864, in a second number of " *New Materials for the History of Man*," entitled " *Astronomical Features in the Mosaic Cosmogony.*" The Ed. of the *Etymological Review* during the past year in a series of articles on " *The Mythical Character of Pre-historic Chronology*," which were favorably noticed in the *Times*, has brought out this point very clearly, but he has apparently not seen the paper of Mr. H., and is not aware that the peculiarities he has noticed in the pre-historic Chronology of ancient nations is still more apparent in that of the Mosaic narrative. Two months after No. 2 was published, the Astronomer Royal for Scot., (Prof. J. Piazzi Smyth) drew attention to the wonderful *Meteorological* Science of the ancients which he ascribed to divine inspiration, in a paper read by him on the Great Pyramid. The *savants* of Napoleon's expedition to Egypt had conjectured that the coffer in the chamber of the Great Pyramid was a standard of measures similar to our own, and built on a knowledge of the exact size of the earth, a view elaborated by the late Mr. Taylor in his work on the Great Pyramid, and supported by the Astromoner Royal for Scot. in the paper referred to. As he was about to spend some months of the winter of 1864 at the Great Pyramid, for the purpose of examining that building with accurate instruments, Mr. H. suggested to him his belief that it was originally an Astronomical Observatory, the window or small opening from the central chamber towards the apex, being probably intended to ascertain with accuracy when the Pleïades were on the Meridian at midnight, a point which could not be with certainty determined by the naked eye. In Oct. 1866, Prof. S. wrote to Mr. H. the following satisfactory intelligence :

" You wished to know if anything about the Pleiades might be found in the Great Pyramid. I believe that an immense deal about them is there, so much so, that without disturbing other important purposes of the building, there is enough to constitute the Great Pyramid the monument of the year of the Pleiades. The proofs are gradually coming out of the mass of observations I made there this spring."

He has recently written to Mr. H. that he intended to read before the Royal Astronomical Soc. (Lon.) a paper " *On the date of the Pyramid from an Astronomical point of view*," adding :

" And there it is that the year of the Pleiades theory by their being *on the meridian at midnight* is so important or receives so much confirmation. I shall undoubtedly allude to you as first giving me the idea, and should be glad to refer to any paper of yours, which by being printed together with mine, (if the Soc. should choose to print either), would be immediately within men's reach."

If the Great Pyramid was, as suggested, an Astronomical Observatory for the purpose supposed by Mr. H., the age of the Great Pyramid can be accurately estimated by calculating how many thousand years must have elapsed since the Pleiades, when in the Meridian, were visible from the chamber of the Great Pyramid.

I. The Past and the Future of Nova Scotia : and address on the 113th Anniversary of the settlement of that Province. *Halifax*, 1862, pp. 27, 8vo.

" The subject-matter of this address is the rise and progress of a colony which, although neither populous nor wealthy, has always claimed the distinction of being pre-eminently loyal."—*Sat. Review*.

II. The Unity of Origin of the Human Race proved by the Universality of certain Superstitions. *Do*. (privately printed,) 1863.

III. New Materials for the History of Man, derived from a Comparison of the Calendars and Festivals of Nations.

No. 1. *The Festival of the Dead. Do.* (privately printed,) 1863, pp. 104.

The first 25 pages appeared in the 1st vol. of *The Trans. of the N. S. Institute ;* the remainder was gradually added giving the results of further investigations.

" I fear you have thought me very neglectful in not thanking you sooner for your paper read before the Nova Scotian Institute. Though late, allow me now to do so, and also to express my pleasure at the great amount of new matter you have brought together bearing on the Festival of the Dead, matter very interesting in itself, and especially valuable as strong corroborative evidence of what I think we cannot be wrong in assuming the common origin of the human race."— Sir Henry Ellis.

" I am truly gratified by your kindness in sending a copy of your remarkable essay on the Festival of the Dead. The Bishop of Natal had lent me a copy some months ago, and I was greatly struck by the novelty of your theory and the amount of learning and research which you have brought to its elucidation."—Sir J. Emerson Tennent.

No. 2. *Astronomical Features in the Mosaic Cosmogony. Do.* (privately printed,) 1864.

" Your researches are certainly of a very interesting character, and in my opinion the result tends strongly to confirm our belief in the common origin of the human race. The traditions as to the Deluge also incline in the same direction, and I trust that your future enquiries may combine with the results in establishing on a firm foundation some of the most striking declarations recorded in Holy Writ."—C. T. Cantuar.

" Mr. Haliburton has long occupied himself with investigations into the unity of those singular superstitious practices which are so widely spread amongst the most various tribes of mankind, in the hope thereby of obtaining evidence of the unity of origin of the human species. His first essay is devoted to the discussion of the almost universal attribution of more or less ominous character to the act of sneezing, and his second treats of the very general prevalence of the custom of holding 'festivals of the dead' at the beginning of the month of November. This practice the author finds prevailing in the Southern hemisphere in connexion with the rising of the Pleiades, which marks the beginning of the year, and he hence supposes that the custom took its rise south of the equator in the form of a New Year's commemoration of departed friends and relatives. In support of this hypothesis, involving, as it does, migration northwards of the ancestors of those European and Asiatic peoples amongst whom a similar custom is to be traced, Mr. Haliburton adduces many curious and interesting facts."—*West. Review*.

IV. Descriptive Catalogue of the Nova Scotia Department for the International Exhibition, 1862. *Do.* 1862, pp. 51.

" The Catalogue * * * although not so large as those of the Indian Empire, and of the Colony of Victoria, contained more interesting information than either of these, and by the press generally was pronounced superior to any of the Catalogues of Departments."—Dr. Honeyman.

V. Report of the International Show Committee of Nova Scotia. *Do.* 1863, pp. 36.

VI. Report of Nova Scotia Commissioners for the International Exhibition, 1862. *Do.* 1864, pp. 38.

VII. Confederation or Annexation ? An address on the proposed Federation of the British North American Provinces. *Do.* 1865.

VIII. Voices from the Street—a Series of Poems. *Do.* (privately printed.) N. D., pp. 20.

Haliburton, *Hon.* Thomas Chandler, *M. A., D. C. L., M. P.* A distinguished novelist and humourist. B. at Windsor, N. S., Dec. 1796. D. at Gordon House, Isleworth, near London, Eng., 27 Aug., 1865. He was descended from an ancient Scottish family of the same name, (with which Sir Walter Scott was also connected,) mentioned in Border History, in the beginning of the 16th century, as "leal, true and honest men, and good borderers against the English." In the early part of the 18th century, towards the close of the reign of Queen Anne, a branch of the family emigrated to Boston, in the now U. S. of Am., whence at the time of the Revolution the grandfather of the subject of this notice, still "leal and true" to his sovereign, removed to Windsor in N. S. Mr. H. was the only child of the late Hon. William Otis Haliburton, a Justice of the Court of Common Pleas, N. S., by Lucy, eldest daughter of Major Grant, an officer of considerable professional reputation, who fell while resisting an attack made by a body of rebels during the Am. revolutionary war. Through his maternal grandmother, the wife of Major Grant, who was a Miss Kent, Mr. H. was connected with the well-known Chancellor Kent, and through his grandmother by his father's side, with the Otis family of Boston. He was ed. first at the Grammar Sch. of Windsor, his native place, and afterwards at the Univ. of King's Coll. in the same province. At the time he was removed to the latter establish-

ment—which was then considered one of the most successful educational institutions in Am., the Rev. Dr. Porter. of Brazenoze Coll. (Ox.) officiated as president, while the Rev. Dr. Cochran. of Trinity Coll. (Dub.) fulfilled the duties of vice-president. Among the scholars under the tuition of these reverend gentlemen contemporaneously with Mr. H., there were several who were destined to achieve celebrity in their respective spheres. One became the chief justice of Gibralter ; four won their way to the Bench, and attained professional distinction in the Supreme Court of N. S. ; two received appointments as Judges in N. B. ; one became distinguished as a Q. C. at the English Bar ; while another, also a native of N. S., after a brilliant military career in the service of Her Majesty in India, won a name of world-wide celebrity by his heroic defence of Lucknow ; we allude, of course, to the gallant General—the late Sir John Inglis, K. C. B. Mr. H. held a prominent place among the pupils of King's Coll. until the year 1824, when he quitted the institution ; before he left he secured various prizes, different marks of esteem from the professors. and had graduated with distinguished honours. At an early period of his studies he evinced a taste for the pursuit of literature. In a closely contested trial for the prize for an English essay, "On the Advantages derived from a knowledge of the Classics "— in which competition many were engaged—Mr. H. came off victorious. Besides this prize, he obtained other honours for his skill in composition.

On leaving Coll. he made choice of the profession of law, and after undergoing the usual period of study, and passing the necessary examinations was admitted to practice as a barrister. His career at the bar was a successful one. After his first visit to Eng. he practised at Annapolis Royal, the former capital of N. S., where he acquired a large and lucrative business. His reputation as an advocate stood deservedly high. A wider sphere of action. was soon, however, to be opened to him ; his services were solicited as a mem. of the Legislature of his native Province, and in compliance with the wishes of his friends he entered the Leg. Assem. as mem. for the county of Annapolis. He took an active part in the different deliberations and discussions of that body, and by his powers of debate and other prominent abilities speedily attained a leading position as a legislator. Speaking of one of his oratorical efforts at this time Mr. Murdoch, in his recent *History of N. S.*, says :

"This speech was the most splendid piece of declamation that it has ever been my fortune to listen to. Mr. Haliburton was then in the prime of life and vigor, both mental and physical. The healthy air of country life in his native Windsor had given him a robust appearance, though his figure was yet slender and graceful. * * * As an orator, his attitude and manner were extremely impressive, earnest and dignified, and although the strong propensity of his mind to wit and humour were often apparent, they seldom detracted from the seriousness of his language when the subject under discussion was important. Although he sometimes exhibited rather more *hauteur* in his tone than was agreeable, yet his wit was usually kind and playful. On this occasion he absolutely entranced his audience with the corruscations of genius playing with classic and historic imagery, and appealing to the kindest feelings of humanity. He was not remarkable for readiness of reply in debate ; but when he had time to prepare his ideas and language, he was almost always sure to make an impression on his hearers."

In 1828, when only 32 years of age, he received the appointment of Chief Justice of the Court of Common Pleas, no small tribute to his merits; and until 1840, he discharged the functions of that important office with unvarying zeal and ability. In the latter year the Court of Common Pleas was abolished, and the services of Mr. H. were transferred to the Supreme Court. In Feby., 1856, he resigned his office of Judge in this Court, and soon afterwards removed to Eng., where he continued to reside till his death.

As an author Mr. H. first came before the public in 1829, as the historian of his native province. His work was widely circulated, well received by both the public and the press, and at once secured for its author a place among the *literati* on this side of the Atlantic. It was thought so highly of in N. S.,

that the House of Assem. of that Province tendered Mr. H. a vote of thanks * which he received in person in his place in Parliament. To the present day his "*Hist. and Stat. Account of Nova Scotia*" is regarded as a standard work in the Province. Judge H. became unconsciously the author of the inimitable works of Sam Slick. For the purpose of preserving, or, at least, reviving some anecdotes and good stories that were then fast dying out, connected with colonial life, he began a series of anonymous articles in the *Nova Scotian* newspaper, then ed. by Hon. Joseph Howe, and made use of a Yankee pedlar as his mouth-piece. The character adopted, or imagined, proved to be a *hit*, and the articles amused the readers of that paper and were copied by the Am. press. They were collected together and published at Halifax anonymously, and several editions were issued in the U. S. A copy was taken thence to Eng. by Gen. Fox, who gave it to Mr. Richard Bentley, the publisher. To Judge H's surprise he learned that

* Extract from the Proceedings of the House of Assembly of Nova-Scotia :

"Resolved, that the thanks of this House be communicated to *Thomas C. Haliburton*, Esquire, for the very laudable and laborious effort which he has made to illustrate the History, Topography, and Resources of the Province, in tho '*Historical and Statistical Account of Nova Scotia*,' now issuing from the press; and that the Speaker be requested to convey to Mr. Haliburton the substance of this Resolution.

"Mr. Haliburton being called into the House, and standing in his place, was thus addressed by Mr. Speaker : Mr. Haliburton, I am directed by this House to communicate to you, that they have had under their consideration a work now issuing from the press, of which you are the author, entitled '*An Historical and Statistical Account of Nova Scotia*,' which they think alike useful to the Province, and honorable to yourself, and that, to mark their approbation of this first effort to describe the country, and develope its resources, they have unanimously passed a vote of thanks to you for this laudable undertaking, which resolution will be read to you by the Clerk. It affords me a great deal of pleasure to add my opinion of the work to that of the Representatives of the people, who deem it an object of this honorable notice, as the production of a native of the Province."

an English edition had been issued and was very favorably received in Eng. For sometime the authorship was assigned to an Am. gentleman in London, until Judge H. visited the mother country and became known as the real author. For his *Sam Slick* he received nothing from the publisher, as the work had not been copyrighted, but Mr. Bentley presented him with a silver salver, on which was an inscription written by the Rev. Richard Barham, better known as the author of the *Ingoldsby Legends*. Between Barham, Theodore Hook and Judge H. an intimacy sprang up. They frequently dined together at the Athenæum, to which they belonged, and many good stories told by Hook and Barham were remembered by Judge H. long after death had deprived him of their society. As regards *Sam Slick*, it was written anonymously; the author never expected that his name would be known, or that his productions would escape the usual fate of Colonial newspaper articles. The character of the Yankee pedlar has somewhat changed since then, or at least, in 28 years, the race of Sam Slick's have as a general rule migrated westward. Mrs. Trollope, Dickens and a host of other severe critics have rubbed off, or rather knocked off, the rough edges of Am. manners in the older states, and have made a change for the better in the *outward* characteristics of the Yankee. But veritable Sam Slick's occasionally visit Can. and the Lower Provinces. About 10 or 12 years ago a Yankee sold a large number of wooden clocks throughout N. S. and Cape Breton. They were warranted to keep accurate time for a year, and hundreds of notes of hand were taken for the price. The notes passed by endorsement into third hands, but unfortunately the clocks would not go. Actions were brought in several counties, and the fact that Seth's clocks had stopped caused as much lamentation and dismay as a money panic. The first case that came up was tried before Judge H. much to the amusement of the public, and to the edification of the Yankee clockmaker, who had a long homily read to him on the impropriety of cheating Bluenoses with Yankee

clocks that would do anything sooner than keep time.

While dealing with subjects that relate to mankind in general and illustrate human nature, in his earlier works, which were intended more for Colonial readers than his later works, which were likely to find a wider circulation in Eng. than here, he continually pressed on his readers the following truths :—

I. That our political institutions secure to us practically a larger amount of freedom than those of the Am. Republic.

II. That the resources of N. S. are very great, and much neglected.

III. That we have as a people been wasting our time and our energies in political contests and discussions, instead of uniting together to promote the material prosperity of the province.

Within the past 5 or 6 years the justice of these views has been practically acknowledged; and in spite of the divisions and lethargy of the people of B. A. (for they apply with equal force to the whole of the Provinces), the agricultural, horticultural and mineral resources of those provinces are making themselves known to the world. In spite of Sam Slick's advice, the farmers of N. S. especially, for more than 20 years devoted all their leisure and thoughts to politics, unconscious that there was gold under the very platforms on which windy nothings were dealt out to them by local rival statesmen. In 1861 a N. Scotian laid down to drink, and put his nose so near a lump of gold that he could not help seeing it. A reward to the man who was so, fortunate as to be thirsty, is contemplated and has been discussed by the Legislature. Now, matters are changing and while questions of a wider scope occupy attention, hundreds are amassing wealth by opening their eyes to the vast and varied resources of the country. Experience is proving that the value attached by Sam Slick to the geographical position and natural advantages of the Provinces, was not a mistaken one. We are, however, more grateful to those who amuse, than to those who instruct us. Many persons, who laughed at Sam Slick's jokes, did not relish his truths ; and his popularity as a writer was far greater out of N. S.

than in it; but it had ceased to depend on the verdict of his countrymen. To illustrate this, we may mention that, the Univ. of King's Coll. (Winds.) his *alma mater*, gave him an honorary M. A. degree, and very soon after the Univ. of Oxford gave him an honorary D. C. L. As we have stated, on Judge H. leaving for Eng. to take up his residence there, he resigned his seat on the Supreme Court Bench. Before leaving he applied for his pension, which he had previous to his appointment enjoyed as a former Judge of the Court of Common Pleas. The pension was £300 a year, and he urged on the government in addition to his legal rights, his claim as the historian of N. S., and a colonial author. The claim was resisted for 4 or 5 years, and when a decision was a second time given in his favor the case was carried to Eng. on appeal. The Judicial Committee decided it in his favour. We give below a list of Judge H.'s various works and productions, together with the opinions of competent critics on them, which will speak to their merits in a literary point of view. Several of his works have been translated and reproduced on the continent of Europe, and have been equally appreciated.

Shortly after Judge H. took up his residence in Eng. he was solicited to come forward as a mem. of the House of Commons, for the County of Middlesex, a proposal which he declined, but at the general election of 1859 he was induced to go into Parliament mainly from his friendship with the late Duke of Northumberland, who offered him his support as a candidate for Launceston, where the Duke's influence was very strong. The borough was small, and the labours imposed on its representative were light. His ambition did not, however, lead him to covet that distinction, and his health and feelings rendered parliamentary life somewhat irksome to him. In his speech of acknowledgement, on the occasion of his election, he thanked the electors, "not merely in his own name, but on behalf of 4,000,000 of British subjects on the other side of the water, who up to the present time had not had one individual in the House of Commons through whom they might

be heard." The new mem. for Launceston took his seat in the House as a Conservative, but at the same time declared himself to be "a representative of all parties rather than a party man." During the session he joined in some of the debates, and spoke occasionally at public meetings. At a large meeting at Tynemouth, Mr. William Lindsay, M. P., having spoken of the *usefulness* of the humourous works of "*Sam Slick*," the following characteristic reply was elicited from Judge H.

"Mr. Lindsay has alluded to my books, and said there was an object of usefulness in them. In that he is right, for I should indeed feel ashamed of myself—it would be very unsuitable and very incompatible with the situation of a judge, which I have held in another part of the world—if I should sit down and write a jest book to make people laugh. That would be a very undignified employment for a judge and a very unprofitable one; but I thought I might do a very great service to my countrymen—for I am a native of the other side of the water—provided I could convey to them certain truths, which, I thought, would either be too homely for them to care much about, or too dry for them, unless, like doctor's pills, they had a little sugar put around them. I therefore wrapt them with a little humour, in order that when people read them for amusement they might find that they had learned something they did not know before. Otherwise I should be ashamed to have written a mere jest-book."

As we have stated, Judge H. died at his residence in Isleworth, on the banks of the Thames. There, during the few years in which he had lived amongst them, he had greatly endeared himself to the people of the place—he was ever ready in contributing to its local institutions, not merely by presiding over the meetings of the Philanthropic Soc., and aiding charitable objects generally, but also by lecturing and assisting in various ways the Isleworth Reading Soc., and other associations of a like character. He was buried in Isleworth churchyard; and, in accordance with one of his last wishes, his funeral was plain and unostentatious. We close our sketch in the words of a local chronicler:—

"The village of Isleworth will henceforth be associated with the most pleasing reminiscences of Mr. Justice Haliburton; and the names of Cowley, Thompson, Pope and Walpole will find a kindred spirit in the world-wide reputation of the author of "*Sam Slick*," who, like them, died on the banks of the Thames."

There is a biography and portrait of Judge H. in Tallis's *National Portrait Gallery*, and Jones, R. A. has executed a very good bust of him, a copy of which is in the Crystal Palace, Sydenham.

I. A General Description of Nova Scotia. New ed. *Halifax*, 1825, pp. 192, 8vo.

II. An Historical and Statistical Account of Nova Scotia (with map and engravings). *Do.* 1829, 2 vols., pp. 340–453, large 8vo.

"Mr. Haliburton has given us a history and description of his native province, which not only do great credit to himself, and to Nova Scotia, but will safely bear a comparison with any of the works of a similar kind, that have appeared in the United States. * * * In closing our remarks upon Mr. Haliburton's work, we would again recommend it to those who are interested in American history. It is written with clearness, spirit, industrious accuracy, and with great candor and justice."—Hon. C. W. Upham: *N. A. Rev.*

III. Kentucky; a tale. *London*, 1834, 2 Vols., 12mo.

IV. The Clockmaker; or, Sayings and Doings of Sam Slick of Slickville. *London* and *Halifax*.

1st series 1837, 2nd series 1838, 3rd series 1840. Reprinted *Do.* 1838–1843, 3 Vols., p. 8vo. New Ed. *Do.* 1845. An. Ed. *Do.* 1862. *Philadelphia*, 1857, pp. 220, 12mo.

"He deserves to be entered on our list of friends containing the names of Tristram Shandy, the Shepherd of the *Noctes Ambrosianæ*, and other rhapsodical discourses on time and change, who, besides the delights of their discourse, possess also the charm of individuality. Apart from all the worth of Sam Slick's revelations, the man is precious to us as a queer creature—knowing, impudent, sensible, sagacious, vulgar, yet not without a certain tact : and overflowing with a humour as peculiar in its way as the humours of Andrew Fairservice or a Protestant Miss Miggs, (that impersonation of shrewish female service !)"—*Athen.*, (Lon.)

V. The Letter Bag of the Great Western ; or, Life in a Steamer. *London*, 1839, p. 8vo. ; *Halifax*, 1840, pp. 180, 8vo.

New Ed., *London*, 1843. An. Ed., *Do.*, 1862, 12mo.

"Original and pithy, it is always refreshing to fall in with this inimitable story teller. His mixture of sound sense with genuine humour, his fund of information and peculiar way of putting it on record, his fun and his force,—the fun being part and portion of that force,—are at the same time qualities so entertaining and instructive, that we know not in the end whether to be better pleased with the intelligence we have acquired or the amusement we have received."—*Lit. Gaz.*, (Lon.)

VI. The Bubbles of Canada. By the author of the Clockmaker. *Do.* 1839, pp. 332 ; *Philadelphia*, do., 12mo.

VII. A Reply to the Report of the Earl of Durham. By a Colonist. *Halifax*, 1839, pp. 28, 8vo., and *London*, pp. 91, 8vo.

"The production is worthy of a man of high talents, excellent judgment, and sound constitutional principles in both Church and State. The writer of those letters takes up *seriatim*, the most objectionable points in the report of the noble earl ; and animadverts upon them in no common style of acrimony and ridicule."—*Gaz.*, (Mont.)

VIII. Traits of American Humour; by Native Authors. *London*, 1843, 3 vols., p., 8vo. ; *Do.*, 1852.

"No man has done more than the facetious Judge Haliburton, through the mouth of the inimitable 'Sam,' to make the old parent country recognise and appreciate her queer transatlantic progeny. His collection of comic stories and laughable traits is a budget of fun full of rich specimens of American humor."—*Globe*, (Lon.)

IX. Sam Slick's Wise Saws and Modern Instances. *Do.*, 1843, 2 vols., p. 8vo.

New Ed., *Do.*, 1853. An. Ed., *Do.*, 1859. *Philadelphia*, 1853.

"Let Sam Slick go a mackarel fishing, or to Court in England—let him venture alone among a tribe of the sauciest singlewomen that ever banded themselves together in electric chain or to mystify man—our hero always manages to come off with flying colours—to beat every craftsman in the cunning of his own calling—to get at the heart of every maid's and matron's secret. The book before us will be read and laughed over. Its quaint and racy dialect will please some readers—its abundance of yarns will amuse others. There is something in the volumes to suit readers of every humour."—*Athen.*, (Lon.)

"We do not fear to predict that these delightful volumes will be the most popular of Judge Haliburton's admirable works. The

'Wise Saws and Modern Instances,' evince powers of imagination and expression far beyond what even his former publications could lead any one to ascribe to the author. We have, it is true, long been familiar with his quaint humour and racy narrative, but the volumes before us take a loftier range, and are so rich in fun and good sense, that to offer an extract as a sample would be an injustice to author and reader. It is one of the pleasantest books we ever read, and we earnestly recommend it."—*Standard*, (Lon.)

X. The Old Judge ; or, Life in a Colony. *Do.*, 1843, 2 vols , p. 8vo.

New Ed., *Do.*, 1849. An. Ed., *Do.*, 1860. *New York*, 1849.

XI. The Americans at Home ; or Byeways, Backwoods and Prairies. *Do.*, 1843, 3 vols., p. 8vo. ; new ed. *Do.*, 1854.

" In this highly entertaining work, we are treated to another cargo of capital stories from the inexhaustible stores of our Yankee friend—all of them graphically illustrative of the ways and manners of Brother Jonathan." —*John Bull*, (Lon.)

XII. Rule and Mis-rule of the English in America. *Do.*, 1843, 2 vols., p. 8vo.

New Ed., *Do.*, 1850, pp. 351-372. *New York*, 1841.

" We conceive this work to be by far the the most valuable and important Judge Haliburton has ever written. While teeming with interest, moral and historical, to the general reader, it equally constitutes a philosophical study for the politicians and statesmen. It will be found to let in a flood of light upon the actual origin, formation, and progress of the Republic of the United States."—*Naval and Military Gaz.*, (Lon.)

XIII. The Attaché ; or, Sam Slick in England. *Do.*, 1843-4, 4 vols., p. 8vo.

New Ed., *Do.*, 1849. An. Ed., *Do.*, 1862, 12mo.

XIV. Yankee Stories and Yankee Letters. *Philadelphia*, 1852.

XV. The Sayings and Doings of Samuel Slick, Esq., together with his Opinion on Matrimony. *New York*, 12mo.

XVI. Sam Slick in Search of a Wife. *Do.*, 12mo. N. D.

XVII. Nature and Human Nature. *London*, 1855, 2 vols., p. 8vo.

New Ed., *Do.*, 1858, 12mo. *New York*, 1855, 12mo.

XVIII. Address at Glasgow, Scotland, on the present condition, resources and prospects of British North America. *London*, 1857, 8vo. ; *Montreal*, 1857, pp. 17.

XIX. Speech in the House of Commons 21 April, 1860, on the repeal of the differential duties on Foreign and Colonial Wood. *London*, 1860, pp. 39, 8vo.

" I have ever read and valued the conversations of Sam Slick not for their humour, exquisite and racy as it is, in many of the chapters—but for the deep instructive moral, the sound lessons of practical education they convey to the country. There is not provincial custom, opinion nor prejudice, opposed to steady and persevering industry, and of course to the progress of individual and general prosperity, which is not exposed and treated with consummate tact and ridicule. The self-sufficiency of Sam Slick—his *larfs* at the Bluenoses and the Englishers— his continual *puffing* of the New Englanders, and the pictures he draws of the superior *cuteness*, industry, and craft of the latter, are no doubt intended to teach the Colonist, that it is in vain to expect that he will even succeed, in the race of national rivalry, till he learns and practices the same habits. The natural advantages of this country, Nova Scotia, are drawn in glowing colours—but these are ever set off with jokes upon indolence and want of energy and speculation, too highly coloured perhaps, but still done with sufficient skill ' to point the moral.' I quote a few extracts to justify these reflections and to elevate our old friend Slick, from the character of a humourist, to that of a lecturer upon habits and the true economy of human life. The knowledge of letters and of books, be it ever recollected, is only a means to an end. The state diffuses education or intelligence to render the population more diligent, virtuous and saving—so that they may become better purveyors to their own fortunes and to the general treasury ; and a moralist or humorist like Sam Slick who satyrizes personal faults and habits, and induces change and amendment, by exhibiting a contrast of a happier state of things, is entitled to the public gratitude— even tho' some will think the sketches may be too strongly drawn, or quarrel with the political tendencies which some of his lectures exhibit,—still the greater virtues ought to excuse the minor offences."—G. R. Young : *Col. Literature*.

HALL, ARCHIBALD, *M. D., L. R. C. S*, (Edin.) B. at Montreal, 8 Nov., 1812. Was ed. chiefly at the Royal Gram. Sch. of his native city, which he attended from 1818 to 1839. Having selected medicine as his profession, he was forthwith apprenticed to the late W. Robertson, M. D., one of the foremost physicians and accoucheurs then in Montreal, under whose auspices his studies were directed, following the lectures of the McGill Univ. for the 3 succeeding years. As Chemical instruction was scarcely obtainable in this country, in those early days of its medical history, in 1832, after the visitation of the Asiatic Cholera had ceased, he was sent to Edinburgh, then generally considered the most celebrated sch. of Medicine in Gt. Brit. to follow up his studies. He passed the Coll. of Surgeons there, in April, 1842 : by the middle of May, he had passed with great *éclat* the 2 examinations demanded by the rules of the Univ., and on the 24th of August he graduated, and immediately after returned to Can. to pursue the active duties of his profession. As a collateral branch of Medical study, Dr. H. was much devoted to the natural sciences, and especially attached himself to Botany, Zoology, and Meteorology. Bringing with him from Edinburgh a fine collection of the plants indigenous to the neighbourhood of that classic city, he began soon after his return the foundation of an herbarium of the plants growing about Montreal, and sent home to his *Alma Mater*, in the course of a few years, a very large and carefully preserved collection. Zoology appears to have been his chief delight, as in 1839, we find him presented with the silver medal of the Natural History Soc. (Mont.) as the successful competitor for a prize offered by that Society for the best Essay " *On the Zoology of the District of Montreal.*" This work is a voluminous one, but in consequence of the limited time allowed to send in the essay, its contents were restricted to the Mammals and Birds, and so generally accurate is it, that we believe only two known species of Birds are omitted, and as many among the quadrupeds, the omission arising entirely from their excessive rarity. This manuscript essay after lying in the closets of the Soc. for nearly 25 years was finally printed in the pages of the *Can. Naturalist*, the publication occupying a considerable portion of the numbers of that valuable

journal for several years. It was concluded in 1864. In 1836 he was called upon to share with the late Dr. A. F. Holmes his Professorship in the McGill Univ. He accordingly lectured that winter upon Materia Medica and Therapeutics. Upon the death of his old preceptor Dr. Robertson, and the consequent change of Professorships, Dr. H. was called to fill the chair of Chemistry which he continued to do until the decease of the late Dr. McCulloch, in 1854, when he was unanimously called upon by his colleagues to discharge the duties of the chair of Obstetrics, previously held by that esteemed gentleman. Attached to this chair is the University Lying-in-Hospital, under the control of the Prof. serving to illustrate the precepts taught in the class room. In 1835 Dr. H. was elected one of the attending physicians to the Mont. General Hospital, the duties of which, sometimes exceedingly onerous, were faithfully discharged for a period of 16 years, when he retired upon the consulting staff, of which he is now the senior mem. He also acted for about 12 years as the Physician to the Ladies Benevolent Society, and to the old House of Industry, during the existence of that institution. Finally in 1856, he was called to the Vice-Presidency of the Coll. of Phys. and Surg. of L. C, and was elected President of the same in 1859. The term of office lasts for 3 years, and is emphatically the highest gift at the disposal of the profession. As a medical writer Dr. H. is best known as the ed. of *The British American Journal of Medical and Physical Science* (Mont.), which he established in April, 1845, and conducted with great credit and ability from that time until its suspension in 1852, and again, from 1860 until it finally expired 2 years afterwards. This periodical was the ablest of its kind ever published in Can., and had for contributors the first medical men in the Province.

I. Letters on Medical Education addressed to the members of the Provincial Legislature of Canada. *Montreal*, 1842, pp. 30, 8vo.

II. Letters on the Medical Faculty of McGill College. *Do.*, 1845, pp. 7.

III. Biographical sketch of the late A. F. Holmes, M. D., LL. D., including a history of the Medical Department of McGill College. *Do.*, 1860, pp. 21.

HALL, *Capt.* BASIL, *R. N.*
I. Voyage dans les Etats-Unis de l'Amérique du Nord et dans le Haut et le Bas Canada, traduit de l'Anglais. *Paris*, 1834, 2 vols, 8vo.

HALL, CHARLES W. A mem. of the Massachusetts Bar. Son of Isaac C. H. of Charlottetown, P. E. I., and a graduate of Cambridge Univ.
' I. Twice Taken ; an historical romance of the Maritime Provinces. *Boston*, 1867, pp. 242.
" We are no great admirers of Romance, whether historical or otherwise ; but the volume before us contains so much that is instructive relative to the fall of Louisburg— the city "Twice Taken"—the horrors of the war-path, the excitement of the chase, and the self-denial of some of the Jesuit missionaries who labored among the Aborigines of these lands,—and at the same time none of the sickening sentimentalism so frequently found in works of fiction, that we can heartily recommend it to our countrymen, especially to the youth of the Colony, who may thereby be stirred up to procure and read every book within their reach bearing upon the early history of these Provinces"— *Patriot*, (Charlott.)

HALL, FRANCIS, *Lieut.14th Light Dragoons.*
I. Travels in Canada and the United States in 1816 and 1817 : *London*, 1818, 8vo.; *Boston*, do.

HALL, FRANCIS, *C. E.*
I. Report on the Shubenacadic Canal. *Halifax*, 1825.

HALLEY, WILLIAM.
I. The Irish Race at home and abroad ; a speech. *Toronto*, 1860.

HALLIBURTON, *Sir* BRENTON, *Kt.* Late Chief Justice of N. S. B. 3 Dec., 1775. D. near Halifax, 16 July, 1860. Was the son of an U. E. loyalist, who removed to N. S. during the Am. Revolution. Ed. in Eng. Served for some years as an officer in the N. S. Regt., and afterwards in the 7th Royal Fusiliers. Resuming the study of the law, which his military duties had interrupted, he was, in 1803, admitted as a Barrister. In 1807 he was elevated to the Bench. In 1816 he was appointed a mem. of the Council, and in 1833

Chief Justice. Sir B. contributed frequently to the press, the most noteworthy of his writings being a series of letters written in 1813, on the course of, and principles involved in the Am. war at that time, which appeared in the *Recorder* (Hal.,) above the signature of " Anglo American," and the others enumerated below which are all republished in Mr. Hill's *Life of Sir B. H.* '
I. Observations on the importance of the North American Colonies to Great Britain. *Halifax*, 1825, 8vo ; 2nd ed. *London*, 1831.
"The value of these colonies to England in her position as mistress of the seas, is set forth with arguments so sound and language so powerful, that it may not be amiss in the present day to call attention to the unalterable facts."—*Rev.* G. W. HILL : *Memoir of Sir B. H.*
II. Critical State of the Bull family.
" It is a humorous account of the changes wrought in the English constitution, under the influence of Earl Grey and Lord John Russell." *Idem.*
III. John Bull and his Calves. (Written previous to the Can. Rebellion.)
IV. Reflections on Passing Events ; a poem. With notes. By an Octogenarian. *Printed for private circulation. Halifax*, 1856.

HALLOWELL, J. S., Student at Law. (Tor.)
I. Digest of Acts passed during sessions of 1860–1–2 which repeal, amend, vary or affect, Consolidated Statutes for Canada. *Toronto*, 1863.

HAMEL, ANDRÉ R.
I. La Question des Fabriques. 1831, pp. 17.

HAMILTON, *Sir* CHARLES.
Report of the Trial of an Action by Mr. W. Dawe, against Vice Admiral Sir Charles Hamilton, Governor of Newfoundland. *London*, 1824, 8vo.

HAMILTON, JAMES EDWARD.
I. Reflections on the Revolution in France, by the Rt. Hon. Edmund Burke, considered ; also observations on Paine's Rights of Man. With remarks on the prospect of a Russian War and a Canada bill. *London*, 1791, 8vo.

HAMILTON, PIERCE STEVENS. A N. S. journ. and writer. B. at Truro, N. S., 1826. Matriculated at Acadia Coll.,

Wolfville, but did not remain to graduate. In 1851 was admitted as an Atty., and, in the next year, was called to the Bar, and practised in Truro, and afterwards in Halifax; but becoming regularly connected with the newspaper press, to which he had previously been an occasional contributor, he from this time abandoned the active pursuit of his profession. From 1853 to 1861 he ed. the *Acadian Recorder*, the oldest journal in N. S., and both before and since has written largely for the local press and for other newspapers in Eng. and the U. S. His main purpose as a journ., in addition to the promotion of various public measures and undertakings, seems to have been to further a Union of the British Am. Provinces. In 1863 he was appointed Gold Commissioner of N. S., and, in 1864, his jurisdiction was extended, and he was appointed Chief Commissioner of Mines for the Provinces.

I. Observations upon a Union of the Colonies of British North America. *Halifax*, 1855.

II. A Union of the Colonies of British North America considered nationally. *Do.*, 1856.

III. Nova Scotia considered as a Field for Emigration. *London*, 1858, pp. 91.

"It contains a condensed statement of the wealth and resources of that colony, which may be commended to any one desirous of knowing the actual material value of these Lower Colonies, now claiming alliance with Canada."—*Can. Nat.*

IV. Letter to His Grace the Duke of Newcastle, upon a Union of the Colonies of British North America. *Halifax*, 1860.

V. Union of the Colonies of British North America; being three papers upon this subject originally published between the years 1854 and 1861. *Montreal*, 1864, pp. 103, 8vo.

"I do not know whether hon. gentlemen of this House have seen some letters on colonial union, written in 1855, the last addressed to the late Duke of Newcastle, by Mr. P. S. Hamilton, an able public writer of Nova Scotia, and the present Gold Commissioner of that Province; but I take this opportunity of bearing my testimony to his well-balanced judgment, political sagacity and the skilful handling the subject received from him at a very early period."—*Hon.* T. D. McGee: *Speech during Debate on Confederation*, 1865.

VI. A Review of Hon. Joseph Howe's Essay, entitled : "Confederation considered in relation to the interest of the Empire." *Halifax*, 1866, pp. 25, 8vo.

HAMILTON, ROBERT DOUGLAS, *M. D.* A contributor to the newspaper press of U. C. B. at Muirhead, Lanarkshire, Scot., 16 Jany., 1783. D. at Scarborough, near Toronto, 2 April, 1857. His father had been a stone-mason but gave up that trade and leased a farm upon which the subject of this notice was born. After receiving his elementary ed. at the Grammar Sch. of Stonehouse, in his native county, he studied the classics and natural philosophy at the Univ's. of Glasgow and Edinburgh, at the latter of which he also studied and completed his medical ed. From April 1808 till Nov. 1809 he was Asst. Surgeon to H. M. Hospital ship *Tromp*. He practised for a short time at Cornwall, Eng.; and during the Peninsular war, having volunteered his services as a surgeon, served with the Brit. army in Spain and Portugal. In 1827 he emigrated to the U. S., and in 1830 he removed to York U. C. and settled at Scarborough, where he continued to reside until his death. Throughout life, he devoted a large portion of his time to literature and literary pursuits. He early cultivated the muses, and was a frequent contributor to the newspaper press, in whatever place he resided. He was the author of several works, a list of which we give below. In Can. he contributed several series of letters on literary, political and other subjects to the newspaper and periodical press, under the *nom-de-plume* of "Guy Pollock," commencing first we believe in the *Can. Literary Mag.* (York) in 1833, and subsequently in the *Courier of Upper Canada*, the *Herald*, the *Palladium* and the *British Colonist*, all, at one time or another, published in Toronto. He left a large number of MS writings, written in both Britain and Am., poems, novels, dramas, essays on politics, agriculture &c. These we understand are soon to be published, together with a memoir of the author, written by his kinsman Dr. J. R.

Dickson, (Glasg.) Dr. H. was a man of large mental endowments and great cultivation. In politics, we believe he was a Tory, or at any rate a Conservative in his leanings, and at one time was a candidate for a seat in the Can. Parliament.

I. Essays. *Truro, Eng.*, 1812.

II. Craignethan Castle ; a poem. *Edinburgh*, 1817, pp. 140.

III. The Principles of Medicine, on the Plan of the Baconian Philosophy. *London*, 1822, pp. 295.

IV. Dr. Shaddow of Goslington. By Mungo Coulter Goggle.

HAMILTON, W. R., *F. R. S.*
I. No Mistake ; or, a Vindication of the negotiators of the Treaty of 1783, respecting the North Eastern Boundary of the United States. In a conversation between John Bull and Jonathan. *London*, 1842, pp. 20, 8vo.

Privately printed.

HANCOCK, J. WEBSTER, *LL. B.* A Practising Barrister at Berlin, U. C.
I. A System of Conveyancing ; comprising the principles, forms and laws, which regulate the transfer of property in Canada. *Toronto*, 1861.

" This is by far the best work on conveyancing ever issued in Canada."—*U. C. Law Journ.*

II. A Synoptical Index of the Statutes of Canada and Upper Canada, with notices of the later acts which affect them. *Do.*, 1865.

" We look upon this as the most useful legal compilation that has recently been published in Canada."—*Do.*

HANSON, ELIZABETH.
I. An Account of the Captivity of Elizabeth Hanson, late of Kachecky, in New England, who with four of her children and servant maid, was taken captive by the Indians and carried into Canada. Setting forth the various remarkable occurrences, sore trials, and wonderful deliverances which befell them after their departure, to the time of their Redemption. Taken in substance from her own mouth, by Samuel Bownas. *London*, 1782, a new ed., sm. 8vo.

HARDIE, *Rev.* ALEXANDER, *B. A.* A Wes.-Meth. Min. (Consecon, U. C.)
I. Infant Baptism ; a sermon. *Peterborough*, 1864, pp. 34.

" Our young brother has handled the subject in a masterly manner. The style is excellent, and the facts and arguments are admirable."—*Christian Guardian* (Tor.)

HARDY, *Capt.* C. C., Royal Artillery. For some years residing in N. S. Wrote a series of " *Letters from the Backwoods of North America.*" — For the *Field* (Lon.,) 1860-61.

I. Sporting Adventures in the New World. *London*, 1855, 2 vols.

Trans. N. S. Inst. of Natural Sciences.
I. The Nocturnal Life of Animals in the Forest. 1863.

II. On the Caplin of Newfoundland. *Do.*

III. On Provincial Acclimatisation, 1864-5.

HARMON, DANIEL WILLIAMS.
I. A Journal of Voyages and Travels in the Interior of North America, between the 47th and 58th degrees of north latitude, extending from Montreal nearly to the Pacific Ocean, a distance of about 5,000 miles, including an account of the principal occurrences, during a residence of nineteen years, (1800-1819) in different parts of the country ; to which are added a concise description of the face of the country, its inhabitants, their manners, customs, laws, religion, &c. : (With portrait and map), *Andover*, 1820, pp. 432, 8vo.

HARRIS, RICHARD.
I. The Seige of Canada, an Epic poem, 12 parts. *London*, 1859-60, 12mo.

HARRIS, WILLIAM. A Can. journ. B. near Hacketstown, Co. Carlow, Irel., 1816. In 1833 emigrated to Can. with his parents, and settled near Ottawa. Three years afterwards entered into partnership with Mr. O. R. Gowan in the publication of *The Statesman*, a newspaper, which first appeared at Brockville and latterly at Kingston, where the partnership was dissolved in 1843. *The Statesman* was the recognized organ of the Orange body, and supported the Conservative party. In 1844 Mr. H. established *The Packet,*

(Ottawa), in the interest of the Reform party and strongly advocated the principle of Responsible Government. In 1846 he disposed of this paper to Messrs. Friel and Bell, and it was afterwards merged in *The Citizen*, of the same city. Mr. H. retired from journalism, and in 1860 was appointed Crown Land Agent for the Co. Renfrew, a position which he still holds.

HARRISON and WINCHESTER, *Generals*.

The Campaign of the North Western Army under Generals Harrison and Winchester, in the winter 1812–13. *Ohio*, 1819.

HARRISON, ROBERT ALEXANDER, *Q. C., D. C. L.* A Can. legal author. B. at Montreal, 1833. Was the first person called to the Bar of U. C. " with honors." He served for some years as Chief Clk. of the Western branch of the Crown Law Dept. Can. Was a contributor to the *Merchants' Mag.*, the *Daily Colonist* (Tor.), and various other periodicals and newspapers. Has been joint ed. of the *Upper Canada Law Journal* (Tor.) since 1857, and is one of the founders and editors of the *Local Courts' Gazette*. He enjoys an extensive practice as a common law lawyer in Toronto, and for some years, has been retained in nearly every important public case before the Courts in the Upper Province. Was for several years President of the Literary Soc., (Tor.), and has been connected with various other bodies of a similar character.

I. A Digest of all the Cases decided in the Queen's Bench and Practice Court for Upper Canada, from 1823 to 1851 inclusive, being from the commencement of Taylor's Reports to the end of Vol. VII., Upper Canada Reports (Cameron's Digest included), with an appendix containing the digest of cases reported in Vol. VIII Upper Canada Reports ; by Robert A. Harrison, Student at Law, under the supervision of James Lukin Robinson, Barrister at Law. *Toronto*, 1852, pp. 580, 8vo.

" A faithful digest of all the decisions of our Courts from the earliest period since which we have an authentic record, must obviously be of great value, not merely to the lawyer, but to officials of all kinds, and to every one who is likely to come in personal contact with the law. • • • • The work before us is not only creditable to Upper Canada as a mere book, but so far as we can judge it has been compiled with much care and skill."—*North American* (Tor.)

II. The Statutes of Practical Utility in the Civil Administration of Justice in Upper Canada. *Do.*, 1857, pp. 296, 8vo.

" These statutes and all the previous and subsequent laws they bear upon, Mr. Harrison has compiled with great care and accuracy, improving and occasionally supplying marginal notes • • • Mr. Harrison deserves well of the profession for his useful and in many respects unattractive labours." *Colonist* (Tor.)

III. A Manual of Costs in County Courts. *Do.*, 1857, pp. 40, 8vo.

" A most useful and reliable manual."— *Leader* (Tor.)

IV. The Common Law Procedure Act, 1856, and the County Courts Procedure Act, 1856, and the New Rules of Court; with notes of decided cases ; together with an appendix, containing the Common Law Procedure Acts of 1857. *Do.*, 1858, pp. 828, 8vo.

" These are the acts which have revolutionised the law of Upper Canada, after their progenitors had exercised a like radical influence in the old country. They are in effect an amalgamation of our Procedure Acts of 1852 and 1854, together with an act applying them in a great measure to the county courts of Canada. The work is therefore almost as useful to the English as to the Canadian lawyer, and is not only the most recent, but by far the most complete edition which we have seen of these important acts of Parliament. The editor has not been content with industriously collecting the numerous decisions which are now scattered through our reports upon these statutes, but has displayed both skill and judgment in their arrangement, and in deducing, wherever it was possible, those principles, of which the decisions are either suggestive or illustrative."—*The Jurist* (Lon.)

" Mr. Harrison's work is, in fact, a full practice for the Upper Canadian Courts, including the County Courts of the Province : and it is but justice to say that no pains have been spared to make the notes as practicable as possible ; and the annotator appears thoroughly to understand his text and to be remarkably well up in the law of the mother country."—*The Solicitor's Journal* (Lon.)

V. Rules, Orders and Regulations as to Practice and Pleading in the Courts of Queen's Bench and Common Pleas in Upper Canada, under the Common

Law Procedure Act, with notes explanatory and practical. *Do.*, 1858, pp. 156, 8vo.

"Mr. Harrison is the Archbold of Upper Canada—painstaking, clear-headed and practical. His present work indicates care and completeness ; and the notes accompanying it are unusually copious."—*Colonist* (Tor.)

VI. Rules, Orders and Regulations of County Courts, with notes. *Do.*, 1858, pp. 110, 8vo.

"Mr. Harrison has supplied very full notes and explanations."—*Globe* (Tor.)

VII. The Municipal Manual for Upper Canada. *Do.*, 1859, pp. 784, 8vo. ; New ed. *Do.*, 1867.

"We have received from the publishers a copy of this most useful work * * * We regret that our reference to the work cannot now be as full as its great and general importance would call for, our time being very limited. Mr. Harrison's well known character as an annotator is however of itself a guarantee that no labor has been spared in making it a desideratum for every lawyer and member or officer of a Municipal Council in this Province."—*U. C. Law Journal*

"Mr. Harrison in his very useful work the Municipal Manual has placed the question fairly in view, &c."—Sir J. B. ROBINSON, in 19 U. C. Q. B. Rep., 472.

VIII. A Digest of all Cases decided in the several Courts of Error and Appeal, Queen's Bench, Common Pleas and Chancery in Upper Canada (since the publication of Robinson & Harrison's Digest). By Robert A. Harrison and Henry O'Brien. *Do.*, 1863, pp. 870, 8vo.

XIX. The Assessor's Guide ; for making the Assessments of Property in the Municipalities of Upper Canada. *Do.*, 1864.

HART, ADOLPHUS M. A Can. author. B. at Three Rivers, L. C., about 1816. Is the youngest son of the late Ezekiel Hart, Esq. Had a large practice as an advocate from 1840 to 1850, when he removed to the U. S., and was admitted by courtesy as a Counsellor-at-Law in the States of Missouri and N. Y. While residing in N. Y. and afterwards at St. Louis was nominated Commissioner of Deeds by the Governors of California and Louisiana respectively. In 1854 he sided with the Democratic party in N. Y., in the memorable contest for the Governorship of that State,

and wrote several electioneering pamphlets in the interest of Mr. Seymour, the candidate of the party, which had a large circulation. In 1857 Mr. H. returned to Can., and is now practising his profession at Montreal.

I. History of the discovery of the Valley of the Mississipi. *Cincinnati*, 1853, 12mo. ; an ed. *Philadelphia*.

"The work is chiefly intended for the use of academies and schools, and for this purpose is invaluable ; but it also contains much information which would interest the general reader. It is supplied with copious notes, and is written in a clear, concise style, with sufficient spirit to render it acceptable in the hands of one who may read merely for amusement. It also displays much labor and research, in the writer, and claims to be, as it undoubtedly is, the only work of the kind in the English language devoted to this interesting branch of History.' "—*Ned Buntline's Novelist*, (St. Louis.)

II. Life in the Far West ; or, the Adventures of a Hoosier. *New York*, 8vo.

III. Practical Suggestions on Mining Rights and Privileges in Lower Canada. *Montreal*, 1867.

HART, A. W.
I. Our Colonies. *Montreal*, 1849.

HART, M. O. (Mont.)
I. Index to the matters contained in the Civil Code of Lower Canada. *Montreal*, 1866.

HARVARD, *Rev.* W. M.
I. Letter to His Excellency Sir George Arthur, K. C. H., Gov. and Commander in-Chief, &c., on that portion of the Clergy Reserve property, (Landed and Funded) of Upper Canada, not specifically appropriated to any particular Church. *Quebec*, 1839, pp. 46, 2nd ed.

II. Five defensive letters in behalf of the British Wesleyan Conference, against the attacks of the *Canada Conference Journal*. *Toronto*, 1846, pp. 44.

HARVEY, ARTHUR, *F. S. S.* A Can. Statist. B. in Eng., 1834. Ed. in France and Holland, and was also for some time at Trinity Coll., (Dub.), but emigrated to Can. before he could take his degree. Was Assist. Ed. of, and Parliamentary Correspondent for, the *Spectator* (Ham.); served also in the latter capacity for . *Gazette* (Mont.) and other journals, and as Can. Correspondent for several Eng. and Am. newspapers. Had editorial charge of the *Morning Chronicle*, (Que.), of which he had previously been shorthand reporter, for a short period prior to his retirement from the press, in consequence of ill health, in 1862. Mr. H. is now Statistical Clk. to the Finance Depart. (Can.) He has been elected a Fellow of the Statistical Soc. (Lon.)

I. On the Appearence and Decline of Malarious disease in the valley of the Lower Grand River. *Can. Journ.*, 1859.

II. The Grain Trade. Extract from a paper on "The Graphical Delineation of Statistical Facts." With Map illustrating the course and comparative magnitude of the principal channels of the Grain Trade of the Lake Regions, 1862. Read before the Lit. and His. Soc. (Que.)

III. The Reciprocity Treaty ; its advantages to the United States and to Canada. [An Essay to which was awarded the first prize by the proprietors of the *Trade Review*, (Mont.)] *Quebec*, 2nd Ed. 1865, pp. 29, 8vo.

IV. Year Book and Almanac of British North America for 1867, being an Annual Register of Political, Vital, and Trade Statistics, Customs Tariffs, Excise and Stamp Duties ; and Public Events of interest in Upper and Lower Canada, New Brunswick, Nova Scotia, Prince Edward Island, Newfoundland, and the West Indies. (With Maps.) [Edited.] *Montreal*, 3rd Ed. 1866, pp. 163, 8vo.

" The best statistical manual of British America, which, with existing sources of information, it is possible to prepare   It is a regular *Multum in Parvo*."—*Journal* (St. John, N. B.)

HARVEY, *Rev.* MOSES. A Presb. Min. B. at Armagh, Irel. Studied in Belfast Coll. Min. of Maryport, Eng., 1844. In 1852 appointed to Free Ch., St. John's, N. F. L., where he still remains.

I. Thoughts on the Poetry and Literature of the Bible. *St. John's*, 1853, pp. 28.

" A very superior production. The writer is thoroughly in love with his subject ; his style finely harmonizes with it ; and over the whole discussion he throws a rich glow of religious fervour, which is very refreshing and instructive. One naturally is led to put this little treatise alongside of a similar thing which lately came from the pen of Dr. Hamilton of London; and it is saying a good deal of Mr. Harvey's tract when we give it as our opinion that it can stand such a comparison. As regards mere style we greatly prefer it."—*Scottish Guardian.*

II. The Testimony of Ninevah to the Veracity of the Bible. *Do.*, 1854, pp. 61.

" An excellent addition to our 'Christian Evidences'—popular in manner, graphic and well put in form. From the religious system, military usages, costumes, architecture, &c., of the Assyrians, Mr. Harvey deduces several telling arguments for the veracity of Scripture."—*Witness*, (Edin.)

III. Lectures on the Harmony of Science and Revelation. *Halifax* and *St. John's*, 1856, pp. 104.

" The man of science who is an enlightened christian, can easily show how his knowledge that came supernaturally from God, and his knowledge attainable by the ordinary exercise of his faculties, on the materials furnished by the surrounding universe, can co-exist and mutually illustrate each other. Mr. Harvey has done so, in the work before us, in a manner that will call forth the admiration and applause of every intelligent reader. He has succeeded in making ' the new familiar and the familiar new.' Topics that are usually looked upon as dry and uninviting, in his hands are fresh, lucid and attractive."—*Presb. Witness*, (Hal.)

IV. Lectures on Egypt and its Monuments, as illustrative of Scripture. *St. John's*, 1857, pp. 95.

V. Lectures, Literary and Biographical. *Edinburgh*, 1864, pp. 512.

" The Lectures embraced in the present work were delivered at intervals, during the past few years, to Literary Institutes in the town of St. John, Newfoundland. They are eleven in number, their subjects have a wide range, and their treatment is in every instance characterised by breadth of view, clearness of thought, and artistic purity and beauty of expression. Mr. Harvey evidently knows how to attract and command popular audiences, and he is certainly not ignorant of the most approved methods of instructing and interesting them. His themes are : 'Edmund Burke and Oliver Goldsmith,' 'Wit and Humour,' ' English, Scotch and Americans,' ' The Poetry of Geology,' ' Ireland— Her History and People,' ' Dr. Kane's Arctic Explorations,' ' Sydney Smith—His Life, Wit and Wisdom,' ' Our Mother Age, or the Times We Live In,' ' Knowledge is Power,' and ' Thomas Hood—His Life and Poetry.' There is not one of the essays which is not equal to the best ordinarily delivered to Literary Institutes in this country, and several are quite superior – the volume, indeed, is a most readable and instructive one."—*Caledonian Mercury*, (Edin.)

HARVEY, W.

I. The Priest and the Novelist : a Requiem ; with a preface on William M. Thackeray and Frederick W. Faber. *Quebec*, 1864, pp. 20.

HASKINS, JAMES, *A. B., M. B.*, (T. C. D.) A poetical contributor to the *Literary Garland*. (Mont.)

The poetical works of James Haskins, A. B., M. B., Trinity College, Dublin. Edited by Henry Baldwin, A.M., Osgoode Hall, U. C., Barrister-at-Law. *Hartford*, 1848, pp. xvii-320.

HATHEWAY, CALVIN.

I. Sketches of New Brunswick ; containing an account of the first settlement of the province, with a brief description of the country, climate, productions, inhabitants, government, rivers, towns, settlements, public institutions, trade, revenue, population, &c. By an Inhabitant of the Province. *St. John*, 1825, pp. 108, 8vo.

HAUGHTON, WILLIAM. A Can. poet. Has written many fugitive pieces, under the *nom de plume* of *Silvicola*, of more or less merit, for the newspaper press. Some of his poems have appeared in *Graham's Mag.* (U. S.) Resides at Keppell, U. C.

HAW, *Rev.* WILLIAM.

I. Fifteen years in Canada ; being a series of letters on its early history and settlement ; its boundaries, divisions, population and general routes ; its agricultural progress and wealth compared with the United States ; its religious and educational institutions ; and its present political condition and relations ; together with the advantages it affords as a desirable field of emigration. *Edinburgh*, 1850, pp. 120.

HAWKINS, ALFRED. A native of Eng. D. at Quebec, 30 June, 1854. Was Shipping Master of the Port of Quebec for some years.

I. Picture of Quebec, with Historical Recollections. *Quebec*, 1834, pp. 477, (Plates), 12mo.

" Endowed with a keen relish for the beautiful and sublime in scenery and art, indomitable perseverance in the acquisition of

12

information, a taste refined by an extensive acquaintance with the best ancient and modern authors, and an ardent love of his subject, we know of but few persons in the province better qualified than the compiler of this work, to carry out to a successful termination the important task imposed upon him."—*Gazette*. (Mont.)

II. The Plan of the Naval and Military Operations before Quebec, and Death of Wolfe. *London*, 1842.

" The plan is the production of Mr. Alfred Hawkins, who has carefully compiled the topographical portion of it from original surveys, and laid down with equal accuracy the operations of the English naval and military forces. He has represented also the defences of the French under Montcalm, and indeed omitted not one single point, however minute, that may serve to explain the proceedings of the attacking and defending parties. The field works of the British troops at the Island of Orleans; the entrenchments and line of battle of the French army ; the redoubts, batteries, and other defences, which extend to a distance of nearly nine miles ; all these various explanatory details are delineated with a skill and accuracy that is truly astonishing. The plan is still further embellished with an exquisite miniature copy of West's celebrated picture, ' The Death of Wolfe on the Field of Battle,' and with a sketch of the troops in the act of ascending the lofty precipices to gain the heights of Abraham. This sketch is one of the most spirited things of the sort we ever remember to have seen, and gives a vivid idea of the perilous nature of the achievement. A vignette, in the corner of the plan, represents Britannia, supported by the lion, pointing out to the victorious troops the citadel of Cape Diamond ; Wolfe's name is inscribed on her shield, on the rays of which are emblazoned the names of the gallant regiments which shared the glories of the day."—*Sun*, (Lon.)

III. The Quebec Directory and Strangers guide to the City and Environs, 1844-5. *Quebec*.

HAWKINS, *Rev.* ERNEST. Preb. of St. Paul's Cathedral, (Lon.) and Secy. to the S. P. G.

I. Annals of the Diocese of Toronto (with Map). *London*, 1848, 12mo.

II. Annals of the Diocese of Quebec (with Maps and Plates). *Do.*, 1849, 12mo.

HAWLEY, WILLIAM FITZ. A Can. poet. B. 1804. D. at Laprairie, L. C, Jany., 1855. In addition to his two published works contributed largely to the Can.

periodical press. He was long actively engaged in collecting the materials for a History of Can. ; an undertaking which he reluctantly abandoned, owing to the destruction by fire of many valuable historical manuscripts and papers which he had acquired.

I. Quebec, The Harp, and other poems. *Montreal*, 1829, pp. 172, 18mo.

The Soc. for the Encouragement of Arts and Sciences (Que.) awarded its annual medal to the author, for this work.

II. The Unknown, or Lays of the Forest. *Do.*, 1831, 12mo.

" The first of these works contains descriptive and other poems for which the author received honorary medals. In the last is found a beautiful and true description of the river St. Maurice and its banks with the falls of Shawenegan."—*Herald*, (Mont.)

HAYDEN, *Rev.* HENRY, " S. T. P., *A. M.* Of Trin. Coll. Dublin. A Presbyter of the United Ch. of Eng. and Irel."

I. Illustrations of Astronomy. *Halifax*, 1836, pp. 39, 8vo.

HAYES, A. A.
I. On Antimony from New Brunswick. *Proc. Nat. His. Soc.* (Bos.), 1863.

HAYWARD, *Mrs.* CATHERINE.
I. The Battles of the Crimea ; with other poems on the most touching and interesting incidents in the campaign, from well authenticated sources. *Port Hope, U. C.*, 1855, pp. 68.

HAZARD, JOSEPH. Of Lincoln Coll., Oxford.
I. The Conquest of Quebec ; a poem. (With Plan of Quebec.) *London*, 1769, pp. 20, 4to.

HAZLITT, W. C.
I. British Columbia and Vancouver's Island. *London*, 1858, 12mo.

II. The Great Gold Fields of Cariboo. *Do.*, 1862, 12mo.

HEAD, *Colonel* CHARLES. An officer in the Brit. Army. B. in N. S. Left his native Province at an early age, and d. abroad.
I. Eastern and Egytian Scenery, Antiquities, &c., with descriptive notes, maps and plans of an Overland Route. *London*, 1833.

This valuable work contains 22 large plates and was published at £3 13s 6d.

HEAD, *Sir* FRANCIS BOND, *Bart., K. C. H.* Lieut. Gov. of U. C. from 1835 to 1838. B. near Rochester, Eng., 1793.

I. Narrative of his Administration in Canada, with the Revolt. *London*, 1839, pp. 526, 8vo.

" A lively, pleasant, self complacent piece of egoism • • • directly opposite in all its characteristics to the Report of Lord Durham : but this we say without reference to the principles advocated by either party." *Athen.* (Lon.)

II. Supplemental chapter to 3rd Ed. *Do.*, 1839, pp. 36.

III. An Address to the House of Lords, against the Canada Re-Union Bill, and disclosing the improper means by which the consent of the Legislature of the Upper Province has been obtained to the measure. *Do.*, 1840, pp. 52, 8vo.

IV. The Emigrant : Scenes in Canada. *Do.*, 1846, post, 8vo : New ed., 1852.

Addresses to Sir Francis B. Head, Bart., from the Legislatures of the British North American Colonies, &c. &c., on his resignation of the Government of Upper Canada. *Toronto*, 1838, pp. 38.

Lord Glenelg's despatches to Sir F. B. Head, Bart., during his administration of the Government of Upper Canada. *London*, 1839, pp. 193.

HEAD, *Sir* GEORGE, *Kt.* An Officer in the Brit. army ; served in Can. and U. S. D. 1855.
I. Forest Scenes and Incidents in the Wilds of North America ; being a Diary of a Winter's Route from Halifax to the Canadas, and during a four months Residence in the Woods on the Borders of Lakes Huron and Simcoe. *London*, 1829, pp. 362 cr. 8vo ; 2nd Ed. 1839, 8vo.

HEADLEY, J. T.
I. The Second War with England. *New York*, 1853, 2 vols., 12mo.

HEARNE, SAMUEL.
I. A Journey from the Prince of Wales's Fort in Hudson's Bay, to the Northern Ocean. Undertaken by the order of the Hudson's Bay Company, for the discovery of Copper Mines, a North-West Passage, &c., in the years 1769, 1770, 1771, and 1772. (With plates.) *London*, 1795, pp. 458, 4to.

Translated into French. *Paris*, 1799. 2 Vols., in-8.

" Cette relation, une de celles qui ont répandu le plus grand jour sur un des points les plus essentiels de la géographie, fait beaucoup d'honneur à son auteur. Le voyage de *Hearne* prouve que le fameux voyage au Nord-Ouest, n'existe pas où on le plaçait jadis : ce voyageur a par là, rendu un service essentiel à la géographie, en faisant disparaître une chimère qui causait bien des disputes. Son expédition et celle de Mc-Kenzie, donnent lieu de présumer que le continent do l'Amérique Septentrionale ne s'étend pas beaucoup au-delà du 71e parallèle, et font souhaiter que des entreprises subséquentes mettent à même de prouver que l'espace de mer, connu sous le nom de Baie de Baffin, est une Manche et non un Golfe."—*Biog. Univ.*

EAVYSEGE, CHARLES. A Can. poet. B. in Liverpool, Eng., 2 May, 1816. Came to Can. in 1853 and took up his residence in Montreal, where he has since remained. On the occasion of the Ter-Centenary celebration of the birth of Shakespeare in 1864, he wrote an Ode in honour of the event which was received with great favour. The titles of his works are given below. Mr. H. has been for several years a local reporter to the *Daily Witness*, (Mont.)

I. Saul : a drama in three parts. *Montreal*, 1857, pp. 315, 8vo.

2nd Ed. carefully revised and amended. *Do.*, 1859, pp. 328, 8vo.

" • • • the work is indubitably one of the most remarkable English poems ever written out of Great Britain. This copy was given to the writer of the present article by Mr. Nathaniel Hawthorne, to whose recommendation of this, to him and to us, unknown Canadian poet, our readers and English literature generally are beholden for their first introduction to a most curious work. 'Saul' is in three parts, each of five acts, and altogether about ten thousand lines long. In it the greatest subject, in the whole range of history, for a drama, has been treated with a poetical power and a depth of psychological knowledge which are often quite startling, though, we may say, inevitably, below the mark of the subject-matter, which is too great to be done full justice to, in any but the words in which the original history is related. • • • There are two things, however, which he proves that he knows, namely, the Bible and human nature; and a poet cannot be said to be really uneducated who knows these well. Shakespeare he also knows far better than most men know him, for he has discerned and adopted his method as no other dramatist has done."—*North Brit. Rev.*

II. Count Filippo ; or, The Unequal Marriage, a drama in five acts. *Do.*, 1860, pp. 153.

• • • •

" Of poetry like this there is very far too much in Count Filippo. We weary of watching this continual strain for the grasp of two thoughts at once, as the eye wearies of long looking at stereoscopic figures, and we long for the simple statement of a great truth, or the hearty and direct expression of strong feeling. This is the great fault of the drama, to which is to be added the defect of characterization first mentioned. Briefly, too, as to the rest, the author does not show in wise or philosophical views of life the fruits of profound knowledge or instinctive comprehension of its relations. This is to judge the play by a very high standard, it is true ; but its merits are so great that it can be gauged by no lower. If it be the work of a young man, and he has the genius to create a style of his own, he may become the first dramatic poet of the age."—*Albion*, (N. Y.)

III. Jephthah's Daughter. *London* and *Montreal*, 1865, pp. 94, 12mo.

" There is great art in the development of the daughter's feelings from her first natural terror of death to the hallowed resignation with which she finally prepares for it, still casting a sad, submissive glance on the fair world she quits." After quoting the passage beginning " Oh! think how hard it is to die when young !" &c., the critic says—" This is very touching, and goes direct to the heart. Nor is there less nature and beauty of expression in the lines that record her first conviction of inevitable doom

' Deep darkness gathers o'er my prospect, mother,' &c.

Pity and filial love at length reconcile the victim to the altar. There is a sense too of noble pride in her sacrifice ; she gives herself for her country no less than for her father. • • • There is no need after our quotations, to say that the character of Jephthah's daughter displays both imagination and feeling."—*Athen.*, (Lon.)

IV. The Advocate ; a novel. *Montreal*, 1865, 8vo.

HECTOR, JAMES, *M. D.*

I. On the Geology of the Country between Lake Superior and the Pacific Ocean (between 48° and 55° parallels of latitude) explored by the Government Exploring Expedition under the command of Captain J. Palliser (1857-60). *Abst. Proc. Geol. Soc.* (Lon.) 1861.

HELLMUTH, *Venerable* I. Archdeacon of Huron. Is Principal of, and Divinity Prof. in, Huron Coll., U. C.

I. A Reply to a letter of the Rt. Rev. the Lord Bishop of Montreal and Metropolitan of Canada, addressed to the Bishops and Clergy of the United Church of England and Ireland in Canada. *Quebec*, 1862, pp. 26, 8vo.

HEMMING, E. J., *B. C. L.* A L C. Advocate (Drummondville, L. C.)

I. On the neglect of Chemistry by practical farmers ; with tabulated results of anayses in Agricultural Chemistry. A prize essay. *London*, 1853, pp. 157, 8vo.

Obtained the prize offered by the Royal Agricultural Soc. (Eng.) in 1851.

II. Digested Index to the Statutes in force in Lower Canada at the end of the Session of 1856. Prepared by order of the Legislative Assembly. *Toronto*, 1857, pp. 508, 8vo.

HENDERSON, ALEXANDER. A Can. artist.

I. Canadian Views and Studies. (Photographs). *Montreal*, 1866.

HENEY. *Hon.* HUGHES. A Can. public man. B. 1790. D. at Three Rivers, L. C., 15 Jany., 1844. Studied at St. Raphael Coll. Sat for Montreal in the Assem. of L. C., from 1820 until 1832. In 1830 accepted office as a mem. of the Ex. Council. In 1842 was appointed a Com. for the revision of the Statutes of L. C., but did not live to complete his share of the work.

I. Commentaires sur l'acte constitutionnel du Haut et du Bas-Canada. *Montréal*, 1832, 8vo.

HENNING, THOMAS.

I. Meteors and Falling Stars. *Can. Journ.*, 1854.

II. Remarks on the Planetoids between Mars and Jupiter. *Do.*, 1855.

III. The applicability of our Educational System to the social condition of large cities. *Do.*, 1858.

HENRY, ALEXANDER. A Can. merchant. B. in New Jersey, Augt., 1739. D. at Montreal, 4 Apl., 1824. Travelled for 16 years in the North-west country in the pursuit of his business as a fur-trader ; the adventures and results of which are told in his work. Subsequent to 1781 carried on business as a general merchant (Mont.), and at the time of his death held the office of King's Auctioneer for that District.

A good biography of him appears in the *Can. Mag.* (Mont.) 1824.

I. Travels and Adventures in Canada and the Indian Territories, between the years 1760 and 1776. With portrait. *New York*, 1809, pp. viii–330, 8vo.

" This little volume, besides the materials it furnishes for his own biography, by displaying the stronger features of his character when placed in many trying and perilous situations, contains a great deal of valuable geographical information relative to the country, and many curious details of the customs and manners of the natives."—*Can. Mag.*

" His enterprise, perils and intrepidity, excite deep interest."—CHANCELLOR KENT.

HENRY, GEORGE.

I. Emigrants Guide. *Quebec*, N. D., 12mo.

HENRY, JOHN JOSEPH. Accompanied Arnold on his expedition to Quebec. B. 1758. D. 1810.

I. Interesting account of the hardships and sufferings of that band of heroes who traversed the wilderness in the campaign against Quebec in 1775. *Lancaster, U. S.*, 1812, 12mo.

HENRY, WALTER, *M. D.* A well known contributor to the press. B. at Donegal. Irel., 1 Jany., 1791. D. at Belleville. U. C., 27 June, 1860. Ed. at Trinity Coll. (Dub.) Studied for the medical profession under Sir Everard Home, and was a mem. of the Medical Soc. of Guy's Hospital, of the Medical Soc., and of the Coll. of Surgeons, (Lon.) During the period of his studies attended St. George's, Guy's and St. Thomas' Hospitals. Entered the army as Hospital Assist. in April, 1811 and rose through the various grades of the service until he was appointed Staff Surgeon in 1839, and Deputy Inspector Genl. of Hospitals in 1845. We learn from *Hart*, that he served with the 66th Regt. from May, 1811, to the close of the Peninsular War at Toulouse ; including the seige of Badajoz ; battle of Vittoria and the action in the Pyrenees: battles of Nivelle and Nive ; engagement at Garris ; battle of Orthes and the action at Acre. He also served with the same corps in the Nepaulese war in India, in 1816–17, and in the two Can. rebellions in 1837–8. Dr. H. was with his regt. in St. Helena during the last 4 years of the life of Napoleon, and at his death was charged with the duty of preparing the bulletin of the *post mortem* appearances of the body, which was published by the British Govt. He was stationed in Can. from 1827 to 1841 when he was removed to Halifax, N. S. Whilst at Quebec he wrote a considerable portion of the work whose title is given below, and had the book printed there. Of his other writings only those published in the *Albion* (N. Y.), from 1837 to 1845, over the signatures of " Miles," " Piscator " and " Scrutator" have come to our knowledge. The 2 letters signed " Miles " are succinct and trustworthy cotemporary accounts of the rebellions in Can. in 1837–8. " Scrutator's " letters were on *The Politics of Nova Scotia* and were dated from Halifax in 1843–44. In one of these a paragraph indicates an early intention of the Doctor, subsequently carried out, to settle somewhere under the British flag on this side of the Atlantic. In a few remarks, Dr. Bartlett, the then ed. of the *Albion*, truly characterized them as " those admirable letters." The letters of " Piscator," 2 in number, are on *Salmon Fishing in Canada*, and evince an intimate and thorough acquaintance with the subject. Dr. H. was also the author of a paper, *Observations on the Habits of the Salmon Family*, in the *Trans. of the Lit. & His. Soc.* (Que.), 1837. In 1852 he was appointed Inspector Gen. of Hospitals in Can. where he remained during the remainder of his life, retiring upon half pay in 1856, and dying at Belleville, where he had carried out his intention of " settling under the British flag."

I. Trifles from my Portfolio ; or, recollections of scenes and small adventures during twenty-nine years military service in the Peninsular War and invasion of France, the East Indies, campaign in Nepaul, St. Helena during the detention and until the death of Napoleon, and Upper and Lower Canada. By a Staff Surgeon. *Quebec*, 1839, 2 vols., 4to.

2nd. Ed. published under the title of " Henry's Military Life." *London*, 1843, 2 Vols., pp. 300–384, 8vo.

" The style of the work throughout, is masculine, correct and classical ; and such as to reflect honour on the author as an officer and a scholar."—*Gazette*, (Mont.)

HERBERT, HENRY WILLIAM. An Am. author. Better known by his *nom de plume* of " *Frank Forester.*" B. in London, Eng., 7 Apl., 1807. D., by his own hand, in N. Y., 17 May, 1858.

" The most scholarly of sportsmen, the most sportsmanlike of scholars."—*Albion*, (N. Y.)

I. The Field Sports of the United States and British Provinces of North America. *New York*, 1849, 2 vols.

II. Fish and Fishing-Book of the United States and British Provinces of North America. *Do.*, 1849, 8vo.

III. Supplement to the above. *Do.*, 1850.

IV. The Horse and Horsemanship of the United States and British Provinces of North America. *Do.*, 1857, 2 vols. 8vo.

HERBERT, *Miss* MARY E. A N. S. authoress. Has written poetry, tales, essays &c., for several Lower Province newspapers, especially for the *Provincial Wesleyan* (Hal.)

I. Scenes in the Life of a Halifax Belle. *Halifax*, 1859, pp. 60.

II. Woman as she should be ; or, Agnes Wiltshire. *Do.*, 1861, pp. 145, 8vo.

III. Flowers by the Wayside. *Do.*, 1865, pp. 78.

" What she writes is always well worth reading and many of her poems and other pieces are really beautiful."—*Presb. Witness*, (Hal.)

HERBERT, *Miss* SARAH. A N. S. authoress and poet. Sister of the preceding. B. in Irel., Oct., 1824. D. at Halifax, N. S., 1844. She was endowed with powers for literary composition of a high order ; as a child she was thoughtful, sensitive and so exceedingly diffident that it was not until her 15th year that her talents became known beyond her own circle.

" It was then," says a writer in the *Provincial Mag.*, (Hal.), " that the voice of song which so long slumbered in her bosom, first essayed its humble notes, and though feeble in its commencement, it grew stronger and sweeter, until passing from earth it mingled in the melody of Heaven."

Her first productions appeared in the *Morning Herald* and the *Nova Scotian*. After the establishment of the *Olive Branch* (Hal.), she became a regular contributor to its pages and eventually ed. of that paper. She also occasionally contributed to the *New Brunswicker* and the *Amaranth Mag.*, (St. John, N. B.) Miss H. manifested a warm interest in Temperance, and wrote several poems and tracts in favour of the cause; as a mem. and office bearer of one or two local benevolent societies, and as a sabbath school teacher a large sphere of useful labour was opened to her in which she accomplished a large amount of good.

I. Agnes Mailard, a temperance tale. *Halifax*.

The Eolian Harp, or Miscellaneous Poems. By Sarah and Mary E. Herbert. *Do.*, 1857, pp. 237.

HERCHMER, *Rev.* W. M., *M. A.* Queen Coll. Oxford.

I. Love, the spirit of Masonry ; an address. *Kingston*, N. D., pp. 12.

HERIOT, GEORGE. Formerly Deputy Postmaster General of British North America.

I. The History of Canada, from its first discovery, comprehending an Account of the original Establishment of the Colony of Louisiana. *London*, 1804, 2 vols, 4to.

" Taken from Charlevoix."—RICH.

II. Travels through the Canadas, containing a description of the picturesque scenery on some of the Rivers and Lakes ; with an account of the productions, commerce, and inhabitants of those Provinces : to which is subjoined, a comparative view of the manners and customs of several of the Indian Nations of North and South America ; illustrated with a map and numerous engravings, from drawings made at the several places by the author. *Do.*, 1807, pp. 602, 4to.

" There are some things, no doubt, in the volume before us, which deserve to be told ; and a person going to Canada might even wish to have *all* that is contained in the first part of the book. But the second half is absolutely useless ; and if we allow the first to stand, we have a detail of the lakes, rivers, and cataracts, the villages, farm-houses, and townships of Canada, considerably more

minute, (need we say how much less interesting ?) than we possess of the county of Northumberland."—*Edin. Rev.*

HENVIEUX, J. A. Register of the Co. of Terrebonne, L. C.

I. Analyse des Lois d'Enrégistrement, etc., suivie d'un Appendice contenant certaines observations sur les défauts et les lacunes de la Loi d'Enregistrement. *Montréal*, 1864, pp. 116, 32mo.

" Voici un excellent travail, que nous recommandons à l'attention de tous ceux que leurs affaires du pays obligent de s'occuper de l'importante question des hypothèques. C'est une analyse intelligente, correctement écrite, sobre de remarques et toute pratique, de la loi actuelle de l'enregistrement. Nul doute que, l'auteur n'atteigne le but qu'il s'est proposé, et qu'il ne rende la connaissance de la loi plus facile, et les lacunes plus évidentes." — JOSEPH ROYAL: *Rev. Can.*

HEY, *Hon.* WILLIAM. Chief Justice of Quebec from 1766 until 1777. Sat in the House of Commons of Great Britain. D. in Eng., 1797.

I. A View of the Civil Government and Administration of Justice in the Province of Canada, while it was subjected to the Crown of France.

II. A Plan for settling the Laws and the Administration of Justice in the Province of Quebec.

Both these papers were published by the *L. C. Jurist*, (Mont.), 1857.

HICKEY, MICHAEL JOSEPH. A Can writer. B. at Nenagh, Irel., 14 Feby., 1827. Drowned at Toronto, U. C., 24 Nov., 1864. Left an orphan at a tender age, he with the independence of spirit so characteristic of his countrymen, emigrated to Can. in 1845. For a short time he was engaged in the lumbering business on the Ottawa, which however he soon relinquished for the study of Law ; he was admitted as an atty., and was preparing for his final examination as a barrister, when he was unfortunately cut off in the flower of his youth. Mr. H. was favorably known as Ed. of the *New Era*, (Mont.) ; he subsequently ed. the *Tribune*, (Ottawa) ; and contributed some descriptive essays to *Blackwood's Mag*. He was a frequent contributor in prose and poetry to several Can.

journals. He left behind him in MS. a work of fiction of considerable length, and many essays and sketches, &c., which are to be published at an early day.

HICKMAN. WILLIAM.

   I. Sketches on the Nissisaguil, a river of New Brunswick. *London*, 1861, folio.

HIGGINS, WILLIAM HENRY. A Can. journ. B. at Limerick, Irel., Jan., 1830. Was connected with the *Colonist*, (Que.) from 1853 to 1855 ; and during same period was Parliamentary Correspondent for the *Leader* (Tor.), *Spectator* (Ham.), and other journals. Ed. the *Reporter* (Whitby) from 1855 to 1866 ; and established and ed. the *Journal* (Oshawa) for a short period. In 1857, founded the *Chronicle* (Whitby), a Liberal Conservative journal, which he still owns and conducts. Is the author of various poetic pieces which have appeared in the newspaper press from time to time.

HILL, *Rev.* GEORGE W., *M. A.* A Min. of the Ch. of Eng. (Hal.) B. at Halifax, N. S., 9 Nov. 1824. Received his primary education in his native city, and attended Acadia Coll., Horton, for 2 years. In early life turned his attention to farming, but gave it up and entered King's Coll., Windsor, to study for the ministry. He graduated B. A. in 1847, and in the same year was ordained Deacon and became curate of St. George's, (Hal.,) where he remained until 1854, having in the meantime been ordained to the priesthood, and been sent to Eng. on a mission on behalf of his *Alma Mater*. In the last named year was appointed Prof. of Pastoral Theology in King's Coll., which position he held until Dec., 1859, when he became Curate of St. Paul's. In 1865 he was appointed Rector (Hal.,) and at the same time Chaplain to the Leg. Coun. of his native Province.

   I. Old Testament History, its Chronology, apparent discrepancies and undesigned coincidences, a lecture. *Halifax*, 1855, pp. 27, 8vo.

"It displayed much careful and accurate research, and was in many parts eloquent."—*Journal*, (Hal.)

   II. A Sermon preached before the Hon. the Board of Governors and the Members of the University of King's College, Windsor. *Do.*, 1855, pp. 13, 8vo.

   III. Nova Scotia and Nova Scotians ; a lecture. *Do.*, 1858, pp. 49, 8vo.

"We have seldom had the satisfaction of listening to a discourse written in a style so classic, and delivered in such an eloquent manner as that by which this lecture was characterized. From the commencement to the close, each period appeared to surpass in classic elegance that which had preceded it ; and the simple narrative was so adorned and embellished, as to appear the sublime conception of the poet and the scholar."— *Express*, (Hal.)

   IV. Review of the Rise and Progress of the Church of England in Nova Scotia ; a Sermon. *Do.*, 1858, pp. 33, 8vo.

   V. Records of the Church of England in Rawdon from its origin until the present date. *Do.*, 1858, pp. 28, 8vo.

   VI. Oration at the Inauguration of the Welsford and Parker Monument. *Do.*, 1860, pp. 24.

"The Rev. Mr. Hill, then, amid the repeated applause of the assembled multitude, delivered an oration of matchless beauty ; tracing with a master hand, the lives and characters of the heroes, and the stirring events in which they were actors. It was replete with information and research, and evinced great knowledge of the early history of our country."—*Express*, (Hal.)

   VII. The Message and Qualifications of the Minister ; a Sermon, with an Address to Candidates for ordination. *Do.*, 1861, pp. 15.

   VIII. Memoir of Sir Brenton Haliburton, late Chief Justice of the Province of Nova Scotia. *Do.*, 1864, pp. 207, 12mo.

"We look upon this volume • • • • as a very interesting contribution to our colonial literature. It deals with the life and actions of a good and great colonist, who distinguished himself, during the most stirring periods of our colonial history, as a soldier, statesman and jurist ; and in the eyes of those who knew him best, he was most admired for the many virtues which adorned his character in social life. In sketching the career of his hero, the author's hand seems to have been tremulous with affection ; but the judgment which characterises his pages is unclouded, and the style is easy, correct, and sometimes eloquent."— *Examiner*, (Charlotte.)

"It constitutes a valuable addition to our provincial literature."—*Chronicle*, (Hal.)

IX. Letter to the Parishioners of St. Paul's, Halifax. *Do.*, 1866, pp. 48, 8vo.

HILL, *Rev.* JAMES J. Rector of St. James's Par., (Newport, N. S.)

I. The Liturgy of the Church of England. *Halifax*, 1861, pp. 21, 8vo.

HILL, *Hon.* PHILIP CARTERET, *D. C. L.* A Halifax Barrister. Brother of the Rev. G. W. H. Has been President of the N. S. Institute of Natural Sciences. Appointed Secy. of the Province of N. S., 1867.

I. Unity of Creation; a Lecture. *Halifax*, 1857, pp. 34, 8vo.

II. The United States and British Provinces contrasted from personal observation; a Lecture. *Do.*, 1859, pp. 30, 8vo.

HILL. S. S.

I. Emigrants Guide to British American Colonies. *London*, 1837, 12mo.

II. A Short Account of Prince Edward's Island. *Do.*, 1839, pp. 96, 8vo.

HILTON, *Rev.* JOHN. Incumbent of Brockton, U. C.

I. Sermon preached at St. Paul's Church, Perrytown, and at St. John's Church, Elizabethville, in October, 1857, on the Church and her Services. pp. 22.

HINCKS, *Hon.* FRANCIS, *C. B.* Formerly Statesman and journ. in Can. B. in Irel. Is the 5th and youngest son of the late Dr. Hincks, of Belfast. Coming to Can. on a visit, in 1830, he determined upon entering into business and taking up his residence in the Province, which he did in the following year. On the appointment of Lord Durham to the Govt. of Can. Mr. H. founded the *Examiner* newspaper (Tor.) of which he became the principal ed. This paper was a special organ of the liberal party and in Mr. H's. hands wielded much influence and power. It furnished such decided evidence of knowledge and ability on his part that it is said Lord Sydenham was most anxious to obtain his services in his lordship's Council in 1841. In that year Mr. H. was first returned to Parliament as a mem. of the Leg. Assem. in which he continued to hold a seat,

with but slight interruption, until his retirement from public life in Can., in Nov., 1855. In 1843 he proceeded to Montreal where he conducted the *Times* for a short time. In the following year he established the *Pilot*, a paper of which he was chief ed. It was a strong party organ and did a vast deal in restoring Lafontaine and Baldwin to power. In 1848, upon returning to office, Mr. H. retired from the press. He was twice Inspector Genl., and for some time Prime Min. of Can. In 1855 he was appointed Governor of the Windward Islands where he remained until 1862, when he was transferred to the governorship of British Guiana.

I. Canada: its Financial Position and Resources. *London*, 1849, pp. viii–32.

II. Speech in Legislative Assembly on the Financial condition of the Province. *Toronto*, 1851, pp. 16.

III. The Seigniorial Question; its present position. By a member of the Legislative Assembly from Upper Canada. *Quebec*, 1854.

IV. Documents relating to the resignation of the Canadian Ministry in September, 1854. Speech of Hon. Inspector General Hincks,—Address to the electors of South Oxford—Correspondence with Mr. Wilson, M. P. P., &c. *Do.*, 1854, pp. 27.

V. Review of Mr. Howe's pamphlet on the Organization of the Empire. *London*, 1855.

HINCKS, *Rev.* WILLIAM, *F. L. S.*, *F. B. S.* (Eng.) Prof. of Natural History Univ. Coll. (Tor.) Brother of the preceding. Was the 1st Prof. of Natural History in Queen's Coll. (Cork). Has contributed papers on Botany to the Brit. Association, of which he was an early mem., and to the Linnæan Soc., of which he has been for many years a fellow.

Canadian Journal.

I. Natural History in its relation to Agriculture; a lecture. 1854.

II. Considerations respecting anomalous vegetable structures. 1858.

III. The Sensationalist Philosophy. 1859.

IV. The Family of Falconidæ. do.

V. On some questions in relation to the theory of the structure of plants of the orders Brassicaceæ and Primulaceæ. 1860.

VI. Remarks on the classification of Mammalia. do.

VII. On the true aims, foundations and claims to attention of the science of political economy. 1861.

VIII. Specimen of a Flora of Canada, with preliminary remarks. do.

IX. An attempt at an improved classification of fruits. do.

X. An attempt at a new theory of human emotions. 1862.

XI. An Injury into the natural laws which regulate the interchange of commodities between individuals and nations, and the effects of interference with them. do.

XII. Observations accompanying the exhibition of a specimen of " *Sula Bassana* " (the Solan Goose or Gannett), lately obtained at Oshawa, C. W., and belonging to the Museum of the University of Toronto. do.

XIII. Materials for a Fauna Canadensis. do.

XIV. The Struthionidæ : the extent and divisions of the family with its systematic position and relations. 1863.

XV. On the families properly belonging to the fissirostral suborder of insessorial birds, and the real position of some which have been referred to it. 1864.

XVI. Remarks on the principles of classification in the Animal Kingdom, in immediate reference to a recent paper by J. W. Dawson, LL.D., F. R. S., Principal of McGill College, Montreal. 1865.

XVII. Thoughts on Belief and Evidence. do.

XVIII. On Chorisis. do.

HIND, HENRY YOULE, *M. A.*, *F. R. G. S.* A Can. Exploror and Geologist. B. in Nottingham, Eng., June, 1823. Until the age of 14, with his cousin, Mr. J. R. Hind, the eminent astronomer, was the private pupil of the Rev. W. Butler, head-master of the Nottinghamshire Grammar Sch. On leaving that institution was sent to the Royal Commercial Sch. at Leipzig, where he remained for 2 years, acquiring a knowledge of German, French, Chemistry, Natural Philosophy, &c. Upon returning home studied for a few years, again with Mr. Butler, and then at Cambridge, entering Queen's Coll. Owing to circumstances over which he had no control, he only remained a single year at the Univ. In 1845 he went to France to acquire a more perfect knowledge of the French language. So much travelling in early life must have created a distaste for sedentary pursuits, for, in 1846, we find him starting for Am., and spending a year or more in wandering through Mexico and portions of the Southern States. In 1847 he came to Can. He was teacher in one of the common sch's. of U. C. for some months, when he became the successful candidate for the office of mathematical master and lecturer in chemistry and natural philosophy in the Provincial Normal Sch. for U. C., then about to be established at Toronto. He remained at this institution for about 5 years when he received the appointment of Prof. of Chemistry and Geology in the Univ. of Trinity Coll. in the same city. Mr. H. was selected by the Govt. of Can. in 1857, to accompany the expedition despatched by that govt. to survey the country between Lake Superior and the Red River of the North, in the capacity of Geologist and Naturalist. In 1858, he was placed in charge of the Assinniboine and Saskatchawan Exploring Expedition, and was instructed to make a Topographical and Geological Exploratory Survey of the country between the Red River of the North and the elbow of the South Branch of the Saskatchawan. His reports on these expeditions have been published by the Can. Govt., and also laid before the House of Commons, and published by command, with several additional maps, both geological and topographical, executed by Arrowsmith, under Mr. H's. supervision. These maps embody all the recent discoveries in that region up to 1860. In the last named year he was elected a F. R. G. S., and superintended personally the publication of his *Nar-*

rative of the Canadian Red River Explor-ing Expedition, &c., which with his other principal works were brought out in London by the Longmans. In 1861 Mr. H. conducted an Exploratory Survey up the Moisie River to the table-land of the Labrador Peninsula, with a view to collect materials for a description of the eastern part of B. A. In 1864 he removed to N. B., and in accordance with instructions from the Provincial Govt., made a Geological Survey of that Province. During the years 1852-3-4-5 he ed. the *Can. Journal*, the organ of the Can. Institute. (Tor.) In 1854 he was the successful compe-titor for a prize of £100, offered by the corporation of Toronto, for a report on the best means of preserving the har-bour of that city. Among minor literary efforts he has written in successive years of the *Canadian Almanac*, (Tor.), the articles on "*The Future of Western Canada*," "*The Great North West*," and "*Our Railway Policy*." Many of his lectures on various subjects have ap-peared in Can. journals and periodi-cals. In 1861 he undertook the ed. management of *The Journal of the Boards of Arts and Manufactures*, (Tor.) which, we believe, he conducted up to his departure for N. B.

I. Lectures on Agricultural Che-mistry ; or Elements of the Science of Agriculture. *Toronto*, 1850.

"Mr. Hind appears to have treated the subject in a succinct and comprehensive manner."—*Gazette*. (Mont.)

II. A Comparative View of the Cli-mate of Western Canada, considered in relation to its influence upon Agricul-ture. *Do.*, 1851, pp. 38.

III. Essay on the Insects and Dis-eases injurious to the Wheat Crops. *Do.*, 1857, pp. 139. 8vo.

"The essay is not of mere temporary in-terest, it is a useful digest on a highly im-portant subject, of what is to be found in various volumes, and in detached essays and observations scattered through periodicals."

IV. Report on a Topographical and Geological Exploration of the Canoe route between Fort William, Lake Superior and Fort Garry, Red River ; and also of the valley of Red River, north of the 49th parallel, in 1857. *Do.*, 1858, pp. 16, 8vo.

V. North West Territory. Reports of Progress ; together with a prelimi-nary and general report on the Assinni-boine and Saskatchewan exploring ex-pedition, made under instructions from the Provincial Secretary, Ca-nada. (With Plates and Maps.) *Do.*, 1859, pp. 201, large, 4to.

"The report embraces an Itinerary, with topographical information rendered in the concisest form ; reports of progress, by dif-ferent members of the exploring party ; Me-teorological and Geological details ; and a narrative embodying descriptions of scenery, native habits, and such incidents of travel as are at once attractive to the general reader, and of value to those who are desi-rous of ascertaining the fitness of the region for a scene of emigration, and a future pro-vince of British North America."—*Can. Journ.*

VI. Narrative of the Canadian Red River Exploring Expedition of 1857, and of the Assinniboine and Saskat-chewan Exploring Expedition of 1858. (Illustrated with 20 chromoxylographs 76 wood cuts, 3 maps, topographical and geological, 4 plans and a sheet of profiles of the country explored.) *London*, 1860, 2 vols, 8vo.

"These explorations were undertaken for the purpose of ascertaining the practicability of establishing an emigrant route between Lake Superior and Selkirk settlement, and of acquiring some knowledge of the natural capabilities and resources of the valleys of the Red River and the Saskatchewan.

"In pursuance of these objects the author has given in these volumes a minute, clear and most readable account of the districts through which his course lay. • • • • Distances, topography, natural productions, geological structure and climatal conditions of these regions are carefully noted."—*Can. Nat.*

"By his excursion up the Moisie River, in Eastern Canada, Prof. Hind has added to our knowledge of the distribution of anorthosite rocks ; and by his explorations in the Red River region he has shown the extension in that direction of the Lower Silurian and Devonian series, without the intervention of the Middle and Upper Silurian."—SIR W. E. LOGAN : *Geo. of Can.*

VII. A Sketch of the Overland Route to British Columbia. *Toronto*, 1862.

"Prof. Hind has here brought together. from his own previous writings and personal knowledge of the country, and from the best authorities relating to that portion which lies beyond the limits of his own travels, an amount of useful information scarcely to be obtained elsewhere, and of the greatest importance to emigrants who are inclined to prefer the overland route."—*Can. Journ.*

VIII. Explorations in the Interior of the Labrador Peninsula, the country of the Montagnais and Nasquapee Indians. (Illustrated with 12 chromolithographs, 24 woodcuts and 2 maps.) *London*, 1863, 2 vols., pp. xxviii–655, 8vo.

" We do not remember to have ever read a book of travels which so completely brings the country before the reader's eyes. The author's natural susceptibility to the savage beauties of the country is seconded by powers of description of the rarest sort; whilst his knowledge of, and sympathy for, the Indian character, kept his mind constantly open to every trait which could throw light upon their customs and superstitions."—*West. Rev.*

IX. Eighty Years Progress of British North America, by Messrs. Hind, Keefer, Robb, Perley and Murray. *Toronto*, 1863, pp. 776, 8vo.

X. A Preliminary Report on the Geology of New Brunswick, together with a special report on the distribution of the Quebec group in the Province. *Fredericton*, 1865, pp. 293, 8vo.

" It brings to bear a great mass of varied information derived from many sources."—*Can. Nat.*

Canadian Journal.

I. Notes on the Geology of Toronto. 1852.

II. On some of the Superstitions and Customs common among the Indians in the valley of the Assinniboine and Saskatchewan. 1859.

III. A glance at the political and commercial importance of Central British America. 1863.

IV. Observations on supposed glacial drift in the Labrador peninsula, Western Canada, and on the south branch of the Saskatchewan. *Proc. Geol. Soc.* (*Lon.*), 1864.

HINGSTON, WILLIAM HALES, *M. D.*, *L. R. C. S.*, (Edin.) Practising at Montreal, where he is Surgeon to the St. Patrick's department of the *Hôtel-Dieu*, and Vice-President of the Medico-Chirurgical Soc. Dr. H. was the first Can. admitted into the Imperial Leopold Academy

(Vienna). He is also a mem. of the *Soc. Medicale de Paris;* of the German Soc. of Naturalists and Physicians, and of the *Pollichia* of Bavaria. He has contributed to the medical press of Can.

Proceedings of the German Soc. of Naturalists and Physicians.

I. Anchylosis.

II. Medical Institutions of Paris.

III. Observations on Chloroform.

IV. Removal of Sub-maxillary gland.

V. Congenital Hydrocephalus.

VI. Uræmic Poisoning

VII. Mental Depression.

VIII. Medical Evidence.

IX. Muscular Fatigue.

X. Traumatic Aneurism.

XI. Re-vaccination.

XII. The Climate of Canada (several papers.)

HIRSCHFELDER, JACOB M. Lecturer on Oriental Literature, Univ. Coll. (Tor.)

I. A Key to German Conversation, consisting of familiar dialogues &c. calculated to facilitate the acquisition of that language. *Toronto*, 1845, pp. 96, 8vo.

II. An Essay on the Spirit and Characteristics of Hebrew Poetry. *Do.*, 1855, pp. 40, 8vo.

This has been adopted by the Senate as a text book in the Univ. of Toronto.

III. The Biblical Expositor. 3 Parts. Introduction ; New translation of Genesis with Critical, Philological and Explanatory Notes. *Do.*, pp. 78.

IV. The Scriptures Defended. Being a reply to Bishop Colenso's Book on the Pentateuch and the Book of Joshua. *Toronto* and *London*, 1863, pp. 216, 8vo.

"In a very candid spirit he meets the Bishop of Natal, and at the same time proves the groundlessness of his specious objections to the inspired records. Mr. Hirschfelder's intimate acquaintance with the Hebrew language, and with the customs of the Jews, gives him no small advantage in exposing the shallow reasoning of Colenso."—*Globe*, (Tor.)

HOBBS, J. S.
I. Sailing Directions for the Gulf and River of St. Lawrence. *London*, 1843, 8vo.

HODDER, EDWARD M., *M. D., M. R. C. S.* (Eng.) A medical practitioner in Toronto. Has written numerous medical and surgical papers for the Eng. medical press, and the *Can. Medical Journal*, (Mont.) Has been President of the U. C. Medical Board.

I. The Harbours and Ports of Lake Ontario ; in a series of [20] charts, accompanied by a description of each, together with the Lighthouses, Harbour lights, depth of water, &c. Compiled from authentic sources, recent surveys and personal observations. *Toronto*, 1857, 8vo.

II. Chart of Lake Ontario. *Do.*, 1863.

HODGE, THOMAS HOUNSELL. Wrote for B. A. Mag. under *nom de plume* of " H. T. Devon."

I. A Tale of the Bay of Quinte. *Brit. Am. Mag.*, Vol. I.

II. Leaves from the Life Romance of Merne Dillamer. *Do.*, Vol. II.

HODGES, JAMES, *C. E.* Engineer on behalf of the contractors, Messrs. Peto, Brassey and Betts, in the construction of the Victoria Bridge, (Mont.) Resides in Can.

I. Construction of the Victoria Bridge at Montreal, in Canada. Elaborately illustrated by Views, Plans, Elevations, and Details of the Bridge ; together with Designs of the Machinery and Contrivances used in the Construction, with a Descriptive Text. *London*, 1860, Imp., folio.

"The present volume was prepared by Mr. Hodges, the Engineer to the Contractors, who was in fact the true *Pontifex Maximus* of this stupendous tube, for the purpose of being presented to His Royal Highness on the occasion. The work has been printed and illustrated with almost unexampled magnificence. It bears the same relation to ordinary books that the Victoria Bridge itself bears to ordinary bridges."—*Edin. Review.*

HODGINS, JOHN GEORGE, *M. A., LL. B., F. R. G. S.* A Can. author. Son of Mr. William Hodgins, of Dublin, Irel. B. there 12 Augt., 1821. Came to Can. in 1833. Was Ed. at U. C. Academy, and Victoria Coll., Cobourg, from which latter institution he afterwards received the degree of M. A. Graduated in the Law Faculty of the Univ. (Tor.) in 1860 and received the degree of LL. B. In Oct., 1844, was appointed Senior Clk. in the Educational Department for U. C.; in 1846 Recording Clk. or Secy. to U. C. Board of Education (now Council of Public Instruction), and in 1855, Deputy Superintendent of Education for U. C., a position which he still retains, with much credit to himself and the Public Service. Mr. H. has written very largely on subjects of Educational and School Reform. Most of his contributions have appeared in the *Educational Journal of U. C.*, of which he has been joint Ed. since its establishment, but many papers from his pen have appeared in other publications, the principal of which are included in the following list :—

I. Geography and History of British America and of the other Colonies of the Empire. *Toronto*, 1857, pp. 128, small 4to. ; 2nd ed. 1860.

"We welcome, with sincere satisfaction, this little product of the Canadian Educational Press, as an attempt—and in most respects a very successful one—to supply a grave defect in the material for juvenile school teaching. * * * It will meet, at once, one of the most obvious wants of our scholastic system."—PROF. D. WILSON ; *Can. Journ.*

II. Sheet Lessons on General Geography. *Do.*, 1859–1865.

III. Lovell's General Geography.— (With Maps and Illustrations.) *Montreal*, 1861, pp. 100, 4to.

Numerous editions since.

"The colony produces many of its own school books, among which may be mentioned Lovell's General Geography, a trustworthy and attractive manual, remarkable for its clear arrangement and for the fullness of its illustrative and statistical contents."— *Report of the Jurors Educational Department International Ex.*, 1862.

"It is a vast improvement upon such works as have heretofore been in circulation in the country. * * * It is very evident that a great amount of labour and expense have been bestowed on the work."—SIR W. E. LOGAN, KT., F. R. S.

IV. Easy Lessons in General Geography. *Do.*, 1864, pp. 80, sm. 4to.

Other editions since.

"Geography is a delightful study, and these Lessons are a delightful method of imparting an interest in it to the young. The sketches are admirable, combining great ingenuity and tact with the use of easy and familiar language, in the treatment of such subjects as the Earth and its appearance, Time and its divisions, Geography, the Hemispheres, the Mariner's Compass, &c. The trips are designed to connect, in the mind of the pupil, the objects and associations of travel with a geographical knowledge of the more important physical features of the principal countries in the world. We are glad to see religion discreetly respected, and loyalty taught as one of its lessons."— *Presbyterian*, (Mont.)

V. School History of Canada and of the other British North American Provinces. *Do.*, 1865, pp. 282, 16mo.

" This little volume contains a vast number of facts about Canada and the British Provinces, the collecting of which must have cost the compiler an endless amount of labor. It can scarcely be called a history of the Provinces, although it contains much that the historian might advantageously avail himself of in writing a history of these countries. In the hands of judicious teachers, it may be found very useful in imparting to the young an outline of the chief events which have occurred in these Provinces since their discovery by Europeans."—*Globe*, (Tor.)

VI. School Manual for Upper Canada, with notes and digest of school cases tried before the Superior Courts. *Toronto*.

VII. The Canadian School Speaker and Reciter, containing a number of Prose and Poetical Pieces and Dialogues, suitable for Grammar and Common School Examinations and Exhibitions. *Preparing*.

VIII. Introductory Sketches and Stories for Junior Classes, based upon the History of Canada and of the other British Provinces in North America, for the use of Schools. (With Illustrations.) *Do.*

IX. First Steps in General Geography. (With Maps and Illustrations.) *Do.*

Periodical Press.

I. Education in Upper Canada. *Am. Journ. of Ed.* 1856.

II. Proteus of the Lakes. *Can. Journ.*, do.

III. Meteorological Statistics in Upper Canada, with Map. *Do.*, do.

IV. Education in Upper Canada : *Eighty Years Progress*, (Mont), 1863.

V. Education in Lower Canada. *Do*.

" A very valuable sketch. Comprises much in a small space."—*Am. His. Mag.*

VI. Educational Resources of Canada. *Can. Almanac*, 1863.

VII. Origin and Character of the Early Trade Contests between Canada and New York—The St. Lawrence *vs.* The Hudson. *Brit. Am. Mag.*, Vol. I.

" A very interesting paper."—*Am. His. Mag.*

VIII. Discoveries and Trade of the Rival French and English Colonists in the Hudson Bay Territories. *Do.*, Vol. II.

HODGINS, THOMAS, *M. A.*, *LL. B.* A Toronto Barrister. Brother of preceding. Is a graduate of the Univ. of that city. Was formerly in the Educational Office, U. C. Wrote " *Letters on University Education in Upper Canada, by a Bachelor of Arts* " and many articles on the same subject, in the newspaper press 1856–58. Contributed various legal articles and reports of cases decided in the Court of Chancery, U. C., and reports of controverted parliamentary election cases to the *U. C. Law Journal* (Tor.), 1858–65.

I. The Right of the Bible in our Common Schools, by George B. Cheever. With an introduction to the Canadian edition. *Toronto*, 1851, pp. 194, 8vo.

II. The Educational Manual for Upper Canada ; containing the Laws and Regulations relating to Common and Grammar Schools, and the University of Toronto, with explanatory notes. *Do.*, 1856, pp. 167, 8vo.

III. The Canadian Educational Directory ; containing an account of the Schools, Colleges and Universities, Scientific and Literary Societies in the Province ; with decisions of the Superior Courts in Upper Canada, relating to school questions &c. *Do.*, 1857, pp. 128, 8vo.

" Unpretending as this work is, it will be valuable to the historian of Canada, hereafter, when the harvest of the good seed-time is beginning to be reaped."—*Can. Journ.*

IV. The Municipal Reports ; containing reports of cases arising under the

Municipal and School Laws of Upper Canada. Edited by Robert A. Harrison, Esq., and Thomas Hodgins, Esq., Barristers at Law. *Do.*, 1863, pp. 774, 8vo.

HODGSON, ADAM.

I. Letters from North America, written during a Tour in the United States and Canada : *London*, 1824, 2 vols. 8vo.

HODGSON, *Rev.* J. F.

I. Plea for united responding in the Public Worship of God. *Toronto*, 1859, pp. 16. Reprinted.

HOGAN, JOHN SHERIDAN. A Can. journ. B. near Dublin, Irel., about 1815. Murdered, near Toronto, Dec., 1859. He early obtained employment as a newsboy in the office of the *Provincial Wesleyan* (Ham.): having learnt the printing trade he was promoted to be foreman of the office, and subsequently was admitted as a contributor to the paper. He studied law, and in 1844 was admitted as an Atty., and practised for some years in Hamilton. Giving up that profession, however, he proceeded to Toronto and established the *United Empire*, a weekly journal, which advocated High Church Toryism. This paper was ably conducted and met with fair support; it eventually became the property of the present prop. of the *Leader.* For some years Mr. H. acted as Parliamentary correspondent for several journals, and owing to his bold, bitter and unsparing style of writing, made few friends and many enemies. About this time (1850) he contributed some able articles on the aspect of affairs in Can: to *Blackwood's Mag.*, which did much to establish his reputation as a public writer. He also wrote *The New Year's Ode* in that year for the same periodical. In 1855 he was awarded the first prize by the Paris Exhibition Committee of Can. for his *Essay on Canada*, and about the same time became Ed. of the *Daily Colonist* (Tor.), a position which he held for some years, and which he only relinquished on account of a difference of opinion with the proprietors of the paper. At the general election in 1857 he was returned as a mem. to the Leg. Assem. in the Reform interest.

I. Canada. An Essay : to which was awarded the first prize by the Paris

Exhibition Committee of Canada.— (With Maps.) *Montreal*, 1855, pp. 110, 8vo.

" Mr. Hogan has furnished us with such an essay, which, though certainly not free from sins of omission and a sprinkling of errors, is capable of creating a very interesting, encouraging and truthful impression of many leading features in Canadian life, and of the encouraging future which lies within the reach of every immigrant, and is the sure destiny of the country at large."—*Can. Journ.*

II. Review of the Proceedings of the Reform Convention, held in the St. Lawrence Hall, Toronto 9th Nov., 1859. *Toronto*, pp. 15.

HOGG, JAMES. A N. B. poet and journ. B. at Leitrim, Irel. D. at Fredericton, N. B., 12 June, 1866. Several of his sketches and tales appeared in the *University Mag.* (Dub.), the *Albion* (N. Y.), and in Eng. journals. Had been Ed. and Prop. of the *New Brunswick Reporter* (Fredericton) for some years prior to his death, and was preparing a volume of original poems for the press.

I. Poems. *St. John, N. B.*, 1825, pp. 270.

II. Poems. Religious, Moral and Sentimental. *Fredericton.*

HOGG, *Rev.* JOHN. A Min. of the Presb. Ch. of Can. In 1854 assisted to establish a monthly religious publication, called : The *Waymarks in the Wilderness*, (Ham.), to which he contributed many interesting and instructive articles.

HOLCOMBE, JAMES P.

I. The Law of Debtor and Creditor in the United States and Canada. *New York*, 8vo, N. D.

HOLIWELL, *Mrs.* M. J. H. A Can. authoress. (Tor.) Contributed to the *Newsboy*, (Tor.), 1854, the *Home Journal*, (do.), 1861, and the *Brit. Am. Mag.*, (do.), 1863-4. (See two essays *The Poetry of Everyday Life*, and *The Love of Reading* in that mag.)

I. The Old World and the New ; a novel. *Globe*, (Tor.), 1859.

II. The Earles in Canada ; a tale. *Do.*, 1862.

III. The Settler's Daughter. *Brit. Am. Mag.*, 1863.

IV. Address to Parents on the Education of Girls. *Toronto*, 1865, pp. 16, 8vo.

HOLLAND, *Rev.* HENRY, *M. A.* Of Queen's Coll. Cambridge. Rector of St. Catharines, U. C.

I. Christ's Prerogative in the choice of His Servants ; a sermon. *Toronto*, 1857, pp. 22.

HOLLAND, SAMUEL. "Surveyor Genl. of Lands for the Northern District of North America."

I. Observations made on the Islands of St. John and Cape Breton, to ascertain the longitude and latitude of those places, agreeable to the orders and instructions of the Rt. Hon. the Lords Commissioners for Trade and Plantations. *Phil. Trans.*, 1768.

II. Astronomical Observations. *Do.*, 1769.

III. Eclipses of Jupiter's Satellites, observed near Quebec. *Do.*, 1774.

IV. Astronomical Observations. *Do.*

HOLLINGWORTH, S.

I. The Present State of Nova Scotia : with a brief account of Canada, and the British Islands on the coast of North America. *Edinburgh*, 1787, pp. 221, 8vo. ; Translated into French : *Paris*, 1787, 8vo.

"The account here given of the rapid growth of the infant settlement of Nova Scotia, especially since the termination of the war with our late colonists, is really astonishing, and leaves us no room to doubt the very great advantages which will, in all human probability, accrue to the mother country from the welfare and prosperity of this her youngest child."—*Mon. Rev.*, (Lon.)

HOLMES, ANDREW FERNANDO, *M. D., LL. D.* A Can. Medical Practitioner. B. at Cadiz, 1797. D. at Montreal, 9 Sept. 1860. Came to Can. with his parents in 1801, and after receiving his ed. at the Royal Grammar Sch. (Mont.), proceeded to Edinburgh, where he took his medical degree. He was an ardent student of Botany, Geology and Mineralogy, and brought with him to Can. on his return, an extensive herbarium of plants, and a large collection of minerals and geological specimens which formed the nucleus of a splendid collection which he subsequently presented to McGill Coll. In conjunction with others he founded and was for a long period an active mem. and office-bearer of the Natural History Soc. (Mont.) His catalogue of the minerals and geological specimens in its museum is a monument of untiring industry. In 1824, with the assistance of some other members of the profession, he established the Medical Institution of the same city, and delivered courses of lectures before it, which were afterwards recognized by the Univ. of Edinburgh, on the principle of two courses for one of that Univ. In 1828 the Institution became merged in the Univ. of McGill, and from that time up to 1844, Dr. H. filled the chair of Chemistry and Materia Medica, when he was called to that of Principles and Practice of Medicine, a position, the duties of which he continued to discharge until his death. From the time of the new organization of the Univ., he was Dean of the Faculty. Besides controversial writings on medical subjects, Dr. H. was the author of many important papers, which, from time to time, appeared in the medical periodicals. Several of them appeared in the *Medical and Surgical Journal* (Bos.), before any medical serial was published in Can ; one paper especially which attracted some notice at the time " *The History of the Cholera at Montreal*, was a contribution to that journal. His first paper " *On the intrauterine crying of the child*," appeared in the *Med. Journal* (Edin.) He contributed some interesting cases on " *Heart Disease*," and an elaborate paper on " *Fatal Jaundice*," to the *Med. Chronicle* (Mont.) To the well-known *Brit. Am. Journal* of the same city, he contributed the following : 1. *On fleshy tubercle of the uterus ;*—2. *A case of wound of the heart without rupture of the pericardium ;*—3. *A case of femoral hernia ;*—4. *Obstruction of the appendix vermiformis ;*—5. *A case of the employment of chloroform.* Dr. H. was an honorary mem. of many scientific and literary bodies on both sides of the Atlantic.

(See *Hall, Dr. A.*)

HOLMES, GERVAS. A Can. journ. B. at Retford, Eng., Jan. 1826. Came to Can. in 1852, and during the 6 months of his stay, ed. the *Gazette* (Ham.) Failing health caused him to return to Eng. in the same year, but in June 1855 he again came to Can. In 1856 he became Ed. of the *Star* (Cobourg), a Liberal Conservative paper, where he remained until 1863, when ill health again compelled him to abandon his connection with the press. Mr. H. has contributed occasionally to the *Rural New Yorker* (Rochester N. Y.), and the *Canada Farmer* (Tor.) He still resides at Cobourg.

HOLMES, *Rev.* JOHN. A R. C. clergym. B. at Windsor, Vermont, 1799. D. at Lorette, near Quebec, 1852. Was studying for the ministry of the Wesl. Ch. when he became a convert to Romanism. Was for a lengthened period prof. of philosophy and a director of the Seminary (Que.) He was considered a very eloquent pulpit orator.

I. Histoire Ancienne des Egyptiens, des Assyriens, des Mèdes et des Perses, des Grecs et des Carthaginois, à l'usage de la jeunesse. *Québec*, 1831.

II. Nouvel abrégé de géographie moderne, suivi d'un appendice, et d'un abrégé de géographie sacrée à l'usage de la jeunesse ; en deux parties. *Do.* 1832, pp. 300, 12mo.; 6th Ed., 1862, pp. 894.

" The geography of Mr. Holmes will replace the school works hitherto imported from abroad, which always contain inaccuracies in descriptions of Canada and America generally."—*L. C. Journ. of Ed.*

III. Conférences de Notre Dame de Québec. *Do.*, 1850, pp. xxiii and 137, 8vo.

HOMER, JOHN, *M. P.* for Barrington, N. S. I. A Brief Sketch of the present state of the Province of Nova Scotia ; with a project offered for its relief. *Halifax*, 1834, pp. 31, 8vo.

HONEY, JOHN. Joint Prothonotary, (Mont.) I. Tables of Fees to Attorneys and Officers of the Courts of Law, exhibiting without calculation the amount of fees and disbursements in suits ; together with Rules of Practice of the Court of Queen's Bench, and Tariffs of Fees for Registrars, Advocates and Officers of the Courts, including schedules of taxes upon proceedings in the Courts of Civil and Criminal jurisdiction, Lower Canada. *Montreal*, 1862.

HOOKER, *Sir* WILLIAM JACKSON, *K. H., D. C. L.* A distinguished Eng. Naturalist. B. 1785. D. 12 Augt., 1865.

I. Flora Boreali-Americana ; or the Botany of the northern parts of British America : compiled from the Plants collected on the late Northern Expeditions under Capt. Sir John Franklin ; to which are added those of Mr. Douglas, from North West America, etc. *London*, 1840, 2 vols. 4to.

II. Suggestions to the Members of the Botanical Society of Canada, with reference to a Colonial Flora. *Trans. Bot. Soc. Can.*, 1861. •

HOOTON, CHARLES. An Eng. writer. I. St. Louis' Isle, or Texiana ; with additional observations made in the United States and Canada. (Portrait). *London*, 1847, 8vo.

HOPE, *Rev.* HENRY, *LL. B.* Ed. the *Old Countryman* newspaper (Tor.) for many years.

I. Letters from Canada. *London*, 1863, pp. 83, 8vo.

" These letters contain that kind of information which will be useful to the intending emigrant ; they give the experience of one who has cast his lot in Canada, and who from it affords all encouragement to others to follow his example."—*The Field*, (Lon.)

HONSNELL, WILLIAM, (Mont.) Has written various fugitive poems for the Can. press.

I. The Ice-bound Ship, and the Dream ; by W. H. *Montreal*, 1860, pp. 48, 8vo.

HORTON. *Sir* R. WILMOT, *Bart.* I. Ireland and Canada ; supported by local evidence. *London*, 1839, pp. 78.

HOSE, G. (Mont.) I. Chemical Tables ; containing a list of the Elementary Substances, with their symbols and atomic weights, and the general principles of the chemical nomenclature, for the use of Students. *Montreal*, 1845.

HOSKINS, BRADFORD S. I. A Few Thoughts on Volunteering. *Quebec*, 1862, pp. 24, 8vo.

HOUGH, FRANKLIN B. I. Papers Concerning the Attack on Hatfield and Deerfield, by a party of

Indians from Canada, September nineteenth, 1677. *New York*, 1859, pp. 82., 8vo. Map.

II. Diary of the Siege of Detroit in the War with Pontiac. Also, a Narrative of the Principal Events of the Siege, by Major Robert Rogers. A Plan for conducting Indian Affairs, by Colonel Bradstreet ; and other authentic documents never before printed. Edited with Notes. *Albany, N. Y.*, 1860, pp. 301, 4to.

How, Henry, *D. C. L.* Prof. of Chemistry and Natural History in Univ. of King's Coll., Windsor, N. S.

I. On the Occurrence of Natroborocalcite in Gypsum of Nova Scotia. *Sill. Journ.*, 1857.

II. Analysis of Faroëlite and some other Zeolitic Minerals occurring in Nova Scotia. *Do.*, 1858.

III. Analysis and Description of Three New Minerals from Trap of Nova Scotia. *Edin. New Phil. Journ.*, 1859.

IV. On an Oil-Coal from Pictou Co., Nova Scotia. *Sill. Journ.* and *Edin. New Phil. Journ.*, 1860.

V. On Gyrolite occurring in Trap of Nova Scotia. *Edin. New Phil. Journ.* and *Sill. Journ.*, 1861.

VI. On Natroborocalcite and another Borate in Gypsum of Nova Scotia. *Sill. Journ.*, 1861.

VII. On Pickeringite occurring in Nova Scotia. *Quart. Journ. Chem. Soc.*, 1863.

VIII. On Mordenite, a New Mineral from Trap of Nova Scotia. *Do.*, 1864.

IX. On some Mineral Waters of Nova Scotia. *Can. Nat.*, 1863.

X. On the Waters of the Mineral Springs of Wilmot, N. S. *Trans. N. S. Inst.*, 1864.

XI. Notes on the Economic Mineralogy of Nova Scotia. Part I. Iron Ores. *Do.*, 1864.

XII. Note on Purification of Ozolic Acid. *Chem. News*, 1864.

XIII. On a Dense Brine from Salt Springs, N. S., 1865.

XIV. On some Brine Springs of Nova Scotia. 1865.

XV. Notes on Economic Mineralogy of N. S. Part II. Ores of Manganese. *Trans. N. S. Inst.*, 1865.

XVI. Do. do. Part III. Limestone and Marble. *Do.*, 1866.

XVII. Contributions to the Mineralogy of Nova Scotia. *Phil. Mag.*, 1866.

XVIII. Sketch of Mineralogy of Nova Scotia, as illustrated by the collection of minerals sent to the Paris Exhibition. *Halifax*, 1867.

Howard, Henry, *M. D., M. R. C. S.*, (Lon.) B. at Nenagh, Tipperary, Irel., 1 Dec., 1815, where he was ed. Studied his profession in Dublin, attending the lectures in the Coll. of Surgeons and the Univ. of Trinity Coll. After practising in Dublin and Co. Leitrim, emigrated to Can., in 1841. For a short time resided upon Amherst Island, U. C., then at Kingston, and finally took up his residence in Montreal. At the latter city he was afforded an opportunity, for which he had always longed, to devote his whole time to Eye and Ear Surgery. In 1861 was appointed Medical Supdt. of the Lunatic Asylum at St. John's, L. C., a position which he still retains. Dr. H. has been a contributor to the *Medical Press* (Dub.,) and from 1845 to 1859, wrote many valuable papers in the *B. A. Journ.* (Mont.)

I. The Anatomy, Physiology, and Pathology of the Eye. *Montreal* and *London*, 1850, pp. 505, 8vo.

"This work is evidently the production of a man thoroughly acquainted with the subject of which he treats. The anatomical section comprises, with a few exceptions, all the discoveries of modern anatomists."— *Lancet*, (Lon.)

Howard, J. H.

I. Laws of the British Colonies in America, concerning Real and Personal Property, and manumission of slaves; with a view of the Constitution of each colony. *London*, 1827, 2 vols. 8vo.

Howard, Middleton, of Wadham Coll., Oxford.

I. The Conquest of Quebec : a poem. *Oxford*, 1768, 4to.

Howe, *Hon.* Joseph. A Can. orator, statesman and journ. B. on the North-West Arm, N. S., 1804.

"Here" says his biographer, "he spent the first thirteen years of his life; and here was nurtured the robust constitution which, for half a century, has seemed to defy mental and bodily fatigue. Here was imbibed the love of nature, of field sports, of the sea, of woodland rides and rambles, which are still retained. Here was nourished the poetic spirit, that, in all the earlier portions of his life, broke out into verse; and which, though chastened and subdued by a severe political training, colors all his speeches and writings still. He received no regular education, having to walk two miles to get to school in summer, and in winter being kept at home. But he had his father to talk to in the long evenings, and books to study. Hard exercise and desultory reading alternated, and a well-stored mind was ever present with him, upon the large resources of which he could at any moment draw."

Of his ancestry Mr. H. gives the following account in one of his speeches in Eng. :

"During the old times of persecution, four brothers, bearing my name, left the southern counties of England, and settled in four of the old New England States. Their descendants number thousands, and are scattered from Máine to California. My father was the only descendant of that stock, who, at the Revolution, adhered to the side of England. His bones rest in the Halifax churchyard. I am his only surviving son."

We may add that his father, who d. in 1835, was for many years King's Printer and Postmaster Genl. of N. S. When 13, he was placed in the *Gazette* office, where he worked for 10 weeks at the printing business, occasionally assisting his brother in the post office, and sometimes, during his absence, taking charge of both offices. Mr. H. made his first appearance in print while still an apprentice, by the publication of a little poem, entitled *Melville Island*, which Mr. Annand informs us attracted general attention :

"This island stands at the head of the North-West Arm. Prisoners were confined there during the last French and American wars. The situation and incidents connected with the island were poetical, and perhaps the most was made of them. Other pieces in prose and verse followed and were published in the newspapers of the period under anonymous signatures. He thus trained himself by the practice of composition, rather than by the study of language."

Whilst on this subject we can state that some of his later poems, written

occasionally during and eventful career, generally admired.
Fathers, breathes a fir
The Song for the Center
ing of Halifax, wri[t]
which has been se
patriotic outburst of
might feel proud :

"Hail to the day ! when tl
And planted their standard
Above and around us thei
Rejoicing to mark how w
Beneath it the emblem
waving,—
The Rose of Old England
The Shamrock and This
braving ;
Securely the Mayflower k

Of his comic squibs
poons *The Lord of*
written on Lord Fa
at one time Lt. Go
most amusing. Fror
room, Mr. H. soon
the ed. sanctum. In
the *Weekly Chronicle;*
name to the *Acadian*
career as a public w
year in which he
made no attempts a[t]
In Jany. 1828, he p
Scotian journal, from
for £1050, a large su
newspaper at that
of his share in the *A*
sole ed. and propri
Scotian, and continue
years. Of his effor
overcome popular pr
youth, supposed inal
rience in the manag
and important an or
undoubtedly no one
tell. Let it suffice
say that by dint of
domitable energy an
surmounted all the
position, and establi[s]
a sure and solid foun
nand draws a lively
and active life duri
tion of his editorial

"British, foreign, and
and periodicals, were
bates in the House o
portant trials in the cc
by his own hand, and
brought him into fami
nearly all the public r
establishment of agenci

tion of business, in the interior, compelled him to travel over the inland districts and to visit all the seaport towns. In these journeys many valuable acquaintances were made, and much information was acquired. Gradually he became familiar, not only with the people best worth knowing, and from whom anything could be learnt, but with the whole face of his native country; and with the political literature of all countries which expressed their opinions in the English language. Such leisure as he had was given to more serious investigations, or to the attractive novelties of the day. I have often seen him, during this period, worn out with labor, drawing draughts of refreshment alternately from Bulwer's last novel or from Grotius on National Law. His constitution was vigorous, his zeal unflagging. It was no uncommon thing for him to be a month or two in the saddle; or, after a rubber of racquets, in which he excelled, and of which he was very fond, to read and write for four or five consecutive days without going out of his house.

" Seven years of this kind of mental training, which preceded his first noticeable display as a public speaker, did much to repair a very defective education. I have glanced over the files of the *Nova Scotian* from 1828 to 1835, and, to any body who will do the same, the process of intellectual cultivation and development, will be very apparent.

" In the volume for 1828, there are almost no politics. Those sketches of country towns and rural scenery, which, under the heading of " Western and Eastern Rambles," enlivened the pages of the *Nova Scotian* for several years, and enlightened a good many worthy people who never go from home as to the beauties and fertility of their own country, were commenced in this year. So was the Club, a series of papers, after the model of Blackwood's Noctes Ambrosianæ, and to which Sam Slick, Doctor Grigor, Lawrence O'Connor Doyle, and Captain Kincaid, all of whom subsequently distinguishhd themselves in other fields, are said to have contributed. There was, perhaps, too much of personality in these dialogues, but there was unquestionably a good deal of wit, humor and vigorous writing. There is also in the earlier files, some beautiful poetry, by Henry Clinch, then a student at King's College, and now Rector of South Boston, a gentleman whose productions I hope yet to see in some collected form in every library in the Province.

" In 1829, Huskisson's system was promulgated, and Mr. Howe, who had previously been an admirer of Adam Smith, became thenceforward an ardent Free Trader, in which faith he has continued down to the present time. In this year he published Haliburton's *History of Nova Scotia*, losing heavily by the speculation, the edition being, at that early period, too large. The book, however was invaluable."

13 *

Henceforth, his pen became a power in the province, and his reputation extended. In 1830 he commenced in his paper a series of " *Legislative Reviews*," which were continued from year to year, and were the means of bringing before the people the short-comings of public men and the necessity of various reforms. In 1836 he was tried for libel by the municipal body of Halifax, under which great neglect, mismanagement and corruption had been generated. He defended his own cause, and had the satisfaction not only of gaining his case, but of arousing such a storm of public indignation against the effete and disordered system of civic govt. as eventually extinguished it, in no very long time. For his public-spirited and fearless conduct on this occasion he was presented with a service of plate by his countrymen. At the end of 1841, Mr. H. retired from the ed. management of the *Nova Scotian*, and disposed of the paper. Subsequently Mr. Annand became its proprietor. In 1844, Mr. H. was induced by the parliamentary leaders of the liberal party, to resume his journalistic functions, and from that time until 1856 he ed. his old paper, and in addition the *Morning Chronicle*, a new journal, which had been established, also the property of Mr. Annand. In both these papers, Mr. H. waged an uncompromising warfare against the unconstitutional administration of Lord Falkland :

" Those who glance over the files for 1844 and 1845, will find in them everywhere traces of the activity and fecundity of a vigorous mind, resolutely directed to one object. Mr. Howe's pen, ever playful and energetic. was wielded with great effect, and the organized band of scribblers that the Governor had gathered around him, soon began to discover that they were to have no child's play. He pelted them with prose one day and poetry the next, so that they were puzzled to decide whether he had studied Junius to most advantage or Hanbury Williams."

Mr. H. first entered the N. S. legislature in 1835, and sat as a mem. of the Assem. with but slight interruption, from that time until 1863, when he received an appointment from Her Majesty as Fishery Commissioner. He was for a lengthened period the leader of the Liberal party, once Speaker of the Assem., a mem. of several administrations, and, we believe, twice Prime Minister of his native province. He laboured long and earnestly for the principle of Responsible Govt., and it was owing to his great and unceasing efforts that that principle was at length conceded to the B. A. Colonies If to have done nothing else for his country, surely that of itself is sufficient to cause his name to be honored while living, and his memory revered, when dead, by all true Canadians, to the latest time. He was one of the first to promote the establishment of steam communication and the conveyance of mail matter by steamships between Europe and Am. He early projected an intercolonial railway between Can. and the Maritime Provinces, and was a strong and able advocate for the Union of all the B. N. A. Provinces. He has also sought for the representation of the Colonies in the British House of Commons. As an orator, Mr. H.'s reputation is not simply provincial. His eloquence is great and overflowing. As a debater, public speaker or lecturer, he has few equals on the Am. Continent.

I. Address before Halifax Mechanic's Institute. *Halifax*, 1834, pp. 23, 8vo.

II. The Practicability and Importance of connecting Halifax with all the counties lying round the Basin of Mines by means of a Railroad to Windsor. *Do.* 1835.

III. " Responsible Government, " Letters to the Rt. Hon. Lord John Russell, on the right of British Americans to be governed by the principles of the British Constitution. *Do.* 1839, pp. 48, 8vo.

IV. Letters to the Right Hon. Lord John Russell on the Government of British America. *London*, 1846.

" He pleads, and justly, for the more general employment of Colonists in offices of trust in the Provincial Post Offices, Customs Department, &c. He urges the raising of Colonial corps—the manning of men-of-war from special colonies and argues for Colonial representation in the Imperial Parliament. He suggests that the five North American Colonies should be allowed to elect ten members—viz: Canada three, Prince Ed-

ward's Island one, and the others two members each."—Sim: *Col. Mag.*

"In Mr. Howe's second letter to Lord John Russell, the personal disabilities of the Colonists are exposed with ability and great freedom. He declares that there is a universal determination to rest satisfied with no inferiority of social or political condition."—*N. A. Rev.*

V. Letters to Earl Grey. *Do.* 1850.

" He could not close without again referring to the Hon. Mr. Howe, and repeating his opinion that no colonist could peruse those magnificent letters addressed by him when in England to Earl Grey on the subject of Colonial interests, without a feeling of pride and gratification ; and whatever may be the issue of the final proceedings that he (Mr. Howe) had performed a noble duty to British America."—Speech of Hon. E. Chandler.

VI. Speech at Southampton, England, on the importance and value to Great Britain of Her North American Colonies. *Do.* 1851, pp. 28.

" The speech delivered by Mr. Howe on this accasion is perhaps one of his best."—Hon. W. Annand.

VII. Speech at Halifax on Intercolonial Railroads and Colonization. *Halifax*, 1851, pp. 24, 8vo.

" It was here that he delivered that speech which Lord Grey informed him was ' one of the best that he had ever read.' "—*Ibid.*

VIII. Speech on the Importance and Value to Great Britain of her North American Colonies. *London*, 1851, 8vo.

IX. A Letter to the people of Nova Scotia against Irish Roman Catholics. pp. 9, 8vo.

X. Letter to the Hon. Francis Hincks. Being a review of his reply to Mr. Howe's speech on the Organization of the Empire. *Halifax*, 1855, pp. 22, 8vo.

XI. Letter to Rt. Hon. W. E. Gladstone. Being a review of the debate on the Foreign Enlistment Bill and our Relations with the United States. *London*, 1856, 8vo.

XII. Letters on the recent Railway Riots, their causes and results ; and the political position of the " Young Ireland Brigade." *Halifax*, 1857.

XIII. Lecture before St. John Early Closing Association. *St. John*, 1859. pp. 17, 8vo.

XIV. Letter to the Rt. Hon. C. B. Adderley, M. P., on the relations of

England with her Colonies. *London,* 1863, pp. 61, 8vo.

Republished by Hon. Isaac Buchanan: *Hamilton,* 1863.

XV. Shakspeare; an oration delivered at the request of the St. George's Society at the Temperance Hall, 23rd April, 1864. *Halifax,* 1864, pp. 25, 8vo,

XVI. Speech at the International Commercial Convention at Detroit. *Hamilton* and *Montreal,* 1865.

Several reprints.

"The oration of Hon. Joseph Howe was undoubtedly the great event of the sessions of that body. It combined, eloquence, argument, and rhetoric in the most masterly manner, and throughout gave evidence of the highest order of oratorical ability."—*Tribune,* (Detroit.)

XVII. The Organization of the Empire. *London,* 1866, pp. 30.

"The Hon. Joseph Howe, of Nova Scotia, has made himself well known as the eloquent and pertinacious opponent of that project for the Confederation of the North American provinces of which we have heard so much lately. Apparently, it is in part with a view to show the world that a statesman may be thoroughly hostile to that scheme and yet a firm supporter of British connection that he has now given us, in the compass of a very short pamphlet, his views on the ' Organization of the Empire.' Whether we agree with him or not, we cannot fail to do justice to the clear, concise masculine manner in which he has treated and really developed so extensive a topic in the space of thirty pages. Accustomed as we are on great colonial questions to the endless see-saw of orators in Parliament, and journalists in this country, always afraid of saying too much or too little, it is a great relief to meet with a colonist who knows what he means and wants, and can put it forward for our consideration in unmistakable English. Nor is it less satisfactory to see the hopeful and courageous frame of mind in which he opens the discussions."—*Pall Mall Gazette,* (Lon.)

XVIII. Confederation considered in relation to the interests of the Empire. *Do.* 1866.

"Any person of ordinary intelligence reading Mr. Howe's pamphlet cannot fail to be struck with its want of logical coherency. It is like a quilt of patchwork, very clumsily put together, without any regard to the harmony of colours * * * In his anxiety to write down Confederation, he has ignored all the rules of logic with the most astonishing recklessness."—*Reporter,* (Hal.)

"Let any reader, be he the most astute of logicians, analyze it as carefully as he may, from beginning to end, and he cannot find one clearly, openly, manfully expressed argument—an argument reasoned syllogistically from premises to conclusion, for or against any thing whatever, throughout the whole of this mass of words. This is assertion. If proof is asked,—Lo ! the pamphlet itself."—P. S. HAMILTON.

The Speeches and Public Letters of the Hon. Joseph Howe. Edited by William Annand, M. P. P. *Boston,* 1858, 2 Vols., pp. 642–558, R. 8vo.

"In the works now before us, we are invited to survey the intellectual proportions of another of her sons, who, in real, practical value, has conferred more service on his native country than any of those we have named. Though for the first time his career is thus brought completely before us, we have not been so distant as not to have caught the echo of his cheering cry, as for the last twenty years he has led the battle of civil and religious liberty in the British Colonies. We have taken sufficient interest in colonial politics to know that, in every one of those arduous conflicts by which Nova Scotia and her surrounding colonies wrung from the parent country independent institutions, his plume waved in front, and that to his undaunted perseverance and energy the final victory was largely due. Free institutions once attained, Mr. Howe appears to have devoted his attention almost entirely to the development of the material resources of the colony, and we find his name for the past few years connected with projects of intercolonial railroads, and other measures of internal improvement. The first volume records his political labours and services from 1828, when he began his career as a journalist, down to 1840, when Responsible Government became firmly established in British America. In the second volume we have his railway and colonization speeches, his public letters on various subjects, two or three admirable lectures delivered before scientific and literary societies, and a few grave and satiric poems."—*Tribune,* (N. Y.)

HOWISON, JOHN.

I. Sketches of Upper Canada, Domestic, Local and Characteristic: to which are added, Practical Details for the information of Emigrants of every class, and some Recollections of the United States. *Edinburgh,* 1821, pp. 356, 8vo.

HUDON, JOSEPH MAGLOIRE, *Q. C.* A Can. journ. B. at Rivière Ouelle, L. C., 1821. Studied for the Bar, and in 1844, while yet a student, founded *L'Artisan* (Que.), a paper devoted to the

interests of home industry and literature. Later he joined Mr. Plamondon
on the well known literary and musical periodical, *Le Ménestrel*.

HUESTIS, *Capt.*
I. Adventures during his banishment
from Canada to Van Dieman's Land.
Boston, 1848, 12mo.

HUME, GEORGE.
I. Canada as it is. *New York*, 1832,
18mo.

HUMPHREY, *Rev.* W. H.
I. The Sabbath : a moral and positive institution ; two sermons. *Halifax*, 1860, pp. 32, 8vo.

HUNT, GILBERT J.
I. History of the late War between
the United States and Great Britain,
from 1812 to 1815, written in Scripture
style. *New York*, 1819, 12mo.

HUNTER, *Rev.* JOHN. Min. of Chalmer's
Ch. (Hal.) Returned to Eng., 1861.
I. Review of E. Maturin's Letter ; a
Lecture. *Halifax*, 1859, pp. 40, 12mo.
II. The Age and its Young Men ; a
Lecture. *Do.*, pp. 11, 8vo.

HUNTER, ROBERT, *M. D.*
I. Hydro-Therapeutics, or a Treatise
on the Water Cure ; being a digest of
the opinions and experience of some
of the most distinguished Physicians
in Europe and America, on the Cura-
tive virtues of Water &c. *Toronto*,
1848, pp. 95.

HUNTER, WILLIAM S.
I. Ottawa Scenery, Canada West.
Ottawa, 1855, 4to.
II. Panoramic Guide from Niagara
Falls to Quebec. (Map and illus-
trations.) *Boston*, 1857, pp. 56, 12mo.

HUOT, L. H.
I. Le Rougisme en Canada. Par un
Observateur. *Québec*, 1864, pp. 79.

HURD, J. C.
I. Lecture on the prospective tri-
umph of the Temperance Reformation.
Halifax, 1855, pp. 17, 8vo.

HURLBURT, J. BEAUFONT, *M. A.*, *LL. D.*,
K. C. T. A Can. Author. B. in Augusta,
Co. Grenville, U. C. His grandparents,
paternal and maternal, were U. E.
Loyalists. Completed his education at
Yale Coll., Conn., U. S. Studied the
Oriental languages under Dr. Nord-

heimer, N. Y. Was for some time
Principal of U. C. Academy, (Cob.) In
1843 was appointed acting Principal
and Prof. of Latin, Greek and Hebrew,
in the Univ. of Victoria Coll., (do.) In
1858 was admitted to the Bar of U. C.
In 1861 served as a Commissioner on
behalf of Can., and was one of the Jurors of the International Exhibition.
(Lon.) During the last 20 years has
written on various subjects for the
Can. press, and occasionally for foreign
reviews. Some of his papers on scientific subjects have appeared in *Silliman's
Journal.*

I. The Forests of Canada. *Montreal*,
1862.

II. Britain and her Colonies. *London*,
1865, pp. 270, Large 8vo.

" A work well worthy the attention of
English statesmen. It gives a history of
colonization, ancient and modern, so far as
it illustrates the object of the author—the
continuance of the relations, and upon a
similar basis, between England and her colonies."—*Athen.*, (Lon.)

HURLBURT, *Rev.* THOMAS. A Wes. Meth.
Min. and Indian Missionary. Is known
for his extensive acquaintance with
the Indian languages. B. in Tp. of
Augusta, U. C., March 1808. Has been
37 years a Missionary amongst the Indians, and in that capacity has travelled
from Texas to Hudson's Bay, and
through most of the intervening regions. Has preached in both Chippewa
and Cree. In 1857 translated and
published the Gospel of St. John, and
7 of the smaller Epistles in the Cree
language ; and in 1860-1 published
and ed. a small paper at Sarnia, in the
Chippewa language, called *Petaubun*,
(Peep-of-Day.) Mr. H. has also contributed to the *Christian Guardian*
(Tor.), on subjects connected with Indian affairs ; and several articles from
his pen have appeared in the *Methodist
Quarterly Rev.* (Bos.)

" It (*Petaubun*) is certainly a novelty in
Canada, and probably such a thing was
never before attempted, as a periodical in
the Chippewa. The editor of *Petaubun* is
probably the only man living, competent to
the task, having written largely and preached
for thirty years in their native tongues. That
he has been a close observer, what he has
already written upon the tribes he has visited, and the able articles he has published

upon the geology and geography of the interior of the continent, abundantly prove. His perseverence has been shown by his casting type, making his press and printing, while in the Hudson's Bay, the Scriptures in the Cree language, and this without having had any previous knowledge of any of these arts."—*Spectator*, (Ham.)

HUSTON, J. Asst. French translator Leg. Assem. Can. D. at Quebec, 21 Sept., 1854.

I. Le Répertoire National, ou Recueil de Littérature Canadienne. *Montréal*, 1848, vol. I., pp. 368 ; vol. II., pp. 376 ; vol. III., pp. 384; vol. IV., 1850, pp. 404, 8vo.

HUTCHINS, THOMAS. Was Gov. of Albany Fort, Hudson's Bay Territory.

I. On the success of some attempts to freeze Quicksilver, at Albany Fort, in Hudson's Bay, in the year 1775 ; with observations on the Dipping Needle. *Phil. Trans.*, 1776.

HUTCHINSON, *Rev.* D. FALOON, *A. M.* Min. of St. Paul's Ch., Bridgewater, N. S. Ed. of the *Burning Bush* (Hal.)

I. A Rhetorical Catechism. *Belleville*, 1850, pp. 156.

II. Satisfaction of Justice ; a poem. *Kingston*, 1851, pp. 50.

III. A Class Book on Rhetoric, wherein are exhibited the graces and style of English composition and Public oratory. *Hamilton*, 1853, pp. 175 ; 2nd Ed. *Chicago, U. S.*, 1861.

IV. Astronomical Philosophy. *Kingston*, 1855.

V. Discourse on Christian Baptism.

VI. The Puseyism and Semi-Popery of the Rev. J. M. Cramp, D. D., being a reply to the literary character of a catechism recently published by that gentleman on Christian Baptism. *Halifax*, 1866, pp. 24.

HUTTON, WILLIAM. Secy. of the Bureau of Agriculture, Can., from 1853 until his death, 19 July, 1861.

I. Canada, a Brief Outline of her Geographical position, productions, climate, capabilities, educational and municipal institutions, &c. *Quebec*, 3rd Ed., 1861, pp. 64, 8vo.

II. Caird's Erroneous View of Canada answered and refuted. *Toronto*, 1858.

HUYGHUE, DOUGLAS S. B. at St. John, N. B. ; now resides in Australia. Contributed largely to Brit. and Am. periodical Literature.

I. Nomades of the West ; or Ellen Clayton. *London*, 1850, 3 vols, post, 8vo.

II. Argimon ; an Indian tale.

I. . .

IBBOTSON, HENRY J. Deputy Clk. of Recorder's Court (Mont.) Has occasionally contributed articles and sketches to the Can. newspaper press, and was ed. of 2 journals for a brief period. Wrote sketch of *Policeman X* in *Brit. Am. Mag.* (Tor.) 1863.

INGALL, *Lieut.*

I. District traversed by the St. Maurice Expedition, in 1829. *Trans. Lit. & His. Soc.* (Que.) Vol. II.

II. Remarks on the Country lying between the Rivers St. Maurice and Saguenay. *Do.* Do.

INGERSOLL, CHARLES JARED. An Am. author.

I. Historical sketch of the Second War between the United States of America and Great Britain, declared by Act of Congress, the 18th of June, 1812, and concluded by peace the 15th of February, 1815. *Philadelphia*, 1845–1852, 8vo., 4 vols.

INGLIS, *Rev.* DAVID. Min. of the Can. Presb. Ch. (Ham.) Has contributed occasionally to the religious press.

I. On the relation of Quantity to the Æsthetic sentiment. *Can. Journ.*, 1858.

II. Righteousness Exalteth a Nation : a thanksgiving sermon. *Hamilton*, 1866, pp. 14.

INGLIS, *Rt. Rev.* CHARLES, *D. D.* First Anglican Bish. of N. S. B. in Pennsylvania, U. S., about 1734. D. at Halifax,

N. S., 24 Feby., 1816. An U. E. Loyalist. Was Asst. Rector of Trinity Ch. N. Y., from 1764 to 1777, when he became Rector, a position which he resigned in 1783. Appointed Bish. of N. S. in 1787, he being the first bish. appointed in the whole Brit. Colonial Empire. In 1809 he was nominated and took his seat as a mem. of H. M. Council, N. S.

I. An Essay on Infant Baptism; in which the Right of Infants to the Sacrament of Baptism is proved from Scripture. *New York*, 1768, pp. 187, 8vo.

II. Discourse concerning the evidences of our knowing Christ; by Rev. Ralph Cudworth. With a preface, notes, and translations of Latin and Greek quotations, by Rev. Charles Inglis. *Do.*, 1770, 8vo.

III. Sermon occasioned by the death of John Ogilvie of New York. *Do.*, 1774, 8vo.

IV. Sermon occasioned by the death of Samuel Auchmuty. *Do.*, 1777, 12mo.

V. Letters of Papinian, in which the conduct, present state and prospects of the American Congress are examined. *Do.*, 1779, 12mo.

VI. Sermon delivered in New York, 26 Oct., 1783. *London*, 1784, 8vo.

VII. A Charge delivered to the Clergy of the Diocese of Nova Scotia, at the Primary Visitation, holden in the town of Halifax, in the month of June, 1788. *Halifax*, 1789, pp. 62, 8vo.

VIII. Charge delivered to the Clergy of Nova Scotia at the Triennial Visitation holden in the Town of Halifax. *Do.*, 1792, 4to.

IX. Steadfastness in Religion and Loyalty recommended; a sermon. *London*, 1793, 8vo.

X. Sermon preached in the Parish Church of St. Paul at Halifax, 25 April, 1794, the Day appointed by Proclamation for a General Fast and Humiliation in H. M. Province of Nova Scotia. *Halifax*, 1794, 8vo.

XI. Charge to the Clergy of the Diocese of Nova Scotia, in June and August, 1803. *Do.*, 1804.

The case of the Right Rev. Chas. Inglis at the Commissioner's Office, 31 July, 1799. *London*, 4to.

INGLIS, *Rt. Rev.* JOHN, *D. D.* Late Anglican Bish. of N. S. D. in London, Eng., 27 Oct., 1850. Ed. at King's Coll., Windsor, N. S. The only son of the preceding. Was for some years Rector of Halifax and Chaplain to the Leg. Coun. Appointed Bish., 1824, and in the following year, a mem. of H. M. Council of the Province. He was a sound scholar and an eloquent speaker.

I. The Rising Village; a Poem. By Oliver Goldsmith, a collateral descendant of the author of the "Deserted Village." With a Preface, by the Bishop of Nova Scotia. *London*, 1825, pp. 48.

"We cannot conclude without expressing our highest approbation of those generous feelings and sentiments which pervade the elegant Preface to the 'Rising Village'; in every line of which we can trace the friend, the scholar and the divine. 'I have pleasure,' says the learned and reverend author; 'I have pleasure in acknowledging myself one of those friends, who take an interest in the success of this little poem, and in the welfare of a person so meritorious and deserving as the Author of it.'"—*Can. Rev. & Mag.* (Mont.)

II. A Sermon preached in the Cathedral of St. Paul's, London, on June 11. 1831, at the yearly meeting of the Children of the Charity Schools in and about London and Westminster. *London*, pp. 14.

III. Memoranda respecting King's College at Windsor, in Nova Scotia, collected and prepared for the purpose of making evident the leading object in suggesting and establishing that Institution. By one of the Alumni. *Do.*, 1836, pp. 31, 8vo.

IV. A Pastoral Address. *Halifax*, 1838, pp. 11, 8vo.

V. Journal of Visitation in Nova Scotia, Cape Breton and along the Eastern Shore of New Brunswick; by the Lord Bishop of Nova Scotia, in the Summer and Autumn of 1843. (With Map.) *London*, 1844, pp. 70, 18mo.

(See *Cochran*, Rev. J. C., *Willis*, Rev. R.)

INONS, JAMES. "Secy. of the Prov. Agricultural Board."

I. Practical directions for the selection and management of Field and Garden Seeds in Nova Scotia. *Halifax*, 1851, pp. 7, 8vo.

IRVING, ÆMILIUS, *Q. C.* An U. C. Barrister. Is Solicitor to the Great Western Railway Co., Can.

I. An Index to the Statutes of Canada, from 3 and 4 to 12 and 13 Victoria, inclusive, 1840 to 1850, &c. *Toronto*, 1850, pp. 72.

IRWIN, *Rev.* JOHN, *A. M.* A Min. of the Ch. of Eng. Incumbent of St. Luke's, (Mont.) B. in Tyrone, Irel., 1817. Ed. at the Univ. (Dub.) where he attained distinction in classics. In 1845–6 ed. the *Western Star* (Galway), and from 1854 to 1859 the *Christian Witness and Church Advocate* (Bos.) Was also a contributor to the *Church Review*. In 1862

Mr. I. became ed. of the *Echo and Protestant Episcopal Recorder* (Mont.), which, however, he soon relinquished. It is understood that he has in preparation a second volume of the *History of Ireland* bringing it down to the present time.

(See *Falloon*, Rev. Dr.)

IZARD, GEORGE. A Maj. Genl. in the service of the U. S., during the War of 1812.

Official correspondence relative to the military operations of the American Army, under the command of Major General Izard, in 1814 and 1815. *Philadelphia*, 1816, pp. 152, 8vo.

J.

JACKSON, C. F

I. Copper-bearing belt of Canada East. *Proc. Nat. His. Soc.* (Bos.), 1863.

JACKSON, CHARLES T., and FRANCES ALGER.

I. Remarks on the Mineralogy and Geology of the Peninsula of Nova Scotia ; accompanied by a coloured map, illustrative of the structure of the Country, and by several views of its scenery. From the Memoirs of the American Academy. *Cambridge*, 1832, pp. 116, 8vo.

JACKSON, *Rev.* GEORGE.

I. A Further Attempt to Substantiate the Legitimacy of Infant Baptism and of sprinkling as a scriptural mode of administering that ordinance, in a series of letters addressed to the Revd. William Elder, intended as a reply to his letter entitled : "Infant sprinkling weighed in the balance of the sanctuary and found wanting." *Halifax, N. D.*, pp. 256, 8vo.

JACKSON, JOHN MILLS.

I. A View of the Political Situation of the Province of Upper Canada, in North America ; in which her physical capacity is stated ; the means of diminishing her burden, encreasing her value, and securing her connection to Great Britain are fully considered, with notes and an appendix. *London*, 1809, 8vo.

JACKSON, *Rev.* WILLIAM.

I. The Portrait of the Rev. Thomas Taylor ; or the Hypocrite unmasked. *Halifax*, 1835, pp. 27, 8vo.

II. The Seven Heads of Arminianism, out of which came the "Ten Horns of Calvinism," examined and refuted by the scriptures of truth. *Do.*, 1837, pp. 24, 8vo.

JACOBS, *Rev.* PETER.

I. Journal of the Rev. P. Jacobs. *Toronto*, 1853, pp. 32.

JAMES, ALEXANDER.

I. Reports of Cases in the Supreme Court of Nova Scotia, commencing with Easter Term, 1853. *Halifax*, 1853.

JAMES, WILLIAM. An Eng. Naval historian. D. 1827.

I. An Enquiry into the Merits of the principal Naval Actions between Great Britain and the United States ; comprising an account of all British and American ships of war, reciprocally captured and destroyed since the 18th of June, 1812. *Halifax, N. S.*, pp. 102, 8vo.

II. A Full and Correct Account of the chief Naval Occurrences of the late war between Great Britain and the United States ; with a cursory examination of the American accounts of their naval actions fought previous to that period, to which is added an appendix with plates. *London*, 1817, pp. 780, 8vo.

III. A Full and Correct Account of Military Occurrences of the late War between Great Britain and the United States. With an appendix and plates. *Do.*, 1818, 2 vols, 8vo.

JAMESON, *Mrs.* ANNA. An Eng. author. Married in 1824, Mr. R. S. Jameson, who, in 1841, became Vice Chancellor of U. C. Resided for some years with her husband at Toronto. D. in London, 17 March, 1860.

I. Winter Studies and Summer Rambles in Canada. *London*, 1838, 3 vols., 8vo. *New York*, 1839, 2 vols., 12mo.

II. Sketches in Canada. *London*, 1852, 12mo.

JARVIS, *Rev.* GEORGE S., *A. M.* Rector of Hampstead, N. B.

I. Three Sermons on different subjects. *St. John*, 1835, pp 29, 8vo.

JARVIS, *Lt. Col.* SAMUEL PETERS. Brevet Major, 82nd Regt. and Asst. Adjutant Genl. Militia, Can.

I. An Historical Record of the 82nd Regt. or Prince of Wales' Volunteers. *London*, 1867.

JENKINS, *Rev.* JOHN, *D. D.* Presb. min. of St. Paul's Presb. Ch. (Mont.) Was, for 10 years, joint ed., with Albert Barnes, of Philadelphia, and others, of the *Presb. Quarterly Review*, now incorporated with the *Am. Theological Review*, to which he largely contributed. Has written and published various sermons, lectures, sketches of travel, &c., not enumerated here. Is President of the Literary Club, (Mont.)

I. A Protestant's Appeal to the Douay Bible and other Roman Catholic Standards in defence of the doctrines of the Reformation. *Montreal*, 1853, 12mo., 4th Edition.

II. The Faithful Minister, a life of the Rev. William Squire. *Do.*, 1853, pp. 120.

III. Pauperism in Great Cities. *Philadelphia*, 1854.

IV. Thoughts on the Crisis. *Do.*, 1860.

V. Two fast day discourses preached in Philadelphia in relation to the Civil War. *Do.*, 1862–3.

VI. Canada's Thanksgiving for National Blessings; a sermon. *Montreal.* 1865.

" Altogether the discourse is an admirable one—well worthy every body's perusal, calculated to produce good to such as lay its monitions to heart."—*Gazette*, (Mont.)

JENNINGS, *Miss* CLOTILDA. A N. S. writer. Has written various prose tales and sketches, and short fugitive poems for the local newspaper press. She was a regular contributor in prose and verse to the *Provincial Mag.*, (Hal.), during its existence, and has lately contributed some interesting sketches to the *Saturday Reader*, (Mont.) At the time of the Burn's Centenary wrote a poem in honour of the event which was submitted to the Committee in London, and is included in *The Burn's Centenary Wreath*, (Lond. 1859). Upon the occasion of a general public exhibition of the products of the Province of N. S., held at Halifax, in 1855, Miss J. carried off the prize offered for the best tale and poem illustrative of the history, manners and scenery of N. S.

I. Linden Rhymes. By Maude. *Halifax*, 1854, pp. 152, 8vo.

II. The White Rose in Acadia ; and Autumn in Nova Scotia, a Prize tale and poem. By " Maude." *Do.*, 1855, pp. 36, 8vo.

JENNINGS, *Rev.* JOHN, *D. D.* A min. of the Can. Pres. Ch. (Tor.) B. at Glasgow, 8 Oct. 1814. Went to Coll. at Edinburgh to study for the ministry both in the United Session, and part of the time in the Established Ch. under Dr. Chalmers. Decided finally in favour of the former, and was ordained by the celebrated George Gilfillan, and inducted to the pastoral charge of Toronto in 1839. Was one of the first, and throughout one of the most earnest advocates of union, of what is now the Can. Presb. Ch. Was an extensive contributor, editorially to the *Colonist*, and to the *Banner*, (Tor.) Took an active part in the overthrow of King's Coll. of that city, and laboured with Mr. Baldwin and Lord Elgin to erect the present provincial Univ., of which he is one of the Senate ; he also laboured and wrote to abolish the Clergy Reserves. In 1851 established, and for 3 years ed., the *Can. Presbyterian Mag.* (Tor.) Received his degree of D. D. from the Univ. of N. Y.

I. Reason or Revelation ; or, the religion, philosophy, and civilization of the ancient Heathen, contrasted with Christianity and its legitimate consequence. *Toronto,* 1852, pp. 48.

II. Say No. *Do.,* 1865, pp. 59.

JERROLD, DOUGLAS E. Son of the celebrated Eng. humorist. Ed. the *News Bag,* a literary periodical (Tor.) 1854.

JOHNSON, GEORGE WASHINGTON. B. at Binbrook, U. C., 19 Aug., 1839. For some years acted in the capacity of a sch. teacher, devoting his leisure moments to self culture and writing for the press. He contributed in prose and verse, under various signatures, to *Harper's Weekly, Frank Leslie's Newspaper, Ledger,* and *Weekly,* (N. Y.); the *Atlantic Monthly* and *Waverly Mag.,* and to several Can. journals. In June 1864, removed to Cleveland, O., U. S., where he became assist. ed. of the *Daily Plain Dealer,* and is an active contributor to the periodical and newspaper press.

I. Maple Leaves. *Hamilton, U. C.,* 1864, pp. 204, 12mo.

" The work contains much good poetry, and breathes a spirit of loyalty through every line."—*Spectator,* (Ham.)

II. The Mente's Secret, or, the Vengeance of Madra ; a novel. *Cleveland,* 1864, pp. 180.

III. The Belle of Bladen's Brook ; a novel. *Do.,* 1865, pp. 200.

JOHNSON, *Miss.* HELEN MAR. A Can. poet. B. at Magog, C. E, 27 Oct., 1835. D. there 13 Mar., 1863. Her first poetical effusions appeared in 1850, in the *Journal,* (Stanstead), and exhibited as the ed. remarked, " a rare poetical talent for one so young." She afterwards frequently contributed to that paper, and to the *Gazette* (Sherbrooke.) In the latter the poems *Through a Glass Darkly ; Our Ship is Homeward Bound; The Song of the Peasant Girl ; Our Native Land ; The Battle-field ;* and *Dost*

thou Remember me ? are from her pen. In 1856 she wrote a serial story called *William Artherton, or the Lord will provide,* for *The Youth's Guide* (Bos.), and also occasionally contributed short poems to the same paper. To *The Advent Herald,* (Bos.), the oldest Prophetical journal in Am. she frequently lent the aid of her pen, as also to the *Witness,* (Mont.) For one of her poems, *The Surrender of Quebec,* in her published volume, she was awarded a medal by the Lit. and His. Soc. of that city. Many of her pieces are to be found in Dewart's *Selections.* She died, the victim of consumption, at the early age of 28.

I. Poems. *Boston,* 1855, pp. 249.

" The whole of the poems display deep poetic ardor, and are rich in imagery ; the diction is rich and varied, and not unfrequently pleasingly figurative, and the versification regular and pleasing." *Sinclair's Monthly Cir.* (Que.)

" Her unpublished poems, from which most of the selections in this work are taken, exhibit a more cultivated taste, and finished style, than we find in her published volume. Many of the pieces, among her unpublished remains, were evidently written under the influence of suffering with the shadow of death gradually darkening her life."— DEWART.

II. The Bride of Christ ; a tract. *Do.,* 1858, pp. 12.

JOHNSON, *Rev.* JOHN H., *M. A.* A Wes. Meth. Min., (Peterborough, U. C.) B. in Tp. of Caledonia., U. C., 1826. Ed. at the District Grammar Sch., and at Victoria Coll. (Cob.) Has taught several Model and Grammar Sch's., and was for some time Principal of the Belleville Academy. Has contributed from an early age to the periodical and newspaper press.

I. The Christian Ministry ; a sermon. *Brockville,* 1850, pp. 24.

II. A Funeral Sermon on Mrs. (Dr.) Clark. *Cobourg,* 1853.

III. Unbelief ; a sermon. *Brighton, C. W.,* 1860.

IV. Inaugural Address as Principal of the Belleville Seminary. *Hamilton,* 1857.

V. Man the Architect of his own Fortune ; a Lecture. *Montreal,* 1862, pp. 24.

JOHNSON, THOMAS R.

I. A Comprehensive System of Book-Keeping by Single and Double Entry; for the use of Schools. Simplified by detailed explanations of the phrases and books in general use, and by numerous examples. With a variety of useful rules, tables and calculations. *Montreal.*

JOHNSON, W. R.

I. The Coal Trade of British America, with researches on the characters and practical value of American and Foreign coals. *Washington*, 1850, 8vo.

JOHNSTON, J. F. W., *F. S. R.*, (L. and E.) A well-known Eng. writer on Agriculture. D. 1855, aged 59. Was Prof. of Chemistry and Mineralogy in the Univ. of Durham.

I. Report on the Natural Capabilities of the Province of New Brunswick. *Fredericton*, 2nd Ed. 1850, pp. 95 ; another Ed. *London*, 1857.

JOHNSTON, *Rev.* SAMUEL F. A Presb. Missionary from N. S. B. at Stewiache, N. S., 1830. D. on the Island of Tanna, New Hebrides, 1861. In 1859 proceeded to the South Seas as a Missionary of the Presb. Ch. N. S. He was the author of various articles on religious and missionary topics in the *Christian Instructor*, (Hal.) Many of his letters were published in the Presb. journals and periodicals of the Lower Provinces. A Memoir of his life has been written by the Rev. Geo. Patterson (whom see.)

JOHNSTON, THOMAS.

I. Travels through Lower Canada, interspersed with Canadian tales and anecdotes, and interesting information to intending emigrants. *Edinburgh*, 1827, pp. 96, 12mo.

JOHNSTONE, WALTER.

I. A Series of Letters descriptive of Prince Edward Island, in the Gulph of St. Lawrence, addressed to the Rev. John Wightman, Minister of Kirkmahoe, Dumfries-shire. By Walter Johnstone, a native of the same country. The author of these letters went out for the express purpose of surveying Prince Edward Island, and collecting information on the subject of Emigration. During two summers and one winter, he was assiduously en-

gaged in the prosecution of this object; and the small volume now presented to the Public will be found to contain a full and particular account of the climate, soil, natural productions and mode of husbandry adopted in the Island ; together with sketches of scenery, manners of the inhabitants, &c., &c.; the whole being intended for the guidance of future emigrants, particularly as to what implements and necessaries it may be proper to provide themselves with before crossing the Atlantic. *Dumfries*, 1822, pp. 72, 12mo.

II. Travels in Prince Edward Island, Gulf of St. Lawrence, North America, in the years 1820-21. Undertaken with a design to established Sabbath Schools, and investigate the religious state of the country, wherein is given a short account of the different denominations of Christians, their former history and present condition, interspersed with notes relative to the various clergymen that have officiated on the Island. (With Map.) *Edinburgh*, 1823, pp. 132, 12mo.

JONES, EDWARD C. A Toronto barrister.

I. Upper Canada Common Pleas Reports. *Toronto*, 1852–64, 13 vols., 8vo.

JONES, J. A.

I. Haverhill; or, Memoirs of an Officer in the Army of Wolfe. *London*, 1831, 3 vols., 12mo. Reprinted : *New York*, 1831.

JONES, JOHN MATTHEW, *F. L. S.* (Hal. N. S.) Is a Barrister of the Middle Temple, (Lon.)

I. The Naturalist in Bermuda ; a sketch of the geology, zoology and botany of that remarkable group of islands ; together with meteorological observations. With a map and illustrations. *London*, 1859, pp. 192, 8vo.

" As a contribution to science containing much that is original and interesting, we cordially recommend this little book to our readers."—*Can. Nat.*

II. The Great Gymnetms, recently captured in the Bermudas. Descriptive particulars, &c. *Proc. Zool. Soc.* (Lon.)

III. Contributions to the Ichthyology of Nova Scotia. *Halifax*, 1863.

IV. On Ocean Drifts and Currents. *Can. Nat.*, 1864.

"An interesting paper."—PRINP. DAWSON.

V. Contributions to the Natural History of the Bermudas. Part I. Mollusca. *Halifax*, 1864, pp. 13.

VI. Contributions to the Natural History of Nova Scotia. Reptilia. *Halifax*, 1865, pp. 15.

VII. On Nova Scotian Fishes. *Do.*, do.

JONES, LEONARD G.

I. Farming and Gardening made easy; or, plain instructions in Agriculture, Horticulture, &c. *Dundas, U. C.*, 1853.

JONES, *Rev.* PETER. An Indian Missionary. B. at Burlington heights, near Hamilton, U.C., 1802. D. at Brantford, U. C., 29 June, 1856. He belonged to the Ogibway tribe of Indians, and was known by the name of "Kahkewaguonaby." He early manifested a thirst for knowledge, and through the aid of his friends and others obtained a good English education. In 1833 he was admitted as a priest in the Wes. Meth. Ch., and up to the time of his death devoted himself with zeal and earnestness to his ministry. He had visited and preached in the U. S. and Gt. Brit., in both of which countries he made warm friends. During his stay in London he rendered very effectual service to the several Indian tribes in N. Am. His industry and application, in everything which he undertook, were great. His services in the cause of Christianity among his countrymen were incalculable.

"Mr. Jones was a man of athletic frame, as well as of masculine intellect; a man of clear perception, good judgment, great decision of character; a sound preacher, fervent and powerful in his appeals; very well informed on general subjects, extensively acquainted with men and things, serious without gloom, cheerful without levity, dignified and agreeable in his manners; a faithful friend, a true patriot, a persevering philanthropist; a noble specimen of what Christianity can do for the Indian Gentiles of Canada, and therefore for the Gentiles of the whole world."—REV. E. RYERSON, D. D.

I. Ojebway Spelling Book. Translation. 1828.

II. Ojebway Hymn Book; translation. *New York*, 1829; 2nd Ed. *Toronto*.

III. The Gospel of St. Matthew; translated into the Ojebway language. *Toronto*, 1829.

IV. The Gospel according to St. John; translated into the Chippeway Tongue by John Jones, and revised and corrected by Peter Jones, Indian Teachers. *London*, 1831, 12mo.

V. Life and Journals. *Toronto*, 1860, pp. 424, 12mo.

VI. History of the Ojebway Indians; with especial reference to their conversion to christianity. With a brief memoir of the writer. *London*, 1861, pp. 278, 8vo.

"Not a few of the incidents and anecdotes of this history of the red man come up to our memory with a pleasing vigour and freshness, from having heard the *viva voce* delineations of its accomplished author. Probably no man could speak with greater authority on the past state and future prospects of the North American Indians than Mr. Jones, having himself been a Chief of one of the tribes. After his conversion to christianity, not only was his life spent as a preacher of righteousness among the various tribes, but he employed every means within his power for the amelioration of their condition. It is to be regretted that a man of such parts as Mr. Jones, was so soon removed from a sphere in which his endeavours to benefit his race were so eminently owned of the 'Great Spirit'; but, in the interesting sketch of his life,—in which are brought out some touching exemplifications of that *inner* life, which marks the character of the true child of God,—there is ample proof of what Divine Grace can accomplish in these dark places of the earth; and a striking reproof and refutation of the views of those who have from time to time maintained the impossibility of morally or spiritually elevating the wandering tribes of North America. Mr. Jones' graphic and interesting narrative, which death prevented his own hand from completing, is of essential value as shewing the native habit and moral tendencies of the mind of the untaught Indian; while to the lovers of philology, and all who take an interest in these remarkable people, his brief account of the different languages in use among the various tribes, cannot fail to be of interest and service."— *Witness* (Edin.)

VII. Additional Hymns, translated a short time before his death. *Brantford*, 1861.

JORGENSEN, A.

I. The Emigration from Europe during the present Century; its causes and effects. Translated from Norwegian Statistics and Reports, and from extracts of "*Historique de L'Emigration Européene, Asiatique et Africaine, au XIX Siècle.*" *Quebec*, 1865, pp. 23, 8vo.

JUKES, AUGUSTUS, *M. D.* A medical practitioner (St. Catherines, U. C.) Has contributed in prose and verse to newspapers and periodicals. In the *Ang. Am. Mag.* wrote various poems:—*Occasional sayings and doings of the Blinks*;

Selections from the Odes of 'Hafiz' the Persian poet, rendered into English verse 1852; *Christmas Eve, a tale of the New York State*, 1853, &c.

JUKES, J. B., *M. A., F. G. S., F. C. P. S.*

I. Excursions in and about Newfoundland during the years 1839 and 1840. *London*, 1842, 2 vols., pp. 322–354, 12mo.

JUNEAU, F. E.

I. Nouvel Alphabet ou Lectures graduées pour les enfants du premier age. *Québec*, 1865.

K.

KALM, PETER.

I. Travels into North America; containing its Natural History, and a circumstantial account of its plantations and agriculture in general; with the civil, ecclesiastical and commercial state of the country, the manners of the inhabitants, and several curious and important remarks on various subjects; translated from the Swedish language into English, by John Reinhold Forster, F. A. S. *London*, 1770, 3 Vols., 8vo.; 2nd Ed., *Do.*, 1772, 2 Vols., 8vo.

"Ce voyage est également curieux et instructif. Il nous donne des notions précieuses sur la géologie et la minéralogie de l'Amérique-Septentrionale. Les Descriptions des minéraux ont cependant le défaut de ne pas être conçues dans des termes assez précis, ce qui tient à l'état de la science d'alors. Kalm n'est pas en général un bon écrivain, mais c'est un observateur judicieux et impartial."—*Bib. de Voyages.*

KANE, PAUL. A Can. painter. B. in Toronto, where he was ed., and received the first lessons in his art. In 1840 proceeded to Europe and studied painting at Rome, Genoa, Naples, Florence, Venice and Bologna. After 9 years absence returned to his native country, and travelled extensively in the Hudson's Bay Territory, taking sketches of, and making notes on, the habits, customs and physical peculiarities of the aborigines. Some of the results of his experiences and studies are

embodied in the volume produced by him. A collection of his paintings has been purchased by the Can. Legislature for the Parliament Buildings, Ottawa; another collection is the property of the Hon. G. W. Allan (Tor.) Mr. K. resides in his native city.

I. Wanderings of an Artist among the Indians of North America, from Canada to Vancouver's Island and Oregon, through the Hudson's Bay Company's Territory, and back again. (With illustrations.) *London*, 1859.

"Mingling among the Indians as a great Medicine-man, respected or dreaded for his supernatural powers, Mr. Kane witnessed many singular rites and customs not often seen, and never before narrated by a traveller. Without being either a critical linguist, or an ethnologist, he has accumulated many facts highly valuable to both."—PROF. D. WILSON: *Can. Journ.*

Canadian Journal.

I. Incidents of travel on the North West Coast, Vancouver's Island, Oregon, &c. 1855.

II. Notes of a Sojourn among the half-breeds, Hudson Bay Company's Territory, Red River. 1856.

III. Notes of travel among the Walla-Walla Indians. do.

IV. The Chinook Indians, 1857.

KATZMANN, *Miss* MARY J. Has written various fugitive pieces in verse for the N. S. press. Ed. the *Provincial Mag.* (Hal.), for 2 years.

KEATING, WILLIAM H. An Am. Historiographer.

I. Narrative of an Expedition to the source of St. Peter's River, Lake Winnepeek, Lake of the Woods, &c., performed in the year 1823, by order of the Honble. J. C. Calhoun, Secretary of War, under the command of Stephen H. Long; compiled from the notes of Major Long, &c. *Philadelphia*, 1824, 2 vols, 8vo.; *London*, 1825, 2 vols., 8vo.

KEEFER, THOMAS COLTRIN, *C. E.* B. at Thorold, U. C., 4 Nov., 1821. Ed. at U. C. Coll. Commenced his profession, in 1838, at Lockport, on the Erie Canal. In 1840 returned to Can. and was employed by the Welland Canal Co. In the following year, the Canal was adopted as a provincial work by the Govt., and its enlargement was commenced. Mr. K., then being in his 20th year, was appointed to the charge of the enlargement of the feeder, and continued to be the only engineer in charge until the appointment of the engineer-in-chief in 1842. Since then he has been employed upon a large number of provincial, municipal and private undertakings, his professional services being sought for in Can., the Lower Provinces, and the U. S. He was one of the first Engineers to prepare the necessary plans for the construction of the Great Victoria Bridge across the St. Lawrence, of which plans several were adopted almost exactly by the Eng. Engineers. It has been claimed by his friends that, "all which is peculiar, all which distinguishes this bridge from any other, is derived from him," while several Can. and Am. writers on the bridge, give him a foremost position in relation to it.

I. The Philosophy of Railroads. 1849; 4th Ed. revised, *Montreal*, 1853, pp. 47.

II. The Canals of Canada; their Prospects and Influence. *Toronto*, 1850, pp. 111.

To this was awarded the premium offered by the Gov. Genl. for the best essay on the subject.

III. Report on a Survey for the Railway Bridge over the St. Lawrence, at Montreal. 1853.

IV. "Montreal" and "the Ottawa:" two lectures. *Montreal*, 1854, pp. 73, 8vo.

V. Report of Survey of Georgian Bay Canal Route to Lake Ontario, by way of Lake Scugog, accompanied with maps, &c. *Whitby*, 1863. pp. 20, 8vo.

KEELE, W. C. A Toronto Attorney.

I. The Provincial Justice, or Magistrate's Manual, being a complete digest of the Criminal Law of Canada and a compendious and general view of the Provincial Law of Upper Canada, with practical forms for the use of the Magistracy. *Toronto*, 1st Ed. 1835; 5th Ed. 1864, pp. 858.

II. District Law Manual. *Do.*, 1844, 8vo.

III. A Brief View of the Laws of Upper Canada up to the present time: including a treatise on the Law of Executors and Wills, and the Law relative to landlord and tenant, distress for rent, constables, assessors, collectors, &c. *Do.*, 1844.

KELLY, WILLIAM, *M. D.* A Surgeon in the Royal Navy.

I. On the Temperature, Mirages, &c., of the River St. Lawrence. *Trans. Lit. & His. Soc.* (Que.) Vol. III.

II. Abstract of Meteorological Journal kept at Cape Diamond, from Jan. 1st., 1824, to Dec. 31st., 1831; with some remarks on the climate of Lower Canada. *Do.* do.

III. On the Medical Statistics of Lower Canada. *Do.* do.

IV. Analysis of Mineral Water, sent from Gaspé by Drs. Skey and Kelly. *Do.* do.

V. On the Temperature of the Springs, at Quebec. *Do.* do.

VI. On some extraordinary forms of Mirage. *Do.* do.

VII. On the Temperature of the surface of the water over the banks and near the shores of the Gulf of St. Lawrence. *Do.* do.

KEMP, *Rev.* ALEXANDER FERRIE, *M. A.* A min. in the Can. Presb. Ch. Held a charge in Montreal for many years. In conjunction with the Rev. D. Fraser (now of Inverness, Scot.) ed. the *Cana-*

dian Presbyter (Mont.) a monthly religious periodical, from its commencement in Jan., 1857, until discontinued in Dec., 1858. Mr. K. wrote the majority of its leading articles. For several years was one of the Ed's. of the *Can. Nat.* We append a list of his contributions to that publication.

I. Digest of the Minutes of the Synod of the Presbyterian Church of Canada, a historical introduction and an appendix of forms and procedures. *Montreal*, 1861, pp. 474, 8vo.

II. Rules and Forms of Procedure in the Church Courts. *Do.*, 1865, pp. 110, 12mo.

Canadian Naturalist.

I. Notes on the Bermudas and their Natural History, with special reference to their Marine Algæ. 1857.

II. The Fresh Water Algæ of Canada, in two parts. 1858.

III. Archaia ; a Review of Prin. Dawson's work bearing that title. 1859.

IV. Classified List of Marine Algæ from the Lower St. Lawrence, with an introduction for amateur collectors. 1860.

V. A Holiday Visit to the Acton Copper Mines. do.

" A good popular exposition of the Geology of this very interesting mining district." —BISHOP FULFORD.

VI. On the Shore Zones and Limits of Marine Plants on the North Eastern Coast of the United States. 1862.

KENDALL, *Rev.* E. K., *B. A.* Late Scholar of St. John's Coll. (Cam.) Was for some time Prof. of Mathematics in Trinity Coll., (Tor.)

I. Note on Euclid, Proposition 5, Book I. *Can. Journ.*, 1858.

II. On the connection between Experiment and Theory in the progress of Scientific Discovery ; a lecture. *Montreal*, 1859. pp. 63, 8vo.

III. Sermon on behalf of the Clergy Sustentation Fund. *Toronto*, 1859, pp. 16.

IV. Christ seen in the Stranger ; a sermon. *Do.*, 1860, pp. 23.

V. Remarks on the negative index of a function. *Can. Journ.*, 1863.

KERR, WILLIAM, *M. D.* Practises at Doon, U. C. Is a corresponding mem. of the Medical and Physical Soc. (Calcutta), and of the Medico-Chirurgical Soc. (Glas.) From 1828 until the present time, has contributed many valuable papers to the Edinburgh and Glasgow medical press.

KERR, WILLIAM H. C., *A. M.* A Practising Barrister and Atty., at Brantford, U. C.

I. The Heroides of Ovid. Carefully edited, with notes. *Toronto*, 1865, pp. 68, 12mo.

KERSHAW, *Mrs.* Ed. of the *Literary Transcript* (Que.) from its commencement, in 1838, until she took her departure for Europe in 1840, when the paper was discontinued.

KERSHAW, PHILIP G., *B. A.* A Graduate of the Univ. of McGill Coll. D. some years since.

I. Reflections on Itinerary Parliaments ; by Marcullus. *Montreal*, 1856, pp. 33, 12mo.

KIDD, ADAM. A Can. poet. B. 1802. D. at Quebec, 5 July, 1831. His work exhibits considerable powers of versification.

I. The Huron Chief, and other poems. *Montreal*, 1830, pp. 216, 8vo.

KING, *Rev.* ANDREW, *A. M.* Prof. of Theology and Church History in the Coll. of the Presb. Ch. (Hal.) Has contributed many articles, and was for some time ed. of, the *Missionary Record of the Free Church of N. S.*

I. Inaugural Lecture at the opening of the first Session of the Free Church College. *Halifax*, 1848.

II. The True Rule of Christian Conduct ; a sermon. *Do.*, 1851, pp. 19.

III. The Papacy : a Conspiracy against Civil and Religious Liberty. First lecture before the Protestant Alliance of N. S. *Do.*, 1859, pp. 30, 8vo.

IV. Christ's Zeal for God's House ; a sermon preached at the opening of the Synod of the Presbyterian Ch. of the Lower Provinces. *Do.*, 1861, pp. 16.

V. Narrative of Events issuing in the Institution of the Free Church of Scotland, in separation from the State. *Do.*, 1861, pp. 30.

VI. The Character of Popery as illustrated in the History of Scotland ; a sermon. *Glasgow.*

VII. The Inspiration of the Books of Scripture ; a sermon. *Do.*

KING, J. H. Has contributed short fugitive pieces in verse to the *Gospel Tribune* 1853–4, and the *Christian Guardian* (Tor.), same period, and since then to various newspapers in U. C. Lives at Artemesia, U. C.

KING, *Major* W. Ross, *F. R. G. S., F. S. A. S.*
I. The Sportsman and Naturalist in Canada ; or, Notes on the Natural History of the Game, Game Birds, and Fish of that country. *London*, 1866.

KINGDOM, WILLIAM.
I. America and the British Colonies ; an Abstract of all the most useful information relative to the United States of America, and the British Colonies of Canada, the Cape of Good Hope, New South Wales, &c. ; exhibiting at one view the comparative advantages and disadvantages each country offers for Emigration. Collected from the most valuable and recent publications ; to which are added a few notes and observations. *London*, 1820, pp. 330, 8vo.

KINGSFORD, WILLIAM, *C. E.* A Can. author and journ. Was for some time ed. of the *Times* (Mont.), the *Colonist* (Tor.), and other newspapers. Now resides in England.

I. The History, Structure, and Statistics of Plank Roads in the United States and Canada. *Philadelphia*, 1851, 8vo.

II. Impressions of the West and South, during a six weeks holiday. Letters which " first appeared in a Toronto newspaper." By W. K. *Toronto*, 1858, 8vo.

III. The Canadian Canals, their history and their cost, with an inquiry into the policy necessary to advance the well-being of the Province. *Do.*, 1865, pp. 191, 12mo.

" Impartially and honestly written, filled with facts and data laboriously collected and carefully put together, and containing many well timed suggestions for future action, based on past errors and present exigencies, it cannot fail, we think, to win for itself a wide and favorable reception."—*Can. Journal* (Tor.)

KINGSMILL, *Colonel.* A retired officer from the Brit. Army.

I. The Greenwood Tragedy. Three addresses delivered to the prisoners in Toronto Gaol soon after the suicide of William Greenwood, and having reference to that event ; to which is added an appeal to the ladies of Canada. *Guelph*, 1864, pp. 35, 8vo.

KINGSTON, G. T., *M. A.* Prof. of Meteorology, Univ. Coll. (Tor.), and Director of the Magnetical Observatory, in same city. Was 1st Class in Mathematics at Cambridge, 1846.

I. Abstract of Magnetical Observations made at the Magnetical Observatory, Toronto, Canada West, during the years 1856 to 1862, inclusive, and during parts of the years 1853, 1854 and 1855. *Toronto.*

Can. Journal.

I. Annual Mean Meteorological Results at Toronto, from 1855 to 1864, in each annual volume.

II. On the Employment of the Electric Telegraph for predicting storms. 1857.

III. On deducing the mean Temperature of a month. 1858.

IV. On the Magnetic disturbances at Toronto during the years 1856 to 1862, inclusive. 1863.

V. Remarks on the Temperature Coefficients of Magnets. do.

VI. On the Annual and Diurnal distribution of the different winds at Toronto. 1864.

VII. On the abnormal variations of some of the Meteorological elements at Toronto and their relations to the direction of the wind. do.

VIII. On the relative durations of the different Winds during rain 'or snow, derived from the Toronto observations, in the years 1853 to 1859, inclusive. do.

IX. Monthly absolute values of the Magnetic elements at Toronto, from 1856 to 1864, inclusive. 1865.

X. The Toronto Observatory. *B. A. Mag.*, 1863.

" A particularly pleasing scientific paper, replete with knowledge and gracefully written."—*Albion*, (N. Y.)

KINGSTON, W. H. G. A favorite Eng. author.

I. Western Wanderings. or a Pleasure Tour in the Canadas. *London*, 1855, 2 vols., p. 8vo.

II. The Log-House by the Lake : a tale of Canada. *Do.*, 1864, 18mo.

KINNEAR, DAVID. A Can. journ. B. at Edinburgh, Scot., about 1807. D. at Montreal, 20 Nov., 1862. Was the son of a banker, and a lineal descendant of the celebrated Col. Gardiner. He was admitted as a mem. of the Scottish bar, but never prac'ised his profession. During his residence in Edinburgh, enjoyed the society of most of the leading literary men of the day, including Sir Walter Scott, James Hogg, and Prof. Wilson. Was for some time engaged in commerce in London, where he also became acquainted with the *literati* of the Metropolis. In 1835, he emigrated to Am., and after visiting some parts of the U. S., made a complete tour of Can., and finally settled as a farmer at Drummondville, L. C. During the rebellion of 1837 he bore arms against the insurgents, and subsequently was appointed a stipendiary magistrate in charge of the police force organized to restore order. At the close of this service he accepted from his old friend, the late Mr. Hew Ramsay, the post of ed. of the *Gazette* (Mont.), at that time owned by the firm of Armour and Ramsay. This position he relinquished to become a partner in the *Herald*, of the same city, then in the hands of Mr. Robert Weir, senior, in consequence of the death of that gentleman's talented and lamented son. He eventually became senior partner and ed. of that newspaper, a position which he held up to the day of his death.

"No one could have had the opportunity of knowing Mr. Kinnear, as it has been our privilege to know him, without feeling that his intelligence, his conscience and his will were alike in sympathy with every noble or loving act by whomsoever it was performed. The very reasons, however, that have impressed us with a deep sense of his worth, make it improper on our parts to allude to the particulars of his life as a journalist. We could hardly write, all that we believe to be true of our late friend, without the appearance—perhaps the reality—of egotism. We shall, therefore, merely say, what his writings abundantly prove, that no difference of race, creed, colour, or social position ever operated to create a prejudice in his mind against either class or individuals.

"We do not believe that, during the many years that he has been the chief editor of this paper, one single allusion has been made by him to insult or wound a human creature on account of those accidents which are so often turned into sources of bitterness and ill-will. If he has not, at all times, completely escaped those personal collisions to which persons who take part in political warfare are unfortunately exposed, he nevertheless, considering the length of his career, had a remarkably small list of enemies. We may add that a man of more independent feeling never lived. We are confident that no one ever pretended to have influenced his opinion by an unworthy motive, nor to have even suspected him, on any grounds which he could allege, of being capable of being so influenced. Of course, like other men, he had faults ; but those most noticeable were chiefly the exaggeration of firmness, in his adherence to convictions which had been formed with care ; which were cherished because he believed they led to what was good as well as true ; and which he had no thought of peddling away for his own interests, or out of complaisance to others. His opinions were expressed and held with manly openness. He committed no errors having their origin in meanness or duplicity."—OBIT. NOTICE : *Herald*, (Mont.)

KIRBY, JAMES, *M. A., B. C. L.* A Montreal Advocate. Has contributed to Appleton's *New Am. Cyclopædia.* Has also written Law Reports for various legal and other publications. In 1865 established the *Lower Canada Law Journal*, (Mont.), of which he is Ed.

I. The British North American Almanac, and Annual Record for 1864. A handbook of statistical and general information. [Edited] *Montreal*, pp. 368. 8vo.

"It is, we believe, the first important work of the kind, relating to the British American Provinces, that has yet been published. No pains have been spared to make it ample and accurate in details. Many scholars, residing in the Provinces, have aided in the labour ; and the result—eminently creditable to editor and assistants—is a complete and very impressive picture of a most interesting country."—*Albion*, (N. Y.)

KIRBY, WILLIAM. A Can. poet and journ. B. in Hull, Eng., 1817. Came to Can., with his parents, in 1832, and has resided at Niagara, U. C., for the last 26 years. Ed. in his native county and in Canada. For many years, up to 1861, ed. the *Mail* (Niagara). He has contributed both in prose and verse to the press of this country and of Eng. In 1846, he wrote his principal poem, *The U. E.*, in 12 Cantos, the longest and as to its subject the most thoroughly distinctive Can. poem we possess. Besides aiming at the common object of all poetry: to profit and delight, the composition of *The U. E.* was mainly prompted by the desire to catch and treasure up for posterity, ere they had wholly vanished from earth, the spirit, form and manner of the brave and devoted U. E. loyalists who founded U. C., and gave that Province a noble ancestry of which any country might be proud.

I. The U. E., a tale of Upper Canada. *Niagara, U. C.*, pp. 178, 16mo.

KIRK, ABDIEL, A Musician.

I. The Two Spirits, a tale : written in imitation of the German. *Halifax*, 1843, pp. 46, 8vo.

KIRK, JOHN FOSTER. An Am. author. B. at Fredericton, N. B., 1824. Spent most of his youth in N. S., where he received a good classical education, under the private tuition of a graduate of one of the English Universities; he has since acquired a knowledge of several modern languages. In 1842 Mr. K. removed to the U. S., and after many years residence in that country has transferred his allegiance, and become a naturalized citizen of the Am. Republic.-- An intimate and most agreeable connection (that of Private Secy. and *amanuensis*,) with Mr. Prescott the historian, extending over the last 10 years of that great writer's life, enabled him to go more deeply into the sources of European history than is common on this continent; and 2 visits to Europe enlarged his opportunities for original research. It was owing to the suggestion of Mr. Prescott, who had himself contemplated writing the work, that Mr. K. undertook *The History of Charles the Bold.* It formed the subject of unremitting labour for many years, a labour, however, which was not devoted to an unworthy or unremunerative object, judging from the large sale the work has had, and the high praise bestowed

14 *

upon it by the press of Gt. Brit., France, and the U. S. Mr. K. contributes occasionally to the *North Am. Rev.* and the *Atlantic Monthly.* He is married, and resides at Dorchester, near Boston, Mass.

I. Life of Charles the Bold, Duke of Burgundy. *London* and *Philadelphia*, 1863, 2 vols.

"Mr. John Foster Kirk, whose familiarity with the history and languages of Modern Europe, has greatly aided me in the prosecution of my researches, while his sagacious criticism has done me no less service in the preparation of these volumes."—PRESCOTT'S *Philip the Second.*

"Mr. Kirk has produced a work which is quite entitled to take rank with the writings of his two predecessors [Prescott and Motley,] with whom he has, both in his merits and his faults, a certain family resemblance. He has studied his subject, not only with patient industry, but with that strong sense of its pre-eminent interest and importance which seems almost disproportionate to a bystander, but which helps him to see and understand much that an equally learned but less enthusiastic student might have overlooked. His extensive and minute knowledge is the learning of a man of vigorous thought, accustomed to bring his mind to consider men and things, not merely as they have been written about, but as they actually were, in the variety and complexity of their real existence. With such characters to deal as Louis XI. and Charles the Bold, and with such a subtle master of the moral aspects of the time as Commines for his guide, Mr. Kirk has ample materials for the most remarkable pictures : and he shows himself competent to handle them. His conceptions of men are clear, discriminating, and well-sustained. When he is most disposed to generalize, he remembers, and allows himself to be checked by facts at variance with the main effect of his judgment : and combinations and contrasts of qualities which do not ordinarily go together keep a character before us which suits no one but the person spoken of. Moreover, he pictures to himself the men in the scenes amid which they moved, and subject to the ideas and customs by which they were ruled. His imagination is active and impressible ; it readily extracts from the monuments of past days the materials of lively delineations, and reproduces them in a shape which, in its completeness, its choice of important features, and its intelligible explanation of causes and motives, satisfies modern requirements as to the way in which a story should be told."—*Saturday Rev.*, (Lon.)

II. Charles the Fifth. *N. Am. Rev.*

III. Mary Tudor. *Do.*

IV. Wilson's New Conquest of Mexico ; (two papers.) *Atlantic Mon.*

- V. Philip the Second. *Do.*

KIRKWOOD, ALEXANDER. A Clk. in the Crown Land Dept. Can.

I. A Short Treatise on the Milk-Weed, or Silk-Weed, and the Canadian Nettle, viewed as industrial resources. *Ottawa*, 1867, pp. 25, 8vo.

KLAUKE. —

I. On North Western American Emigration ; with a supplement. 1867, pp. 22—22, 12mo.

KNIGHT, *Rev.* R. "Wes. Meth. Missionary."

I. Address before the Horton and Cornwallis Temperance Societies.— *Halifax*, 1846, pp. 22, 8vo.

II. The Genuineness and Authenticity of Revelations ; a Lecture. *St. John, N. B.*, 1850, pp. 24, 8vo.

KNIGHT, THOMAS FREDERICK. A N. S. writer. Has contributed articles to the *Methodist Monthly Mag.* (See *Characteristics of St. Paul,* a id *Memoir of the Rev. Dr. Knight,* in that periodical.) From 1851 to 1865 wrote many miscellaneous articles for the *Provincial Wesleyan,* and has also contributed on political topics to the *Reporter,* both of (Hal.) Mr. K. is the author of a *National Ode* of great power and beauty. He is a clk. in the Receiver Genl's. Office, (Hal.)

I. Nova Scotia and her Resources ; a prize essay. *Halifax* and *London*, 1862, pp. 87, 8vo.

" A valuable essay."—*Quar. Rev.*, (Lon?.)

" It is a production which, as a whole, conveys a valuable amount of information respecting our Province, which was urgently required, in order to set our Colony and its native resources in a proper light before the world. The essay is written in a plain and, generally speaking, clear style, and has the merit of giving a greater variety of details than we remember to have seen in any similar work on Nova Scotia."—*M. Chronicle,* (Hal.)

" Very able essay."—R. G. HALIBURTON.

II. Our British North American Colonies. *Quart. Rev.*, 1864.

III. The American War: with some suggestions towards effecting an honorable peace. *Halifax*, 1864, pp. 16.

IV. Descriptive Catalogue of the Fishes of Nova Scotia. *Do.*, Part I. 1866, pp. 54 ; Part II, 1867, pp. 113, 8vo.

KNOX, *Captain* JOHN, *R. N.*

I. An Historical Journal of the Campaigns in North America, for the years 1757-58-59 and 1760 ; containing the most remarkable occurrences of that period, particularly the two sieges of Quebec, &c., &c., the orders of the Admirals and General Officers ; description of countries where the author has served, with their forts and garrisons, their climates, soil, produce, and a regular diary of the weather. As also several Manifestos, a Mandate of the late Bishop of Canada, the French Orders and Dispositions for the defence of the Colony, &c. (With portraits of Generals Amherst and Wolfe). *London*, 1769, 2 vols. pp. 870, 4to.

" A valuable collection of materials towards a history of that period, with a description and natural history of those parts in which Knox personally served."—LOWNDES.

" These are two heavy tedious volumes. The first one particularly, being principally taken up with a journal of his garrison residence in Nova Scotia and New Brunswick, where he was locked up in small forts, from which they could not venture a mile, without risk of attack from the Acadians and Savages. The war between the English and French in this quarter, seems to have been carried on by both parties with the utmost barbarity. It had all the horrid features of Indian warfare, plundering, burning, and scalping. The second volume, which narrates the operations before Quebec, the battle in which Wolfe and Montcalm lost their lives, the capture of the city, and the final capitulation of the Marquis de Vaudreuil, and surrender of the Canadas to General Amherst, is interesting in spite of the author."—*N. A. Rev.*

KOHL, J. G.

I. Travels in Canada and through the States of New York and Pennsylvania. Translated from the German, by Mrs. Percy Sinnett. *London*, 1860, 2 vols., pp. 345—357, 8vo.

KOHLMEISTER, BENJAMIN, and GEORGE KNOCH. Missionaries of the Ch. of *Unitas Fratrum,* or United Brothers.

I. Journal of a Voyage from Okkak, on the coast of Labrador, to Ungava Bay, westward of Cape Chudleigh ; undertaken to explore the coast, and visit the Esquimaux in that unknown region. (With Map.) *London*, 1815, pp. 83, 8vo.

L.

LABELLE, *Rév.* M. F.

Biographie et oraison funebre du Rév. M. F. Labelle, et autres documents relatifs à sa mémoire, ainsi qu'à la visite de P. A. De Gaspé, écuier, au Collége de L'Assomption. *Montréal*, 1865, pp. 85.

LABRIE, **JACQUES**, *M. D.* A French Can. writer. B. in Can., 1783. D. at St. Eustache, L. C., 26 Oct., 1831. Ed. at the Quebec Seminary. Graduated in medicine at Edinburgh. Sat for several years in the Assem., L. C., of which he was an active mem. In 1807 established the *Courrier* (Que.,) of which he was ed. He wrote a History of Can. which, however, was never published, although the money for that purpose was voted by the L. C. Legislature. The MS. was afterwards destroyed in the sacking and burning of St. Benoit. Some historical fragments from his pen appeared in *La Bibliothèque Can.*

I. Les Premiers rudiments de la Constitution Britannique, traduits de l'Anglais de M. Brooke, précédés d'un précis historique, et suivis d'observations sur la Constitution du Bas-Canada. *Montréal*, 1827, 8vo.

LACASSE, **NAPOLÉON**. Prof. in Laval Normal Sch. (Que.)

I. Tenue des Livres en Partie simple et en Partie double, ou comptabilité générale. *Québec*, 1866, pp. 212, 8vo.

Approved by the Council of Public Inst. L. C.

LACHLAN, *Major* ROBERT. A retired officer from the Brit. Army. Served for a lengthened period in the 17th Regt., of Foot. Was for several years President of the Nat. His. Soc. (Mont.) Now resides in U. S.

I. A Discourse read before the Western District Literary, Philosophical and Agricultural Association. *Sandwich, U. C.*, 1842, pp. 17.

II. Remarks on the State of Education in the Province of Canada. By "L." [Reprinted from *B. A. Journ.*] *Montréal*, 1848, pp. 72.

"The work bears evidence of much reflection and considerable research." — *B. A. Journ.*

III. Renewed remarks on same subject. *Do.*, 1849, pp. 48.

IV. A Retrospective Glance at the Progressive State of the Natural History Society of Montreal, with a view to ascertaining how far it has advanced the important objects contemplated by its founders; a lecture. *Do.*, 1852, pp. 24.

V. Narrative of the Failure of an attempt to establish a Great National Institution for the reception of Orphan Children of Officers of the British army. *Do.*, 1854, pp. 45.

VI. How Patriotic Services are rewarded in Canada; exemplified in the case of Major Lachlan, late of Montreal. *Cincinnati, O.*, 1856, pp. 16.

VII. Paper and Resolutions in advocacy of the establishment of a uniform system of Meteorological Observations throughout the whole American continent. *Do.*, 1859, pp. 14.

Canadian Journal.

I. On the Establishment of a System of Simultaneous Meteorological Observations &c., throughout the British American Provinces. 1854.

"A clear and well considered paper."— SIR J. B. ROBINSON, BART.

II. On the Periodical Rise and Fall of the Lakes. *Do.*

"Highly interesting collection of facts * * * * furnishes a large amount of instructive information respecting the history of one of those remarkable inland seas."— *Can. Journ.*

III. Account of an Extraordinary sudden fall in the Waters of the Niagara River. 1855.

IV. On the Formation of a Canal between Lakes St. Clair and Erie; and the foundation of a town and harbour at the mouth of the two creeks, in the Township of Romney, in connection with the establishment of an extensive system of Drainage, by which near a million of Fertile Acres would be redeemed in one District do.

V. Supplementary Remarks in behalf of the establishment of a Provincial System of Meteorological Observations. do.

LACOMBE, PATRICE, *N. P.* D. at Montreal, 6 July, 1863, aged 56.

I. La Terre Paternelle. Roman de mœurs. *Rep. Nat.*, 1848.

LAFLÈCHE, *Rt. Rev.* LOUIS. Coadjutor R. C. Bish. of Three Rivers, L. C. B. at St. Anne de la Pérade 4 Sept., 1813. Ordained priest 1844. Was during 12 years a missionary in various parts of the Hudson's Bay Territory; his letters and reports from that region, embodied in the *Rapports sur les missions du Diocèse de Québec*, from 1846 to 1856, contain a large amount of valuable information as to the general value and resources of the North-west country. For some years he was Superior of Nicolet Coll. Mgr. L. has written letters to the French Can. press on various subjects. Several of his pulpit discourses, delivered on special occasions, such as the *Oraison funèbre des soldats morts à Castelfidardo; Éloge funèbre de feu l'Hon. J. E. Turcotte; Discours sur la Nationalité &c.*, which have appeared in the newspapers, are well thought of.

I. Quelques Considérations sur les Rapports de la Société Civile avec la religion et la famille. *Montréal*, 1866, pp. 268, 12mo.

" Chez les hommes du monde et surtout les Canadiens, la lecture de ces écrits produirait peut-être autant de bien qu'en firent en Angleterre les instructions onctueuses et les livres pieux du père Faber. Nos destinées providentielles y sont indiquées avec une justesse frappante."—*Echo du Cab. de Lec.*

LAFONT, J. B. ANGELVY. French Master, Grammar and Central Sch. (Hal.)

I. Treatise on French Pronunciation and Genders. *Montreal*, 1865.

LAFONTAINE, *Hon.* Sir LOUIS H., *Bart.* Late Chief Justice of L. C. B. at Boucherville, L. C., Oct., 1807. D. at Montreal, March, 1864. He was returned to the Assem., L. C., in 1830, and sat in that body until the events of 1837, when martial law was proclamed.

In 1838 he proceeded to Eng. After the Union in 1841 he again entered the Legislature, and was a mem. of the Assem. until 1851. He was twice Attorney Genl., for some time Prime Minister, and took part in introducing Responsible Govt. into Can. Previous to the Union he contributed occasionally to the ed. columns of *La Minerve*, (Mont.)

(See *Royal*, Joseph.)

I. Notes sur l'Inamovibilité des curés dans le Bas Canada. *Montréal*, 1837, pp. 56.

(See *Lartigue*, Mgr. J. J.)

II. Analyse de l'Ordonnance du Conseil Spécial sur les Bureaux d'Hypothèques, suivie du Texte Anglais et Français de l'Ordonnance, des lois relatives à la Creation des ci-devant Bureaux de comtes, et la Loi des Lettres de Ratification. *Do.*, 1842, pp. 244. 8vo.

III. Seigniorial Questions: Containing the Observations of Sir L. H. Lafontaine, Bart. *Do.*, 1856, 8vo.

LAFRANCE, C. J. L.

I. Abrégé de Grammaire Française. *Québec*, 1865, pp. 122, 12mo.

LA FRENAYE, PIERRE RICHARD, *B. C. L.* Since 1855 has been Prof. of Jurisprudence and Legal Bibliography in McGill Coll. (Mont.) Was President of *L'Institut Canadien*, of same city, in the years 1855 and '58. Has been a mem. of the Ed. Committee of the *Lower Canada Jurist* (Mont.), since its commencement in 1857, and contributed Law Reports to its pages.

I. Contrainte par corps. *Rev. Can.*, 1866.

LAGACÉ, *Rév.* M. P. Prof. of Music in the Coll. (St. Anne, L. C.)

I. Les Chants d'Eglise en usage dans la Province Ecclésiastique de Québec. harmonisés pour l'orgue suivant les principes de la Tonalité Grégorienne. *Québec*, 1860.

LALOURCE', M., *Avocat.*

I. Mémoire pour M. François Bigot, ci-devant Intendant de Justice, Police. Finance et Marine en Canada, Accusé; contre M. le Procureur Général du Roi en la Commission, Accusateur. Partie 1re. contenant l'Histoire de l'Administration du Sieur Bigot dans la Colonie, et des réflexions générales sur cette Administration. Partie 2c. contenant la discussion et le détail des Chefs d'Accusation. *Paris*, 1763, in-4.

"Ce mémoire est intéressant, parce qu'il fait connaître le dernier état du Canada sous les Français, qui l'ont cédé aux Anglais en 1763, avec la partie Orientale de la Louisiane."—M. DE FONTETTE.

LAMARCHE, *Rév.* M.
I. L'Église Anglicane et le Rationalisme. *Rev. Can.*, 1864.

LAMBERT, JOHN.
I. Travels through Canada and the United States of North America, in the years 1806, 1807 and 1808; to which are added biographical notices and anecdotes of some of the leading characters in the United States; with a map and numerous engravings. *London*, 1810, 3 vols., 8vo.

LAMBLY, *Capt.* JOHN.
I. Sailing directions for the River St. Lawrence, from Cape Chat to the Island of Bic, &c. *Quebec*, 1808.

LANDERS, ANTHONY.
I. Remarks on the impolicy and injustice of laying a duty on Timber, imported from British America, or taking off the Baltic duty. *London*, 1821.

LANE, EDWARD.
I. The Fugitives; or, a Trip to Canada. *London*, 1830, 12mo.

LANGEVIN, *Very Rev.* E. Vicar Genl. (Rimouski). Brother of the two following.
I. Notice historique sur la mission de Ste. Croix de Tadoussac. (With photograph). *Québec*, 1864, pp. 40.

LANGEVIN, *Hon.* HECTOR LOUIS, *Q. C.* A Can. statesman. B. at Quebec, 25 Augt., 1826. Admitted to the Bar, L. C., 1850. Was Mayor (Que.) from 1858 to 1860. Sat in Leg. Assem. Can., from 1857 until the Union of 1867. Was Solicitor Genl., L. C., from March, 1864, to Oct., 1866, when he was appointed Postmaster Genl. Is now Secy. of State for the Dominion of Can. Ed. *Les Mélanges Religieux* (Mont.) from 1847 to 1849, and also *Le Journal d'Agriculture*, for a brief period.
I. Canada, ses Institutions, &c.; [an essay, to which was awarded an extra

prize by the Canadian Paris Exhibition Committee.] *Québec*, 1855, pp. 186, 8vo.

II. Droit Administratif, ou Manuel des Paroisses et Fabriques. *Do.*, 1862, pp. 206, 8vo.

"L'ouvrage de M. Langevin, quelqu'élémentaire qu'il soit, contribuera sans aucun doute à répandre des notions précises sur cette matière [l'Organisation Paroissiale du Bas Canada], à populariser un sujet que tout citoyen doit connaître, puisque dans cet ordre de choses non seulement tout citoyen est gouverné, mais tout citoyen peut devenir gouvernant."—E. L. DEBELLEFEUILLE: *Rev. Can.*

LANGEVIN, *Rt. Rev.* JEAN. R. C. Bish. of Rimouski, L. C. Was for some years principal of Laval Normal Sch. (Que.) In 1849–50 delivered a series of lectures before *L'Institut Canadien* there, with the title *Aperçu de l'histoire de Québec sous la domination Française* 1659 à 1759, which appeared in *Le Journal* (Que.)
I. Notes sur les Archives de Notre Dame de Beauport. *Québec*, 1860, pp. 128-xxxvi, 12mo.

"Is a work of great interest to our Canadian Genealogists and Antiquaries."—*Journ. of Ed. L. C.*

II. L'Histoire du Canada en tableaux. *Do.*, 1860, pp. 8; 2nd Ed., 1865.

III. Réponses aux Programmes de Pédagogie et d'Agriculture pour les diplômes d'écoles élémentaires, d'écoles modèles et d'académie. *Do.*; 2nd Ed., 1864, pp. 51.

This has been translated into English, and both editions have been approved by the Council of Public Inst., L. C.

IV. Cours de Pédagogie, ou principes d'éducation. *Do.*, 1865, pp. 409.
"The most important work of the kind which has issued from the Canadian press."—*Idem.*

LANGTON, JOHN, *M. A.* Auditor Genl. of Public Accounts, Can. Is a graduate of Cambridge Univ. Sat in Leg. Assembly, Can., from 1851 to 1855. Was Vice Chancellor of the Univ. (Tor.), for some years.
I. Statement before the Committee appointed by the Legislative Assembly to investigate the affairs of the University of Toronto. *Toronto*, 1860, pp. 50.

II. On the age of Timber Trees and the prospects of a continuous supply of Timber in Canada. *Trans. Lit. & His. Soc.* (Que.), 1852.

III. Address before Literary and Historical Society of Quebec at the opening of the session of 1862–3. *Quebec*, pp. 20. do.

IV. Do. do. 1863–4, pp. 34, *Do.* 1864.

V. Note on an Incident of Early Canadian History. *Do.* do.

VI. The Census of 1861. *Do.* do.

VII. Opening Address. *Do.*, 1865, pp. 28.

VIII. Early Records of the Magnetic Declination in North America. *Do.* do.

IX. On the Measurement of Heads in Ethnological Investigations. *Do.*, 1866.

Canadian Journal.

I. The Importance of Scientific Studies to Practical men; a lecture. 1854.

II. On a small Capillary Wave not hitherto described. 1857.

III. On the Early Discoveries of the French in North America. Do.

LANIGAN, G. F. A Can. writer. B. at St. Charles, River Richelieu, L. C., 10 Dec., 1846. Has contributed largely, in prose and verse, to the Can. and Am. periodical and newspaper press. His writings are composed principally of humorous and descriptive sketches of men, nature and things; critical essays; translations from the French and German poets; and short epic and fugitive pieces in verse. Mr. L. has written for *Wilkes' Spirit*, and *Porters' Spirit of the Times* (N. Y.), under the *nom de plume* of "Toxophilite," to the *Western Journal* under that of "El Penseroso," and to the *Albion*, (N. Y.), and other periodicals as "Allid," which latter name he has adopted permanently. In 1867 he joined the staff of the *Gazette* (Mont.), as the ed. of the Sporting department of that journal. He is regarded as one of the most promising of the rising *literati* of Can.

I. National Ballads of Canada, imi-

tated and translated from the originals, by "Allid." *Montreal*, 1865, pp. 15, 12mo.

"Several of these translations have already appeared in the *Albion*, and attracted our attention at the time by the admirable fidelity and poetic taste with which they had been turned into English. We wish him the success which he deserves in such a spirited undertaking; and we must say that the few specimens of his ability which he has given to the world confirm us in the belief that he is qualified to a rare degree for the performance of such a task. His knowledge of the language of the original ballads is evidently perfect, and his appreciation of the rare beauties which many of these old rhymes contain bears testimony to his poetic temperament."—*Chronicle*(Que.)

II. Etudes sur la Poésie Anglaise. *Rev. Can.*, 1866.

LANIGAN, GEORGE. A Can. journ. In 1853, in conjunction with his brother, Richard, established the *Inquirer*, (Three Rivers, L. C.), in the interest of the Conservative party. This he ed. until 1859, when the paper was purchased by the present prop. From 1863 to 1865 he ed. the *Daily News* (Que.), and subsequently, for a short period, the *Transcript* (Mont.) He founded the *Leader*, (Sherbrooke), of which he was ed. Mr. L. is generaly recognized as one of our foremost public writers.

LANMAN, CHARLES. An Am. author. B. in Monroe, Mich., 14 June, 1819. In early life was engaged in mercantile affairs, which he abandoned for Literature. Was for some years private secy. to Daniel Webster. Is now librarian to the House of Representatives, (Washington).

I. A Tour to the Saguenay, in Lower Canada. *Philadelphia*, 1848, 8vo.

II. Adventures of an Angler in Canada, &c. *London*, 1848, 8vo.

III. Adventures in the Wilds of North America. *Do.*, 1854, 12mo.

IV. Adventures in the Wilds of the United States and British American Provinces; with an appendix by Campbell Hardy. *Philadelphia*, 1856, 2 vols., 8vo.

LANTON, *Rev.* HENRY. A Wes. Meth. Min. (Ham.)

I. Lectures on the Second Advent of Christ. *Montreal*, 1855, pp. 452, 8vo.

LAPERRIÈRE, AUG. A Clk. in the Library of Parliament, Can.

I. Canadian Parliamentary Precedents ; a collection of the decisions of the Hon. the Speakers of the House of Assembly, from 1859 to 1866. In English and French. (*In preparation.*)

LA ROCHEFOUCAULT-LIANCOURT, FRANÇOIS ALEXANDRE FRÉDÉRIC, *Duc* de. A French statesman and philanthropist. B. 1747, D. 1829.

I. Travels through the Unites States of North America, the country of the Iroquois, and Upper Canada, in the years 1795, 1796 and 1797 ; with an authentic account of Lower Canada. Translated from the French. (With Maps) *London*, 1803, 4 vols., 4to.

Orignally published in Paris in 1799.

" A tolerably fair picture of America at this period, with respect to agriculture, statistics, manufactures, commerce, national and domestic habits."—LOWNDES.

LAROCQUE, *Rev.* CHARLES. A R. C. Clergym.

I. Notice biographique de Mgr. Lartigue, premier Evêque de Montréal. Suivie de son oraison funèbre. *Montréal*, 1841, pp. 23.

II. Revue des Dogmes Catholiques. *Do.*, 1852, 8vo.

LARTIGUE, *Rt. Rev.* J. J. First R. C. Bish. of Montreal. B. 20 June, 1777. D. 19 Apl., 1840.

I. Mémoire sur l'inamovibilité des curés en Canada, suivi de remarques sur les notes de M. Lafontaine, avocat, relativement à l'inamovibilité des curés dans le Bas Canada. *Montréal*, 1837.

II. Mandement contre l'insurrection particlle du Bas Canada. *Do.*, do.

(See *LaRoque*, Rev. C.)

LARUE, F. A. H., *M. D.* A French Can. author. Contributed to *La Ruche Litteraire* in 1859 under the *nom de plume* of " Isidore de Meplats." He was one of the originators of *Le Foyer Can.* for which he sometimes wrote. His writings are highly esteemed by the French Can. press.

I. Du Suicide ; thèse pour le doctorat en médecine. *Québec*, 1859, pp. 128, 12mo.

I. Le Défricheur de langue, tragédie bouffe (en vers) en trois Actes et en trois Tableaux. *Do.*, 1859, pp. 8.

III. Voyage autour de l'Isle d'Orleans. *Soirées Can.* 1861.

V. Éloge funèbre de M. L'Abbé L. J. Casault, Premier Recteur de l'Université-Laval. *Do.*, 1863, pp. 29, 18mo.

" An eloquent and noble tribute to the lamented and gifted Rector of the University Laval, whose life, spent in the cause of University Education, has made his name one of the most honored in the land of Champlain, Iberville, and Vaudreuil."—*Am. His. Mag.*

VI. Chansons Populaires et Historiques du Canada. *Foyer Can.*, 1863-4.

LASKEY, R. K. (N. B.)

I. Alethes ; or, the Roman exile. 1840.

LA TERRIERE, PIERRE DE SALLES.

I. Dissertation on the puerperal fever. *Boston*, 1789, 8vo.

LA TERRIERE, PIERRE DE SALLES, *M. D.* A French Can. medical practitioner.— Was for sometime a mem. of the Leg. Assem., L. C. D. at Les Eboulements, L. C., 12 Dec., 1834.

I. A Political Account of Lower Canada ; with remarks on the present situation of the People, as regards their manners, character, religion, &c., by " A Canadian." *London*, 1830, 8vo.

LATHERN, *Rev.* JOHN. Wes. Meth. Min. (Hal.)

I. Havelock's last Campaign ; a Lecture. *Halifax*, (*N. D.*), pp. 27, 8vo.

LATOUR, L. A. HUGUET, *N. P.* In 1848 contributed a number of articles to the *Journal d'Agriculture.* Mr. L. has long been a mem. and office-bearer of the Natural History Soc., (Mont.,) and, in 1857, offered a gold medal as a prize for the best essay, in French or Eng., on any subject connected with Can. Nat. History.

I. Annales de la Tempérance. *Montréal*, 1854, pp. 80.

II. Annuaire de Ville-Marie, origine, utilité et progrès des institutions catholiques de Montréal. *Do.*, 1864, pp. 192, 8vo.

" The historical, biographical and statistical information * * * in this little book, is very valuable."—*Journ. of Ed. L. C.*

LAURIN, JOSEPH. Sat in Leg. Assem. Can., from 1844 to 1854.

I. Traité d'Arithmétique et d'Algèbre. *Québec*, 1836.

II. Traité sur la tenue des livres de compte, en partie simple, et en partie double. *Do.*, 1837, 12mo.

III. Géographie Élémentaire par demandes et par réponses. *Do.*, 1839.

LAVAL, *Mgr.* FRANÇOIS DE MONTMORENCY. First R. C. Bish. of New France. B. at Laval, Maine, France, 23 March, 1622. D. at Quebec, 6 May, 1708.

Mémoire sur la vie de M. De Laval, premier Evêque de Québec. Par l'Abbé Bertrand de la Tour. *Cologne*, 1761 ; 2nd Ed., *Paris*, 1762.

Esquisse de la vie et des travaux apostoliques de Mgr. Xavier de Laval Montmorency, premier Evêque de Québec, suivie de l'éloge funèbre du prélat. *Québec*, 1845, pp. 145, 8vo.

Esquisse biographique sur Mgr. de Laval. Par l'Abbé Brasseur de Bourbourg. *Do.* 1855.

Notice historiographique sur la fête célébrée à Québec le 16 Juin 1859, jour du 200me anniversaire de l'arrivée de Mgr. de Montmorency Laval en Canada. Par J. C. Taché. *Do.* 1859, pp. 72.

LAWSON, JOHN, Barrister.
 I. Letters on Prince Edward Island. *Charlottetown*, pp. 76, 8vo.

LEA, I.
 I. Twenty-four new species of Physa of the United States and Canada. *Proc. Aca. N. S. (Phil.)* 1864.

LEACH, *Ven. Archdeacon* W. T., *D. C. L., LL. D.* Fellow, Dean of the Faculty of Arts, Prof. of Logic and Moral Philosophy, and Molson Prof. of English Literature, in Univ. McGill Coll. (Mont.)

 I. Discourse on the Nature and Duties of the Military Profession, delivered to the 93rd Highlanders. *Toronto*, 1840.

" We sincerely wish that this excellent, pious, and patriotic discourse could be put into the hands of every soldier in the British Army. It points out, as its title bears, not only the nature and duties of the military profession, but impresses upon the soldier the honour and respectability of his station, not less as a defender of his country from foreign aggression than a legal conservator of its institutions."—*Gazette,* (Mont.)

 II. Observations on the Hypothesis of the former existence of a great Fresh-water Inland Sea within the Continent of America. *B. A. Journal,* 1845.

III. On the Uses and Abuses of Phrenology ; a lecture. *Do.*, 1846.

IV. Sermon on Advent Sunday, 1851, appointed, by authority, for the celebration of the third semi-centennial jubilee of the S. P. G. F. P. *Montreal,* 1851, pp. 20.

V. A Great Work left Undone ; or the desideratum in systems of Education ; a lecture. *Do.*, 1864, pp. 32.

" The views of the lecturer are very ably and vigorously set forth, and appear to be the result of long and deep meditation."—*Journ. of Ed. L. C.*

LEAMING, JEREMIAH.
 I. Dissertations on True Religion. *Montreal,* 1819, pp. 68.

LEAVEN. *Rev.* THOMAS.
 I. The Authority and Transmission of the Ministry in Christ's Church ; a sermon. *Halifax,* 1848, pp. 16, 8vo.

LEBRUN. ISIDORE. A French author.
 I. Tableaux Statistiques des Deux Canadas. *Paris,* 1833, 8vo.

 (See *Maguire,* L'Abbé.)

LE CONTE, J. L.
 I. Notes on the Coleoptera found at Fort Simpson, Mackenzie River. *Proc. Aca. N. S. (Phil.),* 1860.

LEEMING, JOHN.
 I. Lecture on the Early Closing Movement. *Montreal,* 1851.

LEFROY, *Brig. Genl.* JOHN HENRY, *F. R. S.,* Royal Artillery. Was director of the Observatory (Tor.) from 1842 to 1853, during a portion of which time he was President of the Can. Institute there, and contributed to its journal and to other scientific publications, both on this continent and in Eng. From 1845 to 1853 he contributed to the *B. Am. Journ.* (Mont.), a monthly Meteorological Register at the Toronto Observatory. His observations on the magnetical survey of portions of the Hudson's Bay Territory were published by Genl. Sabine in the *Philosophical Trans.* (1846,) and are in part included in Evan's *Variation Chart of the World,* published by the Admiralty, 1858.

 I. Terrestrial Magnetism ; a lecture before Mechanics' Institute, Toronto. *B. A. Journ.*, 1851.

 II. Remarks on Thermometric Registers. *Can. Journ.*, 1852.

III. Address as President of the Canadian Institute. *Do. do.*

IV. On the Probable Number of the Native Indian population of British America. *Do.*, 1853.

Also published in pamphlet form.

V. Observations made at the Magnetical and Meteorological Observatory at Toronto, from 1840 to 1842. *London*, 1845, 4to.

This work has been continued down to the year 1848. It was published under the name and superintendence of General Sabine, President of the Royal Society.

VI. Magnetical and Meteorological Observations at Lake Athabaska and Fort Simpson and at Fort Confidence. By Col. J. H. Lefroy and Sir John Richardson. *Do.*, 1855, pp. 391, Imp. 8vo.

" We possess * * * * similar results at Lake Athabaska, deduced by Col. Lefroy from observations made by himself, and which although derived from a shorter series of observations are of the highest scientific value."—DR. LLOYD : before *Roy. Irish Aca.*

LEGGE, CHARLES, *C. E.*, (Mont.)

I. A Glance at the Victoria Bridge, and the men who built it. *Montreal*, 1860, pp. 153, 12mo.

LEHMANN, J. F.

I. Remarks on Insanity and the Management of Insane Persons. *Montreal*, 1840.

LEIDY, *Prof.* JOSEPH, *M. D.*

I. Notes of the remains of a species of Seal, from the Post pliocene deposit of the Ottawa River. *Proc. Aca. of Nat. Scien.* (Phil.), 1856.

LEISTE, C.

I. Beschreibung des Brittischen Amerika. *Wolfenbüttel*, 1778, sm., 8vo.

LEITCH, *Very Rev.* WILLIAM, *A. M., D. D.*, Sometime Principal of Univ. of Queen's Coll., (Kings.) B. at Rothesay, Island of Bute, 1814. D. at Kingston, U. C., 9 May, 1864. Received his primary education at the parish sch. of Rothesay, and afterwards entered Glasgow Univ., where he graduated A. M. In 1838 he was licensed as a preacher in the Ch. of Scot. In 1859 he was selected for the office of Principal of the Univ. of Queen's Coll., which he held from that time up to his death. An ardent lover of science he while still a student lectured on astronomy, and for several years acted as assist. to Prof. Nichol in the Univ. Observatory ; he was a diligent contributor to *Kitto's Journal of Sacred Literature, McPhails Mag., The Christian Mag.* (Edin.), *The Scottish Quarterly Rev.* and *Good Words*, in which latter periodical the papers composing his published work first appeared. Shortly after arriving in Can. he was elected Moderator of the Synod of the Ch. of Scot. He had a seat in the Senate of the Univ. (Tor.), in which he was also an examiner. In the enunciation of his views on Univ. reform in Can., Dr. L. showed himself to be a man far removed above the envious assailant and unprincipled leveller. He was a man universally beloved by all people and classes. For some years he held the office of President of the Botanical Soc. of Can., before which he read several papers of interest.

I. God's Glory in the Heavens. *London*, 1862, pp. 360 ; 3rd Am. Ed., *New York*, 1866.

" Dr. Leitch's book is illustrated with some of the most remarkable views of the moon, Spiral nebulæ, and other heavenly bodies. The style in which the work is written is very attractive, and as a popular exposition of the present condition of our knowledge of astronomy, it commends itself to the attentive perusal of all to whom God has given the power to appreciate ' His Glory in the Heavens.' "—*B. A. May.*

II. Opening Address. *Trans. Bot. Soc.*, 1861.

III. On the Sexual Development and Economy of Bees. *Do. do.*

LEITH, ALEXANDER. A Toronto Barrister.

I. Commentaries on the Law of England applicable to Real Property (by Sir William Blackstone, Knight), adapted to the present state of the Law in Upper Canada. *Toronto*, 1864, pp. 416, 8vo.

" Mr. Leith has thoroughly adapted the first volume of the work of the great commentator, or that which treats of real property, to the law of Upper Canada. His task was no ordinary one. Since 1792 the laws of England and of Upper Canada have been, to a certain extent, diverging. A thorough knowledge of the law of England as it was in 1792 was necessary to a correct understanding of the law of Upper Canada as it now exists.

"We know of no man at the bar better fitted than Mr. Leith to point out the differences between the two in such a manner as to instruct the law student and guide the professional man in active practice. He has made the law of real property his especial study. * * * The result, so far as the first volume is concerned, is a Canadian Blackstone, equal to the original as touching its style, and more reliable than the original as touching the present state of the law."—*U. C. Law Journ.*

LELIEVRE, SIMON, *Q. C.* A Quebec Advocate. D. at Quebec, Sept., 1866. Was one of the Ed's. of *La Revue de' Législation,* (Quebec and Montreal), from 1846 to 1848, 3 vols. From 1851 up to his death was on the Ed. Committee of the *Lower Canada* (Law) *Reports.*

LEMAY, LEON PAMPHILE. A French Can. poet. B. at Lotbinière, L. C., 1837, Ed. at his native place and at the Seminary (Que.), at which latter institution he studied for the priesthood, but owing to continual ill-health, abandoned his intention of entering the Ch. He next studied law, which was also in a short time thrown up. Returning from the U. S., whither he had gone in search of fortune, we find him engaged for a brief period as a merchant's clk. at Sherbrooke, L. C. That employment proving uncongenial, he was a second time invested with the cassock, and for two years piously and diligently studied theology at Ottawa ; an attack of dyspepsia prostrated his energies and compelled him to retire from the cloister, never to return. He resumed his legal studies, for a short time was employed in the French translator's office of the Leg. Assem., and at this period married. For some years he has been residing at the village of St. Emelie de Lotbinière. Although his contributions to the chief French Can. periodicals have deservedly attracted the notice and commendation of the *liberati* of this country, the U. S. and France, his literary reputation rests mainly on the work which he has lately produced.

I. Essais Poetiques. *Québec,* 1835, pp. 320, 8vo.

"The volume before us contains a translation of Evangeline, very well rendered, and losing in the French the cumbersome measure to which Longfellow wrote it, and a number of lesser original poems. The poet

shows a keen appreciation of the beauties of nature, and some of his descriptive passages are very fine. We wish him every success, and hope this may not be the last contribution he will make to Canadian literature."— *Gazette,* (Mont.)

LE MOINE, JAMES MACPHERSON. A Can. author. B. at Quebec, 1825. Ed. at the Seminary of that city, where he enjoyed the instruction in his classical course of the Abbé Bouchy, a Parisian teacher. He adopted the profession of law and practised for sometime as an advocate. He has been for some years Collector of Revenue (Que.) Mr. L. has contributed many interesting papers on Natural History and Can. historical transactions and episodes to the Eng. and French periodicals and journals in Can. He has devoted much time and attention to collecting and bringing out rare and valuable manuscripts relating to the early history of his native country. His chief contributions have appeared in *Le Foyer Can.* and *Les Soirées Can.* (Que.,) *La Revue Can.* and the *Saturday Reader* (Mont.)

I. Notes on Land and Sea Birds observed around Quebec. *Can. Nat.,* 1859.

II. L'Ornithologie du Canada. *Québec,* 2nd Ed., 1851, pp. 400.

"I consider it a very desirable addition to the popular Ornithology of North America." —PROF. S. K. BAIRD : Smithsonian Instit.

III. Etude sur les Explorations Arctiques de McClure, de McClintock, de Kane. *Do.*

IV. Les Pecheries du Canada. *Do.,* 1863, pp. 146, 8vo.

"It supplies the most interesting information with regard to the new science of Pisciculture. and the wonderful results which have followed from its cultivation in Europe; it furnishes an accurate list of the rivers in Canada which produce salmon and trout, and of the artificial flies which are best adapted for taking them. It also affords the fullest information from the most authentic sources, of the deep sea fisheries, including the cod, the seal, the whale, the porpoise, the herring and the oyster, giving a calculation of the value of the whole, which ought, most undoubtedly, to attract the attention not only of capitalists and political economists, but of all philanthropic and benevolent men, who would wish to see our population furnished with a wholesome article of food, which nature has so abundantly provided, which is so necessary to a Catholic population, and which has until very lately been altogether neglected."—*Chronicle*, (Que.)

V. La Mémoire de Montcalm vengée, ou le massacre au Fort George, documents historiques recueillis. *Do.*, 1864, pp. 91.

VI. Tableau Ornithologique raisonné. *Do.*, pp. 40.

VII. Maple Leaves: a Budget of Legendary, Historical, Critical and Sporting Intelligence. *Do.*, 1863, pp. 104, 8vo.

"The 'Maple Leaves' here collected are the genuine growth of our own soil, and several of them of our own romantic neighborhood. The Quebec sketches proper are, the 'Legends of Chateau Bigot, or the Hermitage,' the 'Legend of the Golden Dog : *Le Chien d'Or*,' the 'Loss of the Auguste,' and '*La Corriveau*, or the Iron Cage.' In 'the Grave of Cadieux,' and in 'DeBrebœuf and Lalemant,' the author, like his ancestors, explores the interior, carries us up the Ottawa, and as far westward as Lake Simcoe. Though he may fairly claim to be the 'Old Mortality' of this peculiar region of the Province, Mr. LeM. is a Canadian in the largest and most liberal sense,—one of those writers ever ready to do justice to men of other origins, and to exhibit interest in all the famous localities far and near, embraced within our frontiers."—*Mercury*, (Que.)

VIII. Maple Leaves ; Second series. *Do.*, 1864, pp. 224, 8vo.

"The original articles which the present volume contains, display the deep research into our ancient historical records, and the thorough knowledge of their contents which characterize all the productions of this author's pen."—*Transcript*, (Mont.)

IX. Maple Leaves ; Third series. *Do.*, 1865, pp. 137, 8vo.

"Eschewing the role of historian, so little understood and so often prostituted to base purposes, Mr. LeM. has applied himself to the task of preserving from oblivion those themes which may be called the unwritten chapters of our history, inasmuch as they are outside the legitimate scope of the narrator of great events though not less interesting to the present age as affording an insight into the inner-life of our ancestors. The author of 'Maple Leaves,' is at present doing for Lower Canada what John Timbs and the author of 'Haunted London' have done for the antiquities of England's metropolis ; what Jules Janin has done for Brittany, that land hallowed by the legends of Arthur and Merlin ; what the antiquarian societies of all Christendom have done for their respective

countries. In the third issue of 'Maple Leaves,' Mr. LeM. has, however, managed to strike upon a new and comparatively untrodden path of literature, albeit it is within the *genre* we have already defined. 'Canadian Homes' form his text, and he has done ample justice to the beautiful theme."—*Chronicle*, (Que.)

X. Nos Maisons de Campagne. *Rev. Can.*, 1865.

XI. Les Dernières Années de la Domination Française en Canada. *Do.*, 1866.

XII. Souvenirs : Augustus Sala-Garneau-Ferland. *Do.* do.

XIII. On the History of Literature. *Trans. Lit. and His. Soc.* (Que.), 1866.

XIV. On the Birds of Canada. *Do.* do.
Also separately printed, pp. 34, 8vo.

XV. Manuscript relating to the Early History of Canada. *Quebec*, 1867.

"The manuscript was only discovered a few years ago, and is one of those attributed to the Chevalier Johnstone ; the subject treated of being the Campaign of Louisbourg, 1750–58." *Idem*.

XVI. Histoire du Canada. Où est mort Montcalm ? *Rev. Can.*, 1867.

LEMOINE, ROBERT. Clk. Assist. to the Leg. Coun., Can.

I. Rules, Orders and Forms of Proceeding of the Upper House of the Parliament of Canada. *Toronto*, 1858. pp. 111, 4to.

LENNARD, *Capt.* C. E.

I. Travels in British Columbia ; with a Yacht Voyage. *London*, 1862, 8vo.

"Afford a good deal of useful and interesting information about both British Columbia and Vancouver Island."—*Sat. Rev.*

LENOIR, JOSEPH. A French Can. poet. B. at St. Henry, L. C., 25 Sept. 1822. D. at Montreal, 3 April, 1861. His poetical genius, which was of the highest order, manifested itself while he was still at Coll. In 1847 he was called to the bar, and after practising for a few years, accepted the office of Clk. of French correspondence in the Dept. of Education, L. C., a position which he held until his death. He was also assist. ed. of the *Journ. of Education*, L. C. For 12 years he was a constant contributor in verse to the French Can. press. Many of his detached pieces appeared in *L'Avenir*, (Mont.) Some of his poems were republished in the *Rep. Nat.* (Mont.), 1848.

LE PAGE, JOHN. A P. E. I. poet. Has written many short fugitive pieces to the local press, and published several political lampoons in verse. Mr. L. contemplates shortly issuing a second volume from the press.

I. The Island Minstrel : a collection of his poetical writings. *Charlottetown*, 1860, pp. 274, 12mo.

LEPROHON, J. L., *M. D.* Founded in 1847, and ed. *La Lancette Canadienne*, the first medical journal published in the French language in Montreal. It was discontinued after 6 months, from want of support.

LEPROHON, *Mrs.* ROSANNA ELEANOR. A Can. novelist and poet. B. and ed. in Montreal. She early evinced considerable talents for literary composition, and when only 14 years of age began to contribute, under the initials of R. E. M. [ullins], her maiden name, to the *Literary Garland*, the well known Can. magazine, published for many years by Mr. Lovell. We give the titles of her larger and more important serial tales, though her various other writings in prose and verse in that periodical, and in almost every other which has been attempted in the Province, are numerous. Mrs. L. has also contributed to the U. S. press. She has done more almost than any other Can. writer to foster and promote the growth of a national Literature ; her exertions and efforts in this direction have been active and unceasing, and not without success. She has aimed principally, in some of her best known works, to depict the state of society which existed in Can. prior to, and immediately after, the Conquest, and by her often graphic descriptions of the refinement and chivalry of that period, has sought to exert a salutary influence over the present matter of fact and "hard money" world in which we live. Her pictures are lively and well-drawn. She married in 1851, Dr. J. L. Leprohon, (Mont.)

" Her poetry is marked by simplicity and gracefulness of style, strong domestic and human sympathies, and high moral sentiment. * * * Her achievements in prose-

fiction have won her higher distinction, and made her still more extensively known than her poetry."—DEWART.

I. Ida Beresford ; a novel. *Lit. Gar.* 1848.

[Translated into the French. See *De Bellefeuille, E. L.*]

" A story written with great power and vigor. The character of Ida, is finely and effectively cast, and with all her faults, there is thrown around her, the fascination of a noble frank independence, which genius alone could imagine and call into existence. The author is still very young—One of the gifted few upon whom ' Fancy smiled in her cradle,' and 'Genius marked her for her own.' As a *Canadian born* we augur for her a bright wreath of fame. Let her keep truth and nature ever in view, and scorn not the slightest teachings of the Divine Mother, and she may become the pride and ornament of a great and rising country."—MRS. MOODIE: *Victoria Mag.*, (Belleville.)

II. Florence Fitz Hardinge ; a tale. *Do.* 1849.

III. Eva Huntingdon ; a tale. *Do.* 1850.

IV. Clarence Fitz-Clarence ; a tale. *Do.* 1851.

V. Eveleen O'Donnell ; a tale. *Pilot* (Bos.) 1859.

VI. The Manor House of De Villerai ; a novel. *Fam. Herald* (Mont.) 1859.

[Translated into the French. See *De Bellefeuille, E. L.*]

VII. Cantata in Honour of the Visit of H. R. H. the Prince of Wales ; translated from the French of Mr. Sempé. *Montreal*, 1860.

VIII. Antoinette De Mirecourt ; or, Secret Marrying and Secret Sorrowing ; a Canadian tale. *Do.*, 1864, pp. 369, 8vo.

[Translated into the French. See *Genand, J. A.*]

" The tale we have said is simple, but the interest never flags. On the contrary, all, or nearly all, is natural and life-like. With no bewildering plot to puzzle the fancy or addle the reader's brain, the main episodes are cleverly pourtrayed, and the distinctive character of the various personages who appear upon the scene vividly drawn and well preserved throughout."—*Gazette* (Mont.)

" We can confidently call it our best Canadian novel, *en attendant mieux.*"—ALLID: *Sat. Reader.*

LÉRY, *Vicomte* FRANÇOIS-JOSEPH CHAUSSE-GROS DE. A celebrated French Genl. B. at Quebec, 11 Sept., 1754. D. near

Meaux, France, 6 Sept., 1824. Commenced his studies in Paris when only 8 years of age, and at 15 was admitted into the School of Engineers. After many years of active service, in which he greatly distinguished himself, he eventually became Lieut-General, and was created a commander of St. Louis and a knight of the grand cross of the legion of honour.

Notice historique sur le lieutenant-général vicomte de Léry, grand-croix de la légion d'honneur, commandeur de l'ordre royal et militaire de St. Louis. Par le Vicomte de Léry, fils.—*Paris*, 1824, pp. 8, in-8.

LESAGE, S. A French Can. writer.

I. Les Récollets en Canada. *Rev. Can.*, 1867.

LESLEY, J. P.

I. Section of Coal-measure rocks on the Cape Breton coast. *Proc. Am. Phil. Soc.*, 1861.

LETOURNEUX, M. O. A Montreal advocate. In 1846 established *La Revue Canadienne*, a journal at first exclusively literary, but which afterwards became political. In connection with it was the *Album de la Revue Canadienne*, commenced in 1847. Both, if we mistake not, were discontinued in 1849. In this last mentioned year, Mr. L. founded *La Revue de Législation et de Jurisprudence* which was subsequently conducted by Messrs. Lelièvre and Angers (Que.), with the assistance of Mr. J. N. Beaudry (Mont.) All these publications were printed at Montreal.

I. La Société Canadienne. *Rep. Nat.*, 1848.

LETT, WILLIAM PITTMAN. Clk. to the Corporation of the City of Ottawa. Since 1845 has contributed, at intervals, short poetical pieces to the newspaper press, some of which are marked by true poetic fire, and breathe a fine spirit of attachment to Can. and the mother country.

LEVINGE, *Capt.* R. G. A.

I. Echoes from the Backwoods ; or, Sketches of Transatlantic life. *London*, 1847, pp. 258.

" Our author is not only a pleasent sporting companion, but he is also a shrewd observer and useful instructor on the advantages and resources of the fine Province of New Brunswick, to which his remarks and notes chiefly apply."—*Sim. Col. Mag.*

LEWELLIN, J. L.

I. Emigration. Prince Edward Island. A brief but faithful account of this fine Colony ; shewing some of its advantages as a place of settlement, &c. *Charlottetown*, 1832, pp. 28, 8vo.

LEWIS, ISRAEL.

I. The Youth's Guardian against Crime. *Kingston*, 1844, 8vo.

LEWIS, *Rt. Rev.* JOHN TRAVERS, *D. D , LL. D.* Lord Bish. of Ontario, U. C. B. in Cork, about 1826. Ed. at Trinity Coll. (Dub.), where he graduated as senior moderator in ethics and logic, and held the distinguished position of gold medallist, having obtained classical and mathematical honors in his undergraduate course, and also obtained the degree of LL. D. Ordained deacon at Cambridge by the Lord Bish. of Chester, 1848. Was Rector of Brockville for some years previous to his election to the new bishopric of Ontario, in 1861. Has contributed the articles *The Church of the New Testament ; The Salaries of the Clergy* (Reprinted in the Diocese of Mississippi and other Dioceses, with preface, by the Rt. Rev. W. Mercer Green.) *Does the Bible need re-translating* in the *Am. Quarterly Ch. Rev ;* and *The Primitive Mode of Electing Bishops* in *The Journ. of Sacred Literature* (Lon.)

I. A Lecture before the Brockville Library Association and Mechanics' Institute, introductory to the course. *Brockville*, 1855, pp. 18, 8vo.

II. Confirmation a Scriptural and a Rational Ordinance ; a sermon.

III. The Daily Service ; a sermon.

IV. A Free Service ; do.

V. Popular Baptist Argument Reviewed ; do.

VI. A Plain Lecture to Enquirers into the meaning of the Liturgy ; do.

" As an argument for Liturgical worship and an answer to popular objections to the Prayer book, this is one of the most valuable works we have ever seen."—*Am. Quar. Ch. Rev.*

LILLIE, *Rev.* ADAM, *D. D.* A congregational min. in Can. For sometime Theological Prof. in the Congregational Coll., (Mont.) Was presented with a gold watch and a sum of money by the citizens of Toronto, in recognition of his services to the country by the publication of his first work.

I. Canada : its Growth and Prospects ; two lectures. 4th Ed. *Edinburgh*, 1852, 18mo.

II. Canada : Physical, Economic and Social. *Toronto*, 1856, pp. 294, 12mo.

" The author has palpably bestowed a vast amount of labour and research upon his task, and the result is a book most valuable to all who desire to be thoroughly indoctrinated with a knowledge of our capabilities and resources."—*Ang. Am. Mag.*

LILLINGSTON, *Rev. E., B. A.*
I. The last Confederacy of the Gentiles against Israel. *Halifax*, 1855, pp. 24, 8vo.

LILLYWHITE, W. F. A celebrated Eng. cricket-player. Accompanied the Eng. 11 to Can. some years ago. B. 1829. D. 1866.
I. English Cricketers' trip to Canada. *London*, 1860, 12mo ; 2nd Ed.. 1861.

LINDSEY, CHARLES. A Can. journ. and author. B. in Lincolnshire, Eng., 1820. Came to Can. in 1842, and proceeding to the Upper Province, shortly afterwards ed. a newspaper at Port Hope. In 1846 he became Mr. Hincks's sub-ed. on the *Examiner* (Tor.), retaining that position for 6 years. It was while on the staff of that journal that he acquired the reputation of an able and painstaking public writer, and attracted notice as a young man of ability in his profession, which led to his appointment, in 1852, as chief ed. of the *Daily Leader*, of the same city, the chief organ of the Conservative party in U. C. In that position he still continues.
I. The Clergy Reserves : their History and Present position, showing the systematic attempts that have been made to establish in connection with the State a dominant Church in Canada. With a full account of the Rectories. Also an appendix containing Dr. Rolph's speech on the Clergy Reserves, delivered in 1836. *Toronto*, 1851, pp. 74, 8vo.
II. Prohibitory Liquor Laws ; their practical operation in the United States. The subject discussed as a question of state policy and legislation, with sug-

gestions for the suppression of tippling houses. *Do.*, 1855, pp. 35.
III. The Prairies of the Western States : their advantages and their drawbacks. *Do.*, 1860, pp. 100, 12mo.
IV. The Life and Times of Wm. Lyon MacKenzie. With an account of the Canadian Rebellion of 1837, and the subsequent Frontier Disturbances, chiefly from unpublished Documents. *Do.*, 1862, 2 vols., pp. 401-400, 8vo.

" Mr. Lindsey has succeeded in throwing a new light upon many points on which provincial politics have heretofore turned. Here lies the real value of the work. It is as a biography, however, that its chief interest consists. * * * * Mr. Lindsey has performed his task carefully and well. He has been pains-taking in his accumulation of material, and prudent in its use. A judicial impartiality runs through the volumes, in a degree to which few of our political writers could have attained."--*Mercury*, (Que.)

LINDSAY, WILLIAM. A Lieut. in the Can. Militia during the War. Was Collector of Customs at St. John's, L. C., for some years. D. 1812.
I. Narrative of the Invasion of Canada, by the American Provincials under Montgomery and Arnold ; with a particular account of the Seige of Quebec, from the 17th Sept., 1775, the day on which the British Militia was embodied in that place, till the 6th of May, 1775, when the seige was raised. *Can. Rev. and Mag.*, (Mont.), 1826.

LINDSAY, W. LAUDER, *M. D., F. L. S.*
I. What to observe in Canadian Lichens. *Trans. Bot. Soc. Can.*, 1861.

LINTON, J. J. E. Clk. of the Peace, Co. of Perth, U. C.
I. A Prohibitory Liquor Law for Upper Canada, with remarks, &c. *Toronto*, 1860, pp. 48.

LISTON, JAMES K. (Clinton, U. C.)
I. Niagara Falls : a poem, in three cantos. *Toronto*, 1842.

LITCHFIELD, J. P., *M. D.* Med. Supdt. of the Criminal Lunatic Asylum, Rockwood, U. C. Was for a lengthened period connected with the newspaper and periodical press of Gt. Brit., and is still correspondent in Can. for a leading London journal. In 1835, contributed his lectures on diseases of the skin, as Physician to the Infirmary for

Diseases of the Skin, and the Westminster General Infirmary (Lon.,) to the *Lancet* and *Med. Gazette.* In the 2 following years was successively a contributor to *The Monthly Chronicle,* then ed. by Sir Bulwer Lytton, *The New Monthly Mag.,* ed. by Theodore Hook, and *Bentley's Miscellany,* ed. by Charles Dickens. In 1837-8 he became a director of the Metropolitan Newspaper Co., and one of the ed's. of the *Constitutional* (Lon.), a daily morning journal. Proceeding to the antipodes we find Dr. L., in 1839, Inspector of Hospitals in South Australia, and ed. of the *South Australian Chronicle,* positions which he retained for some years. Returning to Europe he served as correspondent at Paris to the *Courier* and the *Court Journal* (Lon.), and in France, Belgium and Holland, in a similar capacity, during 1844-5, for the *League* (Lon.) From the last named year, up to 1852, he held the appointment of Medical Supdt. of the Walton Lunatic Asylum, Eng., and contributed papers on the treatment of the Insane, to the *Museum* and the *Med. Times.* Soon afterwards he emigrated to Am., and for a short time ed. the *International Journal* (N. Y. and Bos.), whence he came to Can., and during 1853-4, was ed. of the *Pilot,* (Mont.) In 1855 he received his present appointment, and for some years has also been Prof. of Forensic and State Medicine in the Univ. of Queen's Coll. (Kings.) Dr. L. is agent in Can. for the Am. Associated Press.

I. Introduction to Library of Popular Instruction. *London,* 1834, pp. 70, sm. 8vo.

II. Outlines of Geology in do. *Do.* 1835, pp. 85, 8vo.

III. Report on the Supply of Water and Salubrity of the city of Adelaide. *Adelaide,* 1840.

IV. Essai sur la raison, et la folie ; thèse inaugurale. *Dewsbury,* 1845, pp. 24.

LITTON, L. J. President of the Sheridan Club, (Tor.,) now defunct.

I. Thoughts on Education, with reflections on the life of R. B. Sheridan ; an Inaugural Address before the Sheridan Literary Society of Toronto. *Toronto,* 1859, pp. 18.

LIVINGSTON, W., *C. M.*

I. An Appeal to the Presbyterians of New Brunswick on the late trial and suspension of the Rev. David Syme, Provincial Missionary. *St. John, N. B.,* 1836, pp. 39, 8vo.

LIVIUS, PETER. Chief Justice of the Province of Quebec, from 1777 till 1786. D. in Eng., 1795.

I. Memorial of Chief Justice Livius. 1778, pp. 52.

Proceedings between Sir Guy Carleton, late Governor of the Province of Quebec, and Peter Livius, Esquire, Chief Justice of the said Province. *London,* 1779, 8vo.

LOCKERBY, *Miss* ELIZABETH N. A P. E. I. poet. B. in Cavendish, P. E. I. Began when quite young to write short pieces in verse, principally on religious topics, many of which she has collected in her published work.

I. The Wild Brier : or, Lays by an Untaught Minstrel, E. N. L. *Charlottetown,* 1866, pp. 196, 8vo.

"The tone is decidedly religious throughout—the muse is generally solemn, if not sad—the versification is pleasant—and the effect always consoling, and at times elevating and stimulating. * * * The descriptive powers of Miss L. are considerable."—*Islander,* (Charlotte.)

LOCKHART, EPHRAIM.

I. Narrative of the oppressive law proceedings, and other measures, resorted to by the British Government, and numerous private individuals to overpower the Earl of Stirling, and subvert his lawful rights ; Also a Genealogical account of the family of Alexander, Earl of Stirling, &c., followed by an historical view of their hereditary possessions in Nova Scotia, Canada, &c. *Edinburgh,* 1836, 4to.

Not printed for sale.

LOCKWOOD, ANTHONY. A Surveyor. Resided in N. S. for some years. In 1819, appointed surveyor genl. of N. B., and a mem. of the Council of that province.

I. A Brief Description of Nova-Scotia, with plates of the principal harbours ; including a particular account of the Island of Grand Manan. *London,* 1818.

"Contains much information."—MURDOCH'S *His. of N. S.*

II. Report on the Projected Canal across the Isthmus, that divides Nova

Scotia and New Brunswick ; explored and levelled in the autumn of 1819. *Fredericton*, 1826, pp. 24, 8vo.

LOGAN, James.

I. Notes of a journey through Canada, the United States and the West Indies. *London*, 1838, 8vo.

LOGAN, *Sir* WILLIAM EDMOND, F. R. S., F.G.S., LL. D. Director of the Can. Geological Survey. B. at Montreal, 1798. Ed. at the High Sch., and the Univ. (Edin.), at which latter institution he graduated. In 1818 he entered the mercantile office of his uncle Mr. Hart Logan (Lon.), and subsequently became a partner in the firm. Returning to his native Province, his attention was attracted to the geological characteristics of Can.; he, however, recrossed the Atlantic, in 1829, and took up his residence at Swansea, South Wales, devoting himself to the study of the coal-fields of that region. He was also, we believe, manager of some copper smelting and coal mining operations there, in which his uncle was interested. Here he remained until 1838, in which year his uncle died. We shall quote from an interesting paper [*] in the *Canadian Journal* (1856) respecting his professional standing and services at this period : —

"Previous to his engagement with the Canadian Government, the reputation of Mr. Logan, (as we shall still call Sir William in referring to his past career,) stood deservedly high, although his merits were then only known and appreciated by the comparatively few scientific men with whom he had direct communication. At an early period he made a very valuable collection of the birds and insects common to Canada, included in which were many species previously unknown, which he subsequently presented to the Institution at Swansea, of which he was one of the founders, and a zealous promoter of its interests during his residence in that locality.

" But it was in the field of geology that Mr. Logan was destined to bear a conspicuous part, and it was during his residence in South Wales, that he performed a work which has been declared by the first scientific men in Europe, to be 'unrivalled in its time, and never surpassed since.' This great work was his Geological Map and Sections of the Glamorganshire Coal-field,

the minuteness and accuracy of which were such, that when the Government survey, under Sir Henry de la Beche, came to South Wales, not one single line drawn by Mr. Logan was found to be incorrect, and the whole was approved and published without alteration. Nor was this all :—the system Mr. Logan had pursued in following out the details of the coal-field was so vastly superior to any hitherto adopted, that the principle has been fully adopted by the British survey. Mr. Logan's map may be said to be the model one of the whole collection. It ought to be borne in mind also, that at this time he was not employed as one of the geological staff, but simply as an amateur, and that—in the same spirit as so many of his Canadian observations have been carried out,—he generously presented the fruits of his labors, without fee or remuneration, to the British Government." [*]

Whilst thus engaged, and up to the time of his appointment in Can., he contributed some very interesting and valuable papers to the Geological Soc. (Lon.), one of which, on "Stigmaria beds" or "under clays" which accompany every coal seam, finally set at rest the long disputed theory as to the origin of coal, and the inferences it led to were universally acknowledged. In 1841 he visited the coal-fields of Pennsylvania and N. S., and communicated papers in reference to them to the same learned body. At this time he began an examination of the older palæozoic rocks of Can.; and in the following year, the Can. Legislature having come to the determination to have the Province geologically explored, Mr. Logan was strongly recommended for the directorship of the survey by the leading geologists of Gt. Brit., from many of whom he received flattering testimonials. He was accordingly applied to by Lord Stanley (now Earl of Derby).

---

* " The Canadian Geological Survey and its director Sir W. E. Logan, by Sandford Fleming, C. E."

* In confirmation of the above we quote from a letter written at the time of Sir William's appointment to the Can. Geol. Survey :—

" His talents, as an accurate mineral surveyor, are of a very high order, and are known to the scientific world by his description of portions of the great coal-fields of Glamorganshire and Pennsylvania. illustrated by most accurate and valuable maps and sections, constructed by himself, which he has laid before the Geological Society of London.

" Moreover, he is not only enthusiastically devoted to, and highly qualified for, field works in geology, but he is also a man of modest and gentlemanly demeanor, and of high principle, and good conduct and right feeling, with whom it is pleasing to have intercourse, and on whom it is quite safe for persons in authority to place confidence."—DR. W. BUCKLAND : *Letter to Bishop of Oxford*.

the then Secretary of State for the Colonies, to accept of the office; which he has since filled with so much credit to himself and the country. In that year (1842) he proceeded to Can., and after making a preliminary survey, completed such arrangements with the Can. Government as he thought requisite at the time, for the full prosecution of the work, and re-crossed the Atlantic in quest of a competent assist., and on other business connected with the undertaking. Previous, however, to leaving for Eng. he examined and accomplished the measurement of the remarkable section of the coal measures at the South Joggins, in N. S.; a work acknowledged to be one of the most important in Am. geology, as the key to the structure of the whole eastern coal basin; and which was published as an appendix to his report of Progress in 1843. Having fully succeeded in the object of his mission, he returned to Can. in 1843, and entered earnestly into the investigation which has since been prosecuted by him steadily and without interruption. From time to time reports of progress of the survey have appeared, and from these may be gathered the important results which have been obtained, notwithstanding the almost insurmountable difficulties and obstacles with which Sir W. has had to contend, in this truly great national work. We again quote from Mr. Fleming's paper:

" The first grant of money made by the Canadian Legislature to carry out the proposed survey for two years, was only £1500, currency, so that it will be obvious it was only by the strictest economy that the salaries could be paid, and travelling and other expenses met; indeed, notwithstanding all the care possible, the necessary work could not be effected with this small grant, and, accordingly, at the expiration of that time, Mr. Logan found himself out of pocket upwards of £800.

" During the summer and autumn of 1843 Mr. Logan was employed in an examination of the coast of the Gaspé Peninsula, while he sent his assistant to make a section of the Upper Province, through the country lying between the lakes Huron and Erie—one grand object of the expedition being to determine what the probabilities were of the existence of coal measures at either end of the Province. In 1844 both Geologists were occu-

pied in exploring and completing a topographical survey of the Ottawa river up to Lake Temiscamang, and of its tributary the Mattawan to Lake Nipissing—his assistant continued the examination and topography in Gaspé. In 1845 the Legislature made a farther appropriation to the Survey of £2,000 currency per annum for five years, and the same was renewed in 1850 for five years more. In 1846, the copper region of Lake Superior occupied the entire attention of the Survey; and since that time an immense amount of country has been examined in various parts of the province, the greater portion of which being entirely wild and unknown, it was found necessary to survey topographically. Besides the geology,—much of it of the very highest economic importance,—which has been followed out on both sides of the St. Lawrence, both above and below Montreal, in the Eastern Townships, and in the region around the confluence of the Ottawa; the courses of all the main rivers of Lake Huron on the one side of the 'height of land,' and of the Ottawa on the other, have been traced and measured to their sources, the lakes and principal features of the interior surveyed, and the elevation of every fall and rapid ascertained trigonometrically or by spirit level. These surveys have since been mapped on a scale of an inch to a mile, with every particular noted thereon.

" Moreover, a regular system of measurements has not been confined to the totally wild and unfrequented part, but has been found absolutely necessary throughout nearly the whole of the settlements, in consequence of the numerous inaccuracies and omissions in the various township plans. Where a more accurate method could not be obtained, all the observations were connected by a registration of each step taken by the observer, the bearings from one point to another being taken by a compass. And as an exemple of the amount of work accomplished by this means—Mr. Richardson (who has been employed as an explorer since 1845) in 1853 registered paces, in his note book, making a total distance during the season of upwards of 1000 miles. The results of this process have also been mapped on a scale of an inch to a mile, and have supplied, on many occasions, much material to fill up deficiencies, and correct discrepancies on the old published maps.

" The result of these investigations is already acknowledged to have been of incalculable benefit to science, as having most essentially thrown light, where there was much misapprehension before, on the whole of American geology; and they have, moreover, beyond dispute, been productive of the most valuable information as regards the distribution of economic materials. While the position of such materials as *do* exist can be readily recognized by reference to the Geological map, in which the various formations are represented by different colours, those that *do not* exist, will be found wanting and, consequently, need not be looked for; such, for example, is the case with regard to Coal—a mineral not likely to be found among rocks recognized as belonging to the Silurian and Devonian epochs. * * * *

"In 1843, Mr. Logan, accompanied by a single Indian with a bark canoe made a thorough examination of the whole of the Gaspé coast, counting every step he took from Cape Rosier to Port Daniel, besides making many pedestrian excursions into the interior—and collecting a large quantity of most valuable fossils and other specimens. And while he was thus employed his assistant, Mr. Alexander, Murray—frequently entirely alone, and often in parts remote from all settlements—collected sufficient information to give a tolerably correct idea of the structure of the whole Western Peninsula. In 1844 and 1845, a triangulation was effected across the Gaspé Peninsula from Cape Chat to Bay Chaleur, a large portion of the range of the Notre Dame or Shick-Shock mountains surveyed, most of the principal rivers measured, the geological character of the rocks ascertained, and specimens collected. This service was performed with a party consisting of only four Indians with two canoes. In making the survey of the Ottawa more assistance was found to be absolutely necessary, but, except in few instances, neither Mr. Logan nor Mr. Murray's party have exceeded the complement of six altogether—inclusive of four Indians and an assistant.

"Since 1845, when the additional appropriation was granted an explorer has been added to the staff whose labors have been incessant and of great value; but while fully admitting the greatly improved circumstances under which the survey was then placed, and the more extensive scale under which the operations were enabled to be carried on, it must be clear to any one at all acquainted with the nature of the service, and of the difficulties to be encountered in a perfectly new country, that the amount of work performed and reported upon never could have been accomplished but by the most indefatigable perseverance and continued application. Accuracy with Mr. Logan is everything—nothing is allowed with him to be of the slightest value that is not essentially correct."

From a recent work *Portraits of Men of Eminence* (Lon.) we gather the following:

"The latest work of Sir W. Logan must be regarded as his greatest. To determine the superposition of such an ancient series of rocks as the Laurentian, is a task which has never been singularly successful in his labours. He has proved the Laurentian rocks to be of two series,—lower and upper,—both highly crystalline, the lower consisting chiefly of orthoclase gneiss, and the upper, instead of orthoclase, containing a great deal of labradorite, both of them holding bands of serpentine and crystalline limestone. In the limestone of the Lower Laurentian limestone, Sir W. L. has found organic remains—the *Eozoon Canadense*, determined by Dr. Dawson, of Montreal, and by Dr. Carpenter, to be one of the Foraminiferæ, a fossil from a zone prodigiously older than any previously known, for it is in the oldest known formation in the world."

In 1854 the *Quarterly Rev.*, (Lon.), spoke of the Can. Survey, as follows:—

"In Canada, there has been proceeding for some years one of the most extensive and important Geological Surveys now going on in the world. The enthusiasm and disinterestedness of a thoroughly qualified and judicious observer, Mr. Logan, whose name will ever stand high in the roll of votaries of his favourite science, have conferred upon this great work a wide spread fame."

As a proof of the two abiding qualities credited to Sir William in the above extract, we may state that on more than one occasion have his services been sought by other governments in a similar capacity. At one time the East India Co. applied to him to undertake an examination of their territory for coal; a work for which, owing to his past experience, he was eminently well fitted. It was a new field too, and great attractions in the form of large emoluments and of great honors to be achieved in the world of science offered themselves. Still, although the temptation was great, it was not sufficient to induce him to desert the work which he had undertaken in Can. and which he considered he was in some way bound to remain and complete.

In 1851 Mr. L. represented Can. at the Great Exhibition (Lon.) and had charge of the Can. geological collection, which had been made by himself or under his immediate direction. It was exhibited with great skill and judgment, displaying to the best advantage the mineral resources of Can. The labour of arranging the specimens was very great, and so enthusiastic was he, that frequently he sallied out at 8 or 10 in the morning, and would work for 12 hours without taking any refreshment. At that Exhibition he also served as a juror, and the value placed on his services in that capacity may be estimated by a very complimentary letter * which he received from the late Prince Consort, as President of the Royal Commission, in conveying to Mr. L. the medal which was awarded him for those services. At this time he was elected a Fellow of the Royal Soc., one of the highest distinctions which could be conferred upon him. At the Paris *Exposition Universelle*, in 1855, Mr. L. was also a Commissioner on behalf of his native Province. On that occasion he received from the Imperial commission the grand gold medal of honor, and was created, by the Emperor, a Knight of the Legion of Honor. In 1856 he received the honor of knighthood from the Queen, and in the same year was awarded by the Geological Soc., of which he had long been a fellow, the Wollaston Palladium medal, for his eminent services in geology. On his return to Can., in the same year, the Can. Institute (Tor.), of which he had been the first president, presented him with an address of congratulation, and had his portrait painted and hung up in the hall of the Institute. The inhabitants of his native city, not to be backward in doing honor to the man whose services and talents their Queen had acknowledged, availed themselves of the opportunity to present him with a handsome testimonial:

" In commemoration of his long and useful services as Provincial Geologist in Canada, and especially his valuable services in connexion with the Exhibition of all Nations in London in 1851, and in Paris in 1855, by which he not only obtained for himself higher honor and more extended reputation,

* Sir,—I have the honour, as President of the Royal Commission of 1851, to transmit to you a Medal that has been struck by order of the Commissioners, in commemoration of the valuable services which you have rendered to the Exhibition, in common with so many eminent men of all countries, in your capacity of juror. In requesting your acceptance of this slight token on our parts of the sense entertained by us of the benefit which has resulted to the interests of the Exhibition from your having undertaken that laborious office, and from the zeal and ability displayed by you in connexion with it, it affords me much pleasure to avail myself of this opportunity of conveying to you this expression of my cordial thanks for the assistance which you have given us in carrying this great undertaking to a successful issue. I have, &c.
(Signed,)   ALBERT.

but largely contributed in making known the natural resources of his native country."

Reports of the Canadian Geological Survey.

I. Report of Progress from 1842 :
1. Preliminary Report in 1842 on the Geology of the Province, by Mr. Logan.
2. Report for 1843, giving a general notion of the Geology of both Eastern and Western Canada so far as then ascertained, by the same.

Montreal, 1845, pp. 159, 8vo.

II. Do. for 1844 :
1. Topographical Surveys of the Cl atte and Great Cascapedia Rivers, by Mr. Logan.

1846, pp. 100, 8vo.

III. Do. for 1845 :
1. Surveys of the Ottawa River and Lake Temiscaming, with various topographical details ; and a description of the Geology of the Ottawa valley, and its economic minerals, by Mr. Logan.

1847, pp. 125, 8vo.

IV. Do. for 1846 :
1. A Geological description of the North Shore of Lake Superior.

1847, pp. 66, 8vo.

V. Two Special Reports on the Mining Region of Lake Superior, addressed by Mr. Logan, the one to the Legislative Council and the other to the Commissioner of Crown Lands. *Montreal*, 1847, pp. 31, 8vo.

VI. Report of Progress for 1847 :
I. A geological and mineralogical description of the Eastern Townships, by Mr. Logan.

1849, pp. 165, 8vo.

VII. Report of a Geological Exploration of part of the North Shore of Lake Huron made by Mr. Logan in 1848; embracing a special examination of the Bruce Mines, with two maps of the Mines and their vicinity. *Montreal*, 1849, pp. 51.

VIII. Report of Progress for 1848. 1850, pp. 65.

IX. Do. for 1849 :
1. Geological examination of St. Paul and Murray Bays, and of portions of the south side of the St. Lawrence.

Toronto, 1850, pp. 115, 8vo.

X. Do. for 1850 :

1. Report on the gold of Eastern Canada, (already described in two previous reports.)

Quebec, 1852, pp. 54, 8vo.

XI. Do. for 1851:

1. Description of the geology of the counties of Beauharnois and Lake of the Two Mountains.

2. A notice of the London International Exhibition of 1851, and of the Canadian Minerals there exhibited.

Do., 1852, pp. 131, 8vo.

" We can only say * * * that the Reports are of the highest value to the commercial and scientific interest of this Province ; and while they reflect great credit upon the Government which provides the means for the prosecution of the researches they detail, they will be a lasting record of the indefatigable industry and rare talent of the gentleman engaged in the arduous work of discovering and describing the geological treasures of Canada."—*Can. Journal* (Tor.)

XII. Do. for 1852 :

1. Geological description of the north shore of the St. Lawrence between Montreal and Quebec, with numerous details of economic minerals.

Do., 1854, pp. 179, 8vo.

XIII. Do. for 1853–54–55 and 56 :

I. Description of the Laurentian rocks of the Ottawa ; with map and remarks on the preparation of a geological map of Canada.

Toronto, 1857, pp. 494, 8vo.

" As in all the labors of the author, there is evidence of careful research and sure progress."—*Silliman's Journ.*

" The report of Sir William Logan relates chiefly to the distribution of the crystalline limestones in the Laurentian rocks at Grenville, Harrington, Wentworth, Chatham, and some adjacent townships. The accurate delineation of these limestone bands is not only of importance in an agricultural and economic point of view, but it is also of essential moment in enabling us to obtain a correct knowledge of the structural peculiarities of Laurentian districts in general."—*Can. Journ.*

XIV. Do. for 1857 :

1. Report on the various labours of the Survey.

Toronto, 1858, pp. 240.

" The body of information collected by Sir William Logan's assistants is valuable in many ways, for, traversing as they do great tracts of imperfectly known country, they are instructed in addition to purely geological researches, to observe the nature of the soil, the heights of Mountains, the rate of the falls of rivers, the state of the timber, and the species of quadrupeds, birds, land, and fresh-water shells, and other points of natural history, the state of agriculture, and any further questions of economics on which they are able to form a just opinion. For the prosecution of such investigations the scientific world is much indebted to the Canadian Government, even though, being subsidiary to geological work, they are necessarily somewhat desultory."—*Sat. Rev.*, (Lon.)

XV. Canadian Organic Remains : Decade III, with woodcuts and plates. *Do.*, 1858, pp. 102, 8vo.

XVI. Do. do. Decade I, with steel plates. *Do.*, 1859, pp. 47, 8vo.

XVII. Do. do. Decade IV, with woodcuts and plates. *Do.* 1859, pp. 72, 8vo.

XVIII. Report of Progress for 1858 :

1. Typographical Survey of the River Rouge, with descriptions of the Laurentian limestones and details of economic minerals —especially lead and copper ores ; with maps.

Do., 1859, pp. 263, 8vo.

" Sir William Logan's report contains the details of an extended exploration of the bands of crystalline limestone in the counties of Argenteuil and Ottawa, examined by him, in part, during the preceding year. These details are chiefly, and necessarily, of local interest, but they contribute much to a correct knowledge of both the geographical and geological features of that portion of the Province. In addition, for example, to the accurate delineation, of about twenty miles of the River Rouge, beyond the area at present surveyed, the position and form, to quote from the report, of thirty-two tributary lakes of various sizes were determined, some being upwards of six miles in length.—*Can. Journ.*

XIX. Geology of Canada, embracing the results of all explorations between 1859 and 1863. *Montreal*, 1863, pp. xxvii–983, Royal, 8vo.

" The preparation of this bulky octavo of nearly a thousand pages has been carried out by the indefatigable director of the survey, Sir William Logan ; and the style in which the work has been got up, the precision of the drawings, and the accuracy of the wood-cuts, may almost challenge comparison with the execution of similar scientific productions on this side of the Atlantic. There has been a steady persistence in the conduct of this remarkable survey, honourable alike to the successive Governments that have encouraged it and to the officers who have carried out the work. No other Colonial Survey has ever yet assumed the same truly national character, and the day may come—if ever the 'Imperial Colony' shall claim and attain independence—when the scientific public of a great nation, looking back upon the earlier dawnings of science in their land, shall regard the name of Logan, a native born, with the same affectionate interest with which English geologists now regard the names of our great geological map-makers, William Smith and De la Beche.

"Neither practical men, in the vulgar sense of the term, nor men of science will ever doubt the value of this anatomizing of the physical structure of Canada. But if, in the colony or elsewhere, there is one so shortsighted as to doubt the wisdom of spending money on researches which do not always suddenly tell on the pockets of the community, let him consider that, in addition to positive benefits, the mere negative results of such a survey have a distinct practical utility; for many a hopeful and unwary speculator, if he will but believe what was expressed by the colours on a geological map, will save himself from the prosecution of undertakings which end in disappointment and ruin to himself and his associates. But, on higher grounds than these, the effect of the encouragement of science in a rising country is surely not to be despised. The foundation of such a survey is like the foundation of those noble universities which have already arisen in the colony, elevating the tone of society by an admixture of a learned and scientific element, commanding the respect of the intellect of their own population, of those 'at home' in the old country, and of foreign *savants* all over Europe."—*Sat. Rev.*, (Lon.)

"After a preface of considerable length, explanatory of the origin, organization and general progress of the survey, the Report opens with a very elaborate sketch of the physical characteristics of the country, from the Gulf of the St. Lawrence and bleak wastes of Labrador, to the plains and forests of the far north west, beyond the shores of Lake Superior. This interesting and exceedingly instructive sketch, from the pen of the Director of the Survey, is followed by a series of chapters in which the various Azoic and succeeding rocks of the Province are described in great length. * * * The undoubted value of the earlier Reports of the survey has long been recognized, both at home and abroad, by all whose judgment, in matters of this kind, can have any claim to our acceptance. The present report, embracing, as it does, the results of all earlier explorations and comprising in itself so much that is new to science cannot fail to meet with equal recognition, and to attract, still farther, the attention of industrial art to the vast stores of mineral wealth that yet remain unworked within the limits of the Province."—*Can Journ.*

XX. Canadian Organic Remains. Decade II, with woodcuts and plates. *Do.*, 1865, pp. 157, 8vo.

XXI. Atlas and Map to accompany the Geology of Canada, 1863. *Do.*, 1865, [letterpress pp. 42,] 8vo.

"In thanking the Government of Canada for this mark of their consideration, I must assure you that these works are of the highest importance in the advancement of Geological Science as well as of Physical Geography, and that in a new edition of my work 'Siluria,' which is in the Press, I shall endeavour to render full justice to their merits."—*Sir R. I. Murchison: Letter to Hon. W. McDougall, Provincial Secretary.*

XXII. Palœozoic Fossils by E. Billings, F. G. S., Palœontologist to the Survey. *Do.*, 1865, pp. 426, royal 8vo.

"For the last twenty years a succession of Reports with the above title, (*Reports of Progress of the Geological Survey,*) has been published, amounting in all to 2,248 pages, 8vo.; illustrated with numerous woodcuts, fifteen sections and maps, and a folio Atlas of twenty-two sheets. In these Reports the results of the preceding year's investigations in Geology, Mineralogy and Palœontology will be found, together with much detailed information as to the Economic Minerals of the Province, and to the Topography, Geography, Soil, Agriculture and Natural History of the districts explored. In the large 8vo. volume on the Geology of Canada will be found condensed the information contained in these Reports, so far as the Geology, mineralogy, and economic minerals of the country are concerned, but for all other subjects the Reports are still important, and often are the only available sources of information on the regions examined. These reports were published both in the Journals of the House of Assembly of the Canadian Parliament, and separately in a demi-octavo form, but are now for the greater part out of print. They have all been translated and published in French as well as in English."—*Appendix to Atlas of Surv.*, 1865.

XXIII. Report of Progress from 1863 to 1866. *Ottawa*, 1866, pp. 321, 8vo.

XXIV. Esquisse Géologique du Canada. Pour servir à l'intelligence de la carte géologique et de la collection des minéraux envoyées à l'Exposition

Universelle de Paris, 1855. Par W. E. Logan et T. Sterry Hunt. *Paris*, 1855, pp. 100, 12mo.

"A better general view of Canadian Geology it is impossible to obtain. Supplying a long felt want, in a manner at once clear, accurate, and entirely free from scientific display, it cannot fail to command for itself the most extensive popularity." — *Can. Journ.*

XXV. Descriptive Catalogue of a Collection of the Economic Minerals of Canada and of its Crystalline Rocks, sent by the Geological Survey to the London International Exhibition of 1862. *Montreal*, 1862, pp. 88, royal, 8vo.

"This catalogue is an admirable work, not merely serving the purpose of a guide of the most useful kind to the collection in the exhibition, but being also a most convenient permanent record of the economic minerals of Canada, and the principal and best known stations in which they occur." — *Idem.*

Canadian Journal.

I. On the Rocks of Canada (Read before the Geological Section of the Brit. Ass., at Ipswich, 1851), 1852.

II. On the Chemical composition of recent and Fossil Lingulæ and some other shells. By W. E. Logan and T. S. Hunt. 1854.

III. On the Physical structure of the Western District of Upper Canada. *Do.*

"A very important addition to our knowledge of Canadian Geology, and seems to dispose of the question frequently raised respecting the existence of workable coalfields in U. C."—*Can. Journ.*

IV. On the division of the Azoic rocks of Canada into Huronian and Laurentian. (Read before the Am. Ass. for the Advancement of Science Montreal.) 1857.

V. On the probable subdivision of the Laurentian Rocks of Canada. (Read before do. do.) 1858.

VI. Relative dates of various intrusive rocks cutting the Laurentian series in Canada. Do.

Canadian Naturalist.

I. On the Track of an Animal lately found in the Potsdam Formation. 1860.

II. Remarks on the Fauna of the Quebec Group of Rocks, and the Primordial Zone of Canada. do.

III. Considerations relating to the Quebec Group and the Upper Copperbearing rocks of Lake Superior. 1861.

IV. On the Rocks of the Quebec Group at Point Levi : in a letter addressed to M. Joachim Barrande, Paris. 1863.

Transactions of the Geological Soc. (Lon.)

I. On the character of the Beds of Clay immediately below the Coal Seams of South Wales, and on the occurrence of Boulders of Coal in the Pennant Grit of that District. 1840.

II. On the Packing of the Ice on the River St. Lawrence ; on a Landslip in the Modern Deposits of its Valley ; and on the existence of Marine shells in those Deposits as well as upon the Mountains of Montreal. 1842.

"The principles laid down in this paper appeared so indisputable to Mr. Stephenson, the eminent engineer, that he has been materially guided by it in reference to the construction and site of the great Victoria Bridge."—SANDFORD FLEMING, C. E.: *Can. Journ.*

III. On the occurrence of a Track and Footprints of an Animal in the Potsdam Sandstone of Lower Canada. 1851.

Correspondence of Joachim Barrande, Sir William Logan and James Hall, on the Taconic System and on the age of the Fossils found in the Rocks of Northern New England, and the Quebec group of Rocks. *Am. Journ. of Scien.*, 1861.

LOMOND, ROBERT.

I. A Narrative of the Rise and Progress of Emigration, from the Counties of Lanark and Renfrew to the new settlements in Upper Canada. *Edinburgh*, 1822, 8vo.

LONG, JOHN.

I. Voyage and Travels of an Indian Interpreter and Trader, describing the manners and customs of the North American Indians. *London*, 1791, 1 vol., 4to.

This work was translated into French : *Paris*, 1794, in-8.

"With a Map of the Western parts of Canada. Volney characterises this work as exhibiting a most faithful picture of the life and manners of the Indians and Canadian traders. Subjoined is 'a vocabulary of the Chippeway language ; names of furs and skins, in English and French ; a list of words in the Iroquois, Michigan, Shawanee, and Esquimaux tongues ; and a table, shewing the analogy between the Algonkin and Chippeway languages.' "—Lowndes.

LORANGER, *Hon.* T. J. J., *Q. C.* A Judge of the Superior Court L. C. B. 1824. Sat in the Leg. Assem. from 1854 to 1863. Was Prov. Secy. 1857-8.

I. Mémoire composé de la Plaidoirie de T. J. J. Loranger, C. R., un des subsituts du Procureur-Général devant la Cour Seigneuriale. *Montréal*, 1855, 8vo.

II. Suite du Mémoire de M. Loranger contenant sa réplique devant la Cour Seigneuriale. *Do.* 1856, 8vo.

LORD, JOHN KEAST, *F. Z. S.* Late Naturalist to B. N. A. Boundary Commission.

I. The Naturalist in Vancouver's Island and British Columbia. *London*, 1866.

LOWE, JOHN. A Can. journ. Served as reporter to *Gazette*, (Mont.), from 1848 to 1850, when he joined the *Colonist* (Tor.) as asst. ed. and reporter. In 1853 re turned to the *Gazette*, as joint ed. and prop., where he still remains. Mr. L. is considered to occupy no inconsiderable place as a Can. journ. In politics he is strictly Conservative.

LOWELL, *Rev.* ROBERT T. S., *D. D.* An Am. Episcopal clergym. B. in Boston, 8 Oct. 1816. Ed. at Harvard Univ. In 1842 went out to Bermuda diocese, and was ordained priest in the following year. He became chaplain to the Bish. of Newfoundland, a position which he afterwards resigned to do missionary work on the Island. He was stationed at Bay Robert in Conception Bay, and it was while holding that charge, that he wrote his well known work, the " *New Priest*," and several of the poems contained in his second volume. Mr. L. remained on the island for nearly 5 years, and was one of the sufferers by the terrible famine which prevailed in a portion of Newfoundland during the time of his residence, towards the alleviation of which he laboured earnestly. For his

services on that occasion, he received the thanks of the then Secy. of State for the Colonies. Since 1859, he has been Rector of Christ Ch. Duanesburgh, N. Y.

I. Story of the New Priest in Conception Bay, (with illustrations by Darley.) *Boston*, 1858 ; new ed. *Do.* 1864.

" The scene of *The New Priest* is placed in a fishing village on the coast of Newfoundland. The main interest of the story turns on the abduction of a young girl by some over zealous Roman Catholics, and her subsequent recovery. The new priest is a convert from the Church of England, who had before the commencement of the book, abandoned his wife to take up the ministry of his new faith. Coming to Peterport in the exercise of his vocation, he finds his wife living in retirement, and is so influenced by her arguments, and by his disgust at the double-dealing of his associates in the conduct of the abduction, that he finally returns to the Anglican communion. He leaves for the mainland to make a public recantation to the Bishop of the diocese, and on his return has to make an overland journey in the depth of winter. The time of his expected arrival having passed, his friends, accompanied by his wife, go out in search, and find him. near his journey's end, frozen to death. The generally grave character of the narrative is relieved by the introduction of a comic character, Mr. Bangs, of the United States, an impertinent Yankee."— DUYCKINCK.

II. Poems. *Do.* 1860. New ed. *Do.* 1864, 16mo.

" In verse, he more than fulfils the promise of his prose. In the few instances in which he betrays the inspiration caught from the scenes of his island-home, and the perils of the sea, he manifests a special appetency and adaptation for that description of imagery, and it is evident that he here opens a view which he might work with the surest and highest profit."—*N. Am. Rev.*

LUCE, JOHN.
I. A Narrative of a passage from Cape Breton across the Atlantic Ocean in 1799. *London*, 1812, 8vo.

LUSHEN, R. L. Wes. Missionary.
I. Recollections of the outlines of a sermon on the death of Mrs. Waterman. *Halifax*, 1827, pp. 8, 8vo.

LUSIGNAN, ALPHONSE. A French Can. journ. B. at St. Denis, River Chambly, 27 Dec., 1843. He completed his classical studies at the Seminary, (St.

Hyacinthe) where, as well as at the Seminary (Mont.), he also studied Divinity. He was admitted to the Bar in 1863. Since then he has been successively ed. of several journals, among others, *Le Journal de St. Hyacinthe*, *La Tribune*, (Que.) and *Le Pays*, (Mont.) ; of the latter, the chief organ of the French Can. Liberal party in L. C., he is now chief ed. Since 1865 he has been Secy. to the *Institut Canadien*, (Mont.) In the same year he was one of the founders of the *Cercle Légal*, of which he was the first President. Various questions of importance, principally, legal, political and local reforms, have engaged his attention as a journ. His style is pure, and he writes with vigour.

I. L'Ecole Militaire de Québec. *Montréal*, 1865.

LYALL, *Rev.* WILLIAM, *LL. D.* Prof. of Logic and Metaphysics, Dalhousie Coll. N. S. Is a Min. of the Presb. Ch. Before coming to this country held a charge in Scot. In 1848 became connected with Knox Coll. (Tor.) as one of its Profs. In 1850 was appointed Prof. of Classics and Mental Philosophy in the Free Church Coll. (Hal.), and on the union of the Free and United Presb. Chs. in N. S. held the same office in the United Coll. On the incorporation of the Collegiate Institution with Dalhousie Coll., received his present appointment. Has contributed an occasional paper on theological and philosophical subjects to *Presbyterian Witness*, (Hal.) and the *Brit. and Foreign Evangelical Rev.*

I. The Intellect, the Emotions and the Moral Nature. *Edinburgh*, 1855, pp. 614, large 8vo.

LYELL, *Sir* CHARLES, *Bart.* A distinguished Eng. geologist.

I. Travels in North America, in 1841-2, with geological observations on the United States, Canada and Nova Scotia. *London*, 1845, 2 vols. 8vo.

LYMBURNER, ADAM. A Quebec merchant.

I. Paper read at the Bar of the House of Commons, by Mr. Lymburner, Agent for the Subscribers to the petitions from the Province of Quebec, bearing date the 24th of November, 1784—23rd March, 1791. *Can. Rev. and Mag.* (Mont.) 1826.

LYON, CALEB.

I. Narrative and Recollections of Van Dieman's Land, during a three years' captivity of Stephen S. Wright, [a political prisoner], with an account of the battle of Prescott. *New York*, 1844, 8vo.

LYSONS, *Col.* D., *C. B.*, Deputy Quarter Master Genl. in Can. for some years.

I. Parting words on the Rejected Militia Bill. *Quebec*, 1862, pp. 14, 8vo.

LYTTLETON, THOMAS, (2nd) *Lord.*

I. A Letter from Thomas, Lord Lyttleton, to William Pitt, Earl of Chatham, on the Quebec Bill. *Boston*, 1774, pp. 17, 8vo ; Reprinted at *New York*, same year ; *London*, same year.

II. Speech on a motion made in the House of Lords for a repeal of the Canada Bill, May 17, 1775. *Do.* 1775, 8vo.

M.

MACARA, MUDIE. (Ham.)

I. A Prize Essay, in the form of an Address, to the members of the Mercantile Library Association of Hamilton, on the advantages, intellectual and social, of associate institutions for literary objects. *Hamilton*, 1855, pp. 19.

Republished in Griffin's *British Eloquence*: *London*.

To this was awarded the Gold Medal of the Association.

"The author evidently possesses powers of a high order; he analyzes, arranges and constructs processes of thought in a masterly way."—*Report of Examining Com.*

MACAULAY, GEORGE HENRY. A Can. writer. From 1862 until the Union of 1867 was Private Secy. to the Speaker of the Leg. Assem., Can. Is an Advocate, L. C.

I. The Political Past, Present and Future of Canada ; an Essay [published in both languages.] *Montreal*, 1858, pp. 40, 8vo.

II. The Landed Credit System, or La Banque du Credit Foncier. *Quebec*, 1863, pp. 66, 8vo.

" Mr. Macaulay has done much to place the system before his readers in its best light· His familiarity with the writings of others on the same subject, gives additional weight to his remarks. His pamphlet is very creditable to him."—*U. C. Law Journ.*

III. The Iron Mines of the St. Maurice Territory ; a series of articles. *Brit. Can. Rev.* (Que.) 1862.

IV. The Union of the Provinces of British North America. Translated from the French of Hon. Joseph Cauchon. *Quebec*, 1865, pp. 154, 8vo.

" Couched in equally accurate and elegant English."—*Gazette* (Mont.)

V. The Proposed B. N. A. Confederation : a reply to Mr. Penny's reasons why it should not be imposed upon the Colonies by Imperial Legislation.— *Montreal*, 1867, pp. 13, 8vo.

MACAULAY, *Rev.* W., *M. A.* Rector (Ch. of Eng.) Picton, U. C.

I. The Portraiture of a True and Loyal Orangemen ; as sketched in a Sermon. *Toronto*, 1854, pp. 26.

MACDONALD, D. G. F.

I. British Columbia and Vancouvers Island. *London*, 1862, 8vo.

MacDONALD, JOHN.

I. Emigration to Canada. Narrative of a voyage to Quebec, and Journey from thence to New Lanark, in Upper Canada. Detailing the hardships and difficulties which an Emigrant has to encounter, before and after his settlement. With an account of the country as it regards its climate, soil and the actual condition of its inhabitants. *London*, 8th Ed., 1826, pp. 36, 8vo.

MACDONALD, *Hon. Sir* JOHN A., *K. C. B., D. C. L., Q. C.* A leading Can. statesman. B. in Scot., 1814. Sat in the Can. Assem. from 1844 until the Union of the Provinces 1867. Has always occupied a foremost position in Can. politics. Previous to the Union of the Provinces had been once Premier, several times co-leader of successive coalition administrations, and held various offices

as a Minister of the Crown. Was chairman of the B. N. A. Conference, held in London in 1866–7, for the purpose of completing the terms of Union between the several Provinces, and submitting the same to the Imperial Govt. In July, 1867, was called upon to form the first Federal Govt. in the Dominion of Can. under the new Union Act. Received his degree of D. C. L. from Univ. of Oxford, 1865. Created K. C. B. 1867.

I. Address to the Electors of Kingston ; with Extracts from Speeches made at Political Demonstrations during a tour through the Province. *Quebec*, 1860, pp. 153, 8vo.

MACDONALD, RONALD. A Can. journ. B. 1798. D. at Quebec, 14 Oct., 1854. He originally studied for the R. C. Ch., and, it is said, that Mgr. Plessis destined him for his suffragan and auxiliary at Halifax. We cannot say what caused him to abandon such bright prospects, but certain it is that he did not continue as a student of Divinity. In 1831 he was entrusted by the Can. Govt. with the management of a sch. for the education of deaf mutes, which he conducted for some years. In 1836 he entered the arena of journalism as ed. of the *Gazette de Québec.* With but one short interruption he was ed. of *Le Canadien* (Que.) from 1847 until his death in 1854. He was one of the most correct and profound writers, as he was one of the most upright and conscientious men in practice and principle, on the French Can. press.

MACDONELL, ALLAN. (Tor.)

I. A Railroad from Lake Superior to the Pacific, the shortest, cheapest and safest communication for Europe with Asia. *Toronto*, 1851.

MACDONNELL, *Rev.* GEORGE. A Min. of the Presb. Ch. of Can., (Fergus, U. C.) B. at Kirkcaldy, Scot., 1811. Early came with his parents to N. S. In 1830 returned to Scot. and studied for the ministry, at the Univ. (Edin.) In 1840 was appointed to the charge of the Scot. Church at Bathurst, N. B., where he remained for 11 years. In 1852 he was settled in the Presbytery of Hamilton, and, in 1855, was appointed to his present charge.

I. Heathen Converts to the Worship of the God of Israel. *Edinburgh*, 1847, pp. 292, 8vo.

"An interesting and edifying volume, in which the scriptural accounts of some of the most remarkable persons who from among the Gentiles became true believers in the God of Israel are collected, explained and commented on, in a manner calculated at once to inform the mind and quicken the spirituality of the reader."— *Watchman* (Lon.)

II. Book of Devotions and Sermons. *Montreal*, 1851.

"It is designed to supply a want to which we think our Church ought long ago to have attended. * * * We esteem it very highly."—*Presb.* (Mont.)

III. Aid to Sacramental Communion. *Do*. 1864, pp. 211, sm. 12mo.

"The subject is one of much moment * * * Mr. Macdonnell has brought to the task the first best requisite, a heart warm with love to the Master of the Feast, and has shewn ability, discretion and an earnest desire to edify his readers, in connecting, illustrating and impressing on the heart and conscience the series of momentous events, commencing with the institution of the Lord's Supper, and concluding with the Ascension, as narrated by the Evangelists."— *Herald* (Guelph.)

MacDonnell, Robert L., M. D. Formerly Lecturer on the Institutes of Medicine, Univ. McGill Coll. (Mont.) Is a Licentiate of the King's and Queen's Coll. of Physicians, and of the R. C. S. (Irel.); mem. of the Pathological and Surgical Societies (Dub..) and Corresponding mem. of the Medical Soc. (Geneva). Was for many years ed. of the *Journal of Medical Science*, (Dub.) From 1845 to 1817 joint ed. of the *Brit. Am. Journal of Medical and Physical Science*, (Mont..) in which periodical many papers from his pen upon Medical and Surgical Science appeared.

MacDougall, *Col.* P. L., Adjutant Genl. of Militia, Can.

I. Emigration ; its advantages to Great Britain and her Colonies. Together with a detailed plan for the formation of the proposed Railway between Halifax and Quebec, by means of Colonization. *London*, 1848, pp. 32, 8vo.

Macfarlane, Thomas. An officer of the Can. Geol. Survey.

Can. Naturalist.

I. The Primitive Formations in Norway and Canada. 1862.

"To Thomas Macfarlane Esq., of Acton, Eastern Townships, L. C., belongs the credit of associating the Huronian of Canada with the semi-chrystallive schists of Norway, in a most valuable memoir published in the *Canadian Naturalist*."—Dr. J. J. Bigsby : *Proc. Royal Geol. Soc.* (Lon.)

II. Extractions of Cobalt. do.

III. Acton Copper Mine. do.

"In the geology and mineralogy of the metalliferous deposits of this group, (Quebec), as they exist at the celebrated copper mine of Acton, Mr. Macfarlane's paper is a great step in advance, more especially in the large number of facts which he chronicles, and which, but for his careful collection of them in the progress of the workings, would have been for ever lost."—Prin. Dawson.

IV. New method of preparing Sulphuric and Muriatic Acids and Bleaching Powder. 1863.

V. On Eruptive and Primary Rocks. do.

VI. On the Extraction of Copper from its Ores in the Humid way. 1865.

VII. Geological sketch of Rossie, N. Y. do.

I. Report on Mineral Deposits and Rocks of the County of Hastings. *Rep. of Pro. Can. Geol. Surv.* 1866.

II. Report on the Geology of Lake Superior. *Do*. do.

Macfie, Matthew.
I. Vancouver Island and British Columbia ; their history, resources and prospects. *London*, 1865, 8vo.

Macgeorge, *Rev.* Robert Jackson. A Min. of the Ch. of Eng. B. near Glasgow, Scot., about 1811. After passing through the usual curriculum of the Univ. (Glas.,) he completed his education at Edinburgh. Ill health obliging him to travel, he went on a voyage to the East Indies, and after spending some months in Bombay, visited the Gulf of Persia. On his return he published an account of his pilgrimage in the *Scot. Lit. Gazette*. He was also a contributor to *Fraser*, and the *Scot. Monthly Mag*. In 1830 he wrote two dramatic pieces which were performed at the Glasgow Theatre. In 1837 he was admitted to Holy orders, and after officiating at Glasgow, came to Can. in 1841, and became incumbent of Christ Ch., Streetsville, U. C. Although his duties there were heavy and widespread, he found time to ed. the *Weekly Review*, which in his hands became one of the most popular, as it was one of the best conducted papers in the Province. In choosing the style of his articles, his object was to attack and expose popular abuses and follies by good natured sarcasm and ridicule. For several years he ed. the *Church* (Tor.) newspaper, the organ of the Episcopal Ch. in Can. He was ed. of the *Anglo American Mag.* (Tor.,) contributing the *Chronicles of Dreepdaily*, the *Purser's Cabin*, and the larger portion of the *Editor's Shanty*, besides many other sketches and tales; he also wrote for the *Globe* and the *Leader* on literary topics. Mr. McG. is the author of several songs which have been set to music. In 1858 he returned to Scot., where he is incumbent of Oban, Argyle.

" Of the very few editors who have endeavored to attach something of a literary character to the newspaper press of Canada, the Rev. Mr. McGeorge, of the Streetsville *Review*, is certainly entitled to the first rank. His efforts have been not only earnest and continuous, but also successful in an eminent degree, and the *Review* though published in a comparatively obscure *cluchan*, has commanded a greater number of hearty, intelligent outside readers than any other journal in the province.

" Mr. McGeorge's efforts as a man of letters, however, have not been confined to the newspaper. He has been a willing and a liberal contributor to the pages of almost every literary periodical published in Upper Canada, during his sojourn in the country. And those who have any acquaintance with the *Anglo American Magazine*, published in Toronto in 1853, must have a favorable opinion of his abilities as a miscellaneous writer. He is verily a literary man, a gentleman, and a scholar, and his thorough knowledge of books and their authors enables his pen to dash on cleverly and successfully through a variety of subjects. His style is terse and vigorous, and his writings generally are distinguished by extensive erudition, facility of diction, much quaint humor, and frequent sparklings of purified wit."—THE LATE THOMAS McQUEEN.

I. The Canadian Christian Offering. *Toronto*, 1848, pp. 102.

II. Tales, Sketches and Lyrics. *Do.* 1858, pp. 269, 8vo.

MACGILL, Rev. ROBERT.
I. Prayers and Devout Meditations, designed to assist the young Christian in the Cultivation of a Devout Temper. *Niagara*, 1842.

MACGREGOR, J.
I. Our Brothers and Cousins, a tour in Canada. *London*, 1859, 12mo.

MACGREGOR, JOHN. A Brit. statist and legislator. Author of "*Commercial Statistics.*" B. at Stornoway, Scot., 1797. D. at Boulogne, France, 23 Apl., 1857. When only 5 years of age was taken to P. E. I., where he lived for many years, serving first as a sch. teacher, next as clk. in a store, and latterly was engaged in ship-building. While residing on the Island he collected the materials for his large work on B. A. From 1840 to 1847 he was Secy. to the Board of Trade (Eng.,) and in that position inaugurated important reforms in the tariff. In the latter year he was returned to the House of Commons as mem. for Glasgow. He was the author of several voluminous works on commerce and history.

I. Historical and Descriptive Sketches of the Maritime Colonies of British America. *London*, 1828, 8vo. ; 2nd Ed. *Edinburgh*, 1832, 2 vols., pp. 1089, 8vo.

" Mr. McGregor has written a very pleasing as well as a highly-valuable book. It teems with kindly feelings and considerable allowances, while nothing is disguised, and every thing is freely commented upon. After briefly noticing the early settlement, advancement, and causes that led to the independence of the Colonies, and also the constitution, policy, military and naval force, and the public institutions of the United States, the author proceeds to give an historical and descriptive view of British America, the whole interspersed with interesting remarks and suggestions on every subject naturally connected with the country and our relationship with it."—*Sun.* (Lon.)

II. Observations on Emigration to British America. *Do.*, 1829, 8vo.

MACINTOSH, JAMES. Has written many sweet little lyrics, some of which have appeared in the *Waverly Mag.* (Bos.,) the

Phrenological Journal (N. Y..) and the *Observer* (Elora, U. C.,) at which latter place he resides.

MACK, W. G.

I. A Letter from the Eastern Townships of Lower Canada, containing Hints to intending Emigrants as to the Choice of Situation, &c. (With map.) *Glasgow*, 1837, pp. 26, 8vo.

MACKAY, CHARLES, *LL. D., F. S. A.* An Eng. poet.

I. Life and Liberty in America; or, Sketches of a Tour in the United States and Canada in 1857-8. *London* and *New York*, 1859, 12mo.

MACKAY, J.

I. Quebec Hill: or, Canadian Scenery; a Poem. *London*, 1797, 4to.

MACKAY, *Rev.* R. D. Late of Wellesley, U. C.

I. The Smoke of the Temple. *Prescott*, 1865.

MACKAY, ROBERT W. STUART. A Montreal publisher. B. in Scot. D. at Montreal, 9 Oct., 1854. Was the son of an officer in the famous Black Watch. At time of his death was preparing a Gazeteer and Directory of the Province generally.

I. The Montreal Directory, corrected in May, 1848. *Montreal*, pp. 355, 8vo.

This useful annual publication is still continued by Mr. Lovell.

II. The Stranger's Guide to the Island and City of Montreal, containing a brief description of all that is remarkable in either (with map). *Do.*, 1848.

III. The Canada Directory. *Do.*, 1851, 8vo.

IV. The Stranger's Guide to the Cities and principal Towns of Canada; with a glance at the most remarkable cataracts, falls, rivers, watering places, mineral springs &c., &c., &c., and a geographical and statistical sketch of the Province, brought down to 1854 (with maps and illustrations.) *Do.*, pp. 136, 12mo.

MACKENZIE, *Sir* ALEXANDER, *Bart.* A Can. traveller. B. in Inverness, Scot. D. 1820. Emigrated to Can. when a young man, and obtained a situation in the counting house of Mr. Gregory, one of the partners in the old North-

West Fur Co. In 1789 his employers sent him on an exploring expedition through the regions of the North-west. He set out from Fort Chippewyan, on Lake Athabaska, where he had been stationed for 8 years, with 4 canoes and a party of 12 persons, to accomplish his mission. For 6 weeks he threaded his way along the rivers and lakes of B. A. till he reached the great northern ocean in lat. 69°. Having returned to Fort Chippewyan, he started in Oct., 1792, to explore the country towards the Pacific, reaching that ocean July 23, 1793, and regaining in safety the point of departure. In 1802 he received the honour of knighthood for his services; and the river by which he had descended from Slave lake to the Arctic ocean was called after him.

I. Voyages from Montreal, on the River St. Lawrence, through the Continent of North America, to the Frozen and Pacific Oceans, in the years 1789 and 1793. With a preliminary account of the rise, progress, and present state of the Fur Trade of that country: Illustrated with Maps and a portrait of the author. *London*, 1801, 1 vol. 4to., pp. 544; *Philadelphia*, 1802, 1 vol. 8vo.

French translation: *Paris*, 1802, 3 vols., in-8.

"Besides the interesting details in this voyage respecting the countries travelled over, and the manners of the inhabitants, it is important, as having effected the discovery of the Polar Sea, by land."—LOWNDES.

"Mr. Mackenzie's narrative, if sometimes minute and fatiguing, is uniformly distinct and consistent; his observations, though not numerous, are sagacious and unassuming: and the whole work bears an impression of correctness and veracity, that leaves no unpleasant feeling of doubt or suspicion in the mind of the reader. Of the importance of his geographical studies we do not think very highly."—*Edin. Rev.*

MACKENZIE, E.

I. An Historical, Topographical and Descriptive View of the United States of America, and of Upper and Lower Canada; with an Appendix, containing a brief and comprehensive sketch of the present state of Mexico and South America; and also of the Native Tribes of the New World; with maps and engravings; 2nd Ed. *Newcastle-upon-Tyne*, 1819, 8vo.

MACKENZIE, THOMAS.

I. Sketches of a Tour to the Great Lakes. *Baltimore*, 1827, 8vo.

MACKENZIE, WILLIAM LYON. A Can. journ. and legislator. B. at Springfield. Dundee, Scot. 12 March, 1795. D. at Toronto, 28 Aug., 1861. William L. was an only son; his father dying shortly after his birth, his mother was left a widow with slender means of subsistence. He was ed. at Dundee. At the age of 17, or thereabouts, he went into mercantile business, to which he added a circulating library, in Ayleth, not far from Dundee. Meeting with only indifferent success, as might have been expected at so early a period of his life, he afterwards went to Eng., where he was for some time in Lord Lonsdale's employment as clk. Before starting for this country, he also spent some time in France. In 1820 Mr. M. came to Canada. For a short period after his arrival he was employed as superintendent over the works of the Lachine canal, but it was not long before he went into partnership with Mr. John Lesslie, now of Dundas, in Toronto, in the book and drug trade. Soon after, the partners established a business at Dundas. The business succeeded remarkably well in both cases. The connection closed early in 1823. Abandoning the mercantile business, very unwisely, as he afterwards often thought, as he would soon have attained a position of wealth had he continued in it, he commenced the career of a journ. and publisher. On the 18th May, 1824, appeared at Queenston, U. C., the first number of the *Colonial Advocate*, very much in the shape of Cobbett's *Register*, and containing 32 pages. The form was, however, altered to the broad sheet in the second or third number. It was published at Queenston until Nov. of the same year, when the paper was removed to Toronto. In those days the govt. was a sort of close corporation, and was not accustomed to have its acts freely criticised. Of the state of things which existed in U. C., we will give Mr. M's. own testimony:

"I never interfered in the public concerns of the colony, in the most remote degree, until the day in which I issued twelve hundred copies of a newspaper, without having asked or received a single subscriber. In that number I stated my sentiments, and the objects I had in view fully and frankly. I had long seen the country in the hands of a few shrewd, crafty, covetous men, under whose management one of the most lovely and desirable sections of America remained a comparative desert. The most obvious public improvements were stayed: dissension was created among classes; citizens were banished and imprisoned in defiance of all law; the people had been long forbidden, under severe pains and penalties, from meeting anywhere to petition for justice; large estates were wrested from their owners in utter contempt of even the forms of the courts; the Church of England, the adherents of which were few, monopolized as much of the lands of the colony as all the religious houses and dignitaries of the Roman Catholic Church had had the control of in Scotland at the era of the Reformation; other sects were treated with contempt and scarcely tolerated; a sordid band of land-jobbers grasped the soil as their patrimony, and with a few leading officials, who divided the public revenue among themselves, formed 'the family compact,' and were the avowed enemies of common schools, of civil and religious liberty, of all legislative or other checks to their own will. Other men had opposed, and been converted by them. At nine-and-twenty I might have united with them, but chose rather to join the oppressed, nor have I ever regretted that choice, or wavered from the object of my early pursuit."

The *Colonial Advocate* soon fell under the displeasure of the ruling party, and every effort, except such as reason and the law might have sanctioned, was made to suppress it. A bitter personal quarrel, carried on by means of the press, between Mr. M. and some prominent members of the official party, led, in 1826, to the violent destruction of the *Advocate* printing office by a mob of irritated friends of the ruling party. The office was forcibly entered, and the types cast into the bay of Toronto. A most inopportune time was chosen for the work of destruction. It was probably not known to the rioters that the last number of the paper which it was intended to destroy had already been published; for if it had the act would have been as stupid and unnecessary as it was wicked and illegal. As the act was done in the face of day, the perpetrators of it were known, and damages were recovered against them, on the case being brought into a court of justice. We must suppose that the object of scattering the types into the bay was to put an end to the existence of an obnoxious newspaper; but the effect was precisely the contrary of what had been intended. The paper, of which the last number had already been issued, received from the violence used to put it down a new lease of existence. The *Colonial Advocate*, instead of expiring in 1826, as it would, if left to itself, continued to be published till 1834, when the press and types were sold to Dr. O'Grady. The "press riot" had another effect, the reverse of what was intended. Through it, not only was Mr. M. brought more prominently into notice than ever before, but that popular instinct which always flies to the succor of any man who is unfairly treated, created for him a large number of enthusiastic friends and supporters. In 1828, the question of his becoming a candidate for the Co. of York, at the election about to take place, was raised, and at the proper time he was returned to Parliament. The violence of the official party was not confined to the destruction of a printing office. Mr. M. had, in his newspaper, used language towards the majority in the Assem., which that majority chose to regard as libellous, and they resolved to punish the representative for the act of the journ. The alleged libel consisted of describing the majority as sycophants fit only to register the decrees of arbitrary power. Admitting the language used by Mr. M. to have been libellous, the proper remedy would have been to bring the case before the jury. But that remedy was hopeless; it was notorious that no verdict could have been obtained against the publisher of the alleged libel. It was treated as a breach of privilege; on that ground the expulsion proceeded, and an attempt was made to render Mr. M. incapable of sitting in the Assem. His re-election could not, however, be prevented, for no mem. of the official party would have had the least chance against him; and as often as he was expelled— 5 times—he was re-elected; once when he was absent in Eng. At this time

of day no one pretends to defend the arbitrary proceedings of the Assem., and it is impossible to read the debates which took place on the occasions of these repeated expulsions, without being surprised at the want of sagacity in the men by whom they were performed. No new offence was deemed necessary to justify each new expulsion—the original breach of privilege, as it was called, was held to incapacitate the person charged with it from taking his seat in the house to which he was so often elected. Other pretexts were, however, found, but it is a remarkable fact that not one of the expulsions proceeded from anything that Mr. M. had done as a mem. of the house. The hostility of that body was directed entirely against a mem. of the press. The printing and distribution at his own expense of 200 copies of the official journals of the house was attempted to be made a cause of expulsion. It was not pretended that the journals had been falsified or interpolated. The motion rested upon an obsolete rule of the house which forbids any one to print the proceedings of that body without authority— a rule that is constantly and systematically violated, and the putting of it into force would be just as absurd as the revival of the Eng. statute, which renders it penal for any person to fail to appear in the Established Ch. once every Sunday. The cause of the liberty of the press became identified in the minds of the people, with Mr. M., and every new expulsion only added to his popularity, and increased his power. At last it was resolved to punish the constituency which had persisted in re-electing the expelled mem., and the Assem. refused to issue the writ for a new election. This refusal contrasted strongly with the official pretence previously set up that it was necessary for the Co. of York to be fully represented in the legislature, and that therefore no time ought to be lost, after an expulsion, in calling a new election. These arbitrary proceedings of the Assem. finally evoked the decided condemnation of the Imperial Govt. The period during which the Co. of York was left without a representative, from this cause, extended from 1831 to 1834. On one occasion the re-election of Mr. M. was followed by a demonstration of menacing character against the Assem. A large escort conducted him to the Assem. to take his seat. Strangers were ordered to be excluded from the galleries, but the doors of the Assem. were burst open, and the order of exclusion set at defiance by the people.

In May, 1832, Mr. M. proceeded to Eng. bearing a petition of grievances to the Imperial Govt., said to have been signed by 19,000 persons. He remained there for a period of 18 months, and was able to effect far more than any one could at that time have done in Can. during the period of a lifetime. While there he had the hearty and energetic assistance of his early and constant friend, the late Mr. Joseph Hume. Mr. Hume had at that time considerable influence in the House of Commons, with the press and with the govt. Mr. M. obtained a patient hearing at the colonial office, and the result of his interviews with Lord Goderich was a long and elaborate despatch from that nobleman, laying down for the guidance of the Can. govt. principles that would effect great reforms and get rid of many of the grievances complained of. His exertions procured the removal of some of the officials who held the first places in the govt., and caused instructions to be sent to the lieut. gov. to appoint 1 member at least of the popular party to a governmental office. To himself a most tempting offer was made by the Colonial Secy. The Post Office in U. C., then under imperial control, yielded about $60,000 a year and the whole of the revenue went into the pocket of the postmaster. Lord Goderich proposed to divide this office, and give Mr. M. half the spoils. The latter replied that if he accepted the offer he certainly should benefit himself individually, but that the abuse of which he was sent to complain would still be continued. He therefore declined to accept the offer. It was at the instance of the Colonial Secy. that Mr. M's. stay was protracted to 18 months in Eng., in order that an opportunity might be afforded to discuss the various questions on which

16

the popular party in U. C. had complained to the Imperial Govt. Perhaps it was his success on this occasion that caused Mr. M. to the close of his life to believe that our political movements could be best influenced by the application of a leverage power in Downing street ; an error which arose from his not making due allowance for the change which our system of govt. has undergone. He had been anxious to make a second journey to Eng., and he was firmly convinced that if he were there he could produce changes as great as those which resulted from his previous visit. From first to last, Mr. M. was elected to the legislature of Upper and of United Can. 14 or 15 times, and he was only once defeated. The first mayor of Toronto—chosen in 1836—he was also one of the first magistrates ever elected in U. C. Before the passing of the charter under which he became mayor, elective magistrates were unknown in the province. For a short time in 1837 he published a journal called the *Constitution*. Of the Insurrection in which Mr. M. bore so prominent a part, in 1837 and 1838, it is impossible within the limits of our space to treat. He always said that he was led into it by the urgent entreaties of the L. Can's., and he left behind him documents in which he frankly confesses the error of the part he played and expresses regret for the course he was induced to take. But even the Rebellion, with all its evils, was not without its incidental advantages. It awakened the attention of the Imperial Govt. to the various abuses of the oligarchial system which had previously existed, and brought about a beneficial change sooner than it could otherwise have occurred. Few men paid more dearly for an error than Mr. M. did in this case. His life was spared, it is true ; but as his *Life* (written by Mr. Lindsey,) shows, it is very doubtful whether 1 person in a 100 would consider life desirable upon such conditions. Under the Van Buren administration, Mr. M. was sentenced to 18 months' imprisonment for a breach of the neutrality laws of the U. S., and he was actually kept in close confinement for 12 months at Rochester. Ruined by the confiscation and sale of his property in Can., and unable to use his exertions for the benefit of his family, he was made to taste the bitter draughts of poverty. He never took root in the U. S. He was not at home there; he was an exile. He found foreigners looked upon with suspicion, and excluded from nearly all the offices in the gift of the Federal Govt. He was long anxious to return to Can. before the issuing of the amnesty which enabled him to do so. He finally received a pardon through the influence of his friend, Mr. Hume, and he always continued of the impression that he had nothing to thank the Can. Govt. for in that respect. He published a journal both at N. Y. and Rochester, intituled : *Mackenzie's Gazette*, and he was for a considerable time connected with the *Tribune*, of whose proprietor, Mr. Greeley, he had the most exalted opinion. The amount of labor that he performed—at one time as Washington correspondent of that journal, at another time its correspondent at Albany while the State Convention was sitting to revise the constitution—was prodigious ; quite enough to have given occupation to almost any other 3 men. He burned the midnight oil and prematurely consumed his own vitality. After his return to Can. in 1850, he offered as a candidate for the first constituency—Haldimand—that became vacant, and was elected. He continued to hold his seat in the Leg. Assem. till 1858, when he resigned. He attached himself to no party, and though he was generally in the opposition, he attended no opposition " caucus " and entered into no party engagements. From 1853 to 1860 he owned and conducted at Toronto a weekly paper called *Mackenzie's Message*. Mr. Lindsey forms the following estimate of his career as a journalist :

" His writings show an uneven temper ; but taken them in the mass, and considering the abuses he had to assail, and the virulence of opposition he met—foul slanders, personal abuse, and even attempted assassination—we have reason to be surprised with the moderation of his tone. In mere personal invective he never dealt. He built all his opposition on hard facts, collected with industry, and subject to the usual amount of error in narration. Latterly he had entirely abandoned the practice of replying to the abusive tirades of business competitors or political opponents.

" 'I part company,' he said, 'with the corps editorial in the best possible humour.' With papers that pursued him with abuse, he ceased to hold any communication ; refusing neither to read or receive them. He borrowed this metaphor to show how he might have failed to come up to his original intentions. 'We begin to cross a strong river, with our eyes and our resolution fixed on the point of the opposite shore on which we propose to land ; but gradually giving way to the torrent, we are glad by the aid perhaps of branch and bush to extricate ourselves at some distance and perhaps dangerous landing place, much further down the stream than that on which we had fixed our intentions.' He generally wrote in the first person ; and his productions sometimes took the shape of letters to important political personages. His articles were of every possible length, from the terse, compact paragraph to a full newspaper page. On whatever objects exerted, his industry was untiring ; and the unceasing labors of the pen, consuming nights as well as days, prematurely wore out a naturally durable frame. Though possessed of a rich fund of humour, his work was too earnest and too serious to admit of his drawing largely upon it as a journalist. Of Robt. Randal, when his constituents had given him a new suit of clothes, he said : 'He now moves among us literally clothed from head to foot with the approbation of his constituents.' He sometimes kept note of time by printing at the head of his labors : 'Midnight Selections and Reflections (half asleep).' Whatever he did, he did with an honest intention : and though freedom from errors cannot be claimed for him, it may truly be said that his very faults were the results of generous impulses, acted upon with insufficient reflection."

It is now universally conceded that, however erroneous his views, Mr. M. did everything from a thoroughly honest motive, and in the belief that it was best for the country. He was no trading politician or office-seeker, and the best test of his political virtue is that he resisted the most alluring temptations when he thought their acceptance would be contrary to the interests of the public. His most intimate friends best know the value he set upon political honesty, and how deep and utter was his detestation of a tendency to dishonesty or corruption.

I. The Legislative Black-List of Upper Canada ; or, official Corruption and Hypocrisy unmasked. *York*, 1818, pp. 40.

II. Sketches of Canada and the United States. *London*, 1833, pp. 500, 8vo.

"It treated of a great variety of subjects, having no necessary connection with one another, and little regard was paid to method in the arrangement. The greater part of the book consisted of notes taken by the author while travelling in the United States and Canada; and if this had been explained, the intermingling of topics would not have appeared incongruous, as it did under the arrangement adopted. Political topics were not forgotten; and there was an agreeable seasoning of racy and remarkable anecdotes."—C. LINDSEY: *Life of Mackenzie.*

III. The Seventh Annual Report of the Select Committee of the House of Assembly of Upper Canada, on Grievances. By W. L. Mackenzie, Chairman. *Toronto*, 1835, 8vo.

IV. Sketches of William L. Marcy, Jacob Barker and others. *Boston*, 1845, 8vo.

V. The Lives and Opinions of Benjamin Franklin Butler, United States District Attorney for the Southern District of New York, and Jesse Hoyt, Counsellor at Law, formerly Collector of Customs for the Port of New York. *Do.*, 1845, pp. 152, 8vo.

VI. The Life and Times of Martin Van Buren, etc., with anecdotes of J. K. Polk. *Do.*, 1846, pp. 308, 8vo.

(See *Lindsey, C.*)

MACKIE, *Rev.* GEORGE, *D. D.* Formerly of Quebec.

I. Sermon preached at Quebec on National Schools in that city. *Quebec*, 1840, pp. 16.

MACKINTOSH, CHARLES HERBERT. A Can. journ. B. at London, U. C., 1843. Ed. at Galt and in Caradoc, U. C. Was connected with the *Free Press* (Lon.,) as reporter, from 1861 to 1864, and with the *Times* (Ham.,) as local ed., from the latter year until May 1865, when he purchased the *Home Guard*, (Strathroy), changing its name to the *Dispatch*, which he still conducts.

MACLEAN, JOHN.
I. Service in the Hudson's Bay Territory. *London*, 1849, 2 vols. p. 8vo.

MACLEOD, *Sergeant* DONALD.
Memoirs of the life and gallant exploits of the old Highlander, Sergeant Donald Mac-Leod, who, having returned-wounded with

16 *

the corpse of General Wolfe from Quebec, was admitted an out-pensioner of Chelsea Hospital in 1759, and is now in the 103rd year of his age. *London*, 1791, 8vo.

MACNIVEN, *Mrs.* C. B. 1823. D. 1865.
I. Aileen; a poem. *Ingersoll, U. C.*, 1865, pp. 52.

MACTAGGART, JOHN. A Civil Engineer in the service of the Brit. Govt. employed in the construcion of the Rideau Canal. D. in Scot. 1830.

I. Three years in Canada: An account of the actual state of the country in 1826-7-8., comprehending its resources, productions, improvements and capabilities; and including sketches of the state of society, advice to emigrants, &c. *London*, 1829, 2 vols., 8vo.

MAGRATH, T. W.
I. Authentic Letters from Canada, with an account of Canadian Field Sports. *Dublin*, 1833, 12mo.

MAGUIRE, *Very Rev.* THOMAS. A R. C. priest. B. at Halifax, N. S. D. at Quebec, 17 July, 1854. Ordained priest 1800. Was on 2 occasions sent as a delegate to Rome on behalf of the Ch. in Can. Had been offered the mitre in one of the inferior Provinces, but declined the distinction. Served as Superior of the Coll. (St. Hyacinthe, L. C.) and at his death was Vicar Genl. of the Diocese of Quebec, and Chaplain to the Ursulines.

I. Observations d'un Catholique sur l'histoire du Canada de l'honorable William Smith. Par Vindex. *Québec*, 1827.

II. Recueil de Notes Diverses sur le gouvernement d'une paroisse, l'administration des sacraments, etc., adressées à un jeune curé de campagne. Par un Ancien Curé du diocèse de Quebec. *Paris*, 1830, pp. 378; New Ed. *Québec*, 1865.

III. Clergé Canadien vengé par ses ennemis; ou observations sur un ouvrage récent, intitulé: "Tableaux Statistique et Politique des Deux Canadas." Par Vindex. *Québec*, 1834.

IV. Doctrine de l'église catholique concernant la soumission aux autorites civiles.

V. Manuel de jurisprudence à l'usage des ecclesiastiques.

VI. Manuel des difficultés les plus communes de la langue Française, adapté au jeune âge, et suivi d'un Recueil de locutions vicieuses. *Québec*, 1841.

MAILLARD, *L'Abbé* PIERRE. R. C. missionary to Cape Breton, N. S.

I. Lettre sur les Missions de L'Acadie et particulièrement sur les missions Micmaques. *Soir Can.*, 1863, pp. 136.

II. Grammaire de la Langue Mikmaque, par M. l'Abbé Maillard, redigée et mise en ordre par Joseph M. Bellenger (Ed. by J. G. Shea). *New York*, 1864, pp. 101, 8vo.

MAILLOUX, *Rev.* ALEXIS. A R. C. clergym. Was Vicar Genl. (Que.,) and for some time Principal of St. Anne Coll., L. C. Rendered great service, as a preacher, to the cause of Temperance.

1. La Croix présentée aux membres de la Société de Tempérance. *Québec*, 1850.

II. Manuel des parents chrétiens, ou devoirs des pères et des mères dans l'éducation religieuse de leurs enfants. *Do.*, 1851, 8vo.

MAIN, DAVID. A N. B. journ. B. in Richibucto, N. B., 13 July, 1835. Ed. in the higher branches at the Univ. of N. B. From 1856 to 1861 was engaged in active business pursuits in St. John. In the last named year undertook the charge of the Eng. and Commercial department of the Collegiate School (Fred.) He first became connected with journalism, in 1863, by joining the staff of *The Morning Telegraph* (St. John,) as legislative reporter, and subsequently became associate ed. of that paper. In 1865 he established the *St. Croix Courier* (St. Stephen,) of which he is ed. and prop. The *Courier* has become the leading journal of the Western district of N. B. In Politics it is independent, but its ed. has always been an unflinching supporter of Colonial Union.

MAIR, CHARLES. A Can. writer. B. in Co. Lanark, U. C. In 1860–62, contributed several short poetical pieces of superior merit to the *Transcript* (Mont.,) which were highly spoken of. In 1862 two descriptive poems from his pen, *The Pines* and *Summer*, were read before the Can. Botanical Soc. which drew from the late Rev. Principal Leitch of Queen's Coll. (Kings.,) the following tribute :

" The Pines is a truly Canadian production, inspired by an acquaintance with and love of the forest, while *Summer* has more of the old world stamp shewing by the impress a style of its Literature. Canada ought to be proud of Mr. Mair's poems."

On this occasion, Mr. M. was elected an honorary mem. of the Society. Since then his occasional poetical efforts have appeared in the *Daily News*, (Kings.,) with the exception of two sonnets, *To the Humming Bird* and *To a Sleeping Child*, which he contributed to the *B. A. Mag.* (Tor.) As a prose writer he is known by a tale *Twelvetrees*, (Mont. *Transcript*, 1861.) and by a sketch, *Frogs and their Kin*, (*B. A. Mag.*, 1863.) Speaking of the tale, the Ed. of the *Transcript* declared it to be " an unrivalled piece of auto-biography." Mr. M. intends bringing out a volume in London shortly. He is still very young ; and should he continue in the field of literature, there is no manner of doubt that, by his superior talents and education, his extensive and varied knowledge, and his refined taste and judgment, he will occupy no inconsiderable place among the literary men of the present day.

MAIR, *Rev.* JAMES, *M. A.* Presb. min. (Martintown, U. C.)

I. The Sabbath ; a sermon. *Kingston*, 1866.

" An able, carefully written sermon, meriting a careful perusal."—*Gazette* (Mont.)

MAIR, JOHN, *M. A., M. D.* A Staff Surgeon (half pay) in the Brit. Army. B. at Aberdeen, Scot., 1798, where he was ed. Studied anatomy in London under Mr. Brookes, and also attended the surgical practice at St. George's Hospital under Mr., afterwards, Sir B. Brodie. In 1851 commenced medical studies at the Univ. (Edin.,) and became ordinary and subsequently extraordinary mem. of Royal Medical Soc. In 1821 studied in Paris under Dupuytren and Broupais, and dissected with Lisfranc. Entered the army as Hospital Asst. in same year, having previously received certificate of qualification from Blizard and Abernethy for Surgeoncy of any regt. in the service. Served in nearly all H. M.'s dependencies, attaining the rank of Staff Surgeon (1st Class), and retired from the army in 1852, settling at Kingston, U. C. Contributed various articles on the Temperance movement to the *Gospel Tribune* (Tor.,) 1851 ; *On Communion wine question*, in letters addressed to the Dean of Carlisle, in the *Temperance Spectator* (Lon.,) 1861 ; *On the Medical Profession in relation to the Temperance movement*, and *The Sacramental Elements*, to the *Journal of Temperance* (Can.,) 1864–5 ; in 1849 to *Med. Times* (Lon.,) *Results of my Experience in the Treatment of Asiatic Cholera as it occurred at Kingston, C. W., in* 1849.

I. "The Cup of the Lord," not "The Cup of Devils." Reprinted from *Gos. Tribune. Toronto*, 1855, pp. 21.

II. Nephaleia ; or, Total Abstinence from Intoxicating Liquors in man's normal state of health, the doctrine of the Bible. In a series of letters, with addenda, to Edward C. Delavan, Esq. With coloured plates of the stomach as affected by strong drink. *Albany*, 1861, pp. 300.

"The entire question of ' Biblical Temperance ' is discussed in Nephaleia, but particularly what is called the ' Sacremental wine question' Dr. Mair has devoted his leisure hours for many years to a painstaking research and a careful study of most passages of scripture bearing upon this important subject ; and the result is a clear and settled conviction that total abstinence from intoxiciating liquors, in man's normal state, is the doctrine of the Bible."—*Temperance Spectator* (Lon.)

MALCOLM, *Rev.* JAMES. A probationer Can. Presb. Ch. B. at Gaddon, Scot. Took the 1st Class Queen's Scholarship, in Normal Sch. (Edin.) Was Head Master of the Port Madoc National Sch., Wales, and has also taught in Can. Previous to coming to Can. wrote *The Poetry of Teaching; or, the Village School, its Subjects and its Rulers* ; (*London*, 1858, pp. 36,) ; which the *Athenæum* (Lon.) declared, "was full of thought and feeling " and had " a Crabbe-like mellowness upon the village pictures." Has contributed to *Good News*, the *Evangelizer*, the *Canada Observer*, and various other periodicals and journals. His 2 best poems are *The Emigrant Ship, or a Voyage across the Atlantic ;* and

Saustauraitzie ; or the Traditional History of the Huron or Wyandotte Indians. Mr. M. is preparing a work to be called, " Side-glances at Men and Things."

MALCOLM, JOHN. (Woodstock.)
I. A Genealogical Tree of the Royal Family of Great Britain.—*Toronto*.

MANLY, *Rev.* J. G.
I. Canada : its Geography, Scenery, Produce, Population, Institutions and Condition. *Dublin*, 1860, pp. 32.

MARCH, JOHN, and T. P. DIXON, Reporters.
I. Reports of the Debates of the House of Assembly, of the Province of New Brunswick, during the 1st and 2nd Sessions of 1866. *St. John*, 1866, pp. 126—86. Folio.

MARCHAND, F. G. A French Can. Poet. His pieces, which are marked by some degree of merit, have appeared in *La Ruche Littéraire* (1853-54); *La Revue Can.* and *Le Foyer Can.* From 1861 to 1863, was editor of the *Franco-Canadien*.

MARCOU, JULES.
I. Geological Map of the United States and British Provinces of North America. *Boston*, 1853, 8vo.

II. On the Black Slate of Braintree, Massachusetts, containing Paradoxides, and on similar strata in Newfoundland, near Lake Champlain, and in the vicinity of Quebec. *Proc. Nat. His. Soc.* (Bos.,) 1860.

III. Notice sur les gisements des lentilles trilobitifères taconiques de la Pointe-Lévis au Canada. (From the *Bulletins de la Soc. Géol. de France.*) *Paris*, 1865, pp. 16.

MARCOUX, *Rev.* JOSEPH. A Priest in the R. C. Ch. Was for over 80 years Missionary to the Iroquois Indians at Sault St. Louis. D. May, 1855. In addition to the following, Mr. M. wrote an Iroquois Grammar, a French and Iroquois, and Iroquois and French Dictionary ; and translated the life of Our Saviour into the Iroquois language ; these, however, have never appeared in print.

I. Livre de Prières et de Cantiques. *Montréal*, 1852, pp. 198, 8vo.

II. Catéchisme. *Do.*, 1854, pp. 48.

MARMETTE, J. E. E.
I. Charles et Eva. Feuilleton Historique Canadien. *Rev. Can.* 1866-7.

MARRIOTT, *Sir* JAMES.

I. Plan of a Code of Laws for the Province of Quebec; reported by the Advocate General. [With Appendix on the Estates of the Jesuits in Canada.] *London*, 1774, pp. 292, 8vo.

MARRIOTT, J. W.

I. India and its Mutiny; a Lecture. *Halifax*, 1858, pp. 36, 8vo.

MARRYATT, *Capt.* FRANCIS, R. N. A well known Eng. Naval Novelist.

I. Diary in America. Part Second: with Canada and the present condition of the Indians. (With a Map of aboriginal America). *London*, 1840, 3 vols. 8vo.

II. The Settlers in Canada. *Do.*, 1844, 2 vols., 12mo.

MARSAIS, A. A French Can. lyric poet. (Ham.) Some of his pieces appeared in *La Ruche Littéraire* (Mont.) In 1854-5 contributed to *La Minerve* (same city.) and in 1855-6 to *Le Canadien* (Que.) He has since written for nearly all of the French Can. newspapers.

I. Romances et Chansons. *Québec*, 1854.

MARSDEN, JOSHUA.

I. Narrative of a Mission to Nova Scotia, New Brunswick and the Somer's Islands, with a Tour to Lake Ontario; to which is added "The Mission," an original poem, with copious notes (portrait). *Plymouth-dock*, 1816, pp. 283, 8vo.

MARSDEN, WILLIAM, *M. D.* A leading medical practitioner (Que.) B. at Bolton, Lancashire, Eng. 18 Feb., 1807. Came to Quebec in 1812, where he has since resided. Ed. at the Royal Grammar Sch. there. Completed his medical education in London and Paris. Has been a medical examiner for more than 30 years; and ranks high as a medical jurist and consulting physician. Before the incorporation of the Quebec Medical Sch. and Laval Univ., he, for many years, delivered with great success courses of lectures on Anatomy and Physiology, Surgery, Materia Medica and Botany. Dr. M. has probably contributed more, as a writer, to the medical press than any other medical man in Can. From 1827 up to the present time, his pen has been devoted to science and literature, poetry and prose. In Medicine and Surgery he has written much for the *Lancet* (Lon.,) *Medical and Surgical Journal*, both quarterly and monthly (Edin.,) the *U. C.* and the *L. C. Medical Journals*, and the *Brit. Am. Journal* (Mont.) He was a contributor, above various signatures and on various subjects, to the *Mercury*, and the *Gazette* (Que.), and to the *Settler* (Mont.) From 1851 to 1854 Dr. M. took a large share in the ed. management of the Quebec *Mercury*. It is understood that he is preparing for early publication a complete history of Asiatic Cholera, its etiology and pathology, commencing with its outbreak in India in 1817. For some years he was President of the Coll. of Phy. and Surg. of L. C. (of which he is a Governor). He is also an Honorary Fellow of the Medical Botanical Soc. (Lon.); a Corresponding Fellow of the Medical Soc. (Lon.); an Honorary Fellow of the Lyceum of Natural His., and of various other learned bodies and societies.

MARSHALL, *Hon.* JOHN G. A N. S. Author. Is the son of a captain in the Brit. army. Born in N. S. 1786. He received a limited classical ed. at the Prov. Grammar Sch (Hal.,); and after going through the prescribed course of legal studies in Halifax, was admitted in 1808 a barrister in the Supreme Court, and other courts of law and equity in the Province. In 1811, when 25 years of age, was elected a mem. of the Prov. Parliament for his native county,—for which his father had been a representative for about 14 years previously,—where he sat for 10 years. While in the legislature, and in extensive practice in his profession, residing in the capital, he was, in the year 1823, selected to fill the special offices then created of Chief Justice of the Courts of Common Pleas, and President of the Courts of Sessions, throughout the Island of Cape Breton, which Island had for many years been a distinct Brit. colony, but had shortly before, by the King in Council, been made a part of the Province of N. S. He was also appointed the Custos of all the Counties of the Island, and a Master in the Court of Chancery throughout the Province. He held these and several other important public offices, for about 18 years. In the year 1841, new arrangements being made by the legislature as to the Courts of Common Law, all the Courts of Common Pleas throughout the Province were abolished, and Judge M., with 3 other divisional Chief Justices of those courts were placed on pensions for life. Within a few months after he was thus withdrawn from the bench, he was called into the public advocacy of the Temperance cause, with which he had for several years previous been identified as a mem. During nearly the whole of the 5 following years until 1846, he was almost constantly and exclusively engaged in the same advocacy, going in regular circuits throughout every part of the Province, and also several times visiting, on the same mission, the Provinces of N. B. and P. E. I. In 1846 for the first time he went with his friends to Gt. Brit., and immediately commenced labouring in the same cause, and continued almost incessantly for nearly 4 years, during which he lectured in upwards of 250 different cities and towns of Eng., Scot., and Irel., in parts of Wales, and in the Islands of Orkney, Shetland, Jersey and Guernsey, and delivered during this period about 560 public addresses, nearly all on the total abstinence subject. In 1850 he returned to N. S., and after remaining there about 2 years, still frequently lecturing in the same cause, he came in 1852 to Can. for the same purpose, where with a short intermission he continued for a like period, almost constantly lecturing, chiefly in the most populous towns and sections of the Western district of country. Again returning to his native Province in 1854, he continued to exert himself there in the same way for the next 2 years; and also visited Newfoundland. In 1856, again went to Eng. for the sole and express purpose of assisting in the advocacy of the movement for the legal prohibition of the common traffic in intoxicating liquors, judging that from his legal standing and attainments, as well as his long experience in the Temperance cause, he could be of some service to that important effort.

On his second visit, which continued for nearly 2 years, he constantly exerted himself by lecturing and otherwise, in very many parts of Gt. Brit., having delivered in all about 180 public addresses, in nearly as many different places. At the very great number of meetings he has addressed, throughout the whole period of his advocacy in the temperance and prohibitory cause, many thousands have been enrolled as members. It is important that we should state that, all Judge M's exertions in the Temperance and Prohibitory movements have been entirely gratuitous, both as to his lectures and travelling expenses.

In addition to the list of his writings which we give below, he has at various times published a large number of tracts on religious and other subjects, which have appeared in Gt. Brit. and N. S. He has also contributed largely to the newspaper press: in 1863 in the *Christian World* (Lon..) *Letters opposing Sir Charles Lyell's supposition as to the age of the world and in support of the Scripture chronology; also reviewing and opposing his notions and argument as to the "transmutation of species and gradual developments in the natural world," as contained in his work "The Antiquity of Man"; in the Morning Chronicle* (Hal.). 1865, *Letters relating to the proposed Union of the North American Provinces.*

I. A Patriotic Call to Prepare in a Season of Peace for one of Political Danger; suggested by reflections on the policy and designs of the United States towards Great Britain and her American Colonies; with a view of the principal advantages of Nova Scotia. *Halifax,* 1819, pp. 151, large 8vo.

II. The Justice of the Peace, and County and Township Officer in Nova Scotia; being a guide to them in the discharge of their official duties. *Do.* 1837, pp. 669, 8vo.; 2d. Ed. 1845, pp. 800.

This work was offered to the Provincial Parliament by the author. It was recommended by message of the Lieut. Gov. to the Legislature, and after examination of the MS by the Commons' Committee, was unanimously accepted and published by them. In 1846, the thanks of the Legislature were tendered to the author for the public benefit, he had conferred upon the Province, by the work in question.

III. Pamphlet in favour of Temperance Reform. *Edinburgh*, 1849, pp. 36, 8vo.

IV. Do. *Aberdeen*, 1849, pp. 86.

V. Impartial View of Causes and Effects in the present Social Condition of the United Kingdom, with practical suggestions. *Halifax*, 1851, pp. 204, 8vo.

VI. The Strong Drink Delusion with its criminal and ruinous results exposed ; with examinations of remedies. *Do.*, 1855, pp. 152, 8vo.

VII. On the Moral Condition of British Society, and how to reform it. *Liverpool*, 1857, pp. 60.

VIII. Pamphlet in answer to one by Rev. Ed. Maturin, M. A., on various theological subjects. *Halifax*, 1859, pp. 72.

IX. Do. *Do.*, 1859, pp. 72.

X. Pamphlet on the Sabbath. *Do.*, 1860, pp. 15, 8vo.

XI. Sermons on some of the principal Doctrines and Duties of Christianity. *Do.*, 1862, pp. 302, 8vo.

XII. Answers to "Essays and Reviews." Each of the seven Essays, &c., answered *seriatim*. *Do.*, 1862, pp. 230, 8vo.

" Your admirable Reply to ' Essays and Reviews' I have read with great delight, and I have no hesitation in stating that, of the various Critiques and Replies to those pernicious productions, I have read none so thorough and satisfactory as yours. I am sure it would be useful if circulated in this country, and be of great value, especially to our young men who may be enquiring after the truth."—Rev. Janez Burns, D. D., (Lon.) *Letter to author.*

XIII. A Full Review and Exposure of Bishop Colenso's errors and miscalculations in his work, "The Pentateuch and book of Joshua critically examined." *London*, 1863, pp. 187, 8vo.

" Mr. Freeman, not satisfied with giving us Dr. Scott, has added to it the exceedingly racy volume of Judge Marshall, of Nova Scotia, which presents aspects of the subject differing from all that have gone before. The rest were either literary laymen or persons, here we have the views of a practical lawyer, who may be said to have supplied at once an argument and a summing up, and the result is the pounding of the poor Bishop as in a mortar. The Hon. Judge, while an adept in law, is not ashamed of the Gospel. This volume will, probably, from the fact of its origin and character, find its way and do its work in many quarters where a more elaborate performance from a clerical pen would be rejected. On that ground, it is eminently fitted to be useful."—*Brit. Standard*, (Lon.)

XIV. A Full Review of Bishop Colenso's profane fictions and fallacies in part 2 of his work. *Do.*, 1864, pp. 205, 8vo.

" The honorable author of this work did good service to the cause of Bible truth in his review of the bishop's first volume, and here he has renewed the attack at all points with weapons of invincible force. His critique is thorough and complete, and he has brought both learning and a ripe knowledge of the word of God to bear on the Natal prelate. We advise all who feel interested in the momentous questions involved to read the judge's work, which, with other excellencies, has those of plainness and brevity."—*Baptist Messenger*, (Lon.)

XIV. An Examination of the proposed Union of the North American Provinces. *Halifax*, 1865, pp. 71, 8vo.

MARTIN, *Père* FÉLIX. A French historical writer. Is a priest of the order of Jesuits. Came to Can. in 1842, and became Rector of the Coll. of St. Mary, (Mont.) He contributed to the newspaper and periodical press. Two of his contributions, *La Dispersion des Hurons* and *Les Récollets au Canada*, appeared in the *Mélanges Religieux*, (Mont.) He is a corresponding mem. of the Historical Soc., (N. Y.)

I. Manuel du Pèlerin de Notre Dame de Bonsecours à Montréal, orné de deux gravures en taille douce. *Montréal*, 1848, pp. 178.

II. Relations des Jésuites sur les découvertes et les autres événements arrivés en Canada et au Nord et à l'Ouest des Etats-Unis (1611-1672), par le E. B. O'Callaghan ; traduit de l'anglais avec quelques notes, corrections et additions. *Do.*, 1850, pp. 79.

III. Relation abrégée de quelques Missions des PP. de la Comp. de Jésus dans la Nouvelle France, par le Père F. J. Bressani ; traduit de l'Italien et augmenté d'un avant-propos de la biographie de l'auteur, de beaucoup de notes et de gravures. *Do.*, 1852.

IV. Relations de la Nouvelle France, (1673-79.) *Québec*, 1860.

V. Relations inédites de la Nouvelle France, (1672-79.) *Paris*, 1861, 2 vols.

VI. Première Mission des Jésuites du Canada. Lettres et documents inédits. *Do.*, 1864.

MARTIN, ROBERT MONTGOMERY. An Eng. Colonial historian. Now dead. Ed. the *Colonial Mag. and Commercial Maritime Journal* (Lon.,) from its commencement in 1840 until 1842.

I. Statistics of the Colonies of the British Empire in the West Indies, North and South America, Asia, Australasia, Africa and Europe ; with Map, Chart and Seals for each Colony. Published by the authority of Government. *London*, 1840, pp. 916, R. 8vo.

II. History of the Colonies of the British Empire in North America, &c. From the official records of the Colonial Office. *Do.* 1843, 8vo. New ed. 1849.

III. The Hudson Bay Territories and Vancouver's Island ; with an Exposition of the Chartered Rights, Conduct and Policy of the Hon. Hudson's Bay Company. *Do.* 1849, 8vo.

MASERES, FRANCIS, *M. A.*, *F. R. S.*, *F. A. S.* Cursitor Baron of the Exchequer in Eng., from 1773 till his death. B. in London, 15 Dec., 1731. D. there 19 May, 1824. After leaving Cambridge Univ. he was called to the Bar. From 1766 to 1769, was Attorney Genl. of the Province of Quebec. On his return to Eng. he acted as agent for the Protestant Settlers in Quebec, in which capacity he wrote a letter to the Lord Mayor of London, expressing the sincere and hearty thanks of the settlers, for the city's mark of their paternal regard, testified towards them by their address to the King, in their behalf, and requesting the Lord Mayor, &c., once more to exert themselves, in order to recover the civil and religious rights of a no inconsiderable number of honest and enterprising subjects of the Crown. In addition to the works enumerated below, Baron M. was the author of many others on a variety of subjects.

I. Mémoires à la défense d'un plan d'Acte de Parlement pour l'Etablissement des Loix de la Province de Québec, contre les objections de Mons. François Joseph Cugnet. *Londres*, 1770, folio, 1773, folio.

II. A Collection of several Commissions and other public instruments, proceeding from his Majesty's royal authority, and other papers, relating to the state of the Province in Quebec, in North America, since the conquest of it by the British Arms in 1760. *London*, 1772, pp. 311, 4to.

III. Quebec Commissions. *Do.* 1774, folio.

IV. An Account of the Proceedings of the British and other Protestant Inhabitants of the Province of Quebec, in North America, in order to obtain a House of Assembly in that Province. *Do.* 1775, pp. 294, 8vo.

V. Additional Papers concerning the Province of Quebec ; being an Appendix to the Book, intituled : An Account of the Proceedings of the British and other Protestant Inhabitants of the Province of Quebec, in North America, in order to obtain a House of Assembly in that Province. *Do.* 1776, pp. 510, 8vo.

VI. The Canadian Freeholder ; in two Dialogues, between an Englishman and a Frenchman settled in Canada, shewing the sentiments of the bulk of the Freeholders of Canada concerning the late Quebec Act, with some remarks on the Boston Charter Act ; and an attempt to shew the great expediency of immediately repealing both those Acts of Parliament, and of making some other useful regulations and concessions to His Majesty's subjects, as a ground for a reconciliation with the United Colonies in America. *Do.* Vol. I, 1776, ; Vol. II and III, 1779, 8vo.

"The title of the 1st volume states "In two Dialogues"; but those of the 2nd and 3rd volumes state "In three Dialogues."

"Cet ouvrage renferme une critique assez amère du Gouvernement Français, et une des Apologies de l'Angleterre."

"Le premier emploi de l'auteur fut celui de Procureur Général de Québec, où il se fit remarquer pendant la guerre d'Amérique par sa loyauté. A son retour en Angleterre, il fut nommé Clerc-Baron de l'Echiquier, place qu'il remplit encore avec une grande réputation."—*Biog. des Hommes Vivants.*

VII. Occasional Essays, chiefly Political and Historical. *Do.* 1809, 8vo.

Contains several pieces relating to Am., and *"An account of the noblesse or gentry in Canada."*

MATHEVET, *Rév.* JEAN CLAUDE. A R. C. priest. D. in Can. 4 Augt. 1781. Was a Missionary amongst the Indians at the Lake of Two Mountains, from 1746 to 1778.

I. Aimie Tipadjimo8in Masinaigan ka ojitogobanen kaiat ka niina8isi mekate8ikonaie8igobanen kanactageng, 8ak8iena8indibanen. (History of the Old Testament, in the Algonquin language.) *Montreal,* 1859, pp. 337, 12mo.

II. Ka Tite Tebeniminang Jezos ondaje aking. (Life of Jesus Christ, in the Algonquin language.) *Do.* 1861, pp. 396, 12mo.

MATHIESON, *Rev.* ALEX., *A. M., D. D.* A Min. of the Presb. Ch. of Can., (Mont.) B. at Renton, Dumbartons., Scot., about 1796. Ed. at Univ. of Glasgow. Licensed to preach 1823. Ordained to St. Andrew's Ch. (Mont.,) 1826. Has been twice Moderator of the Synod, and is now senior min. of the Presb. Ch. in Can.

I. Sermon on death of Mr. Robert Watson. *Montreal,* 1827.

II. Introductory Remarks by a member of the Church of Scotland in Canada to "Thoughts on personal and family religion, by Rev. George Tod, Dundee." *Do.* 1833.

III. Sermon on St. Andrew's Day. *Do.* 1837.

IV. Discourse delivered on board Transport ship *Java,* off Quebec, to 1st Batt. 71st Highland Light Infantry, en route for the West Indies. *Do.* 1843, pp. 41.

V. The Christian's Death no cause for Sorrow; a sermon. *Do.* 1848, pp. 33.

VI. The Moral and Religious Influences of Autumn; a sermon in three parts. *Do.* 1849, pp. 72.

VII. A Tribute of Respect to the memory of a Good Man; a sermon on death of Hugh Brodie, Esq. *Do.* 1852, pp. 44.

VIII. Sermon preached at opening of Synod at Quebec. *Do.* 1861, pp. 29.

IX. Anniversary Sermon before St. Andrew's Society. *Do.* 1863, pp. 19.

X. The Beauty of Earthly Objects of attachment A sermon. *Do.* 1864, pp. 26.

MATTHEW, G. F. A N. B. geologist.
I. List of mineral locations in New Brunswick. *Sill. Journ.,* 1863.

II. Observations on the Geology of St. John County, N. B. *Can. Nat.* Do.

III. Contributions to Prof. Bailey's Report on the Geology of N. B. 1865.

IV. Azoic and Palæozoic Rocks of Southern N. B. *Quar. Journ. Geol. Soc.* (Lon.) Do.

MATTHEWS, R. F.
I. Poems. *London, U. C.,* 1866.

MATURIN, *Rev* EDMUND. . A clergym. of the Ch. of Eng. in N. S. Was a native of Irel., and ed. at Dublin Univ. In 1859 he abjured Protestantism and went over to the Ch. of Rome. His pamphlet defending the change occasioned a good deal of religious discussion, and many pamphlets were published in answer to it. Subsequently he returned to the Protestant faith, publishing his reasons for so doing. He was a fine scholar, and as a preacher possessed talents of a high order.

I. The Claims of the Catholic Church; a letter addressed to the parishioners of St. Paul's Church, Halifax. *Halifax,* 1859.

"It is written in the style which allures to betray and dazzles to blind, and which, by cool assumption and confident assertion. leads the reader, ere even he is aware, to conclusions which, had they been arrived at in any other form, would have been repelled as an insult to the understanding. and a libel on the veracity of evidence and the teachings of history."—*Christian Instructor,* (Halifax.)

II. A Defence of "The Claims of the Catholic Church," in reply to several recent publications. *Do.,* 1859.

MAUDUIT-DUPLESSIS.
I. Description nautique de la côte du Labrador, depuis le Cap St. Louis jusqu'à la Grande Pointe, comprenant le détroit de Belle Ile; traduit de l'Anglais. *Paris,* 1852, 8vo.

MAUNAULT, *L'Abbé* J. A. A missionary of the Ch. of Rome at St. François, Co. Yamaska, L. C.

I. Histoire des Abenakis depuis 1605 jusqu'à nos jours. *Sorel*, 1866, pp. III—631, R. 8vo.

"Ce livre, dit l'auteur, est l'histoire d'une tribu sauvage qui aujourd'hui compte à peine 350 âmes en Canada. Descendants d'une nation, qui pendant cent cinquante ans, a rempli un rôle très considérable dans les guerres de la Nouvelle-France et de la Nouvelle-Angleterre, et s'est toujours constamment montrée l'alliée fidèle et infatigable des français, ces restes d'une grande peuplade méritaient de voir les services de leurs ancêtres retracés dans un ouvrage spécial.

"Nos historiens ne rendent guère aux héroïques Abénakis le tribut de gloire et de reconnaissance qui leur est dû, ils paraissent oublier que si cette nation, autrefois nombreuse et puissante, se trouve maintenant réduite à quelques familles, c'est que pendant près de quatre-vingts ans elle a mis au service de la cause catholique et française dans l'Amérique du Nord, le plus pur de son sang et les plus beaux coup de sa vaillance. M. l'abbé Maurault, qui a été vingt-cinq ans, le pasteur des derniers rejetons de cette tribu, s'est ému de cet oubli. Il leur a consacré le livre que nous avons sous les yeux.

"Ecrit sans prétentions, cet ouvrage n'aborde aucune des questions de haute philosophie chrétienne contenues dans l'histoire des nations sauvages de l'Amérique du Nord : quand, dit l'auteur, la tombe sera fermée sur le dernier des Abénakis, on lira avec intérêt l'histoire de cette antique tribu qui, pendant si longtemps unit ses armes à celles des Français, pour combattre un ennemi commun. Et quand le temps, qui détruit tout, aura effacé en Canada la dernière trace du dernier de ces sauvages, les Canadiens aimeront encore à relire les anciennes traditions et les intéressantes légendes de ces amis de leurs ancêtres.' C'est ce caractère légendaire qui rend si attrayante la lecture de l'ouvrage de M. l'abbé Maurault.

"Le style est simple, naturel, clair; les détails abondent, quoique les sources varient peu; l'ordonnance de l'ouvrage est faite avec soin, et le lecteur en suit toutes les divisions avec facilité et sans confusion. Par sa manière, par le choix de sa narration, par la multiplicité des faits particuliers, par son goût des légendes, ce côté si vrai et si populaire de l'histoire, M. l'abbé Maurault appartient à la même classe d'historiens que les abbés Faillon et Ferland, il est moins mystique que le premier, n'a peut-être pas la phrase ni la philosophie du second, mais il est évidemment de la même école.

"L'histoire des Abénakis est un beau livre qui a sa place dans toutes les bibliothèques canadiennes; il est encore mieux que cela, il est un monument national élevé à la gloire de nos anciens alliés, et ses 600 pages

prouvent une fois de plus que la vraie civilisation des sauvages n'a été comprise et amenée que par la doctrine et les enseignements catholiques."—JOSEPH ROYAL : *Rev. Can.*

MAY, *Rev.* JOHN, A. M. A min. of the Ch. of Eng. (March, U. C.) Some very sweet little poems have proceeded to the newspaper press from the pen of Mr. M. In 1861, *A Summer Ramble in the Woods*, a descriptive poem written by him, was read before the Bot. Soc. of Can. and is to be found in the *Trans.* of that body.

I. An Ode to the Prince of Wales. *Kingston*, 1860.

II. Sermon on the 12th July, 1865. *Do.*

MAYERHOFFER, *Rev.* V. P. A clergym. of the Ch. of Eng. Officiated for some time, up to the period of his death, in the Diocese of Toronto.

I. Twelve years a Roman Catholic Priest; or, the autobiography of the Rev. V. P. Mayerhoffer, M. A. Late Military Chaplain to the Austrian army, and Grand Chaplain of the Orders of Freemasons and Orangemen in Canada, B. N. A. *Toronto*, 1861, pp. 340, Demy 12mo.

A posthumous work, published after the death of the author.

MAYNE, DANIEL HAYDN.
I. Poems and Fragments. *Toronto*, 1838, pp. 123.

MAYNE, *Commander* R. C., *R. N.*, *F. R. G. S.*
I. Four years in British Columbia and Vancouver's Island; an account of their Forests, Rivers, Coasts, Goldfields and Resources for Colonization. (With map and Illustrations.) *London*, 1863, pp. 468, 8vo.

McADAM, ADAM.
I. Communications, originally published in the *Montreal Herald*, in reply to letters inserted therein under the signature of Archibald Macdonald, respecting Lord Selkirk's Red River Colony. *Montreal*, 1816, pp. 57, 8vo.

McADAM, J. L.
I. Essai pratique sur la manière de réparer et entretenir les chemins publics. *Québec*, 1819, pp. 12.

McCALLUM, ARCHIBALD, *M. A.* Principal of Central Sch. (Ham.)

I. A Chart of Natural History, with synopsis, or hand-book of Natural History. *Toronto,* 1866.

McCALLUM, DUNCAN C., *M. D.* Was one of the ed's. of the *Medical Chronicle* (Mont.)

I. Introductory lecture to the winter courses of the Faculty of Medicine of the University of McGill College. *Montreal,* 1860.

McCARA, JOHN. Barrister at Law.

I. The Origin, History and Management of the University of King's College, Toronto. *Toronto,* 1854, pp. 101.

McCARROLL, JAMES. A Can. poet, humourist and miscellaneous writer. B. in Lanesbora, Co. Longford, Irel., 3 Augt. 1815. He obtained a good Eng. education, including a knowledge of the classics. In 1831 he came with his family to Can. and settled in the wild forests of the Upper Province. He had a natural taste for Literature, and soon began to contribute scraps of prose and verse to the provincial journals, which were received with much favour. In 1843 he became ed. and prop. of the *Chronicle* (Peterboro,) and in 1847 purchased the *Newcastle Courier,* (Cob.,) of which he was also Ed. Since then there has scarcely been a periodical or newspaper of any note published in U. C. with which he has not had something to do, either as Ed., literary critic, ed. or ordinary contributor, or correspondent. His more important pieces have appeared in the *Canadian Gem,* (Cob., 1848,) the *Anglo Am. Mag.* (Tor., 1855,) the *Leader,* the *Home Journal* and *Brit. Am. Mag.* (Tor.) A short time since he owned and ed. a humourous weekly publication called the *Latchkey,* and it was in that sheet that the letters of *Terry Finnegan* were first published. As a humourous lecturer, he is regarded as holding no uncertain position—his lecture on " The House that Jack Built" has been delivered in almost every city and town in Can., and has invariably drawn from the press the highest eulogiums. His literary reputation however will rest chiefly upon his poems; and we are glad to learn that he contemplates soon bringing out a collection of them in book form.

I. The New Guager; a tale. *Ang. Am. Mag.*

II. The New Life Boat; *Do.*

III. The Adventures of a Night; *Do.*

IV. Letters of Terry Finnegan to the Hon. T. D. McGee. *Toronto,* 1864, pp. 104, 12mo.

" Who has not laughed over the remarkable humour of ' Terry Finnegan,' wondered at his acute discrimination and felt proud that Canada could boast of having at least one real wit, whose genius, force and fine imagination are a happy blending of the leading characteristics of Dickens and Lover?"—*Times,* (Ham.)

McCARTHY, JUSTIN. D. Que., July, 1832.

I. Dictionnaire de l'Ancien Droit du Canada, ou compilation des Edits, Declarations etc., concernant le Canada. *Québec,* 1809, 12mo.

McCAUL, *Rev.* JOHN, LL. D., *M. R. I. A.* President of Univ. Coll. (Tor.) B. in Dublin in the early part of the century. Ed. at Trinity Coll. there, were he obtained the highest honors in his class. Subsequently served as classical tutor and examiner. In Nov. 1838 he was appointed, by the late Archbishop of Canterbury, principal of Upper Can. Coll. (Tor.,) and entered upon his duties in the following year. In 1842 he became vice-president, and prof. of classics, logic, rhetoric and *belles-lettres* in King's Coll., same city; in 1853 was elected president of the new Univ. Coll., and appointed to the vice-chancellorship of the Univ., both of which he still continues to hold. Is a distinguished classical scholar. Dr McC. was, during its existence, ed. of a literary monthly periodical, the *Maple Leaf,* (Tor.) which he conducted with much ability. He is also the composer of several anthems and other pieces of vocal music. In 1863 was elected President of the Canadian Institute.

I. Remarks, Explanatory and Illustrative, on the Terentian Metres, with a sketch of the History, &c., of Ancient Comedy. *Dublin,* 1828, 8vo.

II. The Metres of the Greek Tragedians, explained and illustrated. *Do.,* 1828, 8vo.

III. Dionysius Longinus on the Sublime, with English notes. *Do.,* 12mo., 1829.

IV. Selections from Lucian, with English notes. *Do.*, 12mo., 1829.

V. Q. Horatii Flacci Satiræ et Epistolæ. Textum recognovit, intisque cum alionum tum suis instruxit. *Do.*, 12mo., 1833.

VI. The First Book of the Histories of Thucydides, &c. with Explanatory and Critical notes. *Do.* 1834, 8vo.

VII. Remarks in the Course of Classical Study, &c. *Do.* 8vo.

VIII. Scansion of the Hecuba and Medea of Euripides. *Do.* 1836, 8vo.

IX. The Metres of the Odes of Horace explained. New Edition. *Do.* 1838, 8vo.

X. Love to God and our Neighbour ; a sermon. *Toronto*, 1840.

"This is a very well written, pious and eloquent discourse, and exceedingly appropriate to the occasion on which it was delivered. The style is severally chaste, the language simple, and the religious doctrines and principles enunciated highly scriptural. What higher praise can be bestowed on any human production. ?"—*Gazette*, (Mont.)

XI. Britanno-Roman Inscriptions, with critical notes. *Toronto and London*, 1863, pp. 338, 8vo.

"The volume will, we are sure, be very acceptable to students of British archæology, who will recognise in it that spirit which ought to animate all similar researches ; namely, not an endeavour to prove who is right or who is wrong in the interpretation of these monuments, but to ascertain what is really the truth. The inscriptions are arranged according to counties, and the work has a good Index."—*Notes and Queries*, (Lon.)

"Dr. M'Caul points out a good many instances where the renderings proposed by earlier writers cannot possibly be got out of the words. He is evidently a better scholar than most of the antiquaries who have taken to his special branch, and brings a much more thorough knowledge of contemporary literature to bear upon the subject."—*Saturday Review.* (Do.)

"As a specimen of Canadian literature this is certainly a very remarkble volume. It is one which, wherever produced, would do credit to the learning, ingenuity and good taste of its author, and could hardly fail to obtain the high approbation of those who can appreciate such pursuits ; but it could scarcely have been expected in the old world, that in the remote capital of Western Canada, a scholar would devote his time to correcting by accurate knowledge and acute

reasoning the errors of those who would seem to have much better means of examining the particulars requiring to be known than himself, and however high our aspirations may be, it is not exactly in this department that we should expect our countrymen to obtain distinction : Yet our judgment is altogether at fault if this work is not received as a valuable contribution to an interesting department of Archæological study, extending the reputation of its author for curious research, accurate scholarship and judicious criticism and proving that materials and encouragement for such pursuits are not altogether wanting to us, far as we may be removed from the objects themselves of whose worn and partially defaced inscriptions we attempt to penetrate the meaning."—*B. A. Mag.*

Canadian Journal.

I. Notes on Latin Inscriptions found in Britain. 1858-59-60-61 & 62.

II. Annual address as President of the Can. Institute, 1863.

III. Tesseræ Consulares. *Do.*

IV. On inscribed sling-bullets. 1864.

McCOLL, EVAN. A Scot. lyric poet residing in Can. B. at Kenmore, Loch-Fyne-Side, Scot., 12 Sept., 1808, where he is known as the "*Clarsair-nam-beann*," or "the Mountain Minstrel." A prominent place has been assigned to him in Mackenzie's "*Beauties of Gaelic Poetry, and Lives of the Highland Bards*" (Glas., 1841). From this sketch we learn that he acquired the rudiments of an Eng. education, and with it a taste for Eng. literature, from a private tutor whom his father out of his slender means had succeeded in engaging. The circumstances in which his father were placed, rendered it necessary for young McC. to engage in the active operations of farming and fishing, and he was thus employed for several years. He had early devoted himself to the poetic muse, and in 1837 became a contributor to the *Gaelic Magazine* (Glas.).

"His pieces excited considerable interest, and a general wish was expressed to have them published in a separate form, by all Highlanders, with the exception of his own immediate neighbours, who could not conceive how a young man, with whom they had been acquainted from his birth, should rise superior to themselves in intellectual stature, and public estimation." *

---

* *Mackenzie.*

His first volume attracted a large degree of attention, and was favourably reviewed by the highest literary authorities. In 1831, his father, with the rest of his family, emigrated to Can.; but McC. himself could not so soon leave his native hills; and when, in 1837, he accepted a clerkship in the Customs at Liverpool, it was not without a painful struggle that he bade adieu to the land of his birth. In 1846 his second work appeared from the press, and was even better received than his first. In 1850, in consequence of ill-health, he visited Can. where he determined to remain, having been appointed to the Provincial Customs, at Kingston. Here he has since resided. He is the Bard of the Caledonian Soc. of that city, and his annual contribution on the anniversary of Scotland's Saint, is always looked for with much interest. His "*Bonnet, Kilt and Feather*," and his "*Lake of the Thousand Isles*" are particularly good. So is his "*Robin*," written for the people's centennial celebration of the favorite Scottish poet's birthday in Kingston. The ed. of the *Daily News* of that city, in noticing this latter song, observed :

"Its melodious and flowing beauty of expression commanded general admiration ; its pervading characteristic—that of being in Burns' own style,—and the subject being throughout in especial relation to the Scottish bard, made it peculiarly appropriate as a birthday ode, and as a specimen of that class of poetry. it must be held in high estimation   *   *   We consider that in *Robin*, Mr. McColl has achieved his greatest success, and as an artistic production, it deserves to be placed on a level with Lady Nairn's celebrated impersonation of Burn's so touching and pathetic, ' *The Land o' the Leal.*' "

We understand that Mr. McC. has in preparation a new volume of poems which is shortly to be published.

I. Clarsach nam Beann ; or, poems and songs in Gaelic. *Glasgow.*

"Mr. McColl's Gaelic pieces are chiefly amorous, and emanate from a heart imbued with the finest feelings of humanity. His ' *Ode to Loch-duich*' is inimitable. Rich in the most splendid imagery of nature, represented to our admiring gaze, through the burning vista of poetic genius, we sit on the author's lips, float with him on its glassy surface, or dive into its transparent bosom.

" As a Celtic bard, Mr. McColl is second to none ; and we trust that a young man, who has commenced his career so auspiciously, will yet be an honour to his country, and to the republic of letters."—*Constitutional*, (Glas.)

" We do not envy the taste of that man who will sit an hour on the mountain side. without the bewitching company of ' *Clarsach nam Beann.*' "—Dr. Norman McLeod.

II. The Mountain Minstrel ; or, poems and songs in English. *London*, 1846, 12mo.

" Evan McColl's poetry is the product of a mind impressed with the beauty and the grandeur of the lovely scenes in which his infancy has been nursed. We have no hesitation in saying, that this work is that of a man possessed of much poetic genius. Wild, indeed, and sometimes rough, are his rhymes and epithets; yet there are thoughts so new and so striking—images and comparisons so beautiful and original—feelings so warm and fresh, that stamp this Highland peasant as no ordinary man. His volume well deserves a niche among the curiosities of modern literature."—Dr. Norman McLeod.

" There is a freshness, a keenness, a heartiness in many of these productions of the Mountain Minstrel which seem to breathe naturally of the hungry air, the dark, bleak, rugged bluffs among which they were composed, alternating occasionally with a clear, bewitching, and spiritual quiet, as of the gloaming, deepening over the glens and woods. Several of these melodies, towards the close of this volume, are full of simple and tender feeling, and not unworthy to take their place by the side of those of Lowland minstrels of universal fame."—P. J. Bailey.

McCord, David R., *B. A.*
I. Notes on the habitats and varieties of some Canadian Ferns. *Can. Nat.* 1864.

McCord, Thomas. An Advocate of L. C. Secy. to the Codification Commission, L. C.
I. Synopsis of the changes in the Law effected by the Civil Code of Lower Canada. *Ottawa*, 1866, pp. 39, 8vo.
II. A Handy Pocket Edition of the Civil Code of Lower Canada. *Montreal*, 1867.

McCulloch, *Rev.* Thomas, *D.D.* A theological and religious controversial author. B. in the parish of Neilston, Renfrew, Scot., about 1776. D. at Halifax, N. S., 1843. He was ed. at the Univ. (Edin..) and studied Theology under Prof. Bruce of the Associate Synod at Whitburn. He was ordained min. of a congregation at Stewarton, Ayrshire, but did not long remain there. In the year 1803 he went to Pictou, N. S., and in the following June, was inducted min. of the harbour of Pictou, or the town, as it was then beginning to be called. The town consisted at that time of only about a dozen houses, the inhabitants of which with a few others scattered around, composed his congregation. The sphere of his labours, as far as his congregation was concerned, was small; but his was a mind that in any sphere must have made its influence felt beyond any single spot where he might be located. Accordingly he soon began to take part in public affairs. As early as the year 1805 he projected an institution for the higher branches of education, especially for the benefit of dissenters. But the scheme died away as visionary. The only institution of the kind in the Province at that time was King's Coll., (Windsor.) One of its by-laws was as follows:

" No member of the University shall frequent the Romish mass, or the meeting houses of Presbyterians, Baptists or Methodists, or the conventicles or places of worship of any other Dissenters from the Church of England, or where divine service shall not be performed according to the liturgy of the Church of England, or shall be present at any seditious or rebellious meeting:

By another by-law degrees, and consequently all the civil privileges which graduation conferred, could only be conferred on those who had previously subscribed the 39 articles of the Church of England. The Institution was modelled after the University of Oxford. The students were compelled, at a heavy expense, to reside within its walls; and the whole management was such, as effectually to exclude the great majority of the youth of the Province, even had its statutes been more liberal.

For some time little attention was paid to these things. The larger portion of the population in the rural districts were still struggling with the difficulties of a first settlement, and as to education, few thought of seeking for their children more than the ordinary training of a common sch. Even that was difficult to obtain, and

when obtained very inferior. A large proportion of the inhabitants did not feel the necessity of any thing better, and many did not value education at all. The population was sparse, and the several portions had but little communication with one another or with the capital. To excite among such men an interest in an institution for the higher branches of education, and to raise among them the contributions necessary for its establishment and maintenance, was no easy task. Dr. McC., however, gave himself to the work with all the energy of his nature. For some years he had taught a grammar sch., or academy, partly as a means of improving his circumstances,—being like most of the ministers of that period but very imperfectly supported by his congregation,—but chiefly with the design of raising the standard of education in the district. The number and progress of those who attended that institution revived the idea of a coll., and accordingly under the leadership of Dr. McC., a soc. was formed for the founding of such a seminary on a liberal basis; and with the cordial concurrence of the then Lieut. Gov., Sir John C. Sherbrooke, an act of incorporation was granted to the trustees in the year 1816.

The intention then was to found an institution for dissenters, not indeed excluding churchmen; but as King's Coll. was entirely under their control, it was expected that only dissenters would take advantage of the new institution, and that as they were excluded from King's, they would combine in favour of the other. The leaders of the Ch. of Eng. in the Province took alarm at the idea of such an institution, which they judged would form a rallying point for dissenters, against the ch. They were willing, at least the liberal minded among them, to allow Presb's. to have an institution in which they might give their children such education as they could. It must be observed that, at that time, the Council of xii, which possessed both Executive and Legislative powers, was then the absolute rulers of the country. Not only was the Assem. not in the commanding position which it has since occupied under Responsible

Govt., it was in a state of complete subserviency to the Upper House. If the former manifested anything like a spirit of independence, the latter had only to refuse to do business with them to cause the latter to give way. Of this body the Anglican Bish. was a mem., and with scarcely an exception the members belonged to that body. The result was that when the bill which had passed the Assem. without any tests, came to the Coun., it received an additional clause, providing that the trustees and teachers must be members either of the ch. of Eng., or of the Presb. body. This threw the institution into the hands of the Presb's. alone, and left it dependent upon them for support. As they then consisted only of about 20 congregations, most of these in thinly settled districts, and the members in humble circumstances, the reader will perceive that Dr. McC. had but a feeble support to rely on. It should have been mentioned that, to avoid exciting the jealousy of King's Coll., it was resolved to assume the modest name of an academy, and not to seek the right of conferring degrees or other privilege of a coll. Hence the name Pictou Academy; though from the first it was intended to impart the education usual in colleges. Under the act of incorporation, the trustees immediately set to work, and raised £1000 for the erection of a building, a large sum under the circumstances; and Dr. McC. was chosen its first president. From that time, his life was chiefly devoted to the interests of the institution. At first almost the whole teaching devolved on him, and that not under the most favourable circumstances. The late Jotham Blanchard thus wrote of the efforts of Dr. McC. during the infancy of the institution:

"Of his daily labours and nightly vigils, after taking charge of the Institution, I am surely a competent witness. I was one of his first students, and have often seen him at 8 o'clock of a winter-morning enter his desk in a state of exhaustion which too plainly showed the labours of the night. To this those who are acquainted with the subject will give credence, when I state that his share of the course was, besides Greek and Hebrew, Logic, Moral Philosophy and Natural Philosophy. In each of these sciences, he drew out a system for himself, which was of course the result of much reading and much thought. When I add to this account of his daily labours, the repairs and additions which were necessary to a half-worn apparatus, and which none but himself could make, I am almost afraid my testimony will be doubted. And for the first 5 or 6 years of the institution, let it be remembered, he had charge of a congregation, and regularly preached twice a day, save when over-exertion ended in sickness."

The Rev. Geo. Patterson, of Pictou writes:

"During the whole time of his continuance in connexion with the Institution, he taught Logic, Moral Philosophy and Natural Philosophy, there being only one other Professor, who taught the classics and mathematics. Diverse as the branches were which he taught, he taught them all. I have since had an opportunity of knowing something of the Professors of Edinburgh University, but never till I saw them did I know the real greatness of Dr. McCulloch. There were men there who in a particular department to which they had chiefly directed their attention would have doubtless excelled him, such as Hamilton in Metaphysics, &c., but there was no man in that university, who could have made the same appearance that he could in all the branches taught. He was in fact a perfect Senatus Academicus. He could have taken any branch included in the faculty of arts, and Theology, and even some reckoned under the faculty of medicine, such as Chemistry and Natural History, and taught it in a respectable and efficient manner. You may think this exaggeration from the partiality of an old pupil, but Dr. Dawson of McGill college, expressed to me some years ago in Edinburgh the same views. I may add that his intellect was of that peculiar clearness, that whatever he knew, he knew accurately and distinctly. It was impossible for him to be obscure."

In teaching the branches named, in such an institution, he would have had abundance of labour, but this was only a small part of what devolved upon him. Besides the charge of a congregation till the year 1824, he took an active part in the business of the synod of the Presb. Ch. of N. S., of which he was a mem.; and most of the public documents of the body came from his pen. As soon as the first class of students were sufficiently advanced, he was requested by the synod to take charge of their studies in Theology. To his other labours were added the instructing of these young men in Hebrew and Theology. We may add here that he was a superior Hebrew scholar, and as such almost entirely self-taught. But his labours were chiefly increased by the opposition which the institution met with. This as forming an important chapter in the history of N. S. we must notice. After the Pictou Academy was commenced, the trustees made application to the Legislature for aid from the public treasury. The large majority of the House of Assem. were willing to grant the necessary assistance, and the first grant was carried in that branch of the legislature with only 4 dissentient voices, but in the Coun. it met with most determined opposition. From the year 1818 till the year 1834, this was the great question before the legislature, the Assem. being favourable, a majority of the Coun. unfavourable. There was a minority of the Coun. consisting of the liberal minded members of the Ch. of Eng., who always favoured the institution; but the majority steadily resisted a permanent endowment, or any attempt to remove the tests from the institution. Upon these questions a battle was fought every year, generally ending in a grant for that year, but even this at at length the Coun. refused, and the trustees resolved to lay their grievances before the King. In these days of religious equality and of good feeling among religious denominations, it is scarcely possible to realize the state of matters which existed then, the dominancy of one ch., and the inferior position of dissenters, the prejudices with which they were regarded even by sensible men, and the difficulties with which Dr. McC. had therefore to contend. Many believed that a dissenter must be disloyal, and letters were actually sent to the highest authority in the Province, charging Dr. McC. and his fellow labourers with disloyalty. But this was not the source of the most virulent hostility which the Academy encountered. Soon after it was founded, several clergym. arrived in the Province from the established ch. of Scotland. Dr. McC. though desirous of having the institution on a liberal basis, and the means of giving such a training as would fit our youth for usefulness in any sphere, attached

17

special importance to the institution as a means of training young men for the ministry. Indeed the difficulty of obtaining min's. to supply the destitute parts of the province was one and the principal moving cause which led him and his fellow labourers to found such an institution. When these min's. arrived, they found the institution commencing to send out the first number of native preachers. They came with all that supreme contempt which it was customary then and long after for old country people to feel for every thing colonial. The idea of training some of the inhabitants of the woods for min's, or giving a collegiate education to a native, seemed to them supremely ridiculous, and they assailed them with every epithet of contempt. They had, too, all the contempt for seceders, which the members of the established ch. in Scot. then entertained for that body. Still they were not long in seeing that the Presb. ch. of N. S., composed principally of seceders who were in the Province before them, had a firm footing in the country, and that such an institution by providing min's. was giving them a great advantage. They therefore opposed the institution as favouring the seceders in opposition to the Kirk of Scot. They did not ask to put it down entirely, but they asked 2 things, that Theology should be removed from the institution, and that the ordinary branches of a common sch. education should be introduced. To meet the former demand Dr. McC. removed his Theol. Class to his own house, instead of using a class room in the institution, the use of which had been granted by the trustees; not content with this they wished to stop him from teaching it at all. This he positively refused. The second was virtually destroying the institution as far as its original purpose was concerned, and was unnecessary, as there was a Grammar Sch. within a few rods of the building. The controversy was carried on with a virulence which it is now scarcely possible to realize. The opposition from these sources involved Dr. McC. in a vast amount of labour. His pen was constantly employed, in various ways, writing appeals and petitions to the legislature, writing appeals to the Presb. congregations, visiting them to collect funds, and carrying on a scarcely interrupted controversy through the press. His writings on this subject were at first generally published in the *Acadian Recorder*, but afterwards in the *Colonial Patriot*. More than once he visited Scot. and appealed to the Secession Synod and other dissenters, from whom he received liberal aid. A soc. was formed through his instrumentality in Glasgow for aiding the institution and the missionary operations of the Ch., which raised liberal contributions for the object. Besides these labours he visited Halifax and the leading towns in the Lower Provinces, delivering popular lectures on science, especially chemistry, illustrated by experiments, with the design of awakening an interest in education. These lectures were probably the first of the kind in B. N. A. With the assistance of his family he collected a museum of Natural History, which was the finest in the province at that time. Audubon pronounced the collection of native birds as the finest or among the finest he had ever seen. To the discredit of N. S., be it said, it was allowed to be sold abroad. The result of all these struggles in the Pictou Academy was that in the year 1834 it was remodelled, and those who were the most active in their hostility were introduced into the trust. This introduced the strife into the Board of Trustees, and exchanged external war for internal dissension. The new trustees succeeded in getting a part of the funds directed to teaching the branches of a common sch. education. This crippled the others so that the trustees were soon involved in difficulties as to paying the professors. The friends of the institution had lost heart and in a measure their confidence, and after a few years struggling Dr. McC. was removed, in the year 1838, to Dalhousie Coll., of which he was the first principal.

We have been thus particular in describing the founding and early struggles of this institution for the following reasons :

1. The institution was the means of training a large number of men for occupying prominent stations of usefulness in every sphere of life. We may only mention such men in Education as Dr. Dawson of McGill College, and Dr. Ross, Principal of Dalhousie College : in the Ministry, the Rev. P.G.McGregor (Hal.) and the late Rev. John McLean (Richibucto); and in the Foreign Mission field, the Rev. John Geddie of Aneiteum in the New Hebrides ; in Medicine, the late W. R. Grant, Professor in Pennsylvania Medical Coll. ; at the Bar and in Politics, the late Jotham Blanchard, the late George R. Young, the present leader of the opposition in N. S., A. G. Archibald, after Mr. Howe, the most eloquent man in that Province, Hugh Hoyles, late Attorney General of Newfoundland, and if we are not mistaken, the present Judge Ritchie of N. B. besides a large number who in less important spheres have been showing the benefits of the training which they received at the Institution. Two min's trained at the institution were sent as missionaries to Can., the late Rev. Aba McKenzie. (Goderich.) and the present Rev. Wm. Fraser, (Bondhead.)

2. It gave an impetus to the cause of education such as can now scarcely be estimated. When Dr. McC. began his labours there was scarcely a respectable common sch. in the rural districts, at all events in the Eastern parts of N. S., and a large portion of the people being originally from the Highlands of Scot. scarcely valued Education at all. The result of Dr. McC's. labours was a prodigious change, which continues to this day. Many who did not succeed in the learned professions did much for the improvement of the country by the sch's. which they taught. Nearly all the young men who entered upon the learned professions were obliged during their collegiate course to teach sch. in order to obtain means to prosecute their studies, so that a large number of good schools were established throughout the various parts of the Province. The sending forth of such a number of young men diffused a desire for knowledge even in the poorest settlements. The keen discussions which the question elicited, excited attention to the subject of education, both in the legislature and among the general public. The other religious bodies were also led to establish institutions for teaching the higher branches and for the training of young men for the ministry.

3. In a religious point of view the influence of the Institution was wide spread. The present influential position of Presbyterianism in N. S. is largely the result of Dr. McC's. labours in connexion with it.

4. In a public point of view, out of the Pictou Academy discussions in the country and in the Legislature arose the popular party which fought against irresponsible power, lodged in the hands of a few, sitting in secret, and controlling the whole affairs of the Province. It was in these dis-

cussions that public opinion began to be brought to bear upon the govt., it was in them that the assem. first began to act an independent part, it was through them that complete religious equality now happily existing was established, and thus the foundations were laid for those changes in their political constitution which took place a few years later.

We may here add a few words from the minute of the Synod of the Presb. Ch. of N. S. at the time of Dr. McC's. decease.

"The many and useful labours in which, for a long series of years, be was engaged, together with his untiring energy and perseverance, often amid no small difficulty and discouragement, they (the synod) would highly appreciate. More particularly, they would advert to his able and meritorious defence of Protestantism, at an early period of his residence in this Province; to his subsequent and arduous exertions in establishing a literary and philosophical Institution in the town of Pictou; to the assiduity and care with which for many years he toiled on behalf of its interests, and presided in its management; and to the success of his exertions, not merely in imparting to many young men such an education as formed a solid preparation to their occupying important stations in life, in a manner creditable to themselves and useful to the public; but also in exciting a decided taste for liberal studies, especially in the Eastern section of the Province.

"But the synod would attach peculiar value to his services as their professor of Divinity. The fruits of his labours in this department are to be found not merely in the Presbyterian Church of Nova Scotia, but even in Canada and the United States, in the ministrations of faithful men who received from him their first lessons in Theology. While the synod admired his varied and extensive learning, they had perfect confidence in his soundness in the faith. These together with his experience, zeal and acknowledged aptitude for imparting knowledge, rendered him an accomplished and successful public instructor."

From an early period, as early as 1807-8, Dr. Mc C. was a contributor to the newspaper press of N. S. He frequently wrote in the *Acadian Recorder*. In that journal some of his writings, which have been published separately, first appeared—such as *William;* the letters of *Stepsure*, a series of light and amusing sketches of the social habits of the people of N. S., particularly in the rural districts; the letters to Dr. Burns, &c. Subsequently he wrote in the *Nova Scotian* and the *Colonial Pa-*
17*

triot. His newspaper writings are diverse in point of style—some grave and some gay, other on local controversies, ecclesiastical and political. We offer the opinion of the Rev. Geo. Patterson, a highly competent critic on his merits as an author and writer:

"The general style of all Dr. McC's. writings is remarkably terse, vigorous and pointed. The sentences are generally short and epigrammatic. In fact they would sometimes read as a series of proverbs. All his writings are marked by logical force and clearness. In his controversial writings he showed himself a master of sarcasm, but this is generally mixed with an irresistible drollery. The style of controversy in those days was bitter, and he hurled his weapons at his antagonists in a manner that was crushing. Even yet his controversial writings may be read without regard to the particular subject of controversy, just as one would read the diatribes of Swift or the satires of Wolcott, merely for the intellectual power and literary skill which they manifest. *Stepsure's* letters again are a mass of drollery, but convey many lessons of practical wisdom. In his more serious writings such as his Lectures on Theology, there is however not the slightest appearance of those qualities, unlike humorists like Rowland Hill, who mingled the comic even with his most serious strains. Nobody in reading these could have imagined that he was the same writer who in another sphere could overwhelm an antagonist by most withering sarcasm, or make all hold their sides by torrents of fun."

I. Popery Condemned by Scripture and the Fathers: being a refutation of the principal Popish Doctrines and Assertions, maintained in the Remarks on the Rev. Mr. Sanser's examination of the Rev. Mr. Burke's Letter of Instruction to the Catholic Missionaries of Nova Scotia, and in the Reply to the Rev. Mr. Cochran's fifth and last letter to Mr. Burke. *Edinburgh*, 1808 pp. 385 12mo.

II. Popery again Condemned by Scripture and the Fathers: being a Reply to a part of the Popish Doctrines and Assertions contained in the Remarks on the Refutation, and in the Review of Dr. Cochran's Letters, by Edmund Burke, V. G. Que. *Do* 1810 pp. 429, 12mo.

III. The Prosperity of the Church in Troublous Times; a sermon preached at Pictou. *Halifax*, 1814, pp. 24, 8:c.

IV. Words of Peace ; being an Address, delivered to the congregation of Halifax, in connection with the Presbyterian Church of Nova Scotia, in consequence of some congregational disputes &c. *Do.*, 1817 pp. 16, 16mo.

V. Report of a Committee appointed by the Synod of the Presbyterian Church of Nova Scotia, to prepare a statement of means for promoting religion in the Church, securing the permanence in the Church, an enlarging its bounds, &c. *Do.*, 1818, pp. 34, 8vo.

VI. The Nature and Uses of a Liberal Education illustrated ; a lecture. *Do.* 1819. pp. 24, 8vo.

VII. Colonial Gleanings. *Edinburgh*, 1826, pp. 144, 18mo.

" It consists of two short tales or rather sketches of colonial life, entitled respectively, ' William,' and ' Melville.' The former represents a Scotchman of the humbler ranks of life emigrating to Nova Scotia, and by his steady habits acquiring a competence and a respectable position in society, but not being of firm religious principle and gradually falling into the dissipated habits then so prevalent, went to ruin and ended his days in the poor-house. The second sketch is a sort of reverse picture. It describes a young man of a respectable but reduced family emigrating with the view of regaining the wealth and position of his ancestors, succeeding in business for a time, but finally meeting with reverses and seeking consolation in religion, which he had previously neglected. The first he says in the preface ' is a faithful delineation of a character not uncommon among Scotchmen abroad.' The second bore more of a fictitious character. Both sketches are interesting, and in some parts extremely touching. The style is the same pithy and epigrammatic style as that of his other writings. I think that he had not the dramatic art that would have been required to make him an accomplished tale writer."—REV. GEO. PATTERSON.

VIII. A Memorial from the Committee of Missions of the Presbyterian Church of Nova Scotia, to the Glasgow Society for promoting the religious interest of the Scottish settlers in British North America ; with observations on the constitution of that Society, and upon the proceedings, and first annual report of the committee of directors. 1826, 8vo.

IX. Calvinism, the Doctrine of the Scriptures, or, a scriptural account of the ruin and recovery of Fallen man ; and a review of the principal objections which have been advanced against the Calvinistic system. *Glasgow* and *London*, 1849, pp. 270, 12mo.

" The subjects discussed involve the most difficult points in Theology, and have called forth the efforts of the most profound philosophers, and the most learned divines, and, yet with the exception of Principal Hills' lucid exposition of the Arminian and Calvinistic systems, we do not remember having seen these subjects more clearly or more satisfactorily discussed.

" We would most earnestly recommend all our readers to get the book and to place it in their library side by side with the Confession of faith. It is in our opinion a standard theological work, not only in its lucid and scriptural exposition of fundamental and vital doctrine, but in its triumphant refutation of error. We were never more thoroughly satisfied, than by the perusal of this volume that the system of Calvinism, is the religion of the Bible." *Presb. Witness,* [Hal.)

X. Letters of Mephibosheth Stepsure. (Reprinted from the *Acadian Recorder* of the years 1821 and 1822.) *Halifax,* 1860, pp. 143, 8vo.

Published anonymously.

McCULLY, *Hon.* JONATHAN, *Q. C.* A N. S. statesman and journ. B. in Cumberland, N. S., 1809. He studied for the Bar, to which he was admitted in 1837, and successfully practised his profession at Amherst, from that time until 1849. In early life he was brought into notice as a contributor to the *Acadian Recorder,* (Hal.,) upon which paper he was afterwards engaged for some years as a regular writer. Mr. McC. commenced public life in 1847, by being selected to fill a vacant seat in the Leg. Council. In 1849 he removed to Halifax, where he has since resided. For some years previous to 1857, he was Judge of Probate for that city and the metropolitan county. In that year he went into opposition with his party, and transferred his services from the *Recorder* to the *Morning Chronicle and Nova Scotian,* a weekly and tri-weekly journal, which was the organ of the Liberal party. This he continued to conduct with much ability up to 1860, when his party came back to power, and he went into office as Solicitor Genl. and Chief Com. of Railways, becoming at same time leader of the Govt. in the Leg. Council. During the existence of the Liberal administration, and after the withdrawal of Messrs. Young and Howe from public life, Mr. McC. still held the position of chief Ed. on the above paper, and through the aid of his powerful and vigorous pen did much for the cause of his party. In 1863 the Liberals again went into opposition. In that year the subject of the Union of the Maritime Provinces was discussed by him in a series of editorials in his paper, in which he submitted the outlines of a scheme, which met with much attention in all the Colonies. Shortly afterwards the subject was taken up in the legislature of N. S., and resolutions passed in favour of a joint Conference with the Provinces interested. As leader of the Opposition in the Upper Chamber, Mr. McC. was appointed a delegate to that Conference which met at Charlottetown in 1864, and to the larger and more important one, arising therefrom, at Quebec, in the same year. In the deliberations of both he bore a prominent part. Up to 1865 he still continued Ed. of the *Morning Chronicle* (which had become a daily,) and gave a strong and hearty support to the Confederation project. Early in that year, however, through differences of opinion with the prop., Mr. Annand, who was throughout opposed to the Union of N. S. with Can., Mr. McC. retired from the paper, and became ed. of the *Morning Journal*, the name of which he changed to the *Unionist.* He is still ed. of that paper. Under his management the *Unionist* has largely extended its circulation, and rendered important aid in effecting Confederation. In 1866–7 Mr. McC. attended the Colonial Conference in London as a delegate. He is still in the active prosecution of his profession at Halifax.

I. British America : Arguments against a Union of the Provinces reviewed ; with further reasons for Confederation. *London,* 1867, pp. 32, 8vo.

McDONALD, *Dr.* A.

I. An Address to the People of British America upon subjects relating to the progress of the people and the improvement of the country. Published by the Author. 1853, pp. 32, 8vo.

McDONALD, ARCHIBALD.

I. Narrative respecting the destruction of the Earl of Selkirk's Settlement, upon Red River, in 1815. *London,* 1816, pp. 14, 8vo.

II. Reply to the letter lately addressed to the Earl of Selkirk, by the Hon. and Rev. John Strachan, D. D., &c. Being four letters (reprinted from the *Montreal Herald*), containing a statement of facts, concerning the Settlement on Red River, in the district of Ossiniboia, territory of the Hudson's Bay Company, properly called Rupert's Land. *Montreal,* 1816, pp. 50, 8vo..

(See *McAdam, A.*)

McDONALD, R. C. " Lieut.-Col. of the Castle Tioram Highlanders, P. E. Island, &c., and paymaster of 30th Regt."

I. Sketches of Highlanders ; with an account of their early arrival in North America ; their advancement in Agriculture ; and some of their distinguised military services in the War of 1812. *St. John, N. B.,* 1843, pp. 70, 8vo.

McDONELL, *Colonel* JOHN. B. at Scottos, 1728. D. at Cornwall, U. C., 1810. Served in the Spanish army in early life.

I. A Narrative of the early life of Col. John McDonell, of Scottos, written by himself, after he came to Canada, at the urgent request of one of his particular friends. Interspersed with numerous anecdotes and historical details of the times. *Can. Mag.* (Mont.), 1825.

McDONELL, *Very Rev.* WILLIAM. A clergym. of the R. C. Ch. in Can. B. in Co. Banff, Scot. D. at Hamilton, U. C. At the time of the Peninsular war was charged with a confidential mission to the Continent of Europe, to rescue King Ferdinand of Spain from the power of Bonaparte. Through the well organized system of *espionage* of the latter, the project failed. Mr. McD. when on his way to the deposed monarch, was seized by the emissaries of the Emperor, brought before that Potentate and sent back to Eng. He enjoyed the friendship of the Royal

Family of Gt. Brit. Coming to Can. he had charge of the congregation of Ottawa. For many years previous to his death, he laboured at Hamilton, with the ecclesiastical rank of Vicar General. He was chiefly distinguished as a pulpit orator and prose writer, though he wrote many beautiful poems, which, however, have never been collected together in a permanent form. For sometime he ed. and published in Can. a newspaper called *The Catholic.*

McDonnell, Alexander.

1. A Narrative of the Transactions in the Red River country ; from the commencement of the operations of the Earl of Selkirk, till the summer of the year 1816. With a map exhibiting part of the route of the Canadian Fur Traders in the interior of North America, and comprising the scene of contest between the Earl of Selkirk and the North West Company. *London*, 1819, pp. 106, 8vo.

McDonnell, John F. A Can. journ. B. at Quebec, 1838. Was on the staff of the *New Era*, (Mont.) Subsequently became reporter, sub. ed. and finally, in 1865, ed. of the *Morning Chronicle*, (Que.) In 1863 he was admitted as an advocate, L. C. He is the author of various poetical contributions to the Am. and Can. press. Mr. Dewart in noticing his poetry says :

"It is to be regretted, that one who can write so musically, and with such deep appreciation of nature's beauty and power, should renounce the muses, to the extent Mr. McD. has latterly done."

McDougall, Hon. A. A N. S. politician and lawyer. B. in N. S., of Scotch descent. Was at one time Sol. Genl. of his native province. Possessed a fine literary taste, and contributed to *Bentley's Miscellany* (Lon.) One little comic poem, "My Sunday Coat of Blue" from his pen, in that periodical, attracted much attention and was commended. Now dead.

McDougall, Hon. William. C. B. A Can. statesman and journ. Is the grandson of an U. E. loyalist. B. at Toronto, 25 Jany., 1822. Ed. there and at Victoria Coll. (Cobourg.) Early in life was admitted to practise as an Attorney, but it was not until 1861 that he became

a Barrister of U. C. In 1848 he established the *Canada Farmer* (Tor.,) a semimonthly agricultural, scientific and literary journal, which in the following year was merged in the *Can. Agriculturist*, a monthly agricultural journal ; this paper he continued to publish and conduct until 1858, when he disposed of the copyright to the Board of Agriculture, U. C. In 1850 he founded the well-known semi-weekly newspaper, called the *North American*, of which he was chief ed. from its first issue until it was merged in the *Daily Globe*, in 1857. The *North American*, as the leading Reform organ of the day, enjoyed a wide circulation and wielded considerable political influence in U. C. Its editorials were forcible, vigorous and trenchant ; and were powerful auxiliaries in attack or defence, to the party whose mouthpiece it was. The extent of its influence was felt by the Prime Minister of the day, who, it is said, waited upon Mr. McD. as ed., to solicit his countenance and sanction to the nomination of a well-known mem. of the Reform party to a seat in the Cabinet. It was owing largely to the superior ability manifested by Mr. McD., while discharging the duties pertaining to his editorial office, and to the intimate and thorough acquaintance with all questions relating to politics and the science of Government generally, which he displayed, that he was regarded, at that time, as one of the "coming men" of his party. It was not, however, until 1858 that he entered the Legislature. During the interval, between the discontinuance of his paper and this latter event, and up to 1860, he acted as political writer to the *Globe*, a part of the time having entire editorial control of the political department of that journal. From 1862 until 1864 he was Commissioner of Crown Lands in the Liberal Administration of Mr. Sandfield Macdonald. In the latter year he took office as Provl. Secy. in the Coalition Administration of Sir E. P. Taché, an office which he held until the Union of the B. N. A. Provinces in 1867, when he was appd. to his present office of Min. of Public Works for the Dominion of Can. At the same time the Queen was pleased to create him a Companion of the Civil division of the order of the Bath. In 1865 he was Chairman of the commission appointed to open Trade Relations with the West Indies, Brazil and Mexico. He was a mem. of the Charlottetown and Quebec Union Conference's, and in 1866 proceeded to Eng. as one of the delegates from B. A. appd. to confer with the Imperial Govt. in the framing of the Confederation Act. Mr. McD. is a very fluent and effective public speaker, and the great success of the Union Govt. at the polls, during the late general election, is largely ascribed to his eloquent public advocacy of the policy of the new Administration. He may be considered as the *bona fide* leader of the Reform party in Can.

I. Address of the Constitutional Reform Association to the People of Upper Canada. *Toronto*, 1860, pp. 48, 8vo.

II. Report of the Commissioners from British North America appointed to enquire into the Trade of the West Indies, Mexico and Brazil. *Ottawa*, 1866, pp. 184, 8vo.

McDowall, *Rev.* James. A Presb. Min. Received license to preach in 1856, and was for some years stationed in the Bermudas, but his health failing him, he came to Can. where he died, 1864, aged 38.

A Brief Memoir and some Remains of the late Rev. James McDowall. Edited by the Rov. James Cameron. *Toronto*, 1866, pp. 54, 8vo.

" The Memoir and Remains, that follow, are published at the request of Members of the Presbyterian Congregation of St. Vincent, Sydenham and Euphrasia, who desire to possess, in the book, a memorial of their late Pastor."—*Preface.*

McGee, *Hon.* Thomas D'Arcy, *B. C. L., M. R. I. A.* A Can. author and statesman. B. at Carlingford, Irel. 13 April, 1825. Descended from an old Ulster family. Ed. at Wexford. When only 17 years of age left his native land, and emigrated to the U. S., where he joined the newspaper press of Boston, delivered lectures on various subjects, and eventually made his mark as a public speaker. In 1845 a newspaper article from his pen, on an Irish subject, having attracted the notice of the late

Mr. Daniel O'Connell, he was offered a position in the ed. staff of the *Freeman's Journal* (Dub.,) which he accepted, and returned to Irel. Of the succeeding events in his career, while he remained there, a good account is given by Mr. Fennings Taylor :

" Ardent by temperament, and enthusiastic by disposition, it was impossible for Mr. McGee to keep within the bounds of moral force which Mr. O'Connell had prescribed, and which the newspaper he served was instructed to advocate. Mr. McGee felt that such fetters galled him, and he became impatient under their restraint. The habit of maintaining his own convictions, was, and is, a necessity of his condition. Following the lead of his feelings, he determined at all hazards to associate himself with the more advanced and enthusiastic of the liberal party, then known by the name of " Young Ireland." This section or *coterie*, for it was scarcely a party, possessed many attractions for such an adherent. Besides the name, and the bright, alluring, misleading quality of youth, which that name symbolized and expressed, the *coterie* was made up of those many-hued forms of intellectual mosaic work which men generally admire and rarely trust ; very charming in our sight and very perishable in our service. It was composed, at least at first, almost altogether of young barristers, young doctors, young college men and young journalists, most of them under thirty, and many under twenty-five years of age. Mr. McGee was probably their most youthful member, for when his association with them commenced he was not of age. Of such hot blood was the ' Young Ireland' party compounded, that little surprise was occasioned, and none was expressed, when its mischievous revels where broken up by the riot act. If we understand the history of those times aright, the policy of moral force which had guided O'Connell was not, in the first instance, discarded by his younger and more ardent disciples. They wished to accomplish the purpose of ' The Liberator,' only they desired to shorten the time and accelerate the speed of the operation. They thought that O'Connell was ' old and slow.' They felt that they were young and active. In their minds the rivalry between age and youth was renewed, provoking the old issues and re-enacting the old results. Keeping in view the great end which they had set themselves to accomplish, they nevertheless sought, in the first instance, to move by literary, rather than by political appliances. Accordingly they planned, among other works, a series of stirring shilling volumes for the people, entitled the ' Library of Ireland.' The famine of 1847 extinguished the enterprize, but not until twenty volumes of this new National Library had been published.

Of the above number Mr. McGee was the author of two. One, a series of biographies of illustrious Irishmen of the seventeenth century, and the other a memoir of ' Art. McMurrough,' a half forgotten Irish king of the fourteenth century. Of course, works published under such circumstances, and forming parts of such a series, would at first, at all events, be well received and widely circulated ; but their merits could not have been of a mere evanescent character, for we are credibly informed that now, after a period of twenty years, the books we have mentioned still retain their popularity.

" Mr. McGee, if we remember aright, has somewhere said, with respect to the transactions of those times, that ' Young Ireland,' not content to restore the past, endeavored to re-enact it; not content to write history, tried to use a familiar phrase of Mr. John Sandfield Macdonald, to ' make it, ' and we have little doubt, could we see the intellectual machinery which preceded those events, we should discover that none more than Mr. McGee have assiduously labored to manufacture history. The coterie grew into a confederation of which Mr. McGee was, we believe, the chief promoter and chosen secretary. It was not without adherents, neither was it without attraction, and especially to the class, a by no means inconsiderable one, whose judgment is controlled by their imagination, and who seem to think that feeling and wisdom are identical qualities. We decline to indicate those transactions by any particular name. We all know that they were failures, and since time tempers judgment, we venture to believe that the actors of that day concur with the critics of the present time in thinking that they were follies."

Having made his escape to Am., Mr. McG. resumed his old occupation as a journ. and lecturer. He published two newspapers in succession, The New York Nation, and The American Celt. But Republican institutions and manners became distasteful to him—with time and reflection a great change had come in his political views. Accordingly, early in 1857, he accepted an invitation, extended to him by his friends in Can., to remove to Montreal, where he has since resided. In the same year he commenced the publication there of the well known New Era newspaper. At the general election which followed, he was returned to Parliament as one of the members for the city of Montreal, which he still represents in the Dominion Parliament. From May 1862 to May 1863 he held office as

President of the Executive Council, and again from April 1864 until the Union of the Provinces in 1867, as Min. of Agriculture, .&c., and as such represented Can. at the late Dublin Exhibition, and the Exposition Universelle at Paris. As a public man in Can., Mr. McG. has identified himself with two prominent and important subjects—Immigration, and the Union of the Provinces, of both of which he has been an earnest and an eloquent advocate. As a public speaker and lecturer he is considered to be without a rival in the new Dominion. He has also strenuously laboured, and with some success, towards the establishment of a B. A. literature. In addition to the works whose titles we give below, Mr. McG. has contributed largely to the periodical literature of the old and new worlds. Of his lectures and addresses we give the titles of some of the principal : Columbus ; Shakspeare ; Milton ; Burke ; Grattan ; Burns ; Moore ; the Reformation ; the Jesuits ; the English Reformation of 1688 ; the Growth and Power of the Middle Classes in England ; the Moral of the Four Revolutions ; the Irish Brigade in the Service of France ; the American Revolution ; the Spirit of Irish History ; Will and Skill ; the Morality of Shakspeare's Plays ; the Future of Canada ; the Land we Live in ; Canada's Interest in the American Civil War ; British American Union ; Character of Champlain ; the Common Interests of British North America ; the Germans in Canada ; the Irish in Canada ; Confederation ; Public Opinion ; Public Life. He is a mem. of the Royal Irish Academy, a corresponding mem. of the Historical Societies of the States of N. Y. and Maine, and a mem. of nearly every literary and scientific soc. and association in Can.

I. O'Connell and his Friends. Boston, 1844.

II. Lives of the Irish Writers of the 17th Century. Dublin, 1847.

III. Life of Art McMurrough. Do. 1848.

IV. Memoir of Duffy. Do., 1849.

V. History of the Irish Settlers in America. Boston, 1851, 12mo.

VI. History of the Attempts to Establish the Protestant Reformation in Ireland. *Do.*, 1853, 12mo.

VII. Catholic History of North America. *Do.*, 1854, 12mo.

VIII. Life of Bishop Maginn. *New York*, 1856.

IX. Canadian Ballads, and Occasional Verses. *Montreal*, 1858, pp. 124, sm. 8vo.

"These ballads are presented to the young people of Canada as an offering of first-fruits, and we are quite sure that those who peruse them will look forward with much eagerness for another instalment in the same direction."—*Globe* (Tor.)

"The Canadas have not yet enriched the realms of poetry. One true poet they have within their borders,—Mr. D'Arcy McGee,—who should not altogether give up to politics that which was meant for poetry. The principle of rebellion with him was fertile in fine and stately verse, when he was in 'Ould Ireland,' and we trust the strong feeling of his conservatism in his new home will yet inspire many a song."—*Athen.* (Lon.)

X. Emigration and Colonization in Canada : a Speech in the House of Assembly. *Quebec*, 1862, pp. 25.

XI. The Internal Condition of American Democracy; considered in a letter to the Hon. C. G. Duffy, M. P. P., Minister of Public Lands of the Colony of Victoria. *London*, 1863, pp. 19, 8vo.

"The source from which this brief letter emanates, and the subject of which it treats, confer upon the opinions expressed considerable interest and importance. From a long residence in the United States, Mr. McGee speaks as an authority who will be listened to with careful attention and respect. The picture he draws of the present Social position of the Boston school of Americans, is anything but flattering to their pride ; the future national character, he half predicts they will attain, is the reverse of encouraging."—*B. A. Mag.*

XII. A Popular History of Ireland : from the earliest period to the Emancipation of the Catholics. *New York*, 1863, 2 vols., pp. 823, sm. 8vo,

"Mr. McGee has done his best to give a fair, impartial, and faithful history of his native country ; and though less accurate in language, and less brilliant in style than we looked for, his work is probably the best popular history of Ireland that has been published." — *Brownson's Quarterly Rev.*

"His narrative, always clear, is often graphic. The reader is shown how much of Irish history is tradition, how much is fact. The annals of Ireland from the death of Queen Elizabeth to the Emancipation Bill of 1829 have never been so clearly written. The history from the death of Queen Anne to the year 1829 is as interesting as a romance, yet thoroughly reliable. Mr. McGee has produced a work that will live."—*Am. Lit. Gaz.*

"No man before Mr. McGee has brought out the *inner life* of Irish history—the poetry of dry facts, and his history is, therefore, beyond all comparison, the most readable Irish history yet given to the world. It is Ireland's *story*, well told, or rather painted, as far as words can paint historical events, historical portraits."—*Tablet*, (N. Y.)

XIII. The Crown and the Confederation. Three Letters to the Hon. John Alexander McDonald, Attorney General for Upper Canada. By a Backwoodsman. *Montreal*, 1864, pp. 36, 8vo.

XIV. Notes on Federal Governments, Past and Present. *Do.*, 1865, pp. 75, 8vo.

"Mr. McGee has thrown together in these sixty pages,—printed with his usual accuracy and elegance by Lovell,—the results of much varied reading, on the subject of Federal Governments. Of these, he gives us a condensed but satisfactory analysis of eight principal examples—ranging over a period of two thousand years, and extending in space from Greece to New Zealand."—*Gaz.* (Mont.)

XV. Two Speeches on the Union of the Provinces. *Quebec*, 1863, pp. 34, 8vo.

XVI. Speeches and Addresses chiefly on the subject of British American Union. *London*, 1865, pp. 308, 8vo.

"These speeches and addresses have been delivered from time to time during the past half-dozen years, and they form an admirable commentary upon the course of events during that period. Indeed, we know of no work more capable of aiding the 'home' reader personally unacquainted with the British North American provinces in forming a proper estimate of the elements which go to make up the aggregate, as the author in his preface terms it, of the present British American society in the western hemisphere, and as a book of reference the volume before us is invaluable." *Can. News* (Lon.)

"Mr. McGee's name has lately been a great deal before the public in connection with sentiments remarkable for sound sense, discrimination, and enlightenment."—*Ill. Lon. News.*

XVII. The Irish Position in British and in Republican North America. A Letter to the Editors of the Irish Press irrespective of party. *Montreal*, 1866. 2nd Ed., pp. 45, 8vo.

" Mr. D'Arcy McGee, the Canadian Minister of Agriculture and Immigration, was a visitor to this country in the spring of last year, and the speeches which he delivered to Irish audiences attracted much attention from their novelty, eloquence, and boldness. He then told a story which no one had ventured to tell before him, and represented Irish life in America without colouring or distortion. He tells us now, through a letter which he has addressed to the editors of the Irish papers across the Atlantic, what are the elements of this Irish life which enter into the compound of Fenianism. If any one in this country wonders why American citizens of Irish extraction should be thinking of a raid upon Canada instead of minding their own affairs, Mr. McGee will furnish a solution of the enigma."—*Times*, (Lon.)

McGILL. *Rev.* RODT.

I. Discourses preached on various occasions. *Montreal*, 1853.

McGREGOR, *Rev.* JAMES, *D. D.* A Presb. clergym. B. in the parish of Comrie, Perthshire, Scot., 1759. D. at Pictou, N. S., 1830. Studied at the Univ. of Edinburgh, and was ordained min. of Pictou in 1786, arriving there in the following year, where he continued to reside until his death. Dr. McG. contributed to the *Christian Mag.* (Edin.,) and to the provincial press, especially to the *Acadian Recorder* and the *Colonial Patriot.* He left a large number of MSS. in Gaelic and English. Three of these, with various other emanations from his pen, have been published in his Remains, ed. by his grandson.

I. A Letter to a Clergyman, urging him to set free a black girl he held in Slavery. *Halifax*, 1783, pp. 12.

II. Letter to the General Associate Synod, April 30th, 1793. *Paisley*, 1793, pp. 16, 8vo.

III. On the Millenium. *Christian Mag.* (Edin.) 1800.

IV. Dain a Chomnadh Crabhuidh, Le Seumas Macghriogair, searmonaich au t-sois geil an America. With a Memoir of the author. *Glasgow*, 1st Ed. 1818 ; 3rd Ed. Do., 1832 ; *Pictou*, N. S., 1861.

The latter ed. contains a memoir by Rev. D. B. BLAIR.

" These poems are smooth in versification, pleasant in their garb, and evangelical in their doctrines. They are chiefly composed after the model of Duncan McIntyre the Breadalbane poet, from whom he borrowed the airs as well as many of his words and expressions. The author's mind was richly stored with gospel truth."—Rev. D. B. BLAIR.

V. An Address to the Congregations under the inspection of the Presbyterian Synod of N. S., exciting them to a public spirit in the cause of Christ. (In conjunction with the Revd. Hugh Graham.)

Remains of the Rev. James McGregor, D. D., edited by his grandson, the Rev. G. Patterson, (whom see) *Philadelphia* and *Edinburgh*, 1859.

" We have perused most of the Remains with much pleasure and we may add edification. They undoubtedly manifest " a vigour of thought, a clearness and simplicity of style, and an acquaintance with Theology and familiarity with scripture, which entitle their author to a high place among Theologians. We have never seen a more thorough and satisfactory discussion of the Imprecations in the Psalms than this volume contains. The essay on Baptism is also singularly candid, clear and conclusive. * * *

" The essay on the Millennium contains many very interesting, and some original and startling speculations.

" We have read the letter on Slavery with heart glowing with admiration for the generosity, the Christian enthusiasm, the fervid eloquence of the man. It is almost forgotten in this Province that ever the slavery question was discussed in our midst with great ability and a good deal of feeling on both sides. Dr. McGregor took an active and honourable part in the discussion. The letter here republished was originally addressed to the Rev. Mr. Cock of Truro, who had two female slaves. Of the £27 received in money by Dr. McGregor for his first years salary, £20 went to pay for the freedom of a woman, held as a slave by Matthew Harris, of Pictou. And he paid £50 in all to effect her liberty. This was an act of charity rarely equalled anywhere and never in Nova Scotia. He subsequently devoted a large portion of his scanty means to relieve and assist such negroes as were within his reach. We should look upon it as a strange anomaly now a days were a Presbyterian minister to possess slaves ; yet Mr. Cock was by no means singular in his day. Slaves were then held in many parts of this Province, and good men were ready to quote scripture in defence of slaveholding and slavetrading, even as it is now done in the

United States. We have never seen the scriptural argument against slavery better put than in Dr. McGregors's letter."—*Presb. Witness*, (Hal.)

A Memoir of Dr. McGregor, with notices of the colonization of the Lower Provinces of British America, &c. By the same. *Philadelphia* and *Edinburgh*, 1859, pp. XV.—543, 12 mo.

" The work contains the story of the life of a remarkable man, who lived in a remarkable period of the ecclesiastical history of the Province, or rather of these Lower Provinces, and who bore a remarkable part in moulding the ecclesiastical and spiritual character of a large portion of their inhabitants, and in organizing and establishing the Presbyterian Church of Nova Scotia.

" The work is most instructive. It cannot fail to be a great lesson teacher to ministers and people ; and through it Dr. McGregor though dead for nearly thirty years, will read many heartstirring admonitions to the ministry of our day, and many an inducement to be instant in season and out of season, assuring them that like minded and like hearted with him, in due time they will reap if they faint not.

" Probably this work will be as interesting and useful to the imported as to the native ministry of these Provinces, whether connected with the Presbyterian or any other denomination of Christians, * * But all ministers must if they read in a proper manner be the better of getting and reading this book. It will teach them in what spirit to minister and for what end. It will present them with an all but perfect specimen of a man at once an evangelist and a pastor. The messenger and the overseer were never more happily combined than in Dr. McGregor, so that while he was ' so journeying oft' from Pictou round about the ' Island,' and to the furthest verge of the other Province, and proclaimed the glad tidings of great joy to the lonely settlers in the unbroken forests, they will see him among his own people as a nurse among her charge, or a father in his family ' warning every man that he might present every man perfect in the day of the Lord Jesus.'

" In the simplicity and godly sincerity of his deportment—in the unselfishness and unworldliness of his spirit, in the absence of all ministerial pride and pretension and the possession of ministerial power to an extent rarely equalled, and based on the qualities just mentioned—in his entire devotedness and unwearying assiduity in the work to which he was committed,—and in his exclusive dependance on God as faithful to his promise manifested every day by his devotional habits—will they see a model minister making full proof of his ministry, furnishing an example there is honour in imitating.

" And the book is full of instruction to the people as well as to the minister. It will show them at what cost their privileges were obtained and how their existence and continuance depended under God, on the toil and travail, on the prayers with strong crying and tears, on the work and the warfare of a man who counted all things but loss, if so be that his kinsmen according to the flesh, who had left the scenes of their birth and the place of their fathers sepulchres for a home in the new world, might have a better and more enduring substance in the heavenly country."—Rev. Robt. Sedwick. *Christian Instructor N. S.*

McGregor, Patrick, A. M. A Toronto Barrister. B. in Scot. A graduate of the Univ. of Edinburgh. Admitted to the Bar of U. C. in 1857.

I. The Genuine Remains of Ossian, literally translated from the original Gaelic, with a preliminary dissertation. *London*, 1841.

" I can safely say that it displays much talent and much interesting research, * * His translations are in good English and I have perused them with much pleasure."—The late Prof. John Wilson, (Edin.)

" I find it singularly exact and faithful, indeed it seems to me, its only fault is its being in some instances too close. The meaning of the original is given with great precision and its spirit and manner preserved with remarkable felicity."—The late Rev. Norman McLeod, D. D.

II. A System of Logic, comprising a Discussion of the various means of acquiring and retaining Knowledge and avoiding Error. Consisting mostly of new matter. *New York*, 1862, pp. 469, p. 8vo.

" We are inclined to think that the author has been entirely successful, so far as the needs of students and general readers are concerned."—*N. A. Rev.*

" Something to make us more accurate thinkers is what we want. We know of no book that so well meets this idea as this work."—*Post*, (Bos.)

McGregor, Rev. P. G., D. D. Prof. in St. Francis Xavier Coll., Antigonish, N. S. Youngest son of the late Dr. McGregor. Since 1843 has been min. of Poplar Grove Ch. (Hali.)

I. Providence of God in reference to Nations ; a lecture. *Halifax*, 1858, pp. 31, 8vo.

II. The Evils of a Superficial Education ; a lecture. *Do.* 1866.

"The subject is handled in a masterly manner and many valuable suggestions are contained therein."—*Reporter* (Hal.)

III. Galileo and the Copernican System—How treated by Rome; a lecture. *Do*. 1867.

McINTOSH, DONALD. Contributed to the *Literary Garland* in 1847, *Hector Kemp and the Fairies of Corrynasheeich ; a Highland Legend*. Some of his poetry is to be found in Dewart's *Selections*.

McKENZIE, *Rev.* J. G. D. A min. of the Ch. of Eng. (Ham.) In 1844 whilst preparing for the ministry at the Diocesan Coll., (Cob., U. C.,) contributed many fugitive pieces to the *Church* journal, of that place, amongst which we may mention *Paul of Samosata ; a tale of the ancient Syrian Church ; A Review of some leading points in the Character and History of Leo X; Life and Writings of Minucias Felix;* and *The Massacre of St. Bartholomew*. After the removal of the paper to Toronto, Mr. M. was associated in the management of it, first with Rev. R. J. McGeorge and subsequently with Rev. A. Dixon.

McKENZIE, *Rev.* WILLIAM. Presb. min., (Ramsay, U. C.)

I. A Gospel within the Gospel ; an exposition of the parable of the prodigal. *Prescott*, 1864, pp. 74.

McKILLOP, ARCHIBALD.

I. Temperance Odes and Miscellaneous Poems. *Quebec*, 1860, pp. 96.

McKINLAY, *Rev.* JOHN. A Presb. min. in N. S.

I. Address of the Synod of the Presbyterian Church of Nova Scotia to the people under their charge. *Pictou*, 1843, pp. 22, 12mo.

McKINNON, *Rev.* WILLIAM CHARLES. A Wesl. clergym. in N. S. Now dead. Before entering the ministry ed. a newspaper at Sydney, C. B.

I. St. Castine ; a legend of Cape Breton. *Cape Breton*, 1850, pp. 72. 8vo.

II. Frances, or Pirate Cove ; a legend of Cape Breton. *Halifax*, 1851, pp. 44, 8vo.

III. St. George ; or, the Canadian League. *Do.* 1852, 2 vols., pp. 283–323, 8vo.

"A greater medley of intrigues, conspiracies, murders and horrifying events, we never saw collected in such compass."—*Prov. Mag.* (Hal.)

IV. The Papacy : the Sacrifice of the Mass ; a lecture. *Do.* 1859, pp. 28, 8vo.

V. The Divine Sovereignty ; a sermon preached at Elmsdale. *Do.* 1861, pp. 19, 8vo.

McLACHLAN, ALEXANDER. A Can. poet. B. at Johnston, Scot., 1820. He is the son of a mechanic, and although in youth sharing but few of the advantages of education, was from the first a voracious reader and soon became acquainted with the works of the principal Brit. authors. In early life he was apprenticed to a tailor, at which trade he worked, for many years. He became connected with the Chartist movement, but like many another, after visiting the neighbouring States, was completely cured of his longing for political changes. In 1840, he took up his residence in Can., and for a short time after his arrival laboured in the bush. Since his advent as an author and lecturer he has lived at the village of Erin, U. C. Mr. McL. has contributed very materially towards the establishment of a national literature in Canada. His chief aim as a poet, is to be considered the exponent of the views of the working classes of this country—to be to us what Burns was to Scot. The desire to ameliorate the condition of his fellow craftsmen is traced in many of his pieces; he shews the mental workings of the working man, for the purpose of getting those of the rich who obtain their living by head work instead of hand work, or without work of any kind, to see that the real distinction between them consists on their part less in intrinsic worth than in fortuitous antecedents. In this noble effort he stands shoulder to shoulder with such men as Burns and Miller. As a proof of the excellence and popularity of his verse, we may mention that some years since he was the winner of the prize, offered by the Glasgow *Workman* newspaper, for a national song for Scot. We may add that the prize was open for competition to the entire world. *The Workman* announced the name of the fortunate competitor in the following terms :—

" We have received numerous contributions from Scotsmen in the Colonies, and have great pleasure in awarding the prize to Alexander McLachlan, for his national song of the *Halls of Hollyrood.* Mr. McLachlan's patriotism and intelligence are a credit to the land of his birth and we hope an acquisition to the land of his adoption."

In 1863, he was appointed by the Can. Govt., to lecture in Gt. Brit. in favour of emigration to this country. He has also lectured in the principal cities and towns of the province on various literary subjects.

"The poet's elocution is really excellent—chaste, simple and earnest—yet, this is the least of his praise. His poetry is of a very high order. The address to Garibaldi is, all national predilections apart, equal to 'Scots wha hae wi' Wallace bled ;' and we cannot help thinking, that were this soul-stirring lyric turned into good Italian, and sung through the streets of Rome and Venice, it would be no feeble auxiliary to the cause of liberty in Italy."—Rev. J. George, D. D.

I. Poems, chiefly in the Scottish Dialect. *Toronto*, 1856, 12mo.

"Within two or three years Mr McLachlan has produced a volume of poems containing pieces not unworthy—of Tannahill or Motherwell."—Hon. T. D. McGee.

II. Lyrics and Miscellaneous Poems. *Do.*, 1858, 12mo.

" We have always taken a deep interest in Canada, and will henceforth take a deeper interest, from knowing that it contains a citizen so truly inspired with the genius of poetry as the author of these beautiful Lyrics."—Sir Archibald Alison.

III. The Emigrant and other Poems. *Do*, 1861, pp. 286, 12mo.

"No one capable of judging of high oetical talent can rise from the perusal of this volume without the conviction, that at length, a poet has arisen among us. The world has innumerable good versifiers, but McLachlan takes his place far above the choir of mere euphonius singers. He is obviously one of those gifted men who add to the real capital of the world's stock of thought. It may take some time, yet assuredly the day will come, when every Scotchman of taste will place these poems in his library, near the poems of Burns, and in doing so, will feel a generous pride in thinking, that if his country produced in the last century the greatest of all lyrical poets, the same country has given birth, in the present century, to another poet, sprung also from the laboring class, whose songs will ere long be sung with delight in many parts of the world, and whose weighty thoughts, in fragments of verse, will yet be woven into the common speech of men."—*Globe,* (Tor.)

McLauchlin, S. Photographer to the Dept. of Public Works, Can.

I. The Photographic Portfolio, a monthly view of Canadian scenes and scenery. *Quebec,* 1859.

McLean, *Rev.* Alexander. A Presb. min. in Can. B. on Island of North Uist, Scot., March, 1827. D at Morriston, U. C., 24 May, 1864. Was Pastor of East Puslinch Ch., at his death, and was engaged in writing two works, one on Baptism, the other on Gospel Salvation, which may yet be published.

I. The more Priests the more Crime. *Toronto,* 1854.

Written in defence of Protestantism.

II. The Tri-Centenary of the Scottish Reformation. *Do.,* 1861.

" The published writings of Mr. McLean, have called forth much attention and awakened inquiry, and on the whole gave promise of eminence in research, criticism and power."—*H. & F. Rec.* of *Can. Pres. Ch.* (Tor.)

McLean, John.

I. Notes of a Twenty-five years' Service in the Hudson's Bay territory. *London,* 1849, 2 Vols. 8vo.

McLean, *Rev.* John, *A. M.* A Presb. clergym. in N. S. B. at the West River of Pictou, N. S., 1 Sept., 1801. D. at Pictou, 20 Jany., 1837. He was ed. at the Pictou Academy, and at Glasgow Univ., where he received his degree. He possessed superior powers as a preacher, and was endowed with a rich and cultivated mind. We believe an intention existed after his death, of publishing a selection of his sermons, with a memoir of his life, but from various causes it has since been abandoned.

I. A Sermon preached in the Court House, Richibucto, on Tuesday, Jany. 13, 1829, before the Magistrates, Juries, and other inhabitants, at the opening of the General Sessions ; being the term at which licenses are granted annually to the retailers of spirituous liquors. *Saint Andrews,* 1829, pp. 19, 12mo.

II. The Truth and Divine Authority of the Scriptures, and the importance of knowing their contents; a sermon. *Pictou*, 1830, pp. 44, 12mo.

III. An Address, delivered at a quarterly meeting of the Pictou and West River Temperance Societies. *Do.*, 1833, pp. 24, 12mo.

McLEOD, *Rev.* ALEX. W.

I. The Methodist Ministry Defended; or, a reply to the arguments in favor of the divine, and the uninterrupted succession of Episcopacy as being essential to a true church and a scriptural ministry. *Halifax*, 1838, pp. 107, 8vo.

McLEOD, DONALD, (Woodstock, U. C.) D.

I. Donald McLeod's Gloomy Memories in the Highlands of Scotland: versus Mrs. Harriet Beecher Stowe's Sunny Memories in (Eng.) a Foreign Land: or a faithful picture of the Extirpation of the Celtic race from the Highlands of Scotland. *Toronto*, 1857, pp. xvi-212, 8vo.

McLEOD, *Rev.* NORMAN, D. D. One of a deputation, in 1845, from the Ch. of Scot. to the B. N. A. Colonies.

I. Religious Sophistry exposed; a letter. *St. Ann's, Cape Breton.*

II. The Disease and the Remedy; a sermon. *Halifax*, 1846, pp. 19, 8vo.

McMAHON, *Rev.* J. B. A R. C. priest, L. C.

I. Dialogue between a Young Gentleman and a Divine. *Quebec*, 1833, pp. 62.

McMILLAN, A. G. Student-at-Law. (Tor.)

I. New Manual of the Costs, Forms and Rules in the Common Law Courts of Upper Canada. *Toronto*, 1865.

"It should be a *vade mecum* to every practising lawyer and zealous law-student."— *U. C. Law.-Journ.*

McMULLEN, JOHN. A Can. historian and journ. Has ed. the *Monitor* (Brockville,) a Conservative journal, since 1856.

I. The Camp and Barrack Room, or the British Army as it it. *London*, 1846, pp. 316, 8vo.

II. History of Canada. *Brockville*, 1856, pp. 506, 8vo.

McNAB, JOHN. Co. Atty. and Clk. of the Peace for York & Peel, U. C.

I. The Magistrates Manual; being a full compilation of the Law relating to Justices of the Peace, &c. *Toronto*, 1865.

"The experience of the author, in his office of County Attorney, must have been of great assistance in the preparation of the book, and would enable him to point out many things that might escape the attention of a merely professional man, however competent otherwise for the task."— *U. C. Law Journ.*

McNAUGHTON, THOMAS, *B. A.* Has ed. the *Sun* (Cobourg, U. C.), a Reform journal, of which he is also prop., since 1856.

McPHERSON, JOHN. A N. S. poet. B. at Liverpool N. S., 4 Feby., 1817. D. at Brookfield N. S., 26 July, 1845. He received an ordinary Eng. education at his native place, where he resided until his 17th year, and afterwards had the benefit of brief tuition from Mr. A. M. Gidney, at Brookfield.

"McPherson's boyhood" as his biographer Thompson tells us, "was distinguished for seriousness, for avoidance of rough boisterous play, for fondness of retirement, and for an ambition to improve his mind, and mayhap to win some literary fame."

A severe personal injury which he received in early life, in a playful contest with a young friend, caused him some months confinement to the house, and frequent subsequent weakness and pain. This, doubtless, exercised an influence over his after career, and gave him still further opportunities of pursuing his favorite studies.

"He had intellectual qualifications for the teacher's avocation," continues Mr. Thompson, "he studied educational topics carefully; he wrote on some departments of the profession; but he loved leisure and meditative peace, his physical health required repose and solace,—his mind was sensitive and yearned for some reasonable wordly competence. Such requirements, natural and praiseworthy in their way, were sadly out of keeping with the noise, and roughness and fagging, and poor pecuniary renumeration of such schools as came within his personal experience. No wonder that under the changes of locality, incident to his teaching years, his prevailing feelings were those of difficulty and gloom: his chief employment was not congenial or productive, and want of daily means for comfort, became almost a daily fear."

Before taking up the employment of sch. teaching, McP. lived in Halifax for a short time, where he was employed as a clk., and shortly afterwards went on a voyage to the West Indies.

In 1841, he married. He taught sch.

for 2 years at Kempt Settlement, and subsequently at Maitland. We are unable to state when he first began to contribute to the press. but it must have been when very young, for his pieces, which generally appeared under his initials, were read and known in N. S., for many years previous to his lamented and untimely decease. They generally appeared in the local journals ; he also wrote for the *Olive Branch*, a mag., which was ed. by his friend Miss Sarah Herbert. His whole life was a series of difficulties, troubles and discontents. An enfeebled constitution rendered him helpless to combat the stern realities of the world—his temperament was quick and uneven, and he was extremely sensitive : an unkind word or criticism having the effect of making him unhappy for a whole day. He had indulged in the hope of having a home of his own, no matter how small and contracted it might be in its dimensions. The Literary Soc., the Highland Soc., (Hal.,) and several friends in the same city, subscribed funds to assist him in his cherished object. He purchased a plot of ground upon which he erected a cottage, in which he lived for a short period ; his pecuniary difficulties forced him to dispose of his newly acquired property, and he shortly afterwards died beneath the roof of a relation. The best of his poems are contained in the volume published under the editorship of Mr. Thompson, 17 years after the death of their author.

I. The Praise of Water ; a prize poem. *Halifax*, 1843, pp. 16, 8vo.

This received a prize as the best poem on Temperance.

" It was one of those efforts whose money reward was by no means commensurate with the labor and talent required for its production."—J. S. T. THOMPSON.

II. The Harp of Acadia ; poems descriptive and moral. With an Introductory memoir by J. S. T. Thompson. *Do.*, 1862, pp. 298, 12 mo.

" John McPherson's inexperience of society and unfitness for the money-making conflicts of this life, combined with weak health, were doubtless the real causes of his unsuccessful lot. Sir Walter Scott said wisely that a man ' might make literature his staff, but not his crutch,' and perhaps our Nova Scotian poet made the mistake not uncommon to young writers, of expecting too much from ' the vision and the faculty divine.' But the story of McPherson's life—delicately and conscientiously told by his chosen biographer—its honest struggle, its unaffected purity and domestic tenderness, its reasonable ambition, and its sad and baffled close, is a more pathetic poem than any he ever wrote. But he who watches over us all did not quite forget him, and the unfailing love and care of his wife enabled him to bear with gentleness and comparative fortitude the gloom, privation and pain of his latter days.

" These poems are not imaginative or pictorial in any great degree,—they are not aglow with gorgeous description, or the fire of sustained passion,—but they are melodious, tender, and original. They are not the reflex of his reading, they are his own genuine utterance. Grace and perspicuity of expression, usually one of the charms last acquired by accomplished and well-trained authors, seems to have been the unconscious possession of this one ; and when we remember how little he was aided in that way by the society of fluent talkers, the suggestions of judicious critics, or the influence of early discipline, we venture to conclude that he was taught and endowed very much as the ravens are fed and the lilies clothed."—Miss CLOTILDA JENNINGS.

McQUEEN, THOMAS. A Can. journ. B. in Scot. D. on his farm, near Goderich, U. C., 25 June, 1861. Before coming to Can. he had published, between 1836 and 1850, three volumes of poetry, which have been so popular that they have run through three editions each. His poetry took a political turn. Mr. W. W. Smith says of his literary efforts in Can. :

" Some of his Canadian pieces in verse, which are not numerous, are very beautiful. Of these, we remember *Our own broad Lake*, and others. He entered heartily, though too late in life to effect much with his own pen, into the plans of those who were and are seeking to establish and build up a native literature among us. Some years ago, he ended an editorial on the subject, with the earnest appeal, ' Will *nobody* write a few songs for Canada.' "

From an affectionate and well-written obituary notice of Mr. McQ. in the *Signal*, which we reproduce, we glean particulars relative to his early career in Scot., and his subsequent labours in Can., not, however, holding ourselves responsible for the political *animus* of the article :

" Thomas McQueen was born of humble parentage in Ayrshire, Scotland. For the position be afterwards acquired, he was but little indebted to educational advantages in early life. He had attended school but a few months, when he was taken from it, to assist his parents in their toil for subsistence. About his tenth year he met with the accident that occasioned the lameness which attended him through life. This disqualifying him for a time for out door-labour, was a circumstance that exerted great influence on his after life, for it inspired him with an inclination to devote himself to books and solitary reflection. His natural genius had thus an opportunity of developing, and by his efforts to cultivate the powers of his mind, and store it with useful knowledge, he grew up a well educated, although in the strictest sense of the word, a self trained man. In his fifteenth or sixteenth year he engaged in the business of a stone mason, and continued in that employment while he remained in Scotland. In his intervals of toil, however, he found time for the cultivation of his intellect, and for devoting a portion of his attention both to literature and politics. During the great agitation for Parliamentary Reform, Mr. McQueen distinguished himself as an ardent and able leader of the class to whom he belonged. As a speaker, and by his contributions to the periodical press, he took conspicuous rank among the advocates of the rights of the working man. He published also several volume of poetry, through which the ardour of his political sympathies constantly burns; and he made vigorous efforts to elevate the minds of the working classes by the weekly issue of a series of essays and lectures on a variety of subjects connected with Political Economy, Education and Morals. Mr. McQueen was but little known in Canada, in his character as a poet. He probably found in coming to this country, that among a practical people such as ours, in contributing his mite towards the procuring of needed reforms he could hit the mark more directly and effectively by the use of plain intelligible prose, than by indulging in imaginative flights of poetry. In 1842 he emigrated from Scotland to Canada, and settling in the county of Renfrew, resumed his occupation as a stone-mason. But he was not long here, ere his sympathies with the popular cause actively enlisted him in the struggle for Responsible Government, which was then agitating the country. He again became a writer for the press, and numerous articles from his pen, published in the *Bathurst Courier* (Perth) on the political questions of the day, attracted much notice, and elicited universal praise from the liberal party. After the election of 1847, he was induced by the Hon. M. Cameron to risk the establishment of a newspaper in the county of Huron, which till then had been unrepresented by the press, and on the 4th February, 1848, Mr. McQueen issued the first member of the *Huron Signal*. The great question of Responsible Government had just been satisfactorily settled by the decisive triumph of the Liberal party at the polls, but, that having been disposed of, there were many practical reforms which it was necessary for the good of the country should be carried out. Among these were the opening of King's College to the community generally, irrespective of creed, the settlement of the principles of a national system of education, and the secularisation of the Clergy Reserves. Into the discussions of these and many other questions of nearly equal importance Mr. McQueen at once threw himself with the whole force and earnestness of his character, and fully maintained the reputation he had acquired as one of the ablest political writers in the Province. In 1852 he assisted in establishing the *Canadian*, a newspaper published in Hamilton, and continued to conduct it till 1854, when he returned to Goderich, and resumed his editorial labours on the *Signal*. In the same year he offered himself as a candidate for the representation of Huron and Bruce, in opposition to Mr. Cayley, but the people had lost confidence in the Hinck's Administration, of which Mr. McQueen at that time was a supporter, and he was defeated. At the general election of 1857, after Mr. Cayley and his friends had been tried and found wanting, Mr. McQueen did not himself re-appear as a candidate, but gave efficient service in securing the defeat of Mr. Cayley, and through that gentleman's defeat, the condemnation by the most popular constituency in the Province of the policy and conduct of the Coalition formed in 1854. During the present contest, although battling with disease, he gave what assistance he could to the Liberal cause, and as we have said, died in harness, the very number of the *Signal* which announced his death, containing an earnest and urgent appeal from his pen to the people of Huron and Bruce to do their duty to their country in the present crisis.

" At a time like this our cause can ill spare the advocacy of so able and fervent a worker as Thomas McQueen. His removal by the hand of death leaves a blank in our ranks which it may be difficult to fill. We speak of him as a party man, for such he was strongly and decidedly. In the struggle of opposite parties and principles, he knew there was a right side and a wrong side, and to what he thought the right party priciples he deliberately attached himself, and worked for them, with wholehearted zeal. It is not, however to his party alone that his a loss : the whole country is the loser when such men as he are taken away. We have amongst us few who unite in so eminent a degree as did Thomas McQueen, the character of the vigorous independent thinker, and the practical efficient worker, and the removal of such a man furnishes good cause for sorrow and regret on the part of the entire community."

McWHINNIE, JOHN. A Can. journ. B. at Glasgow, Scot., 1807. Came to Can. 1821. Was connected with the *British American* (Woodstock.) as local ed., from 1849 to 1853. In 1854 established the *Sentinel* (same place,) a weekly journal, of which he became ed., a position which he still holds. *The Sentinel*, up to 1858, supported the Reform party, but has since advocated the Liberal Conservative cause.

MEDLEY, *Rt. Rev.* JOHN, *D. D.* Lord Bish. of Fredericton, N. B. B. in Eng. 1804. Ed. at Wadham Coll. Oxford, where he was 2nd class in classics, 1826; graduated M. A., 1830; D. D. 1845; Vicar of St. Thomas's, Exeter, 1838; Prebendary of Exeter Cath. 1842; consecrated 1st Bish. of Fredericton, 1845.

I. Sermons, published at the request of many of his late parishioners. *London*, 2nd ed. 1845, 12mo.

II. The Episcopal Form of Church Government; its antiquity, &c. *Fredericton*, 1845, pp. 46, 8vo.

III. The Reformation, its Nature, its Necessity and its Benefits; a sermon. *Do.* 1847, pp. 27, 8vo.

IV. A Charge delivered in the Cathedral of Christ's Church, to the Clergy of the Diocese, at the 2nd Triennial Visitation.. *St. John*, 1850, pp. 63, 8vo.

V. Good Taste; a lecture. *Do.* 1857, pp. 31, 8vo.

VI. Sermon preached before H. R. H. the Prince of Wales on his visit to Fredericton, in Christ Church Cathedral. *Fredericton*, 1860, pp. 13, 8vo.

VII. The Mission of the Comforter; two sermons. *Do.*, 1867.

MEECHAM, A. G.
I. Rise and Progress of Methodism in Canada. *Picton; C. W.*, pp. 900.

MEEK, F. B.
I. Descriptions of new Cretaceous fossils collected by the Northwestern Boundary Commission, on Vancouver and Sucia Islands. *Proc. Aca., N. S.*, (PHIL.) 1861.

18

MEEKE, *Rev.* W.
I. For a small Parish in Newfoundland; A Plain sermon to Plain people. *Halifax*, 1845, pp. 10, 8vo.

MEIGS, *Major* R. J.
I. Journal of the Expedition against Quebec, under command of Col. Benedict Arnold, in the year 1775. With an introduction and notes by Chs. I. Busnell. (With plates.) *New York*, privately printed, 1864.

This, we presume, is a reprint, under a different title, of the pamphlet credited to Maj. Meigs, by Rich, p. 211.

MEIKLE, W.
I. The Canadian Newspaper Directory. Containing a complete list of all the newspapers in Canada, the cirlation of each, and all information in reference thereto. *Toronto*, 1858, pp. 60, 12mo.

MEILLEUR, JEAN BAPTISTE, *M, D., LL. D.* A writer on Education &c., B. at St. Laurent, L. C., 9 May, 1796. Ed. at Coll. of Montreal. Studied law for a short time, but abandoned it, entering the Coll. of Castletown, Vt., U. S., for the study of Medicine; he also studied philosophy at the Coll. of Middlebury, N. H. Received degree of M. D. in 1825. In 1834 was returned to Parliament of L.C. He was the first Supdt. of Education for L. C., and during his occupation of that office established 45 superior educational institutions. He was also for sometime Postmaster (Mont.,) Inspector of Post Offices for the District of Montreal, and is now Agent for the Sale of Law Stamps in that city. Shortly after his admission to his profession, Dr. M. contributed several interesting papers on Medical science to *Le Journal de Médecine* (Que.); many papers from his pen on subjects connected with Education, Geology, Botany, Agriculture &c., are to be found in the pages of the French Can. periodical and newspaper press during the last 30 years. In 1834, he ed. *L'Echo du Pays*. Dr. M. was one of the founders of L'Assomption Coll. He is a mem. of the Am. Association for the Advancement of Science, of the Medico-Philosophical Soc. of Vermont, and a corresponding mem. of the Historical Soc. of Michigan, &c.

I. Treatise on the Pronunciation of the French Language, with Practical Irregularities Exemplified. *U. S.*, 1823 ; 2nd Ed. *Montreal*, 1841, pp. 108, 8vo.

"The author has taken the question at its root, and followed it through with a skill and industry which is as honorable to himself as it must be useful to those who will avail themselves of the result of his labors."— *Lit. Garland.*

II. Cours abrégé de Leçons de Chimie, contenant une exposition précise et méthodique des principes de cette science. *Do.*, 1833, 8vo.

III. Nouvelle Grammaire Anglaise. *St. Charles, L. C.* 1833 ; 2nd Ed. *Montréal*, 1854, pp. 206, 8vo.

IV. Circular, containing instructions to the School Commissioners in Canada East, and a Precis of their duties. *Montreal*, 1844.

"It is a lucid and concise exposition of the requirements of the [Education] Act, accompanied by remarks and suggestions from the Superintendent himself."—*Lit. Garland.*

V. Traité sur l'Art Epistolaire, par un Canadien. *Do.*, 3rd Ed., 1853, pp. 150, 12mo.

VI. Memorial de l'Education. *Do.*, 1860, pp. 400, 8vo.

MELLISH, J.
I. Military documents concerning the Operations of the British Army, under General Wolfe, in 1859-60; and concerning the War of 1812. *Philadelphia*, 1814, 8vo.

II. Travels through the United States of America, in the years 1806-7 and 1809-1811, including an account of passages betwixt America and Britain, Ireland and Canada, with corrections and improvements till 1815. (With Maps and plans.) *Philadelphia*, 1818, pp. 648, 8vo. First ed. published in 1812.

MELLISH, JOHN T.
I. An address delivered at Amherst, N. S., Nov. 29, 1866, on the occasion of the opening of Cumberland County Academy. 1867.

"Both eloquent and stirring."—*Bulletin,* Charlottet.)

MELSHEIMER, F. V.
I. Tagebuch von der Reise der Braunschweigischen Auxiiartruppen von Wolffenbüttel nach Quebec. *Minden*, 1776, 8vo.

MELVILLE, HENRY, *M. D.* Was a contributor to the *Anglo Am. Mag.* (Tor..) during its existence. Now resides in the U. S.
I. The Rise and Progress of Trinity College, Toronto ; with a sketch of the life of the Lord Bishop of Toronto, as connected with the Church Education in Canada. *Toronto*, 1852, pp. 265, 8vo.

MELVIN, JAMES.
I. A Journal of the Expedition to Quebec in the year 1775, under the command of Col. Benedict Arnold. *Philadelphia*, Franklin Club, 1865, 8vo.

MENZIES, GEORGE. A Can. journ. Was by birth a Scotchman. D. at Woodstock, U. C., 4 March, 1847. Previous to the Rebellion of 1837, ed. the *Reporter* (Niagara ;) subsequently assisted Mr. Simpson in the management of the *Chronicle*, of same place, and afterwards was associated with Mr. Dalton on the *Patriot*, (Tor.) In 1840, with another, established the *Herald* (Woodstock,) it being the first newspaper ever published in the Co. Oxford. He was the author of some very sweet pieces of poetry. After his death his widow published a volume of his poems, with the following title :
I. The Posthumous Works of the late George Menzies, being a collection of poems, sonnets, &c., written at various times when the author was connected with the provincial press. *Woodstock, U. C.*, 1850.

MERCER. *Major, R. A.*
I. Catalogue of remarkable coincidences, inducing a belief in the Asiatic Origin of the North American Indians. *Trans. Lit. and His. Soc.*, Vol. I.

MERCIER, HONORÉ. A French Can. journ. B. at St. Athanase, L. C., 1840. Studied at St. Mary's Coll. (Mont.) Is an advocate. Ed. *Le Courrier de St. Hyacinthe* from 1862 to 1864.
I. L'Héroisme, and La Patrie ; two lectures delivered at St. Hyacinthe. 1865, pp. 80, 8vo.

MEREDITH, EDMUND ALLEN, *LL. B., LL. D.* Asst. Secy. of State for the Provinces. Can. Son of the Rev. Dr. Meredith, Fellow of Trin. Coll. (Dub..) and grandson of the Very Rev. Dean Graves, Fellow and Regius Prof. of

Divinity, in the same Univ. B. at Ardtrea, Co. Tyrone, Irel. Studied at Trin. Coll., where he obtained high honours, including a scholarship, mathematical medal, first prize in Political Economy, also the degree of LL. B. Was called to the Irish Bar in 1844 ; in the same year was admitted to practise at the Bar in U. C., and in 1846, to the Bar of L. C. Held for upwards of a year the office of Principal of the Univ. of McGill Coll. (Mont.) Was for 2 years President of the Lit. and His. Soc. (Que.) In 1847 was appointed Asst. Provl. Secy. U. C., an office which he held until the Union of the Provinces of B. N. A. in 1867, when he was appointed to his present office. Has been for some years Chairman of the Board of Inspectors of Asylums, Prisons, &c. Received the hon. degree of M. A. from the Univ. of Bishop's Coll. Lennoxville, L. C., and that of LL. D. from the Univ. of McGill Coll. Is an hon. mem. of the Am. Ass. for the Promotion of Social Science.

I. An Essay on the Oregon Question ; read before the Shakspeare Club. *Montreal*, 1846, pp. 43, 8vo.

II. Influence of Recent Gold Discoveries on Prices. *Can. Journ.*, 1856, pp. 17.

II. An Important but Neglected Branch of Social Science. *Trans. Lit. and His. Soc.* (Que.) 1861, pp. 24.

IV. Note on some Emendations (not hitherto suggested,) in the text of Shakspeare, with a new explanation of an old passage. *Do.* 1863, pp. 8.

V. Glance at the Present State of the Common Gaols of Canada ; the individual separation of prisoners (with shortened sentences) recommended on moral and economic grounds. *Do.* 1864, pp. 18.

Also in pamphlet. form.

VI. Short School Time, with Military or Naval Drill, in connection especially with the subject of an efficient Militia System. *Do.* 1865, pp. 26 ;

Also in pamphlet form.

"Mr. Meredith deserves thanks that in this as in other directions he is labouring to promote social and educational reforms. We are happy in having men in the public ser-

18 *

vice whose hearts are so thoroughly in their work as he has shown his is in the giant task of the amendment of our disgraceful prison life and prison discipline, and in cognate subjects."—*Gazette* (Mont.)

"An able and instructive address."—*Journ. of Ed. U. C.*

MEREDITH, EDWARD.
I. Letter to the Earl of Chatham on the Quebec Bill. *London*, 1774, 5th ed., 8vo.

MERRITT, J. P. Son of the following.
I. The Historic Tree of British North America, an emblematic tree, shewing the various periods of British American Colonial History, from 1492 to the present time. *St. Catharines*, 1866.

MERRITT, *Hon.* WILLIAM HAMILTON. A Can. statesman B. at Westchester, N. Y., 3 July, 1793. D. on the River St. Lawrence, 6 July, 1862. Was the son of an U. E. loyalist. Ed. at Ancaster, U. C., and at Windsor Coll., N. S. Served as a Can. Militia officer during the war of 1812. He projected the Welland Canal and the Welland Railway, and it was through his instrumentality that both were finally constructed. Mr. M. designed many other equally important works and schemes for the improvement of trade, and the development of the natural resources of Can. He sat in the U. C. legislature from 1832 till the Union, and subsequent to that event held a seat in the two branches of parliament, in succession, at his death being a mem. of the Leg. Coun. We understand that a memoir of his long, eventful and useful life, is being prepared for the press, and will shortly be given to the public. Mr. M. contributed largely to the Can. newspaper press, especially to the *Niagara Gleaner*, on subjects connected with the development of the trade and industrial resources of the Province.

I. A Brief Review of the Revenue, Resources and Expenditure of Canada, compared with those of the neighbouring State of New York. *St. Catharines, C. W.*, 1845, pp. 22.

II. Letter addressed to the Inhabitants of the Niagara District on Free Trade, &c. *Niagara*, 1847, pp. 32.

III. A Concise View of the Inland Navigation of the Canadian Provinces. *St. Catharines*, 1832, pp. 20.

IV. Review of the Origin, Progress, Present State and Future Prospects of the Welland Canal. pp. 48.

V. Journal of Events principally on the Detroit and Niagara Frontier, during the War of 1812. By Capt. W. H. Merritt, of the Provincial Light Dragoons. Published by the Historical Society of British North America. *St. Catharines*, 1863, pp. 82.

MERRY, W. A.

I. The Mercantile Calculator for the British Colonies, adapted to the Forwarding, Iron, Grocery, &c., Trades. *Montreal*, 1847, 8vo.

METCALFE, *Rt. Hon.* CHARLES THEOPHILUS, *Lord*. Gov. Genl. of B. N. A. from 1843 to 1845. B. 30 Jany., 1735. D. in Eng., 5 Sept., 1846. Had been successively Gov. Genl. of India and Gov. of Jamaica.

Report of the Proceedings of a meeting of the friends and admirers of Lord Metcalfe in Montreal, 1st Feby., 1847. *Montreal*, 1847, pp. 15.

Life and Correspondence, from unpublished letters and journals. By J. W. Kaye. *London*, 1854, 2 vols. 8vo.; 2nd Ed., 1858.

Selected Papers and Correspondence. Edited by J. W. Kaye. *Do.*, 1855, 8vo.

(See *Ryerson, Rev. E.*

(" *Wakefield, E. G.*)

MICHAUX, F. A. A celebrated French Botanist. B. at Versailles 1770. He was employed by the French Govt. on a scientific mission to N. A., to decide what species of the forest trees of that country might profitably be introduced into Europe, and made 3 voyages to this country, whence he sent to France large quantities of valuable seeds.

I. The North American Sylva ; or, a Description of the Forest Trees of the United States, Canada and Nova Scotia, considered particularly with respect to their use in the Arts, and their introduction into Commerce ; with a description of the most useful of the European Forest Trees. Translated from the French. (Illustrated by 156 finely coloured copper-plate engravings, by Redouté, &c.) *Philadelphia*, 1817, 3 vol., Imp. 8vo. (See *Brunet, Rev. O.*)

The original ed. appeared at Paris, 1810, 3 vols. R. 8vo. *London ed.* 1819.

(See *Nuttall, P.*)

MIDDLETON, H.

I. A Clear Idea of the Genuine and uncorrupted British Constitution, in an address to the Inhabitants of the Province of Quebec, from the 49 Delegates in the Continental Congress at Philadelphia. 1774, 8vo.

MIDDLETON, ROBERT. A Can. journ. B. at Berwick-upon-Tweed, 1810. Assisted in establishing the *Chronicle* (Que.,) of which he was ed. for a short time. Has been connected with the *Gazette* of same city, the oldest newspaper published in Can., for the last 33 years, and is now Ed. and Joint Prop. of it.

MILES, H. H., *M. A., LL. D.* Secy. to the Educational Dept. (Que.) Until recently was Prof. of Mathematics and Natural Philosophy in, and Vice-Principal of Bishop's Coll., Lennoxville. Served as a Commissioner on behalf of Can. at the International Exhibition (Lon.) 1862.

I. On the Ventilation of Dwelling Houses and Schools. Illustrated by diagrams, with remarks upon sanitary improvements. *Montreal*, 1858, pp. 68, 8vo.

" The whole of public hygiene is dealt with, in this little work, in a most able and scientific manner."—*Journ. of Ed. L. C.*

II. Canada East at the International Exposition. [With maps.] *London*, 1862, pp. 88, 8vo.

MILES, *Rev.* STEPHEN. A Can. journ. B. at Royalton, Vt., U. S., 19 Oct., 1789. His career as a Can. journ. has been long and eventful. In 1807 came with Mr. Nahum Mower to Montreal, and in May of that year, assisted him in establishing the *Canadian Courant* there. In 1810 proceeded to Kingston, U. C., the journey from Montreal to that place then occupying 12 days, and in Sept. issued the first newspaper printed in Kingston and the third in U. C., called the *Gazette*, of which he became ed. In 1813 the 2 other existing printing establishments in U. C., one at Newark and the other at York, were destroyed by fire, the papers ceased publication, and Mr. M.'s paper, the *Gazette*, remain ed the only journal published to the west of Montreal, up to 1816. In 1818 he disposed of his office and the goodwill of the paper, and after serving on 1 or 2 other journals, commenced, in 1828, the *Gazette and Religious Advocate*, of which he continued ed. and prop. until 1830. He then undertook the management of the *Canadian Watchman*, and in the following year moved to Prescott, where he founded and ed. the *Grenville Gazette*, the first paper published in that place. In 1833 he disposed of that paper, returning to Kingston, where after some slight connection with 1 of the papers he was, in 1835, received into the Meth. Ch. as a traveling min., the duties of which he still discharges. Mr. M. may be considered the oldest living journ. in Can.

MILES, WILLIAM AUGUSTUS. Author of many English tracts.

I. Remarks on the Act for the Encouragement of the Newfoundland fishery. *London*, 1779, 4to.

MILLER, *Mrs.* MARIA, (formerly Miss Morris). B. in Halifax, N. S., where she still resides. Whilst still quite young, attracted attention by the indications she gave of artistic taste and power. Besides exhibiting skill in the various departments of painting and drawing, her tastes led her to make a special study of flower-painting, and in this branch of art she has achieved remarkable success. Animated by a spirit of originality and a praiseworthy pride of country, she devoted her talents to the task of portraying the beautiful Wild Flowers of her native land. Those who consider themselves best acquainted with the rich and varied Flora of the Acadian provinces, will be hardly able to appreciate the magnitude of the labour involved, or the excellence of the result achieved by Mrs. M. until they see the volumes of her work, containing as they do one of the most pleasing and valuable contributions made to modern Botanical Science and Floral Art. Specimens of her later paintings were sent to the Exhibition (Lon.) of 1862, but unfortunately arrived too late for competition with other works of art; their merits, however, were highly praised by the London Press. We understand

that Mrs. M. proposes to continue the publication of the Flora of N. S. and N. B., and may hereafter paint that of Canada.

I. The Wild Flowers of Nova Scotia, (with coloured plates). *London*, 1840. 4to.; 2nd Series, 1853.

MILLEN, ROBERT. Of the Middle Temple. Barrister at Law.

I. The Law and the Love of Unity exhibited in Creation ; a Lecture. *Halifax*, 1858, pp. 40, 8vo.

II. True Greatness; a Lecture. *Do.*, 1859, pp. 29, 8vo.

MILLS, ARTHUR.

I. Colonial Constitutions; an outline of the constitutional history and existing government of the British Dependencies ; with Schedules of the Orders in Council, Statutes, and Parliamentary Documents relating to each Dependency. *London*, 1856, 8vo.

MILNE, *Rev.* JAMES, A. M. (Fredericton, N. B.)

I. Remarks on Dr. Burns's View of the Principles and Forms of the Presbyterian Kirk as by law established in Scotland. *St. John*, N. B., 1818, pp. 40, 8vo.

MILTON, *Rev.* CHARLES WILLIAM.

I. Narrative of the Gracious dealings of God in the Conversion of W. Mooney Fitzgerald and John Clark, two malefactors, who were executed on Friday, Dec. 18, 1789, at St. John's New Brunswick, for Burglary; in a Letter from the Rev. Mr. Milton to the Rt. Hon. the Countess Dowager of Huntingdon. *London*, 1790, pp. 22, 12mo.

MILTON, *Viscount*, F. R. G. S., F. G. S., and CHEADLE M. A., M. D., Cantab., F. R. G. S.

I. The North-West Passage by Land ; Being the Narrative of an Expedition from the Atlantic to the Pacific, undertaken with the view of Exploring a Route across the Continent to British Columbia through British Territory, by one of the Northern Passes in the Rocky Mountains. (With maps and numerous Illustrations.) *London*, 5th Ed. 1866, 8vo.

"Extremely interesting book."—*Reporter*, (Hal.)

MOLESWORTH, *Rt. Hon. Sir* WILLIAM. An Eng. statesman. D. 1855. Was for sometime Secy. of State for the Colonies.

 I. Speech on the Canada Bill, 23 Jany., 1838. *London*, 1838, 8vo.

MONCRIEF. *Major.*

 I. A Short Account of the Expedition against Quebec, commanded by Major-General Wolfe, in the year 1759. By an Engineer upon that Expedition, *N. D.*

MONDELET, *Hon.* CHARLES JOSEPH ELZÉAR. A Judge of the Court of Queen's Bench L. C. B. at St. Charles, L. C., 27 Dec. 1801. Has served on the Bench since 1842.

 I. Lettres sur l'Education Elémentaire et pratique. *Montréal*, 1841, pp. 60.

 Published in both languages.

 II. Essai Analytique sur le Paradis Perdu de Milton, par Charles Mondelet et William Vondelvenden. *Répertoire Nat.*, 1848.

 III. Address before the American Association for the Advancement of Science. *Montreal*, 1857, pp. 9.

MONDELET, *Hon.* DOMINIQUE. A Can. Judge. D. 1863. Had sat in Parliament and held office before the Union.

 I. Traité sur la Politique Coloniale du Bas-Canada. Réflexions sur l'état actuel du Pays. Par un Avocat. *Montréal*, 1835, pp. 67.

MONRO, ALEXANDER, *P. L. S.* A N. B. writer. B. in Banff, Scot., 1813. Emigrating with his father when quite young, his early years were devoted to clearing and cultivating a farm near Bay Verte. He is almost entirely self-ed. Mr. M. has written extensively for the newspaper press of the Lower Provinces, and from 1838 to 1860, ed. and published a monthly serial called *The Parish School Advocate*, devoted to education and general literature. In his professional capacity, he has been engaged in making many important public surveys, and some years since was selected by the Provinces of N. S., and N. B. to establish the long disputed boundary line between the two Provinces.

 I. A Treatise on Theoretical and Practical Land Surveying, demonstrated from its first principles, and adapted to woodland surveys, with diagrams. *Pictou*, N. S., 1844, pp. 269, 12mo.

The New Brunswick Legislature contributed £50 towards the publication of this work.

"It is original in its contents, and many of its problems and diagrams have never before appeared in a work of the kind."—*Mechanic and Farmer* (Pictou).

 II. History, Civil divisions, Geography and Productions of Nova Scotia, New Brunswick and Prince Edward Island, with maps. *Halifax*, 1855, pp. 392, 8vo.

"Mr. Monro has done for New Brunswick and its lesser neighbors what was done by Mr. Montgomery Martin, many years ago, for more extensive regions of our colonial empire. He has collected and arranged data valuable to the statesman, the merchant, the emigrant, and the philosopher; and the realization of his hopes in the adequate peopling and cultivation of these fair provinces will materially contribute to the prosperity and happiness of a considerable portion of the human race."—*European Times*, (Liverpool).

 III. Statistics of British North America. *Do.* 1862, pp. 228.

 IV. History, Geography and Statistics of British North America. *Montreal*, 1864, pp. 324, 8vo.

MONTCALM, LOUIS JOSEPH DE SAINT VÉRAN. *Marquis* DE. A celebrated French military general. B. in France, 1712. D. at Quebec, when in command of the French forces, from the effects of wounds received at the taking of that city by the Eng., 14 Sept., 1759.

 I. Lettres de Monsieur Le Marquis de Montcalm, Gouverneur-Général en Canada; à Messieurs de Berryer et de la Molé, écrites dans les années 1757, 1758 & 1759. Translated into English. *London*. 1777, pp. 28, 8vo.

MONTGOMERIE, HUGH E. Author of the novels and translations, which appeared in the *Literary Garland*, under the *nom de plume* of "Edmond Hugomont". Was a Vice President of the Shakspeare Club (Mont.) Returned to Scot., his native country, 1849.

MONTIZAMBERT, EDWARD L., *M. A.*, Law Clk. to Leg. Coun., Can.

 I. Lecture on the Mercantile Law of Lower Canada, delivered at Montreal, 27th Jany., 1848. *Montreal*, 1848, pp. 28.

MOODIE, JOHN WEDDERBURN DUNBAR, formerly lieut in the 21st Regt. of Fusiliers, and latterly Sheriff of the Co. of Hastings U. C. Served with his regiment in Holland, and was at the night attack on Bergen-op-Zoom, in 1814, where he was wounded. In 1819 emigrated to Cape of Good Hope. Returning to Eng. in 1829, he there married, in 1831, Miss Susanna Strickland, and in the following year came to Can., where he has since resided. In 1831 he wrote an account of his adventure with an elephant in Africa, for the *Library of Entertaining Knowledge*, and about same time, an account of the Campaign in Holland, for the *United Service Journal*, which was afterwards published in book-form, together with other narratives of the war from different pens. He contributed to the *Literary Garland*, (Mont.,) and assisted his wife in the ed. of the *Victoria Magazine*.

I. Ten Years in South Africa. *London*, 1835. 2 vols. 8vo.

II. Scenes and Adventures, as a Soldier and Settler, during half a century (with Portrait). *Montreal*, 1866, pp. 299, 12 mo.

MOODIE, *Mrs*. SUSANNA. A Can. authoress. Wife of the above. Well known in Can. and Gt. Brit. for her works, and as an extensive contributor to the periodical Literature of both countries. B. at Bungay, Co. Suffolk, Eng., 6 Dec., 1803. She is a mem. of the talented Strickland family of Beydon Hall, in the above county ; four of her sisters, Elizabeth, Agnes, (the best known), Jane, and Mrs. Traill, (whom see,) have each contributed to the Literature of the day. Both Mrs. M. and her sisters were ed. by their father, who is represented to have been a gentleman of education, refined taste, and some wealth. Mrs. M. was only in her 13th year, when her father died. As early as her 15th year, she began to write for the press, generally for annuals and periodicals, contributing short poems and tales for children. About 1820, she produced her first work of any pretension—a juvenile tale, which was well received by the public and press. In the following year she married Mr. Moodie, a half pay officer from the 21st Fusileers, and in 1832, emigrated with

her husband, to Can. They bought a farm near Port Hope, which, however, they only held for a short time, removing to the back-woods 10 miles north of Peterborough, where they settled. Here they remained for a period of 8 years, experiencing all the trials, mishaps and troubles incident to early settlers, and which are so graphically narrated and depicted by Mrs. M. in her *Roughing it in the Bush*. In 1839, Mr. M. was appointed Sheriff of Hastings, (an office from which he retired a few years since,) and, with his wife, took up his residence at Belleville, where they have since lived. During the existence of the *Literary Garland*, (Mont.,) Mrs. M., was the principal contributor of fiction to its pages. For some years she ed. the *Victoria Magazine*, (Belleville). Her contributions to these and other annuals, magazines and newspapers would fill many volumes.

Juvenile works published from 1820 to 1826.

I. Spartacus ; or, the Slave's Struggle for Freedom.

II. Josiah Shirley ; the Little Quaker.

III. Hugh Latimer ; or, the Schoolboy's Friendship.

IV. Precept and Practice ; or, the Vicar's tales.

V. Rowland Massingham ; the Boy that would be his own Master.

VI. The Little Prisoner.

VII. Little Black Pony, and other stories. *Philadelphia*, 18mo.

Since 1830.

VIII. Enthusiasm and other Poems. *London*, 1830.

"The volume bears throughout the impress of a mind which has drank deeply at the fountain of genius."—*Lit. Garland.*

IX. Flora Lindsay ; or, Passages in an Eventful Life. *Do.* 1854, 2 vols, 8vo. ; *New York*, 1854, 12mo.

" Had this work been written as a personal narrative of the trials and difficulties of a gentlewoman obliged to emigrate, it would have possessed not only a genuine interest which must have appealed to all readers, but coming from a woman of Mrs. Moodie's practical knowledge, it would have been a useful manual of information to all in similar circumstances. But the attempt to make it into a novel, by giving it a catching title has rendered it ineffective for either use or amusement."—*Athen.* (Lon.)

X. Mark Hurdlestone, the Gold Worshipper. *Do.* 1853, 2 vols. p. 8vo. *New-York,* 1853, 12mo.

XI. Geoffrey Moncton; or. the Faithless Guardian; a novel. *Do.* 1856, 2 vols. p. 8vo. *New York. Do.* 12mo.

XII. Matrimonial Speculations. *Do.* 1854, p. 8vo.

XIII. Roughing it in the Bush; or, Life in Canada. *Do.* 1852, 2 vols. p. 8vo.; new ed. *Do.* 1853; another ed. *Do.* 1857; *New York,* 1854, 12mo.

"Mrs. Moodie is unquestionably one of the most distinguished pioneers of Canadian literature. She has wrought hard with heart and hand to advance her adopted land in the Republic of Letters, and the work of which we are speaking will add fresh laurels to her already goodly coronet of merit."—*Ang. Am. Mag.* (Tor.)

"Written in a lively, amusing and most interesting style, and full of incident and adventure."—*Col. Mag.* (Lon.)

XIV. Life in the Clearings, *versus* the Bush. *Do.* 1853, p. 8vo.; *New York,* 1854, 12mo.

"It consists of some account of the authoress's own life, with her preparation for emigration and her voyage across the Atlantic, ending where her 'Roughing it in the bush,' begins. Without any very great pretentions, it is a very lively pleasant book, just the sort of companion for a summer tourist. It well sustains Mrs. Moodie's reputation, and we predict for it a good deal of popularity on this side of the Atlantic."—*Gazette,* (Mont.)

XV. Dorothy Chance; a serial story. (published in the Montreal *Daily News,* 1867.)

MOORE, *Hon.* PHILIP H., late M. L. C. Can.
I. Address delivered at the Annual Fair, held at Stanbridge in Sept. 1859, pp. 16.

MOONSOM, *Captain* W.
I. Letters from Nova Scotia; comprising sketches of a young country. *London,* 1830, pp. 371, 12mo.

MOREAU, CHARLES HENRI. A Canadian comic writer and caricaturist. B. at Paris, France, 1835. D. in France, 1867. Entered *L'École Impériale des Beaux Arts,* 1852. Served as an officer in the army of the Potomac, in 1860.

In 1865, established and ed. *Le Perroquet* (Montreal,) a pictoral comic weekly, which enjoyed great popularity during its brief existence.

MORETON, *Rev.* JULIAN. Late Missionary at Greenspond, Newfoundland. Now Colonial Chaplain, Labuan.
I. Life and Work in Newfoundland; Reminiscences of thirteen years spent there. *London,* 1863, pp. 166, 8vo.

MORGAN, *Lieut.* J. C. Royal Marines.
I. The Emigrant's Note Book and Guide; with Recollections of Upper and Lower Canada, during the war. *London,* 1824, pp. 348, 12mo.

"A partial, though at the same time, a useful work."—*Quar. Rev.* (Lon.)

MORIN, *Hon.* AUGUSTIN NORBERT. A Can. journ., statesman and judge. B. at St. Michel, near Quebec, 12 Oct., 1803. D. near St. Hyacinthe, L. C., 27 June, 1865. Ed. at the Seminary (Que). He studied law at Montreal, and was admitted to the Bar in that city. He was first returned to Parliament in 1830, as a mem. of the L. A. of L. C., and speedily took his place as one of the foremost politicians of the French Can. party. In 1834 he was selected to proceed to Eng. as the bearer of petitions from his countrymen to the throne. After the Union he sat in the Assem. of United Can., occupying various offices in successive administrations, and was for some time co-leader of the Govt. with Mr. Hincks. In 1855, he was raised to the Bench. He was a mem. of the commission appointed for the codification of the Laws of L. C. In 1826, founded *La Minerve* (Mont.), a newspaper of which he was ed. for many years, which still survives and enjoys a high place amongst French Can. journals. Mr. M. was the author of some poems and songs which were reproduced in the *Rép. Nat.* (1848.)

I. Lettre à l'Honorable Ed. Bowen. Ecr., un des Juges de la Cour du Banc du Roi de Sa Majesté pour le District Québec. *Québec,* 1825, pp. 16.

"The style was said, at the time, to be very correct, though the reasoning, according to opinions, would appear ill-founded or conclusive."—*Can. Rev.,* (Mont.)

II. Lecture sur l'Education, devant l'Institut Canadien, le 18 Décembre, 1845. *Montréal*, 1845, pp. 30.

MORPHY, J.   A Clk. in the Crown Land Department, Can.

I. Recollections of a Visit to Great Britain and Ireland, in the Summer of 1862. *Quebec*, 1863, pp. 95, 8vo.

II. Ned Fenton's Portfolio. *Do.*, 1863, pp. 139, 8vo.

MORRIN, JOSEPH, *M. D.* Founder of Morrin Coll., (Que.) B. in Dumfriesshire, Scot., in the early part of the century. D. at Quebec, 1861.

I. Inaugural Address at the opening of the Quebec School of Medicine. *Quebec*, 1849, pp. 31.

" The principal part of the address is occupied by a history of medicine, written in the terse, forcible, epigrammatic style, for which the author is so remarkable, but which gives to the narrative a zest, which the very dryness of the subject would otherwise preclude. The most interesting portion of the lecture is the concluding part, in which some statistical information is afforded of the early medical history of the country."— *B. A. Journ.*

MORRIS, ALEXANDER, *D. C. L.*   A Can. Essayist. Son of the late Hon. W. Morris, (whom see.) B. at Perth, U. C., 17th March, 1827.   Pursued his studies at the Univ's. of Glasgow and of McGill Coll., (Mont.,) of which latter institution he is a governor. Is an advocate of L. C., and a barrister of U. C. In 1861 was returned to the Leg. Assem., Can., where he sat until the Union of 1867. He is a mem. of the House of Commons of the Dominion.

I. The Railway Consolidation Acts of Canada. *Montreal*, 1854.

II. Canada and her Resources ; an Essay to which was awarded the second prize by the Paris Exhibition Committee of Canada. *Do.*, 1855.

" Mr. Morris has • • succeeded in disarming criticism, by limiting himself strictly to the duties of a compiler, without entering into any speculations or descriptions, which give a charm to Mr. Hogan's essay, and contribute so much to make it a readable book."— *Can. Journ.*

III. Nova Britannia ; or, British North America, its extent and future ; a lecture. *Do.*, 1858, pp. 67, 8vo.

" Mr. Morris • • • is at once statistical, patriotic and prophetic. The lecturer sees in the future a fusion of races, a union of all the existing provinces, with new provinces to grow up in the west, and a railway to the Pacific. The design of the lecture is excellent, and its facts seem to have been carefully collected."— *Can. Nat.*

IV. The Hudson's Bay and Pacific Territories ; a lecture. *Do.*, 1859, pp. 57.

MORRIS, *Rev.* A. P., and JAMES RAVEN.

I. Arithmetic for use in Colleges and Schools. *Hamilton*, 1860.

MORRIS, B. R.   *M. D.*   Formerly of Toronto, U. C.

I. Observations on the construction of an Hospital for the Insane. Pamphlet.

II. Theory as to the cause of Insanity. *Do.*

III. Description of an Intestinal worm from the duodenum of the white fish of the Canadian Lakes. *Can. Journ.*, 1859.

IV. On the power that certain water-birds possess of remaining partially submerged in deep water. *Do.*, 1862.

MORRIS, JAMES H., *M. A.*

I. Notes of Travel in China. *Can. Journ.*, 1857.

MORRIS, M. and M. C.   (Hal.)

I. Metrical Musings. *New York*, 1856, pp. 188, 8vo.

MORRIS, *Hon.* PATRICK.   A Newfoundland politician. Was for some time leader of the Liberal party, and Colonial Treasurer in that Island.   Contributed largely to *Sim. Col. Mag.* (Lon.,) on subjects concerning the trade relations and resources of Newf.

I. Arguments to prove the policy and necessity of granting to Newfoundland a constitutional government ; being a letter to the Right Hon. W. Huskisson, Esq.   *London*, 1828.

" The letter displayed considerable ability on the part of the writer."—REV. C. PEDLEY : *His of N.*

II. A Short Reply to the Speech of Earl Aberdeen, and also a letter to the Most Noble the Marquis of Normanby, on the state of Newfoundland. By a Member of the House of Assembly of Newfoundland. *Liverpool*, 1839, pp. 49.

III. Short Review of the History. Government, Constitution, Fishery and Agriculture of Newfoundland, in a series of letters addressed to Earl Grey. *St. Johns, N. F. L.*, 1848.

"A considerable portion of this work is occupied with an able *exposé* of the pernicious effects of the unwise concessions made to the French and Americans, of fishing on our coast, bolstered up as the fisheries of these nations are by enormous bounties."—*Newf. Paper.*

MORRIS, W.
  I. The Accountant's Guide, for elementary schools in Canada. *Quebec,* 1833.

MORRIS, HON. WILLIAM. A Can. Legislator. B. at Paisley, Scot., 1786. D. at Perth, U. C., 1858. Sat as a mem. of the U. C. Assem., from 1820 until the Union, when he was called to the Leg. Coun. of the United Provinces. Was a mem. of the Ex. Council, from 1844 to 1848.

  I. A Letter on the subject of the Clergy Reserves and Rectories, addressed to the Very Rev. Principal Macfarlan and the Revd. R. Burns, D. D. *Toronto,* 1838, pp. 74.
  II. Reply to Six Letters addressed to him by John Strachan, D. D., Archdeacon of York. *Do.*, 1838, pp. 54.

MORRISON, DANIEL. A Can. journ. B. in Inverness, Scot. He is the son of a Scotch clergym. Coming to Can. at an early age, he for some years, was engaged in agricultural pursuits in U. C. Subsequently, for a brief period, he ed. the *Dundas Warder*, and, by the vigour of his pen and his enterprise and force of character, raised that paper from a comparatively obscure and insignificant position to one of considerable standing and influence in the country. His reputation as a public writer extended, and he became ed. of the *Daily Leader* (Tor.) For some time up to 1859 he conducted, and for a short time, was joint prop. of the *Daily Colonist* of the same city. After Quebec became the seat of government of Can., he undertook the ed. control of the *Daily Chronicle*, then the leading government organ there. In 1861 he removed to London U. C., where he had ed. charge of the *Daily Prototype.* Subsequently he left the Province; and has since been for some years connected with the N. Y. daily newspaper press. As a public writer and journ. Mr. M. had very few superiors in Can. To great skill, and readiness was united the power of a well stored mind, great literary capacity, and a thorough acquaintance with the history, resources, and capabilities of his adopted country. His departure from Can. left a wide gap in the ranks of Provincial journalists, which it has been hard to fill.

MORRISON, *Rev.* DUNCAN. (Brockville, U. C.)
  I. God's Providence in Calamity. *Prescott,* 1865.

MOUNTAIN, *Colonel* A. S., *C. B.*, A. D. C. to the Queen. Brother of the following. B. at Quebec, 4 July, 1797. D. on the march from Cawnpore to Futtyghur in India, 8th Feb. 1854. Saw considerable active service in India and China.

  Memoirs and letters edited by Mrs. Mountain. (With portrait.) *London,* 1857, 12mo.

MOUNTAIN, *Rt. Rev.* GEORGE JEHOSHAPHAT, *D. D., D. C. L.,* Late Lord Bish. of Quebec. B. in Norwich, Eng. 27 July, 1789. D. at Quebec, 6 Jany. 1863. He was the second son of the late Dr. Jacob Mountain, the first Anglican Bish. of Quebec. The family is of French extraction. When only 4 years of age accompanied his parents and family to Quebec, on the appointment of his father to the then newly created, and, for many years afterwards, the only See of the Ch. of Eng. in Can. There he received the early portion of his education. At 16 he proceeded to Eng., where, until he entered Cambridge he pursued his studies under a private tutor. He graduated at Trinity Coll. in 1810. Returning to Can. in the following year, he studied for Holy Orders under his father (whose secy. he became ;) was admitted to Deacon's Orders in 1812 ; to the Priesthood in 1814 ; and received the appointment of evening lecturer at the cathedral. From 1814 to 1817 he was Rector of Fredericton, N. B., when he returned to Quebec as rector of that parish, and bishop's official. In 1821, he became archdeacon of L. C. In 1836 he was consecrated Bish. of Montreal, as coadjutor to Bish. Stewart, who had succeeded his father in the See of Quebec. Bishop S. shortly afterwards leaving for Eng., the charge of the entire diocese (which has since been divided into 6,) was under his care and direction until 1839, when U. C. was made a separate See. It was through his earnest exertions and remonstrances that Rupert's Land was also, in 1849, erected into an Episcopal See. He continued to have the entire spiritual charge of L. C., until 1850, when he succeeded in having the diocese of Montreal constituted, he retaining the diocese of Quebec, by far the poorer and more laborious of the two. No one at this day can form any proper idea, or realize the enormous labours, the wide range and greatness of the duties which fell to the lot of our early spiritual rulers. Long before Bish. M. was elevated to the Episcopal bench, he performed long, tedious and oftentimes dangerous journeys, into the interior of what was then in most places almost a wild and unsettled country, to minister to the religious wants of the children of his Ch., and otherwise advance the cause of Christianity. And these journeys and expeditions were continued down to within a few years of his death,—no undertaking appearing to this intrepid man of God too hazardous or dangerous. Whether it was as an apostle to the Indians of the North-West Territory, (in the days when the bark canoe afforded to the traveller the only mode of conveyance,) or among the untutored people of the Ottawa, in remote settlements in the Eastern Townships and surrounding country, amidst the rude inhabitants of the Magdalen Islands, or on the barren and inhospitable shore of Labrador—wherever the peril was greatest, and the labour to be performed most arduous and exacting, there was this great Christian hero to be found doing the work of his Master. On 4 or 5 occasions, he crossed the Atlantic in the interest of the Ch., at a time when ocean navigation was not so safe and so rapid as it has since become. Churches, schoolhouses, and asylums sprang into existence throughout his diocese through his instrumentality and prospered under his fatherly hand. The Church Soc. was founded by him. But perhaps the greatest of his works,

in one way, was the establishment, in 1844, of the Univ. of Bishop's Coll., Lennoxville, L. C., for the education of clergymen for the Ch. of Eng. Bishop M. was the first principal of, and prof. of divinity in, the Univ. of McGill Coll.; he was also one of the first members of the Royal Institution for the Advancement of Learning in Can., and long discharged the duties pertaining to those positions. In closing this brief and imperfectly written sketch of Bishop M's. life we cannot do better than quote the words of a writer in the *Quebec Mercury*, who said on the occasion of his death, that he " was universally known as a learned theologian, an elegant classical scholar, an able writer, an eloquent and, in the best sense, powerful preacher, and a most polished gentleman."

In addition to the productions from his pen which we give below, we may state that many of his sermons, charges, &c., have appeared in the Eng. work entitled, *The Churches in the Colonies.*

" None who have enjoyed the privilege of knowing the Bishop personally will ever forget his tall and slender form, reverend with meek dignity; his singular modesty and courtesy of demeanor, the gentleness of his voice, the kind considerateness of his thoughts for others, his ready and unaffected hospitality, and the ripe scholarly tone that was apparent in all that he said and all that he wrote. Unselfishness was never more strongly marked in any character, and those who know his life-long labours........ in short, his faithful and quiet devotion to duty at all times—none who have known all this will ever cease to remember the departed Bishop as one of the rarest examples of the Christian, the scholar and the gentleman united, as they always ought to be, in the person of a Bishop."—*Church Journal*, (N. Y.)

I. Sermon preached as an Appeal on behalf of the Waterloo sufferers. *Fredericton*, 1816.

II. Sermon on the Occasion of the Death, from Hydrophobia, of His Grace the Duke of Richmond, Governor General of B. N. A. *Quebec*, 1819, pp 17.

III. The Education of the Poor, the Duty of Diffusing the Gospel, and particularly on the importance of family religion; a sermon. *Do.*, 1822, pp. 28.

" Contains evidence of his anxiety for the spiritual growth of his flock, and its promotion by the use of the ordinances of the Church, which he was firm in the conviction that Christ had appointed as the means to that end."—*Memoir of Bp. M.*

IV. A Letter to Mr. S. C. Blyth, occasioned by the recent publication of the narrative of his conversion to the Romish Faith, by a Catholic Christian. *Montreal*, 1822, pp. 290, 8vo.

V. Sermon on the occasion of the first Ordination by the Hon. and Rt. Rev. C. J. Stewart, Lord Bishop of Quebec. *Quebec*, 1826.

VI. Sermon at the Visitation of the Hon. and Rt. Rev. the Lord Bishop of Quebec. *Montreal*, 1833.

VII. A Retrospect of the Summer and Autumn of 1832, a sermon; with an appendix of facts concerning the late awful visitation of the Cholera Morbus. *Quebec*, 1833. pp. 33.

"This excellent sermon was preached on the conclusion of the year 1832—— a year, the most disastrous ever known in the history of Canada. * * * Of the sermon itself we will merely say, that independent of the melancholy interest belonging to the subject to which it is devoted, it demands universal attention for its plain and energetic pathos, its passages descriptive of the fearful scenes exhibited during the prevalence of the pestilence, its touching, yet manly exhortations, its simplicity and strength of language."— *Can. Lit. Mag.* (York U. C.)

VIII. The Journal of the Bishop of Montreal, during a visit to the Church Missionary Society's North-West America Mission. To which is added, by the Secretaries, an appendix, giving an account of the formation of the mission, and its progress to the present time. *London*, 1845, pp. 236; 2nd Ed. *Do.* 1849, 12mo.

IX. Songs of the Wilderness, being a Collection of Poems, written in 1844, with illustrative notes. *Do.* 1846, 12mo.

X. Sermon on the Responsibilities of Englishmen in the Colonies of the British Empire. Preached before the St. George's Society. *Quebec*, 1847, pp. 18.

XI. Journal of Visitation in a portion of the Diocese, by the Lord Bishop of Montreal. *London*, 1847, pp. 103.

XII. Thoughts on "Annexation," in connection with the duty and the interest of members of the Church of England; and as affecting some particular religious questions. Printed for private circulation. *Quebec*, 1849, pp. 28.

"Towards the close of 1849, the Bishop, who very rarely indeed took any part in political affairs, felt it his duty to print, for private circulation among members of the church, some 'Thoughts on Annexation,' which he had originally drawn up in the shape of a pastoral letter. The necessity, however, for sending it forth in this form had happily passed away, before it could be issued, but he was anxious, as far as possible, to exhibit the duty of Churchmen towards the Church and Realm of England, to which he was himself thoroughly and devotedly attached, and to dissuade them from being carried away by any passing excitement of discontent."—*Memoir of Bp. M.*

XIII. A Pastoral Letter to the Clergy and Laity of the Diocese of Quebec, in connection with the subject of the Bill introduced into the Imperial Parliament, during the last season, for the conveyance of certain privileges to the Colonial Churches, &c. *Do.* 1853, pp. 14.

XIV. A Charge delivered to the clergy of the Diocese of Quebec, at the Triennial visitation held in the Cathedral of Quebec. *Do.* 1854, pp. 46

XV. The Duty of the Christian Minister in following Christ; the sermon preached at an ordination of Priest and Deacons held by the Provisional Bishop of New-York, in Trinity Church, New-York. *New-York*, 1854, pp. 32, 8vo.

XVI. Letter respecting Synodical Action in his Diocese; together with considerations relative to certain interruptions of the peace of the Church in the parish of Quebec. *Quebec*, 1858, pp. 27.

XVII. Sermons. Published at the request of the Synod of the Diocese. *London*, 1865, pp. 262, p. 8vo.

[*Contents:* The Ten Virgins; The Judgment of Man; The Burden of Dumah; The Unproductive Vineyard; Compliance with Ordinances; The Joy of Christians; Christ coming to His Own; The Punishment·of Sodom; The History of Joseph; The Choice of Moses; The Threefold Witness in Earth; The Prince of this World; Prayer; The Journeyings of Israel a Type of the Christian · Pilgrimage; Confirmation and the Sacraments; Words and Thoughts acceptable before God ; The Mystery of Godliness ; Sins and Good Works manifest beforehand ; God in Creation and Providence.]

A Memoir of George Jehoshaphat Mountain, D. D., D. C. L. Late Bishop of Quebec. Compiled (at the desire of the Synod of that Diocese) by his son, Armine W. Mountain, M. A., Incumbent of St. Michael's Chapel, Quebec, *Montreal*, 1866, pp. 477, 8vo.

" There are few greater pleasures in these days, than to get hold of a really good book— a book not only thoroughly and conscientiously well done from beginning to end, but distinguished also by some peculiarity of subject, opening a fresh field of interest, and breaking a door for the reader into a realm of outlying knowledge. Such pleasure we have experienced in perusing the volume before us, in reading this memoir of the active, hard, and energetic life, and struggles to build up the Church of England in this Province, of one who has now passed to his reward—the very beau-ideal of a Christian Bishop. The work is remarkable in another sense—as giving us an excellent idea of what Canada was half a century ago—what hardships and difficulties its settlers, at that comparatively recent period, had to contend with, while building up their home in the great primeval forests, and clearing the land, now rich and fertile, and yielding abundant crops, of the trees and bush which then cumbered it. But what the volume beyond anything else practically shows is, how God has been pleased to bless and prosper this portion of His Catholic Church since 1793, when Dr. Mountain, the first Bishop of Canada, and father of the subject of the present memoir, was, at the instigation of Mr. Pitt, consecrated and sent to Quebec to take possession of his immense See. One cannot help thinking, while perusing chapter after chapter of the memoir, on the words of the great missionary apostle, and how appropriately they might be applied, though doubtless in a very much restricted sense— ' in much patience, in afflictions, in necessities, in distresses;' ' in journeyings often, in perils of waters, in perils in the wilderness, in weariness and painfulness, in hunger and thirst.' "—*Transcript* (Mont.)

MOUNTAIN, *Rt. Rev.* JACOB, *D. D.* First Anglican Bish. of Quebec. B. at Thwaite Hall, Norfolk, Eng., 1750. D. at Quebec, 16 June, 1825. Appointed to the See of Quebec, 1793.

    I. Thanksgiving Sermon. *Quebec*, 1799, 8vo.

MOWAT, *Hon.* OLIVER, *Q. C.* One of the Vice Chancellors, U. C. Sat for some years in Leg. Assem. Can., and was a mem. of several Govt's.

    I. A Letter on the Bill for quieting titles to Real Estate in Upper Canada, addressed to the Hon. John A. Macdonald, Attorney General for U. C. *Toronto*, 1865, pp. 17, 8vo.

    II. Annual Address as President of the Can. Institute. *Can. Journ.*, 1865.

MOYLAN, JAMES GEORGE. A Can. journ. B. near Maynooth, Irel., 1826. Entered St. Jarlaths Coll., Tuam, 1837. Studied at Maynooth Coll., from 1842 to 1847, and completed the course of Rhetoric, Logic, Metaphysics and Natural Philosophy there. In 1848 received an appointment in H. M. Customs in London, which he resigned in 1851, and emigrated to Am. Was Asst. Secy. to the Chilian Embassy at Washington, and, in 1852, became Secy. to the Whig Executive Committee at same city. Served as Washington correspondent, in 1853–4, for the *Times* (N. Y.) ; *Mercury* (Charleston) ; *Picayune* (New Orleans); *Examiner* (Richmond,) and other journals ; and in 1854–5, as reporter to *Times* (N. Y.) In 1858 established the *Canadian Freeman* (Tor.,) a weekly Catholic, but not ecclesiastical, journal, Conservative in politics, of which he is ed. and prop., and as such has rendered important services to the cause of his countrymen in Can. and Am. Mr. M. is regarded as one of the most able and talented writers on the Can. press.

MUDIE, ROBERT.

    I. The Emigrants Pocket Companion ; containing : what emigration is, who should be emigrants, where emigrants should go ; a description of British North America, especially the Canadas, and full instructions to intending emigrants. *London*, 1832.

MULKINS, *Rev.* HANNIBAL.

    I. Report to the Canada Temperance Society on the working and effects of Prohibitory Legislation to suppress Intemperance in the New England States. *Kingston*, 1855, pp. 28.

MULLALY, JOHN.

    I. A Trip to Newfoundland ; its scenery and fisheries; with an account of the laying of the Submarine Telegraph Cable, (with engravings). *New York*, 1856, pp. 108, 12mo.

    II. The Laying of the Cable ; or, the Ocean Telegraph ; a Narrative of the attempt to lay the cable across the entrance to the Gulf of St. Lawrence in 1855. *New York*, 8vo.

MULLOCK, *Rt. Rev.* JOHN THOMAS. R. C. Bish. of St. John's, Newfoundland. B. in Limerick, 1806. Ed. at Seville. Belonged to the Franciscan order of Monks. Was Superior of the Franciscan House in Dublin. Consecrated Bish. of St. John's, 1847. Has written various articles in Home reviews, and occasionally contributed letters &c., to the newspaper press of N. F. L.

I. Life of Saint Alphonsus M. Liguori. *Dublin*, 1846.

II. History of Heresies, translated from the Italian of Saint Liguori ; 2nd Ed. corrected, revised and continued to the present time. *Do.*, 2 vols.

III. Lectures on Newfoundland, delivered at St. Bonaventure's College. *St. John's* and *New York*, 1860, pp. 60, 8vo.

" These lectures give a brief but able historical sketch of the island of Newfoundland, and of its soil, climate, mineral, and commercial wealth and resources."—*Am. His. Mag.*

IV. A Sermon preached in the Cathedral, St. John's. *St. John's*, 1861, pp. 15.

MULOCH, *Rev.* JOHN A. I. Defence of the Church of England against the Methodists. *Carleton Place, U. C.*, 1850, pp. 54.

MURAT, EUGENE. I. Papeta ; a story, abridged and arranged from the diary and private papers of Mr. Eugene Murat. *St. John, N. B.*, 1867.

MURDOCH, BEAMISH, *Q. C.* A N. S. historian. B. at Halifax, N. S., 1800. Admitted as an Attorney 1821, and as a Barrister, 1822. In 1826 was returned as a mem. of the Assem. of N. S., for Halifax. From 1850 to 1860 held the office of Recorder (Hal.) In his younger days, contributed to local newspaper press on subjects of passing interest.

I. A Narrative of the Late Fires at Miramichi, New Brunswick ; with an Appendix containing the statements of many of the sufferers, and a variety of interesting occurrences; together with a Poem entitled 'The Conflagration.' *Halifax*, 1825, pp. 48, 8vo.

II. An Essay on the mischievous tendency of Imprisoning for Debt, and in other civil cases. *Do.*, 1831, 2nd Ed., pp. 60, 8vo.

III. Epitome of the Laws of Nova Scotia. *Do.*, 4 vols., 1832–33, 8vo.

IV. Celebration of the Centenary Anniversary of the Settlement of the City of Halifax : Oration by Beamish Murdoch ; Poem by Joseph Howe. *Do.*, 1849,

V. A History of Nova Scotia, or Acadie. *Do.*, vol. I., 1865, pp. 543 ; vol. II., 1865–6, pp. 624 ; vol. III., 1867, pp. xxiii–613, 8vo.

" Though the style of the author is that of the Annalist or Chronicler, rather than of the Historian, this work is valuable and indispensable for reference."—*Journ.* (St. John, N. B.)

" Having traced the progress of Acadie from its first inception as a French colony in 1605, to its conquest by Nicholson in 1710,—thence to the British settlement at Chebucto in 1749, and marked the establishment of representative government in 1758,—having watched it through the phases of the old French war, the exile of the Acadians, the revolution in the older English provinces on the continent, and their uprising into a nation and an Empire,—having seen the immigration from New England in 1760 upon the vacant lands originally occupied by the French on the bay of Fundy and basin of Mines,—the advent also of the loyalists in 1783, and the founding of the governments of New Brunswick, Cape Breton and Prince Edward Island :—having seen the progress made by this country during the wars of Napoleon and the second American war, gradually but certainly advancing in the march of intellect and industry, with occasional additions to its population from the British isles :—having noticed the large sums of money given by parliament to aid our endeavours, and the extensive military and naval protection constantly afforded us :—under all these transactions there is a broad and deep foundation of gratitude laid that we cannot keep out of view, due on our part to the latest generation to the monarchs and parliaments of Great Britain for unlimited and unstinted favor and support."—*Author's Preface.*

MURDOCH, *Rev.* JOHN L., *A. M.* Presb. min., Windsor, N. S.

I. The Causes which since the Reformation have led to the revival and increase of Popery ; a lecture. *Halifax*, 1859, pp. 35, 12mo.

MURDOCK, WILLIAM. A N. B. poet. B. at Paisley, Scot.,1823. Has written poetry from an early age. Came to N. B. in 1854. Is now on the staff of the *Morning News*, (St. John.)

I. Poems and Songs. *St. John*, 1860, pp. 152, 8vo.

MURPHY, HENRY.

I. The Conquest of Quebec. An Epic Poem. In eight books. *Dublin*, 1790, pp. 308, 12mo.

MURRAY, Hon. A. M.

I. Letters from the United States, Cuba and Canada. *London*, 1856, 2 vols., p. 8vo.

MURRAY, HUGH, *F. R. S. E.*

I. Historical Account of Discoveries and Travels in North America; including the United States, Canada, the Shores of the Polar Sea, and the Voyages in search of a North-West Passage ; with Observations on Emigration ; (illustrated by a map of North America.) *London*, 1829, 2 vols., 8vo.

II. An Historical and Descriptive Account of British America, comprehending Canada, (Upper and Lower,) Nova Scotia, New Brunswick, Newfoundland, Prince Edward Island, the Bermudas and the Fur Countries ; their history from the earliest settlement ; the Statistics and Topography of each district ; their Commerce, Agriculture and Fisheries; their social and political condition ; as also an account of the manners and present state of the Aboriginal tribes; to which is added a full detail of the principles and best modes of Emigration. With illustrations of the Natural History, by James Wilson, R. K. Greville and Professor Trail. (With 16 maps and plates. *Do.* 1839–40, 3 vols., 12mo.

MURRAY, J. D. A Can. journ. B. in parish of Small Isles, Invernesshire, Scot., Feby. 1825. After attending the Parochial Sch. in his native parish, entered a Model Sch. at Edinburgh, and there won the first prize in the English Composition class, against 43 competitors. Was for some time a Free Ch. teacher in Small Isles ; and during the great destitution in the Highlands and Islands, he served as a Relief Inspector. In 1849, visited the Western States, where he first became permanently connected with the press; and in 1851 came to Can. In 1854 he was entrusted by the late Mr. W. L. Mackenzie with the general management of the *Message* (Tor.,) during the absence of the latter at the Seat of Government to fulfil his parliamentary duties. Previous to this, however, Mr. M. had contributed articles on literary subjects to the *Family Herald*, (Tor.) In 1855 he established the *Gazette*, (Thorold,) which he conducted up to 1860. In that year he purchased the *Post*, (St. Catharines,) and merged the former journal in it, under the name of the *Post*. Early in 1866 he disposed of this paper, and gave up his connection with the newspaper press. Mr. M. was a bold and forcible writer of the Reform School ; though in many things he took strong grounds against his party.

MURRAY, JOHN.

I. The Emigrant and Traveller's guide to and through Canada by way of the River St. Lawrence, &c. *London*, 1835, pp. 63, sm. 8vo.

MURRAY, *Miss* LOUISA. A Can. author. B. at Carisbrook, Isle of Wight, 1822. Is the daughter of an officer, who, as a Lieut. in the 100th, or Prince Regent's Regt., served in Can. during the War of 1812 ; he distinguished himself in many actions, particularly at the capture of Fort Niagara, the battle of Chippewa, and the storming of Fort Erie, at the latter of which he was wounded and taken prisoner. Miss M. contributed to the *Literary Garland* (Mont.,) during its existence. She also contributed to *Once a Week* (Lon.,) and to the *British American Mag.*, (Tor.) Her writings consist of novels, tales, and essays, are characterized by great purity and elevation of thought and elegance and originality of style. Although chiefly known through her prose compositions, she has from time to time come before the world as a writer of verse, some of the sweetest as well as the most tender little lyrics that we have seen in the Can. periodical press, having emanated from her pen.

I. Fauna ; or, the Red Flower of Leafy Hollow ; a novel description of Canadian life and scenery. *Lit. Garland*, 1851.

II. The Settlers of Long Arrow ; a novel. *Once a Week*, 1861.

III. The Cited Curate ; a novel. *Brit. Am. Mag.*, 1863.

" Her productions in this department of literature [prose-fiction] will compare favourably with those of the most eminent writers of the day. " *The Cited Curate*," evinces more genuine intellectual power than any similar production we have seen from a Canadian pen."—Dewart.

" She is a poetess of a high order, if I am at all capable of judging, a good romance writer, and one of the most discriminating of critics and essay writers, taking bold, large, original views on almost every subject of human thought, and capable of shewing, with vivid distinctness, and clearness of unmixed outlines, the indiosyncrasies of each writer, so that they may stand out in their individualities in bold relief. • • • She is among the genuine gold productions of great mother nature, and will yet have (if only she can be made to covet it highly) the stamp of current sterling stamped upon her by the judgment of mankind, if my opinion be worth much."—Rev. J. A. Allan : *Letter to Author.*

Murray, *Rev.* Robert. A N. S. journ. and writer. B. in Colchester Co., N. S., about 1833. Is a min. of the Presb. Ch. When quite young evinced a strong taste for Literature, and began writing for the press. In 1855 became chief ed. of the *Presbyterian Witness* (Hal.,) a position which he still retains. He has also been joint ed. of the *Home and Foreign Record* (Hal.,) a monthly periodical and the official organ of the Presb. Ch. in N. S., since 1861. In 1860, and again in 1864, he made a tour through Can. and the U. S., and in 1862 visited Europe, on each of which occasions he wrote a series of graphic and instructive letters to the *Witness* and other journals, describing the various places of historic interest he had seen and visited, and the several remarkable personages he had met.

So highly have these letters been thought of, that permission has frequently been solicited, and liberal offers made to their author for their publication in book-form. Mr. M. is acknowledged to be the best descriptive, as well as one of the most industrious writers on the press of the Lower Provinces. He excels as a keen and effective political writer, and throws himself warmly into whatever cause he espouses. Of late years he has given strong support to Confederation. In addition to the journals with which he is connected, he has contributed articles on literary, social, economic and scientific subjects to the following : *Christian Work, Daily Review* (Edin.) ; *Weekly Review* (Lon.) ; *Morning Journal* (Glas.) ; *Evangelist* (N. Y.) ; *Presbyterian* (Phil.) ; and *Recorder* (Bos.)

Murray, *Rev.* William. A min. of the Presbyterian Ch., N. S., (Cornwallis.) Eldest brother of the preceding. Contributed *The History, Resources, &c.*, of *Nova Scotia, Newfoundland and Prince Edward Island,* to *Eighty Years Progress,* (Tor.,) 1863. From 1854 to 1856 ed. the *Presbyterian Witness* (Hal.,) to which he still contributes. Is now preparing an historical work to be published abroad.

Myers, *Colonel.*

I. Notes on the Weather at Halifax, during 1863, with comparisons of the temperature of that place with some other parts of British North America. *Trans. N. S. Inst.,* 1864.

II. Notes on the Weather at Halifax, during 1864. *Do.* 1864–5.

Myrand, Dominique Prosper. B. at Quebec 1815. D. there 1860. Was chief French translator to Leg. Assem. Can.

I. Etude sur l'instruction publique chez les Canadiens Français. *Québec,* 1857, pp. 24.

N.

NARRAWAY, *Rev.* J. R. A Wes. Meth. Min., N. S.

I. Sermon on the occasion of the death of Charles F. Allison, founder of Mount Allison Academy. *Halifax*, 1859, pp. 19, 8vo.

NANTEL, *Rev.* A. A R. C. priest.

I. M. L'Abbé Ducharme, orateur. (Souvenirs.) *Rev. Can.*, 1865.

NEAL, JOHN. An Am. author.

I. The Battle of Niagara, with other Poems, by Jehu O'Cataract. *Baltimore*, 1818; 2nd Ed. *Do.*, 1819.

NEILSON, *Hon.* JOHN. A Can. Statesman and Journ. B. at Dornald, parish of Balmaghie, stewartry of Kircudbright, Scot., 17th July, 1776. D. at Quebec, 1st February, 1848. Ed. at one of the parish schools in his native country.

When about 14 years of age, his family sent him to seek his fortune in Can., placing him under the care of his elder brother, Samuel N., who had just then succeeded his uncle, Mr. W. Brown, in the property and editorship of the *Gazette* (Que..) which had been first published by him and his partner, Mr. Gilmour, on the 21st June, 1764. Mr. S. N. died in 1793, and Mr. J. N. being yet a minor, the publication of the *Gazette* was conducted by the late Rev. Dr. Sparks, his guardian, until 1796, when, Mr. N. coming of full age, he assumed the direction of the paper, and from that period it took a new character of interest and importance. In 1810, the increasing demand for political intelligence and the importance of the public questions which began to be discussed in the legislature, induced Mr. N. to enlarge the size of the paper, and to publish it twice a week, and, as had formerly been the case, in both languages. Under the management of its judicious ed., the *Gazette* acquired a perceptible and increasing influence on public opinion, by the ability and discretion with which political subjects were discussed in it; the personal influence of its ed. naturally increased with that of

19

his journal; his capacity for civil affairs, attracted the attention of his fellow citizens, and in 1818, he was brought forward as a candidate and elected to the provincial assem., as a mem. for the Co. of Quebec; he thus entered upon a new and more important political career; he was now in the full vigor of his age and ripened intellect, and, as might be expected from his character, he soon took a lead in the active business of the legislature. At an early period after he became a legislator, he turned his attention to the measures necessary for the promotion of two of the most important and enduring interests of civil society—education and agriculture; and, as an auxiliary to the latter, he sought to effect an improvement in the system of granting the waste-lands, to encourage the survey and exploration of unknown territory within the limits of the province, and thus to assist the development of the resources of the country. He bore a leading part also in the discussion of the grave questions which, after 1818, occupied the public mind, and led to differences between the executive govt. and the Assem., as to the control and appropriation of the public revenues—the accusations brought against public functionaries—the plurality of offices, and the alleged abuses or evils in the administration of govt., Mr. N's conduct was marked by firmness and impartiality, and by that spirit of justice which was part of his individual character. But as the *Gazette* was employed by govt. as the vehicle of public notifications, and might thus be represented as in some sort its organ, Mr. N., in 1822, in order to be free in his political capacity from even the appearance of any such connection, transferred the whole establishment to his son, Mr. S. N., who, shortly afterwards, accepted a commission from govt. as king's printer and ed., and for about a year that paper bore the imprint, " by authority." But the commission having been revoked in 1823, the *Gazette* resumed and thenceforth retained the character of an independent paper, which it had borne since its establishment. The disputes between the executive govt. and the Assem., on financial matters, had, in 1822, apparently become so irreconcilable, that the Imperial Govt., pressed at the same time by U. C. to interfere in a question of finance pending between the 2 provinces, determined to propose to parliament to re-unite the provinces. The intelligence of this measure created general uneasiness among a large part of the people of L. C., and a strenuous spirit of opposition to it being aroused, it was determined by those adverse to it to send delegates to Eng. with representations against it. Mr. N. was chosen as the delegate from the district of Quebec, and Mr. Papineau, for that of Montreal, and through their remonstrances, supported by the influence of Sir J. MacIntosh in Parliament, or rather by his withdrawal of the assistance which the govt. had understood him to have promised, the measure was, in 1823, abandoned for the present. In 1828, the discussions between the local govt. and the Assem. having become more and more exasperated, a petition of grievance was sent to Eng., addressed to the Sovereign and Parliament, complaining of the administration of the govt., and bearing the names of upwards of 80,000 inhabitants of the province. Mr. N. was again chosen as a delegate jointly with Mr. D. B. Viger and Mr. Cuvillier, to support the complaints and demands of the petitioners before the imperial authorities; and a committee of inquiry having been appointed by the House of Commons, Mr. N. and the other delegates were examined, with many other witnesses; and a report was made favorable in the main to the views of the petitioners. The testimony given by Mr. N., with respect to the Leg. Coun., gave occasion subsequently to a charge against him of having recommended that that body should be made elective; but an unprejudiced perusal of his evidence, taken as a whole, will shew that then, as at all times afterwards, both in his ed. articles and in his place in the Assem., he discountenanced all

suggestions of fundamental changes, and maintained that the existing constitution and frame of govt., if properly administered, were sufficient 'for the peace, welfare, and good govt. of the province.' In like manner, both before and after that celebrated inquiry, Mr. N. always expressed his entire confidence in the good intentions, liberality and justice of the British Govt., in every thing that concerned the welfare of the people of L. C.; and the recommendations of the report then made, being carried into execution, in a spirit of concession and conciliation by a new gov. (Sir James Kempt), had the effect of producing a greater degree of tranquillity, in the province. On the 29th March, 1830, Mr. N. received the thanks of the House of Assem. for his services on this mission to Eng. Nor was this vote of thanks the only public mark of approbation which Mr. N.'s services to the people called forth. In Jan., 1831, a silver vase, which cost 150 guineas, (raised by public subscription) was presented to him at a public dinner, given to him by a large number of his fellow citizens, in testimony of their gratitude for his services in Eng. in 1823 and 1828. It was about this period that a difference of opinion on points of political importance began first to shew itself between Mr. N. and the leaders of the party with whom he had generally hitherto acted. His career was in nothing more remarkable than for his constant desire to maintain the ancient institutions, usages, and social arrangements of the French Can. portion of the population; and he vigorously opposed the measure called *Le Bill des Fabriques*, in 1831, which he considered as a needless and mischievous encroachment on the laws and customs by which the parochial ch. corporations had hitherto been governed, and, as tending to create disorder and confusion, where tranquillity and contentment had generally prevailed before. The separation thus made was widened still further at the same period, and the political quiet partially restored by the measures of administration in 1829 and 1830, was again disturbed by the agitation of the question of an elective Leg. Coun., by the imprisonment of 2

publishers of newspapers for alleged libels on that body, and, by the deplorable events·at the Montreal election, in 1832, when the ed. of one of those papers was elected to the Assem. When this unfortunate occurrence was made the subject of investigation before the committee of the Assem., and the feelings of party and origin were aroused into irritated action, Mr. N. abstained from taking any part in the proceedings, and his conduct on that occasion was justly considered as indicating his marked disapprobation of the course pursued by his political friends, who strove to cast the whole odium of the occurrences in question upon the civil and military authorities. He looked with ill-boding and prophetic eye on the measures of his party, as mischievously intermeddling with what ought to have been left to the proper tribunals of justice; and from that period may be dated his entire separation from that party. The consequences of that separation to himself personally were soon evident; for, on the occasion of the general election of 1834, he was thrown out of the representation of the Co. of Quebec, for which he had sat for 15 years. In the session of 1834, the celebrated 92 resolutions on the state of the country, (which a min. of the crown described as a "paper revolution," but which have now almost become a reality,) were adopted, and were brought before the Imperial Parliament, in a petition, calling for organic changes in the constitution, and the general adoption of the elective principle. Those who desired to maintain the constitution of the country unimpaired, formed themselves into "Constitutional Associations," throughout the province; and sent home petitions to the govt. and parliament in Eng. True to his principle of seeking administrative and opposing needless constitutional changes, Mr. N. accepted the appointment of a delegate from Quebec, associated with Mr. W. Walker, an advocate, of Montreal, (whom see,) to carry these petitions to Eng., and urge the objects of them there. Upon this third mission, Mr. N. proceeded to Eng. in the spring of 1835, and communicated with the new Colonial Secy., Lord
19*

Glenelg; but, in the month of July, the Brit. cabinet determined to transfer the further inquiry into these political distractions to the province itself, by recalling Lord Aylmer, and sending out Lord Gosford, as gov.-in-chief, with a commission also, jointly, with 2 others, as com's. of inquiry. Mr. N., consequently, returned immediately to Can. In this year, the health of his son, the ed. of the *Gazette*, which had been for some time failing, sank under the labor of a daily publication, (a change which had been adopted in 1832. when the *Gazette* appeared alternately in the two languages,) and he was obliged to go to the south of Europe;— and, having died at N. Y., on his return to his family, his father, at the age of 3 score, while suffering under this afflicted bereavement, and the disappointment of his hopes, resumed his ed. labors, in order to maintain the old establishment. Amongst the events of 1837 and 1838, Mr. N. was found true to those loyal principles, which he had always inculcated—recommending order and obedience to the laws, and respect to the constituted authorities. Notwithstanding the deplorable revolt of a portion of the population, he still showed himself the firm and constant friend of the French Can's., and maintained that the mass of the people were untainted by disloyalty or disaffection. He was, in truth, attached to them *as a people*—he loved to talk of their primitive manners and customs, their simple character and habits, and the peculiar changes and occurrences of their history; for their clergy, too, he entertained a high respect; which respect was returned by equal respect and regard, on their part, which followed him, it is believed, to the last moments of his life, and still attends his memory. The Union of the Provinces, which followed upon the events of 1837-8, was opposed by Mr. N., so long as he conceived that opposition could be of any avail;—having been called to the Special Coun. in 1839, after the suspension of the constitution, he there voted against the Union, being supported only by 2 other members, and in June, 1849, at a general meeting of the inhabitants of Quebec, he prepared a series of resolutions, which were embodied in a petition sent to Eng., remonstrating against the measure. When the Act of Union passed, Mr. N. came forward, and was elected without opposition, as mem. for his old county in the united legisl. Mr. N.'s rooted desire to stand by old institutions, and even usages, again manifested itself in his constant disapprobation of what is called " Responsible Govt. ;" and, his opinion upon this innovation upon the old system of colonial govt. are to be found thickly scattered through his ed. articles in the *Gazette*, from the adoption of the resolutions upon this subject in the Assem., in 1841. On the formation of a new govt. in November, 1843, he was urged to accept the honorable post of Speaker of the Leg. Coun. ; but he declined it, as he had uniformly declined every office of emolument, in fulfilment of a public declaration he once made to his constituents, and it was not till the session of 1844, that he consented, though the offer had before been frequently made to him, to become a mem. of that branch of the legisl. He was now verging to the appointed period of 3 score years and 10, and his constitution betrayed the inroads of age. He had already seen many contemporaries go before him to the grave, with whom he had been connected in the relations of sincere friendship, or in those of political life; but he still continued to take that active part which he considered to be his duty, as a mem. of society, in all public measures, either within the legisl. or without, which appeared to him conducive to the public weal; on such occasions, he shrunk not from meeting or co-operating with those who might be of an adverse political party, and the respect with which his suggestions were received in the public assemblies of his fellow citizens, shewed the weight attached to his opinions, and the confidence reposed in his ripened judgment and long experience in public affairs. It was at last in discharging a voluntary duty that he had taken upon himself, by attending with his brethren of St. Andrew's Soc. to receive the representative of his sovereign with due honor on his visit to Quebec,

in Oct. 1847, that Mr. N. brought on himself the malady which proved ultimately fatal to him ; he was on that occasion exposed for a considerable time to a chilling rain, but persisted in remaining to read the address of his fellow citizens, to His Excellency, on his first arrival in the ancient capital of Can. He was shortly after taken ill. and never fully shook off the disease ; but in spite of increasing weakness, his spirit failed him not, nor his habits of application to business ; so that neither his family nor his medical attendants perceived the full extent of his danger, and it may be said that he " died in harness," for the very evening before his death, he wrote off for the next issue of the *Gazette*, and with a steady hand, and almost without obliteration, the 2 remarkable articles, his last impressive words to his fellow citizens, which appeared in the *Gazette* of 21st Jan., 1848 ; the following day he was no more. As a public journ. his labors, spread over 30 volumes of the *Gazette*, attest his industry, ability, firmness and moderation, in delivering to the public the opinions upon the various subjects of political discussion which occupied the public attention oftentimes during periods of great difficulty and agitation. In his style of writing he was a model for journalists—plain, simple, concise, terse and idiomatically Eng. When the occasion required, as may be seen in some of his communications to the *Gazette*, then conducted by his son, in the summer of 1832, after the fatal occurrences at the Montreal election, he threw into his compositions a degree of eloquence and force seldom surpassed in any public journal. His *forte* lay in compressing into a small compass of well arranged thoughts and well chosen words, what ordinary writers would spread over columns with a *flux de paroles*. To his earnest pursuit, as a legislator, of what seemed to him to be for the public good, ample testimony is afforded by the statute book of the province, and the journals of the legislative bodies to which he belonged.—

(See *Papineau*, Hon. L. J.)

NEILSON, JOSEPH.

I. Observations upon Emigration to Upper Canada, with a brief topographical sketch of the different districts of the Province ; a prize essay, to which was awarded a Gold Medal from the Upper Canada Celtic Society. *Kingston, U. C*, 1837, pp. 74, 12mo.

NELSON, JOSEPH.

I. Political and Commercial Importance of completing the Line of Railway from Halifax to Quebec. (With map.) *London*, 1860, 8vo.

NELSON, HORACE, M. D. Son of Wolfred N. D. at Montreal, Jan. 1863. Was at one time Prof. of Surgery in the Univ. of Vermont, and ed. of *Nelson's Am. Lancet.* Contributed many valuable and interesting papers on medical and surgical science to the *Brit. Am. Journ.*, (Mont.)

I. Structure of the Rectum, its history, symptoms, diagnosis, pathology and successful treatment by incision. *Montreal*, 1861.

NELSON, WOLFRED, M. D. A Can. medical practitioner and writer. B. at Montreal, 10 July 1792. D. there 17 June, 1863. He was ed. for the Medical profession. In 1811, he received his degree ; and settled at St. Denis, L. C., where he practised for some years. In 1827, he was returned as a mem. to the Assem., L. C., and thenceforward occupied a prominent position in politics. In the Rebellion of 1837 he took up arms as a leader of the insurgents, and won the victory of St. Denis. Soon after that event, however, he was captured and sent into exile. On his release he recommenced the practice of his profession in the U. S., and as soon as the amnesty permitted returned to his native country. In 1844 he was elected to the Can. Parliament, in which he sat until 1851. In that year he was appointed an Inspector of Prisons, and in 1859, Chairman of the new Board of Inspectors of Prisons, Asylums, &c., which he held up to his death. He held various other offices of honour and emolument, and was twice elected President of the Coll. of Phys. and Surg., L. C. His reports on the Penitentiary, Prisons, and Public Health, contain many valuable suggestions towards the improvement of our prison discipline in the care of convicts, and the preservation of public hygiene, many of which were adopted by the Govt. Dr. N. contributed a large number of interesting papers on medical science to the public organs of his profession in Can. and the U. S. We give below a list of such of them as we have been able to obtain :

I. On Charbon (Carbuncle) or, as commonly called, Pustule Maligne, with numerous cases. *Med. Gaz.* 1844.

II. On Inguinal Hernia, with cases. *Med. Jour.* 1844.

III. On Acute Laryngitis, with cases. *Med. Gaz.* '45.

IV. Letters on Medical Literature. *Tessier's Med. Journal*, 1826.

V. On a plan to be adopted for the administration of medicine to obstreperous children and patients affected with tonic spasms. *Med. Intelligencer*, (Phil.) '45.

VI. On the administration of medicines by the nose in certain cases. *Med. Journal*, (Bos.) '45.

VII. On Acute Peritomtis (6 Articles). *Med. Gaz.* '45.

VIII. On Wounds of the Intestines. *Can. Med. Journal*, '52.

IX. On very pecular cases of inflamation of Appendix Vermeformis, with cases. *Journ. of Med. Science*, '47.

X. Cases (11) illustrative of the treatment of Puerperal Convulsions with extensive and interesting observations in two papers. *Northern Lancet*, 1853.

XI. On Wounds of Blood Vessels with cases. *Northern Lancet*, 1853.

NESBITT, THOMAS, T.

I. Directions de Navigation pour l'Ile de Terreneuve et la Côte du Labrador et pour le golfe et le fleuve St. Laurent. Compilées spécialement d'après les inspections faites par ordre des Gouvernements Anglais et Français. Par L'Amiral Bayfield, et les Capitaines Bulloch, Cook, Lane, Les Barres, Lockwood, Lambly et autres ; et par le Capitaine Lavand, de la Marine Française. Traduit de l'Anglais. *Québec*, 1864, pp. 203, large 4to.

" Mr. Nesbitt has supplied a want which must have made itself felt greatly and for a long time by the French Canadian navigators."—*L'Ordre*, (Mont.)

NETTLE, RICHARD. Formerly Supdt. of Fisheries L. C.

I. The Salmon Fisheries of the St. Lawrence and its Tributaries. *Montreal*, 1857, pp. 144, 12mo.

NICKALLS, JAMES, Jr. An U. C. Barrister.

I. Statutes of Upper Canada. Together with such British Statutes, Ordinances of Quebec, and Proclamations, as relate to the said Province. Revised. *Kingston*, 1832.

NICOLLS, *Rev.* JASPER H. *D. D.* A Clergm. of the Ch. of Eng. Is Principal of, and Prof. of Classics in Bishop's Coll., Lennoxville, L. C,

I. The End and Object of Education ; a lecture. *Montreal*, 1857.

II. Address to the Convocation of Bishop's College, at its annual meeting. *Sherbrooke*, 1860, pp. 21.

NOBLE, *Capt.* A., *R. A., F. R. A. S.*

I. Monthly Meteorological Register at Quebec. By Capt. Noble and Mr. W. D. C. Campbell, *Can. Journ.* 1854-5-6.

II. Mean Results of Meteorological Observations taken during the winter of 1853-4. *Trans. Lit. His. Soc.* (*Que.*) 1855.

III. On the value of the Factor in the Hygrometric Formula. *Can. Journ.* 1856.

NOBLE, *Rev.* LOUIS L.

I. After Icebergs with a Painter; A Summer Voyage to Labrador and around Newfoundland. *New York.* 1861, pp. 326, 12mo.

"Mr. Noble has a painter's eye and a poet's soul. His voyage carried him among the grandest coast and water scenery of our western world, and his descriptions reproduce what he saw with singular vividness. The volume is made still more attractive by engravings of a high order of excellence."—*N. A. Rev.*

NOEL, MRS. J. V. A Can. authoress. B. in Irel. Emigrated to Can., in 1832, whence in a short time she removed to the Southern States, residing some years in Savannah. Here she was eminently successful in conducting a seminary for young ladies. In 1847, she returned to Can., and has since resided at Kingston, U. C. Mrs. N's. literary talent early manifested itself, and some of her writings elicited the praise

of literary people in the C native country. She has ries and tales for various both in Can. and the U. S.

I. The Abbey of Rat other tales. *Kingston*, 18: 12mo.

" These tales are three in nu in very choice and elegant la Abbey of Rathmore is a tal Rebellion full of stirring incider story of the series, Madeline Be also of deep interest, and the c scenery as the characters pass and Scotland into Italy, are stri tiful. In the third story of Gr or, the Slave's Revenge, the sc Southern States of the Union, illustrates southern life and instructing in the impending c the impression made upon t intelligent and observant str peculiar institutions of the sou closes with some very prettily-light Thoughts, by Miss Ellen ? sesses much of the charmin talent of her mother."—*Daily*

II. The Cross of Pride ; *Ill. News*, 1863.

" There is displayed in thi literary taste both in its cc execution which entitle it to than the majority of the no blished."—*Herald and Advertii*

III. The Secret of S *Sat. Reader.* (*Mon.*) Vol. I.

NORRIS, *Rev.* R. Missionary F. P.

I. A Candid Discussion cipal Tenets of the Romar *John, N. B.*, 1806, pp. 114,

NORTON, *Rev.* ROBERT.

I. Maple Leaves from the grave of Abraham I *Catharines*, 1865, pp. 40, 8v

(See *Burns*, Rev. R. F.)

NOTMAN, JOHN.

I. The Law and Practic Controverted Parliamenta in the Province of Cana 1863, 8vo.

NUTTALL, THOMAS, *A. M., F. .*

I. A Manual of the Or the United States and of C Birds. *Cambridge* 1834, 12 12mo.

II. The North American Sylva; or, a Description of the Forest Trees of the United States, Canada and Nova Scotia, not described in the work of F. Andrew Michaux, and containing all the Forest Trees discovered in the Rocky Mountains, the Territory of Oregon, down to the shores of the Pacific, &c., (Illustrated by 112 plates.) *Philadelphia*, 1849, 3 vols. R. 8vo.

O.

O'BRIEN, GODFREY S., *P. L. S.*
  I. The Tourist's Guide to Quebec. *Quebec*, 1864, pp. 70, 4to.

O'BRIEN, J. W.
  I. Excursion aux Provinces Maritimes. Impressions de Voyage. Par le correspondant du *Canadien*. *Québec*, 1864, pp. 52.

O'CALLAGHAN, EDMUND B. *M. D., LL. D.* An Am. historian. B. in Irel. Prior to the Rebellion in Can. in 1837, held a prominent position in L. C.; was a mem. of Parliament, and ed. of the *Vindicator* (Mont.) After the uprising, in which he participated, he fled to the U. S., where he has since resided, and has devoted himself principally to literary pursuits. He has published many valuable and interesting works bearing on the early history of the State of N. Y., of which the principal is *The Documentary History of the State of New York*. 4 vols., 1849-51.

  I. Jesuit Relations of Discoveries and other Occurrences in Canada and the Northern and Western States of the Union. From the Proceedings of the New York Historical Society. *New York*, 1847, pp. 22, 8vo.

  (See *Martin, R. P.*)

O'CONNOR, PATRICK.
  I. The Arabian Art of Taming and Training Wild and Vicious Horses. *Dundas, U. C.*, 1857.

OGDEN, *Hon.* C. R. For some years Atty. Genl., Isle of Man. D. 1865.
  I. Petition of Charles Richard Ogden, Esq., late Attorney General of Canada, to Her Majesty. *Liverpool*, 1860, 8vo.

OGDEN, J. C.
  I. Tour through Upper and Lower Canada. *Wilmington, U. S.* 1800, 12mo.

O'GRADY, *Rev. Dr.* WILLIAM J. A priest of the R. C. Ch. Ed. the *Correspondent* (Tor.,) with which, in 1834, was incorporated the *Advocate*, which latter paper had been previously owned and ed. by M. L. Mackenzie.

OLIVER, M. H., *M. D.* A Can. journ. B. at Bayswater, Lon., 1826. Was one of the original contributors to *The Man in the Moon*, ed. by the late Albert Smith, and to other Eng. periodicals. Was for sometime connected with the *Sun* (Lon.) Wrote a *Handbook to Lowestoft*, in 1849. In following year commenced the publication of *The East Anglican Record*, a monthly narrative of local events (Lowestoft,) which was one of the first attempts to establish an unstamped newspaper in Eng. Came to Can. in 1854. Was ed. and publisher of the *Star*, (Paris, U. C.) from 1855 to 1858. Established the *Erie News*, (Simcoe,) in 1858, which he subsequently disposed of. Ed. the *Times*, (Ham.) in 1860, and in following year undertook the ed. control of the *Freeholder*, (Cornwall,) which he relinquished in 1865 in order to practise his profession.

OLIVER, W. S.
  I. Lecture on the Social Evil, delivered to the men of the 60th Rifles, March 7, 1862. *Quebec*, 1862, pp. 20.

OLIVIER, *Hon.* L. A., *Q. C.* A Can. Senator.
  I. Essai sur la Littérature du Canada. *Rép. Nat.*
  II. Le débiteur fidèle. *Do.*

O'LOUGHLIN, *Rev.* A. J. Incumbent of Sydenham, C. W.
  I. Man, a Material, Mental and Spiritual Being; a lecture. *Kingston*, 1860, pp. 66.

O'MEARA, *Rev.* FREDERICK A., *LL. D.* A Min. of the Ch. of Eng., (Port Hope, U. C.,) In addition to the following is the author of several tracts in the Ojibwa language.

I. A Translation of the Book of Common Prayer, in the Ojibwa language. Published by the Society for Promoting Christian Knowledge. *Toronto*, 1853, pp. 628. d. 12mo.

II. A Translation of the New Testament·into the same language. *Do.* 1854, pp. 766, d. 12mo.

III. A Short Account of the Missions of the Church of England, among the Ojibwa and Ottahwah Indians of Lakes Huron and Superior. *London.*

IV. American Philology; a review of Schoolcraft's large work on the Indians of N. A. *Can. Journal.* 1858.

The two following translations were made by Dr. O'M., in conjunction with the late Rev. Peter Jacobs :—

IV. A Translation of the Five Books of Moses, commonly called the Pentateuch, into the Ojibwa language. *Toronto.*

V. A Hymn Book for the use of Ojibwa Indian Congregations of the Church of England. *Do.*

O'REILLY. *Father.* A R. C. Clergym. in N. S. Now d. ·

I. The Letters of Hibernicus. Extracts from the pamphlet entitled: *A Report of the Committee of St. Mary's, Halifax,* and a review of the same. *Pictou,* 1842, pp. 160, 8vo.

ORONHYATEKHA. A Mohawk Indian.

I. On the Grammatical Structure of the Mohawk Language. *Can. Journ.* 1865.

ORROCK, *Rev.* J. M. A writer on religious topics. B. at Murchall, Linlithgowshire, Scot., 1830. Has resided in Can. from an early age. Ordained to the ministry of the Second Advent Conference, 1851. Has contributed many articles to the *Advent Herald* (Bos.,) and was joint ed. of the *Millennial News* (Mont.) Since 1865 has been ed. of the *Youth's Visitor* (Bos.) Resides at Waterloo, L. C.

I. The Hope of the Church ; a tract. *Boston,* 1852.

·II. The Glory of God Filling the Earth. *;Do.,* 1853.

III. The Return of the Jews. *Do.,* 1854.

IV. The Army of the Great King ; short sermons on short texts; miscellaneous pieces and poetic musings. *Do.,* 1855, pp. 224.

" The Army of the great King is an allegorical sketch of the Church in the world. The short sermons are pithy and evangelical. The miscellaneous pieces are all of a practical character, whilst the poetical musings evince respectable poetical talent in their author."—*Can. Rev.* (Mont.)

V. Our Position ; a tract. *Do.,* 1856.

VI. Jerusalem in Gloom and Glory, with a review of the Rev. G .B. Bucher's " Objections to Error." *Do.,* pp. 48.

OSSAGE, F. M. F.· An associate prof. in Jacques Cartier Normal Sch. (Mont.)

I. Les Veillées Canadiennes ; traité élémentaire d'agriculture, à l'usage des habitans Franco-Canadiens. *Québec.* 1852, pp. 150.

II. Nouveau Système de Comptabilité Agricole ; ou méthode sûre et facile pour bien gérer les opérations d'une ferme. *Montréal,* 1853, pp. 35.

OSUNKHIRHINE, *Rev.* P. P.

I. Metaphysical Inquiry, deducing many self-evident truths from the very nature of things of what God's nature and will require. 1857.

OUELLET, *Rev.* M. R. A French Can. priest.

I. Mouseigneur Hughes (Etude) *Rev· Can.* 1864.

II. Le Cardinal Wiseman. *Do.* 1865.

OUTRAM, JOSEPH.

I. Nova Scotia; its Condition and Resources. *Edinburgh,* 1850, pp. 35. 16mo.

II. A Handbook of Information for Emigrants to Nova Scotia. *Halifax,* 1864, pp. 36, 8vo.

OWEN, C. B. A mem. of the Legislature N. S. Contributed to *Simmond's Col. Mag.* (Lon.)

I. Epitome of the History, Statistics &c., of Nova Scotia. By a Nova Scotian. *Halifax,* 1842, pp. 147, 12mo.

OWEN, *Prof.*

I. On a Fossil embedded in a mass of Pictou Coal. *Geol. Journ.* (Lon.) 1853.

P.

PACKARD, A. S., Jr.

I. A list of Animals dredged near Caribou Island, Southern Labrador, during July and August 1860. *Can. Nat.*, 1863.

PAINCHAUD, A., *M. D.* (Que.)

I. Cours de Lecture sur l'univers. *Rep. Nat.*, 1850, pp. 98.

PAINCHAUD, *Rev.* CHARLES FRANÇOIS. A R. C. clergym. in Can. B. on Crane Island, L. C., 9 Sept. 1783. D. at Ste. Anne de la Pocatière, L. C., 9 Feb. 1838. In 1814 was appointed *curé* of the latter place, where he founded the Coll. of St. Anne. He was the author of several canticles, and left behind him in *MS*. " *Remarques sur la philosophie du Comte de Bonald ; des observations sur les théories du Comte de Maistre.*"

Eloge de Messire C. F. Painchaud, Fondateur du Collége de Ste. Anne, suivi de diverses notices sur la vie de ce digne prêtre, (with portrait.) Par Charles Bacon, élève de philosophie.—*Ste. Anne de la Pocatière*, 1863, pp. 96, 8vo.

PALLISER, *Capt.* An Eng. Explorer.

I. Papers relative to the Exploration by Capt. Palliser, of that portion of British North America which lies between the Northern Branch of the River Saskatchewan and the frontier of the United States, and between the Red River and Rocky Mountains, (with map and geological plates.) *London*, 1859, Folio.

II. Report of his Exploration on the River Saskatchewan, and between the Red River and the Rocky Mountains. (With Maps.) *Do.*, 1860, Folio.

III. Journals relative to the Exploration of that portion of British North America between Lake Superior and the Pacific Ocean. (With map and many geological sections.) *Do.*, 1863, Folio.

PALMER, H.

I. On the application of localized Galvanism in the treatment of disease. *Toronto*, 1863, pp. 48.

PALMER, JOHN.

I. Journal of Travels in the United. States of North America and Lower Canada, performed in the year 1817 : containing particulars relating to the prices of land and provisions, remarks on the country and people, interesting anecdotes, and an account of the commerce, trade and present state of Washington, New York, Philadelphia, Boston, Baltimore, Albany, Cincinnati, Pittsburg, Lexington, Quebec, Montreal &c. To which are added a description of Ohio, Indiana, Illinois and Missouri, and a variety of other useful information, &c., (with a map.) *London*, 1818, 8vo.

PANET, JEAN CLAUDE.

I. Journal du Siége de Québec en 1759. *Montréal*, 1866, pp, 24, 8vo.

PAPIN, JOSEPH. A French Can. journ. and politican. B. at L'Assomption, L. C., 14 Dec. 1825. D. at same place, 23 Feby. 1862. Admitted to the Bar, 1849. President of *L'Institut Canadien*, 1847, (Mon.) He sat in the Leg. Assem. from 1854 till 1857. He was one of the ed's. of *L'Avenir*, and one of the founders of *Le Pays*, two liberal, or *Rouge* journals (Mon.,) the former of which is now defunct. As a newspaper writer he possessed great ability, though it is chiefly as a popular orator that he will be best remembered.

PAPINEAU, *Hon.* LOUIS JOSEPH. A Cau. statesman. B. at Montreal, Oct., 1789. Ed. at the Seminary, (Que.) Called to the Bar of L. C. 1811. While yet a law student, was, in 1809, returned to Parliament. Represented the west ward of Montreal for 20 years. In 1812, he became leader of the Can. Opposition party, a position which he held up to the rebellion of 1836-7. Was, from 1817, for 20 years, Speaker of the Leg. Assem. In 1820 he was elevated to a seat in the Ex. Council. In 1822 he, in conjunction with the late Mr. Neilson, was chosen as a delegate to proceed to Eng. to oppose the Imperial plan for the Union of U. and L. Can., a mission which resulted in complete success and the withdrawal of the obnoxious measure. He was the leader in the Rebellion of 1837 ; after its failure he fled to the U. S. and thence, in 1839, to France, where he resided for 8 years. On his return to Can. he was again returned to Parliament, but exercised little or no influence over parties, and, in 1854, retired altogether from public life.

I. Letter to His Majesty's Under Secretary of State, on the subject of the proposed Union of Upper and Lower Canada. By I. J. Papineau and John Neilson. *London*, 1824; 8vo.

II. Speech on the Hustings at the opening of the Election for the West Ward of the City of Montreal, 11th August, 1827. *Montreal*, 1827, pp. 48.

III. Histoire de l'Insurrection du Canada, en réfutation du rapport de Lord Durham. (Extracted from *La Revue du Progrès*, Paris.) *Burlington, Vt.*, 1839, pp. 35.

" Has nothing historical in it, but may be read as a political pamphlet."—*Bibaud Jeune.*

(See *DeBleury*, Hon. *S.*)

IV. Address to the Electors of the Counties of Huntingdon and St. Maurice, December, 1847.

".The first letter of Mr. Howe to Lord John Russell, and Mr. Papineau's Address to his constituents, also relate to the subject of ' Responsible Government.' But these two political leaders disagree. The former is its advocate, while the latter stigmatizes it as a mockery, a delusion, and a cheat."—*N. A. Rev.*

" Une immense auréole d'orateur entoure le nom de M. Papineau, mais en relisant ses discours, sans doute mal rapportés, et où d'éternelles redites ne contribuent pas peu à faire paraître interminables des phrases déjà longues par elles-mêmes, on ne conçoit de son éloquence qu'une idée bien au-dessous de l'admiration qu'elle inspirait à ses contemporains."—HECTOR FABRE : *Can. Lit.*

PAQUIN, *Dr.* J. M.

I. Questions générales sur l'Agriculture à l'usage des écoles. *Montréal*, 1859, pp. 24.

PAQUIN, *Messire. Curé* of St. Eustache, L. C., at the time of the revolt in 1837.

I. Journal historique des évènements arrivés à St. Eustache pendant la rebellion du Comté du Lac des Deux Montagnes. *Montréal*, 1838, 32mo.

PARENT, ETIENNE. A French. Can. journ. B. at Beauport, near Quebec, 2 May, 1801. Received his education at the Seminary of that city, and at the Coll. of Nicolet, at both of which he distinguished himself in Classics, Political Economy, and *Belles Lettres*. On completing his studies he retired to his father's farm, on which he had been born, to assist his parent in the arduous duties of his calling. The clear and able reputation which he had left behind him at Coll., combined with the talents for literary composition and polemical discussion which he had early evinced, and since cultivated and improved, had secured strong and influential friends in his favour, who were anxious that his talents should not be lost to the province and to his countrymen. Accordingly in his 21st year we find him installed as chief Ed. of *Le Canadien*, the oldest French newspaper in the Brit. Provinces, a position which he ably filled until 1825, when the publication of the paper was suspended. In that year he entered upon the study of the law, and after having undergone the usual clerkship, and passed his final examination, was admitted a mem. of the Bar. He did not practice for any length of time, having shortly after his admission accepted the appt. of French translator and Law Clk. to the Assem. of L. C. ; he also for a short time filled the office of Librarian to that body. On the abolition of the old constitution of L. C., his employment by the Assem. of that Province necessarily ceased, and he devoted himself entirely to the conduct of *Le Canadien*, the publication of which he resumed in 1831 and continued up to 1842. During the troublous times of 1836–37, he took sides with the majority of his countrymen, and suffered imprisonment in the Quebec Jail, for a too bold and injudicious expression of his political opinions. At the Union of the Provinces he was returned to Parliament, where he sat for some years, but resigned to accept office under the Crown. When Responsible Govt. was conceded, he received the appt. of Clk. to the Ex. Council, and, in 1847, was transferred to the office of Assist. Secy. for L. C. In 1867 he received his present office of Acting Asst. Secy. of State for Can. Since 1847 he has occasionally acted as ed. of his old newspaper, and contributed to other journals. He is now the Nestor of the French Can. press. Mr. P. writes with great ease and ability—he possesses great reasoning and argumentative powers, and with these are united a force and energy of expression which few of our public writers have possessed. In his hands *Le Canadien* became a powerful organ of public opinion, and it was owing to his long and unwearied exertions in connection with it, and the determined stand which it took that many of the reforms which have been since effected in our political system were granted. We may add that Mr. P. was the originator of French Public Lectures in L. C.

I. Pierre Bedard et ses deux fils. *Journ. de l'Inst. Pub.*, 1859.

"An excellent biography, from the pen of one of our first writers, and of one of those who have given the most powerful start to the literature, and we might say to the intellectual revival of Lower Canada."—Hon. P. J. O. Chauveau.

II. L'Industrie considérée comme moyen de conserver notre Nationalité. A lecture delivered before *L'Institut Canadien*, Montréal, 1848. Republished in *Rép. Nat.*

III. Importance de l'Etude de l'Economie Politique. *Do.*

IV. Du Travail chez l'Homme. *Do.* 1847.

V. Du Prêtre et du Spiritualisme dans leurs rapports avec la Société. *Do.* 1848.

VI. Considérations sur notre système d'Education Populaire, sur l'Education en Général, et les moyens Législatifs d'y pourvoir. *Do.* 1848.

VII. De l'Importance et des Devoirs du Commerce ; a lecture. 1852. Repub. in *Lit. Can : Le Foy. Can.*

VIII. De l'Intelligence dans ses Rapports avec la Société ; a lecture before *l'Institut Canadien*, Quebec, 1852. *Do. do.*

IX. Ditto. 2nd Part, 1852. *Do. do.*

X. Considérations sur le sort des Classes Ouvrières ; a lecture, 1852. *Do. do.*

"When Mr. Rameau was in Quebec, I took occasion to ask him what he thought of our best writers. 'Sir,' said he, 'I will relate to you what occurred to me in Paris last winter. I was acquainted with Canadian literature before I came here, and in order to test the correctness of my own opinion, I assembled some literary friends and told them that I intended reading them a chapter out of two new books which they had never seen before ; they assented ; this done, and replacing the books in my book case, I requested them to tell me candidly where they could have been written. 'Why in Paris, where else,' they replied ; ' none but Parisians could write such French.' Well, gentlemen, said I, you are much mistaken, these books were written on the banks of the St. Lawrence, at Quebec, Etienne Parent and Abbé Ferland are the authors. My friends could scarcely be convinced of the fact.' I take pleasure in recording this, as both the works alluded to are re-published in the New-Year Volume, presented to subscribers, by the publishers of the *Foyer Canadien*, and because such a circumstance does honor to the country. I take particular pleasure in noticing this honorable fact, because it also effectually bears on a stupid assertion not altogether uncommon, viz : That French Canadians speak nothing but *patois*—whereas, if the whole truth were known, it would appear that our peasantry talk better French, than does one-half of the rural population of France ; in fact, it is not rare to find the French peasantry of one Department, scarcely able to understand the idiom of the corresponding class in another Department."—J. M. Lemoine: *Maple Leaves.*

"Auprès de nos historiens, supérieur à eux par l'étendue et la force de son esprit, se place le premier de nos publicites, M. Etienne Parent, journaliste, et journaliste toujours en vue pendant trente ans, ses écrits touchent d'ailleurs à l'histoire et forment la plus solide partie de nos annales politiques. Personne n'a déployé parmi nous dans ce métier de la presse, dont les conditions sont rendues si difficiles par la passion des partis, l'intolérance des intérêts personnels, l'indifférence du public et les nécessités de l'improvisation quotidienne, personne n'a déployé des vues plus larges et plus justes, une perspicacité aussi rarement en défaut, une sagesse aussi profonde. L'inspiration nationale a été égale du premier jour au dernier. Deux œuvres de cet éminent esprit donnent à elles seules une idée exacte de sa rare puissance et de sa haute originalité. La première a pour titre : *Du Prêtre et du spiritualisme*, la seconde : *De l'intelligence dans ses rapports avec la société.* Il y a dans ces deux lectures le résumé d'une constitution sociale admirable, fondée sur les vues les plus neuves et les plus profondes. C'est là une œuvre digne de la méditation des esprits philosophiques et dont on ne comprendra que plus tard, lorsque les études et l'expérience politique seront plus avancées parmi nous, la valeur et la portée."— HECTOR FABRE : *Lit. Can.*

PARKE, SHUBAEL. An U. C. Barrister.

I. The Smuggler, a Poem. *Hamilton*. 1852, pp. 79.

PARKMAN, FRANCIS. An Am. historical author. B. at Boston, 16 Sept., 1823.

I. History of the Conspiracy of Pontiac, and the war of the North American Tribes against the English Colonies, after the conquest of Canada, (with maps) *Boston*, 1851, 8 vo., *London*, *Do.* 2 vols. p. 8vo.

II. France and England in North America—a series of historical narratives. Part I.—Pioneers of France in the New World. *Boston*, 1865, pp. 420, Part II. The Jesuits in North America in the 17th Century, *Do.* 1867. pp.

XIX—pp. 463, 8vo.

PARSONS, U., *M D.*

I. Battle of Lake Erie ; a discourse before the Rhode Island Historical Society. *Providence*, 1854, 8vo., 2nd Ed.

II. Speech at Put-in Bay, Sept., 10, 1858, the 45th anniversary of the battle of Lake Erie. (*No title page*) 8vo.

PATON, *Rev.* A. Min. of the Presb. Ch. of Can., (Mont.)

I. O Wheel ! or, Thanksgiving Thoughts ; a sermon. · *Montreal*, 1865, pp. 18.

PATRICK, ALFRED. Clk. Assist., Leg. Assembly, Can.

I. Digest of "Precedents or Decisions" by Select Committees appointed to try the merits of Upper Canada Contested Elections. *Montreal*, 1849, 8vo.

"Invaluable to all persons engaged in politics, or practising law."—*Gazette* (Mont.)

PATTERSON, *Rev.* GEORGE. A N. S. author. Pastor of the Presb. Ch. Greenhill, Pictou, N. S. B. at Pictou, 30 Apl., 1824. Ed. at the Academy there and at Dalhousie Coll. (Hal.) Was an early contributor to the press. In 1843, when only 19 years of age, became ed. of the *Eastern Chronicle* (Pictou,) a respectable country journal, which he founded in the place of 2

other papers which had previously existed there. In 1846, he terminated his connection with journalism, for a time, and proceeded to Brit. to prosecute his Theological studies for the Presb. Ch. On his return, in 1849, he was ordained pastor of Greenhill, where he has since remained. From 1850 to 1856, was ed. of a small monthly sheet, the *Missionary Register of the Presb. Ch. in N. S.*, which in the last mentioned year became enlarged to a magazine of 48 pages and assumed the name of the *Christian Instructor and Missionary Register of the Presb. Ch. of N. S.*, Mr. P. continuing to occupy the ed. chair, the duties of which he discharged with ability for the next 5 years. While holding this position he wrote a large number of essays and articles, biographical and historical, and particularly devoted himself to tracing out the histories of the early ministers of the Lower Provinces. In 1860, the Presb. Ch. and the Free Ch. of N. S. were united, and the *Instructor* ceased at the end of that year ; a new periodical, however, was established called the *Missionary Record of the Presb. Ch. of the Lower Provinces*, and Mr. P. was appointed ed. of it, cojointly with the Rev. R. Murray (Hal.) He still continues to hold that position. Mr. P. in addition to his ed. duties has found time to contribute frequently to other periodicals and journals. He is a very graceful and instructive writer, possessing a ripe experience and cultivated taste, which manifest themselves in all his productions. The services which he has rendered to the Presb. Ch. in his ed. and literary labours are incalculable.

I. A Brief Sketch of the Life and Labors of the late Rev. John Keir, D. D., S. T. P., *Pictou*, 1859, pp. 43. 8vo.

II. The Present Truth ; a synod sermon. *Do.*, 1859.

III. Memoir of the Rev. James McGregor, D. D., Missionary of the General Associate Synod of Scotland to Pictou, Nova Scotia ; with notices of the Colonization of the Lower Provinces of British America, and of the social and religious condition of the early settlers. *Philadelphia*, 1859, pp. 548, 12mo. 3 ed's.

" The authorship and the author claim a passing notice. The author is the eldest grandson of Dr. McGregor, and as for many reasons, so for engaging in such a work, he deserves to be hailed as ' A worthy son of a worthy sire.' Filial veneration and love coupled with a natural desire to preserve the memory of such a life as his grandfather's, has prompted him to undertake a work for which the churches in America and Britain will thank him, and for which they will as they ought to hold themselves his debtors. He has done for Dr. McGregor what McCrie has done for Knox, what Fraser has done for the Erskine's, what Hanna has done for Chalmers, and McGill for Dr. Heugh.

" A Presbyterian minister of a country congregation of any extent in these colonies, has barely time for his congregational duties. He has not time at all, if he were to devote that attention to the literature of his profession to which it is entitled ; otherwise he must be a slave, and would soon wear out in mind and body and be laid down in an early grave. To write a volume such as this would be a task to any man, no matter how favourably situated and well qualified by general literary culture and habits. For Mr. Patterson to write such a work, and do his other work as he does it, can only be accounted for on the principle embodied in the Italian adage *con amore*, only because he felt it to be emphatically a work and labour of love. • • • Of the varied merits and demerits of the work as a literary production, it is not necessary to write almost any thing. The subject of the work is its recommendation. The theme is the eulogy. Still there are not a few excellencies distinguishing the volume which may be simply mentioned. As in similar works of standard merit, the author makes his subject to a very great extent tell his own story. It is Dr. McGregor rather than his biographer with whom the reader has mostly to do. And then there is an utter absence of every thing like ostentation, or a straining after effect. The author leaves his story to exert its own influence, be it powerful or puny on the mind of its readers, and as a result of this mode of treatment, when proceeding on with the narrative the author is for the time being forgotten, and the only anxiety is to get from chapter to chapter, till the last page is perused and a tear suffered to fall on the honoured grave where lies the precious dust of the faithful servant, in the sure and certain hope of a blessed resurrection. • •

" As it is, the work is creditable all round— creditable to the memory of a good and a great man ; creditable to the author, both as a commanding example of filial piety and an abiding addition to our colonial literature ; creditable to the church which had such a name prominent among her fathers, and such a writer among her sons. And it will be to the further credit of the children of our people, if they put this work on the shelves of their libraries and write its contents on the fleshly tables of their hearts."— REV. ROBT. SEDGWICK : *Instructor*, (N. S.)

IV. Remains of the Rev. James McGregor, D. D. Edited by his grandson, the Rev. George Patterson. *Philadelphia* and *Edinburgh*, 1859.

" A welcome companion to the Memoirs." — *Presb. Witness* (Hal.)

V. Memoirs of the Rev. S. F. Johnston, the Rev. J. W. Matheson and Mrs. Mary Johnston Matheson, Missionaries on Tanna, with selections from their diaries and correspondence, and notices of the New Hebrides, their inhabitants and Missionary work among them. *Pictou*, 1864, pp. 504, 12mo. 2 ed's.

" It is not often the case that we feel such an interest in reading works of a biographical nature as we have felt in the perusal of this work. True it presents before us the character of those who were not distinguished by any very shining talents, and in their lives we see but few very thrilling incidents; yet there is something pervading the whole book which we can hardly describe, but which we think will make it peculiarly attractive to the heart of every true child of God. Open it in what part we may we feel that we are holding converse with one whose heart was warm with love to the Saviour, and we read but a few lines before we become sensible of corresponding emotions.

" Mr. Patterson has done a good work in presenting these biographies to the church. They will prove memorials honoring to the names of three departed servants of Christ, and creditable to the Presbyterian church of Nova Scotia.

" The work is also interesting on account of the information it imparts relative to the New Hebrides, and the work of those missionaires there.

" The author has exhibited good taste in the selection of his materials and we sincerely hope that his labours will be duly appreciated by the christian public."

PATERSON, ROBERT STEWART. B. in Belfast, Irel. Has written numerous descriptive and other poems for various journals in the Province, some of which are to be found in Dewart's *Selections*. He contemplates publishing a volume of his contributions to Canadian poesy.

PATTON, *Ven.* HENRY, *D. C. L.* Archdeacon of Ontario and Rector of Cornwall, U. C.

I. Attachment to the Church of God : a sermon. *Toronto*, 1853, pp. 24.

II. The Salaries of the Clergy ; an article from the *Church Review*; with an introduction. *Do.*, 1857, pp. 31.

PATTON, *Hon.* JAMES, *LL. D., Q. C.* A Can. lawyer. B. at Prescott, U. C., 10th June, 1824. Ed. at U. C. Coll., and at Kings Coll. (now Univ. of Toronto.) Called to the bar, 1845. In 1852, established the *Herald*, (Barrie,) a Conservative journal, which he ed. for 2 years. In 1855, in conjunction with others, founded the *Upper Canada Law Journal*, which still survives. He sat in the Leg. Coln from 1856 until 1863, and was for a short time, Sol. Gen. for U. C.

I. Canadian Constable's Assistant. *Toronto*, 1852.

PAVIE, THEODORE.

I. Souvenirs Atlantiques : Voyage, aux Etats-Unis et au Canada : *Paris*, 1833, 2 vols. *in*-8.

PECH, JAMES, *Mus. Doc. Oxon.* Served as musical critic to *Gazette*, (Mont.) in 1864–5. Now resides in N. Y.

I. An Analytical and Critical Synopsis of a Selection of Piano-Forte Literature &c., given before the Montreal Literary Club, 25th May, 1865. *Montreal*, 1865, pp. 72, 8vo.

"In addition to a very select musical *repertoire* the programme contains some melodies very gracefully written, which appeal touchingly to the public heart. The songs intituled ' The Spring' and 'The Streamlet,' prove that Dr. Pech is not only a musician, but a poet ; and a poet of no mean order either. The imagery is appropriate, the sentiments peculiarly affecting and the poetry harmoniously strung and highly rythmical."—S. P. DAY.

PEDLEY, *Rev.* CHARLES. A Min. of the Congregational Ch. Can. B. in Staffordshire, Eng., 1820. Studied for the Ministry at the Independent Coll. Rotherham. Pastor at Chelsea-le-Street, 1848. In 1857 emigrated to St. John's, Newfoundland, to take charge of the Congregational Ch. in that city, and while residing there undertook, at the suggestion of the then Gov., Sir Alexander Bannerman,

to overlook the public archives with the view of preparing an authentic history of the Colony. In 1864 Mr. P. came to Can., and is now officiating at Cold Springs, near Cobourg, U. C. Has contributed to the *Eclectic* (Lon.)

I. The History of Newfoundland, from the earliest times to the end of 1860. (With map.) *London*, 1863, pp. 531, 8vo.

" This growth of a colony in less than three centuries is illustrated and supported in the present volume by copious details, extracted from official records preserved in the archives of the Island. The work derives from them an authentic character which enhances its value. It is a faithful and interesting picture of the exertions by which some peculiar gifts of nature, under an unpromising aspect, amidst artificial difficulties, and occasionally impaired by accidental disasters, have been steadily improved to the advantage alike of those who enjoy and of those who provide them. It is an encouraging lesson for the British public to persevere in supporting that line of colonial policy which, while it diffuses civilisation, perpetuates its blessings by the security of a well-regulated freedom and well-adjusted institutions."—*Morning Post*, (Lon.)

PELLETIER, *Rev.* THOMAS BENJAMIN. A R. C. priest. B. at Kamouraska, L. C., 8 June, 1807. D. at Levis, L. C., 25 April, 1865. Ed. at Quebec and at the Coll. of Nicolet. He studied law, but eventually entered the Ch. and was ordained priest in 1837. He had been *Préfet des Etudes* at St. Anne's Coll. and director of the Coll. Masson. In 1829 he contributed some articles to the French Can. newspaper press on a proposed change in the law respecting *Fabriques*, which had the effect of doing away with the contemplated measure. He was the author of several lengthy poems, one or two of which have been published, written in the heroic-comic style. From 1861 to 1864 he was virtually the ed. of the *Gazette des Campagnes* (St. Anne,) a farmer's journal.

I. Considérations sur l'Agriculture Canadienne au point de vue religieux, national et du bien-être materiel. Par un ami de l'Education. *Québec*, 1860, pp. 50.

Notices biographiques de Messire C. Gauvreau, V. G., Ancien Supérieur du Collége de Saint Anne, et de Messire Ths. B. Pelletier, Ancien Préfet des Etudes. Avec portraits. *Ste. Anne de la Pocatière*, 1865 pp. 46.

PELTIER, ORPHIR. A French Can. poet and writer. B. 7 Sept., 1825. D. at Montreal, 1852. Ed. at the Coll. (Mont.) At the age of 22 was called to the Bar. Previous to this, however, he had studied music and eventually became organist of St. Patrick's Ch. He contributed various literary essays and poetical effusions to the French Can. press. He composed a piece of sacred music, *O Salutaris Hostia*, which was published in the *Album Musical de la Minerve*. At a tender age he had to submit to a dangerous surgical operation which, left an incurable infirmity of which he eventually died. Some of his poetical pieces are to be found in the *Rép. Nat.*, and one, *Travail et Paresse*, in *La Littérature Can.* (Que.) 1864.

" Un autre jeune poète, M. Orphier Peltier, est mort presqu'au sortir de ses études classiques. Quoique la pièce de vers que nous donnons de lui soit loin d'être parfaite, elle révèle cependant un talent poétique que l'âge et l'étude n'auraient pu que développer."—*Litt. Can.*

PENNY, EDWARD GOFF. A Can. journ. B. in Eng. Came to Can. in 1844, and immediately joined the staff of the *Herald* (Mont.) as reporter. He proved so able and efficient in that position that in a few years he was promoted to the position of joint ed., the late Mr. Kinnear being chief ed., and was admitted into the proprietorship of the paper. On the death of Mr. K. he succeeded him as chief ed. and prop. of the *Herald*, and as such still continues. Mr. P. is considered to be a clear and painstaking writer—and is undoubtedly the ablest journ. connected with the *Rouge*, or Liberal, press in Can.

I. The Proposed British North American Confederation : Why it should not, be imposed upon the Colonies by Imperial Legislation. *Montreal*, 1867, pp. 24, 8vo.

PEPPERRELL, SIR WILLIAM, *Bart.* A Brit. Genl. Commanded the troops at the reduction of Louisburg in May, 1745. He was rewarded with a Baronetcy, and, in 1759, appointed Lieut. Genl. B. at Kittery Point, Maine U. S., 1697. D. there 6 July, 1759.

I. An Accurate and Authentic Account of the taking of Cape Breton, in the year 1745 ; together with a computation of the French fishery in that part of the world. *London*, 1788, 8vo.

Sermon on the death of Hon. Sir. W. Pepperrell, Bart, by Dr. Stevens. *Boston*, 1759, 8vo.

Life of Sir William Pepperrell, Bart., the only native of New England who was created a Baronet during our connection with the Mother country. With a Plan of Louisburg. By Usher Parsons. *Boston*, 1855, 12mo ; 3rd Ed. 8vo.

PERCY, *Rev.* GILBERT, *D. C. L.* Formerly of Quebec.

I. Letter to the Rt. Rev. the Lord Bishop of Quebec, on subjects connected with Tractarianism in the Church. *Quebec*, 1858, pp. 26, 8vo.

PERKINS, SAMUEL.

I. History of the Political and Military Events of the late war between the United States and Great Britain. *New York*, 1825, 8vo.

PERLEY, HENRY F. (Hal.)

I. Gold Mines and Gold Mining in Nova Scotia. *Can. Nat.* 1865.

PERLEY MOSES HENRY. A N. B. author. B. in N. B. 1804. D. at Forteau, Labrador, 17 Augt. 1862. Ed. in his native province. In 1828 was admitted as an Atty. of the Supreme Court, and was called to the Bar in 1830. For several years was largely engaged in the milling and lumbering trade, was the means of introducing much capital into N. B., and of bringing prominently before Eng. and the U. S., the natural capabilities and resources of the province. For some time prior to the consideration of the Reciprocity Treaty of 1854, laboured with Hon. Daniel Webster and other eminent Am. and Can. public men, in collecting and compiling trade and other statistics of the B. A. colonies and the U. S., and in completing those measures which ultimately tended to the adoption of the treaty. So highly were his services on this occasion regarded, and so much were his talents and abilities appreciated by Lord Elgin, the then Gov. Genl., who negotiated the Treaty, and the Imperial Govt., that he was immediately appointed Com. under its 1st and 2nd Articles to carry out the terms of the Treaty, an office which he held up to the period of his decease. Previous to holding that office, he had filled the positions of Com. of Indian Affairs and Emigration Officer, respectively. Mr. P. was the founder of the Natural History Soc. of N. B. He was a man possessed of a thorough and extensive knowledge of the geography and resources of B. N. A.; had considerable skill as a public lecturer, and evinced a warm interest in everything having a tendency to advance the literary, scientific and general standing of his country. Mr. P. contributed to many Eug. and Am. periodicals and journals.

"We can speak ourselves, from general knowledge, of Mr. Perley's great zeal, energy, and enterprise on behalf of the Colony, of which he is a distinguished member, for during his short sojourn (just ended) in this country, to which he was officially deputed, no man labored harder to bring prominently forward the importance, the value, and the resources of the Province. In public and private, in the city and at the Colonial Office and West End, his object was to inform, suggest, and enlighten, and he had the satisfaction, after labouring most assiduously, of accomplishing the ends he had in view, by bringing to maturity several important undertakings, full and complete arrangements of which he took back with him."—*Sim. Col. Mag.* (1847.)

I. Reports on the Condition, &c., of the Indian Tribes in New Brunswick.

II. Report on the Fisheries of the Gulf of St. Lawrence. *Fredericton*, 1849.

"This Report although issued ten years ago, contains the best account of the Fisheries of the Gulf at present extant.— E. BILLINGS: *Can Nat.* 1859.

III. Report on the Fisheries of the Bay of Fundy. *Do.* 1851.

IV. Reports on the Sea and River Fisheries of New Brunswick. 2nd Ed. *Fredericton, N. B.,* 2nd Ed. 1852, pp. 294, 8vo.

"Replete with curious facts and well digested details. To the statesman and the naturalist, Mr. Perley's work equally commends itself."—*Ang. Am. Mag.* (Tor.)

V. Hand-Book of Information for Emigrants to New Brunswick. *St. John,* 1854 ; 2nd Ed. *London,* 1857, pp. 94, 8vo.

VI. Report on the Forest Trees of New Brunswick. 1847.

Published *in extenso* in *Sim. Col. Mag.* (Lon.)

VII. Observations on the Geology and Physical Characteristics of Newfoundland. *Can. Nat.* 1862.

Sporting Review, (Lon.)

I. The Camp of the Owls. 1839.

II. The Forest Fairies of the Milicetes. 1840.

III. Ottowin and Lola. *Do.*

IV. The Stream-Drivers. *Do.*

V. The Lawyer and the Black Ducks. 1841.

VI. The White Spectre of Weepemaw. *Do.*

VII. The Indian Regatta. *Do.*

VIII. The Bear and the Lumberman. *Do.*

"Mr. Perley was a man eminent for his powers of observation, and possessed a vast store of information on the physical features and resources of the maritime provinces, which he was ever ready to render useful to his countrymen. He is well known in British America, and abroad, as the author of valuable reports on the fisheries, on timber trees, on emigration, and on other subjects of public importance."—*Can. Nat.* (Mont.)

PERRAULT, JOSEPH FRANÇOIS. A French Can. author. B. about 1750. D. at Quebec, 5 April, 1844. Held the office of Prothonotary of the Court of Queen's Bench for the District (Que.) for many years. Was an earnest labourer in whatever conduced to the intellectual advancement and elevation of his country ; he was President of two societies established to promote education, and founded an elementary sch. in Quebec, which did much public good in its time. He was awarded a silver medal by the Lit. and His. Soc. of that city for his " Digested plan of general and permanent education, calculated to promote the prosperity of Can. under its present circumstances."

I. Le Juge de Paix et Officier de Paroisse pour la Province de Québec. *Québec,* 1789.

II. Lex Parliamentaria de George Pettyt, ou traité de la loi et coutume du Parlement. Traduite en Français. *Do.,* 1803, 8vo.

III. Dictionnaire Portatif et abrégé des Lois et Règles du Parlement Provincial du Bas Canada. *Do.,* 1805.

IV. Manuel des Huissiers de la Cour du Banc du Roi du District de Québec. *Do.*, 1813.

V. Questions et Réponses sur le Droit Criminel du Bas Canada. *Do.*, 1814, pp. 491, 12mo.

VI. Cours d'Education Elémentaire. *Do.*, 1822, pp. 163.

VII. Extrait ou Précédents tirés des Régistres de la Prévôté de Québec. *Do.*, 1824.

" The work appears to have been compiled with much industry and judgment, and is a curious and valuable acquisition to the libraries of our legal practitioners."—*Can. Mag.* (Mont.)

VIII. Extraits ou Précédents des Arrêts tirés des Régistres du Conseil Supérieur de Québec. *Do.*, 1825.

" It comprises a period from April 1727 to May 1759. The publication of this work, which will prove a valuable acquisition to the libraries of our professional men, affords a further proof of the active zeal of the worthy Prothonotary, who at an age when most men seek only ease and retirement, devotes his time and labour to the service of the community."—*Idem.*

IX. Traité de la Grande et de la Petite Culture. *Do.*, 1830, pp. 300.

" He appears to adduce the philosophy of his art from great experience; he teaches a judicious practice and a wholesome theory. He treats his subject with charming simplicity, and joins a clear method with such purity of language, that his work deserves a place in the ranks of standard books."—PASCALIS.

X. Plan Raisonné d'Education Générale et Permanente. *Trans. Lit. and His. Soc.* (Que.) 1831.

XI. Moyens de conserver nos Institutions, notre Langue et nos Lois.

XII. Abrégé de l'Histoire du Canada, en cinq parties. Première partie : Depuis sa Découverte jusqu'à sa Conquête par les Anglais, en 1759 et 1760. Second partie : Depuis sa Conquête par les Anglais, en 1759 et 1760, jusqu'à l'Etablissement d'une Chambre d'Assemblée, en 1792. Troisième partie : Depuis l'Etablissement d'une Chambre d'Assemblée, jusqu'à l'année 1815. Quatrième partie : Depuis le départ du Général Prevost jusqu'à celui du Comte Dalhousie. Cinquième partie : Depuis le départ du Comte Dalhousie jusqu'à

l'arrivée de Lord Gosford et la Commission Royale, en Août 1835, pour le redressement des Griefs. Dédié à l'usage des Ecoles Elémentaires. *Do.*, 1832–1836, 4 vols., 18mo.

XIII. Traité de Médecine Vétérinaire.

XIV. Code Rural à l'usage des habitants tant anciens que nouveaux du Bas Canada. *Do.*, 1832, pp. 33.

XV. Traité d'Agriculture adapté au climat du Bas-Canada. *Do.*, 1839, pp. 69.

PERRAULT, JOSEPH FRANÇOIS. A Can. writer on agriculture, &. Is grandson of the preceding. B. at Quebec, 28 May, 1838. Ed. at the Seminary there. He studied the agricultural systems of Eng., Scot., France, Germ., Italy, Switzerl. and Holland in each of those countries, and was for some time, a pupil at the Royal Agricultural Coll., Cirencester, Eng., and of the Imperial Agricultural Sch., Grignon, France. He ed. L'*Agriculteur* and the *Farmer's Journal* (Mont.,) monthly periodicals, from 1857 until 1860. In 1861 he founded La *Revue Agricole* and the *Lower Canada Agriculturist*, as the official organs of the Board of Agriculture, L. C. (of which he was for some years Secy.) and has continued to ed. them up to the present time. Sat in Leg. Assem. Can. from 1863 to 1867.

I. Compte-rendu de l'Exposition Provinciale agricole de Montréal en 1858, pp. 100.

II. Compte-rendu de l'Essai général des machines et instruments aratoires de Montréal en 1859, pp. 55.

III. Histoire du Canada, 1859, pp. 50.

IV. La Carrière Agricole, 1860, pp. 24.

V. Le Crédit-Foncier. 1860, pp. 32.

VI. Le Colonisateur, 1860, pp. 22.

VII. Compte-rendu de l'Exposition Provinciale Agricole de Québec en 1860, pp. 24.

VIII. Amendements à la loi d'Agriculture, 1860, pp. 46.

IX. Le Rapport du Ministre de l'Agriculture pour l'année 1859, 1860, pp. 40.

X. Compte-rendu d'une excursion agricole dans les Etats de l'Ouest, 1860, pp. 36.

XI. Exploration de Québec au Lac St. Jean. *Montréal*, 1864, pp. 57, 8vo.

XII. Traité d'Agriculture Pratique. *Do.* 1865, pp. 300.

XIII. Four years in Parliament. *Do.* 1867.

PERRO, B. French Teacher.

I. A B E C E D A I R E, an elementary work on the French Language. *Halifax*, 1817, pp. 38, 8vo.

PERROT, NICHOLAS. An early Can. traveller and trader amongst the Indian tribes of N. A. B. 1644. Came early in life to Can. He was ed. in Quebec by the Jesuits. He rendered considerable service to the French Govt. during his intercourse with the aborigines. D. subsequent to 1718. An excellent sketch of his life and services is given in the *Am. His. Mag.*, (N. Y.) 1865.

I. Mémoires sur les Mœurs, Coustumes et Relligion des Sauvagés de l'Amérique Septentrionale. *Leipzig* and *Paris*, 1865, pp. 341, 12mo.

"There has long existed in manuscript a work, embarrassed in style, confused in matter, but still authentic and valuable * * * written by Nicholas Perrot, towards the close of the 17th century. De la Potherie used it, Charlevoix used it, Ferland used it, Shea used it, and still it lay unpublished. It has at last appeared * * * edited by Rev. J. Tailhan, of the Society of Jesus, who has overwhelmed Perrot's 156 pages of text with nearly 200 of notes, which do not seem to us of sufficient value to have so added to the work."—*Am. His. Mag.*

PERRY, GEORGE H., *C. E.* Was on the staff of Govt. Engineers, Irel. In this country has served as an Engineer on the Great Western Railway; surveyed on the projected Ottawa Ship Canal and other important public works. Wrote lately a series of valuable and interesting articles on Defence, in the *Volunteer Rev.* (Ottawa.)

I. Lecture on the Ottawa River. *Ottawa*, 1861.

II. The Staple Trade of Canada; a lecture. *Do.*, 1862, pp. 45.

"A hasty glance at this little pamphlet convinces us that it contains matter of considerable interest. It treats of the Ottawa trade from the day when the first raft swung at its mooring at the village of Hull. (11th June, 1806,) preparatory to proceeding on its perilous voyage to Quebec, down to the present time, when lumber forms such an important item, in our exports that it is with truth called the staple of Canada,"—*Leader* (Tor.)

III. British North America at the Detroit Convention. *Do.*, 1865.

IV. River Communications of the B. N. A. Provinces. *Do.*, 1865.

PERRY, COMMODORE OLIVER H. An Am. Naval Officer. Commanded the Am. squadron on Lake Erie, Sept. 1831. where he succeeded in defeating the Brit. Naval force under Capt. Barclay. B. 1785. D. 1819.

The Life of Commodore O. H. Perry, with an appendix. By John M. Niles.—*Hartford* 1821, 2nd Ed., 12mo.

Life of Commodore O. H. Perry. By Capt. A. S. Mackenzie. With an appendix containing a reply to J. Fennimore Cooper's account of the battle of Lake Erie.—*New York*, 1840, 2 vols., 18mo.

PETERSON, C. J.

I. Military Heroes of the War of 1812, and of the War with Mexico. *Philadelphia*, N. D., 8vo.

PETIT.

I. Dissertations sur le droit public des colonies Françaises, Espagnoles et Angloises, d'après les Loix des Trois Nations, comparées entr'elles; dans la 1ère. on traite de la guerre entre l'Angleterre et ses colonies; et de l'état civil et religieux des Canadiens catholiques. *Genève*, 1778, 8vo.

PETITCLAIR, PIERRE. A French Can. dramatist and poet. B. at Quebec. D. in 1860. Was for sometime a resident of Labrador and of Gaspé. Many of his poems are republished in the *Rép. Nat.* 1848.

I. Griphon, ou Vengeance d'un Valet. Comédie. 1837.

II. Une partie de campagne, comédie en deux actes. *Québec*, 1865, pp. 61.

"Not without vivacity and wit."—*L. C. Journ. of Ed.*

Répertoire National.

I. Une Aventure au Labrador. 1848.

II. La Donation. Comédie en deux actes. *Do.*

"They lack neither spirit or originality." *Idem.*

PHELAN, *Rt. Rev.* PATRICK. R. C. Bish. of Kingston, U. C., 1862.

Life of Right Reverend Patrick Phelan, third Bishop of Kingston, to which is added a synopsis of the lives of the two first Bishops of Kingston. By the Clergyman who served Bishop Phelan's last mass. *Kingston*, 1862.

PICHÉ, E. U. Mem. of the Leg. Assem., Can., from 1858 to 1861.

I. Aux habitans du Comté de Berthier ; réponse aux injures de la *Minerve*, &c. *Toronto*, 1859, pp. 55, 8vo.

PICKARD, *Rev.* HUMPHREY, *D. D.* President of the Mount Allison Educational Institution, N. B. Has contributed occasionally to the religious press of the Lower Provinces.

I. Inaugural Address delivered on the occasion of the opening of Mount Allison Academy. 1843.

II. Sermon in honour of the Founder of the Institution on the 16th anniversary of that event. 1859.

PICKEN, ANDREW L. Was a contributor to the *Museum* in 1833 ; and to *Literary Garland*, both of (Mont.,) in 1845. In the latter wrote *Hindallah, a Metrical Romance, in 3 cantos.* D. at Montreal, 2 July, 1849.

I. The Canadas, as they at present commend themselves to the enterprise of Emigrants, Colonists, comprehending a variety of Topographical Reports concerning the quality of the land, &c., in different districts : and the fullest general information : compiled and condensed from original documents furnished by John Galt, Esquire, and other authentic sources; with a map : *London*, 1832, 8vo ; 2nd Ed. *Do.*, 1836, pp. 349, App. lxxxvii, sm. 8vo.

PICKERING, JAMES.
I. Inquiries of an Emigrant. Being the narrative of an English farmer, from the year 1824 to 1830, with the author's additions to March, 1832, during which period he traversed the United States and Canada, with a view to settle as an emigrant; 4th edition, including information, published by H. M. Commissioners of Emigration. *London*, 1832.

PICKERSGILL, *Lieut.* RICHARD. "Commander of H. M. Brig *Lion.*"
I. Track of His Majesty's Brig *Lion,*

from England to Davis' Streights and Labrador in 1776, &c. *Phil. Trans.*, 1778.

PILOTE, *Rev.* F. A French Can. priest and writer. B. at St. Antoine de Tilly, L. C., 4 Oct., 1811. Ed. at the Seminary, (Que.) Ordained priest in 1825, he proceeded to Nicolet Coll. in the same year to teach theology. In 1836 had charge of the parish of River Ouelle. In same year became lecturer on theology in the Junior Department of St. Ann's Coll., in which institution he has remained up to the present day, rising from his first position in the Coll. to the office of Vice Superior in 1850, and Superior in 1853. This latter office he resigned, in 1862, through ill-health. On the foundation of the sch. of agriculture in connection with the coll., in 1859, he proceeded to Europe to examine the various agricultural institutions and systems in France. He also visited Eng. and Irel. for the same purpose. For some years he has been chief ed. and director of *La Gazette des Campagnes.* He has contributed to other French Can. journals on subjects connected with agriculture, colonization, &c.

I. Le Saguenay en 1851 ; histoire du passé, du présent et de l'avenir du Haut Saguenay au point de vue de la colonisation. *Québec*, 1852, pp. 147.

II. Manuel des Congréganistes des Saints Anges. *Do.*, 1862.

PLAMONDON, LOUIS. A Quebec Advocate. D. many years since. Was Secy. of the *Société Littéraire de Québec*, and afterwards Vice-President of the Soc. for the Encouragement of Arts and Sciences.

I. Discours prononcé devant la Société Littéraire de Québec, à l'ouverture de la Séance du 3e Juin. *Québec*, 1809.

PLAMONDON, MARC-AURÈLE. A Quebec Advocate. Ed. and published in that city for several years *Le Menestrel*, a literary and musical miscellany. Was during its existence, ed. of *Le National*, (Que.,) a liberal journal, which he conducted with great ability and success.

20 *

PLAYFAIR, *Lieut.-Col.* A. W. A retired officer from the Brit. army. Was mem. of the Leg. Assem., Can., from 1858 to 1861.

I. The Pacific Railway on British Territory. 1852.

II. A Letter from a Volunteer of 1806 to the Volunteers of 1860, with suggestions on the defence of England, her weakness and her strength. *Montreal*, 1860, pp. 30.

III. Suggestions on the Defence of Canada, by the formation of Flank Companies from the Sedentary Militia. 1861, pp. 8.

IV. Comparison between the march of the 43rd Light Infantry, in 1837, and that of the late 104th Regiment in 1813, from New Brunswick to Quebec; also remarks on the best winter route for troops from the British Isles to Canada. 1862.

V. Suggestions on the Defence of the Canadas, on the most economical principles of blood and treasure; with an appendix on the subject of the great lakes, their defences, etc., being an article copied from the "Atlantic Monthly." *Perth, U. C.*, 1865, pp. 13.

PLAYTER, *Rev.* GEORGE. A Wes. Meth. Min. (Frankford, U. C.) Ed. the *Christian Guardian*, (Tor.,) the organ of the Meth. body, in 1844-6, and the *Prince Edward Gazette*, (Picton.) in 1847-9. Contributed many articles of interest to the *Guardian*, both before and since his ed. connection with that journal. Wrote a sketch: *Wesley as a Man of Literature:* for *Meth. Quarterly Rev.*, (N. Y.)

I. Chronological Table, shewing the names, dates and countries of the most noted of the Ancient and Modern poets, and why celebrated or remembered; also notices of the most famous Dramatic authors. 1851.

II. The History of Methodism in Canada; with an account of the rise and progress of the work of God among the Canadian Indian Tribes; and occasional notices of the Civil affairs of the Provinces. *Toronto*, 1862, vol. I.

"Mr. Playter has spared no trouble to make his work a store-house of facts, to which reference may be made by ministers and others interested in the early history of Methodism in Canada. The present volume ends with 1828."—*Globe*, (Tor.)

PLESSIS, *Mgr.* JOSEPH OCTAVE. A distinguished R. C. Prelate. B. at Montreal, 3 March, 1762. D. at Quebec, 4 Dec., 1825. Ordained a priest, 1786. Appointed condjutor in 1800, and succeeded to the bishopric of Quebec in 1806. He was called to the Leg. Coun. L. C., in 1818.

I. Discours à l'occasion de la victoire remportée par les forces navales de Sa Majesté Britannique dans la Méditerrannée, le 1er et le 2 Août, 1798, sur la flotte Française. Prononcé à Québec, le 10 Janvier, 1799. *Québec*, 1799, pp. 24.

II. Journal de deux Voyages Apostoliques dans le Golfe Saint-Laurent et les Provinces d'en bas, en 1811 et 1812. *Foy. Can.* 1865, pp. 206.

(See *Ferland*, Rév. J. B. A.)

PLINGUET, J. A.

I. Souvenirs sur les commencements de l'Union St. Joseph Montréal. *Montréal*, 1866, pp. 72.

POOLE, ALFRED.

I. On the characteristic Fossils of the coal seams in Nova Scotia. *Trans. N. S. Inst.*, 1863.

POOLE, HENRY. Engaged in mining operations at Glacé Bay, Cape Breton. N. S. Has contributed largely to the scientific literature of both the new and the old world. We give a list fo his writings:

In England.

I. Journals of Exploratory Works at the Albion Coal Mines, Pictou, N. S. *Proc. Geo. Soc.* (Lon.), 1853.

II. Meteorological Tables of Climate. Albion Mines. *British Ass.* (Liverpool), 1854, pp. 12.

III. Coal of North Western districts of Asia Minor. [Communicated by the Foreign Office]. *Journal Royal Geo. Soc.* (Lon.), 1855.

IV. Report of a Journey in Palestine, with map. *Do.*

V. Sir John Richardson's Remarks on fish obtained by H. Poole, from Asia Minor, Palestine and the Dead Sea. *Do.*, 1856.

Mr. P. was the first person who saw fish (*Sebias Cyprinodon*) swimming in the Dead Sea, at two distinct places upwards of 20 miles apart—Em Barjeck and Ain Terebeh.

VI. Exploration of Dead Sea. *Do.*, 1857.

VII. Observations with the *Ancroid Metallique* during a tour through Palestine and along the shores of the Dead Sea. *Brit. Ass.* (Cheltenham,) 1856.

VIII. Letters in *Mining Journal.* (Lon.)

  I. Explosions in Collieries 1857.

  II. Relative value of Nova Scotia coals. 1858.

America.

I. Contributions to *Eastern Chronicle.* (Pictou.)

  1. Statistics of snow storms at Albion Mines. 1851.

  2. Periods of Vegetation and yield of crops at do. 1852. [Reprinted in Dawson's Agriculture in N. S.]

II. On the advantage of Local Museums of Practical Geology. *Trans. Lit. and Scien. Soc.* N. S., 1859.

III. Observations to explain table of Mean Temperature of 10 years, Albion Mines. *Smis. Inst. Trans.* (Washington), 1860.

IV. Notes on Coal Field of Pictou, N. S. *Can. Nat.*, 1860.

V. Report on Nova Scotia Gold Fields. *Halifax*, 1862.

VI. On Characteristic Fossils of different coal fields. *Trans. N. S. Inst.*, 1863.

POOLE, THOMAS W., *M. D.*

  I. Sketch of the Early Settlement and subsequent progress of the Town, and County of Peterboro'. *Peterboro'*, *U. C.* 1867, pp. 150.

POPE, *Hon.* W. H. Ed. of the *Islander*, (Charlottetown.) Has held the office of Colonial Secy., P. E. I.

  I. Address on Confederation before Charlottetown Library and Debating Society. *Charlottetown*, 1865.

  II. The Confederation Question considered from a Prince Edward Island point of view. *Do.*, 1866.

PORTEOUS, *Rev.*, WILLIAM. A Presb. min. B. at Napan, Miramichi, N . B., 17 Oct., 1837. D. at Glasgow, Scot. 28 Nov., 1864. Was the son of parents who emigrated

from Lockerby, Dumfriesshire. Ed. in N. B. and at Lockerby. Obtained a Bursary from the Scotch National Ch. in N. B. for 8 years, and enrolled himself as an Arts Student at Glasgow Univ., attending Greek and Latin classes. In 1855, he went to Edinburgh, and, in 1858, became a student of Theology. In 1861, he gained the first prize for an essay *On the Adaptation of Christianity to the Wants of Man*, and in the following year obtained another prize for an essay *On the Nature of Faith.* Being licensed as a preacher in 1862, he was for some time assist. to the Rev. R. Archibald, Monkland, formerly of N. B. In 1863 was appointed min. of Inellan. In 1864 was elected min. of Bellahouston, near Glasgow, but in consequence of opposition from some of the congregation was not inducted.

  I. Sermons by the Rev. W. Porteous, edited with Memoir by the Rev. Alfred

  II. Newwere. *Glasgow and London*, 1865, 12mo.

PORTEN, *Rev.* W. G.

  I. Christ and the Church ; a sermon *Sydney C. B.* 1843, pp. 24, 8vo.

POUCHOT, M.

  I. Mémoires sur la dernière Guerre de l'Amérique Septentrionale entre la France et l'Angleterre. Suivis d'Observations, dont plusieurs sont relatives au théâtre actuel de la guerre, et de nouveaux détails sur les mœurs et les usages des Sauvages, avec des cartes topographiques. *Yverdon*, 1781, 3 Vols. in-12.

  "A modest and valuable work."—J. G. SHEA.

  "This work relates to the War in Canada from 1754 to 1760. The author was commandant of the French forts at Niagara and Levis in Canada. The third volume is devoted to a topographical account of what was at that time called Canada."—RICH.

POUTRÉ, FÉLIX.

  1. Souvenirs d'un prisonnier d'Etat Canadien en 1838. *Montréal*, 1861, pp. 68.

  Also published in Eng.

PRENTISS, S. W. Ensign 84th Regt.

  1. Narrative of a Shipwreck on the Island of Cape-Breton, in a voyage from Quebec, 1780. *London*, 1782, 12mo.

" An interesting narrative, related with moderation and good sense; several times reprinted."—Rich.

PRESCOTT, Miss HENRIETTA. Daughter of Capt. Prescott, Gov. of Newfoundland, in 1834.

I. Poems written in Newfoundland. *London*, 1839, 12mo.

PRESTON. T. R.

I. Three year's residence in Canada. from 1837 to 1839. *London*, 1840, 2 Vols. 8vo.

PREVOST, *Lieut. Genl. Sir* GEORGE, *Bart.* Was Gov. Genl. and Commander in Chief in B. N. A. from 1811 to 1815. B. 19 May, 1819. D. 5 Jany, 1816.

The Letters of Veritas, re-published from the Montreal Herald; containing a Succinct Account of the Military Administration of Sir George Prevost, during his Command in the Canadas; whereby it will appear manifest, that the merit of preserving them from conquest, belongs not to him : *Montreal*, 1815, pp. 157, 8vo.

The following work was written in answer to the preceding one :

The Canadian Inspector, No. 1, containing a Collection of Facts, concerning the Government of Sir George Prevost, in Canada: *Montreal*, 1815, pp. 80, 8vo.

Some Account of the Public Life of the late Lieut. Genl. Sir George Prevost, Baronet; particularly of his services in the Canadas; including a reply to the strictures on his military character, contained in an article in the Quarterly Review for Oct., 1822. *London*, 1823, pp, 197, app. 92, 8vo.

Attributed to E. B. Brenton, Esq., who was assist. secy. to Sir George Prevost.

" This pamplet was published in consequence of an article in the *Quarterly Review* (XXVII. p. 405), on the Campaigns in the Canadas in which all the misfortunes that happened to the English on the Lakes are attributed to Gen. Prevost. The charges against him were, it seems, principally made in the 'Letters of Veritas,' originally published in a weekly paper printed at Montreal, which the reviewer says, within a small compass. contains a greater body of useful information upon the compaigns in the Canadas than is any where else to be found."—Rich.

(See *Christie, R.*)

PREVOST, *Rev.* MICHEL.

Notice sur la vie et la mort de M. Michel Prévost, prêtre du Séminaire de St. Sulpice, Curé d'Office de Montréal [with portrait.] *Montréal*, 1864, pp. 126, 12mo.

PRIEUR. F. X.

I. Notes d'un condamné politique. *Soir. Can.* 1864, pp. 236.

PRIME, BENJAMIN YOUNG, *M. D.* (N. Y.)

I. The Patriot Muse, or Poems on some of the principal events of the late war; together with a poem on the Peace. Vincit amor patriæ : By an American Gentleman. *London*, 1764, pp. 94, 8vo.

II. Columbia's Glory, or British Pride Humbled ; a poem on the American Revolution : some part of it being a parody on an ode intituled : Britain's Glory, or Gallic Pride Humbled ; composed on the capture of Quebec. A. D. 1759, 1791.

PRITCHARD, JOHN.

I. Petition of John Pritchard, of the Red River Settlement. *London*, 1819, pp. 8, Fol.

PROCTOR, JOHN J. A Can. poet. B. at Liverpool. Eng. 1833. Ed. at Sedbergh. in Yorkshire, and passed 2 years at Cambridge. Came to Can. in 1856. Was for some time a teacher in the Junior Dept. of the Univ. of Bishop's Coll., Lennoxville L. C. Has written in prose and verse for various newspapers in the Province, principally, for the *Gazette* (Mont.) Wrote the *Essays of a Ragged Philosopher* in the *Freeman* (Sherbrooke.) Some of his pieces are to be found in Dewart's *Selections.*

I. Voices of the Night; and other poems. *Montreal*, 1861, pp. 118, 8vo.

" Mr. Proctor is a disciple of Tennyson. and the tone and style of the master is almost everywhere apparent in this volume. A large—we had almost said too large a—part of the book is given up to lamentation over the loss of loved ones. There is scarce a merry note in the whole of it. One seems almost to hear a plaining voice even in its most nearly blythe strains, and in parts vent is given to the wildest anguish, the maddest despair. * * *

" Mr. Proctor has great command of good English. a marvellous skill in versification—nor lacks he a goodly portion of that gift which must be born with the poet. which can be brought out by no toil. Almost every where the verses are more than verse—they are vivified with the soul of poetry, and when he casts off the dark shadow which tinges so much of his song and comes out into the healthful light of the working day he sings cheerily enough. Witness his 'Warnings,' and the 'Parody' upon 'A Life on the Ocean Wave,'

"We can heartily commend the book to our readers. We have told them its faults. They will find in it many beauties which we have perforce passed over unnoticed. Mr. Proctor's muse has been silent for some time past; but we hope not idle. We have not too many song-birds in this Canada of ours. Our forests do not seem to breed them plenteously. We would not willingly see genius like Mr. Proctor's suffered to rust."—*Gazette* (Mont.)

PROULX, *Rév. L., A. R. C.* priest. *Curé* (St. Marie de Beauce, L. C.)

I. Défense de la Religion et du Sacerdoce. *Québec*, 1853.

PROVANCHER, *Rév. L.* A French Can. Botanist. Is a priest in the Ch. of Rome, and *Curé* of Portneuf, L. C.

I. Essai sur les Insectes et les Maladies qui affectent le blé. Par Emilien Dupont. *Montréal*, 1857, pp. 38.

II. Traité Elementaire de Botanique à l'usage des écoles. *Québec*, 1858, pp. 118, 12mo.

"This is, we believe, the first of the kind ever published in Canada. It contains many useful references to the Canadian Flora, and is illustrated by 84 wood cuts."—*Jour. of Ed. L. C.*

III. Tableau Chronologique et Synoptique des principaux faits de l'Histoire du Canada, tant civile et politique que religieux, depuis sa découverte jusqu'à nos jours, avec les synchronismes de l'Histoire de France, d'Angleterre et de l'Eglise. *Do.*, 1859, pp. 100, 12mo.

IV. Le Verger Canadien, ou culture raisonnée des fruits qui peuvent réussir, dans les vergers et les jardins du Canada. (Illustrated,) *Do.*, 1862, pp. 153, 12mo ; 2nd Ed. 1864, pp. 190.

V. Flore Canadienne, ou description de toutes les plantes des forest, champs, jardins et eaux du Canada, accompagnée d'un vocabulaire des termes techniques et de clefs analytiques. [With 400 Engravings,] 1862, 2 vols., pp. 842, 8vo.

PROVENCHER dit VILBRUN, JOSEPH ALFRED NORBERT. A French Can. journ. and *littérateur*. B. at La Baie du Febvre, L. C., 6 Jany. 1843. Ed. at the Seminary of Nicolet. In 1861 left coll., entered on the study of law, and for a

time contributed to *L'Echo du St. Maurice*. In the following year established *La Sentinelle* (Three Rivers,) which he ed. This paper enjoyed but a brief existence, but was the means of bringing Mr. P. into favourable notice as a political writer. On proceeding to Montreal, during the winter of 1862-3, he was offered and accepted the position of sub-ed. of *La Minerve*, the leading organ of the Conservative party and the most influential of the French daily press in L. C. For sometime conducted *L'Echo du Cabinet de Lecture*. In Jany. 1866 succeeded as chief ed. of *La Minerve*, in which position he still remains, and has greatly elevated the position of that journal by the superior character of his writings. In 1864 was admitted to the Bar, but has never practised his profession. Mr. P. was one of the founders of *La Revue Canadienne*, in which several able contributions from his pen have appeared. He is regarded as a young man of much promise by the political party to which he belongs.

La Revue Canadienne.

I. Crédit Foncier. 1864.

II. Territoire du Nord-Ouest. *Do.*

III. Recensement Agricole du Bas Canada. *Do.*

IV. Etudes Américaines. 1866.

PRYOR, WILLIAM.

I. The Halifax and Quebec Railway considered with a view to its cost, as well as the prospective business on the Road. *Halifax*, 1851, pp. 40, 8vo.

PRYOR, WILLIAM & J.

I. Paul, no Man of our Time. A Sermon, by F. W. Krummacher, D. D. author of Elijah the Tishbite, etc. Translated from the German. *Halifax*, 1814, pp. 27, 8vo.

PURSH, FREDERICK.

I. Flora Americæ Septentrionalis ; or a systematic arrangement and description of the Plants of North America; containing, besides what have been described by preceding authors, many new and rare species, collected during twelve years travels and residence in that Country. *London*, 1814, 2 vols., 8vo.

PYCROFT, J. W.

    I. Correspondence with Government on the Construction of the Nova Scotia, New Brunswick and Canadian Intercolonial Railway. *London*, 1862, 8vo.

    Privately printed.

PYE, THOMAS.

    . I. Canadian Scenery: District of Gaspé. (With 19 lithographed sketches.) *Montreal*, 1867.

PYKE, *Rev.* J. N.

    I. The Believer Asleep in Jesus: a sermon preached in St. James' Church. Pointe à Cavagnol, on the occasion of the death of Mrs. Francis De Lesderniers. *Montreal*, 1860, pp. 11.

PYPER, JAMES.

    I. Animadversions upon Rev. John Roaf's, two sermons on Baptism. *Toronto*, 1851, pp. 37.

Q.

QUESNEL, JOSEPH. A Can. poet and dramatist. B. at St. Malo, France, 15 Nov. 1749. D. at Montreal, 3 July, 1809. Destined for the Naval service, he, at an early age, followed a sea-faring life, and visited various countries. In 1779, whilst in command of a vessel, bound for N. Y., his ship was captured by an Eng. frigate, and he, with the crew, were taken prisoners and conveyed to Halifax. After his release he proceeded to Can., where he determined to settle. He married at Montreal, and after a voyage made to explore the valley of the Mississippi, eventually fixed his residence at Boucherville, L. C. He was the author of a number of fugitive poems in his native language, many of which have been published in *Rép. Nat.*, (Mont. 1848.) He left behind him several MS. dramatic pieces. He also composed a considerable number of musical pieces, religious and secular.

    I. Lucas et Cécile. Opéra. *Québec*.

    II. Colas et Colinette, ou le Bailli Dupé. Comédie-vaudeville. *Do.* 1788. [Republished in the *Rép. Nat.*]

    III. Les Républicains Français. Comédie en prose. *Paris*.

QUINN, JOHN. Supervisor of Cullers, (Que.)

    I. Ready Reckoner for Contents of Timber. *Quebec*, 1860.

R.

RACINE, *L'Abbé* A. A R. C. clergym. (St. John's Ch. Que.)

    I. Discours à l'occasion du service solennel pour les Soldats Pontificaux qui ont succombé dans la défense du Saint-Siége. *Québec*, 1860, pp. 39.

    II. Discours prononcés à Saint Roch de Québec, au Triduum de la Société de St. Vincent de Paul. *Do.* 1865, pp. 52, 8vo.

RACINE, LOUIS JOSEPH.

    I. Souvenirs Historiques du Canada. *Montréal*, 1865, 18mo.

RAE, JOHN.

    I. New Principles of Political Economy, exposing the fallacies of the system of Free Trade, and other doctrines maintained in the Wealth of Nations. *Boston*, 1834, l. 8vo.

    "The circumstance of its publication in this country is quite accidental. The author, a native of Great Britain, informs us in his preface, that his views received their final development during a residence of several years in Canada, under a full opportunity of comparing the theories of the free trade writers with the phenomena which he witnessed in the expanding resources of the British Provinces."—*N. A. Rev.*

RAMBAU, ALFRED XAVIER. A French Can. journ. B. at Châlain d'Usore, near Montbrison, Department of Loire, France, 22 Feby., 1810. D. at Montreal, 30 Oct., 1856. Studied at the Coll. of Clermont, in Auvergne, where he greatly distinguished himself. On leaving that institution his parents sent him to Italy to complete his education, whence, on his return, impelled by the longing desire of most youths of an ardent temperament for travel and adventure, he sailed for Am. For some years he ed. a Franco-Am. journal in N. Y. In 1832 good French writers were in demand in Can., and a request having been made to the prop. of Mr. R's. paper by a leading Can. politician of the day, (Mr. Debartzch,) to obtain an ed. for a paper which he owned, led to Mr. R. taking up his residence in the Province. In addition to an honorable ambition to achieve some distinction as a writer for the press, Mr. R. was impelled to cast in his fortunes with Can, from the great interest which he felt in the history and the general affairs of a Colony which had formerly belonged to France, and whose people were largely composed of descendants of his own countrymen and compatriots. He regarded Can. in the light of a second Fatherland. We do not know the name of the paper upon which he was engaged on his arrival in Can., but in 1837–8 he ed. L'Ami du Peuple, (Mont.) On this journal he displayed distinguished talent as a writer, and soon won the confidence and approbation of the party he served. His style was pure and classic, possessing the power of conveying truth and instruction in simple and unpretending language. In discussing the momentous affairs and topics of that eventful period, he evinced great boldness and firmness in his utterances. Shortly after his marriage, Mr. R., we believe, entered on the study of the law, and was admitted to practise as an Advocate. Whether he followed his profession, or whether up to 1854 he continued to ed. any newspaper, or contribute to the press in any way, it is not in our power to state. From that year, however, up to the time immediately preceding his death, he was one of the ed's. of La Patrie (Mont..) in which position he manifested all his accustomed ability and those noble and elevated views which always characterized his writings, and which have left him so honourable and so enviable a reputation as a French Can. journ.

I. Le Bill Seigneurial exposé sous son vrai jour par le journal "La Patrie." Refutation victorieuse du rapport soumis a la Convention Anti-Seigneuriale. Montréal, 1855, pp. 31, 8vo.

"Gifted with an ardent imagination, a brilliant intellect, Rambau was one of the literary glories of Canada. If he had lived in France his name would be figuring, perhaps, to-day, in the gallery of illustrious contemporaries. * * * * *
"A flowing pen, a caustic humour; obstinacy in controversies, rendered him a precious friend and a formidable enemy. His relations were legitimatists. From his infancy he had been taught the motto 'Dieu et mon roi.' He remained faithful to it to the end of his existence. Alfred Rambau ranked himself, then, from the first in the Conservative body. He became its standard-bearer.

* * * * *

"In private life he was generous, kindly— a charming narrator; as a public man, he handled the French tongue with grace. His style clear and neat pleased his readers. The erudite found there historical allusions evincing solid information; the little enlightened habitant liked his way of telling things without pretension, but with extraordinary precision; which did not prevent him from sprinkling his compositions with light touches, pleasing and piquant according to circumstances.
"We can affirm that Alfred Rambau conduced in a very great degree to encourage here the taste for sterling French literature. If his attacks were occasionally biting, he knew how to increase the spirit by the softness of his relations. He has contended with energy in defence of his flag; he has marked his career on the press by remarkable works; he died in the midst of them. May the sod lie light upon him; and may this tribute, paid to his memory be an alleviation to the unfortunate family and the friends who have lost him."—La Patrie.

RAMEAU, ST. EDME. A French littérateur. Visited Can. some years since.

I. La France aux Colonies, Acadiens et Canadiens. Paris, 1860, 8vo.

II. Notes Historiques sur la Colonie Canadienne de Détroit. Montréal, 1861, pp. 68.

RAMSAY, *Prof.* ANDREW C., *F. R. S., F. G. S.* Local Director of the Geol. Survey of Gt. Brit.

I. On the Geological causes that have influenced the Scenery of Canada, and the North Eastern States ; read before Royal Institution, (Lon.) 1858.

II. On some of the Glacial Phenomena of Canada and the North Eastern Provinces of the United States, during the drift period. *Journ. Geol. Soc.* (Lon.) 1859.

" Although containing nothing absolutely new, this paper may be consulted with much profit, as an able *resumé* of the known facts of the subject, classified and discussed with great perspicuity."—*Can. Journ.*

RAMSAY, J. R.

I. The Canadian Lyre. *Hamilton,* 1859, pp. 126.

RAMSAY, THOMAS KENNEDY, *M. A., Q. C.* A Can. legal author. Is an Advocate of L. C., practising in Montreal, Prof. of Civil Law in Morrin Coll. (Que.,) and a Fellow of the Univ. of McGill Coll. (Mont.) He held the appt. of Secy. to the Codification Commission L. C., for some years. Of late he has been retained as Crown prosecutor before the Courts at Montreal. Was the originator of the *Lower Canada Jurist,* (Mont.)

I. The Law Reporter, or Journal de Jurisprudence. 1 Vol. *Montreal,* 1854, pp. 213.

II. Notes sur la Coutume de Paris, indiquant les articles encore en force avec tout le texte de la Coutume à l'exception des articles relatifs aux Fiefs et Censives, les titres du Retrait Lignager et de la Garde noble et bourgeoise. *Do.* 1863 ; 2nd Ed. *Do.* 1864, pp. 98, 8vo.

" We have before us a very useful little book under this title. It is a compilation of the articles of the Custom of Paris which are still in force in this Province. The book is very little larger than a catechism, and its utility may be understood when we say that it contains the basis of almost the entire code of law regulating property in Lower Canada, except in so far as special contracts are concerned."—*Herald* (Mont.)

III. Government Commissions of Enquiry. *Do.* 1863, pp. 18.

" To us it seems that Mr. Ramsay establishes satisfactorily in the *brochure* before us, that the Government may not issue Com-

missions to any but the Judges to inquire of crimes and misdemeanors affecting the liberty or lives of Her Majesty's subjects."—*Gazette* (Mont.)

IV. A Digested Index to the Reported Cases in Lower Canada. *Quebec,* 1865, pp. 428, 8vo.

" A much needed work, performed with the ability and zealous assiduity which Mr. Ramsay bestows upon all he undertakes."—*Idem.*

" Le ' Digested Index of Lower Canada Reports' est destiné à rendre d'immenses services aux praticiens du Bas-Canada."—E. L. DEBELLEFEUILLE: *Rec. Can.*

RAND, *Rev.* S. T. A Baptist Min. Is Missionary to the Micmac Indians, (Hantsport, N. S.)

I. An Historical Sketch of the Nova Scotia Baptist Association. *Charlottetown,* 1849, pp. 31, 8vo.

" A very useful and interesting document."—*Messenger* (Hal.)

II. The History, Manners, Customs, Language and Literature of the Micmac Tribe of Indians in Nova Scotia and P. E. Island ; two lectures delivered at Halifax. *Halifax,* 1850, pp. 40, 8vo.

III. The Book of Matthew translated into Maliseet language. *Charlottetown,* 1853.

IV. The Book of John do. do. *Halifax,* 1855.

V. The Ten Commandments, the Lord's Prayer, &c., do. do. *Do.* 1863.

VI. The Books of Genesis, Psalms and Acts, do. do. *Bath, Eng.*

RAND, T. H. Provincial Supdt. of Education, N. S.

I. An Address on an Outline of a System of Public Schools for the City Halifax. *Halifax,* 1866, pp. 14, 8vo.

RANKEN, *Major.* An Officer in the Royal Engineers, who was for some years stationed in Can. Killed, by the explosion of a mine at Sebastopol, in 1855. He had contributed occasionally to the Can. press on subjects of practical reforms and improvements in the Province.

I. The Experiment ; a farce, in one act. By X, author of Nothing, and properly represented by the above unknown quantity. *Quebec,* 1854, pp. 25.

II. Canada and the Crimea ; sketches of a Soldier's life. *London*, 1862, p. 8vo.

RATTRAY, A.
I. Vancouver Island and British Columbia; where and what they are, &c. *London*, 1862, 8vo.

RAWLINGS, THOMAS, *F. R. G. S.*, (Lon.)
I. The Confederation of the British North American Provinces. *London*, 1865, 8vo.

II. What shall we do with the Hudson's Bay Territory ? Colonize the Fertile Belt, which contains forty millions of acres. *Do.* 1866.

RAYMOND, *Very Rev.* J.S. A R. C. clergym. Is Vicar Genl. (St. Hyacinthe, L. C.) In 1849–50 contributed 2 series of interesting articles to the *Melanges Religieux* (Mont.) *Etude sur le moyen âge ;* and *Discussion sur la Civilisation ancienne et la Civilisation moderne ;* in 1853 another series of articles from his pen appeared in the *Courrier* (St. H.,) on *Rome et la Civilisation.* We give his various other contributions below :

I. Importance des Etudes Religieux. Vol. II., *Lit. Can : Foyer Can.*, 1864.

II. Devoirs envers le Pape ; a lecture.

III. Discours prononcé à la translation du corps de Messire Girouard. *St. Hyacinthe*, 1861, pp. 33.

IV. Discours sur la nécessité de la force morale. *Montréal*, 1865.

V. Discours sur l'amour de la vérité. *St. Hyacinthe*, 1866, pp. 47, 8vo.

Revue Canadienne.

I. Destinée Providentielle de Rome (6 articles) 1864.

II. De l'Eglise et de l'Etat, à propos de l'Encyclique du 8 decembre 1864. 1865–66.

III. Entretien sur Naples, 1866–67.

READ, H. Y. (Hopefield, U. C.) Has written for the Provincial Press on subjects connected with Agriculture, Emigration and Colonization.

I. Suggestions on the propriety and practicability of securing Colonization through the means of adoption of the Allotment system. By an Actual Settler. *Montreal*, 1865, pp. 22.

READE, *Rev.* JOHN. Ch. of Eng. min. (Potton, L. C.) In 1856, when 18 years of age, ed. the *Montreal Literary Mag.*, a monthly periodical, which was discontinued from want of support. He is the author of many fugitive and other poems, in Latin and Eng., of considerable merit, which have appeared occasionally since 1856 in the *Gazette, Transcript* and *Witness* (Mont.,) above the signature and initials of " J. F. Home", " R. J. C." and " J. R." He has also translated with success various selections from Homer's *Iliad*, and the French of Beranger; for the first named journal. He contributed a prose essay : *Our Canadian Village,* to the *Brit. Am. Mag.* (1863–4).

"His poetry contains true poetic feeling, and is replete with promise."—DEWART.

REEVES, *Hon.* JOHN. Chief Justice of the Supreme Court of Newfoundland, 1792.

I. History of the Government of the Island of Newfoundland. With an appendix, containing the Acts of Parliament made respecting the trade and fishery. *London*, 1793, pp. 167–cxvi., 8vo. A French ed. appeared in the same year.

"Though a book of small dimensions, it is by far the ablest and most reliable work on the country existing in the present day."— REV. C. PEDLEY :- *His. of Newf'd.*

According to Lowndes this gentleman was the author of a " History of the English Law, from the time of the Saxons to the reign of Philip and Mary. *London*, 2nd Ed. 1787, 4 vols. 8vo."

REID, ALEXANDER P., *M. D.*
I. An Inaugural Dissertation on Strychnia, presented to the Medical Faculty of McGill College, May 1st, 1858, prior to receiving the degree of Doctor of Medicine and Surgery. *Montreal*, 1858, pp. 39.

REID, HUGO. Formerly Principal of Dalhousie Coll., N. S.
I. Elements of Geography, adapted for use in British America. *Montreal*, 1856.

II. Remarks on University Education in Nova Scotia. *Halifax*, 1859.

RENAULT, E. Ed. of *Le Courrier du Canada* (Que.)
I. Souvenirs de ma Paroisse Natale *Soir. Can.*, 1864.

REYNOLDS, *Rev.* HENRY DUNBAR. A clergym. of the Ch. of Eng. B. in Dublin, Irel., 1820. D. at Greenock, Scot., 23 July, 1864. Called to the Irish Bar, 1842. Studied Divinity at Lennoxville, L. C., and was admitted to Holy Orders in 1834. Eventually left the Ch., and became a mem. of the U. C. Bar. Author of miscellaneous contributions to newspaper and periodical press of Irel. and Can., consisting chiefly of fugitive poems, (*Dub. Univ. Mag.*) sketches, tales, &c.

I. The Niagara Church Case; containing the whole of the Correspondence and the Comments of the Toronto press thereon, with a Preface, &c. *Toronto*, 1857, pp. 113, 8vo.

RHEES, W. J.
I. Manual of Libraries, Societies and Institutions, in the United States and British Provinces of North America. *Philadelphia*, 8vo.

RICARD, LOUIS. A French Can. writer. In 1854-5 was on the staff of *La Patrie* (Mont.,) and while acting as honorary com. from Can. at the *Exposition Universelle de Paris*, in the latter year, served as correspondent for that journal. In Dec., 1865, established *L'Echo de la France*, (Mont.,) a weekly publication, the design of which is to reproduce choice extracts from the best French authors and writers of the present day, and which, we believe, is the only periodical of the kind in Am. Is an Advocate of L. C.

RICHARDS, J. H.
I. Vancouver's Island Sailing Directions. *London*, 1861, 8vo.

RICHARDSON, *Hon.* JOHN.
Some Memorials of the Hon. John Richardson. *Kingston*, 1831.

RICHARDSON, *Major* JOHN. A Can. novelist and journ. B. near Niagara Falls, U. C., 1797. D. in the U. S. some years since. Was the son of the late Dr. Robert Richardson, of the Can. Indian Department. His youth was passed at Amherstburg, U. C., where he received his education. At the commencement of hostilities between Gt. Brit. and the U. S., in 1812, he volunteered into the 41st Regt., then serving in Can., and was present, we believe, at many of the engagements, which he afterwards described in his *History of the War*. Being taken prisoner by the enemy he was carried into the U. S., where he remained until exchanged. During the war he received his commission as an ensign in the 41st, afterwards served in the West Indies and in various parts of the Empire, and it was while so employed that he wrote the well-known novel of *Wacousta*, many of whose scenes are laid in and around his early Western home in Amherstburg. In 1835, he joined the Brit. Legion in Spain, under Sir DeLacy Evans, concerning the operations of which he has given us a narrative. For his services in Spain he received the order of St. Ferdinand. He had retired upon half pay from the 92nd Highlanders, to which gallant corps he had latterly belonged, and in Feby., 1838, returned to his native country, as the Special Correspondent of the London *Times*. In that capacity he strongly defended the public administration of the late Earl of Durham (to whose confidence he was admitted;) his views, however, being opposite to those held by the journal in question, he after some time, was relieved of his situation, by the proprietors of the *Times*. The remainder of his career seems to have been be set with troubles and difficulties. In 1840, he established the *New Era, or Canadian Chronicle* (Brockville,) a weekly journal, more literary than political, which only existed for 2 years. In that paper appeared his *Jack Brag in Spain*, a novel of whose merits the late Theodore Hook spoke highly, but which we believe, has never been published in book-form. Major R. had strong claims on the then Can. Govt., and urged his appt. to some suitable position, which was never given to him. Feeling strongly the injustice done him, he established, in 1843, at the then seat of Government, Kingston, another journal, called *The Native Canadian and Spirit of 1812*, which he devoted mainly to the discussion of politics; he was a keen Conservative and strongly hostile to the administration then in power. In this paper he offered strenuous opposition to the Cabinet. In 1845, Lord Metcalfe, obtained for him the appointment of Supdt. of the Mounted Police on the Welland Canal, which he held until the force was disbanded. Subsequently he proceeded to the U. S., where he died.

I. Wacousta ; or the Prophecy : an Indian tale. *London:* — *Philadelphia*, 1833, 2 vols., 12mo.

"The merit of this novel consists in the spirit of its historical pictures, which possess at least the consistency of truth. The writer displays no ordinary share of graphic power, and he has the rare talent of rendering a fearful battle in music. His descriptions of scenery are well executed, but unfortunately they are rare."—*Athen.* (Lon.)

"The perusal of this novel has afforded us more satisfaction than anything of the kind which has fallen within the range of our reading for many a long day. Perhaps we may have met with volumes containing a deeper seated interest, but rarely any that have united so much simplicity with eloquence of style. It will require but slender thought to perceive, by the enthusiastic ardor of the pen, that the author has been bred to a military life, and that he is a man of very superior acquirements, and possessed of intellect and taste that must render him an ornament in the tented field as well as the field of literature."—*Satirist.* (do.)

II. Ecarté ; or, the Salons of Paris. *New York,* 1829, 2 vols., 12mo ; subsequent ed.

III. Movements of the British Legion [in Spain] with strictures on the conduct pursued by General Evans. 2nd Ed., with a continuation from May, 1836, to March, 1837. *London,* 1837, 8vo.

IV. The Canadian Brothers ; or, the Prophecy Fulfilled. A tale of the late American War. *Montreal,* 1840, 2 vols, small 8vo.

"The book is eloquently and vigorously written, as all Major Richardson's novels are, and is full of startling incident."—*Lit. Garland.*

"It is not within our scope to descant on a work which has charmed us from other pursuits, but we can sincerely recommend all who wish for a faithful portraiture of events which characterized the last war between Great Britain and the United States, to read Major Richardson's graphic tale ; throughout which sound principles, manly feelings, and an intimate knowledge of human nature abound."—*Col. Mag.* (Lon.)

V. War of 1812. First series, containing a full and detailed Narrative of the Operations of the Right Division of the Canada Army. *Brockville,* 1842, 8vo.

"Written in a strain of impartial justice, which stands in favourable contrast with some of the histories which have before been written of the same events."—*Lit. Garland.*

"One great advantage which this work possesses over similar publications, is, that the narrative is authenticated by the official documents having reference to the scenes and events of the times, and which of themselves, form valuable records of the war. These documents and the narrative mutually aid one another in developing the true state of facts ; and thus placed in juxtaposition, the reader is assured that he stands on safe and unerring ground."—*Gazette* (Mont.)

VI. Eight Years in Canada, embracing a Review of the Administrations of Lords Durham and Sydenham, Sir Charles Bagot and Lord Metcalfe, and including numerous letters from Lord Durham, Mr. Chas. Buller, and other well-known public characters. *Montreal,* 1847, pp. 232, 8vo.

"Much of the present narrative is of a personal character ; but while we follow the Major in his progress and peregrinations, we are, at the same time, introduced behind the scenes, on many occasions, at Government House, particularly during the lifetime of the late Lord Durham."—*Sim. Col. Mag.*

VII. The Guards in Canada ; or, the point of honor. *Montreal,* 1848, pp. 54.

VIII. Matilda Montgomerie ; or, the Prophecy Fulfilled. *New York,* 1851, 8vo.

IX. Wau-na-gee ; or, the Massacre of Chicago : A Romance. *Do.,* 1852, 8vo.

X. The Monk Knight of St. John. 1854.

XI. Westbrook ; or, the Outlaw. *New York.*

XII. Tecumseh ; a novel.

RICHARDSON, *Sir* JOHN, *M. D., F. R. S., F. L. S.* An eminent Arctic explorer. B. at Dumfries, Scot., 1787.

I. Fauna Boreali-Americana ; or the Zoology of the Northern parts of British America : containing descriptions of the objects of Natural History collected on the late Northern Expeditions, under the command of Captain Sir John Franklin, R. N. ; (illustrated by numerous plates.) Published under the authority of the Right Honorable the Secretary of State for Colonial Affairs. (Part 1, containing the Quadrupeds.) *London,* 1829-37, 4 vols., 4to. Am. Ed. *Norwich, U. S.,* 1837.

II. Journal of a Boat Voyage through Rupert's Land and the Arctic Sea in search of Sir John Franklin, with Appendix on the Physical Geography of North America. *London*, 1851, 2 vols, 8vo.

RICHEY, *Rev.* J. A.   A min. of the Ch. of Eng., (New London, P. E. I.) Has contributed to *Ladies Repository*, and *Waverly* (Bos.), *Transcript* and *New Era* (Mont.), and to the *Sun*, *Church Record*, &c., (Hal.)

I. Poems ; by J. A. R. *Montreal*, 1857, 12mo.

RICHEY, *Rev.* MATTHEW, *D. D.*   President of the Wesl. Meth. Ch. in Eastern B. A. B. in Ramelton, Irel. When a young man emigrated to N. B., where he served for a short time as a sch.-teacher. Ordained a min. of the Meth. Ch. in 1825, and laboured for one winter in Charleston, S. C. Returning to the British Provinces he resided at Halifax, from 1832 to 1835. From 1836 to 1839 he was Principal of the U. C. Academy. He remained in Can. at various stations until 1851, when he returned to N. S. In 1849 he was appointed Acting President of the Can. Conference, and in the 3 following years President of the Conference. From 1856 to 1860, was President of the Methodist Conference of Eastern B. A. Since 1864 has laboured at Charlottetown, P. E. I. Is an eloquent and impressive preacher. Ed. for some time *The Wesleyan*, a weekly paper, published in U. C.

I. The Internal Witness of the Spirit the Common Privilege of Christian believers ; a discourse delivered at Halifax. *Charlottetown*, 1829, pp. 27, 8vo.

II. A Sermon preached for the Benefit of the Poor. *Halifax*, 1833, pp. 23, 8vo.

III. Sermon on the death of the Rev. William McDonald, late Wesleyan Missionary. *Do.* 1834, pp. 32, 8vo.

IV. A Short and Scriptural method with Antipædobaptists, containing strictures on the Rev. E. A. Crawley's Treatise on Baptism in reply to the Rev. W. Elder's Letters on that subject. Part I. *Do.* 1835, pp. 52, 8vo.

V. A Memoir of the late Rev. W. liam Black, Wesleyan Minister, Hali-

fax, N. S., including an account of the rise and progress of Methodism in Nova Scotia. *Do.* 1839, pp. 370, 8vo.

VI. Sermons delivered on Various Occasions. *Toronto*, 1840, 12mo.

VII. Two Letters addressed to the Editor of the *Church*, exposing the intolerance and bigotry of that journal. *Do.* 1843, pp. 18.

VIII. An Address at the Inauguration of the Young Men's Christian Association. *Halifax*, 1854, pp. 26, 8vo.

IX. Britain's Refuge ; a discourse preached on the first Sunday after the arrival of the intelligence of the Fall of Sebastopol. *Do.* 1855, pp. 8, 8vo.

X. A Sermon occasioned by the death of the Rev. W. Croscombe. *Do.* 1860.

XI. A Plea for the Confederation of the Colonies of British North America, addressed to the people and Parliament of Prince Edward Island. *Charlotte-town*, 1867.

" Dr. Richey is deeply impressed with the importance of Confederation, and, in language eloquent and argumentative, he urges an acceptance of the Union which is desired by our Sovereign, and is calculated to promote the interests of the subjects in this Island,—a compact, from which Dr. Richey firmly believes, ' Prince Edward Island has everything to hope, and nothing to fear.' "— *Islander.*

RICHEY, MATTHEW H.   A Barrister of N. S., and at present, Mayor of Halifax.

I. The Spirit of Popery and the Duty of Protestants, in regard to Public Education ; a lecture. *Halifax*, 1859, pp. 36, 12mo.

RICHMOND, W. HARRISON.

I. A Comprehensive System of Book-keeping by Double Entry, &c. *Montreal*, 1846.

II. A Book of Legal Forms, for the legal transaction of business, adapted to the use of Merchants, Clerks, Mechanics, Farmers, &c. *Do.* 1850, pp. 291, 8vo.

Several ed's. of this useful book have since been published.

RITCHIE, *Rev.* DAVID.

I. A Discourse delivered on the death of John Fillis, Esq. *Halifax*, 1792, pp 14, 8vo.

RITCHIE, *Hon.* WILLIAM J. Judge of the Supreme Court of N. B.

    I. The Chesapeake ; before Mr. Justice Ritchie, with his decision thereon. *St. John, N. B.*, 1864.

ROAF, *Rev.* JOHN.

    I. Two Sermons on Baptism. *Toronto*, 1850, pp. 31.

ROBB, CHARLES, *C. E.*, (Mont.)

    I. Observations on the Physical Geology of the Western Districts of Canada. *Can. Journ.* 1860.

    II. Descriptive List of the principal Canadian Timber Trees. *Do.* 1861.

    III. On the Petroleum Springs of Western Canada. *Do.* do.

    IV. Some Observations relating to the physical condition of the superficial deposits in Canada. *Can. Nat.* 1862.

    (See *Willson*, James L.)

ROBB, *Dr.* JAMES. A N. B. geologist and naturalist. B. in Scot. D. in N. B. Was for some years Prof. of Chemistry and Natural Science in the Univ. of N. B., the museum of which he founded. This collection illustrative of the geology, mineralogy and natural history of the Lower Provinces, is by far the most complete in existence. His most important published contribution was a Geological Map of N. B., which accompanied Prof. Johnston's report on that Province (1849.) In that report also appears *Notices of the Geology of New Brunswick*, from his pen.

    I. Oration delivered at the Encænia in King's College, Fredericton, June 28, 1849. *Fredericton*, 1850, pp, 16, 8vo.

    II. Report of the New Brunswick Society for the Encouragement of Agriculture, Home Manufactures and Commerce. *Do.*, 1851.

    III. An Outline of the Course of Improvement in Agriculture considered as a business, on art, and a science, with special reference to New Brunswick. *Do.*, 1856, pp. 64, 8vo.

ROBERTSON, ALEXANDER. A Can. journ. Established the *Daily Evening Herald* (Ham.,) in 1861, which lasted but for a short period. Was Ed. of the *Examiner* (Mount Forest U. C..) from 1862 to

1865. Has ed. the *Daily Times* (Ottawa,) since May 1866. As a public writer is forcible, logical and exact, and we hope ere long to see him occupying a leading position on the Can. press.

ROBERTSON, ALEXANDER, *Q. C.* A Montreal advocate. Is one of the Ed's of the *L. C. Jurist.* (Mont.)

    I. A Digest of all Reports published in Lower Canada to 18 .!. *Montreal*, 1864, pp. 514, R. 8vo.

ROBERTSON, *Rev.* JAMES, LL. D. A clergym. of the Ch. of Eng. Is Rector of Wilmot, N. S. Has been a contributor to the local periodical and newspaper press for many years. In 1835 wrote an essay *On the Application of Science to the Arts*, (*Nova Scotian*, Hal.,) which obtained a prize medal from the Mechanic's Institute of that city. In 1837, *Pastoral Conversations*, a series of papers. (*Churchman*, Lunenburg) ; in 1838, *Essays on Provincial Education* (*Times*, Hal.) ; in 1856-7 a series of *Essays on Church Government* (*Church Witness*, St. John N. B.) ; in 1858-9 *Essays on Politics and Religion* (*Examiner*, Bridgetown,) besides many fragmentary pieces in other journals and magazines.

    I. A Sermon preached at Fredericton before the Clergy of New Brunswick. *St. John*, 1832, pp. 32.

    II. A Treatise on Baptism. *Halifax*, 1836, pp. 316, 12mo.

    III. Sermon preached at St. Pauls, Halifax, before the Clergy of N. S. *Do.*, 1837, pp. 34.

    IV. The Rise and Progress of Error in the Church of Rome ; a lecture before the Protestant Alliance. *Do.*, 1859, pp. 28, 8vo.

    V. Letter to the Rt. Rev. Dr. Binney, Bishop of Nova Scotia ; containing Observations on the origin of the Synodical Movement, and a defence of the position and action of its opponents. *Do.*, 1866, pp. 38, 8vo.

ROBERTSON, *Miss* MARGARET. (Sherbrooke.)

    I. An Essay on Common School Education ; the Galt prize essay. *Sherbrooke*, 1865, pp. 26.

ROBERTSON, THOMAS JAFFREY, *M. A.* A Can. Educational author. D. at Toronto, 26 Sept., 1866, aged 62. Was

Head Master of the Normal Sch. for some years. Had served as Head Inspector of the Irish National Sch's.

I. General Principles of Language; or, the Philosophy of Grammar. *Montreal*, 1860.

Several Editions.

II. An Easy mode of Teaching the Rudiments of Latin Grammar to Beginners. *Do.*

III. Rudiments of Grammar for beginners. Do.

The above belong to Lovell's series of Can. Sch. Books.

IV. Chronological Chart of contemporaneous dates in the history of Judea, Israel, Nineveh, Babylon, Egypt, Syria, Persia, Greece, Phœnicia, Carthage, Troy and Rome. *Toronto*, 1856.

V. Grammar School Tables for parsing Latin and English. *Do.*, do.

ROBINSON, CRISTOPHER, *Q. C.* Reporter to the Court of Queen's Bench U. C. Son of the following. Is a barrister U. C.

I. Practice Court and Chambers Reports. *Toronto*, 1856-60, 2 vols. R. 8vo.

II. Reports of Cases decided in the Court of Queen's Bench, containing the cases determined, with a table of the names of cases argued and a digest of the principal matters. *Do.*, 1857-66, 12 vols. R. 8vo.

ROBINSON, *Sir* JOHN BEVERLY, *Bart.*, *C. B.*, *D. C. L.* Late Chief Justice of U. C. Was the son of a Brit. Officer who served in the first Am. Revolutionary war, and afterwards came to reside in the B. Colonies. B. at Berthier L. C. 26 July, 1791. D. at Toronto, 31 Jany. 1862. Sat for 18 years in the Legislature of U. C. Was Atty. Genl. of that Province for a lengthened period. Appointed Chief Justice in 1829. Received the degree of D. C. L. from the Univ. of Oxford.

I. Charge to the Grand Jury, at Toronto, Thursday, March 8th, 1838, at the Trial of Prisoners for High Treason. *Toronto*, 1838, 8vo.

II. Correspondence between the Right Hon. Sir R. W. Horton, Bart., and J. B. Robinson, Esq., Chief Justice of Upper Canada, upon the subject of a pamphlet intituled ; " Ireland and Canada." *London*, 1839, 8vo.

III. Canada, and the Canada Bill; being an examination of the proposed measure for the future Government of Canada; with an introductory chapter containing some general views respecting the British Provinces in North America. *Do.*, 1840, pp. 223, 4to.

" The main object of Judge Robinson, in this calm and able *brochure*, is to prove that the division of the Canadas into Upper and Lower Provinces, has been extremely beneficial to the valuable province of which the learned author is a native, and that the reunion of the provinces could not cure existing evils—while many ills would flow from the measure. The subject requires an elaborate article, and Judge Robinson's station and character will command a wide perusal of his opinions.—*Col. Mag.*, (Lon.)

IV. Annual Address as President of the Canadian Institute. *Can. Journ.* 1854.

V. Do. do. *Do.*, 1855.

VI. Correspondence of a recent date, between Sir J. B. Robinson, Bart., and Henry Allan, Esq., late Judge of the London District Court. *Do.*, 1857, pp. 8.

(See *Sewell*, Hon. J.)

ROBINSON, *Sir* JAMES LUKIN, *Bart.* Eldest son of the preceding, whose title he succeeded to. Is Surrogate Clk. (Tor.)

I. Upper Canada King's and Queen's Bench and Practice Court Reports, from Michaelmas Term, 3 Will. IV, to Easter Term, 2 Vic. *Toronto*, 1850-55, 3 vols., R. 8vo.

In continuation of Reports in the *U. C. Jurist.*

II. Upper Canada Queen's Bench and Practice Court Reports. *Do.*, 10 vols., R. 8vo.

III. Reports of Points of Practice, &c., determined in Chambers by the Judges of the Court of Queen's Bench and Common Pleas. *Do.*, 1851, 2 vols., 12mo.

IV. Reports of Cases determined in the Practice Court and Chambers ; with points of pleading and practice determined in the Courts of Queen's Bench and Common Pleas. *Do.*

(See *Harrison*, R. A.)

ROBINSON, *Major.* Royal Engineers.
I. A Narrative of a Survey by the British Commission of the Boundary between the British Possessions in

North America and the United States. *Corps' Papers Royal and East India Company's Engineers.* Vol. I, 1849-50.

II. Explanations of the Operations for marking the Boundary. *Do.*, do.

ROBINSON, *Rev.* STUART.
I. Discourses of Redemption, as revealed at "Sundry times and in divers manners." *Toronto*, 1866, 8vo.

ROBSON, *Rev.* JAMES. A Presb. Min. in N. S. A native of Kelso, Scot. D. at Pictou, N. S., 1838.
I. A Selection of Scripture Doctrines for the use of families and sabbath schools. *Pictou*, 1840 ; 2nd Ed. 1845 ; 3rd Ed., 1855, pp. 16, 16mo.

ROBSON, JOSEPH.
I. An Account of six years residence in Hudson's Bay, from 1733 to 1736, and 1744 to 1747; with an Appendix, containing a short History of the discovery of Hudson's Bay, and the proceedings of the English there since the grant of the Hudson's Bay Charter; the soundings of Nelson's River, &c. *London*, 1752, 8vo.

ROCHE-HERON, CHARLES DeCOURCY DE LA. A French writer. Resided in Can. and the U. S. for several years. D. at Cannes, France, 14 May, 1861.
I. Les Servantes de Dieu en Canada. Essai historique sur les communautés religieuses de femmes de la Province. *Montréal*, 1855, 8vo.

ROCHE, ALFRED R. For some time in the Civil Service, Can ; now residing in London, Eng. Served as Can. Correspondent to the *Morning Post*, (Lon.,) for some years.
I. Suggestions on the Military Resources of Canada ; and the means of organizing a small Provincial army in the event of its being determined by the Imperial authorities to diminish or recall the Royal troops, so as to render such an organization essential to the defence of the Country. By the Canadian correspondent of the London *Morning Post*. *Quebec*, 1853, pp. 18, 8vo.

II. Notes on the Resources and Capabilities of Anticosti. *Trans. Lit. and His. Soc.*, (Que.), vol. IV.
"An interesting and instructive paper."— *Can. Journ.*
21

"A graphic and valuable paper."— *Gazette*, (Mont.)

III. A View of Russian America in connection with the present War (with Russia) ; a paper read before Lit. and His. Society of Quebec. *Montreal*, 1855, pp. 70, 8vo.

ROE, *Rev.* HENRY, *B. A.* A Min. of the Ch. of Eng. (St. Matthews, Que.) Is Examining Chaplain to the Lord Bish. (Que.) Has written frequently for the religious periodical and newspaper press of Can.
I. Farewell Sermon to the congregation of St. Stephens, L. C. *Montreal*, 1854.

II. Letter on Tractarianism to the Congregation of St. Matthews. *Do.*, 1858, pp. 23.

III. Review of the "Address of the Lay Association, in a letter from a churchman in town to a churchman in the country. *Quebec*, 1859, pp. 62.

IV. Bicentenary Sermons ; two sermons on the History and Scriptural authority of the Book of Common Prayer. *Montreal*, 1862, pp. 32.

V. Purgatory Transubstantiation and the Mass, examined in three sermons, by the light of Holy Scripture, Right Reason and Christian Antiquity. *Quebec*, 1863, pp. 96, 8vo ; 2nd Ed. *Montreal*, 1863, 8vo.
"The Rev. Dr. Cahill, a Romish controversialist of some fame, visited Quebec, and gave a series of public lectures. The first two lectures * * * were followed by three controversial lectures, addressed to Protestants, upon Purgatory, Transubstantition and the Mass. Dr. Cahill's lectures having been heard by many church-people, and moreover reported at much length in the newspapers, I was requested by several members of my congregation to lay before them the grounds on which the Anglican Church rejects the distinctive teachings of the Church of Rome on those points. I did so in these sermons."—*Advertisement to 1st Ed.*

VI. Prayer, a Confirmation lecture. *Do.*, 1864, pp. 19.

VII. Advantages and Means of keeping up Habits of Reading among the Clergy; a paper read before the clergy at the Visitation of the Lord Bishop of Quebec. *Montreal*, 1864, pp. 23.

VIII. Introduction to Observations on the best mode of providing for the support of the Clergy. *Ottawa*, 1866, pp. 6.

(See Irving, Rev. G. C. *Supplement*.)

ROEBUCK, JOHN ARTHUR, *M. P.* An Eng. statesman. B. 1801. When a boy came to Can., but left the Province, in 1824, to study law in Eng. He was elected a mem. of the Eng. House of Commons, after the passing of the first Reform Bill, and has continued to hold a seat in that body, with but slight interruption, ever since. In 1835, was appointed agent in Eng. for the House of Assem., L. C., during the dispute pending between the Executive Govt. and the House of Assem. In 1838 he ed. together with " other friends of Canada " in London : *The Canadian Portfolio. Containing a faithful exposition of the causes that have produced the Civil War in Canada, together with the various Official Documents necessary to elucidate and support the history of this disgraceful Contest.*

I. Existing Difficulties in the Government of the Canadas. *London*, 1835, 8vo.

II. A Plan for the Government of some portion of our Colonial Possessions. *Do.*, 1849, 8vo.

ROGER, CHARLES. A Can. historian and journ. B. in Dundee, Scot., 14 Apl., 1819. Studied for the Ministry, and afterwards for the Medical profession, and gave up both. Served in the Brit. army in various parts of Eng. and her dependencies ; obtained his discharge in 1842, and settled at Quebec. From 1849 to 1853 he Ed. the *Chronicle* there. For a short time he was ed. of the *Gazette*, in the same city. In 1854 some friends subscribed sufficient funds to establish a daily newspaper, called the *Observer*, the ed. of which they entrusted to Mr. R. The enterprise did not prove successful, and at the expiration of 10 months the publication of the paper ceased. In 1856 he again ed. the *Gazette*, and, in the following year, removed to Port Hope, U. C., where he established the *Atlas*. Mr. R. also established the *Observer*, (Millbrook,) which he conducted for some years. He is now a clk. in the Civil Service, Ottawa.

I. The Rise of Canada from Barbarism to Wealth and Civilization. *Quebec*, 1856, pp. 426, 8vo.

" Few of our readers, who take any interest in Canadian literary matters, can be ignorant of the name and pretensions of Charles Roger. The first volume of his " *History of Canada,*" which appeared some years ago, attracted general attention from the vigour, and originality of its style, and the lucidness of its details.—All persons capable of forming a judgment on the matter, confessed that the work was a credit to the Province, and many have been anxiously looking out for its continuation."—REV. R. J. McGEORGE : *Rec.* (Streetsville.)

ROGERS, *Major* ROBERT. An officer in the Brit. Army. In addition to the following works, was the author of a tragedy called *Ponteach*, published without his name.

I. A Concise Account of North America, containing a description of the several British Colonies on that Continent, including the islands of Newfoundland, Cape Breton, &c. ; as to their situation, extent, climate, soil, produce, rise, government, present boundaries, and the number of inhabitants supposed to be in each. Also, of the interior or westerly parts of the country, upon the rivers St. Lawrence, the Mississippi, Christino, and the great lakes. To which is subjoined an account of the several nations and tribes of Indians residing in those parts, as to their customs, manners, government, numbers, &c., containing many useful and entertaining facts, never before treated of. *London*, 1765, pp. 264, 8vo.

II. Journals of Major Robert Rogers, containing an account of the several excursions he made under the generals who commanded on the Continent of America during the late war. From which may be collected the most material circumstances of every campaign on that continent, from the commencement to the conclusion of the war. *Do.* 1765, pp. 236, 8vo.

" Reminiscences of the French War, containing Rogers' expeditions. To which is added the life of Stark. *Concord N. H.* 1831, 12mo.

" Robert was the son of James R. Rogers, an early settler of the town of Dumbarton, New Hampshire, entered the military service during the French war, and raised a Company of Rangers.

In 1760 Rogers received orders from Sir Jeffrey Amherst to take possession of Detroit and other western posts ceded by the French after the fall of Quebec. He ascended the St. Lawrence and the lakes with two hundred of his rangers, visited Fort Pitt, had an interview with the Indian chief, Pontiac, at the site of the present Cleveland on Lake Erie ; received the submission of Detroit, but was prevented from proceeding further by the approach of winter. He afterwards visited England, where he suffered from want until he borrowed the means to print his Journal and present it to the King, when he received the appointment of Governor of Michilimackinac in 1765. He returned and entered upon his command, but was afterwards, on an accusation of a plot to deliver up his post to the Spaniards, then the possessors of Louisiana, sent to Montreal in irons. In 1769 he revisited England, was presented to the king and imprisoned for debt. He afterwards, according to his account of himself to Dr. Wheelock at Dartmouth, 'fought two battles in Algiers under the Dey.' "—DUYCKINCK.

For the remainder of the story of his singular career see Duyckinck.

ROGERS, WILLIAM B. and HENRY D.
   I. Observations on the Geology of the Western Peninsula of Upper Canada and the Western part of Ohio. *Trans. Am. Phil. Soc.*, 1843.

ROLPH, *Hon.* JOHN, and CHRISTOPHER A. HAGERMAN.
   I. Speeches on the Bill for appropriating the proceeds of the Clergy Reserves to the purposes of General Education. *Toronto*, 1837, pp. 31.

ROLPH, THOMAS. For many years engaged in promoting Emigration to Can. Formed Emigration Societies in U. Can., and frequently visited Gt. Brit., first, we believe, in 1839, where he addressed meetings and contributed to the press in favour of the movement. Wrote many articles in the *Colonial Mag.* (Lon.), respecting Can. and Can. affairs.
   I. A Brief Account, together with Observations made during a visit to the West Indies, and a Tour through the United States of America, in parts of the years 1832–33 ; together with a statistical account of Upper Canada. *Dundas, U. C.*, 1836, pp. 288, 8vo. ; 2nd Ed., *London*, 1842, pp. 300, 8vo.
   II. Canada and Australia. *London*, 1840.

21 *

"This is a short, but interesting pamphlet, called for by the institution of a most unnecessary and disparaging comparison between the above valuable and important colonies, by an author whose zeal evidently outran his discretion. Dr. Rolph's long residence in Canada, and intimate acquaintance with its settlement, population, territorial division, climate, soil, &c., has enabled him to expose the errors of the pamphlet which has provoked this reply."—SIM. *Col. Mag.*

   III. Emigration to the Canadas ; a paper read before the London Colonial Society. *Col. Mag.* (Lon.) 1840.

   IV. Comparative Advantages between the United States and Canada for British Settlers considered, in a letter addressed to Captain Allardyce Barclay, of Ury. *London*, 1842, pp. 32, 8vo.

   V. Emigration and Colonization, embodying the results of a Mission to Great Britain and Ireland during the years 1839–40–41–42, including a correspondence with many distinguished noblemen and gentlemen, several of the Governors of Canada, &c. ; Descriptive accounts of various parts of the British American Provinces. With Observations, Statistical, Political, &c. *Do.* 1844, pp. 883, 8vo.

"Dr. Rolph's work consists mainly of a narrative of his own personal exertions in the promotion of emigration, in which sphere of action all the proof and arguments of the necessity and advantages of emigration are constantly, vigorously and pleasingly elucidated."—*Idem.*

RORDANS, J. Law Stationer, (Tor.)
   I. The Upper Canada Law List, or Directory. *Toronto*, 1857, pp. 150 ; 5th Ed., 1866, pp. 183, 12mo.
   II. The Canadian Conveyancer ; a selection of conveyancing precedents, adapted to Canadian practice. *Do.* 1859, pp. 280 ; 2nd Ed. 1867, 12mo.

"There is an introductory chapter of 27 pages, 'On the laws affecting real property in Upper Canada,' which gives much useful information on the subject, which it would require much time and not a little knowledge of Canadian law to extract from the text-books and statutes. We can recommend the book for its utility."—*U. C. Law Journ.*

ROSE, *Capt.* ALEXANDER. 52nd Regt.
   I. Abstract of a journal of the weather at Quebec, 1st Apl., 1765, and 30th Apl., 1766. *Phil. Trans.*, 1766.

ROSEBRUGH, A. M., *M. D.* Toronto.

I. A new Ophthalmoscope, for photographing the posterior internal surface of the living eye ; with an outline of the theory of the ordinary Opthalmoscope. Reprinted from *Can. Journ.*, 1864.

II. An Introduction to the Study of the Optical defects of the Eye, and their treatment by the scientific use of spectacles. *Do., do.*, 1866, pp. 31.

ROSIER, E.

I. The Emigrant's Friend in Canada. *London*, 1839, 18mo.

ROSS, ALEXANDER. A Brit. Am. author. B. in Nairnshire, Scot., 9 May, 1783. D. at his residence, "Colony Gardens," Red River Settlement, 23 Oct, 1856. Emigrated to Can. in 1805, and for some years taught sch. in the Co. of Glengarry, U. C. In 1810, joined Mr. Astor, in his celebrated expedition to Oregon. The expedition, after a long voyage round Cape Horn, safely reached the mouth of the Columbia river ; and the Fur business was entered upon in a region, where previously there had not been a single white or civilized being. The whole western slope of the Rocky Mountains was wild as in the days of Cortez ; primeval solitude reigned, save where the tramp of the red man or the roar of the wild beast was heard. Naturally adventurous and daring, Ross soon rose in the field of operations. The war of 1812-14 disturbed the enterprize, but he continued a fur-trader until 1824, part of the time in the service of the Hudson's Bay Co. In the following year, on retiring from the active service of the Co., he received a grant of several hundred acres of land in the immediate vicinity of Fort Garry, the capital of the country, upon which he settled. He was appointed a mem. of Council for the district, became Sheriff of Red River settlement and Gov. of the Gaol, holding these positions for a quarter of a century. He was an honorary mem. of the Minnesota Hist. Soc.

I. Adventures of the First Settlers on the Oregon or Columbia River. Being a narrative of the expedition fitted out by John Jacob Astor to establish the Pacific Fur Company ; with an account of some Indian tribes on the coast of the Pacific, with a map. *London*, 1849, 1 vol., pp. 352.

" One of the most striking pictures of a life of adventure which we have read for a long time ; and as full of instruction as of amusement : few will lay it down who have once taken it up, till the closing page is reached. To the lovers of Wild Adventure and perils by flood and field, we know of few books likely to prove more welcome than this work of Mr. Ross. It also possesses an interest of another kind for the historical reader and politician."—*Athen.* (Lon.)

" Mr. Ross has lived for forty years among the fur-traders, and consequently is enabled to present to us a very correct description of the country they traverse, the animals they hunt, and of the natives and their habits of life ; and a very curious and interesting picture it is. Mr. Ross has added considerably to our knowledge of the Oregon territory and its famous river; and we are enabled to form a fairer estimate of Mr. Astor's daring scheme and the causes of its failure, than any that is afforded by any publication that has appeared."—*Critic.* (Do.)

II. The Fur Hunters of the Far West. A narrative of adventures in the Oregon and Rocky Mountains. *Do.*, 1855, 2 vols., pp. 593, 8vo.

" Many accounts of hardships and adventures with savage men and beasts will be found in these volumes. There are some striking sketches of landscape and Indian life and character, as well as a great deal of information about the old Fur trade. The book is of considerable value as a picture of an almost past mode of human existence, as well as for its information upon the Indians of Oregon."—*Spectator.* (Do.)

III. The Red River Settlement ; Its Rise, Progress and Present State, with some account of the native races, and their general history to the present day. *Do.*, 1856, pp. 146, p. 8vo.

IV. Essay on Agriculture.

ROSS, BERNARD ROGAN, *H. B. C. S.*

I. A Popular Treatise on the Fur Bearing Animals of the Mackenzie River District. *Can. Nat.*, 1861.

II. An Account of the Animals useful in an economic point of view to the various Chipewyan Tribes. *Do.*, do.

III. An Account of the Botanical and Mineral products, useful to the Chipewyan tribes of Indians, inhabiting the McKenzie River District. *Do.*, 1862.

Ross, Dunbar, *Q. C.* A Quebec Advocate. B. at Clonakilty, Irel., about 1800. D. at Quebec, 1865. Sat in the Assem., Can., for many years ; Sol. Gen. for a short period. Left behind an unpublished pamphlet on Slavery.

I. The "Crisc" Metcalfe and the Lafontaine-Baldwin Cabinet defended. Letter of Zeno to the Legislative Assembly of Canada. *Montreal*, 1844, pp. 44, 8vo.

II. The Seat of Government of Canada, its Legislative Council, and "Double Majority" Question. *Quebec*, 2nd Ed., 1853, pp. 35, 8vo.

Ross, *Rev.* Duncan. A Presb. Min. B. in Tarbert, Rosshire, Scot. D. at West River, Pictou, N. S., 25 Oct., 1834. He passed through the usual curriculum at Edinburgh Univ., and studied Theology under Prof. Bruce at Whitburn. In 1795 was ordained as a missionary to N. S., whither he proceeded in the following summer. Soon after, settled at West River, Pictou, where he remained as pastor until his death. In addition to his theological and controversial productions given below, wrote largely for the newspaper press of N. S., principally for the *Colonial Patriot* and the *Acadian Recorder*, (Hal.) To the latter in 1826–27 he contributed a series of valuable letters entitled the "*Busy Body*," under the *nom de plume* of "*Solomon Wisewood*," in which he discussed a variety of matters connected with the advancement of the Province. Some of these letters are light and amusing, laying bare the prevailing social follies of the day ; among them are several on Temperance, to promote which he labored earnestly and was the first to advocate Temperance Societies.

I. The Subject and Mode of Baptism ascertained from Scripture ; being a conversation between a private Christian and a Minister ; in which the truth is illustrated, and the sentiments of the Baptists on these points are reviewed. By a Committee of the Associate Presbytery of Pictou. *Edinburgh*, 1810, pp. 50, 12mo.

II. Righteousness and Peace, the Fruits of the Gospel ; or, a relation of the Christian experience and triumphant death of Jane Cameron, in a letter addressed to the Rev. James McGregor, D. D. *Pictou*, 1824.

III. Baptism Considered in its Subjects and Modes, in three letters to the Rev. William Elder. *Do.*, 1825, pp. 78, 8vo.

IV. Strictures on a publication entitled : "Believer in Immersion as opposed to Unbeliever Sprinkling," in two letters addressed to Alexander Crawford. *Do.*, 1828, pp. 38, sm. 8vo.

V. A Reply to a pamphlet lately published, signed X ; or, Reasons for denying that Christ, by his death, purchased common benefits for his people. *Do.*, 1832, 12mo. pp. 12.

Ross, *Rev.* Ebenezer E. (Londonderry, N. S.)

I. The Manliness of Piety ; a Lecture. *Halifax*, 1860, pp. 24, 8vo.

Ross, James, *M. A.* A Can. journ. Son of Alex. Ross (whom see). B. at Red River Settlement, 9 May, 1835. Studied at St. John's Coll., at that place, holding a classical scholarship for 3 years. In 1853 matriculated at the Univ. (Tor.) where he took 2 scholarships, 1 for classics and the other for Modern Languages and History, which he held until 1857. At the final examination for B. A. obtained in addition to his degree 1 silver and 2 gold medals. In 1858 Mr. R. taught as Assist. Classical Master in U. C. Coll. Returning home in the following year he was appointed Postmaster, Sheriff and Gov. of the Gaol at Red River. From 1860 to 1864 he was joint ed. and prop. of the *Nor' Wester*, the only newspaper published on Brit. Territory between Lake Superior and the Pacific. Served for several months in 1864 as associate Ed. of the *Spectator* (Ham.,) when he accepted a like position on the *Globe* (Tor.,) where he still remains. Is regarded with much promise as one of the rising public writers of the New Dominion.

Ross, James. (Rawdon, N. S.)

I. Remarks and Suggestions on the Agriculture of Nova Scotia. *Halifax*, 1855.

Rouxel, *Rév.* H. A R. C. priest. Attached to the Seminary of St. Sulpice, (Mont.)

I. Les Premiers Colons de Montréal. *Montréal*, 1857, pp. 8.

II. La Vocation de la Colonie de Montréal. *Do.*, 1857, pp. 16.

ROWE, G.
I. The Colonial Empire of Great Britain : the Atlantic group. *London*, 1865, 18mo.

ROY, Mrs. JEANNET.
I. History of Canada, for the use of schools and families. *Montreal*, 7th Ed., 1864, pp. 279, 12mo.

Has been translated into French.

ROY, THOMAS, *C. E.*
I. Remarks on the Principles and Practice of Road-making, as applicable to Canada. *Toronto*, 1841, pp. 42.

ROYAL, JOSEPH. A French Can. *littérateur* and journ. B. at Repentigny, L. C., 7 May, 1837. He was a pupil of the Jesuits, (Mont.) Admitted to the Bar, L. C. in 1864. For some years he has been one of the Asst. French translators to the Leg. Assem.. Can. Mr. R. has probably done more than any other of his countrymen towards furthering the cause of French Can. Literature. Without mentioning the time and means he has devoted to the encouragement of commendable literary exertion and enterprise, we may state that by the action of his own pen he has contributed in no common degree towards the establishment of Letters in L. C. In 1857 he rendered no inconsiderable service to his young countrymen in Montreal, by aiding in the formation of the *Cercle Littéraire*, a debating and literary soc., before which as well as before many other associations and institutions of a like character, he has delivered numerous addresses and lectures on various subjects connected with Literature, Science, Art, History and Politics. As a journalist he made his *debut* in 1857, as chief ed. of *La Minerve*, the leading Conservative organ of L. C.. upon which he remained until 1859. Previous to this he had contributed to the French press, but it was not until he had taken possession of the ed. chair that he manifested any great power as a writer. In the latter year he founded, at Montreal, a journal of his own, *L'Ordre*, which he conducted until 1860, when he disposed of the paper, and accepted the ed. of *L'Echo du Cabinet de Lecture Paroissial*, of the same city, a literary and religious periodical. This he conducted with success and ability. His greatest achievement, however, in connection with the press, and a most important auxiliary to our nascent literature, was in founding in Jany. 1864, *La Revue Canadienne*, a monthly literary and political review and mag., which under his editorship and that of a committee of literary gentlemen, has prospered with unexampled success. Previous to the establishment of this useful and valuable periodical the French Can. portion of the population had no work of the kind worthy of the name. It is true that two other French Can. magazines were published at Quebec, but they did not combine the same amount of varied and useful matter which is exhibited in the pages of the *Revue*, nor had they on their respective *corps* of editors and contributors the names of so many writers of a varied and diversified talent and character. Were it for nothing else, and the service we venture to assert was an important one. than the establishment of such an able exponent of the views and opinions of the Gallic race in the new Dominion, and such a considerable literary work as the *Revue* has proved itself to be, Mr. R. should, in our opinion, hold a high place among the benefactors of his nationality. To this periodical he is still a constant contributor. We give below the titles of his principal essays and writings in the *Revue*. In 1867 he was the chief founder of a new daily journal, published at Montreal, called the *Nouveau Monde*, of which he is an associate ed. As a writer. Mr. R. has displayed no common degree of excellence. He is considered to be a perfect French scholar; and we know that there are very few in this country so well acquainted with French literature. As a critic he holds the scales with an even hand. His style is pure, fervent, unstudied. and is often very captivating. It is so clear that the dullest mind would find his writings intelligible. He wields a vigorous pen, strong for good or against evil. We have often heard it expressed that several of his essays and newspaper articles, would do no discredit to some of the leading French writers of the present day. Mr. R., has so far, contributed nothing in a permanent form to our literature, but we hope the day is not far distant when we, in common with the rest of the world may have the pleasure of welcoming a volume from his accomplished and versatile pen.

La Revue Canadienne.

I. Le Traité de Réciprocité. 1864, pp. 15.

II. Vie Politique de Sir Louis II. La Fontaine. Do., pp. 40.

III. Considérations sur les nouveaux changements Constitutionnels de l'Amérique Britannique du Nord. 1865, pp. 38.

IV. L'Aqueduc de Montréal. Do., pp. 20.

V. Considérations sur les nouveaux changements Constitutionnels de l'Amérique Britannique du Nord—L'Annexion. 1866, pp. 27.

VI. Notes pour un Nicolétain. Do. pp. 12.

VII. La Colonisation en 1866. Do. pp. 11.

VIII. Le Sacrifice et L'Egoisme. 1867, pp. 8.

IX. Le Gout. Théorie. Do. pp. 8.

RUSSELL, WILLIAM HOWARD, LL. D. An Eng. author, journ. and newspaper correspondent.

I. Canada; its Defences, Condition and Resources. (With Maps.) *London*, 1865, pp. 352, 8vo.

RUTTAN, *Hon.* HENRY. A Can. inventor. B. in U. C., 12 June, 1792. Is the son of an U. E. Loyalist, of French extraction. Sat in the Legislature, U. C., and during 1 Parliament was Speaker of the Leg. Assem. of that Province. Held the office of Sheriff of the Newcastle District for over 30 years, which he resigned in 1857. Was ed. of the *Star* (Cobourg) from 1847 to 1854. During the greater part of his life the subject of ventilation has engaged his particular attention, and we are firmly convinced that no man has had larger

experience on this subject, or has given more time and expended more money upon it than he has done.

I. Lectures on the Ventilation of Buildings, delivered at the Cobourg Mechanics' Institute. Printed for private distribution. *Cobourg*, 1848, pp. 99, 8vo.

II. Ventilation and Warming of Buildings, Illustrated by fifty-four plates, exemplifying the exhaustion principle; to which is added a complete description and illustration of the ventilation of railway carriages for both winter and summer. *New York*, 1862, pp. 532, 8vo.

" More than nineteen years of the author's life have been devoted to the researches and experiments of which the results are set forth in the present volume. He is evidently a man of original ideas, and at the same time combining no small degree of practical sense with uncommon inventive genius. The plans of warming and ventilation which he proposes, especially in their application to Railway cars, have the merit not only of novelty, but of successful operation, * * * Mr. Ruttan has earned the thanks of the travelling community in particular for the valuable suggestions which he has brought forward."—*Tribune*, (N. Y.)

"Contains much useful information."— *Scientific American.*

RYAN, CARROLL. A Can. poet. B. at Toronto, 1840. Saw service in the Turkish Contingent during the late Russian War. Served in the 100th, or Prince of Wales' Royal Canadian Regiment, from its formation until 1867. Is now ed. of the *Volunteer Review*, (Ottawa.)

I. Oscar and other poems. *Hamilton*, 1857, 12mo.

"'Oscar' is a picture of the Crimean War, written by a young Canadian, who witnessed and bore a part in the scenes he describes. The plan of his poem, however, embraces a sketch of Canadian scenery, as noted by the imaginary hero, on his way to the seat of war."—*Can. Journ.*

II. The Songs of a Wanderer. *Ottawa*, 1867.

RYAN, F. B.

I. The Spirit's Lament; or, The Wrongs of Ireland: a poem. *Montreal*, 1847, pp. 194.

RYAN, MATTHEW. A Can. journ. B. at St. John's, Newfoundland. At an early age commenced contributing to the newspaper press of his native colony, principally to the *Public Ledger* and the *Newfoundlander*, some of his articles attracting a good deal of attention and procuring for him the friendship of leading public men. In 1842 removed to Can., and for a short time was connected with the *Times* (Mont..) but owing to a difference of opinion with the publisher on the political questions and events of the day, threw up his position and soon afterwards (1844) became associate ed. with Mr. Hincks on the *Pilot*. He remained on that paper until 1848, when he was appd. to office under Govt. Mr. R. occupied various positions of trust and importance under the Crown, the last (which he resigned in 1859,) being the Inspectorship of Customs for L. C. During the whole of his residence in Can. has been more or less a writer for the press, invariably taking the Reform side in politics. As a writer he is clear, polished and unlaboured. He ought to take a prominent place on the Colonial press. In 1849 he was admitted to the Bar of L. C., but did not practice until 10 years afterwards.

I. Six Letters in Defence of the Order of Jesuits, originally addressed to the editor of the "Montreal Herald," in reply to a series of articles published by him against the principles and practice of that Order. *Montreal*, 1843, pp. 30.

RYERSON, *Rev.* ADOLPHUS EGERTON, *D. D.*, *LL. D.* A Can. controversial writer and journ. Is Supdt. of Education for the Province of Ontario. B. in the Tp. of Charlotteville, London. afterwards the Talbot District (now Co. Norfolk, U. C.,) 24 March, 1803. His father, Col. Joseph Ryerson, was an U. E. Loyalist, in the British Service at at the time of the Am. Revolution, and was one of the 550 volunteers who went to Charleston, South Carolina. For his activity in bearing despatches about 200 miles into the interior, he was promoted to a Lieutenancy in the Prince of Wales' Volunteers. Subsequently Col. Ryerson was in 6 battles, and was once wounded. He came to Can. from New Jersey, by way of N.

B. in 1783, and enjoyed his half-pay until the time of his death. Egerton was the fourth son of Col. Ryerson. He was named after two intimate friends of his father in the Army, (Capt. Adolphus and Dr. Egerton, we believe.) His youth was passed in his native county, and at its Grammar Sch. and at that of the Gore District, in Hamilton, he received his early education, after which he became an assistant to his brother-in-law, Dr. Mitchell in the Talbot District Grammar Sch. His mother was a woman distinguished for her clearness of intellect, for her strong religious principles, and her kindness of disposition. Egerton was her favorite son, and she sought to inoculate into his ardent mind all those noble principles which lie at the basis of all true excellence of character. Three of his brothers having entered the sacred ministry, he also, after due preparation, followed their example, and on his 22nd birth day (24th March, 1825,) was ordained by Bishop Hedding a Deacon of the Meth. Episcopal Ch. in Can. It being Easter, his first sermon was on the appropriate subject of the Resurrection of Christ. He was first stationed on the Niagara Circuit, embracing many miles; then on the Yonge street Circuit, including the town of York, (now Toronto,) and, in succession at the Credit, Indian Mission, Toronto, Cobourg, Ancaster, &c. Circuits in those days rarely embraced less than 30 or 40 miles. with settlers few and far between. In 1829, (the year after the Am. General Conference constituted the Can. branch a separate annual Conference,) he took a prominent part in the establishment of the *Christian Guardian* newspaper (Tor.,) now in its 37th year, as an organ of that conference and became its first ed. In 1833, he was appointed a delegate to Eng. to confer with the Brit. Conference on a projected union with that Conference. In 1836, he was again appointed to proceed to Eng. to procure a Royal Charter for the U. C. Academy which had been established by the Conference at Cobourg, in the Newcastle District, and to solicit subscriptions in aid of the institution. In these objects he was successful. On his return he was again appointed ed. of the *Christian Guardian*, and was afterwards stationed at Kingston and Toronto. In 1840, the Brit. Conference having dissolved the union, he was a third time appointed as a delegate to that Conference respecting the matter in dispute. In 1841, the U. C. Academy having been by Act of Parliament constituted a Univ. Coll., he was appointed its first Principal ; and, in the same year, received the honorary degree of D. D., from the Wesl. Univ. at Middletown, Connecticut. In 1844 he was appointed by Lord Metcalfe, then Gov. Genl., Supt. of Public Schools in U. C., and, in 1844-5, he made an extensive tour in the U. S. and Europe, with a view to collect information to bring into operation a satisfactory system of Public Elementary Education in U. C. In this he was singularly successful. In 1846, he published an elaborate Report on the subject, and submitted to the Govt. a draft of Bill to carry out his views. The bill became law, and has ever since formed the basis of the U. C. Common Sch. system. In 1853, he submitted to the Govt. another draft Bill to improve the condition of the Grammar Sch's. This also became law, and, from time to time he has sought by legal enactments to build up and perfect that system of public sch's, the foundation of which was so successfully laid in 1846. In 1848 he established *The Journal of Education of Upper Canada*, which still continues, he being its Chief-Ed. from its first appearance. As a writer, a statesman, and a controversialist Dr. R. has confessedly few, if any, equals in Can., while in his successful administration of the now important Educational Department of U. C., he has elicited the highest commendations from men of every shade of political opinion. As yet his purely literary efforts have not been numerous, but his controversial pamphlets are many. His earliest were written in 1827-8, (when he was 25 years of age,) in reply to the attacks on the Wesl. body by the Rev. Dr. Strachan, then Archdeacon of York, but now the Venerable Bish. of Toronto. They at once established his

reputation as a writer and have been the forerunner of the many equally able and successful pamphlets in the accompanying list.

At present Dr. R. contemplates writing (if spared) a History of the United Empire Loyalists, and of his native country. It is looked for with much interest, and will, when issued, form a highly valuable contribution to Historical Literature. As an appreciation of his public labours, the Univ. of Victoria Coll., (Cobourg,) conferred on him in 1861 the degree of LL. D. Dr. R. is also a corresponding mem. of the N. Y. Historical Soc.

I. Claims of the Churchmen and Dissenters of Upper Canada brought to the test in a controversy between several members of the Church of England and a Methodist Preacher, founded on Rev. Dr. Strachan's Sermon on the death of the Lord Bishop of Quebec. *Kingston*, 1828, pp. 232.

II. Letters to the Hon. and Reverend Doctor Strachan, published originally in the *Upper Canada Herald*, in reply to Dr. Strachan's speech in the Legislative Council, 7 March, 1828. *Kingston, C. W.*, 1828, pp. 42.

III. The Affairs of the Canadas in a series of letters to the *London Times*. By a Canadian. *London, Eng.*, 1837, pp. 75.

" A series of powerful letters."— *Gazette*, (Mont.)

IV. Wesleyan Methodism in Upper Canada, a sermon preached before the Wesleyan Conference in Toronto, June, 1837, pp. 27.

V. Civil Government, the late Conspiracy. A Discourse delivered in Kingston, U. C., December, 31, 1837. *Toronto*, 1838, pp. 20.

VI. Petition to the House of Assembly, together with a Message from His Excellency the Lieutenant Governor, and correspondence between the Right Hon. Lord Glenelg, His Excellency, and Mr. Ryerson, relative to the Upper Canada Academy. Printed by order of the House of Assembly. *Do.*, 1838, pp. 78.

VII. Methodist Chapel Property Case. Report of the trial of an action brought by persons calling themselves

"The Methodist Episcopal Church in Canada," to obtain possession of the Wesleyan Methodist Chapel in Belleville. Tried before the Hon. Mr. Justice Jones at Kingston, October 11th, 1837. With brief notes and remarks, by Rev. E. Ryerson. *Do.*, 1837, pp. 103.

VIII. The Clergy Reserve Question; as a matter of History—A question of Law—And a subject of Legislation; a series of letters. *Do.*, 1839, pp. 156.

IX. Wesleyan Methodist Conference, its union with the Conference of the Wesleyan Methodist Church in Canada, in August, 1833, and its seperation from the Canada Conference, in August, 1840, consisting of the official proceedings and correspondence of both bodies and their representatives. By Rev's. W. and E. Ryerson, Representatives of the Canada Conference. *London, Eng.*, 1840, pp. 115.

X. Reply of the Canada Wesleyan Conference, June, 1841, to the proceedings of the English Wesleyan Conference and its Committees, August and September, 1840, with an Appendix containing the Rev. E. Ryerson's replies to the Wesleyan Committee, Rev. Dr. Alder, Rev. W. Lord, &c. *Do.*, 1841, pp. 102.

XI. Petition to the House of Assembly, together with a message from His Excellency the Lieut. Governor and correspondence between the Right Hon. Lord Glenelg, His Excellency, and Mr. Ryerson in relation to the Upper Canada Academy. Printed by order of the House of Assembly. *Toronto*, 1838, pp. 78.

XII Explanatory and Practical Observations made by the Rev. E. Ryerson, at the preparatory opening of Victoria College, Cobourg, in October, 1841. *Do.*, 1841, pp. 16.

XIII. Inaugural Address on the Nature and Advantages of an English and Liberal Education; delivered at the opening of Victoria College, June, 21, 1842. *Do.*, 1842, pp. 34.

XIV. Some Remarks upon Sir Charles Bagot's Canadian Government. *Kingston*, 1843, pp. 12.

XV. Sir Charles Metcalfe defended against the Attacks of his late Counsellors. *Toronto*, 1844, pp. 186.

XVI. Hon. R. B. Sullivan's attacks upon Sir Charles Metcalfe refuted; being a reply to the letters "Legion." *Do.*, 1844, pp. 63.

XVII. Report on a System of Public Elementary Instruction for Upper Canada. Printed by order of the Legislative Assembly. *Montreal*, 1846-7, pp. 191, 12mo.

XVIII. Special Report of the measures which have been adopted for the establishment of a Normal School, and for carrying into effect generally, the Common School Act, (9th Vict. Cap. XX), with an Appendix. Printed by order of the Legislative Assembly. *Do.*, 1847, pp. 72.

XIX. Christians on Earth and in Heaven; the substance of a discourse delivered in the Adelaide street Wesleyan-Methodist Church, Toronto, on Sabbath evening, October 29th, 1848, on the occasion of the death of Mrs. Sanderson, late wife of the Rev. Geo. R. Sanderson, Editor of the *Christian Guardian*. By the Rev. E. Ryerson, D. D. *Toronto*, 1848, pp. 34.

XX. Correspondence with the Government in regard to the School law and the exclusion of the Bible from the Public Schools, 1846-50. *Do.*, 1850, pp. 50, Im. 4to.

XXI. Address to the members and friends of the Wesleyan Methodist Church in Canada, in behalf of Victoria College. (Adopted by the Wesleyan Conference.) *Do.*, 1851, pp. 8.

XXII. A Few Remarks on Religious Corporations and American examples of them. *Do.*, 1851, pp. 8, large 8vo.

XXIII. Correspondence between the Roman Catholic Bishop of Toronto, and the Chief Superintendent of Schools, on the subject of Separate Common Schools in Upper Canada. *Do.*, 1853, pp. 33.

XXIV. Return to an Address shewing in detail, what Books, Maps, and other articles for Schools or Teachers have been purchased or sold, by the Superintendent of Education, West. Printed by order of the Honorable the Legislative Assembly. *Quebec*, 1853, pp. 65.

XXV. Scriptural Rights of the members of Christ's visible Church, or correspondence containing the reasons of Dr. Ryerson's resignation of office in the Wesleyan Methodist Church. *Toronto*, 1854, pp. 32.

XXVI. Law of Separate Schools in Upper Canada, by the Roman Catholic Bishops and the Chief Superintendent of Schools, being the first part of the Correspondence ordered to be printed by the Legislative Assembly. *Do.*, 1855, pp. 40.

XXVII. Copies of Correspondence between the Chief Superintendent of Schools for Upper Canada and other persons, on the subject of Separate Schools, (being a continuation of the return laid before the House, and printed on the 17th September, 1852.) Printed by order of the Legislative Assembly. *Do.*, 1855, pp. 256.

XXVIII. Dr Ryerson's letters in reply to the attacks of foreign ecclesiastics against the Schools and Municipalities of Upper Canada, including the letters of Bishops Charbonnel, Mr. Bruyere, and Bishop Pinsonneault. (Anonnyously compiled from Dr. Ryerson's letters on the subject.) *Do.*, 1857 pp. 104.

XXIX. Special Report on Separate School provisions of the School law of Upper Canada, and the measures which have been adopted to supply the School Sections and Municipalities with school text books, apparatus and libraries by the Chief Superintendent of Education for Upper Canada. Printed by order of the Legislative Assembly. *Do.*, 1858, pp. 76.

XXX. The Educational Museum and School of Art and Design for Upper Canada, with a plan of the English Educational Museum, from the Chief Superintendent's Report for 1856, to which is added an Appendix. *Do.*, 1858, pp. 72.

XXXI. Dr. Ryerson letters in reply to the attacks of the Hon. George Brown, M. P. P., "Editor-in-Chief and Proprietor" of the *Globe*. *Do.*, 1859, pp. 110.

XXXII. Wesleyan Conference Memorial on the question of liberal education in Upper Canada, explained and defended by numerous proofs and illustrations, by a committee. *Do.*, 1860, pp. 72.

XXXIII. University Question. The Rev. Dr. Ryerson's defence of the Wesleyan petitions to the Legislature, and of denominational colleges as part of our system of public instruction, in reply to Dr. Wilson and Mr. Langton, before a select committee of the Legislative Assembly. With an Appendix containing replies to Statements by the Hon. George Brown, M. P. P. *Quebec*, 1860, pp. 49.

XXXIV. University Question: Being a report of a Public Meeting held at the Kingston Conference in reference to the University Question and Victoria College, to which is added Rev. E. Ryerson's defence of the Wesleyan Petitions to the Legislature, and of Denominational Colleges as part of our system of Public Instruction. *Toronto*, 1860, pp. 54.

XXXV. University Reform—Dr. Ryerson's reply to the recent pamphlet of Mr. Langton and Dr. Wilson, on the University Question in five letters to the Hon. M. Cameron, M. L. C., Chairman of the late University Committee of the Legislative Assembly. *Do.*, 1861, pp. 64.

XXXVI. University Reform defended in reply to six editorials of the "Globe" and "Leader," on the University Commissioners and the Advocates for University Reform in Upper Canada. *Do.*, 1863, pp. 17.

XXXVII. Remarks on the new Separate School Agitation. *Do.*, 1865, pp. 26.

XXXVIII to LVII. 20 Annual Reports of the Normal Model Grammar and Common Schools in Upper Canada, from 1845 to 1864 inclusive, by the Chief Superintendent. Printed by order of the Legislative Assembly. *Quebec*. (Averaging about 200 pages each.)

LVIII. The New Canadian Dominion : Dangers and Duties of the People in regard to their Government. *Toronto*, 1867, pp. 35, 8vo.

"Dr. Egerton Ryerson is no mean pamphleteer, and his opinions, 'based on fifty years' reading and meditation, and more than forty years' occasional discussion,' are entitled to. and will carry with them, considerable weight. But besides embodying the personal views of the writer, the little treatise before us is replete with apt and striking quotations from the writings of Lord Bacon, Lord Brougham, Dr. Wayland. Dr. Channing, Robert Hall. Fennimore Cooper, Judge Story, M. de Tocqueville, the historians Hume and Rollin, and from the speeches of three of the most eminent governors who have ever been entrusted with the administration of affairs in Canada : Lord DURHAM, Lord SYDENHAM and Sir CHARLES BAGOT. The whole scope of Dr. RYERSON's pamphlet is embraced in an endeavour to demonstrate that a partisan system of government is productive of the most baneful results to a country ; a proposition which one might suppose to be self-evident, but which, we are sorry to say, is not recognized by a certain portion of the press and people of Canada." *Gazette*, (Mont.)

RYERSON. *Rev.* JOHN. A Wesl. Meth. Min. (Brantford, U. C.)

I. Hudson's Bay ; or, a missionary tour in the territory of the Hon. Hudson's Bay Company. *Toronto*, 1855, 12mo.

" The work abounds in graphic descriptions of a district but little known, and is written in a popular style.   *   *   * It abounds in illustrations which greatly enhance its attractiveness, and is altogether such a book as an intelligent person would wish to become possessed of."—*Journ of Ed., U. C.*

RYLES, *Rev.* MATHEW.

I. Sermon delivered at St. John, New Brunswick, 2 December, 1798, on the late Signal Success granted to His Majesty's Arms. *St. John*, 1798, 8vo.

S.

SABATIER, W.

I. Letter to the President of the Board of Trade, on the proposed Timber Duties, and on the value and importance of the British North American Colonies. *London*, 1821.

SABINE, *Genl.* EDWARD. Royal Artillery. President of the Royal Soc. (Eng.)

I. Observations made at the Magnetical and Meteorogical Observatory at Toronto, in Canada. Printed by order of Her Majesty's Government, under the Superintendence of Lt. Col. Ed. Sabine, Vol. I. 1840-41-42. *London*, 1845.

" The officer appointed to Canada was Lieut. C. J. B. Riddell, who, being obliged to return to England in Feby., 1841, in consequence of ill-health, was temporarily succeeded by Lieut. Younghusband, who acted until the arrival of Lieut. Lefroy in Sept. 1842. The latter officer proceeded in April, 1843, on a magnetic survey within the Hudson's Bay territories, and was succeeded, de novo by Lieut. Younghusband, who continued in charge to nearly the end of 1844."— *B. A. Journ.*

(See *Lefroy*, Brig. Genl.)

II. On the periodic and non-periodic variations of the Temperature at To-ronto, in Canada, from 1841 to 1852, inclusive. *Trans. Roy. Soc.* 1853.

III. Magnetical and Meteorological Observations made at Toronto, Canada 1846-7 and 8, with abstracts to 1855, inclusive. *London*.

SABINE, LORENZO, A. M. An Am. historical and biographical author. B. at Lisbon, N. II., 28 Feby., 1803.

I. The American Loyalists ; or, Biographical Sketches of adherents to the British Crown in the war of the Revolution, alphabetically arranged ; with a preliminary historical essay. *Boston*, 1849, 8vo. ; 2nd Ed. *Do.* 1864. 2 vols.

" The work has taken its place as an independent and original contribution to the American historical library."—DUYCKINCK.

II. An Address before the New England Historic-Genealogical Society, Sept. 13th 1859 ; the hundredth Anniversary of the Death of Major General James Wolfe, with passages omitted in the delivery, and illustrative notes and documents. *Do.*, 1859, 8vo.

" This discourse presents a minute examination of the incidents preceding and attending the seige of Quebec, with an impartial investigation of the part borne by Wolfe in that memorable transaction. It is something beside a eulogy of the great hero; it is an important study of an extraordinary historical epoch."—*Idem.*

SAINSBURY, W. NOEL.

I. Calendar of State Papers. Colonial Series 1574—1660, preserved in the State Paper Department of Her Majesty's Record Office. [Edited.] *London*, 1862.

SAMPSON, *Rev.* JOHN M. A. Rector of Croscombe, Somersetshire, and Fellow of Merton Coll. Oxford.

I. Sermon on a general thanksgiving for the Conquest of Quebec, on Ps. cxliv. 15. *London*, 1771, 8vo.

SANBORN, *Hon.* JOHN SEWELL, *Q. C.* A Can. Senator.

I. University Education in Lower Canada; an address delivered at the annual meeting of the convocation of Bishop's College, Lennoxville. *Montreal*, 1857, pp. 14.

SANGSTER, CHARLES. A Can. poet. B. at the Navy Yard, Point Frederick, Kingston, 16 July, 1822. Is the grandson of an U. E. Loyalist, who served in the Royal Army during the Am. Revolutionary War. His father, who was employed in a subordinate capacity at one of the Naval Stations on the Upper Lakes, died when the future poet was only in his second year. Although sent regularly to sch. in his younger days, the education which he received was very meagre, and it was not until he had reached man's estate that he acquired any knowledge of a superior character or became acquainted with general literature. When only 15 years of age was forced to leave sch. and home, to contribute to the support of his widowed mother. For some time he obtained employment in the naval laboratory at Fort Henry, where he assisted in making the cartridges with which Capt. Sandom, R. N., battered the windmill at Prescott, during the uprising in 1837; and for 10 years he fulfilled the duties of a humble position in the OrdnanceOffice, Kingston. Seeing, however, little or no chance of preferment or advancement and knowing, as he must have known, that he was capable of far higher and more congenial work, he, in 1849, relinquished the situation which he held

and proceeded to Amherstburg, where he ed. the *Courier*, a Conservative journal, then published in that town. Returning to Kingston in the year following, owing to the death of the publisher of the *Courier*, he entered the office of the *Whig*, his position being, or supposed to be, that of sub-ed., but in reality Book-keeper and Proofreader of the establishment. Here he remained during the best part of his life, until 1861. In February, 1864, he joined the staff of the *Daily News*, of the same city, as reporter, on which paper he still continues. Our readers will thus perceive that the life of the national poet of Can., as he is justly regarded, has been a very quiet, laborious and uneventful one, offering few occurrences or points for his biographer to expatiate upon. As a writer of verse Mr. S. began to cultivate the muses when very young—he wrote poems for his play-fellows, which were as far removed from poetry as the earth is from the heavens. But this was not to continue; he possessed the genius of poetry, and the harmony of song must come forth. With years came education, experience and art—his style became less rugged and more finished, as his mind became more cultivated, and his powers as a writer of verse were more exercised. He early wrote for the newspapers and periodicals, his contributions appearing chiefly in the Kingston papers, the *Literary Garland*, *Barker's Mag.* and the *Anglo-American*, until his name and his poems grew familiar, and his reputation extended beyond the boundary lines of his native Can.

Mr. S's first volume " *The St. Lawrence and the Saguenay, and other Poems*," was not generally distinguished for that artistic finish to which he has attained in his more recent publication, " *Hesperus and other Poems, and Lyrics.*" In noticing this, we note also the pleasing fact that his muse is progressive, which is not always the case with poetry. We might instance the author of " *Festus* " and " *The Angel World*," whose latest works show a decided falling off; the author of " *The Angel of the House,* " and others who have sadly retrograded since the publication of their first successful efforts. But while there are traces of genuine poetry interspersed through Mr. S's earlier poems, there is also an observable lack of true artistic skill. The leading poem, particularly, abounds with false rhymes, false accent, and false quantity; but with all its faults, the volume contains poems which are extremely beautiful and full of poetic sentiment and fire. There are stanzas in " *The St. Lawrence and the Saguenay*," which, were the entire poem as free from fault as they, would make it worthy of the subject, and a living addition to Can. literature. Our present intention, however, is more to point out and to prove that Mr. S. is fairly entitled to the designation bestowed on him, that of being a strictly Canadian Poet. In 1860 appeared his second volume *Hesperus and other Poems and Lyrics*, which is decidedly the best of his productions, and was very favorably received by the press of Can., Gt. Britain and the U. S. A Scottish writer, in reviewing the work, places Mr. S. alongside of such poets as Coventry Patmore and Charles Mackay. Since the appearance of this last named work he has occasionally contributed to the press. Some of his pieces appeared in the short lived *Brit. Am. Mag.* (Tor.); others in the *Saturday Reader* (Mont.) He also contributed a poem on the occasion of the "Bryant Festival" at N. Y., which was published in the work issued by the Century Club of that city. Mr. Dewart in his recent volume on Can. Poetry gives his estimate of our national poet :—

" Among those who have most courageously appealed to the reading public, and most largely enriched the poetic literature of Canada, the first place is due to *Charles Sangster*. The richness and extent of his contributions, the originality and descriptive power he displays, the variety of Canadian themes on which he has written with force and elegance, his passionate sympathy with the beautiful in nature, and the chivalrous and manly patriotism which finds an utterance in his poems, fully vindicate his claim to a higher place in the regard of his countrymen, than he has yet obtained. Alexander McLachlan has also evinced that he possesses in a high degree the gift of song. In the opinion of many, he is the sweetest and most intensely human of all our Canadian bards. As Sangster and McLachlan are quite unlike, and each possesses a strongly marked individuality of his own, any comparison between them is inappropriate, and might be unfair to both. In elaborate elegance and wealth of descriptive power, in the success with which he has treated Canadian themes, and in something of Miltonic stateliness and originality of style, Sangster has certainly no equal in this country. But in strong human sympathy, in subtle appreciation of character, in deep natural pathos, and in those gushes of noble and manly feeling which awaken the responsive echoes of every true heart, McLachlan is peerless. That they should both be so little known to the reading public of Canada, is a matter of sincere regret. Taking into consideration the subtle delicacy of thought and elevation of style which distinguishes much of his poetry it is not so difficult to understand why Sangster should be comparatively unappreciated by the great mass of readers ; but that the sentiments of sympathy with humanity in all conditions, and the protests against every form of injustice and pretension, so simply and earnestly expressed in McLachlan's poetry, should secure so few admirers, is a fact that, in spite of all possible explanations, is by no means creditable to the taste or intelligence of Canada."

I. The St. Lawrence and the Saguenay and other Poems. *Kingston* and *New York*, 1856, pp. 262, 8vo.

" Western Canada is enabled to boast, and does boast somewhat loudly, of Charles Sangster, who has celebrated in Spenserian Stanzas, the beauties and the sublimities of the St. Lawrence and the Saguenay. Well may the Canadians be proud of such contributions to their infant literature, well may they be forward to recognise his lively imagination, his bold masterly style, and the fullness of his imagery. *   *   *   There is much of the spirit of Wordsworth in this writer, only the tone is religious instead of being philosophical. *   *   *   *   * In some sort and according to his degree, he may be regarded as the Wordsworth of Canada."—*National Mag.* (Lon.)

" His whole soul seems steeped in love and poesy, and finds utterance in expressions generally eloquent, bold and musical. He is thoroughly sentimental, teeming with ideas of the sublime and beautiful, and his poetry bears evident marks of enthusiastic poetical conception. Mr. Sangster is a Poet of no mean order, and his volume is by far the most respectable contribution of Poetry that has yet been made to the infant literature of Canada."—Thomas McQueen.

" It is a pleasant and tasteful depiction of the scenes and associations of our noble river, written in the same stanza as Childe Harold, and with some echo of its mode of thought, though lacking the force and pathos of its passionate utterances."—Prof. D. Wilson : *Can. Journ.*

II. Hesperus, and other Poems and Lyrics. *Montreal, 1860, pp. 186, 8vo.*

"About four years ago we greeted the appearance of a Canadian versifier, recognizing in him at his advent the germ of a future poet. Nor have we been disappointed. Charles Sangster is now, we think, fairly entitled to a place upon ' Parnassus' Hill.' He writes as though he had stepped up thither himself, unconcious and perhaps uncaring whether those around him sanction the move, or rebuke him for presumption. We mean that he seems to live and breathe mainly in a spiritual atmosphere ; sometimes to be yearning for communion with things not of the earth, earthy—but good and comely and of good repute ; and to hold converse with fantastic beings of his own imagining, as though they were his chosen and most sympathetic associates. Yet, would it be injustice to suppose that Mr. Sangster affects to be above, or even to keep himself aloof from, his fellow men. By no means. Love, as we poor mortals know it, is his frequent theme. The domestic affections prompt him oft. In rural life he revels. His patriotism glows, from contact with local associations and specific events. He can look upon the Apocalypse with unshrinking gaze ; but he has an eye for the daisies under his foot. In a word, his mind is apparently suffused with the divine afflatus, so difficult to analyse or describe, so readily understood by the initiated.

* * * * *

This is not the golden age for poetry. The world is too busy, too impatient, too much titillated by the clever ministering of the daily press ; it can scarcely abstract itself from the realities of life, and the abounding movement of our day. Still, to the faithful few, we commend this comparatively unknown lyrist, and shall be glad indeed if what we have said and quoted shall aid in giving him his proper rank."—*Albion*, (N. Y.)

"His verse adds new interest to the woods and streams amidst which he sings and embellishes the charms of the maidens he celebrates."—DR. O. W. HOLMES.

"Miss Ingelow admires some of the poems very much, especially that on the Comet, and the very beautiful song called 'Young Again,' also the ' Wren.' Mr. Sangster is evidently a true poet and his verses are all the more pleasant to read because he is never careless and never affected."—MISS JEAN INGELOW.

"I think it (*Hesperus*, etc.) a decided improvement upon your first volume, showing both more freshness and more *art*, which is the highest requisite of poetry. I am glad to see that you are thus helping to lay the foundations of a Canadian Literature, and hope you will give us many more corner-stones.

There is quite a mine of poetic wealth in Canada, if it were properly worked."—BAYARD TAYLOR.

SANGSTER, JOHN HERBERT, *M. A., M. D.* Mathematical Master and Lecturer on Chemistry and Natural Philosophy in the Normal Sch., U. C.

I. National Arithmetic, in theory and practice ; designed for the use of Canadian Schools. *Montreal*, 1860.

"From the brief examination we have been enabled to give it, we are inclined to think, it will give a more thorough knowledge of the science of numbers than any other Arithmetic we remember."—*Gazette*, (Mont.)

II. Key to the National Arithmetic, containing the Solutions of all the more difficult problems. *Do.* 1860.

III. Elementary Arithmetic, in Decimal Currency ; designed for the use of Canadian Schools. *Do.* 1860.

"In this little book the subject is taught so clearly and simply as to be suited to the comprehension of the most juvenile tyro, while adapted to secure his interested attention."—*Colonist*, (Hal.)

IV. Key to the Elementary Arithmetic, including the Solution of nearly all the problems. *Do.*

"Mr. Sangster's Arithmetics appear to us to be models of arrangement and good teaching. The rules are in all cases illustrated by operations fully worked out, and explained step by step in such a way that the pupil can have no difficulty in mastering and comprehending the *rationale* of every process employed." —*Educational Times.* (Lon.)

V. Elementary Treatise on Algebra ; designed for the use of Canadian Schools. *Do.* 1861.

VI Key to Elementary Treatise on Algebra, containing full Solutions to all the problems and examples, with numerous explanatory remarks. *Do.*

VII. Natural Philosophy. Part I ; including Statics, Hydrostatics, Pneumatics, Dynamics, and Hydrodynamics. Designed for the use of Normal and Grammar Schools, and the Higher Classes in Common Schools. *Do.* 1860.

VIII. Natural Philosophy. Part II ; Being a Hand-Book of Chemical Physics, or the Physics of Heat, Light and Electricity. *Do.*

IX. Student's Note-Book on Inorganic Chemistry ; including brief notices of the Properties, Preparation and Chemical Reactions of the Principal Elements and their Compounds. *Do.*

X. Human Physiology. (*In press.*)

XI. Simple Exercises in Mensuration. (*In press.*)

All the above works belong to Lovell's Series of Canadian school-books.

SANSOM, JOSEPH.

I. Sketches of Lower Canada, historical and descriptive ; with the Author's Recollections of the soil and aspect, the morals, habits and religious institutions of that isolated country ; during a Tour to Quebec, in the month of July, 1817. *New York*, 1817, p. 8vo.

SANSON, *Rev.* A.

I. Hymns for the use of Sunday Schools ; selected from approved authors. *Toronto*, 1857, pp. 66.

SARGENT, WINTHORP, *M. A.* An Am. historical writer. B. at Philadelphia, 23 Sept., 1825.

I. The History of an Expedition against Fort du Quesne, in 1775, under Major General Edward Braddock, Generalissimo of H. B. M. Forces in America. Edited from original manuscripts. (With illustrations.) *Philadelphia*, 1855, 8vo.

  "Under the modest title we have cited, Mr. Sargent has not only given the most thorough history of Braddock and his expedition that has ever appeared, but furnished one of the best written and most valuable historical volumes in the country."—DUYCKINCK.

SARRASIN, MICHEL.

I. Notice Biographique et Historique sur Michel Sarrasin, médecin du Roi, à Québec, conseiller au conseil supérieur, etc. *Québec*, 1857, pp. 12.

SAUSSERET, *L'Abbé.*

I. La Sœur Bourgeoys. *Troyes*, 1865 (?)

SAVAGE, *Mrs.*

I. Watch : the Prophecy of the Scripture and Truth which came to pass in the year 1851. *Toronto*, 1857.

SAWTELL, *Mrs.* M. ETHELIND. A contributor to the *Literary Garland.*

I. The Mourner's Tribute ; or, Effusions of Melancholy Hours. *Montreal*, 1840.

SAYER, ROBERT.

I. The North American Pilot for Newfoundland, Labrador, the Gulf and River St. Lawrence ; being a Collection of sixty accurate Charts and Plans, drawn from original surveys : taken by James Cook and Michael Lane, Surveyors, and Joseph Gilbert, and other Officers in the King's Service : published by permission of the Right Honorable the Lords Commissioners of the Admiralty. Chiefly engraved by the late Mr. Thomas Jefferys, Geographer to the King ; on 36 copper plates. *London*, 1775, folio.

SCHMOUTH, J. E. Prof. in the Agricultural Sch., St. Anne, L. C.

I. Direction pour la Culture du Tabac. *Québec*, 1865, pp. 24.

SCHULTZ, JOHN C., *M. D.* Ed. of the *Nor' Wester* newspaper, (Red River Settlement.)

I. Botany of the Red River Settlement and the Old Red River Trail. *Trans. Bot. Soc. Can.*, 1861.

SCOBIE, HUGH. A Can. journ. B. at Fort George, Co. Inverness, Scot., 29 Apl., 1811. D. at Toronto, 4 Dec., 1853. Ed. at the Academy of Tain. On the death of his father, in 1832, he emigrated to Can. with his family. For some time he followed the occupation of a farmer in U. C. He became an active and zealous mem. of the Established Ch. of Scot. in this country, to which he had always belonged ; and, in 1838, that body induced him to establish and ed. a journal in their interest, which was called the *Scotsman*, (Tor.)

  "Only two numbers of the paper, however," says a sketch of Mr. S. which appeared in his paper "bearing this name, was issued, as how well soever *Scotsman* might have designated the immediate object of the journal, it was not patriotic enough in the broadest sense of that term, to meet the liberal views of Mr. S., and he therefore changed it into the *British Colonist*."

The paper was first published weekly. It gradually increased in public favour, and from the first took rank as a leading organ of public opinion in the Province.

We again quote from the sketch before mentioned :

  "After the Church of Scotland had obtained those rights she struggled for."

"The *British Colonist* ceased to be the organ of a party or to have connection with ecclesiastical affairs of any kind, further than the publication of news of every denomination of religion. It neither suited the tastes nor the character of Mr. S., to do the drudgery of organship, or to support any ministry or set of men, without reference to their proper and particular merits. He therefore determined to assume the position of an independent journalist; and he has ever and consistently maintained that character, up to his last hour. He knew and calculated the price he had to pay for daring to be independent. He met, as he expected, the disingenuous attacks of the men of all the extreme parties. Again, he had his motives deliberately and elaborately misconstrued; and slander did its worst. It was said he was 'on the edge,' only to see which way the 'cat might jump,' in order to advance his own interest. No imputations could be more false, as his friends knew; and as is well proved by the fact, that he never did become the organ of any set of men, or any Government. We say, well proved, because when we have seen it has been the interest of each succeeding government, to buy up little prints all over the Country, it was with stronger reason their interest, to secure, if they could, the services of a journal so influential as the *British Colonist*. So it follows that, their not doing it was proof they could not; and we do not go too far, when we say, that for this thing the independent journalists of Canada, owe Mr. S., more than respect,—they owe him gratitude, for an example of the success of an independent journalist in times when every engine of corruption was used against him, is a proof of a trial, and proof that integrity and independence will ever meet their fitting reward. It required much in all the circumstances of the case to establish this, but the truth elicited, was worth more than the cost. We have said it did not suit Mr. S's. taste to do the drudgery of a party or a ministry. We might with truth have used a strong expression, and said that, it did not accord with his nature. He was a man of independence as stern, and rugged, and well defined, as his native mountains. Born of the race of mountaineers he shewed those virtues for which history has made them famous. He gloried in being independent and he often laughed with quiet scorn, at the efforts which party politicians, time and again, made to crush him. Up to his last hours, it was his delight to tell to his friends the story of his struggles and the plots of divers politicians to destroy his influence; and how signally he had foiled them. He dwelt with pride, as he had good cause, on all those things; yet not with empty boasting."

22

From a weekly paper, the *British Colonist* became a semi-weekly; then, in addition Mr. S. published the *Daily Colonist*: and to that he added a weekly paper, the *News of the Week*. All these papers survived their originator and founder for some years. He also established the *Canadian Almanac*, which has been continued, first by Mr. Maclear, and latterly by Dr. Chewett, (Tor.) In politics Mr. S. was a Liberal Conservative.

SCOTT, CHARLES, (Mont.)
I. Thoughts on the Government, Union, Danger, Wants and Wishes of the Canadas; and on the proper line of policy of the British Parliament in these respects: being a Letter to Mr. Hitchings, of Toronto, occasioned by, and containing strictures on one addressed to him by Dr. Dunlop, conveying his thoughts on the subject of Responsible Government. *Montreal*, 1839, pp. 135, 8vo.

"Dr. Dunlop wrote a letter to Mr. Hitchings, on Responsible Governments, which was published in the Toronto *Patriot*, and in the Montreal *Gazette*, which gave great offence to Mr. Charles Scott, 'late manager of the Bank of British North America,' at Montreal, who thereupon wrote this pamphlet in reply."—RICH.

SCOTT, *Rev.* JONATHAN. A Wes. Meth. Min., (Tor.) Has contributed to the religious press on both sides of the Atlantic. Was ed. of the *Christian Guardian* (Tor.), the organ of the Wesl. Meth. body in Can., from 1839 to 1843.

SCOTT, *Rev.* JONATHAN.
I. A Brief View of the Religious Tenets and Sentiments lately published and spread in the Province of Nova Scotia; which are contained in a book entitled, *Two Mites on some of the most important and much disputed points of Divinity*. And in a sermon preached at Liverpool, Nov. 19, 1782; and in a pamphlet entitled, *The Antitraditionist*, all being publications of Mr. Henry Alline, with some brief Reflections and Observations; Also, a view of the ordination of the author of these books: together with a discourse on external order. *Halifax*, 1784, pp. 334, 8vo.

SCOTT, *Rev.* WILLIAM.

I. Letters on Superior Education, in its relation to the progress and permanency of Wesleyan Methodism. *Toronto*, 1860, pp. 70.

SCUDDER, SAMUEL H.

I. Account of a recent visit to Lake Winnipeg and the Saskatchawan River. *Proc. Nat. His. Soc.*, (Bos.) 1860.

II. List of Orthoptera on a Trip from Assiniboia to Cumberland. *Can. Nat.* 1862.

SCADDING, *Rev.* HENRY, *M. A., D. D.* A Min. of the Ch. of Eng. Although his family emigrated to Can. in 1792, at the first organization of the Upper Province. having obtained grants of land in Whitby and in the neighbourhood of York (Tor.) Dr. S. was born in Devonshire in 1813. His first sch. education was acquired in the York Grammar Sch., then in charge of the Rev. Dr. Strachan. In 1833 he became a mem. of St. John's Coll., Cambridge, where he obtained the degree (in Mathematics) of B. A. in 1837; and in due course proceeded to M. A., in 1840. On revisiting Cambridge in 1852, he received the degree of D. D. In 1837 he was admitted to Holy Orders, at Quebec, by Bish. Mountain. In 1840 he was apptd. one of the domestic chaplains to the Anglican Bish. of Toronto (Dr. Strachan). From 1838 to 1862 he held a classical professorship in Upper Canada Coll. From 1847 to the present date (1867), he has been Rector of the Ch. of the Holy Trinity, (Tor.) Dr S. has contributed many papers on subjects connected with philology, numismatics &c., to the *Canadian Journal of Industry, Science and Art*, (Tor.) In the 1st Series " *On Vesuvius and its Neighbourhood ;*" " *On Occidental Discoveries.*" In the 2nd Series " *On Phonetic Anomalies observed in the Modern Forms of Ancient Proper Names ;*" " *On the Etymology of Ontario ;*" " *An Annotated Catalogue of the Greek and Roman Coins in the Collection of the Canadian Institute ;*" and the essays " *Errata Recepta, written and spoken.*" Dr. S. contributed to the *Brit. Am. Mag.*, and has written some elaborate critical reviews of books in a Toronto daily journal.

I. The Eastern Oriel Opened ; an address on the laying of the Foundation Stone of the University of Toronto. *Toronto*, 1842, pp. 11.

II. The President's Valedictory Address, delivered before the Athenæum of Toronto. *Do.* 1846, pp. 12.

III. A Memorial of the Rev. William Honeywood Ripley, Classical Master in Upper Canada Coll. *Do.* 1849.

IV. A Dead Christendom Reviving ; an address delivered at the close of the Crimean War. *Do.* 1855, pp. 16.

" Distinguished by that right feeling, correct principle, and careful collation of facts, which we should have expected from the Reverend Incumbent."—*Colonist,* (Tor.)

V. English Civilization Undemonstrative ; an address on the visit of the Prince of Wales to Canada. *Do.* 1860. pp. 23.

VI. Early Notices of Toronto. [Reprinted from the *Brit. Am. Mag.*] *Do.* 1853.

VII. Shakspeare, the Seer—the Interpreter. *Do.* 1864, pp. 88, 8vo.

" There is much thoughtful writing in the address and the highest appreciation of Shakspeare. Unlike many of the Tercentenary addresses Dr. Scadding's is especially deserving of attention, as it takes a comprehensive view of Shakspeare's influence and his prophetic character. It is the most philosophic and suggestive paper we have seen on a subject of universal interest."—*Public Opinion* (Lon.)

" Not only greatly eloquent, but profoundly true, to our thinking.—MRS. COWDEN CLARKE.

VIII. Truth's Resurrections ; a memorial of Easter. *Do.* 1865, pp. 61.

IX. Christian Pantheism ; an address on Thanksgiving Day. *Do.* 1865. pp. 11.

SEATON, *Field Marshal Lord.* Formerly Sir John Colborne. Was Lt. Gov. of U. C., from 1829 to 1835, and subsequently Gov. Genl. and Commander in Chief in B. N. A.

Addresses presented to Major General Sir John Colborne, Lt. Governor of Upper Canada. *Toronto*, 1836, 8vo.

SECCOMBE, *Rev.* JOHN, *A. M.* The Eng. colonization of N. S. must be dated from the settlement of Halifax in 1749. A few years later the Co. of Lunenburg was settled by Protestants from Germany and other parts of the Continent of Europe ; and about the year 1760 several townships were settled by immigrants from Connecticut and other places in New Eng. The Min.'s in the Province were chiefly either Episcopalians or New Eng. Puritans, generally called in N. S., Presbyterians, but being in reality Congregationalists. To the latter Mr. S. belonged. He was a min. for some time of the Protestant Dissenting Meeting House in Halifax, called Mather Ch., in honor of Cotton Mather, and now known as St. Matthews Ch., and also of Chester in Lunenburg, at which place he resided at the time of his death in 1793. He was min. in Halifax as early as 1769. In the latter part of last century he was looked up to with great veneration as the father of the dissenting ch.'s, and generally esteemed for his high Christian character, as well as respected for his scholarship and literary attainments. Mr. S. was b. at Medford, Mass., April, 1708. He graduated at Harvard in 1728, and in 1733 was ordained min. of the town of Harvard, where he remained until his resignation in 1757. Six years afterward he went to N. S. In general literature he is well known as the author of *Father Abbey's Will*, a comic poem containing much native humour.

I. An Ordination Sermon, on John 21 : 15, 16 ; preached at the ordination of Mr. Briun Romcas Comingoe, as Minister of the Dutch Calvinists at Lunenburg, in the year 1770. *Halifax*, 1770.

II. A Sermon occasioned by the Death of the Honorable Abigail Belcher, late Consort of Jonathan Belcher, Esq., late Lt. Governor and Commander in Chief and His Majesty's present Chief Justice of His Province of Nova Scotia, delivered at Halifax, in the said Province, Oct. 20, 1771 ; with an Epistle by Mather Byles, D. D. *Boston*, N. D.

III. A Sermon, occasioned by the Death of Mrs. Margaret Green, consort of the late Honorable Benjamin Green, Esq., delivered at Halifax, in the Province of Nova Scotia, Feby. 1st, 1778. *Halifax*, pp. 21.

SEDGEWICK, *Rev.* ROBERT. Presb. Min. (Musquodoboit, N. S.)

I. The Proper Sphere and Influence of Woman in Christian Society ; a Lecture. *Halifax*, 1856, pp. 47, 8vo.

II. Amusements for Youth ; a Lecture. *Do.*, 1858, pp. 29, 8vo.

III. The Papacy : the Idolatry of Rome ; a Lecture. *Do.*, 1859, pp. 59, 8vo.

SEEMANN, B.

I. Flora of Esquimaux Land. *London*, 1852, r. 4to.

SELKIRK, *Rt. Hon.* THOMAS, *Earl of.* The founder of the Red River Settlement, H. B. Territory. B. 1774. D. 8 Apl., 1820. Besides the pamphlets given below he was the author of a treatise on Emigration and several political tracts.

I. Sketch of the British Fur Trade in North America ; with observations relative to the North-West Company of Montreal. *London*, 1816, pp. 130, 8vo ; *New York*, 1818.

II. A Letter to the Earl of Liverpool from the Earl of Selkirk, accompanied by a Correspondence, with the Colonial Department (in the years 1817, 1818, 1819), on the subject of the Red River Settlement in North America. *London*, 1819, pp. 224, 8vo.

Printed for private distribution only.

Narrative of Occurrences in the Indian Countries of North America since the connexion of the Rt. Hon. the Earl of Selkirk with the Hudson's Bay Company, and his attempt to Establish a Colony in the Red River ; with a detailed account of His Lordship's Military Expedition to, and subsequent proceedings at Fort William, in Upper Canada. *London*, 1817, pp. xiv and 152. ' Appendix ' pp. 87, 8vo.

A Statement respecting the Earl of Selkirk's Settlement upon the Red River, in North America, its destruction in 1815 and 1816, and the massacre of Gov. Semple and his party. With observations upon a recent publication, entitled " *A Narrative of Occurrences in the Indian Countries*," &c. *D.*, 1817, pp. 194, Appendix 100 (Map) 8vo.

"The statement contained in the following sheets was, some time ago, printed and circulated among Lord Selkirk's personal friends, and some other individuals to whom it was thought proper to communicate the facts which it contained." *Preface.*

The Communications of "Mercator," upon the contest between the Earl of Selkirk and the Hudson's Bay Company on one side, and the North-West Company on the other. Republished from the *Montreal Herald*. *Montreal*, 1817, pp. 100, 8vo.

Trials of the Earl of Selkirk versus the North-West Company in 1818. *Montreal*, 1819, 8vo.

Report of the Proceedings connected with the Disputes between the Earl of Selkirk and the North-West Company, at the Assizes held at York, in Upper Canada, Oct. 1818. From minutes taken in Court. *London* 1819, pp. 404, 8vo.

A Narrative of the Transactions in the Red River country; from the commencement of the operations of the Earl of Selkirk till the summer of the year 1816. By Alexander McDonnell (whom see). *London*, 1819, pp. 106, 8vo.

(See *Amos*, A.)

(" *McDonald*, Archibald.)

(" *Strachan*, Rt. Rev. John.)

SELLAR, THOMAS. A Can. journ. B. in Elgin, Scot., 1828. In 1857 purchased the *Times* (Brampton, U. C.,) which he conducted until the following year, when he assumed the management and ed. control of the *Echo*, the organ of the Evangelical or Low Ch. party in the Ch. of Eng. Mr. S. published this paper in Toronto up to 1861, when he removed it to Montreal, where it still continues under his control. In addition to his regular duties on the press, he has at various times corresponded for the *Daily Telegraph*, *Daily News*, *Constitutional Record* (Lon.), the *Courier* (Liverpool) and the *Herald* and *Reformers' Gazette* (Glas.) He has also contributed to several provincial periodicals. Mr. S. has been connected with the Can. Press Association for a considerable period, was for 4 years Secy. and is now 1st Vice President of that body. He is also President of the Mercantile Literary Association (Mont.)

SEMPÉ, EDOUARD. A native of France. Resided in Montreal for a short time, where he contributed poetical pieces to the French newspapers. Many of his poems have appeared of late in *La Revue Canadienne*.

I. Cantate en l'Honneur de Son Altesse Royale le Prince de Galles à l'occasion de Son voyage au Canada. *Montréal*, 1860.

SÉNÉCAL, D. H. A French Can. writer. Has contributed in prose and verse, to different French Can. newspapers and periodicals, the titles of the more important of which we give :

I. Etude historique et biographique sur Pothier. 1858.

II. Introduction à un cours d'histoire du droit ; lecture. 1864.

III. Histoire de la Coutume de Paris en Canada. *Revue Can.* 1864.

IV. L'Encyclique et la brochure de Monseigneur Dupanloup. *Do.* 1865.

V. Quelques mots sur l'album de F. Jehin-Prume. *Do.* do.

VI. M. F. Jehin-Prume. *Do.* do.

SERRILL, E. W., *C. E.*

I. Report on a Railway Suspension Bridge over the St. Lawrence River at Quebec. *Quebec*, 1852.

SEWELL, *Hon.* JONATHAN, *LL.D.* Chief Justice of L. C., from 1808 to 1838. B. at Cambridge, Mass., 6 June, 1766. D. at Quebec, 12 Nov., 1839. Ed. at the Grammar Sch., Bristol, Eng., and afterwards entered Brasenose Coll., Oxford. He emigrated to N. B. in 1785, where he studied his profession. In 1789, was admitted to practice, and in the same year removed to Quebec. In 1793, was appointed Solicitor, and in 1795, Attorney Gen. and Judge of the Court of Vice-Admiralty. He sat in the Parliament of L. C. during 3 consecutive Parliaments. Harvard Univ. conferred upon him the degree of LL.D. In 1844, the prospectus of a work bearing the following title, was issued by one of his sons : "Notes of Decisions in the Court of King's Bench for the District of Quebec, collected by Jonathan Sewell, Esq., late Chief Justice of Lower Canada." This work was never published, owing to the destruction of the MS. in a fire which afterwards occurred.

"Not only was Mr. Sewell a profound lawyer, but he was a good dramatist, a fair musician, a critical student of poetry, and a very facile writer of verse."—FENNINGS TAYLOR : *Poet s. of Brit. Am's.*

I. A Plan for the Federal Union of the British Provinces in North America. *London*, 1814.

II. On the Advantages of Opening the River St. Lawrence to the Commerce of the World. *Do.*, 1814.

"His Royal Highness the Duke of Kent appreciated the importance of both projects, and gave Mr. Sewell great assistance in laying them before the King's Government."— FENNINGS TAYLOR: *Idem.*

III. An Essay on the Juridical History of France so far as relates to the law of Lower Canada. *Quebec*, 1824, 8vo.

IV. Plan for a General Legislative Union of the British Provinces in North America, by Messrs. Sewell, Stuart, Robinson and Strachan. *London*, 1824, 8vo.

V. On Stoves used in Russia for warming dwelling houses. *Trans. Lit. and His. Soc.* (*Que.*,) 1831.

VI. Notes upon the Dark Days of Canada. *Do.*, do.

Proceedings in the Assembly of Lower Canada on the Rules of Practice in the Courts of Justice and the Impeachment of Jonathan Sewell and James Monk, Esqrs., 1814, pp. 64, 4to.

SEWELL, WILLIAM GEORGE. A Can. and Am. author and journ. B. at Quebec, 1829. D. there, 1862. Was a grandson of the above. Mr. S. was bred to the Bar, but although well read and very much attached to his profession, its practice was irksome and disagreeable to him. In 1853 he removed to N. Y., where he became translator and law reporter to the *Herald* newspaper, "the duties of which position," says that journal in its obituary notice, "he discharged with ability." Shortly afterwards he joined the ed. staff of the *Daily Times*, of the same city, "where his good service, sound judgment and varied accomplishments were ever appreciated." Some years previous to his death he retired to the West Indies, in order to guard against the inroads of tubercular consumption, a disease which he had contracted whilst performing his arduous newspaper labours. While residing there he wrote a series of letters to the *Times* on the Emancipation Question and the position of the blacks on those islands, which attracted considerable attention, both at home and abroad; they were considered exceedingly valuable, both for the large amount of information which they contained and the spirit of fairness in which they were written. In compliance with the demands of many parties, Mr. S. afterwards reproduced these letters in book-form and through this work established a high reputation for himself as an author both in Am. and Europe. In addition to his writings in the newspaper press he contributed many papers to the leading periodicals in the U. S., on various subjects, which were marked by more than ordinary literary talent. Had he lived, there is no doubt but that with his great ability and his intense powers of application he would have attained a high place amongst the *literati* of the present day.

"His death has deprived the New York press of an able, honest and most industrious member; it has robbed a very large circle of journalists of an affectionate, faithful and whole-souled friend."—*Herald*, (N.Y.) "Mr. Sewell was a writer of ability. His work on the West Indies contains matter and reflections of the greatest interest which we remember to have seen on this important question." *Express* (*Do.*)

I. Ordeal of Free Labour in the British West Indies. *New York*, 1861, pp. 325, 12mo.; *London*, 2nd ed., 1862, 8vo.

"It contains a mass of facts and testimony extremely valuable both for their completeness and the intelligence with which they are grouped."—*Post* (Bos.)

"This is, as it seems to us, a work of very great value. It gives the result of personal examination, and puts on record specific facts and statistical details. The author is trammelled in his observations neither by preconceived theories nor by the desire of generalizing his results. He, in fact, declines presenting general conclusions, on the ground that each island had its own history, its peculiarities of position, soil, and adaptation, its commercial facilities or hindrances, its numerical proportions and social relations between the dominant and the enslaved races, and that there is not one of the particulars comprehended under these heads that has not modified the effects of emancipation."—*N. A. Rev.*

SHALER, N. S.
I. On the Geology of Anticosti Island, in the Gulf of St. Lawrence. *Proc. Nat. His. Soc.* (Bos.,) 1861.

SHANLY, WALTER, *C. E.*, *M. P.* B. in Stradbally, Queen's Co., Irel., where he was ed. Has held appointments under Dept. of Public Works, Can., and been employed as Chief Engineer on various works of importance. Was General Manager of the G. T. Railway, Can., from 1858 to 1862. Sat in the Leg. Assembly, Can., from 1863 until the Union of the Provinces, 1867, when he was returned as a mem. of the new House of Commons.

    I. Report on Toronto Harbour. *Toronto*, 1853.

    II. Report of the Toronto and Guelph Railway. *Do.*, 1852.

    III. Report on the Ottawa and French River Navigation Project. *Montreal*, 2nd ed., 1863, pp. 56, 8vo.

SHANNON, WILLIAM.

    I. The United Empire Minstrel, with a chronological table of National Events. *Toronto*, 1852, pp. 300.

    II. Narrative of the Proceedings of the Orangemen of Kingston during the visit of H. R. H. the Prince of Wales. *Kingston*, 1860, pp. 50.

SHARPE, LYNCH LAWDON.

    I. The Viceroy's Dream ; or, The Canadian Government not "wide-awake," a mono-dramatico poem. 1838.

    It is in 5 scenes and appears to have reference to the Can. Rebellion of 1837-8. A copy is in the Bodleian Library, Oxford.

SHAW, JOHN.

    I. Ramble through the United States, Canada and the West Indies. *London*, 1856, 8vo.

SHEA, JOHN GILMARY, *LL. D.* An Am. historical writer. B. in N. Y. 1824. Passed a period of 6 years in the Soc. of Jesus, and was for some time a prof. in St. Mary's Coll. (Mont.) Duyckinck says that " the third volume of Bancroft's History drew his attention to the former French colonies in North America, and their romantic interest, and he has since cultivated that field, and incidentally the Spanish colonies, with true antiquarian zeal." He has written and ed. a large number of historical and other works. " From his studies and researches in the history of French colonization, he gathered many manuscripts, from which he

published a series of twenty volumes in antique style, with the type, tail-pieces, initials, and heads of Cramoisy, the French printer of the Seventeenth century." For the last 7 years Dr. S. has ed. the *Historical Mag.* (N. Y.) We append a list of such of his works and publications as relate to our history or affairs :—

    I. Discovery and Exploration of the Mississippi Valley with the original narratives of Marquette, Allouez, &c., (with Map).—*New York*, 1852, 8vo.

    II. History of the Catholic Missions among the Indian Tribes of the United States. 1529—1854, (with plates), *New-York*, 1855, pp. 514, 12mo.

    The portion French missions pp. 123 to 483, is devoted to missions emanating from the mission centre at Quebec. A German translation has appeared at Wurzburg.

    III. Relation de ce qui s'est passé de plus remarquable dans la Mission Abenaquise de Saint Joseph de Sillery, et dans l'établissement de la nouvelle mission de Saint François de Sales, l'année 1684, par R. P. Jacques Bigot, de la Compagnie de Jésus. (Edited,) *Manate*, pp. 61, post 8vo.

    IV. Relation de ce qui s'est passé de plus remarquable dans la Mission Abenaquise de Saint Joseph de Sillery et de Saint François de Sales, l'année 1685. Par le Père Jacques Bigot, de la Compagnie de Jésus. (Edited,) *Manate*, pp. 22, p. 8vo. 1858.

    V. Relation de ce qui s'est passé de plus remarquable dans la Mission des Abenaquis à l'Acadie l'année 1701. Par le Père Vincent Bigot, de la Compagnie de Jésus. (Edited.) *Manate*, pp. 34, p. 8vo.

    VI. Relation de ce qui s'est passé dans la Mission de l'Immaculée Conception au Pays des Illinois, depuis le mois de Mars, 1693, jusqu'en Février, 1694. Par le Père Jacques Gravier, de la Compagnie de Jésus. (Edited.) *Manate*, pp. 65, p. 8vo.

    VII. Copie d'une Lettre écrite par le Père Jacques Bigot de la Compagnie de Jésus, l'an 1684, pour accompagner un collier de pourcelaine envoyé par les Abenaquis de la mission de Saint François de Sales dans la nouvelle au tombeau de leur Saint Patron à Annecy. (Edited,) *Manate*, 1858, pp. 9, 8vo.

    VIII. La Vie du R. P. Pierre Joseph Marie Charmonot de la Compagnie de Jésus. Missionnaire dans la Nouvelle France. Ecrite par lui-même par ordre de son Supérieur. (Edited.) *Nouvelle York*, 1858, pp. 108, 8vo. (plate.)

    IX. Suite de la Vie du R. P. Pierre Joseph Marie Chaumonot de la Compagnie de Jésus, par un père de la même Compagnie avec la manière d'oraison du vénérable Père, écrite par lui-même.—[Edited.] *Nouvelle York*, 1858. pp. 66, 8vo.

X. Relation du Voyage entrepris par feu M. Robert Cavelier, Sieur de la Salle, pour découvrir dans le golfe du Mexique, l'embouchure du fleuve de Mississipy. Par son frère M. Cavelier, prêtre de St. Sulpice, l'un des compagnons de ce voyage.—[Edited,] *Manate*, 1858, pp. 54, 8vo.

XI. Relation de ce qui s'est passé de plus remarquable aux Missions des Pères de la Compagnie de Jésus, en la Nouvelle France, les années 1673 à 1679. Par le R. P. Claude Dablon, Recteur du Collége de Québec et Supérieur des Missions de la Compagnie de Jésus en la Nouvelle France. [Edited,]— *New York*, à la presse Cramoisy, 1859, pp. XIII, p. 290, 8vo.

XII. Relation ou Journal du Voyage du R. P. Jacques Gravier, de la Compagnie de Jésus, en 1700, depuis le pays des Illinois jusqu'à l'embouchure du Mississipi. [Edited.] *Nouvelle York*, 1859, pp. 67, 8vo.

XIII. Relation du Voyage des Premières Ursulines à la Nouvelle Orléans et de leur établissement en cette ville. Par la Rev. Mère St. Augustin de Tranchepain, Supérieure, avec les lettres circulaires de quelques unes de ses sœurs et de la dite Mère, [Edited.] *Nouvelle York*, 1859, pp. 62, 8vo.

XIV. Régistre des Baptêmes et Sepultures qui se sont faits au Fort Duquesne, pendant les années 1753, 1754, 1755 et 1756, [Edited]—*Nouvelle York*, 1859, pp. 61, 8vo.

XV. Journal de la Guerre du Mississippi contre les Chicnchaz, en 1739 et finie en 1740, le 1er n'Avril. Par un Officier de l'armée de M. de Noaille.—[Edited] *Nouvelle York*, 1859, pp. 92, 8vo.

XVI. Relations Diverses sur la Bataille du Malanguoulé, gagné le 9 Juillet, 1755, par les Français sous M. de Beaujeu, Commandant du Fort du Quesne, sur les Anglais sous M. Braddock, Général en chef des troupes Anglaises. Recueillies par Jean Marie Shea, [Edited.]— *Nouvelle York*, 1860. pp. 51, (Portrait,) 8vo.

XVII. Relation de ce qui s'est passé de plus remarquable aux Missions des Pères de la Compagnie de Jésus, en la Nouvelle France, les années 1672 et 1673. Par le R. P. Claude Dablon, Recteur du Collége de Québec, et Supérieur des Missions de la Compagnie de Jésus en la Nouvelle France.—[Edited.] *Nouvelle York*, 1861, pp. 219, 8vo.

XVIII. Relation de la Mission du Mississipi du Séminaire de Québec, en 1700. Par M. M. de Montigny, de St. Côsme et Thaumur de la Source,—[Edited,] *Nouvelle York*, 1861, pp. 66, 8vo.

XIX. Extrait de la Relation des Avantures et Voyage de Mathieu Sâgeau.—(Edited,] *Nouvelle York*, 1863, pp. 32, 8vo.

XX. Grammaire de la langue Mikmaque, par M. l'Abbé Maillard, redigée et mise en ordre par Joseph M. Bélanger, Ptre. [Edited.] *New York*, 1864, pp. 101, 8vo.

XXI. Epistola Rev. P. Gabrielis Dreuillettes, Socretatis Jesu Presbyterè ad Dominum Illustrissimum Dominum Joannem Wintrop, Scutarium heo Eboraci in insula, [Edited,]—*Manhattan*, 1864, pp. 13, 8vo.

XXII.—Relation de sa Captivité parmi les Onneiouts en 1690-1, par le R. P. Pierre Milet, de la Compagnie de Jésus, [Edited.] *Nouvelle York*, 1864, pp. 56, 8vo.

XXIII. Relation des Affaires du Canada, en 1696, et des missions des Pères de la Compagnie de Jésus jusqu'en 1702, [Edited] *New-York* 1865, pp. 73, 8vo.

XXIV. Relation de la Mission Abenaquise de St. François de Sales, l'année 1702. Par le Père Jacques Bigot, de la Compagnie de Jésus [Edited] *Nouvelle York*, 1865, pp. 26, 8vo.

XXV. Lettre du Père Jacques Gravier, de la Compagnie de Jésus, le 23 Février, 1708, sur les affaires de la Louisiane [Edited] *Nouvelle York*, 1865, pp. 18, 8vo.

XXVI. History and General Description of New-France. By the Rev. P. F. X. de Charlevoix, S. J. Translated with notes by John Gilmary Thea. In six volumes, *New York*, 1866, vol. I, pp. 287, 8vo. (maps and plates.)

SHEPPARD, GEORGE. A Can. journ. B. at Newark-on-Trent, Eng., about 1820. Was apprenticed to a book-seller and printer, and from an early age cultivated literary tastes and habits. In his 18th year originated a literary periodical, intituled *The Idler*, which he conducted until the discussions of a Debating Soc., of which he was a mem., awakened an interest in more exciting topics. Godwin's " *Political Justice*," which William Hazlitt says, produced a more profound impression on the youth of his day than any book published, fell into his hands and laid the foundation of extreme views in politics and some peculiarities in religion. He became a contributor to the *Dispatch*, (Lon.,) then under the ed. of Dr. Beaumont, *The New Moral World*, an organ of the co-operative and quasi-communistic movement, which at the time held sway among the industrial classes of Eng., and the

Monthly Repository, an outspoken liberal, journ. then under the management of Mr. W. J. Fox, the eloquent lecturer and afterward mem. for Oldham in the House of Commons. A stenographic report of a political address delivered by Sir Bulwer Lytton, (then Sir E. L. Bulwer,) led to his engagement as reporter of a local radical journal. In 1840 he became reporter of the *Courant,* (Newcastle-on-Tyne,) a commercial non-party paper, of which he soon rose to be ed. In 1843 he visited the Western States, and passed several months on the remote frontier of Wisconsin, then a sparsely settled territory. On his return to Eng. in the spring of the following year he resumed the ed. of the *Courant.* He also became ed. of the *Advertiser,* (Newcastle,) a political journal of the liberal stamp, issued from the *Courant* office; at the same time contributing to the *Morning Chronicle,* and to the *Daily News,* (Lon.,) from the period of its establishment. An oral discussion with Mr. Edward Baines of the *Mercury,* (Leeds.) on the question of voluntary as opposed to state education, brought him into notice as a public speaker; and sharing the excitement generated by the Revolutionary outbreaks on the Continent in 1848 he removed to Hull, where he took an active part in public meetings, and lectured upon the labor question, with a view to mitigate the hostility with which the plans of Louis Blanc and the French Republicans were regarded by the propertied classes. He ed. the *Eastern Counties Herald,* a Hull journal. A series of articles on organized emigration, contributed to a London periodical, and the publication of his book on the North-Western States resulted in the formation of an Iowa Emigration Soc., of which he was chosen leader. Resigning the ed. of the *Herald* early in 1850, he proceeded to Iowa, and during the remainder of the year was occupied with the affairs of the infant settlement. There he formed connections which took him to Washington as associate ed. of the *Daily Republic,* where he remained until the close of the Fillmore administration of which that journal was the organ. From 1854 to 1857 he was retained in the actuarial department of the Can.

Life Assurance Co., (Ham. U. C.) In the autumn of the last mentioned year he re-entered the ranks of journalism as ed. of the *Daily Colonist,* (Tor..) soon afterward, however, coming to a rupture with the ministry of the day, and finally separating from the *Colonist* on the occasion of the Brown-Dorion quarrel with Sir Edmund Head. He next attached himself editorially to the *Globe,* (Tor..) and in Nov. 1859 was the mover of a resolution in favor of dissolution of the Union, in the Reform Convention held there. Through the *Times,* (Ham.,) he continued the advocacy of this and other constitutional changes in the direction of independence. In 1860-61, he was again at Washington, having gone there in the summer of the former year under an engagement with one of the central committees concerned in the then Presidential election. While thus employed he corresponded with various journals, the *Leader,* (Tor.,) amongst others. From 1862 to 1864, he was at Quebec pursuing his profession, first on the *Chronicle* and latterly on the *Mercury.* He was for 12 months occupied as a mem. of the Financial and Departmental Commission, of which he was also Secy. He now resides in N. Y. Mr. S's. reputation as a Can. journalist stood very high; indeed he may be placed in the front rank with the few other gifted and brilliant minds who have, from time to time, held that position. In style clear, nervous and trenchant, often inclined to the sarcastic, he was no uncommon opponent in a controversial warfare; whilst as a partizan he could render the most telling and at the same time the most serviceable assistance. Not a few of our public men and writers for the press have experienced the force of his pen in some chance attack or encounter, and of these there has rarely been found one who possessed the power or the ability or cope successfully with him. We append a list of his several book publications.

I. What have the Whigs done? a political pamphlet by Caleb Wilkins. *Newark,* 1838, pp. 96.

II. A Glimpse of the Far-West. *Newcastle,* 1844; 2nd Ed. *London.*

III. A Handbook of the North-West. *London*, 1849, pp. 300, 12mo.

IV. The Theory and Practice of Life Assurance. *Hamilton*, 1856.

" An ably written pamphlet. • • • It appears to be the substance of a lecture delivered to the members of the Mechanic's Institute, Toronto; and is far superior in matter arrangement, defined objects, and argument, to the generality of lectures of the kind delivered in this country. • • • This is by far the best and most useful little tract on Life Assurance that has yet been published."—*Post Mag.* (Lon.)

V. The Cyclopedia of Biography ; a record of the lives of Eminent Persons, brought down to the present time. [Edited.] *New York*, 1865, pp. 980, Cr. 8vo.

SHEPPARD, *Mrs.* Wife of Hon. William S. Now dead. .

I. On the Recent Shells which characterise Quebec and its environs. *Trans. Lit. and His. Soc.* (Que.,) 1829.

. The authoress received the medal of the Soc. for the above essay.

II. Notes on some of the Song Birds of Canada. *Do.*, 1837.

SHEPPARD, *Mrs.* J. C.

I. Chants Canadiens avec accompagnement de piano. *Québec*, 1856.

SHEPPARD, MAXFIELD. (Que.)

I. Tables for converting deals, planks and staves into Quebec standard. *Quebec*, 1859.

SHEPPARD, *Hon.* WILLIAM, *D. C. L.* (Fairymead, E. T.) D. 1867.

I. Observations on the Plants of Canada described by Charlevoix in his History. *Trans. Lit. His. Soc.* (Que.) 1829.

II. Notes on the Plants of Lower Canada. *Do*, 1831.

III. On the Geographical Distribution of the Coniferæ in Canada. *Annals Bot. Soc. Can.* 1861. Reproduced in *New Phil. Trans.* (Edin.)

IV. Notes on the Trees and Scrubs of Canada. *Can. Nat.* 1865.

SHERWOOD, HAROLD.

I. A Welcome to Albert, Prince of Wales, and other poems. *Toronto*, 1860, pp. 48, 8vo.

SHERWOOD, *Hon.* HENRY. A Can. legislator. Sat. in Can. Parliament from 1843 to 1854. Held office as Sol. Genl. and Atty. Genl., successively.

I. Letter to the President of the Board of Trade, Toronto, on the Usury Laws : by a Citizen. *Toronto*, 1847, pp. 16.

II. Federative Union of the British North American Provinces. *Do*, 1850, pp. 8, 8vo.

SHENSTON, THOMAS S. Registrar of the Co. of Brant, U. C.

I. The County Warden, and Municipal Officer's Assistant. *Brantford*, 1851, pp. 111, 8vo.

II. The Oxford Gazetteer ; containing a complete history of the County of Oxford, from its first settlement, &c. *Hamilton*, 1852, pp. 216, 8vo.

SHIELS, ANDREW, (Dartmouth, N. S.)

I. The Witch of the Wescot ; a tale of Nova Scotia in three cantos ; and other Waste Leaves of Literature. *Halifax*, 1831, pp. 224, 8vo.

SHIRIFF, A. Son of the following.

I. Topographical notices of the Country lying between the Rideau and Penetanguishene. *Trans. Lit. and His. Soc.* (Que.) vol. II.

SHIRIFF, CHARLES.

I. Thoughts on Emigration and on the Canadas as an opening for it. *Quebec*, 1831.

SHIREFF, PATRICK.

I. Tour through North America, with a Comprehensive View of the Canadas and United States, as adapted for Agricultural Emigration. *London?* 1835, 8vo.

SHORTT, *Rev.* JONATHAN, *D. D.* A clergym. of the Ch. of Eng. B. on the Island of Jersey, 1809. D. at Port Hope 24 Augt., 1867. Ordained, 1832. Was Rector of Port Hope U. C. from 1837 until his death. Founded the *Echo and Protestant Episcopal Recorder*, a religious organ of the " Low Church" party of the Ch. of Eng., at Port Hope, in 1850, of which he was ed. for several years. Several of his sermons, addresses and lectures have been printed in pamphlet form.

SHORTT, W. P.

I. Gesta Anglo-Americana scilicet et progymnasmata Novæ Franciæ Pelasgicæ. Liber singularis. *Exeter*, N. D. 8vo.

" This volume is lithographed in Greek : with a preliminary notice, analysis of the work, and notes, in English. The author says, 'the following Greek treatise on America, is perhaps the only historical Greek classic since the days of Procopius.' "—*Cat. Lib. of Parlt. Can.*

SHORTT, W. T. P.

I. Journal of the Principal Occurrences during the Siege of Quebec by the American Revolutionists under Generals Montgomery and Arnold, in 1775-76; containing many anecdotes of moment never yet published; collected from some old manuscripts originally written by an officer, during the gallant defence made by Sir Guy Carleton, afterwards Lord Dorchester. To which are added a Preface and Illustrative Notes. *London*, 1824, pp. III, 8vo.

SHREVE, *Rev.* CHARLES J., *A. B.* " Rector of Christ's Ch., Guysborough, N. S."

I. The Divine Origin and uninterrupted Succession of Episcopacy maintained. In a series of letters addressed to the Rev. A. W. McLeod, in answer to his letters intituled: "The Methodist Ministry defended." *Halifax*, 1840, pp. 163, 8vo.

II. A Sermon preached in Christ Church, Guysboro', on behalf of the Bishopric Endowment Fund. *Do.*, 1852, pp. 15, 8vo.

SIBBALD, — Ed. of the *Canadian Mag.* (York, U. C.) 1832.

SIDDONS, J. H. Formerly of the H. E. I. Co's Artillery. Contributed a short article " *The Canadian on his Travels* " to the *B. A. Mag.* (Tor.,) 1863.

I. The Canadian Volunteer's Handbook; a compendium of military facts and suggestions adapted to Field Service. *Toronto*, 1863, pp. 75.

SILLIMAN, BENJAMIN.

I. Remarks made on a Short Tour between Hartford and Quebec. *New Haven*, 1824, 12mo.; 2nd Ed.

SIMMONS, J. L. A., *C. B.* Colonel Royal Engineers, and Major Genl. in the Ottoman Army.

I. Defence of Canada considered as an Imperial question with reference to a War with America. *London*, 1865, pp. 27.

SIMPSON, *Sir* GEORGE, *Kt.* For many years Gov. of the Hudson's Bay Co. B. in Rosshire, Scot. D. near Montreal, 7

Sept., 1860. Came to Can. in 1820, and proceeded to the North-West in the employment of the H. B. Co., in whose service he remained until his death. Evinced much interest in the cause of geographical discovery on the northern coast of the Am. Continent and was instrumental in having several successful expeditions of discovery fitted out.

I. Narrative of a Voyage round the World in 1841-2. *London*, 1847, 2 vols. 8vo; *Philadelphia.* Do.

SIMPSON, J.

I. Preliminary Report on the projected Railway between the ports of Halifax and Quebec. *Montreal*, 1847 (?) pp. 22, 12mo.

SIMPSON, *Hon.* JOHN. Assist. Auditor of Public Accounts, Can. Was ed. of the *Chronicle* (Niagara.) for some years.

I. The Canadian Forget-me-not for 1837. *Niagara*, pp. 157.

II. The Canadian Mercantile Almanack. *Do.*, 1844.

"A neat and useful compendium."— *Sim. Col. Mag.*

SIMPSON, J. B. Son of the above.

I. Memorials of the late Civil Service Rifle Corps. *Ottawa*, 1867, pp. 118, sm. 8vo.

SIMPSON, THOMAS. Nephew of Sir G. Simpson (whom see.)

I. Narrative of the Discoveries on the N. W. coast of America, effected by the officers of the Hudson's Bay Company, during the years 1836-9. (With Map.) *London*, 1843, pp. 440, 8vo.

SIMPSON, W.

I. Synopsis of the Marine Invertebrata of Grand Manan; or, the Region about the mouth of the Bay of Fundy, New Brunswick. (With three Plates.) *Smith. Con. to Know.*, 1854, pp. 68.

SIMPSON, W. S.

I. Report of the Trial of DeReinhard and McLellan, for murder, committed in the Indian territories, in 1818. *Montreal*, 1819, 8vo.

SKEY, FRANCIS W.

I. Red Riding Hood, an operatic interlude, in two acts. *Quebec*, 1854, pp. 20, 8vo.

SLADDEN, WILLIAM. Formerly a Parliamentary Agent in Can.

I. Synopsis in the form of a Comprehensive Index of the Common Law Procedure Act 1856 and the Common Law Procedure Act 1857 combined. *Toronto*, 1857, pp. 184.

II. The Registry Laws affecting lands in Upper Canada, with an analytical index shewing them in combination, with judicial Dicta and Index. *Do.*, 1857.

" His book is of a class which is eminently useful and practical."—*U. C. Law Journ.*

SLADE, ARTHUR.

I. The Conflagration; comprising two poems. *St. John's, N. B.*, 1837, pp. 32, 8vo.

SLEIGH, *Colonel.*

I. Pine Forests and Hacmatack Clearings; or, Travels, Life and Adventures in the British North American Provinces. *London*, 1853, 8vo.

SLEIGH, W. W.

I. Brief Remarks on the projected Re-union of Lower and Upper Canada. *Montreal*, 1822, pp. 16, 8vo.

SLIGHT, *Rev.* BENJAMIN, *A. M.* A Wesl. Min. of the Can. Conference, now deceased.

I. Indian Researches, or facts concerning North American Indians. Including notices of their present state of improvement in their social, civil and religious condition, with hints for their future advancement. *Montreal*, 1844, pp. 179, 8vo.

" Mr. Slight has been a careful student of Indian character, and he has brought to the task a mind naturally acute, and enriched with the stores of learning which fit the man to become the minister of God."—*Lit. Garland.*

II. The Apocalypse explained in two series of discourses on the entire book of the Revelation of St. John. *Do.* 1855, 12mo.

SMALL, H. BEAUMONT. Is a graduate of Lincoln Coll., Oxford, and a Fellow of the Radcliffe Soc.; Master of the Grammar Sch., Buckingham, L. C. Has contributed to *Household Words, Harper's Mag.*, and the *Can. Patriot*, (Mont.) Is preparing for the press a descriptive history of Can.

I. The Animals of North America Series I. Mammalia. *Montreal*, 1864, pp. 112, 8vo.

" The object of this work is to enumerate the different species of animals of the Northern Continent of America. The author has been very successful in the task he undertook."—*Herald*, (Mont.)

" An unimposing, neatly printed volume, well worthy of perusal, and written in a style seldom met with in concise hand-books."—*Athen.* (Lon.)

II. The Animals of North America. Series II. Fresh Water Fish. *Do.* 1865, pp. 72, 8vo. *

" The angler will find it an invaluable companion, and had it been published in his day, we can almost fancy quaint 'old Izaak' recommending it to his pupil 'Venator' as they sat under shelter, while a 'smoking shower passes off.' "—*Gazette* (Mont.)

III. The Canadian Hand-book and Tourist's guide; giving a description of Canadian lake and river scenery, and places of historical interest, with the best spots for fishing and shooting. (With photographic illustrations by Notman.) *Do.* 1866, pp. 196, 8vo.

SMALL, JOHN.

I. The Farmer's Fruit Book; or, the the practice of fruit growing in the orchard and garden, adapted to the climate of Canada West and the Northern States. *Woodstock*, 1852.

SMALLWOOD, CHARLES, *M. D, LL. D., D. C. L.* Prof. of Meteorology Univ. McGill Coll. (Mont.) B. at Birmingham, Eng. 1812, where he was ed. Graduated at Univ. Coll. Came to Can. in 1833, and in following year went to reside at Isle Jesus, L. C., where he established a meteorological and electrical observatory, and made some important discoveries in meteorology. Since 1858 he has been Prof. of Meteorology in McGill Coll. He resides in Montreal, and has charge of the Univ. Observatory. Has contributed largely on subjects connected with his favourite study and on medical science to periodicals in Gt. Brit., the U. S. and Can. Has sent papers to the Brit. Meteorological Soc. on Ozone and Snow Crystal, and to the Am. Ass. for the Advancement of Science, on Meteorology,

* Mr. Small is now preparing the Third Series comprising.—" *The Birds of North America.*"

Astronomy and Anemometry. Many papers from his pen have appeared in *Silliman's Journal*. In Can. the chief periodicals to which he has contributed, are the *Brit. Am. Journal* (Medical), the *Can. Naturalist* (Mont.), and the *Can. Journal* (Tor.) We append a list of his papers in the 2 latter. Dr. S. has taken a warm interest in the Literary and Scientific Associations in the Province, to nearly all of which he is in some way attached. He is also a mem. of the *Soc. Météorologique de France*, of the *Observatoire Physique Central*, (St. Petersburg,) of the *Académie Royale des Sciences des Lettres des Beaux Arts* (Belgium.) of the National Institute of the U. S., and of the Academy of Natural Science, (Philadelphia.)

I. Contributions to Canadian Meteorology. Reduced from Observations taken at St. Martin, Isle Jesus, C. E. *Montreal*, 1860.

Canadian Naturalist.

I. Monthly Meteorological Register at St. Martin, Isle Jesus, from 1857 to 1862.

II. On Ozone. 1857–1859.

III. On the Meteorology of the Vicinity of Montreal, being reduced from observations taken at St. Martin. Do.

IV. Contributions to Meteorology. 1858.

V. The Observatory at St. Martin, Isle Jesus ; with notes. Do.

VI. Some Observations on Donati's Comet of 1858. 1858.

VII. On the Cold Term of January, 1859, from observations taken at St. Martin, Lat. 45° 32′ N., Long. 73° 36′ W., 118 feet above the level of the sea. 1859.

VIII. Contributions to Meteorology, from observations taken at St. Martin. Do.

IX. On the Aurora Borealis of the 28th of August, 1859. Do.

X. Contributions to Meteorology for the year 1861. 1862.

Canadian Journal.

I. Mean Results of Meteorological observations made at St. Martin, Isle Jesus. 1853.

II. Monthly Meteorological Registers at Isle Jesus, from 1853 to 1862.

III. Description and Notes on the Observatory at Isle-Jesus. 1858.

IV. Contributions to Meteorology, from observations taken at St. Martin, Isle Jesus. 1859–1860.

SMART, C.

I. The Emigrant's Guide to Upper Canada ; or, Sketches of the present state of that Province, collected from a Residence therein during the years 1817, 1818, 1819. Interspersed with reflections. *London*, 1821, pp. 335, 12mo.

SMILEY, ROBERT REID. A Can. journ. B. in Irel. D. at Hamilton, U. C., 10 May, 1855. When a mere boy came with his parents to Can., and was apprenticed to the printing business in the *Herald* Office, (King.), where by dint of energy, perseverance and hard work, he raised himself from being the roller-boy to the position of foreman of the establishment. Subsequently served in the latter capacity in the office of the *British Whig*. Leaving Kingston in 1844, he went to Montreal, where he was employed as foreman in the printing establishment of Starke & Co. While in Montreal, in the summer of 1846, was induced by some of the leading men of the Conservative party to establish the *Spectator* (Ham.,) a semi-weekly journal, whose first number was issued on the 9 July of that year. From a very full and affectionate obituary notice of Mr. S., written by his colleague, Mr. Gillespy, we extract the following, which in addition to furnishing our readers with an account of the labours and services of the subject of this notice in the cause of Can. journalism and constitutional government, will also afford a brief view of the early history of the *Spectator* :

"The manly, independent and straightforward course it [the *Spectator*] pursued, soon earned for it the esteem of all parties, and though recognized as the organ of the Upper Canadian Conservatives, it continued to maintain the independent position it had assumed. When the Draper Ministry came into power, it was soon found that their truckling policy was not calculated to advance the interests of the party, of which the *Spectator* was the organ, and it consequently waged an uncompromising warfare against them. In a very short time Mr. Draper found his way to the bench; the ministry fell to pieces, and the party became almost annihilated. To raise up the party again was indeed a hopeless task, still the *Spectator* pursued its undeviating course, under the able management of Mr. Smiley. Then it was that the great and all-absorbing question of the Clergy Reserves was brought prominently before the people. The Reformers whilst clamoring for the abolition of the Reserves, submitted to be duped by their leaders, and the question, through the selfish aims of the men in power, was permitted to be kept in abeyance from Parliament to Parliament, until at length the pressure from without compelled them to take a more decided stand, although they never intended to bring it to a final settlement. All this time the *Spectator* earnestly labored on the liberal side of this great question, and by its able advocacy, won the support of the moderate men of both the Conservative and Reform parties. It took a prominent stand in opposition to the late ministry, and no doubt contributed greatly to their defeat. The views it enunciated on the leading questions of the day were being gradually adopted by the leaders of the Conservative party, and on the disruption of the late ministry, Sir Allan McNab and his present Conservative colleagues in the Government readily gave way, thus virtually adopting the very principles the *Spectator* had all along been contending for, and acting on its advice they assumed the reins of Government.

"In 1852, the daily issue of the *Spectator* was commenced under very discouraging circumstances. The first year, however, more than realized the expectations formed of its success. * * * So flattering were its prospects that it was found necessary to enlarge its dimensions, which change took place on the very day of Mr. Smiley's death. He accomplished what had long been his ambition, namely: to place the *Spectator* in such a position as would give it a standing unsurpassed by any journal in the Province. But alas, how uncertain is life!—little did he think that the day on which his journal was enlarged should witness his death—Although his mission may be said to have been accomplished, he was actively engaged in planning arrangements for the future up to the last day of his life."

We may add that Mr. S. was entirely a self-educated man. As a public writer he was an ornament to the Can. press, as he would have been to that of any country. Of him it might well be said that he possessed the pen of a ready writer. His style combined strength and vigour with great clearness and precision. In the cause of truth and on the side of the weak and oppressed, he was always to be found, and his general life was so blameless, tolerant and charitable, that he went out of the world leaving scarcely a single enemy behind him. His premature death was regarded as a public calamity by people of all classes and opinions.

SMITH, COKE. Draughtsman to the late Earl of Durham.

I. Views in the Canadas. *London*, 1839, fol.

SMITH, DOUGLAS SHELDON.

I. Selections from Lucien : comprising Charon, Vita, and Timon. Translated with copious annotations. *Toronto*, 1865.

"The translation though pretty literal is spirited, and shows a good appreciation of Lucien's meaning."—*Globe*, (Tor.)

SMITH, GUSTAVE. Organist to St. Patrick's Ch. (Mont.) Was joint-ed. of *Les Beaux Arts*, a journal published there.

I. Abécédaire musical contenant la théorie simplifiée des principes élémentaires appliquée à l'étude d'un instrument ou de la voix. *Montréal*, pp. 32.

SMITH, JAMES. Prof. of Agriculture in the Agricultural and Industrial Coll., (Rimouski, L. C.)

I. Havre de Refuge. Rimouski *vs.* Bic et chemin de fer des Trois-Pistoles. *Québec*, 1856, pp. 15.

II. Les Eléments de l'Agriculture. *Do.* 1862, pp. 117, 12mo.

SMITH, J. F., Jr., Toronto.

I. Note on the more characteristic fossils of the Hudson River group of Toronto and its vicinity. *Can. Journ.*, 1859.

II. Note on a new species of Triarthrus from the Utica Slate of Whitby, Canada West. *Do.* 1861.

SMITH, M.

I. A Geographical View of the Province of Upper Canada, and promiscuous remarks upon the Government; in 2 parts, with an appendix ; containing a complete description of Niagara Falls, and remarks relative to the situation of the Inhabitants respecting the war. *Philadelphia*, 1813, pp. 118, 12mo.

SMITH, MARTIN F.

I. American and Canadian Poems. *Hamilton*, 1863, pp. 314, 18mo.

SMITH, TITUS   A N. S. Naturalist. Now D. Received a classical education and followed agricultural pursuits, residing in the Dutch Village, near Halifax. He frequently contributed to the newspapers of Halifax on subjects connected with his favorite studies Natural History and Geology, and for some time conducted an agricultural periodical in N. S. As early as 1802 was employed by the N. S. Govt. to make a survey of the interior parts of the Province.

"Mr. Smith was remarkable for the vast and varied information he acquired in botany, natural history, &c. With a familiar knowledge of most that nature and books could teach an acquiring mind, he united the unfeigned simplicity and kindness that rendered him an agreeable visitor as well in the families of our citizens as in the cottages of the most humble."—B. MURDOCH's *Hist. of N. S.*

I. Lecture on Mineralogy before Halifax Mechanic's Institute. *Halifax*, 1834, pp. 36, 8vo.

II. The Vegetation of Nova Scotia. *Mag. of Nat. His.* 1835.

SMITH, *Hon.* WILLIAM. "Formerly Surgeon-Physical on the military establishment of Cape Breton, and late Chief Justice thereof."

I. A Caveat against Emigration to America with the state of the Island of Cape Breton, from the year 1784 to the present year; and suggestions for the benefit of the British Settlements in North America. *London*, 1803, pp. 158, 8vo.

SMITH, *Hon.* WILLIAM, *A. M.* An Am. historian. B. at N. Y. 1728. D. at Quebec, 1793. Was the son of an eminent lawyer in the Province of N. Y., a mem. of the King's Council, afterwards raised to the Bench. Ed. at Yale Coll. Studied law in N. Y., and after his admission to the Bar enjoyed an extensive practice. After the Am. Revolution, during which he was a firm adherent to the Crown, was appd. Chief Justice of Can., and as such continued until his death.

I. Review of Military Operations in North America, from the commencement of French hostilities on the frontier of Virginia in 1753, to the Surrender of Oswego, on the 14th August, 1756, in a letter to a Nobleman. *London*, 1757, 4to; *New York*, 1770, pp. 170.

II. The History of the Province of New York, from the first discovery. To which is annexed A Description of the Country, an Account of the Inhabitants, their Trade, Religions and Political State, and the Constitution of the Courts of Justice in that Colony. *London*, 1757, 4to; 2nd Ed. *Do*, 1776, 8vo; *Philadelphia*, 1792, 8vo; *Albany*, 1814, 8vo; *New York*, 1829, 2 vols., 8vo. Translated into French, 1777, 8vo.

"This work which the author in his preface modestly gives to the world as a plain narrative, and not a regular history, contains many valuable materials for the historian." *N. A. Rev.*

SMITH, *Hon.* WILLIAM. A Can historian. B. in 1770. D. many years since. Son of the preceding. Came to Can. with his father in 1786. Was Clk. to the Leg. Assem. L. C., a master in Chancery. and, in 1814, was appointed an Ex. Councillor of same Province.

I. The History of Canada, from its first discovery to the Peace of 1773; and from the establishment of the Civil Government in 1764, to the establishment of the Constitution in 1796. *Quebec*, 1815, 2 vols. 8vo.

"This work was printed in this year (1815), but did not appear until a few years afterwards. It is compiled from the Colony Records, the Jesuits' Journals, and Charlevoix's History."—*Pol. State of L. C.*

SMITH, *Rev.* WILLIAM, *D. D.* Provost of the coll. and academy of Philadelphia.

I. An Oration in Memory of General Montgomery, and of the officers and soldiers who fell with him, Dec. 31. 1775, before Quebec; drawn up (and delivered Feb. 19th, 1776), at the desire of the honourable Continental congress. *Philadelphia*, 1776, pp. 36, 8vo; Reprinted: *London*.

SMITH, WILLIAM H.

I. The Canadian Gazetteer; comprising statistical and general information respecting all parts of the Upper Province, or Canada West (With Map.) *Toronto*, 1846, pp. 287, 4to.

"This is a work, the want of which had been long felt, not only by residents in the Colony, but also by merchants and proprietors in this country."—SIM's *Col. Mag.* (Lon.)

II. Canada, Past, Present and Future, being a historical, geographical, geological and statistical account of Canada West (With Maps.) *Do*, 1851, 2 vols., 8vo.

"We recommend this work to all who desire a knowledge of the present condition of Upper Canada."—*Globe* (Tor.)

SMITH, *Rev.* WILLIAM WYE. A Can. poet and journ. B. at Jedburgh, Scot. 18 March 1827. When quite a child came with his parents to Am., and for some time lived in the city of N. Y., where he attended sch. In 1837 the family removed to Can., and young S. taught sch. at St. George, U. C. With the savings of the year he went back to N. Y. and studied in the Univ. Grammar Sch. there, principally to acquire a knowledge of classics and modern languages. It was there he first became a contributor to the press by writing for the "Poet's Corner" of the *Saturday Emporium*. Returning to Can., in 1849, Mr. S. after a short period of Sch.-teaching commenced business at St. George. In 1855, he removed to Owen Sound. Having been for some years a paid contributor to the *Times* of that place; he, on the retirement of the then prop. in 1863, assumed the control and prop. of that journal; a position however which he soon relinquished. From 1860 to 1864 he was ed. and prop. of the *Sunday School Dial*, the first illustrated children's paper in U. C. Mr. S. has written short lyrical and other pieces for various periodicals and newspapers. He was a contributor to the *Anglo Am. Mag.* and wrote in it *A Tale of the Old Spanish Wars. In the Bush* and *The Woods* in the *Brit. Am. Mag.* are from his pen. In 1865 he accepted the invitation of the Congregational Ch. in Listowel U. C. to become its Pastor, and is now considered a min. of that denomination. Mr. S. is understood to be preparing a Can. poem in blank verse, upon which he professes the intention to rest his literary reputation.

I. Alazon and other poems. *Toronto*, 1850, pp. 125, 16mo.

"It exemplifies correct taste, elegant diction and true genius."—*Pilot* (Mont.)

"Many of the stanzas have a beauty and richness of imagination that well sustain the characters."—*Globe* (Tor.)

II. Shall we have a Prohibitory Liquor Law? [An essay which received a prize of $100 from the Grand Division of the Sons of Temperance.] 1854.

"The author carries his readers as irresistably to his conclusions as the demonstration of a problem in Euclid."—*Gospel Tribune,* (Tor.)

III. Gazetteer of the County of Grey for 1865-6. *Owen Sound*, 1865, pp. 332.

SMITHHURST, GAMALIEL. A mem. of the Assem. of N. S., and Comptroller of of Customs in same Province, for some years.

I. A Narrative of an Extraordinary Escape out of the hands of the Indians, in the Gulph of St. Lawrence, interspersed with a description of the coast, and remarks on the customs and manners of the savages there. Also a providential escape after a shipwreck, in coming from the island of St. John, in said Gulph; with an account of the fisheries round that island. Likewise a plan for reconciling the differences between Great Britain and her colonies. *London*, 1775, pp. 48, 4vo.

"There is nothing very extraordinary or providential in either of the author's escapes."—*Mon. Rev.*

SMYTH, *Sir* DAVID WILLIAM, *Bart.* B. 1764. D. 1837. Early in life an Officer in the Brit. Army. Subsequently removed to U. C. where he was called to the Bar. Was Surveyor Gen. of that Province, one of the Trustees of the Six Nation Indians, a mem. of the Leg. Assem. and Speaker of that body, with a seat in the Ex. Council. Created a Baronet in 1821.

I. A Short Topographical description of His Majesty's Province of Upper Canada, in North America. To which is added a Provincial Gazetteer. *London*, 1799, pp. 166, 8vo; 2nd Ed. *Do*, 1813, pp. 123, 8vo.

"The second edition was revised by Francis Gore, Esq., [Lt. Gov. of U. C.]"—RICH.

SMYTH, *Genl. Sir* JAMES CARMICHAEL, *Bart., C. B., K. C. H., K. M. T, K. S. W.* An Eng. Officer, now dead.

I. Letter to the Author of the Clock-maker, respecting a British Colonial Railway communication between the Atlantic and the Pacific, from Halifax, N. S., to the mouth of Fraser's River. *London*, 1849, pp. 68.

II. Precis of the Wars in Canada, from 1755, to the Treaty of Ghent in 1814. With Military and Political Reflections. (Edited by his son Sir James Carmichael, Bart.) *Do.*, 1862, 8vo.

"This volume originally appeared in 1826 (pp. 185, 8vo) by desire of the Duke of Wellington, the then Master General of the Ordnance " for the use and convenience of official people only."

"The author had been employed to inspect and report upon the state of the defences of the Canadian frontier, and he drew up a brief sketch of the wars to which that frontier had been exposed, in order to exhibit the strategic value of the measures of defence which he recommended. He states in the preface to his work, that the events of the wars of which it treats afford, in his opinion, a demonstration of the impossibility of the conquest of Canada by the United States, provided the British Government should avail itself of the military precautions which were in its power to adopt, ' by establishing those communications and occupying those points' which had been principally suggested by the Duke of Wellington. The author was an officer of engineers of great experience and reputation."—*Sat. Rev.*

SNELLING, RICHARD, *LL. B.* A Toronto Barrister.

I. A Proposal for an Act to authorize issue of Land Debentures, in connection with the quieting of titles to Real Estate in Upper Canada, and with sales made by the Court of Chancery. *Toronto*, 1862, pp. 18.

II. The Grand Trunk Railway of Canada. Proceedings of the Preference bondholders historically, legally and financially considered ; with a concise review of the position of all parties in connection with the present embarrassments of the Company. *Do.*, 1862, pp. 74, 4to.

III. The General Orders, and Statutes, relating to the Practice, pleading and jurisdiction of the Court of Chancery for Upper Canada, with copious notes compiled from the English Reports, and containing a summary of every reported Canadian decision thereon, and a book of Forms.

By R. Snelling and F. T. Jones. *Do.*, 1863, pp. 623, 8vo.

"The editors have done much to popularize the Court of Chancery, by not only collecting in one volume the orders of that Court hitherto to be found, if found at all, in several volumes of the Reports, but by appending to these orders exhaustive notes on every point of doubt or difficulty likely to arise to a practitioner in the course of his practice. No man who studies this work can be otherwise than well up in the practice of that Court. It is, so far as we can learn, decidedly the best work of the kind, on the subject to which it relates, that has been issued in Upper Canada."—*U. C. Law Jour.*

IV. A Treatise on the Law and Practise in Ejectment, comprising the Statutes, with copious notes compiled from the English Reports, and containing a summary of the Reported decisions of the Canadian Courts relating to the subject ; together with a complete collection of Forms. *Do.*, (*In press.*)

SNODGRASS, *Rev.* WILLIAM, *D. D.* A Min. of the Presb. Ch., Can., and Principal of the Univ. of Queen's Coll., (Kings.) B. in the Barony of Cardonald, Abbey Parish, Paisley, Scot. Ed. at Renfrew Academy and the Univ. of Glasgow. Licensed a min. of the Gospel, 1852. Immediately commissioned to P. E. I. and called to St. James's, Charlottetown. Called to St. Paul's, (Mont.) about 1857, and remained in charge until appointed successor to late Dr. Leitch as Principal of Queen's Univ., in 1864. Had degree D. D. from Glasgow Univ., same year. Has contributed on religious topics to the *Monthly Record* (Picton), and the *Presbyterian* (Mont.)

I. An Address at the Inauguration of the Young Men's Christian Association. *Charlottetown*, 1856, pp. 32.

II. Sermon on the Death of Hew Ramsay, Esq. *Montreal*, 1857, pp. 27, 8vo.

III. The Night of Death ; a sermon on the occasion of the death of Hon. Peter McGill ; with biographical notice of the deceased. *Do.*, 1860, pp. 37, 8vo.

IV. The Good Centurion, an example for Scotchmen in Canada ; a sermon. *Do.*, 1862, pp. 15, 8vo.

V. The Two Builders ; or, the conclusion of the matter ; a sermon. *Do.*, 1863, pp. 23, 8vo.

VI. A Minister's Farewell; a sermon. *Do.*, 1864, pp. 20, 8vo.

VII. The Sacredness of Learning; an address on opening the session at Queen's University. *Kingston,* 1864, pp. 15, 8vo.

SNOW, THOMAS HAILES, *M. R. C. S.* (Lon.)
I. Reflections on the Moral and Civil condition of the British Provinces in North America; with observations on the important advantages which must accrue to Canada from the establishment of the Canada Emigration Association. *Niagara,* 1841, pp. 78.

SNOW, W. P.
I. British Columbia considered. *London,* 1858, 12mo.

SOMERVILLE, ALEXANDER. A Can. writer. B. at Springfield, Co. Haddington, Scot., 15 March, 1811. Was in the 2nd Dragoons in 1831-32. Served in the Brit. Auxiliary Legion in Spain, under Sir DeLacy Evans, from 1835 to 1838. Came to Can. in 1858. Was long connected with the press in Gt. Brit., where he was known by the *nom de plume* of " *One who has whistled at the Plough.*" Author of various works and pamphlets there on different subjects, principally directed towards political reforms. Ed. the *Canadian Illustrated News* (Ham.) in 1863; and has contributed some very interesting and graphic sketches under the heading of *Recollections* to the *Spectator* of same city, and the *Gazette,* (Mont.) One of these on the early life and character of the Queen, was spoken of by the ed. of the former paper as evincing "a simple beauty and pathos, which he had seldom seen excelled."

I. Conservative Science of Nations, being the first complete narrative of Somerville's Diligent Life in the service of Public Safety in Britain. *Montreal,* 1860, pp. 320, 8vo.

II. Canada a Battle Ground. *Hamilton,* 1862, pp. 64, 8vo.

III. A Narrative of the Fenian Invasion of Canada, with a Map of the Field of Combat at Limestone Ridge. *Do.*, 1866, pp. 128. 8vo.

"I know nothing in our language which for graphic narrative and picturesque des-

cription of men and things surpasses some of the letters of ' one who has whistled at the plough.' "—RT. HON. R. COBDEN, M. P.

"An able, courageous, manly Reformer."—CHARLES KNIGHT.

"Mr. Somerville writes plainly and forcibly, and with a power of interesting his readers." *Examiner* (Lon.)

SOMMERVILLE, *Rev.* J.
I. A Discourse delivered in the Scotch Church, at Montreal, on the 21st April last, being the day appointed for a general thanksgiving. *Montreal,* 1814, pp. 12.

SOMMERVILLE, Mrs. JANETTE. A Can. poet. Has contributed many short fugitive pieces to the Can. press, principally to the *Witness* (Mont.,) from 1850 to 1857; to the *Observer* (Ayr,) from 1855 to 1858; and to her husband's journal, the *True Banner,* (Dundas,) from the latter year up to the present time. Mrs. S. intends publishing a collection of her poems during the present year.

SOMMERVILLE, *Rev.* WILLIAM. A min. of the Reformed Presb. Ch.. (Cornwallis, N.S.) B. in Irel., Feby., 1800. Graduated at Glasgow Coll., 1819. Ordained in 1831, with a view to labour as a missionary in B. A. Provinces, and took up his residence at St. John, N. B., same year. In 1832 removed to N. S. where he still labours.

I. The Psalms of David designed for standing use in the Church. *Halifax,* 1834, pp. 76, 8vo.

II. Antipedobaptism; a letter to the Rev. John Pryor, Prin. of the Baptist Seminary, Horton. *Do.*, 1838, pp. 53, 12mo.

III. A Dissertation on the Nature and Administration of the Ordinance of Baptism. Part I. *Do.*, 1845, pp. 57, 8vo.

IV. The Exclusive Claims of David's Psalms. *St. John, N. B.,* 1855, pp. 189, 12mo.

This is a reprint of No. I, with a change of arrangement and an appendix of notes.

V. The Study of the Bible adapted to promote Intellectual improvement; a lecture. *Do.*, 1858.

VI. The Rule of Faith; a lecture. *Halifax,* 1859.

VII. Southern Slavery not founded on Scripture Warrant. *St. John*, 1864.

" We have perused it with interest. Like all the productions of its author it is clear, logical and sound."—*Reformed Pres.* and *Covenanter* (Pittsburg, U. S.)

SOULARD, AUGUSTE. A French Can. *litterateur*. B. at St. Roch des Aulnais, L. C., 1819. D. there 28 June, 1852. He was the son of a farmer. After a brilliant course at the Coll. of St. Ann, he went to Quebec to enter on the study of the Law. Here he joined a literary coterie composed almost entirely of young men of his own nationality, to whose exertions and talents is due the start which the growing French Can. literature received at that time, and which it has since well maintained. Mr. S. became one of the most enthusiastic and zealous of this trusty little band of pioneers. Besides contributing on literary subjects to the newspaper press of the day, they organized several literary associations, and a national body—the *St. Jean Baptiste Société*—which has since attained an important position amongst similar fraternities in the Province. In 1840 several gentlemen, among whom were the late Judge Morin and the historian Garneau, determined on establishing a literary and scientific journal the name of which should be *Le Journal des Familles*. So highly were S's. abilities as a writer thought of by them that he was offered the joint ed. management of the new paper. *Le Journal*, however, owing to difficulties unknown to us, never appeared, except in prospectus. He continued to write as an amateur, principally in *Le Canadien* and *Le Fantasque*, in which latter many humourous pieces from his pen appeared. In 1842 he was admitted to practice as an Advocate, and at once took his place as a leading mem. of the bar. He was a fluent and ready speaker, and was generally chosen as the " orator of the day " at the annual banquets of the *St. Jean Baptiste Société*. About this time he delivered, before *l'Association de la Bibliothèque*, 2 lectures on the Gauls and 1 on the Commerce of the Ancients, which were well thought of and solicited for publication in permanent form, a request which their author's retiring and modest disposition prevented him from acceding to. Several of his minor contributions to literature are to be found in *Le Rép. Can. S.* was distinguished for his extensive reading, exquisite taste and sure judgment ; as a literary critic very few in his day could approach him. He died young, much and sincerely regretted. We conclude our notice by an extract from a sketch of S. in *Le Foy. Can.* (1866) written by Messrs. Derome and Chauveau :

"Lorsqu'on songe à tous les efforts que doivent faire nos jeunes gens au sortir du Collége pour se conquérir une position, aux obstacles sans nombre dont la carrière professionnelle est hérissée, aux difficultés que présente surtout l'étude du droit dans le vaste chaos de notre jurisprudence qui se compose des débris de trois ou quatre systèmes de législation, lorsqu'on songe à tout ce que la première jeunesse présente d'illusions, d'aspirations poétiques, de mirages trompeurs ; on ne peut voir sans un bien violent serrement de cœur une tombe ouverte sous les pas d'un jeune homme sur le point d'arriver à la maturité de son talent, à l'âge où l'on commence à recueillir le fruit de son travail, à trouver quelque compensation à tous les sacrifices que l'on a faits. Cette douleur sera encore plus vivement partagée par les amis intimes de M. Soulard, par ceux qui l'ont connu dans nos salons, jeune homme estimé et admiré, causeur aimable et brillant, par ceux qui ont goûté et apprécié cette urbanité exquise, cette gaîté voilée de mélancolie qui donnaient à sa conversation tant de charmes, cette douceur inaltérable de caractère qui n'excluait cependant point le courage et la fermeté lorsqu'une injustice vivement sentie le forçait à sortir de ses habitudes, par ceux qui ont été ses derniers compagnons dans la retraite qu'il s'était formée au milieu de ses auteurs favoris, où il pouvait dire avec Horace :

> Spatio brevi
> Spem longam reseces !

"Longue espérance en effet dans un petit espace, resserré de jour en jour par la mort qui s'approchait, la mort qu'amenait la pulmonie, cette maladie lente mais sûre, qui vous descend dans la tombe en vous entourant d'illusions comme une femme qui berce son enfant dans ses bras avant de le coucher dans son berceau.

"Ce sera pour eux une consolation de savoir que depuis longtemps leur ami se préparait à mourir ; que les trésors de son imagination ont été employés à méditer sur des pieuses lectures; qu'il a laissé la vie au milieu de tous les secours de la religion ; qu'il a même eu le courage de consoler et de fortifier à la mort son père atteint, par une incroyable fatalité, de la même maladie, et qui laissa ce monde quatre ou cinq jours avant son fils vérifiant sous ce toit, hélas ! comme sous tant d'autres, le proverbe que les Arabes ont traduit si poétiquement en disant : Les malheurs sont des oiseaux qui volent toujours par couples !"

SPARK, *Rev.* ALEXANDER, *M. A.* Min. of St. Andrew's Presb. Ch. (Que.) for many years. Ed. the *Gazette* of that city, from 1793 to 1796. Dead.

I. Oration delivered at dedication of the Free Masons Hall. *Quebec.* Published at the request of the Society, 1791 (?).

II. Sermon preached on the Day appointed for a General Fast. *Do.*, 1804, pp. 25.

III. Sermon on the Connection between the Civil and Religious State of Society. *Do.*, 1810, pp. 28.

IV. Sermon preached on the day appointed for a General Thanksgiving. *Do.*, 1814, pp. 18.

V. Sermon preached, 7th March, 1819, the day of his death. *Do.*, 1819, pp. 17

Sermon preached in St. Andrew's church, Quebec, on 14th March, on the occasion of the death of the Rev. Alex. Spark. — *Do.* 1819, pp. 26.

SPEDON, ANDREW LEARMONT. A farmer in Chateauguay, L. C. B. in Edinburgh, Scot., 21 Augt., 1831. Was for some years a teacher in public sch's. L. C. Has contributed in prose and verse to various journals in L. C.

I. The Woodland Warbler ; a collection of original songs, poems, &c. *Montreal,* 1857, pp. 132.

II. Tales of the Canadian Forest. *Do.*, 1860, pp. 260.

III. Rambles among the Blue Noses ; or, Reminiscences of a tour through New Brunswick and Nova Scotia, during the year 1862. *Do.*, 1863, pp. 229, 8vo.

IV. Canadian Summer Evening Tales. *Do.*, 1866, pp. 208, 8vo.

SPENCER, *Rev.* JAMES, *A. M.* A Wes. Meth. Min. and writer. B. in Can. D. at Paris, U. C., 10 Oct., 1863. Ed. at Victoria Coll. (Cob.) Ed. the *Christian Guardian* (Tor.,) for several years.

Was a powerful writer on subjects of controversy. His sermons are written in a plain style, but they are replete with thought and argument, and will amply repay the reader for a careful perusal.

I. Sermons by the Rev. James Spencer, A. M.; with an introduction by the Rev. W. S. Griffin. *Toronto,* 1864, 12mo.

SPRINGER, JOHN S.

I. Forest Trees and Forest Life ; comprising Winter camp-life among the Loggers and wild-wood adventure ; with descriptions of lumbering operations on the various rivers of Maine and New Brunswick, (with woodcuts.) *New York,* 1851, 8vo.

STANNAGE, *Rev.* JOHN. "Rector of St. Margaret's Bay, N. S." Was a Missionary for S. P. G. F. P.

I. On Dissent; a sermon. *Halifax,* 1838, pp. 12, 8vo. ; 2nd Ed. *Do.*, 1840, pp. 18, 8vo.

II. Some Account of the Mission of St. Margarets Bay, Nova Scotia. *Jersey,* 1844, pp. 20, 8vo.

III. Annual address to his Friends in Jersey and other places. *Do.* 1851, pp. 10, 8vo.

IV. What is Popery ? A lecture. *Halifax,* pp. 16, 8vo.

STANSBURY, P.

I. A Pedestrian Tour of 2300 miles in North America, to the Lakes, the Canadas and the New England States, performed in the autumn of 1821, (With engravings.) *New York,* 1822, 12mo.

STANSER, *Rt. Rev.* ROBT., *D. D.* Consecrated Anglican Bish. of N. S. 1816.

I. An Examination of the Rev. E. Burke's pamphlet on Roman Controversy. *Halifax,* (Published between 1805 & 1810) pp. 95, 8vo.

STARR.

I. In Memoriam. Biographical sketches of Mrs. David Starr, her daughter Sarah Elizabeth Starr and her daughter-in-law Mrs. D. Henry Starr. *Halifax,* 1861, pp. 45, 8vo.

STEARNS, *Hon.* SAMUEL, *LL. D.*

I. The American Oracle, comprehending an account of recent discoveries in the arts and sciences, with a

23

variety of religious, political, physical, and philosophical subjects, necessary to be known in all families, for the promotion of their present felicity and future happiness. *London*, 1791, 8vo.

" The author styles himself Astronomer to the provinces of Quebec and New Brunswick ; also to the commonwealth of Massachusetts and the State of New York."— Ricu.

STEELE, *Rev.* H. D. Presb. min., (Cornwallis. N. S)

I. Discourse delivered at Bridgewater, N. S. *Halifax*, 1859, pp. 16, 8vo.

STEELE, *Lieut.* ROBERT. Of the Royal Marines.

I. Tour through part of the Atlantic, Madeira, the Azores and Newfoundland [with chart of the ship's track.] *London*, 1810, 8vo.

STEINHAUER, *Rev.* MR.

I. Notice relative to the Geology of the coast of Labrador. *Geol. Trans.* 1814.

STEPHENS, WILLIAM A. Collector of Customs, Owen Sound, U. C. B. in Belfast, Irel. 1809. Contributed in verse to the *Gleaner*, (Niagara,) the *Casket* and the *Garland*, (Ham..) the *Advocate*, *Palladium*, *Examiner* and the *Leader* (Tor.) the *Albion*, (N. Y.,) the *Saturday Courier*, (Philadelphia,) the *Review*, (Streetville.) the *Baptist Mag.* (Mont.) and various other journals. In 1853 ed. the *Lever*, (Owen Sound.)

I. Hamilton and other poems. *Toronto*, 1840, pp. 180, 12mo.

" We conceive there is both original thinking and much poetic feeling in this effort, and we believe that here are exhibited promises of future excellence in the world of poetry."—*Emigrant and Old Countryman* (N. Y.)

II. Poetical Geography and Ryming Rules for Spelling. *Toronto*, 1848, pp. 36.

STEPHENSON, ROBERT, *C. E.*, *M. P.*

I. Report on Victoria Bridge, Montreal. 1855.

STEPHENSON, RUFUS, *M. P.* A Can. journ. B. at Springfield, Mass., U. S., Jan., 1835. Came with his parents to Can. shortly after the Rebellion in 1837. Was ed. at the Grantham Academy U. C., and early in life apprenticed to the printing business and wrought at his trade in various newspaper offices in the Upper Province. He began contributing to the newspaper press in the columns of the *Kent Advertiser* (Chatham.) In 1852 he became connected with the *Planet*, published at the same place, as assist. ed. In 1856 he succeeded to the editorship and in the following year to the proprietorship of that journal. Mr. S. is a journ. of the Liberal Conservative sch., and is possessed of very considerable talent and power as a political writer. He favours the present Coalition, and has been a strong advocate of the Confederation of B. N. A. Since 1865 has been Mayor of Chatham. In 1867 was returned to Parliament as a mem. of the new House of Commons.

STEPHENS, J. G.

I. On the Agricultural History and Condition of Charlotte County ; a Prize Essay. *Fredericton*, 1861, pp. 8, 8vo.

STEVENS, ONTARIO B. B. Ed. the *Magnet*, (Ham..) a weekly paper, devoted to literature, science and politics, 1840. In 1842 became ed. and prop. of the *Examiner*, (Tor.)

STEVENS, PAUL. A Can. writer. B. in Belgium. Was Ed. of *La Patrie*, (Montreal,) for sometime, and held the chair of Literature in Chambly Coll. Was associated with Messrs. Sempé and Sabatier in conducting *L'Artiste*, (Montreal,) 1860.

I. Fables (en vers) *Montréal*, 1857, pp. 120, 8vo.

II. Contes Populaires. *Ottawa*, 1867, pp. 252, 8vo.

STEWART, *Hon.* ALEX., *C. B.* Late Judge of Vice-Admiralty Court N. S. Formerly Master of the Rolls same Province.

I. Letter addressed to the Chief Justice on the state of the Court of Chancery in Nova Scotia. *Halifax*, N. D. pp. 16, 8vo.

STEWART, *Hon. and Rt. Rev.* CHARLES JAMES. *D. D.* 2nd Anglican Bish. of Quebec. Was the 5th son of John, 8th Earl of Galloway. B. 13 Apr., 1775. D. in London, 13 July, 1837. Graduated at Oxford as M. A. in 1799, having previously been elected to a Fellowship, and was afterwards ordained to the holy ministry. After holding a living in Eng. for upwards of 8 years offered himself to the S. P. G., and was appointed to the mission of St. Armand, L. C. Here, having built a ch. at his own expense and aided in the erection of others, he remained until 1819, when he was appointed visiting missionary in the diocese (Que.) The diocese then included the whole of Can. and his labours were exceedingly heavy. On the death of Bish. Mountain, in 1825, he was appointed Bish. of Quebec, and in the following year was consecrated at Lamheth Palace by Archbishop Sutton. He died in Eng., whither he had gone for the benefit of his health, and was buried in Kensal Green.

I. Two Sermons on Family Prayer, with extracts from various authors, and a collection of Prayers. *Montreal*, 1814, pp. 394, 8vo.

II. New Years Sermon, reviewing the events of the war with the United States, during the year 1814. *Do.*, 15, pp. 22.

III. A Short View of the Eastern Townships in the Province of Lower Canada, bordering on the line 45°: with hints for their improvement. (Map.) *London*, 1817, pp. 20, 8vo.

" First printed at Montreal."—RICH.

IV. Missionary Report. *Do.*, 1821, pp. 24.

V. Letter on the Differences of opinion respecting the Clergy Reserves, and other points. *Quebec*, 1827, 8vo.

The Stewart Missions, a series of letters and journals, calculated to exhibit to British Christians, the spiritual destitution of the emigrants settled in the remote parts of Upper Canada, to which is prefixed a brief memoir of the late Hon. and Rt. Rev. C. J. Stewart, Lord Bishop of Quebec. By Rev. W. J. D. Waddilove, M. A.—*London*, 1838, pp. 252.

Life of Bishop Stewart, of Quebec. By Rev. J. N. Norton.—*New York*, 1859, pp. 137, 12mo.

STEWART, Hon. JAMES. For some years Sol. Genl. and afterwards Puisné Judge of the Supreme Court, N. S.

I. Reports of Cases argued and determined in the Court of Vice-Admiralty at Halifax in Nova Scotia, from 1803 till 1813. *London*, 1814, 8vo.

These are the reports and decisions of the well known Sir Alexander Croke, chiefly, we believe, cases in Prize Court.

STEWART, JOHN. A P. E. I. politician. B. about 1758. D. on P. E. I., 1834. Went to the Island in 1778. Was Speaker of the House of Assem. from 1795 till 1798, and again from 1824 until the death of Geo. IV.

I. An Account of Prince Edward Island, in the Gulf of St. Lawrence, North America, containing its Geography, a description of its different divisions, soil, climate, seasons, natural productions, cultivation, discovery, conquest, progress, and present state of the settlement, government, constitution, laws and religion. *London*, 1806, pp. 320, 8vo.

" Is valuable as a history and creditable to him as an author."—REV. GEO SUTHERLAND.

" This work, which is deficient in zoology, contains a good deal of information on the soil, agriculture, productions, climate, &c."—LOWNDES.

ST. JOHN, CHARLES HENRY. A Newfoundland author. B. on the Island. Now resides in U. S. Edited the *Anglo-Saxon*, (Bos.,) for some years.

I. Poems. *Boston*, 1859.

ST. JOHN, W. C.
I. Catechism of the History of Newfoundland. *Boston*, 1855.

ST.-LUC DE LA CORNE, M.
I. Journal du Voyage de M. St.-Luc De La Corne, dans le Navire L'Auguste, en 1761; avec le détail des circonstances de son naufrage, des routes difficiles qu'il a tenues pour se rendre en sa patrie (Canada), et des peines et traverses qu'il a essuyées dans cette catastrophe affligeante. *Montréal*, 1778, 12mo; 2nd Ed. *Do.*, 1863, pp. 23.

STODDARD, JOHN and JOHN WILLIAMS.
I. Journal of a Diplomatic Visit to the Marquis de Vaudreuil, Governor General of Canada, in 1713, by John Stoddard and John Williams, Messengers, commissioned by His Excellency Joseph Dudley, Governor of Massachusetts.

Being pages 21-42 of the *New England Historical and Genealogical Register*, for the year, 1851, furnished for the *Register* by S. Judd, Esq., of Northampton, who states that it is printed from the original MS. in the handwriting of Captain Stoddard.

With 6 pages of introduction, containing among other matter an account of Capt. Stoddard's family and of John Williams, who was no other than the famous "Redeemed Captive."

STONE, EDWARD MARTIN. Secy. of Rhode Island Historical Soc.

I. The Invasion of Canada in 1775 : including the Journal of Captain Simeon Thayer, describing the perils and sufferings of the army under Colonel Benedict Arnold, in his march through the wilderness to Quebec : With Notes and Appendix. *Providence*, 1867, pp. xxiv–104, 8vo.

Printed for private circulation.

STONE, WILLIAM LEETE. An Am. historical author. B. at New-Paltz, Ulster Co., N. Y., 20 April, 1792. D. 1865.

I. Maria Monk, and the Nunnery of the Hôtel Dieu, being an account of a visit to the Convents of Montreal, and Refutation of the " Awful Disclosures." 1837.

II. The Life of Joseph Brant, Theyendanega, &c. *New York*, 1838, 2 vols., 8vo.

III. The Life and Times of Sa-go-ye-wat-ha, or Red Jacket ; being the sequel to the History of the Six Nations. *Do.*, 1841, 8vo.

IV. The Life and Times of Sir William Johnson, Bart. *Albany*, 1865, 2 vols, pp. XV–555 and 531, 8vo.

:STORER, H. R.
I. Observation on the Fishes of Nova Scotia and Labrador, with descriptions of New Species. *Journ. Nat. His.* (Bos.,) 1850.

:STRACHAN, JAMES.
I. A Visit to the Province of Upper Canada in 1819. *Aberdeen*, 1820, 8vo.

:STRACHAN. R:. *Rev.* JOHN, *D. D.*, *LL. D.* Lord Bish. of Toronto. B. at Aberdeen, Scot., 12 Apl., 1778, at the Grammar Sch., of which city he received his primary education. In 1793 he matriculated at King's College, Aberdeen, and proceeded to the degree of A. M. He prosecuted his theological studies at the Univ. of St. Andrews, and had for fellow collegians Mr. (afterwards Prof.) Duncan, and Mr. (afterwards Dr.) Chalmers, with both of whom he formed strong and lasting friendship, which only ended with death. In 1797, he obtained charge by public competition of the parochial sch. of King's Kettle, and had for one of his pupils the late Sir David Wilkie. In 1799, he received an offer to proceed to Can. to organize and take charge of a Coll. or Univ., which Gov. Simcoe had determined on establishing in U. C. This offer Mr. S. accepted, and in the same year sailed for Can. On arriving in the Province, however, he found that the Gov. had left for Eng., and that the Univ. scheme had been abandoned. Under these circumstances he opened a sch. of his own at Kingston, for the education of a select number of pupils ; which he afterwards removed to Cornwall, where it was attended by many young gentlemen who afterwards attained high distinction in the Province, one of these being the late Sir J. B. Robinson, and another the late Sir J. B. Macaulay. While at Kingston, Mr. S., studied divinity with the view of entering the Ch. of Eng., and in 1804 he was admitted to holy orders and appd. to the mission of Cornwall. In 1812, he was appd. rector, and in 1825, archdeacon of York, (now Tor.) In 1839, he was created Bish. of Tor. In 1818, he had been, by Royal Warrant, called to a seat in the Ex. and Leg. Councils of U. C., and took a prominent part in the discussions and deliberations of those bodies. He resigned both positions shortly before the Union of the 2 Provinces. He is the founder of Trinity Coll., (Tor.) As a writer, Bish. S. is known as the author of seventy essays embracing various subjects, which appeared in the *Gazette*, (Kings.,) in 1811, above the signature of " *Reckoner*." Of his other writings a list is given below.

I. A Sermon preached in Upper Canada. 1812, 12mo.

II. Thanksgiving Sermon during the War with the United States, preached at York. *Montreal*, 1814, pp. 38.

III. Letter to Thomas Jefferson, Esq., Ex-president of the United States, in reference to a comparison of certain proceedings of the British and Americans during the war. 1815, pp. 16.

IV. A Letter to the Right Hon. the Earl of Selkirk, on his Settlement at the Red River, near Hudson's Bay. *London*, 1816, pp. 76, 8vo.

V. Report of the Loyal and Patriotic Society of Upper Canada. *Montreal*, 1817.

VI. A Speech in the Legislative Council, Thursday, 6th March, 1828, on the subject of the Clergy Reserves. *York, U. C.*, 1828, pp. 43.

VII. Letter to the Rev. Thomas Chalmers, D. D., Prof. of Divinity in the University of Edinburgh, on the 'Life and Character of the Rt. Rev. Dr. Hobart, Bishop of New York. *New York*, 1832, pp. 56.

VIII. A Letter to the Congregation of St. James' Church, occasioned by the Hon. John Elmsley's publication of the Bishop of Strasbourg's observations on the 6th chapter of St. John's Gospel. *York*, 1834.

IX. Journal of a Visitation to the Western portion of his Diocese, in the Autumn of 1842. (With Map.) *London*, 1844, pp. 64, 18mo.; 3rd Ed., *Do.*, 1846.

X. Letter to Lord John Russell on the Present State of the Church in Canada. *Do.*, 1851, pp. 22.

XI. Triennial Visitation and Proceedings of the Church Synod of the Diocese of Toronto. *Toronto*, 1853, pp. 49.

XII. The Clergy Reserves; a Letter to the Hon. A. N. Morin, Commissioner of Crown Lands. *Do.*, 1854, pp. 27.

XIII. Charge at the Visitation of the Clergy (containing an autobiographical sketch of his Life.) *Do.*, 1860, pp. 34.

XIV. Pastoral Letter to the Laity of the Diocese of Toronto, on the Maintenance of the Clergy. *Do.*, 1861.

XV. Address delivered to the Clergy and Lay Delegates of the Diocese of Toronto, in justification of Trinity College from recent attacks made upon that institution. *Do.*, 1861, pp. 32.

STRAITH, *Rev.* JOHN. A Min. of the Can. Presb. Ch. (Ingersoll, U. C.)

I. The Fidelity of the Bible: being a Review of Colenso's writings against the Pentateuch and Book of Joshua. *Ingersoll*, 1864, pp. 64.

"It is fitted to be useful, not only by its brevity and precision, but also by the skilful use which its author has made of the language and literature of the Old Testament which distinguishes him amongst his equal in standing * * * In point of argument and intelligence Mr. Straith has no occasion to be ashamed of his book."—*Home & Foreign Record of the C. P. C.*

STRATFORD, S. P., *M. R. C. S.*, (Eng.) Was ed. of the *Upper Canada Journal of Medical, Surgical and Physical Science*, (Tor.) Now of Auckland, New Zealand.

I. Historical Sketches of Louisburg. Cape Breton. *Can. Journ.* 1852.

II. Notes on the Natural History of New Zealand. *Do.*, 1857.

STRATTON, THOMAS, *M. D., L. R. C. S.* (Edin.) Surgeon R. N., Cor. mem. Lit. and Hist. Soc. (Que.), and of other Can. societies. He contributed several papers on medical science, &c., to the *B. A. Journ.* (Mont.,) 1848. In 1840 published and ed. at Kingston, a Gaelic newspaper called *Quairtear nan Coille* ("*Ranger of the Woods*,") which enjoyed but a brief existence. Dr. S. was subsequently employed by the Imperial Govt. in N. S.

I. Proofs of the Celtic Origin of a great part of the Greek Language; founded on a comparison of the Greek with the Gaelic or Celtic of Scotland. *Kingston*, 1840.

"We cannot, indeed, dilate on the learning and research displayed in the little work before us; but we recommend it to the attentive perusal of every scholar interested in tracing the affinity of two such ancient and aboriginal languages as the Gaelic and Greek."—*Gazette* (Mont.)

II. Illustrations of the Affinity of the Latin Language to the Gaelic or Celtic of Scotland. *Toronto*, 1840, 8vo.

III. Remarks on the Sickness and Mortality among the Emigrants to Canada in 1847, with suggestions for an improved method of regulating future emigration. *Sim. Col. Mag.*, 1848.

STREET, ALFRED B. An Am. poet. B. at Poughkeepsie, N. Y., 18 Dec., 1811.

I. Frontenac, or the Atotarho of the Iroquois, a Metrical Romance. *London* and *New York*, 1849; new ed.

"A poem of some seven thousand lines in the octosyllabic measure, founded on the expedition of Count Frontenac, governor-general of Canada, against the powerful Indian tribe of the Iroquois. The story introduces many picturesque scenes of Indian life, and abounds in passages of description of natural scenery, in the author's best vein of careful elaboration."—DUYCKINCK.

STRICKLAND, *Lt. Col.* SAMUEL. Brother of Mrs. Moodie and Mrs. Traill. B. in Eng., 1804. D. at Lakefield, U. C., Jany., 1867. Emigrated to Can., where he continued to reside until his death. Served in the Militia during the Rebellion of 1837.

I. Twenty-Seven Years in Canada West, or the Experience of an Early Settler, edited by Agnes Strickland. *London*, 1853, 2 vols., 8vo.

St. THOMAS, *Mother.* A sister of the Religious Order of the Ursulines (Que.)

I. Les Ursulines de Québec, depuis leur établissement jusqu'à nos jours. (With portraits of the Mother de l'Incarnation and Mad. Peltrie.) *Québec*, vol. I, 1863, pp. 579 ; vol. II, 1864, pp. xv., 38, 362 ; vols III and IV., 1866, pp. 741, 8vo.

"Bancroft has made all American readers familiar with Mother Mary of the Incarnation, and Madame Peltrie, as well as with the romantic story of the early labors of the Ursulines in Quebec. This volume is a carefully prepared and highly interesting history of the convent during the first century of its existence, and contains much matter of general interest to students of American annals."—*Am. His. Mag.* (1863.)

STUART, ANDREW. A Can. statesman. B. at Kingston, U. C., 1786. D. at Quebec, 21 Feby., 1840. Was a son of the well-known Rev. John Stuart, D. D., a clergym. of the Ch. of Eng., who for sometime previous to his decease resided at Kingston, and brother of the late Sir James Stuart, (whom see.) He received his education at Cornwall, under the present Bish. of Toronto, and afterwards continued his studies at Union Coll., Schenectady, U. S. In 1807 he was admitted to the bar, and speedily rose to an extensive practice. In 1810 he defended Judge Bedard, who was exposed to a state prosecution, and from that time his assistance was sought for in every difficult and important case that came before the Courts.

His pleading was conducted with convincing and overpowering eloquence. In 1815 he entered public life, being returned to the Assem., L. C., as one of the members for Quebec, for which city he continued to sit in that chamber until the suspension of the Constitution in 1838. In the last mentioned year he was appointed Sol. Genl. During the course of his public life he took part in the discussion of every important question that arose, and sat on every committee before which any important matter was brought up. His vast and varied information furnished assistance in all these inquiries. His views were on all occasions those of a liberal mind. In 1838 he proceeded to Eng. on behalf of the Constitutional Association of which he was chairman, for the purpose of forwarding the Union of the two Provinces. This was his last public mission. Mr. S. possessed literary attainments of a high order. During the existence of the *Star* newspaper (Que.,) he was a frequent and able contributor to its ed. columns. His taste in the fine arts was just ; his knowledge of the literature of the day, extensive. He possessed an intimate acquaintance with ancient learning, especially with the works of the great model of Roman eloquence. To all institutions promoting literary cultivation he was an ardent friend, and especially to the Lit. and His. Soc. (Que.) He exerted himself with great zeal to forward the *Transactions* of that body, and found the means from the Legislature which enabled it to publish several original documents, procured from various quarters in Europe and Am., illustrative of the previous history of Can.

"A man distinguished by his unceasing advocacy of a liberal and enlightened policy, highly esteemed by all parties in the Province, and who, as a statesman or a jurist, has not left his equal behind him."—*Letter of Zeno*: (DUNBAR ROSS.)

I. Notes upon the South Western Boundary Line of the British Provinces of Lower Canada and New Brunswick, and the United States of America. *Quebec*, 1830, 8vo ; 2nd Ed. *Montreal*, 1839.

II. Review of the Proceedings of the Legislature of Lower Canada in the Session of 1831 ; with an Appendix containing some Important Documents now first given to the public. *Montreal*, 1832, pp. 523, 8vo.

" This work is replete with profound views of government, and contains ample warning of the perilous encroachments of the misguided democratic influence then evidently drawing to a crisis."—*Gazette* (Que.)

III. Account of the Endowments for Education in Lower Canada and of legislative and other public acts for the advancement thereof, from 1763 to the present time. By Andrew Stuart and William Badgley. *London*, 1838, pp. 132, 8vo.

" It gives an able summary of the Acts passed by the House—their political bias and tendency, and contains a defence of the Legislative Council, in the rejection of the system proposed by the Lower House in 1836. The talents, influence, and high public character of Mr. Stuart are well known in Canada, and the impress of his mind has been deeply written in the public policy and history of the Lower Province. His powers were great and commanding. This work on Education, and a work published by him on the sound principles of a Colonial Government, entitled ' *A Review of the Proceedings of the Legislature of Lower Canada in* 1831,' indicated a classical and profound mind. He died amid the universal regret of his brother members of the bar and of his friends—his grave is yet uncovered, but it is still expected that his memory will be honoured and enshrined by some public monument. By rewards of this kind the patriotic dead impart an inspiring and useful influence to the living."—G. R. YOUNG : *Col. Literature.*

Transactions of Lit. and His. Soc.

I. Notes on the Saguenay Country. Vol. I.

II. On the Ancient Etruscans, Tyrrhenians or Tuscans. *Do.*

III. Journey across the Continent of North America, by an Indian chief, from M. Le Sage du Pratz. *Do.*

IV. Canadian Etymologies. Vol III.

V. Detached Thoughts upon the History of Civilization. *Do.*

" It indicates great comprehension of thought, and a vast extent of reading. Though not finished according to the evident intention of the author, and rather the opening up only of the subject, it has the effect of fixing the readers attention upon a number of the most important peculiarities of ancient manners."—*Idem.*

STUART, C.

I. The Emigrants Guide to Upper Canada or Sketches of the present State of that Province, collected from a residence therein during 1817, 1818 and 1819. *London*, 1820, 12mo.

STUART, *Venerable* GEORGE O'KILL, *D. D.*, *LL. D.* Dean of Ontario, U. C. for some years. Now dead.

I. A Charge delivered to the Clergy of Upper Canada, at York, Niagara and Cornwall respectively. *Can. Mag.* (Mont.,) 1824.

STUART, GEORGE O'KILL, *Q. C.* A Quebec advocate. Sat in Leg. Assem. Can., from 1851 until 1857.

I. Reports of Cases argued and determined in the Courts of King's Bench, Vice-Admiralty and Appeals of Lower Canada ; and of Appeals before the Privy Council. *Quebec*, 1834, 8vo.

II. Cases selected from those heard and determined in the Vice-Admiralty Court for Lower Canada ; relating chiefly to the Jurisdiction and Practice of the Court ; or involving Questions of Maritime Law of frequent occurrence in the trade and navigation of the River and Gulf of St. Lawrence, &c. [Edited.] *London*, 1858, 8vo.

These cases were tried before the Hon. Henry Black, C. B., who is still Judge of the Court.

STUART, *Hon. Sir* JAMES, *Bart., LL. D.* A Can. statesman and jurist. B. at Fort Hunter, N. Y., 2 March, 1780. D. at Quebec, 14 July, 1853. Ed. at Schenectady and at the Coll. (Windsor, N. S.) In 1801 he was called to the bar of L. C. From 1805 to 1809 he was Sol. Genl., and from 1822 to 1831, Atty. Genl. of L. C. He sat in the Assem. of that Province almost continuously from 1808 up to his elevation to the bench as Chief Justice in 1838. Besides acting in 1822 as delegate to Eng. from the Brit. inhabitants of Montreal, to advocate the re-union of the Canadas, Sir James rendered many important services to the people and the Govt. of Can. Lord Sydenham availed himself of his talents in preparing the Act of Union between the two Provinces, which until lately formed the Constitution of Can. He was created a Baronet in 1840.

I. Observations on the Proposed Union of the Provinces of Upper and Lower Canada, under one Legislature, respectfully submitted to Her Majesty's Government, by the Agent of the Petitioners for that measure. *London*, 1824, pp. 114, 8vo.

(See *Sewell*, Hon. J.)

II. Correspondence between Lt. Col. Glegg, Secretary of His Excellency Lord Aylmer, Governor in Chief of Lower Canada, and James Stuart, Esq., Attorney General for the said Province, relating, [1.] to the case of Cowie, Davis & Boucher, in the service of the Hudson's Bay Company, against whom actions had been brought for penalties supposed to have been incurred by them, by the sale of spirituous liquors to Indians without a license : [2.] respecting the establishment of boundaries between the King's Posts Territory, and the Seigniory of " Mille Vaches :" [3.] relating to the suspension of Attorney General Stuart from his office, pursuant to an Address of the House of Assembly :—with a Memorial from Mr. Stuart to the Colonial Secretary, Lord Goderich, thereupon. Bound in 1 Vol. Folio. 1827-1831.

The above title is taken from the *Cat. Lib. of Parlt. Can.*

SULLIVAN, ROBERT, *M. A.*, Barrister-at-Law, and CHARLES MOSS, Student-at-Law, (Tor.)

I. A Handy Book of Commercial Law for Upper Canada. *Toronto*, 1866, pp. 270.

" One of the best text books ever written, Smith's Mercantile Law, has been taken as a model, and not only as a model, but the arrangement of that work, as the authors state in the preface, has been closely followed and the language often used."—*U. C. Law Journ.*

SULLIVAN, *Hon.* R. B. A Can. statesman. B. at Toronto. D. there 14 Apl., 1853. Held prominent positions in successive Liberal Administrations before and after the Union of 1840. Was noted for his eloquence at the Bar and in Parliament. Raised to the Bench, U. C., in 1848, where he continued to sit until his death.

I. Letters on Responsible Government. By Legion. (Republished from the *Examiner*.) *Toronto*, 1844.

(See *Ryerson*, Rev. E.)

II. The Connection between the Agriculture and Manufactures of Canada ; a lecture before the Mechanics' Institute of Hamilton. *Hamilton*, 1847, pp. 42.

III. Emigration and Colonization considered. pp. 32, 8vo.

The above appears in *Sim. Col. Mag.* (Lon.) 1847.

SULLIVAN, W. B. A Toronto barrister.

I. Sketch of the Montreal Celebration of the Grand Trunk Railway of Canada. *Toronto*, 1856, pp. 24.

SULTE, BENJAMIN. A French Can. poet. B. at Three Rivers, L. C., 17 Sept. 1841. Has contributed very materially towards the movement for the cultivation of Letters and the elevation of Literature generally, which has been noticeable of late years among his countrymen. Was founder and President of the Three Rivers Literary Institute, a flourishing association in his native city. Mr. S. has been a writer of verse and poetry to most of the principal French Can. newspapers and periodicals, notably to the *Revue Canadienne ;* the *Journal de l'Instruction Publique ;* and the *Echo du Cabinet de Lecture Paroissiale*, all published in Montreal. His style is simple, natural and graceful, redolent of a thousand sources of thought and inspiration, and is clear and intelligible to all minds. He will occupy a high place among the gifted sons of song of his country. We understand that he is preparing a volume of poems for early publication. It is probable that he will also shortly publish a prose work of historical importance on Three Rivers and its Environs, upon which he has been for some time engaged. Since the summer of 1866, Mr. S. has been editor of *Le Canada*, (Ottawa,) a tri-weekly Conservative journal.

" M. Benjamin Sulte, qui a déjà prélude sur la lyre par de mélodieux accords et qui en tirera plus tard des sons puissants."—HECTOR FABRE : *Can. Lit.*

SUTHERLAND, *Rev.* ALEXANDER, (Ham.)

I. Politics and Christianity ; a sermon. 1866.

SUTHERLAND, *Rev.* GEORGE. A Min. of the Presb. Ch. B. in N. S. Ed. at Free Church Coll. (Hal.) Proceeded to New

Zealand in 1867. Has contributed on various subjects to the N. S. and Island press, and was for a short time in 1865–6 ed. of the *Islander*, (Charlottetown.)

I. Oration on the Temperance Reform. *Charlottetown*, 1858, pp. 16.

II. A Manual of the Geography and Natural and Civil History of Prince Edward Island. *Do.* 1861, pp. 164.

" In arrangement, execution, elegance of style, completeness and accuracy of information it leaves nothing to be desired."— *Witness*, (Hal.)

III. The Magdalen Islands ; their Typography, Natural History, Social Condition and Commercial Importance. *Do.* 1862, pp. 50, 8vo.

" An interesting pamphlet."—*L. C. Journ. of Ed.*

Suzon, *Lieut. Col. L. T.* Late Deputy Asst. Adjutant General of Militia, Can. B. in L. C. 1834. D. at Quebec, 18 Aug. 1866. Entered the Volunteer Militia in 1855. Received course of musketry instruction with the regular force, 1861. Drill instructor to 7th District, 1862. Brigade Major of same District, 1863. Lieut. Col. and Interpreter to Military Sch. (Que.) 1864. Depty. Asst. Adjt. Genl. of Mil., 1865. Within a short time of his death was engaged in translating into French Col. McDougall's work on the " *Tactics of War.*"

I. Aide-Mémoire du Carabinier Volontaire, comprenant une compilation des termes de commandement usités dans l'armée Anglaise avec quelques notes explicatives. Aussi : Le manuel du Sergent et la manière de se perfectionner dans l'art du tir, précédés d'un Historique des armes. *Québec*, 1862, pp. 52, 8vo.

II. Tableau Synoptique des Mouvements d'une compagnie. *Do.* 1863, pp. 18.

III. Tableau Synoptique des Evolutions de Bataillon. *Do.* 1863.

IV. Exercices et évolutions d'Infanterie tels que révisés par ordre de sa Majesté 1862. *Do.* 1863, pp. 215, 8vo.

V. Code Militaire. *Do.* 1864, pp. 250, 64 s.

" The zealous and talented author of this work deserves the gratitude of his fellow-countrymen if ever man deserved it. For the last three years his efforts to promote the efficiency of the volunteer force, to foster a military spirit among the young men of his district, and to instruct them in their duties should they be called upon to defend their country, have been unceasing. Not content with the strict discharge of his official duties alone, he has devoted his leisure hours to the task of military instruction in every possible manner in which it could be conveyed. One of the fruits of his labors has been the publication, in the French language, of a series of valuable works such as the volunteer rifle drill-book, the table of company movements, the table of battalion movements, the hand-book of infantry evolutions, etc. The last work from Major Suzor's pen has just been issued from the press, under the title of " Code Militaire." It is in every respect a credit to the writer, and calculated to be extremely useful to officers either of the Volunteer or Service Militia who wish to attain a thorough knowledge of the routine duties which they will have to perform if called out for service. • • •

" The work contains full information as to internal economy, regulations, clothing and arms of a regiment—pay, extra allowances, regimental rank, pensions, penalties and punishments, medals and marks of distinction, courts-martial, barrack regulations, good conduct rewards, &c., &c. There are, moreover, forms of monthly and weekly and other reports, forms of regimental books, &c. In fact every department of military routine and responsibility is fully explained and illustrated. There is also a series of musketry instructions, divided into eight lessons, with directions for ' sighting,' and a summary of the new regulations for target practice—besides a few chapters on the sword exercise."—*Chronicle* (Que.)

" These works now constitute the library of the French Canadian Militia Officer."— *Can. Illustrated News.*

VI. Maximes, conseils et instructions sur L'Art de la Guerre, ou aide-mémoire pratique de la guerre, à l'usage des militaires de toutes armes et de tous pays. *Do.* 1865, pp. 159.

VII. Guide théorique et pratique des manœuvres de l'infanterie, précédé d'un historique de l'origine, de la composition et de l'administration, &c. *Do.* 1865, pp. 303, 8vo.

" I know of no work of the sort that renders the drill so perfectly plain and comprehensible to any capacity."—COL. W GORDON, C. B. *Letter to Author.*

VIII. Traité d'Art et d'Histoire Militaires suivi d'un traité de fortifications de Campagne. *Do.* 1865, pp. 472, 8vo.

SWEENEY, ROBERT. A Can. poet. D. at Montreal, 15 Dec., 1840.

I. Odds and Ends : Original and Selected poems. *New York*, 1826, 12mo.

SYDENHAM, *Rt. Hon.*, (Charles Poulett Thompson,) *Lord*, *K. G. C. M.* Gov. Genl. of B. N. A., from 1839 till 1841. B. at Wimbledon, Eng., 1793. D. at Kingston, U. C., Sept. 1841.

Memoirs of his Life, with a Narrative of his administration in Canada. Edited by his brother, G. Poulett Scrope, M. P. (with portrait) *London*, 1843, 8vo.

Notices of the Death of the late Lord Sydenham, by the press of British North America, with prefatory remarks. *Toronto*, 1841.

(See *Adamson*, Rev. W. A.)

SYMONS, JOHN. Secy. to the Can. Landed Credit Co. (Tor.)

I. Narrative of the Battle of Queenston Heights. *Toronto*, 1859.

II. Letter to the Hon. J. S. Macdonald, Attorney General U. C., on Landed Credit. *Do.* 1862, pp. 43, 8vo.

SYNGE, *Capt.* M. H., Royal Engineers. Was employed on the works at Bytown, 1848.

I. Canada in 1848 ; an Examination of the Existing Resources of British North America ; with considerations on colonization. *London*, 1848, pp. 32.

(See *Ferrie*, Hon. A.)

II. The Colony of Rupert's Land : Where is it, and by what title held ? A dialogue. *Do.* 1863, pp. 56, 8vo.

T.

TACHÉ, *Mgr.* ALEX. Evêque de Saint Boniface. Brother of Sir E. P. T.

I. Vingt années de Missions dans le Nord-Ouest de l'Amérique. *Montréal*, 1866, pp. 245, 8vo.

TACHÉ, *Sir* ETIENNE PASCHAL, *Kt.*, *M. D.* A Can. statesman. B. at St. Thomas, L. C., 1795. D. there, 30 July, 1865. Served as an officer in the Can. *Chasseurs* during the war of 1812. Sat for many years, first in the popular branch of the Legis., and subsequently in the Leg. Coun. of Can. Held many important offices in successive administrations and was Premier for the second time at his decease. He was a Knight of the Roman Order of St. Gregory, and an Aide-de-Camp to the Queen.

I. Du Développement de la Force Physique chez l'homme ; discours. *Rép. Nat.*, 1820, pp. 40.

II. Quelques Réflexions sur l'Organisation des Volontaires et de la Milice de cette Province. Par un Vétéran de 1812. *Québec*, 1863, pp. 45.

TACHÉ, JEAN CHARLES, *M. D.* A French Can. author. B. at Kamouraska, L. C., 1821. Ed. at the Seminary, (Que.) Subsequently studied medicine and received his degree ; for some time attended at the Marine and Emigrant Hospital, (Que.) He sat in the Leg. Assem. Can., from 1847 until 1857. He represented Can. at the Paris Exhibition, 1855, where he did much to bring his native country into favourable notice. On this occasion he received from the Emperor of the French the Cross of the Legion of Honor. From 1859 till 1863 was a mem. of the Board of Prison Inspectors, and in the last named year, was appd. to his present office of Deputy Min. of Agriculture and Statistics. In 1867 he again represented Can. at the *Exposition Universelle* held in Paris. In addition to the list of his writings which we give below, Dr. Taché has contributed largely on various subjects to the French Can. press. He is also the author of several Parliamentary and administrative reports. He ed. *Le Courrier du Canada*, (Que..) from 1857 to 1859. We understand that he is preparing a new and important work for the press.

I. De la Tenure Seigneuriale en Canada, et projet de commutation, suivi de Tableaux relatifs aux Fiefs et

Seigneuries du Bas-Canada. *Québec*, 1854, pp. 82.

The Can. Legisl. published a 2nd Ed. in French and an Eng. translation of the above.

II. La Pléiade Rouge. Par Gaspard Lemage. *Do.*, 1854, pp. 22.

" There is a good deal of ability in the thing, and some sharp hits mixed with not a little injustice. That which is the most reprehensible in it is the style of personal attack, and caricature, indulged in; but that is very common in the Parisian political pamphlet, and political pamphlets you are aware, have always been formidable weapons in Paris. *La Pléiade* is an imitation of *Timon*, but although spicy, it will yet bear no comparison with the brilliant productions of M. Cormenin."—QUEBEC CORRESPONDENCE: *Gazette* (Mont.)

III. Esquisse sur le Canada, considéré sous le point de vue Economiste. (With Map.) *Paris*, 1855, pp. 180, 8vo.

" Ce livre de M. Taché contient une foule de renseignemens aussi utiles que curieux surtout ce qui touche à la géographie et à la configuration physique du Canada, à sa constitution géologique et météorologique, à ses productions naturelles et manufacturées, à ses voies de communication, fleuves, canaux, chemins de fer, et enfin à ses ressources commerciales et financières. Ce livre dont le but est d'appeler l'émigration vers le Canada, où les bras manquent au travail, sera consulté avec fruit par tous ceux qui auraient le désir de quitter l'Europe et d'aller s'établir sur les rives du St. Laurent, dans ce pays hospitalier qui ressemble à la Normandie et qui s'appela longtemps la Nouvelle-France."—E. GALLIEN.

IV. Le Canada et l'Exposition Universelle. *Toronto*, 1856, 8vo.

In both languages.

V. Des Provinces de l'Amérique du Nord et d'une Union Fédérale. *Québec*, 1858, pp. 252, 8vo.

" C'est ce qu'il y a eu de mieux dit et de plus complet sur la matière."—E. RAMEAU.

" Nearly about the same time (1858) Mr. J. C. Taché, wrote a work which was almost prophetic of a question of the B. N. A. Provinces."—J. G. BLANCHET, M. P.: *Speech on Confederation.*

" Veuillez en faire mes compliments à M. Taché, son livre est plus qu'un bon livre, c'est une bonne action."—M. BIOT.

VI. Notice Historiographique sur la Fête Célébrée à Québec, le 16 Juin, 1859, jour du 200me Anniversaire de l'arrivée de Mgr. de Montmorency de Laval en Canada. *Do.*, 1859, pp. 72.

VII. Le Défricheur de Langue, Tragédie Bouffe (en vers), en trois actes, en trois tableaux. Par Isidore Méplats. *Do.*, 1859, pp. 8.

Les Soirées Canadiennes.

I. Trois Légendes de mon Pays :

    (1. L'Ilet au Massacre. 2. Le Sagamo du Kapskouk. 3. Le Géant des Méchins.) 1861.

II. Forestiers et Voyageurs ;

    (1. Les Chantiers. 2. Histoire du Père Michel.) 1863.

III. Le Braillard de la Montagne, légende en vers. 1864.

TALBOT, EDWARD ALLEN. Five years residence in the Canadas : including a Tour through part of the United States of America, in the year 1823. *London*, 1824, 2 vols., 8vo. French translation : *Paris*, 1825, 3 vols., 8vo.

TALBOT, *Major* GEORGE.

I. A Selection of the Psalms of David for Morning Service ; with Chaunts and Responses : the music arranged in four parts, with accompaniment for organ or piano-forte, by W. H. Warren. *Montreal*, 1848, 4to.

TALBOT, MARCUS. A Can. journ. B. in Irel., 1831. Lost on board the str. *Hungarian*, near Portland, U. S., 1860. After receiving his education, came to Can. in 1853, served on the staff of the *Globe*, and afterwards on that of the *Leader*, (Tor.) In 1855, became joint prop. and ed. of the *Prototype*, (London, C. W.), a position which he retained up to his death. In 1857, he was returned to the Can. Parliament. He early manifested considerable literary knowledge which with subsequent study and cultivation, served him well in his after brief journalistic career. He possessed a fair amount of intellectual power, and wielded a pen of considerable vigour and firmness.

TAYLOR, FENNINGS. A Can. biographical author. B. in London, Eng. Is the third son of the late George Taylor, Esq., of Camberwell, Surrey, who was the eldest son of George Taylor, Esq., of Dovercourt, Co. Essex, Eng., by Catharine Fennings, his wife. Ed. at Radley, near Oxford. Arrived at Toronto in 1836, and was in that year apptd. a Clk. in the Office of the Leg.

Council, U. C. Has been an officer of the Leg. Council, Can., since the Union of the two Provinces in 1840. Is now Deputy Clk., Clk. Assistant, and Master in Chancery of that body. Has from time to time made desultory contributions in prose and verse to various periodical publications; and is the author of several songs, two of which have been set to music : the most recent being a very spirited and patriotic national anthem entitled : *God Bless Our New-Born Nation*, of which we quote the second verse :

"God bless our new-born Nation, stern
    Empire of the North;
Pure offspring of high counsel, fair child of
    patriot worth;
The dear old flag is our flag, to bear
    through fame or loss;
Britannia's flag of freedom! the glorious
    triple cross!

I. Portraits of British Americans by W. Notman. With biographical sketches by Fennings Taylor. *Montreal*, Vol. I, 1865, pp. 436; Vol. II, 1867, pp. 360, r. 8vo.; Vol. III, (*in press.*)

"Biography, under the most favorable circumstances, requires no ordinary tact and ability. But the difficulties are greatly enhanced when living contemporaries are the subjects; more especially, when the writer is one personally known to and in almost daily contact with most of the individuals whose characters he has to delineate. Over and above these lets and hindrances in the path of the author of contemporary biography is another, which the editor himself specially notices, the difficulty of treating fairly, or rather pronouncing judgment safely on, an incomplete career. The Grecian sage declined to answer the question of the Persian King, as to whether he thought him entitled to be called 'happy.' The questioner, the wealthy Crœsus, was surrounded by every thing which could render life enjoyable; but the wise man declared himself unable to answer the query because the interrogator was still living, and until 'the end,' no safe opinion could be given. Mr. Taylor cannot imitate the prudent reticence of the sage; he is compelled to pass judgment without waiting for the end. We cannot wonder, therefore, that the Editor approached his task with some little hesitancy. He very possibly recalled to mind the warning of Horace to this accomplished friend Pollio, when the latter was entering upon a not dissimilar literary enterprise.

Periculosæ plenum opus aleœ
Tractas, et incedis per ignes
Suppositos cineri doloso.

"When we remember the many pitfalls which beset the editor's path; that the ground on which he moves is treacherous ground, which craves wary walking on his part; we think we may congratulate him on the ease and freedom with which he treads. * * *

"The sketches are necessarily and properly very brief. But the editor has happily selected and graphically pourtrayed, in each case, the characteristic and salient features. So far as he has yet gone, the Editor has admirably succeeded, in following the *via media* which he sought to attain : The sketches before us being "free alike from extravagant eulogy on the one hand, and from cynical ill-nature on the other." Under the circumstances, the former danger was perhaps more likely to be feared than the latter. But of both the Editor has happily steered clear. * *

"Mr. Taylor's style is polished, graceful and easy."—*Gazette*, (Que.)

"The biographies are very interesting, and great labor must have been bestowed by the editor, Mr. Fennings Taylor, in collecting the materials necessary to write them. They will at some future date be better appreciated, when the statesmen, divines, jurists and merchants have passed away. They have one rare quality, in being written truthfully, and they also contain many historical facts not embodied in the ordinary history of Canada."—*Daily News*, (Mont.)

TAYLOR, HENRY. A Can. author. D. lately.

I. Journal of a Tour from Montreal, through Berthier and Sorel, to the Eastern Townships, &c. *Quebec*, 1840, pp. 84.

"We have been much amused in perusing it, and would strongly recommend a similar indulgence to every one fond of descriptions of rural scenery, and the incidents and accidents of flood and field, especially in a country like this, where there are so few writers capable of doing justice to such important and interesting subjects."—*Gazette* (Mont.)

II. On the Cession of the two Canadas. *Montreal*, 1841, 12mo.

III. On the Forthcoming Union of the Two Canadas, addressed to the Canadian public and their representatives, in the honorable legislature of United Canada. *Montreal*, 1841, pp. 88.

IV. A System of the Creation of our Globe, Planets and Sun as proved by the discoveries of Lavoisier, Arago, Faraday, and others. *Quebec*, 1841, 12mo; 9th Ed. *Do.* 1855, 12mo.

"This edition contains observations on the new discovery, that the magnetic variations of the marine compass are dependent on, and derived from the sun, as their primary source—a discovery which is said to have been made in consequence of observations taken at the Toronto Observatory."— *Colonist* (Tor.)

V. The Present Condition of United Canada, as regards her Agriculture, Trade and Commerce. *Toronto*, 1850, pp. 188, 8vo.

VI. On the Intention of the British Government to unite the Provinces of British North America, and a review of some events which took place during the last Session of the Provincial Parliament. *Hamilton*, 1857; New Ed. *Toronto*, 1858, pp. 117.

TAYLOR, HUGH. A Montreal advocate.
I. Manual of the office duties and liabilities of a Justice of the Peace, with practical forms for the use of Magistrates out of Session. *Montreal*, 1843.
"It supplies a great desideratum."—*Lit. Garland.*

TAYLOR, JAMES W. Special Agent of the Treasury Depart., Washington, for the District of Minnesota, U. S.
I. North-west British America and its Relations to the State of Minnesota. *St. Paul, Minn.*, 1860, pp. 42.
II. The Canadian Reciprocity Treaty. A Plea for its Extension. Report to the Secretary of the Treasury, Washington.
III. Report to the Secretary of the Treasury on the Commercial and Political Relations of the United States with the British American Provinces. *Washington*, 1866, pp. 36.

TAYLOR, S. M. Now d.
I. An Essay suggestive of a Scheme of Colonization adapted to the wild lands of British North America and especially recommended to the consideration of the Government and people of Canada. *Montreal*, 1860.
"This Essay suggests a scheme to promote the settlement of our wild lands by the formation of a Company with sufficient capital to clear a portion of the land, and thus enable the early settler to commence operations under much more favorable circumstances than he can now do."—*Can. Merch. Mag.*

TAYLOR, THOMAS. A Barrister of U. C.; admitted in 1819.
I. Cases argued and determined in the 4th year of Geo. IV. No. I. *York*, 1824, pp. 243.
II. Reports of Cases argued and determined, commencing 4th year of Geo. IV and ending 8th year of Vic. *Do.*, pp. 728.

TAYLOR, Rev. THOMAS.
1. The Baptist Commentator Reviewed; two letters to the Rev. William Jackson, on Christian Baptism, and an Appendix containing strictures on an article entitled the "Baptismal Controversy," in the Nova Scotia Baptist Magazine. *Halifax*, 1835, pp. 137, 8vo.

TAYLOR, T. WARDLAW, *M. A.* A Barrister at Law of U. C. Now a clk. in the Court of Chancery, (Tor.)
I. Orders of the Court of Chancery for Upper Canada, with notes. *Toronto*, 1860.
"Will be of very great service to that portion of the profession who are engaged in Chancery practice."—*U. C. Law Journ.*
II. General Orders of the Court of Chancery of 6th February, 1865, with notes and form; by T. Wardlaw Taylor and G. M. Rae, Barristers at Law. *Do.* 1865.
"The practice in the Court of Chancery was varied in many material points by these orders, and the profession will be much aided in understanding them by this annotated edition. In it the editors have thrown together many valuable notes, have published some useful forms, and prepared an excellent index."—*Globe,* (Tor.)

TELFORD, THOMAS.
I. Report respecting the Bay of Vert Canal, directed to Sir Howard Douglas, Lt. Gov. of N. B., *N. D.*

TELLIER, *Rev.* PÈRE. Belonged to the Jesuit Fathers. D. at Montreal, Feby., 1866.
I. Discours prononcé en chaire, le jour de la célébration de la fête de St. Jean Baptiste. *Toronto*, 1851, p . 17.

TEMPLE, *Rev.* ISAAC, *A. B.*, "of Queen's College, Cambridge, Domestic Chaplain to the Right Hon. the Earl of Dalhousie."
I. Two Sermons preached in St. Matthew's Church, Halifax, on the 9th

and 16th Apl., 1820, on the death of His Late Most Gracious Majesty George 3rd and the accession of George 4th. *Halifax*, 1820, pp. 24, 8vo.

Teuscher, Jacob.

I. Letters on Western Canada, with an Appendix, containing information on the Eastern Townships of Lower Canada ; a guide for Emigrants, (in German.) *Basle*, 1854, pp. 176.

Tessien, François Xavier, *M. D.* A French Can. medical writer. B. at Quebec, 1800. D. there, 24 Dec., 1835. Ed. at the Seminary of his native city, where he acquired a thorough knowledge of classics and *belles lettres;* he afterwards became acquainted with several modern languages. Commenced his studies for the medical profession under Dr. Von Iffland (Que.,) and concluded them in N. Y., where he received his degree. He was admitted a mem. of the profession in Can. on his return to the Province in 1823. At that time he established the first medical serial publication ever attempted in Can. *Le Journal de Médecine de Québec*, which was continued for 3 years, but failed from the usual cause, want of support. *Le Journal* was published in both languages and was eminently useful in its day ; in its pages are to be found many contributions on Medical Science from the pen of its chief ed., who brought to his chosen task talents of a very high order, and an industry and application to further the interests and raise the standard of his periodical very rarely to be found in one so young. In 1826 he left Can. to take up his residence in N. Y. ; here in addition to the translation of Begin's large medical work, he contributed occasionally to the *Morning Courier and Enquirer;* he also issued the prospectus of a *Journal des Sciences Naturelles de l'Amérique* which, however, from some cause unknown to us never appeared. He was a mem. of the Medical Soc. of N. Y., of that of Massachusetts and an honorary mem. of the Am. Institute. Returning again to his native country in 1829, he was appointed Health Officer of the Port of Quebec, a position which he only held for a few years, owing to some political animosity which he had incurred. From 1833

up to the period of his early and lamented death, he served as a mem. of the Leg. Assem. He was the founder of the Medical Soc. (Que.) He also contributed in a great measure towards the formation of the *Soc. des Sciences et des Arts en Canada*, of which for some years he was general secy.

I. The French Practice of Medicine ; a translation of Begin's Therapeutics, with notes and observations illustrative of the treatment of diseases in the climate of North America. *New York*, 1829, 2 vols. in I. pp. 500, 8vo.

Tessier, L. W.

I. Colonisation. *Rev. Can.* 1864.

Tessier, Hon. Ulric Joseph, LL. D., Q. C. A French Can. Senator. B. at Quebec, 1817. Admitted to the Bar, L. C., 1839. Sat in Leg. Assem. from 1851 to 1853. Was a mem. of the Leg. Coun., of which he was Speaker for some years, from 1858 until 1867. Was also a mem. of Can. Govt. for a short period. Served for a term as President of *L'Institut Canadien*, (Que.) Is Prof. of Law Procedure in Laval Univ.

I. Emma, ou L'amour Malheureux, épisode du choléra à Québec en 1832. *Rép. Nat.* 1848.

II. Essai sur le Commerce et l'Industrie du Bas Canada. *Québec*, 1854, pp. 23, 8vo.

Tetu, Charles, *N. P.*

I. Analyse et Observations sur les Droits relatifs aux Évêques de Québec et de Montréal et du Clergé du Canada. *Montréal*, 1842, pp. 240.

Teyoninhokarawen.

I. Address to the Six Nations ; recommending the Gospel of St. John, (In the Indian language.) *London*, 1805, pp. 7

II. The Gospel in Indian, pp. 250, 12mo.

Teulon, *Rev.* W. F.

I. The Death of Christ, the only and sufficient basis for the world's salvation ; a discourse. *Halifax*, 1838, pp. 40, 8vo.

Thellen, Dr. E. A. An Am. sympathizer with the Can. insurgents of 1837.

I. Canada in 1837-38, showing the causes of the late attempted Revolution and of its failure, together with the personal adventures of the author. *Philadelphia*, 1841, 2 vols. 8vo.

THOM, ADAM, *A. M., LL. D.* A Can. journ. B. in Scot. about the commencement of the present century. Ed. at Marischall Coll., Aberdeen, and emigrated to Can. about 1832, joining the newspaper press of Montreal. He established in that city a small paper, called *The Settler*, of which he was chief ed., aided by some members of the " *Beefsteak Club*," which then existed there, of whom the late Mr. C. J. Grant was one. He studied law with that gentleman, and in 1837, or thereabouts, was admitted to the Bar. Throughout the Rebellion of 1837-8, Mr. T. ed. the *Herald*, (Mont.) and apart from the leading ed. articles was a contributor to that paper of many political essays, under one or other of the pseudonyms :—" *Camillus*," " *Brittanicus*," " *Anti-Bureaucrat*" &c., or with the letters " *com*." (communicated) at the end. The most remarkable of these were the letters signed " *Camillus*," addressed to the Earl of Gosford, then Gov. Genl. They were afterwards published in a small volume, with the author's name on the title-page. Shortly after the arrival of the Earl of Durham in Can. as Lord High Commissioner, Mr. T. was added to the literary staff of his lordship, and proved most efficient. We believe that he was the author of a large portion of the celebrated report of Lord Durham on the state of Can. He was one of the earliest advocates of a Confederation of all the B. N. A. Provinces. In 1837 he was appointed Recorder of Rupert's Land, and took up his residence at Red River Settlement, where he remained until he resigned his appointment in the spring of 1855. Since then he has resided in Eng. In addition to his other literary performances, we understand Dr. T. wrote the larger part of Sir George Simpson's *Voyage Round the World*.

I. The Complete Gradus ; comprising the Rules of Prosody succinctly expressed and rationally explained, on a new plan ; and a comprehensive view of middle syllables. *London*, 1832, pp. 107, 12mo.

24

II. Letter to the Right Hon. E. G. Stanley, Secretary of State for the Colonies. By an Émigrant. *Montreal*, 1834, pp. 16.

III. Remarks on the Convention, and on the Petition of the Constitutionalists. By Anti-Bureaucrat (Republished from the Montreal *Herald*.) *Do.*, May 1835, pp. 192, 12mo.

IV. Review of the Report made in 1828, by the Canada Committee of the House of Commons (Republished from the Montreal Herald.) *Do.*, August, 1835, pp. 72, 12mo.

V. Anti-Gallic Letters ; addressed to His Excellency, the Earl of Gosford, Governor-in-Chief of the Canadas. By Camillus. *Do.*, 1836, pp. 226, sm. 4to.

VI. The Claims to the Oregon territory considered. *London*, 1844, pp. 44.

VII. Chronology of Prophecy, tracing the various courses of Divine Providence, from the flood to the end of time, in the light as well of national annals as of scriptural predictions. *Do.*, 1848, pp. 300, 12mo.

THOMAS, C.

I. The Eastern Townships. *Montreal*, 1867.

"These contributions to the history of the Eastern Townships give an account of the early settlement of St. Armand, Dunham, Sutton, Brome, Potton and Bolton ; with a history of the principal events that have transpired in each up to the present time. The work is simply but cleverly written, and has evidently cost the author considerable time and trouble."—*Transcript* (Mont.)

THOMPSON, DAVID. A geological and geographical surveyor and explorer. Was from 1790, for 13 years, in the service of the Hudson's Bay Co., and afterwards, for 15 years, in that of the North West Co. At the time of the Commission relative to the boundary between the Brit. Possessions and the U. S., he was employed by it as Astronomer and Surveyor. He left 37 volumes of his explorations, which are retained in the archives of the Hudson's Bay Co. Many copies of his field books are in the records of the Crown Land Dept. Can.

THOMPSON, DAVID. Late of the Royal Scots. Now living at Niagara, U. C.

I. History of the late War between

Great Britain and the United States of America; with a retrospective view of the causes from whence it originated: collected from the most authentic sources. *Niagara*, 1832, pp. 300, 12mo.

THOMPSON, *Rev.* J. H., *M. A.* Late Canon of Christ Ch. Cath. (Mont.)

I. The Conditions of Christ's Presence with Church Synods; A sermon. *Quebec*, 1858, pp. 12.

II. The Angel of the Church; a sermon preached in 1863 on the consecration of the Rt. Rev. J. W. Williams, D. D., Lord Bishop of Quebec. *Montreal*, 1863.

"An eloquent and able sermon which elicited the admiration of those who heard it delivered. * * * It mainly treats of the office of Bishop."—*Gazette* (Mont.)

THOMPSON, JOHN S. T. A N. S. author and journ. Ed. two or more journals in N. S., with the names of which we are unacquainted. Has also been a contributor to the periodical literature of that Province. Holds a situation in the Post Office (Hal.).

I. Scripture Sketches. *Halifax*, 1829, pp. 280, 18mo.

II. The Building and its Objects; an essay, read in the New Temperance Hall. *Do.*, 1850, pp. 11, 8vo.

III. The Harp of Acadia; poems, descriptive and moral by John McPherson. With an Introductory Memoir of the author by the editor J. S. T. Thompson. *Do.*, 1862, pp. 298, 12mo.

"To realize the cherished wish and hope of McPherson's life, by placing his writings before the public of his native land,—for he contemplated no foreign fame, — much friendly labor and gratuitous pains have been expended upon the rather chaotic mass of manuscript he left behind him, by the gentleman who, with little leisure, has performed his double task as editor and biographer with much zeal, kindness and ability."—MISS CLOTILDA JENNINGS.

THOMPSON, THOMAS PHILLIPS. An U. C. Atty. B. in Eng. Was Ed. of the *Post* (St. Catharines,) for a short time.

I. The Future Government of Canada: being arguments in favor of a British American independent Republic, comprising a refutation of the position taken by the Hon. T. D'Arcy McGee, in the British American Magazine for a Monarchical Form of Government. *St. Catharines*, 1864, pp. 24.

"His political theories are even more impracticable than those of Mr. McGee."—*Constitutional.* (St. Catharines.)

THOMSON, *Rev.* JOHN, *A. M.* "Min. of the Free Ch. of Scot."

I. The Prayer of Jesus for the Oneness of his People; being the substance of discourses delivered in St. Stephen's Hall, St. John. *St. John, N. B.*, 1850, pp. 28, 8vo.

THOMSON, JOHN LEWIS.

I. Historical Sketches of the late war between the United States and Great Britain, blended with anecdotes &c. *Philadelphia*, 1816, 12mo; 5th Ed. 1818.

THOMSON, HUGH C. A Can. journ. D. at Kingston, U. C., 23 April, 1834. In 1819, established the *Upper Canada Herald*, (Kings.,) which we believe he conducted up to the time of his death. Was for some years a mem. of the Leg. Assem. U. C.

THOMSON, WILLIAM ALEXANDER. Vice-President and Manager of the Erie and Niagara Railway Co., U. C. Has contributed occasionally to the newspaper press on subjects connected with Money and Production.

I. An Essay on Production, Money and Government; in which the Principle of a Natural law is advanced and explained. whereby credit, debt, taxation, tariffs and interest on money will be abolished; and National debt and the current expenses of Government will be paid in Gold. *Buffalo*, 1863, pp. 47, 8vo.

THOREAU, HENRY D. An Am. author. D. 1862.

I. A Yankee in Canada. With Anti-slavery and Reform Papers. *Boston*, 1866.

THORNTON, J.

I. Diary of a Tour through the Northern States of the Union and Canada. *London*, 1850, 12mo.

TILL, WILLIAM. Was for many years ed. of the *New Brunswicker*, on which paper he displayed much ability. D. 1860.

I. New Brunswick as a Home for Emigrants &c. A Prize Essay. *St. John*, 1860, pp. 25.

TOCQUE, *Rev.* PHILIP. A min. of the Ch. of Eng. in L. C. A native of Newfoundland. Was originally engaged in mercantile affairs, which he abandoned for the Ch. Studied at Trinity Coll., Hartford, U. S., and was admitted to the order of Deacons by Bish. Williams of Connecticut. Was for some time assist. to Bish. Southgate (Bos.) Admitted to the Priesthood by Bish. Binney of N. S. Incumbent of Tusket, N. S., for more than 8 years. He is now stationed in Hopetown, L. C. Contributed articles on a great variety of subjects to the Newfoundland papers, from 1835 to 1849 ; to the Hartford and Boston papers, from 1850 to 1853, to the *Wesleyan* (Hal.) and other N. S. journals, from 1849 to 1863 ; and to the *Can. Churchman* from the latter year until 1866. He has also written for *Littell's Living Age* (Bos.,) and the *Youth's Instructor* (Lon.)

I. Wandering Thoughts ; or, Solitary Hours. *London*, 1846, pp. 397, 12mo.

II. A Peep at Uncle Sam's Farm. *Boston*, 1851, pp. 287, 12mo.

III. The Mighty Deep. *New York*, 1852, pp. 87.

IV. If I say the truth why do you not believe me ? a sermon. *Yarmouth*, *N. S.*, 1858, pp. 16, 8vo.

TODD, ALFRED. Chief Clk. of the Private Bill Office, Leg. Assem., Can. B. in Eng. 15th March, 1819. Came to Canada in 1833.

I. A Treatise on the Proceedings to be adopted in conducting or opposing Private Bills in the Parliament of Canada ; and the Standing Orders of both Houses in relation thereto. *Quebec*, 1862, pp. 122, 12mo ; 2nd Ed. embracing the latest changes in the Practice, same year.

TODD, ALPHEUS. A Can. Constitutional writer. B. in Eng., 30th July, 1821. Came to Can. in 1833. Was Assistant Librarian to the Leg. Assem., U. C., before the Union of the two Provinces in 1840, and was appointed to same office to Leg. Assem. of United Can. at the Union. In March, 1856 received his present appt. of Librarian to the same House.

24 •

I. Engraved Plan of the City of Toronto, in 1834 : with letter-press references to public buildings, &c. *Toronto*, 1834.

II. The Practice and Privileges of the Two Houses of Parliament. *Do.*, 1839, pp. 337–xliv., 12mo.

III. Brief Suggestions in regard to the Formation of Local Governments for Upper and Lower Canada, in connection with a Federal Union of the British North American Provinces. *Ottawa*, 1866, pp. 15.

IV. On Parliamentary Government in England ; its origin, development, and practical operation. 2 vols., *London*, 1867, vol. I., pp. xx–621, r. 8vo. Vol. II, (*nearly ready for the press.*)

"More than twenty-five years ago, when in the service of the House of Assembly of Upper Canada, as an assistant in the Provincial Library, I was induced to compile a Manual of Parliamentary Practice for the use of the Legislature. The valuable treatise of Mr. May, on the 'Usage of Parliament,' had not then appeared ; and no work then published was sufficiently elementary and comprehensive to be of any service to our colonial legislators in the performance of their parliamentary duties. My little volume, although the crude and imperfect production of a very young man, was received with much favour by the Canadian Parliament. At the first meeting of the Legislature of United Canada, in 1841, the book was formally adopted for the use of the members, and the cost of its production defrayed out of the public funds.

"It was in the same year, and immediately after the union of the two Canadas, that 'Responsible Government' was first applied to our colonial Constitution. In carrying out this new, and hitherto untried, scheme of colonial government, many difficult and complex questions arose, especially in regard to the relations which should subsist between the popular chamber and the ministers of the Crown. Upon these questions, my known addiction to parliamentary studies, together with my official position as one of the librarians of the Legislative Assembly, caused me to be frequently consulted. I speedily became aware that then, as now, no work previously written on the British Constitution undertook to supply the particular informations required to elucidate the working of 'responsible' or 'parliamentary' government. For all preceding writers on this subject have confined themselves to the presentation of an outside view, or general outline, of the political system of England. There is nowhere to be found a practical treatment of the questions involved in the mutual relations between the Crown and Parliament, or any adequate account of the growth, development, and present functions of Cabinet Council. In the words of Lord Macaulay (History of England, iv. 437), 'no writer has yet attempted to trace the progress of this institution, an institution indispensible to the harmonious working of our other institutions.'

"My own researches in this field enabled me to accumulate a mass of information which has proved of much utility in the settlement of many points arising out of responsible government. I was frequently urged, by persons whose opinions were entitled to respect, to digest and arrange my collections in a methodical shape. The fact that the greater part of my notes had been collected when engaged in the investigation of questions not of mere local or temporary significance, but capable of general application, led me to think, that if the result were embodied in the form of a treatise on parliamentary government as administered in Great Britain, it might prove of practical value both in England and her colonies; and that in the constitutional states of continental Europe, it might serve to make more clearly known the peculiar features of that form of government, which has been so often admired, but never successfully imitated. I therefore determined to avail myself of the resources of the well stored library under my charge, and attempt the compilation of a work which, while trenching as little as possible on ground already worthily occupied by former writers, should aim at supplying information upon branches of constitutional knowledge hitherto overlooked."—*Author's Preface.*

"It is a remarkable circumstance that we should be indebted to a resident in a distant colony, the librarian of the Canadian House of Parliament, for one of the most useful and complete books which has ever appeared on the practical operation of the British Constitution. The colonies have not hitherto added much to the literary wealth of the Empire, though they are continually extending the range of our political experience. But a work like this, which has been undertaken and perfected by Mr. Todd, proves with what nice and eager attention the more cultivated minds in the colonies watch every movement of opinion and every inflection of the great parliamentary engine in the mother country. Without any claim to the philosophic depth of Hallam, or the personal authority of Sir Thomas May in treating of the law of Parliament, Mr. Todd contents himself with the humbler, but not less serviceable, task of collecting and enregistering all that has been said and done by the best authorities and the latest decisions on the

practice of the Constitution. His aim has been, not to explore the stream to its sources in mediæval antiquity, but to place in the hands of the public a compendium of its most recent applications. The precedents he cites do not extend beyond the reign of George III; the opinions on which he relies are chiefly those of the statesmen and writers of our own time. We ourselves are bound to look with gratitude on his labours, for he has succeeded in distilling the essence of Whig principles from the pages of this journal, and in digesting a multitude of scattered propositions thrown out at various times in the course of our political discussions. The late Sir George Lewis, the present Earl Grey, and the late Professor Austin (in his '*Plea for the Constitution*') are the three writers to whom Mr. Todd is most largely indebted for the principles of his work. He could have chosen no better guides, for in these men the most sincere attachment to the cause of liberty and progress is ever united to a fearless moderation, and none of them would have sacrificed one jot of his political convictions to the adventitious rewards of public life. Mr. Todd probably knew nothing personally of these eminent men, and his sphere of action lies far apart from theirs. It is therefore with the greater satisfaction that we see their opinions and example operating beyond the Atlantic, and reflected back upon ourselves from the American side of the Empire. We trust the publication of so sensible a book by a Canadian gentleman, at this time, may be propitious to the constitutional welfare of the Great Northern Confederation now about to be inaugurated with the cordial good wishes of the British people; and we hope that the future statesmen of that nation will never forget that if their independence is to be maintained, it will be by contrasting the principles of British Parliamentary Government in Canada with the purely republican and democratic institutions of the United States." *Edin. Rev.*

"For those who are more interested in the practice than in the principles of parliamentary government, the work of Mr. Alpheus Todd will be full of interesting matter. Originating as it did in a collection of parliamentary precedents made by him in his official capacity, it has grown up to be the most complete treatise extant on the limits and extent of the royal prerogative, and on the theory and practice of parliamentary privilege. As a work of reference it is most valuable for every practical politician or writer on political questions. The author having been brought up under the uncontrolled influence of a democratic state of society, longs, as we all do, for a state of things with which we are not sufficiently familiar rightly to appreciate, and expands very naturally upon the value of every check to the growing influence of the democratic element in English society. This, however, in no way detracts from the value of his books, for whatever his predilections, his subject hardly admitted of a partial treatment; and his copious references to original authorities gives the means to all his readers of pursuing the enquiries with which he has occupied himself to such good purpose."— *West. Rev.*

"Mr. Todd is the Librarian of the Legislative Assembly of Canada, and having for upwards of five-and-twenty years had occasion both to study constitutional practice and to give advice in points of procedure to practical legislators, he has undertaken a work upon parliamentary government, the first-volume of which is now before us. At first sight there appears a certain boldness in the notion of one whose experience is exclusively colonial venturing to instruct people at home in the nature and scope of the system by which they are governed. But Mr. Todd has kept himself so accurately informed of all that is said and done in the Mother Country, he has so diligently read everything that has been written here at all likely to throw light on his subject, that nobody will detect the least colonial or provincial flavour in his book. Mr. Beales will find in these pages that his has already become an historic name, for though it was as recently as last August that the Lord Chief Justice declined to re appoint him as revising Barrister, Mr. Todd has immortalized him as an illustration of the 'well understood rule of constitutional government, that all such functionaries should abstain from taking an active part in political contests.' The Colenso case, the retirement of Lord Chief Justice Lefroy, the Edmunds or Westbury case, and even Mr. D'Israeli's remarks on the supplementary Budget of last year, are all duly recorded in their places. Even the provisions of last year's Act for consolidating the duties of the Exchequer and Audit Departments are all set forth. Nobody need fear, therefore, that in buying Mr. Todd's book he is getting anything stale or obsolete. On the contrary, he may refer to it with perfect confidence of finding the last precedent and the newest illustration. The fact that the book was not written at home proves, in some respects, an advantage. It would be difficult to most of us, in the time of strong political passion, to write upon Government with the serenity or impartiality requisite above all things in the composition of a text book. * * * If the second half is as well done as the volume before us, the entire work will be a most valuable addition to our constitutional literature."—*Sat. Rev.* (Lon).

TOLFREY, T. FREDERICK.
I. The Sportsman in Canada. *London*, 1845, 2 vols. 8vo.

TOMKINS, W. GRÆME, *C. E., P. L. S.*
I. Comparative Tabular Meteorological Observations in Canada, England and Russia. *Can. Journ.*, 1859.

TORRANCE, F. W.
I. The Roman Law; a lecture. *Montreal.*

TOUSSAINT, F. X. Prof. of Mathematics in Laval Normal Sch. (Que.)
I. Traité d'Arithmétique. *Québec*, 1865, pp. 238, 12mo.
An abridgment was published in 1866.

TOWNLEY, *Rev.* ADAM, *D. D.* A Ch. of Eng. clergym. (Paris, U. C.) As early as 1837 Dr. T. contributed to the religious and secular press of the Province. He also wrote frequently for the *Churchman* (N. Y.) and was a regular contributor to the *Church* newspaper (Tor.) In 1843 a series of 7 dialogues appeared in the latter called : *Reasons for Returning to the Catholic Church of England*, which at their termination drew from the Ed. the following remarks :

"The conversations between Mr. Seeker and Mr. Brown are brought to a close in this number, and those who have read them through, we think, will pronounce them the most clear and minute exposure of the evils and schismatical character of the methodist system which they have ever met. We part from the excellent and able writer with regret, in the hope, however, that his plain and forcible logic will soon be exercised upon some other interesting and important subject."

In 1862 he contributed a series of letters to the *Leader* (Tor.,) addressed to the Gov. Genl., on the *Principles Involved in the Connection between Canada and England.* Dr. T. in conjunction with the Revs. Messrs. Dewar and Darling, ed. the *Churchman's Friend.* Many of his charges and letters to his parishioners have also been published separately. Referring to the partial distribution of the honours of a certain Univ. in U. C., a correspondent to a daily newspaper thus writes of him:

"But the most industrious and powerful of our clerical writers — Dr. Townley, of Paris — was left out. Although he has written and published on ethics and on the school question, and always been ready with his pen and purse to defend the church of which he is an ornament; yet,—had no honours for him. Was he too 'high' or too 'low,' or too 'broad' or to 'dry?'

On the same subject the late Bish. Doane of New Jersey, writes to a friend :—

"Dr. Townley is well known to me, and richly deserves the highest honours of any College."

I. Ten Letters addressed to the Hon. W. H. Draper, M. P. P., on the Church and Church Establishments, in answer to certain letters of the Rev. E. Ryerson. By an Anglo Canadian. *Toronto*, 1839, pp. 79, 8vo.

II. Denominational Schools, the best and cheapest; being one of a series of letters on the Common School question, extracted from the "Church" newspaper. *Do.*, 1853, pp. 12.

III. Seven Letters on the Nonreligious Common School system of Canada and the United States. *Do.*, 1853, pp. 55, 8vo.

IV. The Church the Channel of Personal Holiness; a sermon. *Do.*, 1856, pp. 14.

"The examination of this sermon has afforded us unmixed satisfaction. It is strongly marked by the clearness of thought and vigour of style which characterize all the writings of the author." *Anon.*

V. The Sacerdotal Tithe. *New York*, 1856, pp. 95, 4to.

"I think it treats a very important and neglected subject in a particularly lucid and forcible way; and I could wish that its statements were brought to the knowledge and the consciences of many in our own country, as well as in America, who need to be awakened and recovered to a sense of the duty which they owe to God and to His ambassadors on earth. I think they could not fail to be convinced if they did but calmly reflect on the truths and facts you have so concisely and clearly put forward."—Rev. H. Bailey, B. D. *Warden of St. Augustines Coll: Cantab: Letter to the Author.*

"Dr. Townley has done a favor not to the Church of Canada merely, but to the whole Church of America."—*N. Y. Church Journal.*

VI. A Report on Ministerial Incomes. *London, C. W.* 1859, pp. 11

VII. Confirmation; the three-fold evidence of its necessity, where it may be had; a sermon. *Toronto*, 1862, pp. 12.

VIII. A Letter to the Lord Bishop of Huron; in personal vindication: and on the inexpediency of a new Diocesan College. *Brantford*, 1862, pp 11.

IX. Plain Explanations No. 1. The Anglican Church not Romanizing. *Toronto*, 1862, pp. 8.

X. Plain Explanations No. 2. "The Rotten Fabric," a remonstrance, in a letter to the Rev. W. S. Griffin, Wesleyan Minister. *London, C. W.*, 1865, pp. 15.

TOWNSEND, JOHN K.
I. Narrative of a Journey across the Rocky Mountains to the Columbia River, and a Visit to the Sandwich Islands, Chili, &c. With a Scientific Appendix. *Philadelphia*, 1839, pp. 352, 8vo.

"Mr. Townsend gives an account of his journey to Vancouver, his excursion in the interior, and up the Columbia, &c."—*N. A. Rev.*

TRACEY, DANIEL, M. D. A Can. journ. Was a native of Irel. D. at Montreal, July, 1832. Established the *Vindicator*, (Mont.) in the Irish and Liberal interest, which he ed. up to his death. A short time prior to that event he had been returned as a mem. to the L. C. Parliament for the West Ward of Montreal. He was a man of general ability, and possessed great strength as a writer.

TRAILL, Mrs. CATHARINE PARR. A Can. authoress. A mem. of the talented Strickland family and a younger sister of Mrs Moodie. B. in Eng. 1805. She was the first of her sisters to commence writing. When only 16 years of age she wrote a series of juvenile books, which were brought out by Harris of St. Paul's Churchyard, (Lon.) and appeared without her name. These were so well received by the public and proved so remunerative to their author that she continued in the same department of literature for many years. Darton the Quaker and other juvenile publishers bringing out her works. In 1832 she married Lieut. Traill of the Scotch Fusiliers, shortly afterwards emigrated with her husband to Can. and settled near Rice Lake in the Upper Province. Here she wrote and prepared most of the works which have since appeared bearing her name. She also contributed a series of tales and sketches under the title of "*Forest Gleanings, illustrative of Life in the Backwoods*" to *Sharpe's London Mag.*, *Chambers Journal* (old series) and the *Anglo Am. Mag.* (Tor.) These with others in MS. would form a large sized volume. Mrs. T. has prepared a work on the Wild Flowers, Shrubs and Forest trees of Can., with a familiar description of the Native Ferns of Can. This she regards as her *magnum opus*. Mrs. T. has rendered very useful and efficient service to her adopted country in her various publications; her *Female Emigrants' Guide* has proved an invaluable boon to many an inexperienced woman in her first years residence in the backwoods. Her husband has been dead for some years.

I. The Backwoods of Canada, illustrative of the domestic economy of British America. *London*, 1835, 12mo; New ed. 1846, 18mo.

II. The Canadian Crusoes, a tale of the Rice Lake Plains. *London*, 12mo, 1852; New ed. *Do.*, 1860; Am. ed. *New York*, 1857.

III. The Female Emigrant's Guide. *Toronto*, 1855; *London*, 1857, 12mo.

IV. Lady Mary and her Nurse; or, a peep into Canadian Forests. *London*, 1856, 12mo.

V. Rambles in the Canadian Forest. *Do.*, 1859.

TREMENHEERE, H. S.
I. Notes on Public Subjects made during a tour in the United States and Canada. *London*, 1852, 8vo.

TROTTEN, *Rev.* THOMAS. A Min. of the Presb. Ch. in N. S. B. in Berwickshire, Scot., about 1781. D. at Antigonish, N. S. 1855. Ed. at Edinburgh Univ. and for sometime prosecuted the study of medicine. He studied Theology under Dr. Lawson, at Selkirk. Was settled for sometime at Johnshaven on the sea-coast of Fife, and, in 1818, removed to N. S., where he became colleague pastor at Antigonish, subsequently succeeding to the entire charge. Here he remained until his death. Previous to going to N. S. contributed to some Scottish religious magazines. For the *Acadian Recorder, Nova Scotian,*

Presbyterian Banner, Eastern Chronicle &c., he wrote much from the time of taking up his residence in N. S. His writings were chiefly on subjects relating to Biblical Criticism, though on one or two occasions he was the author of political articles written in favour of his party, the Whigs or Liberals.

I. A Lecture on Meteorology, delivered before the Pictou Literary and Scientific Society. *Pictou*, 1835.

II. A Treatise on Geology, in which the discoveries of that Science are reconciled with the Scriptures, and the ancient revolutions of the earth shown to be sources of benefit to man. *Do.*, 1845, pp. 224, 12mo.

"The principal peculiarity of this work is an attempt to bring the changes on the surface of the earth described by Geologists within the periods, described in the books of Moses. There is much ingenuity employed in this, and there is some very interesting developements of scripture passages, bearing upon the physical history of the globe. But his theory of course will not be accepted by Geologists. Those portions of the work, however, which treat of the benefit to man of the changes on the earth's surface, and wisdom and benevolence of the creator as thus displayed are admirable."—REV. GEO. PATTERSON.

III. Letters on the meaning of Baptized in the New Testament, in reply to the views of the Rev. Charles Tupper. *Do.*, 1848, pp. 76, 12mo.

TRUDELLE, *Rév.* THOMAS. A French Can. priest, (Que.) Contributed in prose and verse to *L'Abeille*, a small serial, brought out under the auspices of the authorities of the Seminary of Que.

I. Les Bois-francs. *Foyer Can.*, 1863.

II. Hoc erat in votis. *Litt. Can*, 1864.

TUBBEE, LACH CEIL MANATOI ELACH.
I. Sketch of the Eventful Life of Okah Tubbee, of the Choctaw nation of Indians. *Toronto*, 1853.

TUCKER, DAVID, *M. B.*, *B. A.*, *M. R. C. S.* (Edin.) B. in Irel. Ed. at the Univ. of Dublin, where he graduated high in arts. During his residence in Dublin ed. some classical works, and was also engaged as a contributor of leading articles to the *Evening Packet*, of that city. Resides at Pickering, U. C. In 1860 competed successfully for a prize offered in the Co. of Ontario for an Essay on Education, which appeared in successive numbers of the *Chronicle* (Whitby.) He was also a contributor to the *British Am. Mag.* and *Canadian Journal*, (the articles in the latter having been read before the Can. Institute,) of the Council of which body he is a mem.

Brit. Am. Magazine.

I. The Ethics of Burns. II. Our Anglo Saxon tongue (poem.) III. The Burial of Lord Clyde, (do.)

Canadian Journal.

I. On secluded Tribes of Uncivilized men. II. On certain modern views concerning the ordinal arrangement of the higher Mammalia.

Tucker, Miss S.
   I. The Rainbow in the North : a short account of the first establishment of Christianity in Rupert's Land, by the Church Missionary Society. *New York*, 1851, 12mo.; *London*, 1854.

Tudor, Henry.
   I. Narrative of a tour in North America, comprising Mexico, the United States and British Colonies, with an excursion to Cuba. *London*, 1834, 2 vols., 8vo.

Tupper, *Rev.* Charles, *D. D.* Baptist Min. (Aylesford, N. S.) B. at Cornwallis, N. S., 6 Augt., 1794. Is self educated ; and has acquired a knowledge of 9 different languages in addition to Eng. Was Principal of the Baptist Seminary, Fredericton, in 1838-9. Early contributed to the *Christian Watchman* (Bos.) From 1827 to 1832 ed. the *Baptist Missionary Mag.* (Hal. ?) Is the author of several printed sermons.
   I. Baptist Principles Vindicated : in reply to the Rev. I. W. D. Gray's work on Baptism. *Halifax*, 1844, pp. 190, 8vo.

II. Prohibition and Anti-prohibition ; being a series of Letters written by the Rev. Charles Tupper in favour of prohibition and replies to the same by John Bent. *St. John, N. B.*, 1856, pp. 40. 8vo.

Tupper, *Hon.* Charles, *C. B., M. D.* A N. S. statesman. Was Provincial Secy. and Premier of that Province, for some years up to July, 1867.
   I. Speech in the Constitutional Debate. *Halifax*, 1858, pp. 22, 8vo.
   II. Speech of the Honorable Provincial Secretary on the Union of the Provinces, April, 1865. *Halifax*, pp. 16.
   III. A Letter to the Rt. Hon. the Earl of Carnarvon, Principal Secretary of State for the Colonies, in reply to a pamphlet, entitled : Confederation, considered in relation to the interests of the Empire. *London*, 1866, pp. 78, 8vo.

Turcotte, L. P.
   I. Histoire de l'Ile d'Orleans. *Québec*, 1867, pp. 164, in-12.

Turgeon, J. O.
   I. Biographie de Camille Urso. *Montréal*, 1865, pp. 34.

Turnbull, W. B.
   I. British American Association and Nova Scotia Baronets. *London*, 1846, 8vo.

Turner, Thomas Andrew. A Can.journ. B. in Aberdeenshire, Scot., about 1775. D. at Montreal, 21 July, 1834. Purchased the *Gazette* (Mont.) in 1825, which he owned and ed. for some years. Had formerly been a leading Montreal merchant, and was afterwards President of the Bank of Canada. A man of education and talent.
   I. Annexation of Canada to the United States. *Dub. Univ. Mag.*, vol., 35.

U.

UMFREVILLE, EDWARD. "Eleven years in the service of the Hudson's Bay Company, and four years in the Canada fur trade."

I. The Present State of Hudson's Bay; containing a full description of that settlement, and the adjacent country; and likewise of the Fur Trade, with hints for its improvement, &c. To which are added, Remarks and observations made in the inland parts, during a residence of near four years; a specimen of five Indian languages; and a Journal of a Journey from Montreal to New-York. *London*, 1790, pp. 230, 8vo.

UNIACHE, *Rev.* RICHARD P., *A. M.* Min. of Ch. of Eng.

I. Sermon preached at Sydney, C. B. *Sydney*, 1861, pp. 15, 8vo.

UNIACHE, *Hon.* RICHARD JOHN. A N. S. legislator. B. in Irel. D. at Halifax, about 1831. Appd. Sol. Gen., 1782, and subsequently became successively Speaker of Assem., Atty. Genl., and Mem. of H. M. Coun.

I. Statutes at large passed in the several General Assemblies. held in Nova Scotia from the First Assembly in 1758 to 1804 inclusive, with complete Index and Abridgment. *Halifax*, 1805, 4to.

UPHAM, *Hon.* CHARLES WENTWORTH. An Am. author and statesman. B. at St. John, N. B., 4 May, 1802. Is the son of the late Hon. Joshua Upham, Judge of the Supreme Court of N. B. His early years were passed partly in what is now the parish of Upham and partly in Sussex Vale, on the banks of the Kennebecasis in that Province. When about 8 years of age was placed in the Latin Sch. at St. John. Leaving that institution, his father having died, he was placed in an apothecary's store, where, for some time, he was employed in preparing medicines, going through the entire Edinburgh Materia Medica, and waiting as an attendant upon the proprietor, who was a physician and surgeon in extensive private practice and in charge of hospitals. The death of the physician broke up the establishment, and young U. was then placed on a farm in N. S., in the valley of the Annapolis, where he performed the work of which a lad of his years is capable. On 14 June, 1816, he left that Province, without any companion for the trip, and, crossing the Bay of Fundy to St. John, made his way to Eastport, then in the possession of the Brit., and from point to point along the coast to Boston, were he arrived on the 27th of the same month. A benevolent relation took him into his family and sent him to a private sch., whence he entered Harvard Coll. in 1817, and received the degrees of B. A., and M. A., in 1821 and 1824, respectively. During his coll. course he taught sch. at different places. After spending the usual time in preparatory studies at the Cambridge Theological Sch., Mr. U., in 1824, was ordained colleague pastor of the First Ch., Salem, Mass. He resigned the pastoral office in 1844, owing to a severe and long continued bronchitis, which prevented the use of his voice in public delivery for 2 or 3 years. He still, however, continues to reside at Salem. The above is taken nearly altogether from *Duyckinck's Am. Literature*, and we are indebted to the the same excellent work for what follows:

"From Aug., 1851, to Aug., 1852, he was employed in the service of the Board of Education of Massachusetts, and visited the Schools, addressing the people in public assemblies in furtherance of that cause, in more than a hundred towns. In 1852, he was elected Mayor of Salem, and during his administration reorganized the police, introducing the system upon which it has since operated efficiently, and also secured the requisite appropriations and arrangements for the establishment of a State Normal School in that City. He was a member of the House of Representatives of Massachussetts in 1849, 1859 and 1860. He reported and carried the measures that made education a regular department of the State Government, with permanent accommodations within the walls of the State House. He was a member of the State Senate in 1850, 1857 and 1858, and chosen president of that body, by unanimous election in each instance, the two last named years. His efforts in the State Legislature were chiefly directed to the interests of education in the district and high schools, and the endowment of colleges, and to the improvement of the language of the statute Law of the commonweath. He was a member of the Massachusetts Constitutional convention in 1853.

"He represented the sixth district of Massachusetts in the Thirty-third Congress of the United States, from 1853 to 1855. He was chairman of a select committee raised to investigate the affairs and condition of the Smithsonian Institute, and in an elaborate report advocated the policy of making it the foundation of a library, on a scale to which its means are fully adequate, worthy of a nation already acknowledged as a first rate power in the world, and whose strength and glory are in the diffusion of universal knowledge among all its people.

"Mr. Upham's political life was distinguished by the utmost fidelity to those interests of his constituents, whether public or private, for which they had any claim on his attention. His course, moreover, was marked by several important services of a more general nature, and some of national bearing and utility."

During the ministry of Mr. U., in Salem, he published a considerable variety of discourses and tracts, and from early life to the present time has been a frequent contributor to periodical works, in literature and theology, as well as to the newspapers. He ed. the *Christian Register*, from 1845 to 1846. His chief contributions to periodical literature have appeared in the *N. A. Review*, *Christian Examiner*, *Hunt's Merchant's Mag.*, and the *National Portrait Gallery*. We have not space to give the titles of the large number of tracts, speeches, orations, sermons, and legislative reports which have emanated from his pen, and think it best to enumerate only his chief works :

I. Letters on the Logos. *Boston*, 1828, pp. 215, 12mo.

"The design of this volume was to show that the true meaning of 'the Word,' in the first chapter of the Gospel of John and in the New Testament Scriptures generally, is to be found, not in Platonizing writings of a later period, but in the literature and usages of language of the Jews themselves at that time. This work was considered a valuable contribution to theological literature by learned men of the author's denomination."—DUYCKINCK.

II. Lectures on Witchcraft, comprising a history of the Delusion in Salem, in 1692. *Do.*, 1831, pp. 280 ; 2nd Ed. *Do.* 1832.

A new ed. is now going through press.

"This volume is considered a reliable and standard account of that wonder of the early times."—*Ibid.*

III. Life of Sir Henry Vane. *Sparks's Am. Biog. Do.* 1835.

Subsequently republished in the Sch. Library of Mass.

IV. Life of General Washington. *London*, 1852, 2 Vols., pp. 443–423.

V. Life, Explorations, and Public Services of John Charles Fremont. (With Illustrations.) *Boston*, 1856, pp. 356, 12mo.

"Independently of its bearing upon the Presidential election, the book has a permanent worth, at once as affording a fresh example of the success that waits on persevering endeavor, and as giving wide currency to a chapter of our country's history, which has to-day an importance that Fremont himself can hardly have imagined when he accumulated the materials for it."—*N. A. Rev.*

URE, G. P. A Can. journ. B. in Scot. D. at Montreal 22 Aug. 1860. Prior to emigrating from his native land he was connected with the *North British Mail*, and other Scottish journals. On arriving in Can. he joined the staff of the *North American*, and subsequently that of the *Globe* (Tor.) He established the *Family Herald* in the same city, which however was discontinued for want of support. For a year prior to his death he ed. a literary weekly of the same name, published in Montreal by Mr. Lovell. He also contributed articles on moral and political subjects to other Can. journals. As an advocate of Temperance reform he lent great assistance to the cause in Can. He was a man of good education, much energy, but little originality.

I. The Maine Law Illustrated : being the result of an investigation made in the Maine Law States in Feb. 1855. By A. Farewell and G. P. Ure. *Toronto*, 1855, pp. 94.

II. The Hand-book of Toronto, containing its Climate, Geology, Natural History, Educational Institutions, Courts of Law, Municipal Arrangements, &c. By a Member of the Press. *Do.* 1858, pp. 272, 8vo.

URQUHART, DAVID.

I. Exposition of the Causes and the Consequences of the Boundary Differences, between Great Britain and the United States, subsequently to their adjustment by Arbitration. Addressed to the Chamber of Commerce of Sheffield. (With Map.) *Liverpool*, 1839, pp. 95, app. 16, 4to.

II. Case of Mr. McLeod, in whose person the Crown of Great Britain is arraigned for Felony (in the case of burning the *Caroline* Steamer in the Canadian Insurrection.) *London*, 1841, 8vo.

V.

VALADE, F. X. An officer in the Educational Department, L. C.

I. Guide de l'Instituteur. *Montréal*, 5th Ed., 1859, pp. 336, 12mo.

VAN CORTLANDT, EDWARD, *M. D.*, *M. R. C. S.* B. in Newfoundland, 1805. Ed. at Quebec. Passed his examination before the Royal Coll. of Surgeons (Lon.) in 1827, and in 1829 was chosen Librarian to the Royal Medical and Chirurgic Soc. Three years afterwards came to Can. and settled at Ottawa, where he has since resided. Has contributed articles on Archæology, Natural History, &c., to the *Can. Journal* and to the local newspapers.

I. Lecture on Ottawa Productions. *Bytown*, 1853, pp. 8.

II. Observations on the Building Stone of the Ottawa Country ; a lecture. *Ottawa*, pp. 12.

III. An Essay on Entozoa. *Do.* 1865, pp. 10.

" Most practical in its aim, and most ably written in every particular. " — *Mercury*, (Que.)

IV. An Essay on the Native Compounds and Metallurgy of Iron. Especially in connection with the Ottawa Valley. *Do.* 1867, pp. 8.

VAN CORTLANDT, GERTRUDE.

I. Records of the Rise and Progress of the City of Ottawa, from the founding of the Rideau Canal to the present time. *Ottawa*, 1858, pp. 23, 8vo.

VANCOUVER, *Captain* GEORGE, *R. N.* A celebrated Eng. navigator and discoverer, after whom the Island of Vancouver in the Pacific is named. B. about 1758. D. May, 1798.

I. A Voyage of Discovery to the North Pacific Ocean, and round the World ; in which the coast of North-West America has been carefully examined and accurately surveyed. Undertaken by H. M's. command, principally with a view to ascertain the existence of any navigable communication between the North Pacific and North Atlantic Oceans ; and performed in the years 1790-1-2-3-4-5. Edited by his brother, John Vancouver. (With Atlas of plates and maps in folio.) *London*, 1798. 3 vols., 4to; 2nd Ed., with corrections, illustrated with 19 views and charts. *Do.* 1802. 6 vols., 8vo. Translated into French. *Paris.*

" Captain Vancouver died while this work was preparing for the press ; it was finished under the editorship of his brother, Mr. John Vancouver. The object of the voyage was to survey the N. W. coast of America, from lat. 30 N. to 60 N., and to ascertain the probability of a northern passage into the Atlantic, together with the additional purpose of executing the articles of the Convention between England and Spain, respecting Nootka Sound."—RICH.

VAN DUSEN, OWEN. A Can. journ. Is an Atty. of U. C. Established the *Comet*, (Owen Sound,) a weekly Reform journal, in 1851, of which he became ed. as well as prop., positions which he still retains.

VANKOUGHNET, S. J., *M. A.* Barrister-at-Law, and Reporter to the Court of Common Pleas, U. C.

I. Reports of Cases decided in the

Court of Common Pleas. of Upper Canada. *Toronto*, Vol. I, 1865, pp. 665. Vol. II, 1866, pp. 639, r. 8vo.

VAN RENSSELAER, *Rev.* MANUSELL.

I. Memoir of the French and Indian Expedition against the Province of New York, which surprised and burned Schenectady, Feby. 9th, 1689-90. *Proc. N. Y. His. Soc.* 1845.

VAN RENSSELAER, SOLOMON.

I. Narrative of the Affair at Queenstown, in the War of 1812. *New York*, 1836.

VASEY, GEORGE.

I. The Beauties and Utilities of a Library, containing an analysis of the Canadian Parliamentary Library. *Toronto*, 1857, pp. 34.

VAUGHAN, *Capt.* D. Light-house keeper at Belle-Isle.

I. Meteorological Journal and Report relative to the Currents, Climate, and Navigation of that portion of the Lower St. Lawrence forming the Strait of Belle-Isle. *Quebec*, 2nd Ed., 1865, pp. 62.

VENNOR, H. G. Contributed many letters of interest descriptive of Can. scenery and places of interest to the *Witness*, (Mont.) 1862-3-4 and 5. We believe he has lately been in the service of the Can. Geological Survey.

I. Notes on Birds wintering in and around Montreal, from observations taken during the winters of 1856-7-8-9 and 60. *Can. Nat.*, 1860.

II. Cave in Limestone near Montreal. *Do.* 1864.

III. A few Notes on the Night Heron. *Do.* do.

IV. A Short Review of the Sylviadæ, or wood warblers found in the vicinity of Montreal. *Do.* 1865.

V. On the Feathered Songsters of the Island of Montreal. *Brit. Am. Mag.*, 1864.

VERREAU, HOSPICE. Principal of the Jacques Cartier Normal Sch. (Mont.)

I. Mémoire présenté à Son Altesse Royale Mgr. le Duc d'Orleans, régent de France, concernant la précieuse plante du gin-seng de Tartarie, découverte en Amérique par le Père Joseph François Lafitau, de la Compagnie de Jésus, &c., précédé d'une notice biographique. [With portrait of the Père Lafitau.] *Montréal*, 1858, pp. 44.

VIGER, *Hon.* DENIS BENJAMIN, *LL. D.* A French Can. statesman. B. at Montreal, 19 Augt., 1774. D. there 13 Feb., 1861. Ed. at Montreal. Was implicated in the Rebellion of 1837, and imprisoned by the Govt. A short time prior to the insurrection became the bearer of a petition to Eng. on behalf of his countrymen in Can. Sat successively in both chambers of the Can. Legislature, after the Union of 1840. Held office, and for some time was leader of the French Can. Conservative party in the Assem. Wrote several poems, which are to be found in the *Rép. Nat.* (1848), and also founded one or two newspapers in his native city. A very full biographical notice of Mr. V., written by Mr. Joseph Royal, appeared in *Le Journal de L'Inst. Pub.* (Mont.) 1861.

I. Considérations sur les effets qu'ont produits en Canada, la conservation des établissemens du pays, les mœurs, l'éducation, &c., de ses habitants ; et les conséquences qu'entraînerait leur décadence par rapport aux intérêts de la Grande-Bretagne. Par un Canadien, M. P. P. *Montréal*, 1809, pp. 51, 8vo.

(See *Cuthbert*, Ross.)

II. Analyse d'un Entretien sur la conservation des Etablissemens du Bas-Canada, des lois, des usages, &c., de ses habitants. *Do.* 1826, pp. 46, 8vo.

III. Mémoire de D. B. Viger et de Marie Amable Foretier, son épouse, appelants, contre Toussaint Pothier, Ecr., et autres, Intimés, à la Cour Provinciale d'Appel, d'un jugement de la Cour du Banc du Roi, de Montréal, du 20 Février, 1827. *Do.* 1827.

IV. Considérations relatives à la dernière Révolution de la Belgique. Par un Canadien. *Do.* 1831.

V. Observations contre la proposition faite dans le Conseil Législatif, le 4 Mars, 1835, de rejeter le bill de l'Assemblée pour la nomination d'un agent de la Province. *Do.* 1835.

VI. Mémoires relatifs à l'Emprisonnement de l'honorable D. B. Viger. *Do*, 1840, 8vo.

VII. La Crise Ministérielle. *Kingston*, 1844, pp. 46.

VIGER, JACQUES. A Can. antiquarian. B. at Montreal, 7 May, 1787. D. there 12 Dec., 1858. Ed. at the Coll. of St. Raphael, in his native city. He served as an officer under De Salaberry in 1812. Most of his life was passed in making a collection of materials relating to the history of Can., which he embodied in two works, one of them named the *Saberlache*, containing 28 volumes, which still remain unpublished. He was the first mayor of Montreal, and in addition to his other honorary titles, was Commander of the Roman Order of St. Gregory, and a corresponding mem. of the Historical Soc. of Michigan. Mr. V. was the founder of the *Soc. Historique de Montréal*.

I. Relation de la Mort de Louis XVI, roi de France, par M. l'Abbé H. Essex Edgeworth de Firmont. [With notes.] *Montréal*, 1812, pp. 46.

II. Observations en amélioration des lois des Chemins telles qu'en force dans le Bas-Canada en 1825. *Do*. 1840, pp. 36.

The same in English.

III. Rapports sur les Chemins, Rues, Ruelles et Ponts de la cité et paroisse de Montréal, avec notes. *Do*. 1841.

IV. Archéologie Religieuse du diocèse de Montréal, 1850. *Do*. 1850, pp. 36.

V. Souvenirs historiques sur la Seigneurie de LaPrairie. *Do*. 1857, pp. 13.

VILLERS, *Rév.* P. D. De.
I. Quelques leçons sur l'Art Epistolaire et la Politesse. *Montréal*, 1859, pp. 55.

VINNING, *Miss* PAMELIA S. A Can. poet. Is a teacher in the Can. Literary Institute, Woodstock, U. C. Has written a very large number of poems, both sacred and secular. Her first pieces appeared in the *Literary Miscellany*, (Detroit,) for which, and the *Evangelical Witness*, (London, C. W.,) she wrote for some time, above the *nom de plume* of *Emillia*. She afterwards became a regular contributor to the *U. S. Mag.*, which was merged in *Emerson's Mag.*, secondly in *Emerson's & Putnam's Mag.*, and lastly, for several years, in the *Great Republic Monthly*. Among her humourous poems in the latter periodical are

" *Uncle Sams Fourth of July Oration*," " *The Live Yankee*," &c. Her graver poems, however, attracted more notice. Miss V. was also a contributor for some time to the *Ladies' Repository*, (Cincinnati,) and to the religious and literary periodicals in the West. During the existence of the *Can. Illustrated News*, (Ham.,) she wrote frequently for its pages. Most of her productions have been written in Can., and the subjects relate to Can. life and experience. It is understood that she is preparing a collection of the best of her pieces for publication in book-form.

" There is no Canadian poet whose poetry we have read, and re.read, with greater interest and delight than Miss Vining's. This piece (*Under the Snow*) is no ordinary production. It contains beautiful imagery; a sound and elevated philosophy of suffering; great depth and tenderness of feeling; and a rich and exquisite rhythmic music, that lingers in the chambers of the brain, like the memory of a speechless joy."—DEWART.

VOGELI, FÉLIX. Formerly of Lyons, France. Was a contributor to *La Ruche Littéraire*, (Mont.) Ed. *Le Courier*, (St. Hyacinthe, L. C.) in 1859.

I. Almanach Vétérinaire de l'économie rurale, ou guide du propriétaire et de l'éleveur d'animaux domestiques, pour l'an 1859. *Montreal*, pp. 84.

II. Journal d'Economie Rurale, de médecine et de chirurgie vétérinaire. *Do*., 1859, pp. 64.

VOLDENVELDEN, WILLIAM, *P. L. S.* Was for some time Deputy Surveyor Genl.

I. Extraits des Titres de Concessions des Terres en Seigneuries. Par William Voldenvelden and Louis Charland. *Québec*, 1803, 12mo.

VOLNEY, *Le Comte* C. F. DE. A mem. of the Institute of France.

I. Tableau du climat et du sol des Etats-Unis, suivi d'éclaircissements sur la Colonie Française au Scioto, sur quelques Colonies Canadiennes et sur les Sauvages; terminés par un Vocabulaire de la langue des Miamis: ouvrage enrichi de quatre planches gravées, dont deux cartes géographiques, et une coupe figurée de la Chute de Niagara: *Paris*, 1803, 2 vols. *in-8*; New Ed. *Do*., 1822, *in-8*.

English translation.—*London*, 1804, pp. 503, 8vo. The same, with occasional remarks by C. B. Brown. *Philadelphia*, 1804, 8vo.

VON IFFLAND, ANTHONY *M. D.*, *M .R. C. S.* (Eng.) A Can. medical practictioner. B. in Can. Received his degree in Eng. where he studied. In 1820, founded the first anatomical sch. established in Quebec. Has held various important positions in connection with his profession under the Crown, and is now Medical Supdt. of the Quarantine, Gross Isle, L. C. In 1824 wrote a history of the town of Sorel, which appeared in successive numbers of an Eng. periodical. Dr. V. has also written a large number of articles and essays for the medical and general newspaper press, both in Am. and Europe, the principal of which we endeavour to enumerate :

Medical Gazette.

On Diabetes Melletus. 1845.

On Injuries of the Head. do.

Peculiar effects of Vision, do.

On the Siamese Twins. do.

Canada Medical Journal.

On Morbus Cordis. 1845.

On Inversion of the Uterus. do.

Observations on Infanticide. do.

Journal of Medical Science and Provincial press.

Medical Statistics on Hospitals and Lunatic Asylum. 1845.

Cynanche Parotidæa. do.

Rupture of the Bladder. do.

Journal of Medical Sciences.

On Small Pox, and the renewal of Vaccination, every 7 or 8 years. 1846.

On Poisoned Confectionery, &c. do.

On the necessity of appointing Medical Coroners. 1853.

On the Incorporation of the Medical Profession, several papers. 1847.

London Medical Times.

On the Use of the Microscope. 1847.

Medical Science, and Provincial press.

Sheets from my Portfolio—in several articles, (40 papers.) 1848. *Quebec Gazette.*

Medical Science and other Periodicals.

The Duties and Responsibilities of Physicians to Lunatic Asylums. 1848.

Observations on Charbon. do. *Boston Journal.*

On Boards of Health, Cholera, Fever, &c. 1848.

Medical and Physical Journal.

On Narvi Materni. 1850.

Quebec Gazette.

On the Amelioration of our Public Institutions, comprising Hospitals, Lunatic Asylums, Prisons, &c., in 20 chapters. 1852-53.

On Juvenile Reformatories, in several chapters. do.

On Quarantine, 4 articles. do.

On Prison Inspection, several articles. 1856.

On the Abuses of Medical Patronage. do.

The False Position of the Medical Profession in the Social System. 1853.

Biography of the late Dr. Joseph Morrin, written at the solicitation of the Coll. of Physicians and Surgeons, appeared in series. 1864.

Canadien.

On the Precipitate Inhumation of the Dead. 1849.

In several Periodicals.

On Sanitary Measures. 1853.

Medical and Provincial press.

On Quackery, several articles. 1856.

Provincial press.

Medical Men and Modern Society. 1856.

Journal of Sciences and Provincial newspapers.

On Medical Benevolent Societies—several papers. 1853.

Provincial press, and Quebec Gazette.

On Vaccination, Several papers. 1850.

On Homœopathy, Several papers. do.

In all the Newspapers.

On the Construction of Gaols. 1850. (Strongly recommended to Government.)

VONLANDSBURG, *Dr.* JOHN G.

I. "The Nobleman's Son." The Life and Adventures of Dr. John G. Vonlandsburg, Baron of Wormstall, Hanover and Hessen Castell. *Halifax*, 1845, pp. 108, 8vo.

VOYER, L. N. Late a Sergeant in the 100th Regt.

I. Les Qualités Morales du bon Militaire. *Québec*, 1865.

W.

WADDILOVE, *Rev.* W. J. D., *M. A.* •
I. Canadian Clergy Reserves.—
Speeches of the Hon. Colonel Burwell,
in the House of Assembly, the Right
Rev. the Lord Bishop of Toronto, and
the Hon. P. D. DeBlaquière, in the
Legislative Council ; together with the
Letters of Gov. Simcoe, 1790 to 1797,
read by Mr. DeBlaquière, in the Debate ;
and the protests entered against the
Bill of Mr. Poulett Thomson, &c. *New-
castle-on-Tyne*, 1840, pp. 46, 8vo.

(See *Stewart*, Rt. Rev. C. J.)

WADSWORTH, *Revs.* R. D., and W. SCOTT.
I. The Teetotaller's Hand-Book. *Toronto*, 1860, pp. 500.

WAKEFIELD, EDWARD GIBBON. For many
years connected with Can. politics and
affairs. D. in Eng., 1862. Came to
Can. with Lord Durham as his lordship's private Secy., and assisted, with
the late Mr. C. Buller, in framing the
Constitution for B. N. A. He sat in the
L. A., Can., from 1842 till 1844, and
took a prominent part in the discussions
of that body. Subsequently proceeded
to New Zealand, where he resided for
many years. He originated and carried out many political reforms in
Colonial self-govt.

I. England and America. *London*,
1837, 2 vols., p. 8vo.

II. A Letter on the Ministerial Crisis.
By an old correspondent of the Colonial
Gazette of London. *Kingston*, 1843.

"The contents are well worthy the attentive perusal of every student of Canadian
politics."—*Mercury* (Que.)

III. View of Sir Charles Metcalfe's
Government of Canada. By a Member
of the Provincial Parliament. *London*,
1844, pp. 43.

"This is a pamphlet which will attract a
great deal of attention, both from the importance of the subject, and the talent and
peculiar views of the clever writer from
whom it emanates. Mr. E. G. Wakefield
here professes to describe the state of
Government which Sir Charles Metcalfe
found on his arrival, and takes a brief retrospect of the affairs of the province from the
time of Lord Durham's mission. He also
essays to give a definition of the various
views of 'responsible government,' entertained by different parties at home and in
the province. Mr. Wakefield further furnishes what appears to be a clear and
explicit account of the rupture between his
Excellency and his executive councillors."—
SIM : *Col. Mag.*

IV. A View of the Art of Colonization
with reference to the British Empire ;
in letters between a Statesman and a
Colonist. *Do.*, 1849, 8vo.

WALES, WILLIAM, *F. R. S.* An eminent
Eng. Mathematician and Astronomer.
D. 1798.

I. Astronomical Observations made
by order of the Royal Society, at
Prince of Wales's Fort, on the north-
west coast of Hudson's Bay. *Phil.
Trans.*, 1769.

WALFORD, THOMAS, *F. A. S., F. L. S.*
I. Journal of a Voyage made by
order of the Royal Society, to Churchill
River, on the north-west coast of Hudson's Bay ; of 13 months' residence in
that country, and of the voyage back
to England in 1768 and 1769. *Archæol.*,
xiii–22, 1770.

WALKER, ALEXANDER. Formerly a non-
commissioned officer in the Brit. Army.
Now employed in the Military Store
Dept. (Que.) Contributed poetical pieces
to the *Literary Garland* in 1848 ; and to
the *Transcript* (Mont.,) about same time.
He was also a contributor to the *News*
(St. John's,) 1850–1. Was assist. ed. of
the *Gazette* (Que.) from 1857 to 1861.

I. The Knapsack, a Collection of
Fugitive Poems. *Kingston*, 1853, pp.
132, 12mo.

II. Hours off and on Sentry ; or,
Personal Recollections of Military Ad-
venture in Great Britain, Portugal and
Canada. *Montreal*, 1859, pp. 256, 12mo.

WALKER, ANNIE L.
I. Leaves from the Canadian Backwoods. *Montreal*, 1861, pp. 174, 8vo.

WALKER, WILLIAM. A Can. journ. B. at
Three Rivers. D. at Montreal, 10 Apl.,
1844. Was the son of a former Judge

in L. C. In 1819 was admitted to the bar, and speedily attained a high position in his profession, in the practice of which he displayed great energy and more than ordinary ability. He was also remarkable for the fluency of his speech and the retentiveness of his memory. He was considered one of the first commercial lawyers in Can. He ed. the *Courier* (Mont.) for some years. In 1835 Mr. W., together with Mr. John Neilson, was appd., by the Brit. Constitutional party of L. C., as delegates to proceed to Eng. in order to lay the grievances of that important section of the people before the Imperial authorities. This service was performed with great address and ability. He sat in the Leg. Assem. for a short time after the Union. During the Sydenham administration he ed. the *Times* (Mont.) Although a man of refined literary taste he has left no work behind him. The most lengthy of his public labours as a writer is the report of his mission to Eng.

WALLACE, ALEXANDER, *C. E., P. L. S.*
    I. The Ventilation of Railway Cars; a paper read before the L. & H. Soc. of Quebec. *Quebec*, 1862, pp. 9.

WALLACE, D. J.   Contributed several poems to *Home Journal* (N. Y.) which were very favourably received. Some of his pieces have also appeared in *Godey's Lady's Book* (Phil.) In Can. he wrote for the *Gospel Tribune* (Tor.) and for several other journals, and for 2 years had the literary management of the *Home Journal* (St. Thomas,) where he resides. Mr. W. contemplates shortly bringing out a volume of poems.

WALLER, JOCELYN.   A Can. journ. B. in Irel. Was the son of an Irish baronet. D. at Montreal, 2 Dec., 1828. He was a well educated and very able man; but, unfortunately for him, his politics in Irel. did not harmonize with those of his truly loyal family, who, on that account alone, all but repudiated him. Came to Can. in 1820. In this country he became, with his countrymen Drs. O'Callaghan and Tracy, linked in politics with the Papineau party, which, by way of shewing its gratitude for his arduous and faithful services, allowed him, almost literally to starve to death. His first connection with the Can. press

commenced in 1822 as a writer for the *Gazette* (Mont.,) from which, however, he soon retired. At the time that the first bill was originated for the union of the two provinces, he was selected by the French Canadians, who were opposed to the measure, to ed. the *Canadian Spectator*, a paper which they had established in order to defend their position towards the Eng. population. This service he zealously and ably performed. In spite of the efforts of the union party he succeeded in forming a party amongst the Eng., who joined the Canadians in resisting the projected union. In effecting this he incurred the displeasure and ill-will of the Govt. of the day, was imprisoned, and underwent several political suits, from out of which he came victorious.

WALSH, *Most Rev.* WILLIAM, *D. D.* First R.C. Archbish. of Halifax. B. at Waterford, Irel., 1804. D. at Halifax, 1858. Conducted the *Halifax Catholic*, a religious journal, which was discontinued in 1858.
    I. Pastoral Letter for the Lent of 1853 to Clergy and Laity of the Archdiocese of Halifax. *Halifax*, 1853, pp. 61, 8vo.
    II. Ordo Divini Officii Recitandi Missamque Celebrandi in usum Venerabilis Cleric A. Diocesis Halifaxiensis, Pro Anno 1854. *Halifaxiens*, 1854, pp. 36, 8vo.
    II. Pastoral Letter for the Lent of 1864. *Halifax*, 1854.

WALTON, J. S.
    I. School Register. *Sherbrooke, L. C.*, 1863.

WAUDBY, JOHN. A Can. journ. B. in Eng. D. at Kingston, U. C., 28 Augt., 1861. Ed. the *Herald* (Kings.) a newspaper of which he eventually became prop. for some years. In 1841 Lord Sydenham, Gov. Genl. of Can., selected him to establish and ed. at Toronto a periodical which was called *The Monthly Review; devoted to the Civil Government of Canada.* This publication although conducted with remarkable ability did not survive its noble founder and patron, who died in Sept. of the same year. Mr. W. for some years, up to the time of his death, was Clk. of the Peace for the United Counties of Frontenac, Lennox and Addington, U. C.

WARBURTON, *Major* GEORGE D. An officer in the Royal Artillery. Was a mem. of the House of Commons.

I. Hochelaga ; or, England in the New World. *London*, 1846, 2 vols., p. 8vo ; An. ed. *Do.*, 1851 ; Another ed. 1854. *New-York*—

II. The Conquest of Canada. (With portraits of Wolfe and Montcalm.) *London*, 1849, 2 vols., 8vo ; An. ed. *Do.*, 1853 ; An. ed., 1857 ; *New York*, 1850.

Both these works were ed. by Eliot Warburton.

" A younger tribe of aspirants first found themselves in that *salon* before the year 1848. Eliot Warburton—gifted, open hearted—the very type of a true Irish Gentleman, was her especial favourite. We saw him at one of her latest *déjeûners*, with that bright eye, that gay smile, which won every heart. His brother, too, the accomplished author of ' Hochelaga ' and the ' History of Canada,' the manly, intellectual soldier—as a man, beloved, respected and mourned—he too, was always one of her most cherished guests. Both are gone hence in their prime : their lives sunshine—their deaths tragedies."— *Sketch of Lady Morgan by the Whartons.*

WARD, EDMUND. " Assistant Emigrant Agent" N. B. Was ed. of the *Sentinel* (Fredericton.)

I. An Account of the River St. John and its tributary Rivers and Lakes. (With Map.) *Fredericton*, 1841, pp. 96, 8vo.

" The work is a plain, unpretending pamphlet, descriptive of the river St. John and its tributaries, and the valley through which they flow, with notices of the towns and villages on their banks."—*Mon. Rev.* (Tor.)

WARD, J. G. Was connected with the Montreal newspaper press ; and also ed. the *Reformer* (Cobourg) U. C. Now d.

I. The Spring of Life, a didactic poem. With historical and illustrative notes. *Montreal*, 1834, pp. 228, 12mo.

WARR, G. W.

I. Canada as it is ; or, the Emigrant's Friend. *London*, 1847, 18mo.

WATKIN, *Sir* E. W. *Kt.* Mem. for Stockport in the House of Commons. Is President of the G. T. Railway Co. of Can.

I. Trip to the United States and Canada. *London*, 1851, p. 8vo.

25

WATTS, WILLIAM JR. Barrister, N. B.

I. Want of Confidence in our Country and Ourselves ; a Lecture. *St. John, N. B.*, 1852, pp. 11.

WEBBER, A.

I. Table of 200 Mechanical motions. *Toronto*, 1864.

WEBBER, GEORGE.

I. The Last of the Aborigines ; a poem in four cantos. *St. John's.*

WEBSTER, JOSEPH H. Teacher in Model Sch., Truro, N. S.

I. The Acadian Minstrel. *Halifax*, 1860.

WEDDERBURN, ALEXANDER. Was Immigration officer at St. John, N. B. Now d.

I. Notitiæ of New Brunswick. *St. John*, 1838.

II. Practical and Statistical Information ; with Hints to Emigrants.

WEEKS, *Rev.* JOSHUA WINGATE, *A. M.*

I. A Sermon preached at St. Pauls, Church, Halifax, on Friday, June 24, 1785, being the Festival of St. John the Baptist, before the Grand Lodge, and the other Lodges of the Ancient and Honorable Society of Free and Accepted Masons. *Halifax*, 1785, pp. 25, 8vo.

WEIR, ROBERT, JR. A Can. journ. B. about 1809. D. at Montreal, 16 May, 1843. In Nov. 1833 purchased the *Herald* (Mont.,) of which he remained ed. and prop. from that time up to his death. He was one of the most unflinching advocates of Brit. supremacy, and during the unfortunate troubles of 1837 ably wielded his pen in support of the connexion with the mother country, and in deprecating the foul spirit of disloyalty then so widely disseminated throughout the Province. He is spoken of as :

" Leaving behind him a name that will ever be fondly remembered by every Englishman in the country, and his death has occasioned a void which his friends will ever regret."

WELD, C. R.

I. Tour in the United States and Canada, 1854. *London*, 1856, p. 8vo.

WELD, ISAAC, *M. R. I. A.*

I. Travels through the States of North America and the Provinces of

Upper and Lower Canada during the years 1795-6 and 7. (Illustrated.) *London*, 1799, pp. 464, 2 vols, 4to ; 4th Ed. *Do*, 1807, 2 vols, 8vo.

Translated into French. *Paris*, 1800, 2 vols, in-8.

"The Author exhibits some prejudice against the Republicans of North America ; but his account of the Country is very interesting and well executed."—*Pinkerton*.

WELLS, WILLIAM BENJAMIN. At one time a Can. journ ; now Judge of the Co. Kent, U. C. B. in the Tp. of Augusta, Co. Grenville, U. C., 3 Oct. 1809. His grandfather was a volunteer under Sir W. Pepperell at the taking of Louisbourg. His father and mother migrated from New Hampshire to U. C. in 1786. He was ed. at the Augusta Grammar Sch. under Dr Bethune, present Dean of Montreal, assisted by Dr. A. N. Bethune, present coadjutor Bish. of Toronto, and afterwards at Quebec and in the U. S. In 1833 he was called to the Bar of U. C. He established the *Vanguard* (Prescott) in the Reform interest, and thenceforth took an active part in Politics. From about 1834 to 1837, he was a mem. of the Legislature of U. C., and both in Parliament and in the press, was a strong and earnest opponent of Sir F. B. Head. During this time, in addition to the ed. management of his own paper, he contributed to all the leading journals in the Upper Province on political subjects, amongst others to the Brockville *Recorder*, the Grenville *Gazette*, the Cobourg *Reformer*, the Kingston *Spectator*, and the *Chronicle* and *Gazette* of the same city, the *U. C. Herald*, the *Colonial Advocate*, the *Correspondent & Gazette*, the Montreal *Advertiser* and the *Courier*, and also to the *N. Y. Tribune*. After the dissolution of Parliament by Sir F. B. Head, Mr. W. taking exception to the manner in which the elections had been carried by the oligarchical party, refused to take his seat, and together with Messrs. Baldwin and Duncombe proceeded to Eng. to enter a protest against the administration of the lieut. gov. There he remained for upwards of a year after the departure for home of his colleagues, during which period he wrote and published his book on the affairs

of the Upper Province, which was favourably noticed in the *Examiner*, (Lon.) He was also a contributor to the *Constitutionalist*, ed. by the late Laman Blanchard, and carried on in the same paper a controversy with Dr. Ryerson, who came out as the defender of Sir F. B. Head. The correspondence between these two gentlemen if reproduced at the present day would certainly be looked upon as a literary curiosity in its way. Mr. W. having continued in his refusal to take his seat in Parliament, it was, during the stirring events of 1837, declared to be vacant. In 1850 he was appointed Judge of Kent and Lambton, and afterwards on the disunion of those counties, of Kent alone. Judge W. was a contributor to *Barker's Mag.* (Kings) ; he was also a sporting contributor under the *nom de plume* of "*Cinna*" to *Wilkes' Spirit of the Times* (N. Y.) He still occasionaly writes on subjects connected with law reform, science, &c. to various journals in U. C. and U. S.

I. Canadiana : containing sketches of Upper Canada, and the Crisis in its Political Affairs. In two parts, *London*, 1837, pp. 202, 8vo.

WELTON, *Rev.* D. M., *A. M.* Bapt. Min. Windsor, N. S.

I. The Imitative Faculty, its use and abuse : a Lecture. *Halifax*, 1858, pp. 27, 8vo.

WEST, *Rev.* JOHN, *A. M.* "Late Chaplain to the Hon. the Hudson's Bay Co."

I. The Substance of a Journal during a residence at the Red River Colony, British North America ; and frequent excursions among the North West Indians, 1820-21-22 and 23. Second edition enlarged, with a journal of a mission to the Indians of New Brunswick and Nova Scotia, and the Mohawks on the Ouse or Grand River, Upper Canada, 1825-26. *London*, 1827, 8vo.

The first edition appeared in 1824.

"We have here two Journals of an English clergyman, while in performance of his duties as chaplain to the Hudson's Bay Company, and afterwards on a mission to the Indians, in some of the other British possessions on this continent. The author appears to have been actuated by a pious spirit, which is constantly shining through his pages ; and his work affords considerable information concerning the territories occupied by the British fur-traders, as also the state of the Indians, which it appears is wretched enough.

* * * * * *

" Our author's second journal contains a brief narrative of his mission to the Indians in New-Brunswick and Nova Scotia, and the remnant of the Mohawk tribe in Upper Canada, under the direction of the New England Company, which was incorporated in the reign of Charles the Second. It contains little of interest, nor have we space for further extracts. We accordingly take leave of him here not however without rendering him due acknowledgment for the entertainment his work has afforded us, which we have great satisfaction in recommending to the perusal of our readers. It relates to portions of our country less explored than almost any other parts of it, and its contents are consequently so much added to the stock of information on the subject of America."—*N. A. Rev.*

WESTON, RICHARD.

I. A Visit to the United States and Canada, 1833 ; with the view of settling in America. Including a voyage to and from New York. *Edinburgh*, 1836, pp. 312, 12mo.

WETHERBY.—

I. Dawn of a New Empire. Being a reply to " Remarks upon the proposed Federation of the Provinces. By a Nova Scotian." By a British American. *Halifax*, 1864, pp. 11, 8vo.

WHELAN, *Hon.* EDWARD, A P. E. I. journ. and politician. Is ed. and prop. of the *Examiner,* (Charlotte.) Sat in the Leg. Coun., P. E. I., for some years.

" Mr. Whelan is said to be one of the best public speakers in the Lower Provinces ; he certainly is one of the best writers, as the pages of the Charlottetown *Examiner* sufficiently testify."—*The Colonists in Council ; Gazette* (Mont.)

I. The Union of the British Provinces. A brief account of the several Conferences held in the Maritime Provinces and in Canada, in September and October 1864, on the proposed Confederation of the Provinces; together with a Report of the Speeches delivered by the Delegates from the Provinces, on important public occasions. *Charlottetown*, 1865, pp. 123, 8vo.

WHITAKER, *Rev.* GEORGE, *M. A.* Provost of and Prof. of Divinity in Univ. of Trinity Coll. (Tor.)

I. Two Letters to the Lord Bishop of Toronto, in reply to charges brought by the Lord Bishop of Huron, against the Theological Teaching of Trinity College. *Toronto,* 1860, pp. 97.

II. The Bishop of Huron's Objections to the Theological Teaching of Trinity College, with the Provost's Reply. *Do.,* 1862, pp. 84.

III. Sermon preached on the occasion of the Death of the Rev. Thos. S. Kennedy. *Do.,* 1863, pp. 12.

IV. Soberness of Mind ; a sermon. *Do.,* 1865, pp. 13.

V. Office of Ritual in Christian Worship; do. *Do.,* 1866, pp. 23.

VI. The Responsibility attaching to National Character ; do. *Do.,* 1866, pp. 20.

WHITCOMB, *Miss* H. L.

I. First Canadian Arithmetic, intended for the Primary Department of Schools. *Montreal,* 1866.

WHITE, HENRY, *P. L. S.* Toronto.

I. Geology, Oil Fields, and Minerals of Canada West : how and where to find them, with a new theory for the production and probable future supply of Petroleum. Accompanied by illustrated Geological Maps of Canada West and of the Oil Regions ; the former giving the Formative Structure of the Province, with Townships, Counties, Lakes, Rivers, Cities, Towns, Roads, Railroads, &c.; and the latter shewing each Lot, Concession, and Oil Bearing Anticlinal. With a copious Glossary, Index, and a Catalogue of 42 different Mineral Species, embracing 400 localities where they are to be found, pointed out by Townships, Lots, Concessions, &c. *Toronto,* 1865.

II. Gold Regions of Canada. Gold: How and where to find it ! The Explorer's Guide and manual of practical and instructive directions for Explorers and Miners in the Gold Regions of Canada. *Do.,* 1867, pp. 108, 12mo.

WHITE, THOMAS. A Can. journ. Is President of the Can. Press Association. First became connected with the press in 1852 as assist. ed. of *Gazette* (Que.) In June of the following year, established the *Review* (Peterborough,) a weekly journal published in the interest of the Baldwin school of Reformers, but which ultimately, after the settlement of the Clergy Reserve question, became a supporter of the Conservative party and has remained so ever since. Mr. W. had the ed. management of that journal. In Jan. 1865 he, with his brother, purchased the *Daily Spectator* (Ham.,) a well known Western Conservative newspaper, of which he has the full ed. control. He is also ed. and prop. of the *Craftsman*, a masonic organ. Mr. W. has acted for a number of years as a Parliamentary Correspondent for various newspapers. His writings display great strength and vigour of style, as well as ornament of diction. He is also a very forcible public speaker and is regarded as a rising man in the ranks of the Conservative party.

I. Directory of the United Counties of Peterborough and Victoria, with a brief history of the Counties, statistical tables, &c. *Peterborough*, 1855, pp. 89.

II. Exhibit of the Progress of the County of Peterborough, based on the Census of 1861.

WHITEAVES, J. F., *F. G. S.* Recording Sec. of the Natural History Soc. (Mont.)

Canadian Naturalist.

I. On the Land and Fresh Water Mollusca of Lower Canada, with thoughts on the general geographical distribution of Animals and Plants throughout Canada. 1861.

II. On the Land and Fresh Water Mollusca of Lower Canada. 1863.

" It nearly exhausts the subject to which it refers, in so far as present material is concerned."—Principal DAWSON.

III. On the Fossils of the Trenton limestone of the Island of Montreal. 1865.

WHITEFORD, *Miss* ISABELLA. A Newfoundland poet. B. in Co. Antrim, Irel. Has resided at St. John's N. F. L. from an early age.

I. Poems. *Belfast*, 1860, pp. 297, 8vo.

WHITLEY, JOHN. Attorney at Law, (Tor.)
I. Canadian Domestic Lawyer, with plain and simple instructions for the merchant, farmer and mechanic, to enable them to transact their business according to law. *Stratford*, 1864, pp. 441, 8vo.

WHITMAN, JAMES, *B. A.* Barrister, N. S.
I. An Inquiry into the Right of Visit or Approach by Ships of War. *New York*, 1858, pp. 31, 8vo.

" The writer's arguments, drawn mainly from the works of the most celebrated writers on international law and from the statements and admissions of Yankee statesmen themselves—when on their good behaviour before strangers — are unanswerable."—*Aca. Recorder.*

WICKSTEED, G. W., *Q. C.* Law Clk. to the Leg. Assem. Can. From 1842 to 1845 was a Commissioner for the revision of the Statutes of L. C.; and from 1856 to 1861 for the Consolidation of the Statutes of the same Province.

I. Index to the Statutes of Canada : from 1841 to 1853 ; Alphabetical and Chronological. *Quebec*, 1854, 8vo.

" This was a much needed work ; it has been most satisfactorily accomplished by Mr. Wicksteed ; only a person who had the statutes already in some order could have produced in the short time allowed a work involving a critical examination of the whole Statute Law of the Province." *U. C. Law Journ.*

II. Index to the Statutes in force in Upper Canada, at the end of the Session of 1854-5 ; with a reference to Acts expired or repealed. By G. W. Wicksteed and W. C. Keele. *Toronto*, 1856, 8vo.

III. Table of the Provincial Statutes in force, or which have been in force in Upper Canada, in their chronological order, showing which of them or what parts of any of them are now in force, and by what subsequent acts they have been amended, continued, repeated or repealed, or otherwise affected ; with a continuation of the Index to the Statutes in force to the end of the Session of 1856. *Do.*, do.

" We have examined it with care, and can speak with confidence of its merits."—*Idem.*

IV. Index to the Statutes in force in Lower Canada. *Do.*, 1857, 8vo.

In English and French.

WIGGINS, *Rev.* A. V. G., *D. D.*
I. On the Agricultural History and condition of Sunbury County ; a prize essay. *Fredericton*, pp. 12.

WIGGINS, EZEKIEL S. A Sch.-teacher in U. C.
I. The Architecture of the Heavens : containing a new theory of the Uni-

verse, and the extent of the Deluge, and the testimony of the Bible and Geology in opposition to the views of Dr. Colenso. *Montreal*, 1864.

WIGHTMAN, GEORGE.

I. Treatise on Roads, in two parts: Part 1st Surveying and Engineering. *Halifax*, 1845, pp. 284.

" My calculations are based upon the report of Mr. George Wightman, who, rough in his manners though he be, self-taught though he be, is a Nova Scotian of whom we may be justly proud."—Hon. Joseph Howe: *Speech on Windsor Railroad.*

WILBY, JOHN ROBIN. An East India Journ. Was a native of Can. D. in India, 1857. When a very young man he suffered from weakness of the eyes, and the doctors advised that the only way to prevent the loss of sight was to have recourse to a long sea voyage. His friends could not well afford to pay for his passage, so he enlisted as a common sailor, and arrived in India in that capacity. Having obtained his discharge from the ship, he remained in Calcutta, a stranger in a strange land, in search of adventure and fortune. Mr. W. tried his hand alternately as reader, reporter and contributor, in connection with the Calcutta press; but it was not long before he was taken on the ed. staff of the *Hurkaru*, where he distinguished himself by writing some of the ablest and most telling articles that appeared in that print. On leaving the *Hurkaru* press, Mr. W., in conjunction with the then Ed. of the *Calcutta Phœnix*, set up the *Bengal Times*, the name of which was afterwards changed to the *Citizen*. The connexion, however, did not last long, as Mr. W. received the offer of a handsome engagement with the *Mofussulite*, and accepted it. He afterwards had ed. charge of the *Delhi Gazette*, and conducted that journal with an ability which was publicly acknowledged by the managing proprietor, on Mr. W's vacating the ed. chair. He next joined the *Lahore Chronicle*, and only a short time previous to his death, returned to Bengal to take his place on the staff of the *Friend of India*. He was a young man of extensive reading and varied information. There was scarcely a department of philology

or the sciences in regard to which he was altogether ignorant. His linguistical and scientific attainments were pretty nearly on a par, a combination, not always to be met with. Above all as a public writer, Mr. W. was one of the boldest and most thoroughly honest that the Indian press ever possessed.

WILKES, Rev. HENRY, D. D. A min. of the Congregational Ch. (Mont.) B. at Birmingham, Eng., 21 June, 1805. Followed mercantile pursuits in Can., for several years, and eventually became a partner in the firm of David Torrance & Co., (Mont.) Entered Glasgow Univ. to study Theology, and was ordained in 1834. Has been pastor of the First Cong. Ch., (Mont.,) since 1836. Author of various publications issued in Eng. Many of his sermons have appeared in the local newspaper press. Contributed letters, &c. on Church Govt. during several years, to the *Puritan Recorder*, (Bos.,) *The British Banner* and the *The Patriot*, (Lon.)

I. The Duties of Christians as Stewards; a sermon. *Kingston*, 1832, pp. 12.

II. Address before Theological Society, Dartmouth College. *Hanover, N. H.*, 1847, pp. 31.

III. The Ruling Passion of Jesus Christ; a sermon. *New York*, 1847, pp. 11.

IV. The Supreme Importance of Practical Godliness; a sermon. *Do.*, 1848, pp. 10.

V. The Afflictions of the Church improved; a sermon. *Montreal*, 1848, pp. 20.

VI. Essay on Christian Nurture of Children. *Do.*, pp. 16.

VII. Death in the City; address at the funeral of the Mayor. *Do.*, 1848, pp. 19.

VIII. On Freedom of Mind; a lecture; with speech of Lord Elgin. *Do.*, 1848, pp. 22.

IX. The Age and Theology; University address. *Burlington Vt.*, 1850, pp. 20.

X. Jesus the Divine Messiah; an address to Jews. *Montreal*, 1851.

XI. Who is Christ? a sermon. *Do.*, 1851, pp. 16.

XII. Knowing the Time; do. *Do.*, 1853, pp. 15.

XIII. How to use this World, do. *Do.*, 1859, pp. 16.

XIV. Christianity the Restorer, do. *Do.*, 1859, pp. 18.

XV. Internal Administration of the Churches. *Do.*, 1859, pp. 80, 12mo.

XVI. The Name above every Name; a sermon. *Do.* 1864.

WILKIE, *Rev.* DANIEL, *LL. D.* A. clergym. of the Presb. Ch. B. at Tollcross, Scot. 1777. D. at Quebec, 10 May, 1851. Came to Can. in 1803 and settled at Quebec, where he was a teacher of youth for over 40 years. Ed. the *Star* newspaper, of that city, from the commencement of its publication in 1827 until its supension in 1829. Recd. his degree from the Univ. of Glasgow.

I. Letter to the Roman Catholic Clergy and the Seigniors of Lower Canada, recommending the establishment of schools. *Quebec*, 1810, pp. 43.

Trans. Lit. & His. Soc. (Que.)

I. On Length and Space. 1831.

II. Grammar of the Huron Language, by a Missionary of the Village of Huron Indians. Translated from the Latin. Do.

III. Theory of Parallel lines, being an attempt to demonstrate the 12th Axiom of Euclid. 1837.

IV. Oration at the anniversary Prize Meeting. Do.

V. Observations on the Importance of Establishing a General System of Education, at this time (1841) 1855.

WILKINS, *Miss* HARRIET ANNIE. A Can. poet. Better known by her christian names, "*Harriet Annie*," they being generally appended to her contributions to the press. Miss W. is the daughter of the late Rev. John Wilkins. (Ham.,) and grand-daughter of the Rev. Dr. David Francis, an eminent classical scholar. The power of expressing her thoughts in verse was possessed by her when quite a child. Most of the pieces contained in her first volume were written before she had reached her 14th year, when she, with her father, were living in the State of Ohio. While there she was

a contributor to the *Ohio Observer*, a religious journal, which was ed. by the Faculty of Hudson Coll. After the removal of her father to Can. "Harriet Annie" transferred the productions of her pen, at the solicitation of the late Mr. Smiley, to the pages of the Hamilton *Spectator*, of which he was ed. and prop. To that paper she has since been a steady contributor. She has written for many other Can. newspapers. With reference to one of her pieces, "*Buried with Music*," the *Advertiser*, (Mont.,) said :

" The city of Hamilton boasts of a poet, or rather poetess, of which it ought to be proud. We give in another column one of her later effusions "Buried with Music" which has the right ring, and it is worth mountains of the trash which daily reaches us in the shape of rhyme without reason."

I. The Holly Branch. *Hamilton*, 1851, pp. 140, 12mo.

" The poem's possess merit of an exceedingly high order."—*Express*, (Ham.)

" The Holly Branch contains pages which possess merit of a more than average amount. The favorable estimate we have formed of the fair writer's detached pieces, is fully confirmed by a perusal of the whole. Harriet Annie possesses high powers of versification, her taste is unimpeachable, and if she seldom reaches the sublime she never fails to move our sympathies and touch our hearts."—*Church*, (Do.)

II. The Acacia. *Do.*, 1860, pp. 120: 2nd Ed., 1864.

" I have read your poems with a great deal of pleasure, and cannot but admire the play of fancy, the poetical feeling and the command both of imagery and language which they possess. In spite of worldly circumstances cling to your poetry for the love you bear it."—DR. CHARLES MACKEY: *Letter to Miss W.*

WILKINS, M. I., *Q. C.*

I. Confederation Examined in the Light of Reason and Common Sense. *Halifax*, 1867.

WILLAN, JOHN HENRY. A Can. lawyer and journ. B. at Quebec, 17 March, 1827. His father sent him to Eng. to receive his education, which having completed he resided for sometime at Falaise, in Normandy. In 1844, being in London, and about to return to his native country, he commenced direct acquaintance with the press by contributing to *Fraser's Mag.*, two interesting papers descriptive of scenes in the neighbourhood of Quebec. Mr. W., made choice of the profession of law, and in 1845 entered the office of the late Mr. Andrew Stuart. In due course he was admitted to practice, and very soon acquired a leading position as a criminal lawyer, a position, which with the advance of time he has by his rare talents as an expounder of the law and his great powers of eloquence greatly served to strengthen. But it is chiefly with his career as a public writer that we have to do. In the same year that he entered on the study of law, Mr. W. became ed. of the *Freeman's Journal*, and remained at his post till 1847, when he left that paper. Can. was then in the throes of the fiercest political strife she has ever felt, that of 1837 alone excepted. The *Journal* had hitherto preserved a cautious neutrality between the contending political parties, but no sooner had Mr. W. taken the ed. chair than it became the fiercest of the Can. Tory newspapers. It was on this paper that he first displayed his ability as a political writer, and won his spurs as a journ. On leaving the *Journal* he became Parliamentary reporter to the *Gazette* and the *Courier*, (Mont.) His reports were written entirely from memory, but in accuracy and copiousness were not considered inferior to the ordinary work of short-hand writers. Again visiting Eng., in the autumn of 1847, Mr. W. gave his attention to the subject of Emigration to Can., and wrote in the *Times, Herald, Standard, Post* and *John Bull* (Lon.,) respecting it. Returning to Can. he followed up the subject in the *Chronicle, Gazette, Spectator* and *Emigrant* (Que.) and for a while occupied the ed. chair of the last named journal. In 1850 he became connected with the *Mercury,* of same city, first as a Law reporter, and subsequently as political ed., which relation continued until the accession to power of the Liberal party in 1863, when the paper became the organ of that party, and Mr. W. retired from it. Shortly after the return of the Conservatives to power, in 1864, he resumed his place on the *Mercury,* by invitation. In this journal his best political contributions have

appeared. Mr. W. is beyond question in all respects the ablest and most powerful political writer on the Can. press. No other journ. that we have possesses the same strength or vigor, pungency of wit, biting satire, copiousness of language and intimate acquaintance with Constitutional history and parliamentary govt. Throughout his whole career as a public writer he has well maintained his consistency as a Conservative of the old school and a rigid supporter of High Church Establishments.

I. To Whom are we to Belong ? 1846.

II. A Manual of the Criminal Law of Canada. *Quebec,* 1861, pp. 58, 8vo.

III. Some Loose Suggestions for the Improvement of the Criminal Law in its present state of transition. *Do.* 1867, pp. 28.

" Few persons are as competent as Mr. Willan to write on such a subject; and without undertaking to approve all the reforms he suggests, we venture to predict that his work will be well received by those who are of authority in these matters, and by those whose mission it is to oversee the operation of the Laws of the land. It is incontestible that there are defects in our penal code, and above all in our criminal procedure. Mr. Willan points out many such."—*Courrier du Canada.*

WILLCOX, JOSEPH. A Can. journ. An Irishman by birth, he emigrated to U. C. when quite young. In 1803 he became Sheriff of the Home District, but was deprived of his office 3 years afterwards, by the ruling party of the day, for voting against their candidate at a Parliamentary election. In 1807 he established a paper called the *Upper Canada Guardian, or Freeman's Journal,* the second newspaper published in the Upper Province. As ed. of this paper he earned a large degree of popularity with the people and the Liberal party. He was sued for libel by Mr. Gore, the Lieut. Gov., was acquitted, and shortly afterwards returned as a mem. to the Leg. Assem. ; by that body he was incarcerated in the Toronto Gaol for a misdemeanor. For some time up to 1812, he ed. another paper at Newark called the *Telegraph.* On the declaration of war between Gt. Brit. and the U. S. in that year, he gave up his journalistic functions,.

joined the Militia, and fought against the Americans at Queenston. His singular and eventful career was closed by an act of treason, in deserting to the enemy, taking a body of Can. Militia with him. He was raised to the rank of Colonel by the Americans, but did not long enjoy the reward of his treachery, being killed at the seige of Fort Erie in 1814.

WILLIAMS, C. R. A Can. author. Resided at Cobourg, U. C. D. about 1859.

I. The Rival Families ; or, Virtue and Vice ; and the Stolen Jewels ; or, the Matchmaking Mamma. *Cobourg*, 1858, pp. 147.

"Exceedingly clever."—*Spectator*, (Ham.)
"The young will find Mr. W's book very interesting and amusing, and at the same time useful."—*Pilot*, (Mont.)

WILLIAMS, *Mrs.* C. R.
I. Neutral French ; or, the Exiles of Nova Scotia. *Boston*, N. D., 12mo ; 2nd Ed., *Providence*, N. D., 12mo.

WILLIAMS, *Capt.* GRIFFITH, *R. A.* Stationed for many years in Newfoundland.

I. Account of Newfoundland ; with Captain Col's Plan to exclude the French from its Trade. *London*, 1765, 8vo.

II. An Account of the Island of Newfoundland, with the nature of its trade, and method of carrying on the fishery ; with reasons for the great decrease of that most valuable branch of trade. *Do.* 1766, 8vo.

Lowndes gives the following title and date : "An account of the Island of Newfoundland, its Trade and Fishery. Printed for Capt. Cole, 1765, 8vo. pp. 35."

WILLIAMS, HERBERT, Mining Engineer. Supdt., Harvey Hill Mine, L. C.
I. Copper Mining in Canada East. *Trans. Lit. and His. Soc.* (Que.) 1864–5.

WILLIAMS, *Rt. Rev.* J. W., *D. D.* Lord Bish. (Que.) ; appointed 1863. Was for some years Rector of the Junior Department, Bishops' Coll., Lennoxville.
I. A Charge delivered to the Clergy of the Diocese of Quebec at the Visitation held in Bishops' College, Lennoxville. *Montreal*, 1864, pp. 21.

II. Lecture on Self-Education. *Quebec*, 1865, pp. 11.

WILLIAMS, THOMAS.
I. Life of Te-ho-ra-gwa-ne-qua, alias Thomas Williams, a Chief of the Caughnawaga Tribe of Indians in Canada. By the Rev. Eleazer Williams, reputed son of Thomas Williams, and by many believed to be Louis XVII, son of the last reigning monarch of France, previous to the Revolution of 1789. (Printed for private circulation.) *Albany*, 8vo, N. D.

WILLIAMSON, *Doctor* A. J. Ed. the *Anglo-Canadian*, (Ancaster, U. C.,) 1829.
I. Poems on various subjects. *Toronto*, 1836, 12mo.

WILLIAMSON, *Rev.* JAMES, *M. A., LL.D.* Prof. of Mathematics and Natural Philosophy, Univ. of Queen's Coll. (Kings.) B. at Edinburgh, at the High Sch. of which city he was ed., obtaining the prize for the best Latin prose and a gold medal for his proficiency in Greek. Afterwards entered the Univ., and was highly successful in Classics and in the Mathematical and Natural Philosophy Classes, taking first prizes in each of them. He studied divinity under Dr. Chalmers, and was licensed by the Presbytery (Edin.) He laboured for a time in Kilsyth and Drummelqier. In 1842 received his present appl. in Queen's Coll., where he has been eminently popular with the students and graduates, and has been the recipient of various testimonials from them. In 1855 the Univ. of Glasgow conferred upon him the degree of LL.D. It was mainly through his instrumentality that an Astronomical Observatory has been established at Kingston, from which for some years he has transmitted to the Ordnance Dept. of Gt. Brit. elaborate monthly meteorological reports. An abstract of the results of 3 years of these has been published, and another for 3 additional years is now ready for the press. These abstracts afford the only correct data yet available for determining the meteorological characteristics of Kingston, and the service has been performed by Dr. W. without any pecuniary recompense whatever. In 1843-4 he published analyses of several saline springs near Kingston, and of the three springs at Caledonia, and during successive years he made and published observations on Donati's comet. In 1831 he was a contributor to the *Presb. Review* (Edin.,) subsequently merged in the *North British Review*. Many of his lectures and addresses have appeared in *The Presbyterian* (Mont.)

I. Sermon before the Kingston St. Andrew's Society. *Kingston.*

II. The Inland Seas of North America ; and the natural and industrial productions of Canada, with the real foundations for its future prosperity. *Kingston,* 1854, pp. 78, 8vo.

"The admirable lectures of Prof. Williamson, give some very interesting particulars on this subject (the traffic of the Lakes), which are freely used in this sketch." —*Hogan's Essay on Can.*

WILLIAMSON, JOHN. At one time a private soldier in the Brit. Army. D. at Edinburgh, Scot., 1840. Resided at Montreal.

I. The Commuted Pensioner. *Montreal.*

" Obliged, while here, to work at his trade for his daily subsistence, he contrived to find leisure to send forth into the literary world the above mentioned work, which was extremely creditable to him, and would have been creditable to any one ; for while interesting events and descriptions, in tolerable number, are dispersed through the work, light incidents are told in such a palatable way, and with such an easy grace, and often so archly, as to make the perusal of the volume a very agreeable relaxation."—*Herald,* (Mon.)

WILLIS, EDWARD. A N. B. journ. B. in Halifax, N. S., Nov. 1835, where he was ed. In 1854 removed to St. John, N. B., where he wrought at his trade as a printer. About 1857 established and conducted *The Western Recorder,* (Carleton,) a weekly political paper, and about the same time started *The Freemasons' Monthly Monitor,* both of which, however, enjoyed but a brief existence. Mr. W. next served on the *Courier* (St. John,) first as assist. ed. and reporter, and ultimately as chief ed. In 1863 he accepted the chief ed. control of the *Morning News,* (same place,) a tri-weekly and weekly Reform journal, a position which he still retains. *The News* was founded in 1839, and is said to have been the first penny paper established in the British Colonial Empire. It has always upheld the interests of the Liberal party in N. B., and was a strenuous advocate of Responsible Govt. from the first inception of that scheme until its final adoption. It gave the project for the Confederation of B. N. A., based on the Resolutions adopted at the Quebec Conference, a strong and unwavering support.

WILLIS, J. H.
I. Scraps and Sketches ; or, the Album of a Literary Lounger. *Quebec,* 1830.

WILLIS, JOHN R. (Halifax, N. S.) Is an honorary mem. of the Am. Academy of Natural Sciences, (Phil.)

I. European species of Shells of Nova Scotia. *Proc. Aca., N. S.,* (Phil.) 1860.

II. Catalogue of the Marine Shells of Nova Scotia. *Proc. Nat. His. Soc.,* (Bos.) 1861.

III. On Littorina littorea on the coast of Nova Scotia. *Trans. N. S. Inst.* 1863.

WILLIS, JOHN WALPOLE.
I. On the Government of the British Colonies. *London,* 1850.

" The main object of this pamphlet is to advocate Colonial representation in the Imperial Parliament."—*Col. Mag.*

WILLIS, *Rev.* MICHAEL, *D. D.* Principal of and Prof. of Divinity in Knox Coll. (Tor.) B. in Scot. Ed. at Glasgow Univ., where he obtained his degree. Came to Can. in 1847 as prof. of divinity in the above institution, in which he has since remained. His professional course, combining his pastorate and his academic services, now exceeds 40 years. Possesses a high reputation as a preacher of the Can. Presb. Ch., a theologian, and a biblical scholar. Several of his sermons, which have all been very much admired and commended, have appeared in the *Scottish Pulpit.* He has contributed reviews, short essays, &c., to the *Christian Instructor* (Edin.,) and to the *Home and Miss. Record of the Presb. Ch. in Can.*

I. Walking with God ; and its happy issue : a sermon on the death of his father, with extracts from his diary. *Glasgow,* 1827.

II. Lecture on Roman Catholic Emancipation : being an exposition of passages in Revelations. *Do.* 1829.

III. Treatise on Church Establishments. *Do.* 1833, pp. 144, sm. 8vo.

" In point of fact, he has produced the most comprehensive and satisfactory defense of the general subjects that has lately met our eye."—*Christian Instructor,* (Edin.)

IV. Remarks on the late Union between the Church of Scotland and the Associate Synod ; in opposition to certain statements of the Dean of Faculty, with the Documents pertaining to the Union. *Do.* 1842.

V. General Assembly and Presbytery Speeches against the Semi-Pelagian error. *Do.* 1845.

VI. Slavery indefensible ; an essay. *Do.* 1847.

VII. Collectanea, Græca et Latina ; or, Selections from the Greek and Latin Fathers ; with notes for the use of Students. *Toronto,* 1865, pp. 224, d. 8vo.

WILLIS, *Rev.* ROBERT, *D. D., D. C. L.* Rector of St. Paul's (Hal.,) and Archdeacon of N. S. since 1824. Formerly a chaplain in the R. N.

I. Sermon preached in St. Paul's Church, Halifax, on the occasion of the death of the Rev. William Cogswell, A. M., Curate of said Parish. *Halifax,* 1847.

II. Sermon preached on the melancholy occasion of the death of the Rt. Rev. the Bishop of Nova Scotia. *Do.* 1850, pp. 10, 8vo.

WILLOUGBY, J.
I. The Land of the Mayflower ; or, the past and present of Nova Scotia contrasted, with a glance at the future. *Halifax,* 1860, pp. 64, 8vo.

WILLSON, HUGH BOWLBY. A Can. writer. B. in Saltfleet, U. C., 1813. Is a son of the late Hon. John Willson, a prominent mem. of the Assem. of U. C. After completing his education in the Gore District Grammar Sch., entered on the study of law, and, in 1841, was admitted to practice. Previous to this, however, he had visited the West Indies, and during his stay in Trinidad contributed several papers on the natural curiosities of the island to the *Standard* there. Some of these having found their way into the columns of the *Albion,* (N. Y.), led to his becoming an occasional contributor to that journal. Mr. W. on his return home threw himself heartily into the discussion of the commercial topics of the day. He wrote many articles on railways, steam navigation, &c., for the leading Hamilton, Kingston and Montreal journals. In 1849 he became connected, editorially, with the *Independent* (Tor.), a paper started by a number of merchants, to advocate the annexation of Can. to the U. S. The policy of this journal being, as a matter of course, unsustained by public opinion, and Mr. W. feeling himself placed in a false position, terminated his connection with it. About this time he assisted in founding the *Spectator,* (Ham.,) a strictly Conservative journal, in whose columns contributions from him have frequently appeared. In the last mentioned year he visited Eng., where he remained until 1855. Many of his letters on Can. topics, written from time to time, during his residence in the Mother Country, found a place in the *Times* (Lon.) In 1857, he for a short time conducted the *Times* (Ham.), his principal articles relating to questions of currency and banking. In 1861-2, he wrote largely for the *Chronicle,* (Que.,) on subjects connected with the trade of that port and the St. Lawrence. Mr. W. has been engaged in various projects and enterprises having for their object the development of the resources of his native country, many of which have resulted successfully and have served to bring the Province under the favorable notice of other countries.

I. The Military Defences of Canada, in a series of letters originally published in the *Morning Chronicle. Quebec,* 1862, pp. 43, 8vo.

II. The Science of Ship-building considered in its relations to the laws of nature. (With Illustrations.) *London,* 1863, pp. 80.

WILLSON, JAMES L. and ROBB, CHARLES. Mining Engineers, (Mont.)

I. The Metals in Canada, a Manual for Explorers. *Montreal,* 1861, pp. 81.

" The work treats usefully of the various conditions of occurrence of metalliferous deposits generally, and gives directions for the carrying on of preliminary and other explorations with regard to these."—*Can. Journ.*

WILMOT, JOHN EARDLEY, *F. R. S.* An Eng. barrister. D. 1851.

I. Historical View of the Commission for Inquiry into the claims of the American Loyalists at the close of the War between Great Britain and her Colonies, in 1783 : With an account of the Compensation granted to them by Parliament in 1785 and 1788. (With plate.) *London*, 1815, pp. viii–204, 8vo.

WILMOT, *Hon.* LEMUEL ALLEN. A Justice of the Supreme Court of Judicature, N. B. Formerly sat in the Parliament, and held office in the Govt. of that Province.

I. Speech in the House of Assembly of New Brunswick, Feby., 1848.

" He possesses brilliant powers, and as a public speaker ranks with the most effective and eloquent in British America."—*N. A. Rev.*

II. Two Speeches before the Mechanic's Institute, St. John, N. B., and the replies of the Rt. Rev. T. L. Connolly, D. D., Bishop of St. John, &c. *St. John*, 1859, pp. 64, 8vo.

WILSON, *Hon.* ADAM. A Puisné Judge of the Court of Common Pleas, U. C. Sat for some years in the Leg. Assem., Can.

I. A Sketch of the Office of Constable. *Toronto*, 1861.

WILSON, C. H.

I. The Wanderer in America, or Truth at Home ; comprising a Statement of Observations and Facts relative to the United States and Canada, North America ; the result of an extensive personal tour, and from sources of information the most authentic, &c. *Thirso*, (Scot.), 4th Ed. 1823, pp. 120, 12mo.

WILSON, DANIEL, *LL. D.* Prof. of History and Eng. Literature, Univ. Coll. (Tor.) B. in Edinburgh, Scot., about 1816, two years before his brother the late Prof. George Wilson, M. D., of the Univ. of Edinburgh. Pursued his studies in his native city, and early gave evidence of his superior intellectual qualities and attainments. For some years previous to coming to Can., was Secy. to the Soc. of Antiquaries, (Scot.), of which he was also a fellow. In 1853, by the death of M. Arago, a vacancy occurred in the class of honorary members of that body, (the members of which are limited to 20, and included at the time we speak of such men as Guizot, Rawlinson, Biot, Bunsen, Lepsius, &c.,) and Dr. W. was elected to the vacant place. This was in the same year as that in which he was appointed to the chair which he still fills in the Univ. of Toronto. Subsequently he was offered the office of Principal of the Univ. of McGill Coll., but declined it. He ed. the *Canadian Journal* (Tor..) for 4 years, and was presented with a silver service, both as an acknowledgment of the service thus rendered the Canadian Institute whose journal it is, and as some appreciation of the great ability and zeal with which he conducted it. In 1859 he was elected President of the Canadian Institute, an honour which was conferred upon him a second time at the annual election in the following year. In 1863 the Natural History Soc. (Mont.) awarded him its first silver medal " for important services to science, especially to science in Canada." Dr. W. was for some years President of the Teacher's Association, U. C. He is the author of many valuable and interesting papers on scientific and historical subjects in different Brit. and Am. periodicals.

I. Memorials of Edinburgh in the Olden Time. Illustrated from his own drawings. *London*, 1847, 2 vols., 4to.

" We cannot bring our notice to a close without pointing out the varied accomplishments which have been exercised in this production : not only in the striking and lucid descriptions of historical and local events, the true antiquarian spirit in which traditionary assignment has been collated, in the laborious collation of title-deeds, charters and other sources of authentic information, and the admirable order of arrangement of dates, but likewise in the graphic illustrations from drawings by the author's own hand, the result of long and earnest research ; and we sincerely trust

that such talent and application will be honorably distinguished and duly rewarded."
—*Journ. Brit. Arch. Ass.*

II. Oliver Cromwell and the Protectorate. *Edinburgh*, 1848, 12mo.

III. The Archæology and Prehistoric Annals of Scotland. With 200 illustrations, including 6 steel engravings, chiefly from drawings by the author. *London*, 1851, 2 vols., pp. 742, r. 8vo. ; 2nd Ed. revised and nearly re-written, *London* and *Cambridge*, 1864.

"A very large and elaborate classification of the earlier antiquities of Scotland. It is a very instructive, interesting as well as a very handsome book."—*Edin. Rev.*

"This is no ordinary book. If we mistake not, it will form an epoch in the study of the earlier antiquities of Scotland, and of Britain at large.   * * *   A work full of original views, bearing everywhere the stamp of independant investigation, and of an independent judgment."—*Brit. Quar. Rev.*

"The Scandinavian antiquaries have geologically deduced some important facts regarding the pre-historic period ; and Dr. Wilson has followed up the enquiry, with regard to Scotland, in a manner worthy of all praise. His work upon the pre-historic antiquities of Scotland contains an immense mass of facts, with a due proportion of rational deduction."—*West. Rev.*

IV. Prehistoric Man : Researches into the origin of Civilization in the Old and the New Worlds. 2 vols., *Cambridge* and *London*. 2nd Ed., 1862.

"This work is worthy of the high reputation won by Dr. Wilson by his previous contributions to literature. It is a thoroughly good book; in its information fresh and ample, in its conclusions wise, in its arrangement judicious and clear, in its style vigorous, expressive and distinct. The topic is not only vast in range, complex in material, and difficult from its nature, but brings the man who ventures to discuss it into contact with momentous and perplexing questions touching the origin of civilization, the unity of the human race, and the time during which man has been a denizen of this planet. Dr. Wilson proves himself at all points equal to his task."—*Witness* (Edin.)

"Dr. Wilson came to Canada with a high reputation, earned in the study of archæology ; and in this country he has pursued with such energy and . success researches in the ethnology and antiquities of America, the results of which have appeared in many papers, published here and abroad, and more recently in his valuable work ' *Prehistoric Man.* '"—PRIN. DAWSON : *Annual Address before Nat. His. Soc.* (Mon.) 1863.

"Although these volumes contain a variety of interesting information respecting the Red Indian of America, yet they cannot be said to embody much that is really new. Dr. Wilson's opportunities have not yet brought him into actual contact with the ' Wild Forest Man.' His travels, he tells us, have not extended beyond Lake Superior, where the Indian has for a hundred years been more or less in contact with the white man, hence his illustrations of really savage Indian life and arts, are all second hand, and as the authorities he quotes may have been men of widely different observant powers, it is probable that much has yet to be learned respecting this interesting race."—*B. A. Mag.*

V. Address before the Committee appointed by the Legislative Assembly to investigate the affairs of the University of Toronto. *Toronto*, 1860, pp. 40, 8vo.

Canadian Journal.

I. Remarks on some coincidences between the Primitive Antiquities of the Old and New World. 1854.

II. Remarks on the Intrusion of the Germanic Races on the Area of the Older Keltic Races of Europe. Do.

III. Observations suggested by specimens of a class of Conchological relics of the Red Indian Tribes of Canada West. 1855.

IV. Hints for the formation of a Canadian collection of Ancient Crania. Do.

V. Some Associations of the Canadian and English Maple. Do.

VI. Displacement and extinction among the Primeval races of man. 1856.

VII. The Ancient Miners of Lake Superior. Do.

VIII. The Southern Shores of Lake Superior. Do.

IX. Discovery of Indian Remains. County Norfolk, Canada West. Do.

X. Narcotic usages and superstitions of the old and the new world. 1857.

XI. Supposed prevalence of one cranial type throughout the American Aborigines. Do.

XII. Some Ethnographic phases of Conchology. Do.

XIII. Early notices of the Beaver, in Europe and America. 1859.

XIV. The Quigrich. Do.

XV. Annual Address as President of Can. Institute. 1860.

XVI. Notice of a Skull brought from Kertch, in the Crimea. Do.

XVII. Annual Address as President of Can. Institute. 1861.

XVIII. Illustrative Examples of some modifying elements affecting the ethnic significance of peculiar forms of the Human Skull. Do.

XIX. Science in Rupert's Land. 1862.

XX. Ethnical forms and undesigned artificial distortions of the Human Cranium. Do.

XXI. Illustrations of the significance of certain ancient British Skull forms. 1863.

XXII. Historical Footprints in America. 1864.

XXIII. Inquiry into the physical characteristics of the ancient and modern Celt of Gaul and Britain. Do.

WILSON, F. A., *K. L. H., G. S.*, and RICHARDS, ALFRED B.

I. Britain Redeemed and Canada Preserved (With Map and Plates) *London*, 1850, 8vo.

" Bringing forward a gigantic plan of a railroad from Halifax to Vancouver's Island, and proposal to incorporate Canada with England, and otherwise to develope its resources."—J. R. SMITH.

WILSON, JOHN, *A. M.* Prof. of Latin and Greek languages, Univ. of Victoria, Coll., Cobourg.

I. Address delivered before the Alumni of the University. *Toronto*, 1861, pp. 22, 8vo.

WILSON, JOSEPH.
I. The Constitution and History of Canada. *Picton, C. W.*, 1833, pp. 200.

WILSON, *Rev.* ROBERT. Cong. min., Sheffield, N. B.

I. The Papal Supremacy examined; a lecture. *Halifax*, 1859, pp. 37, 12mo.

WILSON, *Rev.* ROBT., *A. M.*
I. Reply to certain calumnious strictures contained in a pamphlet recently published, and intituled : " *An Appeal to the Presbyterians of New Brunswick on the late trial and suspension of the Rev David Syme. St. John*, 1837, pp. 32, 8vo.

WILSON, THOMAS, *B. A.*
I. Transatlantic Sketches ; or, Travelling Reminiscences of the West Indies and United States. *Montreal*, 1860, pp. 179, 12mo.

WILSON, *Rev.* WILLIAM. A Wesl. Meth. min. (Milltown, N. B.) Was for 14 years a missionary in Newfoundland.

I. The Modern Crusade, or the present Russian War, its termination and its results, viewed in connection with Scripture prophecy. *Boston*, 1854, 3rd Ed., pp. 192.

II. Newfoundland and its Missionaries ; in two parts. To which is added a Chronological Table of all the important events that have occurred on the Island. *Cambridge, Mass.*, 1866, pp. 448, 12mo.

" It is written in a chaste, perspicuous style, without ostentation or flourish of any kind, and ought to occupy a place in the library of every intelligent Colonist."—*Bulletin* (Charlottet.)

WILTON, J. H. " Late 23rd Royal Welch Fusiliers."

I. Scenes in a Soldier's Life ; being a connected narrative of the principal military events in Scinde, Beloochistan and Affghanistan, during 1839, 1840, 1841, 1842 and 1843, under Generals Lord Keane, Brooks, Sale, Pollock, Nott and Sir Charles Napier. *Montreal*, 1848.

" The Author was actively engaged with our army in the east, in the fierce struggles which took place during the years from 1839 to 1843, and was an eye-witness to many of the stirring scenes which were enacted during that terrible epoch. Of all that took place, he has prepared a connected narrative which being well and vigorously written will be read with much interest."—*Lit. Garland.*

WILY, *Lieut.-Col.* THOMAS. Chief Superintendent of Stores, Adjutant General's Dept., Can. Is Lt. Colonel of the Civil Service Rifle Regt., Ottawa.

I. The Annual Volunteer and Service Militia List of Canada. 2nd year, *Quebec*, 1865 ; 3rd year, *Ottawa*, 1866 ; 4th year, *Do.*, 1867.

" A Militia *Vade Mecum* in point of fullness and accuracy."—*Transcript* (Mon.)

" In the fact that it has been compiled by Col. Wily we have a guarantee for its correctness."—*Globe* (Tor.)

WINDSOR, *Rev.* SAMUEL B., *M. A.* A clergym. of the Ch. of Eng. Is Chaplain to the Forces (Kings., U. C.)

I. Three Sermons on the Parable of the Prodigal Son—preached in the Cathedral Ch. of St. George. *Kingston*, 1867.

WINTHROP, JOHN. Was Hollisian Prof. of Mathematics and Astronomy, Cambridge, Mass.

I. Relation of a Voyage from Boston to Newfoundland, for the observation of the Transit of Venus, June 6, 1761. *Boston*, pp. 24, 8vo.

II. Observation of the transit of Venus, June 6, 1761, at St. John's, Newfoundland. *Phil. Trans.*, 1764.

WISHART, *Rev.* WILLIAM THOMAS. A min. of the Established Ch. of Scot., in N. S. B. in Scot. After his arrival in N. S. was first settled in Shelburne, whence he removed to St. John, N. B., where he d. in 1853. Having adopted views on the Sabbath and the Christian Ministry at variance with his Ch., he was expelled from that body. He possessed fine talents and a highly cultivated literary taste. *The Provincial Mag.* (Hal.,) to which he occasionally contributed, says of him :

"For scholastic attainment, originality of mind, and strong vigorous intellect, few in these Provinces have equalled this gentleman."

He contributed papers on literary subjects to others of the Provincial press and it is with reference to some of these that the late Mr. G. R. Young alludes in his work on *Colonial Literature :—*

"Before passing from the features of this age, it would be unjust, in a work avowedly devoted to Colonial Literature, if reference were not made to a series of beautiful original papers which appeared in the Halifax *Nora Scotian*, (1840) intituled : "*A Rough Sketch of English Literature, from its first commencement to the age of Elizabeth.*" They are from the pen of the Rev. Mr. Wishart. * * * * These rough notes, and the masterly sketches of the Nineteenth Century by the same hand, contained in the earlier numbers of the *Nora Scotian* for 1840, have been regarded, and justly so, as the evidences of a richly cultivated mind, and superior powers of analysis and comprehension."

I. The Decalogue the best system of Ethics. *Halifax*, 1842, pp. 100, sm. 8vo.

II. Extracts of Lectures on Political Economy, delivered during the Session of 1844 and 1845 before Mechanics' Institute. *St. John*, 1845, pp. 24, 8vo.

III. A Series of Outlines, or Theological Essays, on various subjects connected with Christian Doctrine and Practice. *Do.*, 1847.

IV. The Female Sex ; a lecture delivered in the St. John Mechanics' Institute. *Do.*, 1852.

"The writer has long been known as a popular lecturer and author of several essays on topics of modern literature. The work before us bears the stamp of originality if nothing more. The female character, its capabilities and deficiencies, with ideas for its improvement, is discussed in a most novel manner, and we are not sure that the author has glanced widely from the truth."—*Provl. Mag.* (Hal.)

V. Six Disquisitions on Doctrinal and Practical Theology. *Do.*, 1853.

"While we confess our admiration for the earnestness and sincerity of the author, and the terse and vigorous style, the chaste and classic language in which his ideas are clothed, it is neither our province nor our desire to enter upon points of controversy involved in the subjects discussed. * * * The pen of the author is now silent for ever. This his latest literary production will therefore elicit no critical severity. Whatever may be thought of the late Mr. Wishart's theological writings, it will not be denied by any who have heard him as a public speaker that he possessed great intellectual ability, and as an essayist or popular lecturer would have ranked high in any country with what subject soever under discussion, he reasoned closely yet clearly, and illustrated his views with copiousness and precision. An ample education afforded material for his ardent fancy, and conveyed the sentiment of his writings in a bold and vigorous style. His diligence and love of study enabled him to master a wide range of erudition and to acquire that vast amount of general information that was the marvel of all his acquaintance."—*Idem.*

WIX, *Rev.* EDWARD. "Archdeacon of Newfoundland."

I. The Guilt of a denial of God's Providence ; a sermon. *St. John's*, 1832, pp. 23, 8vo.

II. Six Month's of a Newfoundland Missionary's Journal, from February to August, 1835. *London*, 1836, pp. 264, cr., 8vo.

WOLFE, JAMES. A celebrated Eng. Gen. B. at Westerham, Kent, Eng., 15 Jany. 1726. Killed while commanding the Brit. force in the capture of Quebec, 13 Sept., 1759.

I. Instructions to Young Officers, also his orders for a Battalion and an Army, with the Orders and Signals in Embarking and Debarking an army by flat-bottomed boats, &c., and a Placart to the Canadians. *London*, 2nd Ed., 1780, 8vo.

Life of General James Wolfe, the conqueror of Canada, or the Elogium of that renowned Hero, attempted according to the rules of Eloquence, by J.*** P.****** *London*, 1760, 4to.

An Apology for the Life of General Wolff, by J. Mauduit.—*London*, 1765, 8vo.

"25 copies printed."—LOWNDES.

The Life of Major General Wolfe, founded on original documents and illustrated by his correspondence. (With Portrait.) By Robert Wright, *London*, 1865, pp. 626, 8vo.

"The storming of Quebec and the death of Wolfe and Montcalm are familiar to every military reader; but we have not before seen any thing like so full and satisfactory an account both of the war, and of the whole surrounding circumstances, as Mr. Wright has here written and compiled for us. The book, in fact, teems with scraps which will be devoured with avidity by the military reader. The battles of Dettingen and Fontenoy, the freaks of 'Johnny Cope,' the town life of the period, camp life, the old-fashioned drill and uniform, form only a tithe of the attractive *morceaux* which will be found in this single volume. Finally, we have the battle of Quebec and the death scenes of the opposing heroes. What could a soldier desire more in choosing a book?" *Un. Service Gaz.*

(See *Bell*, Andrew ; *Sabine*, Lorenzo.)

WOOD, Rev. JOHN. A Congregational clergym. (Brantford, U. C.)

I. A Manual on Christian Baptism, its mode and subjects; being the substance of six lectures delivered in the Congregational Church, Brantford, in 1856. *Toronto*, 1857, pp. 123.

II. Prize Essay on the best mode of managing Sabbath Schools, and of conducting the Devotional Exercises. *Hamilton*, 1865, pp. 12.

WOODHOUSE, JAMES.

I. Tables for the calculation of twenty different rates of interest from ten pounds to ten shillings per cent. per annum for any number of days or to any amount. *Toronto*, 1853.

WOODS, N. A. Correspondent of the *Times*, (Lon.,) during the visit of H. R. H. the Prince of Wales to B. A., in 1860.

I. The Prince of Wales in Canada and the United States. (With Map.) *London*, 1861, pp. 438, 12mo.

WOODS, SAMUEL, *M. A.* Head Master of the Grammar Sch., (Kings.,) U. C.

I. The first three Philippic Orations of Demosthenes. With notes, critical explanatory and historical. *Toronto*, 1866, pp. 200, 12mo.

"The notes which Mr. Woods appends to the Philippics are most valuable, and are certain to be appreciated by the student. Though he has made use of the labors of previous editors, he has added to and improved upon them; and his references to parallel readings and forms of expression in other authors have evidently been made with great care."—*Transcript* (Mon.)

WOODWORTH. S.

I. The War; being a faithful record of the transactions of the war between the United States of America and the United Kingdom of Great Britain and Ireland. *New York*, 4to.

WORKMAN, BENJAMIN, *M. D.* A Can. journ. Now Assist. Physician to the Provincial Lunatic Asylum, (Tor.) In 1829, undertook the ed. management of *The Canadian Courant*, (Mont.,) of which he was part prop. *The Courant* pursued an independent policy neither leaning to one nor the other of the political parties of the day. It advocated Temperance and other reforms, and was very useful in its sphere of duty. Dr. W's. connection with it ceased in 1834.

WORKMAN, JOSEPH. *M. D.* Supdt. of the Provincial Lunatic Asylum, (Tor.) Brother of the preceding. Was for some years ed. of the *Mirror* of the same city.

I. Van Der Kolks Pathology and Therapeutics of Insanity. Translated. (Reprinted from the *Am. Journal of Insanity.*) pp. 91.

"We have selected for publication in the present number of the *American Journal of Insanity*, the second part of Schroeder Van

Der Kolk's work, being the portion of the highest practical importance to our readers; and if we may say so, without derogation from the merits of the author, the portion most free from theoritic speculation. The first part is devoted to the Anatomy and Physiology of the Brain, and includes a most valuable section on Imflammation of the Dura Mater."—*Translator's Preface.*

II. Report on British and Irish Lunatic Asylums. *Hamilton,* 1859.

"The report embraces the result of his observations during a ten weeks absence, in which he visited no less than nineteen of the chief Asylums of the mother country, twelve in England, four in Scotland, and three in Ireland."—*B. A. Journ.*

WORKMAN, MATTHEW F. In 1837, when only 17 years of age, wrote an essay " *On the Connection between the Language and the Character of a People,*" for the Natural History Society, Montreal, for which he was awarded the silver prize medal of that body. The author showed in this effort great powers of analysis and comparison on a subject of an abstruse nature, worthy of an advanced scholar with acute intellectual powers. He was a youth of great intellectual attainments and an ardent student. D. of consumption, May 1839. In noticing his death the *Gazette,* (Mont.) said :—

"His premature and lamented death, caused by an overstrained application to study, the result of a too fervent thirst after knowledge, has deprived his parents and relatives of one endeared to them by his virtues and merits, no less than by the ties of nature; and has withdrawn from the world, talents, which, had they been permitted to ripen into maturity, might have been a blessing and ornament to society."

WRAY, *Rev.* H. B.
I. The Mysteries of the Kingdom; a sermon. *Montreal,* 1860, pp. 19.

WRIGHT, FREDERICK. A Can. poet. B. in Irel. Came to Can. 1833. Followed the calling of school teacher for some years. Has contributed largely to the periodical and newspaper press of Can. and the U. S. Resides at Delta, U. C.

I. Wayside Pencillings. *Ogdensburg, U. S.,* 1855, pp. 200.

"He is one of nature's own poets, and draws his inspiration from an unpolluted fountain."—*Globe,* (Tor.)

II. Lays of a Pilgrim. *Brockville,* 1864, pp. 150.

WRIGHT, J. Ed. of the *Parliamentary History of England.*

I. Debates of the House of Commons in the year 1774, on the bill for making more effectual provision for the government of the Province of Quebec. Drawn up from the notes of the Rt. Hon. Sir Henry Cavendish, Bart., Member for Lostwithiel. Now first published. [With Maps.] *London,* 1839, pp. 303. Another Ed. 1841.

WRIGHT, PHILEMON. An early settler on the Ottawa River, Can. B. at Woburn, Mass. U. S., 1760. D. at Hull, 2 June, 1839.

I. An Account of the first Settlement of the Township of Hull, on the Ottawa River, L. C. *Can. Mag.,* 1824.

WRIGHT, THOMAS. " Deputy Surveyor Gen. of Land for the Northern District of Am."

I. Description of the Island of Anticosti. *London,* 1768, 8vo.

II. Immersions and Emersions of Jupiter's first Satellite, observed at Jupiter Inlet, on the Island of Anticosti. *Phil. Trans.,* 1774.

WRIGHT, WILLIAM, *M. D.* Prof. of Materia Medica and Pharmacy, Univ. McGill Coll. (Mont.)

I. The Cranial Nerves, their leading points arranged for the use of Students. *Montreal,* 1851.

II. The Spinal Nerves, their disposition and distribution ; arranged for the use of Students. *Do.,* do.

"Students will find them a very valuable assistant in their anatomical studies."—*B. A. Journ.*

WURTELE, ARTHUR, *C. E., P. L. S.*
I. Tables for reducing English, old French, and metrical Measures. *Montreal,* 1862, pp. 47.

WYLIE, DAVID. A Can. journ. B. at Johnstown, Scot. 23 March, 1811. Was apprenticed at an early age to the printing business, and worked at his trade in several offices in Gt. Brit.; his love of reading and habits of application soon however prepared him for higher duties. He contributed both prose and poetry to one or two Scottish journals, and was employed as reporter on the *Liverpool Mail.* In 1845, he came to Can. and returned to his trade, occasionally writing for the newspaper and periodical press. Shortly afterwards he was engaged as a Parliamentary reporter for the *Herald* (Mont.) In 1849, he purchased the *Recorder* (Brockville) a weekly Reform journal, of which he became ed. as well as prop., positions which he still retains.

I. Recollection of a Convict, and miscelleanous pieces in prose and verse. *Montreal*, 1847, pp. 200.

WYNNE, JOHN HUDDLESTONE.

I. A General history of the British Empire in America, including all the countries in North America and the West Indies ceded by the Peace of Paris. *London*, 1770, 2 vols. 8vo.

Y.

YOUNG, ARTHUR.

I. L'Exemple de la France, avis à la Grande-Bretagne. *Québec*, 1794, 8vo.

YOUNG, *Hon.* CHARLES, *LL. D.* A Judge in P. E. I. Youngest son of the late John Young, ("Agricola.")

I. Inaugural Lecture before Mechanics' Institute. *Charlottetown*, 1839, pp. 20.

II. Address to the Electors of the Third District of Queen's County, by their late Representative. *Do.*, 1840, pp. 12.

YOUNG, *Rev.* GEORGE PAXTON, *A. M.* A Minister in the Can. Presb. Ch. Was for sometime Prof. of Logic and Metaphysics in Knox Coll., (Tor.,) and is now Inspector of Grammar Schools, U.C.

I. Miscellaneous Discourses and Expositions of Scriptures. *Edinburgh*, 1854, pp. 348.

II. The Philosophical principles of Natural Religion ; a lecture. *Home & For. Rec. of C. P. C.* 1862.

Canadian Journal.

I. An Examination of Professor Ferrier's Theory of Knowing and Being. 1856.

II. A New Proof of the Parallelogram of Forces. Do.

III. An Examination of Legendre's proof of the properties of Parallel Lines. Do.

IV. On Sir David Brewster's supposed law of visible direction. 1857.

V. Resolution of Algebraical Equations. 1860.

26

VI. The Relation which can be proved to subsist between the area of a plane triangle and the sum of the angles, on the hypothesis that Euclid's 12th Axiom is false. Do.

VII. Notes on passages in the Platonic Dialogues. 1862.

VIII. Formulæ for the cosines and sines of multiple arcs. 1863.

IX. A New proof of the existence of the roots of Equation. 1864.

X. Remarks on Professor Boole's Mathematical theory of the Laws of Thought. 1865.

" Remarkable researches."—*Can. Journ.*

YOUNG, JAMES, *M. P.* A Can. journ. B. 1835. In 1853 purchased the *Dumfries Reformer* (Galt,) of which he subsequently became ed. As its name indicates, the *Reformer* was, and still is, a supporter of the Liberal party, and as such has lent efficient aid to the great Reform body. In 1863 Mr. Y. retired from the *Reformer*, and subsequently had ed. connection with the *Trade Review* (Mont.) In 1867 he was returned to the House of Commons of the Dominion of Can. He is favourably known as a lecturer, and has held various public positions of importance in his county.

I. The Agricultural Resources of Canada, and the inducements they offer to British labourers intending to emigrate to this Continent ; an essay which obtained the first prize ($50) offered by the Mercantile Association of Hamilton. 1857.

" The essay contains a great deal of useful information, and is written in a conspicuous and masterly style that would reflect credit on some of the best authors of the day."—THE LATE A. MACKINNON.

II. Essay on the Reciprocity Treaty, to which was awarded the second prize by the proprietors of the *Trade Review. Montreal*, 1865.

YOUNG, JOHN. The author of the letters of "Agricola." B., we believe, in or near, Falkirk, Scot. D. at Halifax, N. S., 26 Oct., 1837. Ed. at Glasgow Univ. He entered into trade, and about 1815, emigrated with his wife and four sons to N. S. In 1818 he succeeded in arousing attention to the dormant condition of Agriculture in that Province, through a series of letters which he wrote in the *Recorder* (Hal.,) under the *nom de plume* of "Agricola." These letters were the means of procuring the establishment by the Legislature of N. S. of the Board of Agriculture, of which Mr. Y. eventually became Secy. It was not, however, until the following year (1819) that he avowed the authorship of the letters. At a dinner given in Halifax in 1818, we find the then Governor, the Earl of Dalhousie, toasting the celebrated unknown, as follows :

" He rose to propose the health of a gentleman, who, though unknown to him, he was certain, from his writings deserved the appellation of a scholar and a patriot; and whose exertions in the cause of the prosperity of the country called forth the esteem of every friend to its welfare? After many other remarks, he gave the health of Agricola and success to his labors ? The toast was received with eclat.*"

In 1825 he was returned to the Provincial Parliament, and continued to sit as a member of the Assem. until his death. In that body he displayed considerable eloquence as a speaker, and large and varied knowledge in the performance of his duties. A N. S. journal, opposed to him in politics during his lifetime, in noticing his death, pays the following well deserved tribute to his memory :

" He has left very few men behind him, combining so much varied and valuable information, with the same power to impart it either orally or through the press. • •
This is not the place nor the occasion for elaborate criticism of his course as a legisla-

* Murdoch : *His. of N. S.*

tor—for nice balancings of praise and censure. We feel that a fine intellect has gone down into the tomb,—that an acute and powerful writer—a logical and eloquent speaker, is lost to a country, where, as yet, talent is not very abundant, and the general mind of which the deceased did much to arouse and enlighten ; and we cannot shake off the feelings of sorrow and regret occasioned by his loss."

I. Report of the Proceedings of the Agricultural Society of Halifax for 1823. *Halifax*, 1824.

" To Mr. Young's exertions as an agriculturist, aided by the co-operation of the first characters in that province, and assisted with as much public support as its financial circumstances would allow, Nova Scotia, is deeply indebted. We remember perusing with a lively interest, his valuable writings on rural economy, diffused through the medium of the public papers, when these letters were not stamped with the authentic characteristic of his name. Their intrinsic worth alone, unaided by the weight of power or interest, drew the attention of the public mind towards them; agricultural societies became in vogue ; government gave them its support; Mr. Y. with unceasing perseverance, lent his time and talents to the best means of advancing their interest ; and, as appears by this report, he has now the proud satisfaction of seeing that his plans have been crowned with success, beyond the most sanguine expectations."—*Can. Mag.* (Montreal.)

II. Letters of Agricola on the principles of Vegetation and Tillage. Written for Nova Scotia. *Halifax*, 1822, pp. 462, 8vo.

YOUNG, GEORGE R. A N. S. journ. and legislator. Now d. Was a son of John Young, "Agricola." (whom see.) Established the *Nova Scotian*, (Hal.,) newspaper in 1824 of which he was ed. for some years. He was a mem. of the N. S. Legislature for a considerable period.

I. The British North American Colonies.—Letters to the Right Hon. E. G. Stanley, Esquire, M. P., upon the existing Treaties with France and America. as regard "Their Rights of Fishery" upon the Coasts of Nova Scotia, Labrador and Newfoundland ; the violations of these Treaties by the subjects of both powers, and their effect upon the commerce, equally of the Mother Country and the Colonies, &c. *London*, 1834, pp. 193, 8vo. (*map*.)

II. The History, Principles and Prospects of the Bank of British North America, and of the Colonial Bank; with an Enquiry into Colonial Exchanges and expediency of introducing British Sterling and British Coin in preference to the Dollar as the money of Account and Currency of the North American Colonies. *Do* 1838, 8vo.

III. On the Escheat Question in Prince Edward's Island, Agitation and Remedies. *Do.* 1838.

IV. The Canadian Question. *Do.* 1839, pp. 83.

V. Letters on "Responsible Government," and an Union of the Colonies of British North America, to the Rt. Hon. Lord John Russell. *Halifax*, 1840, pp. 28.

VI. Letters to the Rt. Hon. Lord Stanley, H. M. Secy. of State for the Colonies, and opinion, shewing that the proposed repeal of the Union existing between the island of Cape Breton and Nova Scotia, would be unconstitutional;—as well as inexpedient, when viewed as a question of general Colonial policy. *Do.*, 1842, pp. 14, 8vo.

VII. On Colonial Literature, Science and Education; written with a view of improving the Literary, Educational, and Public Institutions of British North America. In three Volumes. *Do.*, Vol. I, 1842, pp. xiv–373, 12mo.

The first volume only appeared.

"This work comes to our notice as a kind of literary curiosity, being the first volume of any pretensions, so far as we remember, which has come to us from the Northern Colonial press. It has further claims to regard as the production of a gentleman well known among his fellow colonists as a barrister of eminence, who, like some distinguished members of the profession in our own and the mother country, devotes his leisure hours to the great public cause of education and literature.   *   *

"The volume before us, which is to be followed by two more, consists of twelve Lectures, part of which were in substance delivered by the author as President of the Institute at Halifax. The publication, when complete, 'is intended to sketch a general outline which the student may afterwards fill up according to natural taste and predilection, of different branches of letters, philosophy, and legislation; and to aid in this useful labor by giving references to the best authors, where the subjects and ques-

tions are fully and elaborately treated.' It is a design worthy of the author, and calculated to be of much use, we should judge, especially in the present condition of literature and education in the British Colonies. Indeed, we learn from the introduction, that Dr. Birkbeck, the late lamented President of the London Mechanics' Institution, expressed to the author his approval of the scheme, together with that of several influential friends of popular education in the mother country, of whom Lord Brougham was one.   *   *   *

"It is gratifying to see a man in Mr. Young's position, instead of aiming at the reputation of an original writer, employing his talents upon a kind of work better adapted for practical usefulness among those for whom it is more particularly intended. He is content to give ample space to the speculations and conclusions of the leading minds in their several departments, and wherein they have spoken wisely, they are often allowed to speak for themselves. The proper course in a work like this 'of a strictly educational character,' is to inform those who need be informed of some of the main facts which have been best ascertained in science, and of the elementary truths which have been most approved and best illustrated in the history of human thought. The author has thus condensed much valuable matter into the first three Lectures, by way of sketching the successive stages of knowledge up to the time of modern civilization. In the two following, the subject of education is treated in a national point of view, and a good abstract is given of the more approved European systems of popular instruction.

"In the three succeeding Lectures, upon the Condition and Prospects of Education in the Colonies, there is much valuable information that can with difficulty be obtained elsewhere. And those amongst us who take a lively interest in the general cause of popular instruction, irrespective of state and national boundary lines, will be under obligations to the author for enabling them to get some insight into this portion of the subject without the labor that he must have taken in collecting and examining large numbers of reports and other official documents."—*N. A. Rev.*

VIII. Articles on the great Colonial project of connecting Halifax and Quebec by a Railroad. *Do.*, 1847.

YOUNG, *Hon.* JOHN. A Can. merchant and legislator. B. at Ayr, Scot., 1811. Having left sch. at the age of 13, he for nearly 18 months kept a sch. in a parish near his native place. In 1826 he emigrated to Can. and settled at Montreal, where he has ever since (with the exception of 5 years at Quebec) resided, doing business, nearly all that time as a wholesale merchant. In 1846 he was instrumental in organizing a Free Trade Association, of which he became President. This body published the *Canadian Economist*, a weekly journal, devoted to its interests, to which he frequently contributed. He represented Montreal in the Can. Parliament from 1851 to 1857, during part of which time he held office as Chief Commissioner of Public Works. He has also held various other important public positions. Mr. Y's. name has been identified with nearly every question for the improvement of the trade, commerce and currency, and for the development of the resources of the Province, which has been brought forward during the last 30 years. His newspaper writings on these and other subjects of public interest, would fill many volumes.

I. Views of the Commercial Policy of Canada. *Montreal*, 1853.

II. Letters to the Hon. F. Lemieux, Chief Com. of Public Works, on Canadian Trade and Navigation. *Do.* 1855.

III. Letters to the Citizens of Montreal, on the Commerce of the City, and the means of its further development. *Do.* 1855.

IV. Letters to the Hon. T. J. J. Loranger, on Harbour Improvements. *Do.* 1858.

V. Reply to J. C. Trantwine, C. E.. on the subject of the construction of Docks at Montreal. *Do.* 1859.

VI. Letters on the Rival Routes from the West to the Ocean ; and Docks at Montreal. *Do.* 1859, pp. 49.

VII. On the changed opinions of the Montreal Board of Trade on the Canal to connect the St. Lawrence with Lake Champlain. *Do.* 1866.

VIII. Montreal. *Ency. Brit.*, 8th Ed.

YULE, PATRICK, (*Major Royal Engineers.*) Now Major General retired on full pay. Served in Canada during the war of 1812.

I. Remarks on the disputed North-Western Boundary of New Brunswick bordering on the United States of North America, with an Explanatory Sketch. *London*, pp. 28, 8vo.

ADDENDA.

ANDERSON, W. J., (p. 9.) add :
IV. Canadian History and Biography, and Passages in the Lives of a British Prince and a Canadian Seigneur : the Father of the Queen and the Hero of the Chateauguay. Read before Literary and Historical Soc. *Quebec*, 1867, pp. 51, 8vo.

BAIRD, *Rev.* JAMES, (p. 17.) add :
Degree of D. D. conferred upon him in 1867 by Univ. of N. Y.

BENNETT, *Rev.* JAMES, (p. 27.) add :
III. The Logical Consequences of the Acquittal of Jesus ; a Synod sermon. *St. John*, 1867.
" A discourse of rare originality, ability as to its matter and of great beauty of style."— *Journal.*

BLAIN DE SAINT AUBIN, EMM. (p. 35.) add :
B. at Rennes, France, 1833. Has resided in Can. during the past 10 years.

CARROLL, *Rev.* JOHN, (p. 63.) add :
V. Case and his Contemporaries. (*In press.*)

CHAMBERLIN, BROWN, (p. 69.) add :
In 1867 was returned to Can. House of Commons, as mem. for Missisquoi.

CHAUVEAU, *Hon.* P. J. O., (p. 72.) add :
In 1867 was called upon to form the first local govt. for the Province of Quebec, under the Imperial Act of Union of that year. He re-entered Parliament as mem. for his old Co. in the House of Commons and the Local Legislature. Holds office in local govt. as Provincial Secy., Registrar and Minister of Education.
IV. Discours prononcé sur la Tombe de M. F. X. Garneau. *Rev. Can.*, 1867.

CODERRE, J. E., (p. 79.) add 1857 as date of pamphlet.

COOPER, *Rev.* H. C., (p. 81.) add :
II. The United Church of England and Ireland ; a sermon. *Toronto*, 1865, pp. 12.

DOUTRE, G. (p. 107.) add :
I. Les Lois de la Procédure Civil, savoir : texte du Code, rapport des codificateurs, autorités par eux citées, lois de faillite, règles de pratique des différents tribunaux, principes et formules de procédure, etc. *Montréal*, 1867, 8vo.

DRAPEAU, STANISLAS, (p. 109.) add :
VIII. Observations sur la brochure de M. M. les Abbés Laverdière et Casgrain. *Do.*, 1866, pp. 28.

FOSTER, W. A. (p. 129.) add :
In 1867 became ed. of *The Canadian Monetary Times and Insurance Chronicle*, a journal recently established in Toronto.

GERIN-LAJOIE, A., (p. 137.) add :
IV. L'Abbé J. B. A. Ferland. *Foy. Can.* 1865.

GRANT, J. A., (p. 158.) add :
In 1867 was returned to Can. Parliament as a mem. of the House of Commons.

HARRISON, R. A., (p. 176.) add :
In 1867 was returned to Can. House of Commons as mem. for West Toronto.

HELLMUTH, *Ven.* I., (p. 181.) add :
II. Divine Dispensations ; Eight sermons preached in the Chapel of Huron College. *London and Toronto*, 1865.

HODGINS, J. G., (p. 190.) add :
X. Summary of Canons and Resolutions adopted by the Synod of the Diocese of Toronto, from 1851, to 1864, inclusive, with an Index to the whole. *Toronto*, 1865, pp. 79, 8vo.

HOUGH, FRANKLIN B., (p. 194.) add :
III. The Northern Invasion of October, 1780. A series of papers relating to the expeditions from Canada under Sir John Johnson and others against the Frontiers of New York, which were supposed to have connection with Arnold's Treason. Prepared from the original, with an Introduction and Notes. *New York*, 1866, pp. 224, 8vo.

HOWE, *Hon.* JOSEPH, (p. 195.) add :
In 1867 was returned to the Can. Parliament as a mem. of the House of Commons.

MILTON, *Viscount*, and W. B. CHEADLE, (p. 279.) add :
Translated into French. *Paris*, 1867 r. 8vo.

SULTE, BENJAMIN, (p. 364.) add :
In 1867 was elected a corresponding mem. of the *Cercle Artistique et Littéraire de Brussell, Belgique.*

SUPPLEMENT.

BRAUN, *Rév.* **P. A.** De la Compagnie de Jésus.

I. Instructions Dogmatiques sur le Mariage Chrétien. *Québec*, 1866, pp. 193, 8vo.

BROKE, *Sir* **P. B. V.,** *Bart,* **K. C. B.** A distinguished Brit. Admiral. B. Sept. 9, 1776. D. 1840. Commanded H. M. S. *Shannon* and captured the American frigate *Chesapeake*, off Boston harbour, in 1813.

I. Admiral Sir P. B. V. Broke, Bart., K. C. B., &c. A memoir. Compiled by Rev. J. G. Brighton, M. D. (With Illustrations.) *London*, 1866, pp. xvi—488, r. 8vo.

BUREAU, JOSEPH.

I. Hand Book to the Parliamentary and Departmental Buildings, Canada, with plans of the buildings indicating the several offices and the names of the officials occupying them ; together with a Plan of the City, and a short Sketch of the Valley of Ottawa and every object of interest in the neighbourhood ; also Lists of Members of the Privy Council,—Local Governments,—Senators,—Members of the House of Commons and Local Legislatures, &c., &c., &c. *Ottawa*, 1867, 8vo.

CARNARVON, *Rt. Hon.* the *Earl* of. Late Secy. of States for the Colonies.

I. Speech delivered in the House of Lords on moving the 2nd Reading of the Confederation Bill, 19th Feb. 1867. *London*, 1867, pp. 24, 8vo.

DAVIS, ROBERT. A Can. journ. B. in London, Eng. Ed. at Winchester and subsequently graduated at Magdalen Coll., Oxford. Emigrated with his family to Am. in 1842. Mr. D. resided in the U. S. for some five or six years, but in 1848 his strong Brit. proclivities brought him to Can., where making the acquaintance of the late Mr. Hugh Scobie, then prop. of the *British Colonist* (Tor.,) he became connected with the press of this country, and with the exception of a short intermission his connection with the *Colonist* continued until the paper passed into the hands of Mr. S. Thompson, and finally collapsed. He was also engaged in correspondence with Eng. periodicals. In 1862 he founded and ed. at Quebec the *Militia and Volunteer Service Gazette*. In 1864 he succeeded Mr. Shepherd as ed. of the *Morning Chronicle* (Que.) and held that position up to the removal of the Govt. to Ottawa, whither he was sollicited to proceed and bring out a new paper under the auspices of the Govt. He aided in successfully establishing the Ottawa *Daily Times*, of which he remained ed. until the summer of 1866, when he retired from the conduct of the paper through a difference of opinion with the prop. He is now living upon his farm in Western Can. and has, we believe, bid adieu to newspaper life. Throughout his newspaper career Mr. D. was a keen and consistent Conservative, and as such laboured with zeal and ability for the benefit of his party.

I. The Currency ; What it is and what it should be. *Ottawa*, 1867, pp. 33, 4to.

DEMILL, *Prof.*, Dalhousie Coll. (Hal.)

I. Helena's Household ; a tale of Rome in the First Century. *New York*, 1867.

DRINKWATER, *Rev.* **C. H.,** *B. A.* Rector of Hamilton.

I. A Short Account of the manner in which the Emancipation Day, 1st August, 1864, was spent in the city of Hamilton. *Hamilton*, 1864.

GANE, WILLIAM LAW. An Eng. and Can. writer. Better kown in Can. by his *nom de plume :* " The Lowe Farmer." B. at Harwich, Essex, Eng., 1815. Educated in Eng., and afterwards proceeded to Sweden, where he studied at the Univ. of Lund. His first contribution to Literature appeared in the *Royal Ladies Magazine* in 1830, and it is a noteworthy fact, that being a first effort, *the author* *was paid for it.* At 18 he had attained a very respectable position as a writer both in prose and verse, and his contributions were welcomed in periodicals in which such eminent authors as Sheridan Knowles, Mary Howitt, Shelton Mackenzie, Miss Pardoe, Agnes Strickland, Miss Jewsbury, John Galt, Hon. Miss Beauclerk, Viscount Glentworth, &c., were regular contributors. Subsequently he wrote for *Blackwood,* the *New Monthly Mag.*, the *Gentleman's Mag.*, *Frazer*, the *Tablet*, *Douglas Jerrold's Mag.*, *Household Words,* and more recently, *Punch.* Among his earlier productions was a sea-tale, which appeared in the *Metropolitan*, a mag. ed. by Capt. Marryatt, and an historical romance, which attracted considerable attention, called *St. Augustines Mission*, published in the *Cabinet.* To *Bentley's Miscellany* he was a constant contributor from its first appearance under the ed. of Chas. Dickens, until Mr. H. Ainsworth succeeded to the proprietorship. Mr. G. during his literary career in Eng. became the ed. of various monthlies, including the *Lady's Mag.*, the oldest publication of its class ; the *Court Mag.*, and the *'Town and Country Mag.*, of which he was at the same time ed. and prop. His labours were not confined to light literature. His political writings procured for him the sub. ed. of the *Morning Chronicle,* (Lon.) a position which had shortly before been vacated by Mr. Dickens. He also wrote for the *Sun* and other dailies and weeklies. As a public writer he was made acquainted with the celebrated William Cobbett, and as a result of the acquaintance he contributed several papers to *Cobbett's Mag.* Mr. G. came to Can. early in 1860 and resided for a short time in the Tp. of Lowe, on the Ottawa, where he held a farm, or "clearance." Invited to Ottawa city, he became connected with the newspaper press there. He has since served as a parliamentary correspondent for various Can. journals, has contributed in prose and poetry in the *Saturday Reader*, (Mont.) ; and on political subjects to several prominent newspapers. In 1865 he ed. a comic weekly called the *Sprite,* (Que.) He is the author of 4 or 5 distinct works. His earliest was the *Child's Own History of France,* which contained portraits of the long line of French monarchs from Pharamond to Louis Phillipe, and trifling as this work was in a literary point of view, it had the singular merit (as would be thought in Can.) of selling well and giving a handsome sum to both author and publisher. His next work was a *History of the Druids* ; which was followed by *The Sailor, Temptation, a poem ;* and *Memoirs of Don Pedro, Ex-Emperor of Brazil.* For sometime from 1843 Mr. G. held a situation in the Admiralty Office, Eng., subsequently in the Customs. Since his residence in Can. he has been employed for some years as a sessional clk. in the Leg. Assem.

GILBERT, A. G.
I. From Montreal to the Maritime Provinces and back. *Montreal,* 1867.

A series of letters originally published in the *Evening Telegraph,* (Mont.)

GOOCH, JOHN.
I. Manual or Explanatory Development of the Act for the Union of Canada, Nova Scotia and New Brunswick, in one Dominion under the name of Canada Synthetical and Analytical : With the text of the Act, &c., and index to the Act and the treatises. *Ottawa,* 1867, pp. 124, 8vo.

IRVING, *Rev.* GEORGE CLERK, *M. A.* Late Rector of Bishop's Coll. Grammar Sch., Lennoxville, and formerly Vice-Provost of Trinity Coll., (Tor.) Drowned in the Lower St. Lawrence, 1866.

I. Parish, School and College Sermons. With a Memoir of the author's life, by the Rev. George Whitaker, M. A., Vice-Provost of Trinity College, Toronto. Ed. by the Rev. Henry Roe, B. A. St. Mathews, Quebec. *Montreal,* 1867.

JOHNSON, FRANK.
I. Lashed to the Mizen, or a Night off the Cape. *Montreal,* 1867.

KIDDER, FREDERICK.
I. Military Operations in Eastern Maine and Nova Scotia during the Revolution, chiefly compiled from the Journals and Letters of Colonel John Allan, with Notes and a Memoir of Colonel John Allan. *Albany,* 1867, pp. xi–336, 8vo.

KNOX, W. J.

I. On the best means of bringing water from the head of the Lachine rapids to St. Pierre River and from thence to connect with the harbour of Montreal. *Montreal*, 1867.

LACROIX, HENRI.

I. Opuscule sur le Présent et L'Avenir du Canada. 1867, pp. 32.

LANCTOT, MEDERIC. A French Can. journ. at Montreal.

I. Indépendance Pacifique du Canada. *Montréal*, 1867.

LANDOR, HENRY, *M. D.*

I. The Fearful Condition of the Church of England in the Diocese of Huron as shown in the Speeches of the Bishop of Huron. *Hamilton*, 1866.

LAVERDIÈRE, *L'Abbé* C. H., *M. A.* Bibliothécaire de l'Université Laval. (Qué.)

I. OEuvres de Champlain publiées sous le patronage de l'Université Laval, *Québec* et *Ottawa*, (G. E. Desbarats.) 1867, 6 vols. in–4o. (*In press.*)

L'ouvrage contiendra: le Voyage aux Indes Occidentales, précédé d'une notice biographique de Champlain; le Voyage de 1603; l'édition de 1613, c'est-à-dire, les Voyages à l'Acadie de 1604 à 1607 et les Voyages au Canada depuis la fondation de Québec en 1608 jusqu'en 1613, avec *fac-simile* photolithographique de toutes les cartes et vignettes, y compris la rarissime *Grande Carte* de 1612, et la *Petite Carte* de 1613,, *en son vray meridiein* (les deux tirages); le Quatrième Voyage; l'édition de 1619, avec le frontispice gravé et les vignettes; l'édition de 1632, première et seconde partie, avec la *Grande Carte* et sa *Table*; le Traité de la Marine; le Cathéchisme huron du P. Brebeuf; l'Oraison Dominicale traduite en montagnais par le P. Massé; une Dissertation sur les Cartes de Champlain; un Dictionnaire topographique du Canada ancien; des Pièces justificatives, et une Table générale des œuvres de Champlain.

Cette nouvelle édition, imprimée en caractères antiques, sur papier superfin, est une reproduction fidèles des éditions originales, avec notes au bas des pages.

The price of the work complete will be $15 or £3 Stg.

MARSHALL, ORSAMUS H.

I. The Niagara Frontier: embracing sketches of its early history, and Indian, French, and English local names. Read before the Buffalo Historical Club. *Buffalo*, 1865, pp. 46, 8vo.

Printed for private circulation.

McEACHRAN, D., *M. R. C. V. S.* (Edin.) and ANDREW SMITH, *V. S.* (Edin.)

I. The Canadian Horse and his Diseases. *Toronto*, 1867.

" A most useful digest."—*Globe.*

McGANN, J. B. (Hamilton.)

I. The Education of Deaf Mutes; Shall it be Articulation and Lip-reading or Dactylology ? (*In Press.*)

PALMER, PETER S.

I. History of Lake Champlain, from its first exploration by the French, in 1609, to the close of the year 1814. *Albany*, 1866, pp. 276, 8vo.

POMEROY, *Rev.* DANIEL.

I. The Methodist Union : being a Vindication of the Establishment of a Union between the Methodist Denominations in Canada, &c. *Brighton, U. C.* 1862, pp. 159, 8vo.

ROSE, GEORGE MACLEAN. A Can. newspaper writer. B. at Wick, Scot., 1829. Came to Can., 1851. Has been connected with the Can. newspaper press in the capacity of ed., reporter and correspondent for the past 16 years. Is Can. correspondent of the *Scottish Am. Journal*, (N. Y.)

SADLIER, *Mrs.* JAMES. A well-known Am. authoress. Some twenty years ago Mr. James Sadlier, a younger member of the well-known publishing house of that name, in N. Y., visiting Can. on business, met with, wooed, and married, a young Irish lady, Miss Mary Anne Madden, then residing in Montreal. Miss Madden was born at Cootchill, Co. of Cavan, Irel., Dec. 31, 1820, from which with some other members of her family she emigrated to Can., shortly before her first acquaintance with Mr. Sadlier. When scarcely 18 she began to contribute to *La Belle Assemblée*, (Lon.,) a mag. published under the patronage of the late Duchess of Kent. One of her first works was a collection of traditionary stories, published by subscription at Montreal, intituled : *Tales of the Olden Time.* In one of her numerous tales of Irish immigrant life and adventure, called *Eleanor Preston*, there are some sketches of lower Canadian rural life and scenery, which go to show that the faculty of close observation had developed itself very early in her case. The literary works of this gifted lady may be divided into three classes, the Historical Irish romance, of which the *Confederate Chieftains* is the best and most elaborate; her didactic and religious works, original and translated, of which *De Ligny's Life of the Blessed Virgin*, may be cited as an example; and, a department, or sub-department of fiction, in which she stands wholly unrivalled, and which we may call, the romance of Irish immigration. Under this last head, we may mention her *Willy Burke*; *the Blakes and Flanagans; Con O'Regan; Eleanor Preston: Aunt Honor's Keepsake*, &c. &c. We have not, we regret to say, a full list of Mrs. Sadlier's numerous writings and translations within reach, but we hazard nothing in adding that their variety and excellence are such as fairly to entitle her to rank with that gifted Irish sisterhood which boasts the names of Maria Edgeworth, Mrs. Jameson, Lady Morgan, and *Psyche* Tighe. This lady's first literary essays in this country appeared we believe in the well-known Montreal periodical called the *Garland*, (now defunct) and all her books up to the year 1860 were written in Montreal, from which she then removed to N. Y., where she still resides.

VETROMILE, *Rev.* EUGÈNE, a Missionary in Maine, U. S. •

I. The Abnakis and their History, or historical notices of the Aborigines of Acadia. [Illustrated.] *New York*, 1866, pp. 172, 12mo.